30 MINUTES SERIES

BOOKS 1-4

MARCUS BLAKE

VOLUME 1

30 Minutes Series Volume 1: Books 1-4

A Mavericknes Media / Truesource Publishing Book

30 Minutes Series Volume 1 was edited by Vicky Guidry

Mavericknes Media : Dallas Texas

Truesource Publishing : Dallas Texas

www.truesourcepublishing.com

ISBN : 978-1-932996-66-1

Printed in the United States of America
Published in Dallas, Texas

For More information on Marcus Blake go to....

www.marcusblake.net
www.facebook.com/themarcusblake
www.twitter.com/marcusblake
www.thatnerdshow.com

ABOUT THE AUTHOR

Marcus Blake was born in Chicago, Illinois in 1977. He grew up in Chicago and East Texas. His education is in History, Literature, Psychology, and Religion & Philosophy. Marcus Blake has studied at many universities throughout the United States, but his Alma Mater is Stephen F. Austin State University in Nacogdoches, Texas, which is also where he wrote his first book, The Music of Life. Marcus Blake is a Poet, Musician, Comedian, Writer, and Historian. His books are The Music of Life, My Reflections, Returning Home. Sex Game. The Lonely Girl, Stories From Wrigley, 30 Minutes: Trust and Lies, 30 Minutes: Guilty Until Proven Innocent, 30 Minutes: A Soldier's Song, and 30 Minutes: A Badge of Honor. . He has taught in the public school system, served in the Army, and been a guest speaker at Education and Literary events throughout the world. Marcus Blake is also a Radio Host, his current show is Saturday Morning Nerd Show which can be heard on Saturday Mornings at www.thatnerdshow.com. He is a veteran of Rock and Roll shows as well as Political shows on the radio. Marcus Blake makes his home in the Dallas, Texas.

Other Books by Marcus Blake...

The Music of Life

My Reflections

Returning Home

Sex Game

The Lonely Girl

Stories From Wrigley

30 Minutes: Trust and Lies

30 Minutes: Guilty Until Proven Innocent

30 Minutes: A Soldier's Song

30 Minutes: A Badge of Honor

Windows

Ring of Warriors: Making a Fighter

The search for truth is more precious than its possession.

~ Albert Einstein

VERUM EST GRADUM PROPIUS

THE TRUTH IS ONE STEP CLOSER

TABLE OF CONTENTS

30 MINUTES

TRUST AND LIES

BOOK 1

1

The rain was falling hard as Agent Donnelly was the leaving the Department of Justice building in downtown Chicago. The storm had come in early that morning making it an all-around shitty day. Agent Donnelly knew that it would be as he had another long day of meetings at the DOJ in Chicago, but the storm made it worse. This is, was not the most glamorous part of his job. He had been an FBI agent for 10 years now, working in the White Collar Crimes division of the Chicago Office, investigating money laundering, and securities and corporate fraud, and sometimes even organized crime. Chicago was a good place for that.

Agent Gavin Donnelly was a money man, a finance geek who tried to stop crimes involving any kind of currency. He was good, very good, and had a real knack for uncovering fraud when it came to money. Agent Donnelly had been investigating a multimillion dollar corporate fraud and Ponzi scheme that involved one of Chicago's most successful investment firms, one of those companies that had a lot of senior citizen retirement benefits tied up in the company. And now he had the task of catching the crooks that would ruin the lives of thousands of retirees who had spent half of their lives saving for retirement. What he didn't know was that one of the partners of the company that he was trying to put away in prison had hired someone to kill him … just like an old school mafia hit. He had become a dangerous man to the firm and the only solution was to see him dead.

As the rain was coming down hard, Agent Donnelly hurriedly walked across the plaza trying to get to his car and stay, somewhat, dry. It was hard to see anything with the rain, but out of the corner of his eye he saw a man with a mask dart from behind a tree and run toward him. Agent Donnelly could see the gun and quickly drew his service weapon, but he slipped and fell backward onto the concrete ground into a puddle of water. The gunman fired two shots, the first missing Agent Donnelly completely and the second grazing the top of his head causing him to fall unconscious. The bullet had just missed him dead center in the head because he had slipped in the rain, but hit him just enough to cause damage. He wasn't dead, just in a coma. Other agents coming out of the DOJ building responded to the gunman after hearing the first shot. Four agents fired their guns, all of them hitting the assassin. He never had time to finish off Agent Donnelly before he fell to ground, dead.

As for Agent Donnelly, he was in serious condition and rushed to the hospital. The bullet had only grazed his head, but he was bleeding and there was no way to tell yet if there was brain damage. He stayed in a coma for seven days and was monitored closely. After two days in a coma, the doctors were able to conclude that he would not have brain damage, but they didn't know for sure if he would come out of the accident as good as he was before. Agent Donnelly was smart, had quick reflexes, and he was an excellent shot … all the things that made him a good FBI agent.   There was above normal brain activity for the last five days that he was in a coma. One doctor made the comment that it appeared that Agent Donnelly had higher brain functions; he was using more than the average brain power exerted by human beings.

Finally, he came out of the coma and everything was back to normal. There were no signs of damage, he remembered who he was, and more importantly, he functioned normally. Agent Donnelly did not feel any changes. The only thing that he could conclude was wrong with him was having a case of cottonmouth from not drinking water for seven days and a splitting headache, which he attributed from the bullet grazing his head. But that's not what it was from. There was a change, a big one.

Agent Donnelly started seeing things in his head, things going on the hospital, as if it were a dream. Every time a nurse or a doctor came into his room he knew what was going to happen, what they were going to say … he was seeing things about 30 minutes before they happened. Agent Donnelly didn't know whether it was dream or some kind of psychic vision. The images were hazy and staring out in front of him as if he were at the movies. While he couldn't make out every little detail in the so-called vision, he could hear what people were saying and that added to the clues within what he was seeing.

It was all confusing and at first he thought it had something to do with the medication he was being given … it was a fair assumption. Finally, a day after he had woken up from the coma, he saw a vision that seemed more real than anything he had experienced before. When his nurse came back into the room and touched the IV inserted into his arm he saw it plain as day. *The same nurse was replacing the IV bag of another patient in another room; she was talking to him at the same time and not paying attention to what she was giving him. "I hope you're feeling better today, Mr. Davidson. It's a beautiful day outside and you should try to go out and enjoy it." The nurse replaced the IV bag and the IV in the patient's arm and then patted him on the hand while smiling at him, trying to make him feel better since he had been in the hospital for two weeks now. The IV started its drip and then she went into the bathroom to fill up his water pitcher. That's when the patient went into shock; he was having an allergic reaction to the medicine … it was the wrong medicine. The nurse had given it to him by mistake.*

Agent Donnelly shook his head to clear his mind, thinking again that he was having a hallucination. Thirty minutes later, he heard nurses and doctors running down the hall to the sound of the nurse he had seen in his vision shouting, "Code Blue." What Agent Donnelly had seen in the vision was happening now, in real time, clear as day. He knew now that he was not dreaming or hallucinating.; this was real. He was seeing a glimpse of the future, 30 minutes to be exact. What he saw were real events and, for the first time in his career, he was scared; not even having his life threatened or being fired could make him this scared. All his life he had relied on numbers and facts, especially in his career as an FBI agent, to make sense of things, to have certainty and it was a comfort to him. Agent Donnelly had always lived a life that was organized and predictable, without any surprises, and he liked it that way. But now he was completely uncertain about the world he lived in. All he could see now was uncertainty and that's when the fear grabbed him, strangling his senses and not letting go.

Agent Donnelly took a deep breath, got out of his bed and started down the hall toward the patient's room. He was a bit woozy and it made it hard to walk, but he made it to the room filled with frantic doctors and nurses trying to revive the patient. All of them were at a loss on what to do for him because they couldn't figure out what was wrong with him. The patient went into V-fib and had to be shocked back to life. When the doctors got his heart working again Agent Donnelly looked at everybody in the room and said, "The nurse gave him the wrong IV, it's the wrong medication." The doctors and nurses gave Agent Donnelly a strange look since he too was a patient standing in the doorway while wearing a hospital gown. Finally, the nurse who had given the patient the IV bag looked on the label and saw that the medication was wrong and that she had made a mistake. She looked around the room and told everybody that Agent Donnelly was right. When Agent Donnelly was asked how he knew that, he said, "I just knew."

He walked back to his room with mixed feelings. He was glad that he saved a life, but there was a growing fear inside of him. Some might think it was cool to see visions, but Agent Donnelly was not one of them. All it did was get in the way of his normal routine … the routine of being an FBI agent, which he wouldn't be any more if the Bureau ever found out he was having psychic visions. And Agent Donnelly loved being an FBI agent.

2

Present Day

Agent Rachel Main sat outside the FBI office of OPR (Office of Professional Responsibility) in Washington. Rarely was she nervous, but today was different. Her career at the FBI hung in the balance with this meeting and she had spent the last 10 years working her ass off to be one of the best FBI agents in the Violent Crimes division; that was the thought running through her mind. Agent Main came to the FBI right out of college when she was 23, fresh from finishing her Master's degrees in Psychology and Behavioral Science. Ever since she was 14 years old, she wanted to work for the FBI and work in the Violent Crimes division profiling the worst kind of murders. The FBI could give her that chance. She wanted to solve the cases that were considered too hard or unsolvable. Agent Main had been that way ever since her grandmother, who she was very close to, was murdered by a serial killer who was never caught. Every great cop has a driving force that reaches to the bone and the death of someone close was hers.

Ever since she began studying behavioral science she trained herself to be the best in profiling. She was at the top of her class at the FBI Academy in Quantico, Virginia and when she came to the FBI she quickly rose to the top ranks of the Violent Crimes division in just a few short years. She had a real talent for seeing beneath the mask that criminals hid behind to find the truth. She was good in every sense of the word at figuring out the puzzle to solve some of the most gruesome murders in America. She also caught one of the most elusive serial killers in our nation's history, Jonny Roger Smith. He killed 30 people from California to New York and, after 10 years on the run, it was her profile that caught him. Because of this, she was considered one of the best. But here she was, going before the OPR, trying to defend the black mark that had been placed on her record. She was finally called into the office and stood before the panel of 5 agents that made up the OPR.

The OPR didn't have many questions for her. The report of what happened was pretty straightforward. She had been tracking a serial killer who was on the run for the past year and half and had to kill the only lead the FBI had in finding him. The lead was a man who was a known associate of the serial killer she had been tracking. He took a pregnant mother hostage and was threatening to kill her and her unborn child. Agent Main had to make a split-second decision when the associate was holding the woman and her child hostage in an abandoned office building. Before he killed the mother she shot him dead center between the eyes, killing him instantly. Agent Main wasn't able to question the guy and perhaps find out where the serial killer she had been tracking was hiding. In the process, Agent Main was shot by the associate's driver when she charged into the building (without backup) trying to rescue the pregnant mother. The driver shot her in the chest when she wasn't looking because she failed to check behind doors and around darkened corners as she was chasing the associate. She would have been dead if she hadn't been wearing her standard-issue FBI bulletproof vest. As she fell to ground she was able to spin around and shoot the driver, killing him instantly.

Agent Brenda Jensen, the head of the OPR, said to Agent Main, "After reviewing the field report, I just have a few questions before we make a decision on your status with the FBI. First: Why and probably the most important, why did you kill this Jack Spivey, the only lead we had to Bruno Maken's whereabouts? Why didn't you just wound him?"

"I had to make a quick decision," Agent Main replied. "He didn't seem too concerned with staying alive, just killing an innocent pregnant mother. I killed him to save her life and her unborn child."

"How do you know that he wouldn't have let her go if you had not waited for backup and he saw that he was surrounded?"

"Jack Spivey didn't respond to anything I said to him after I shot his driver. He brought his hand up and was going to stab her. It was the only chance to save her life."

Agent Jensen said to her, "But you didn't even try to bargain with him; you just killed him and broke an FBI rule of engagement. It wasn't the only rule of engagement you broke in trying to catch Jack Spivey. "

"He didn't give me time to bargain with him and I decided the mother's life was more important than his." Agent Main was stern with her answer.

Agent Jensen leaned forward and said, "Agent Main, your actions compromised this investigation and now we have no leads on Bruno Maken, which is going to set us back on catching him. He is still out there and could kill even more people. If we have to assign blame then it's with you. Your record with the FBI has been exemplary up to this point, but this isn't just one mistake we can ignore and let you go on. You made several. You didn't wait for backup after you went charging into the building. You didn't check all the primary hidden areas for other suspects, causing yourself to get shot, and then you killed another associate that we could have questioned. These are big mistakes and we still have a very dangerous criminal on the loose. What do you say to all of this?"

Agent Main took a moment to cool down and not lose her temper. In her mind she did the right thing; saving a mother and an unborn child was the best choice. She finally replied, "I still believe I did the right thing and we can still find Bruno Maken. Yes, I didn't wait for backup and that may have been a mistake, but there was no time. Somebody had to go in there and rescue the mother. And of course I did break a rule of engagement by not checking hidden areas for other suspects and got shot. There wasn't time to reason with the man who shot me so I killed him to save my life. But I would like the record to state that I have had plenty of interference in this case that has impeded our investigation. I told you that seeking help from Jack Spivey wasn't a good idea because he would just toy with us and not give us leads. And I was right; he didn't give us anything substantial to help catch Maken. I stand behind my decision to save an innocent life and kill Jack Spivey as well as his driver . I have not given up on this investigation. and I ask that you don't either by taking me off this case. We can still catch Bruno Maken." That was all she said to the OPR panel. They dismissed her and she went back to her office. Agent Main didn't know whether or not she should be cleaning out her desk, but she wasn't going to change her mind in her decisions … she was stubborn that way and it was both a good thing and bad thing. Most of the time, it made her a good agent.

About an hour later her superior, Assistant Director Douglas, came to her office to deliver the bad news. She wasn't being fired or even suspended even though that's what the OPR wanted to do. AD Douglas managed to save her job, although it wasn't easy since she was not very apologetic in the meeting or humble about her mistakes, two things the OPR hated from agents they had to review. He told her:

"They wanted to suspend you, but I had a long talk with them and convinced them not to … you're too valuable to the FBI."

Agent Main sarcastically smiled at the notion and responded, "So what is my sentence?

"You're going to be transferred. You won't be coming back to Washington for a long time if at all. "

"Transferred to where, some hick town like Salt Lake City where I'll be investigating election fraud? "

"No, not at all. I still got them to leave you in Violent Crimes investigating what you're good at. You're being transferred to Chicago and they're sending someone here to replace you."

"Chicago, what the hell am I going to do there?"

"They have a busy Violent Crimes division and serial killers do exist in the Midwest. This is also the city of Al Capone and murder wrapped up with organized crime that still runs rampant there so there's excitement for you. Besides, you're getting a new partner. They have a new agent being transferred to Violent Crimes in Chicago and they need a senior agent to be paired with him. "

Agent Main gave her boss a disgruntled look and said to him, "I have to baby-sit some rookie now?!"

"He's hardly a rookie; he has been with the Bureau for 12 years. He was at the top of his class and has an impeccable record. But they moved him over from White Collar Crimes. "

"Oh, this just gets better, a finance geek solving murders. How the hell did he land that gig?"

"He helped them solve a couple of profile murders in the last year by finding clues that nobody else could. Kind of like you. However, you are getting teamed with him because he is new to the division."

"It's a babysitter job."

"Maybe, but at least you still have a job with the FBI and he can help you see things that you don't always catch in an investigation … yes, you're not perfect."

Agent Main gave him another dirty look. "Why is this happening, is it because I don't play politics?"

"Part of it, but they really don't like you because you don't play well with others. You're too smart and a bit of a narcissist. They only tolerate you because you're successful. You did break some rules of engagement; it might have been the right choice, but you still broke the rules and you have to pay for it. It's their excuse to get you out of Washington. Today you get saddled with the catch-22 of this job, but Chicago might be a good thing for you."

"I don't even like Chicago."

"You better get used to it because if you want to stay with the FBI then you're going to be there for a while. And we both know you're too smart and stubborn to be on some local police force. "

She thanked him for his help with the OPR and then told him, "By the way, I am that good. I don't need anybody.

He smiled at her. "Yeah, you're right, you are that good, but you do need someone to help you and you're going to get it even though you don't want it. Good luck with that."

AD Douglas shook Agent Main's hand and wished her luck.
In a couple of days she would be moving to a new town, a new life,
and for the first time there was uncertainty in her career. That was a
new one for her. She was too good at her job to be uncertain. She
didn't know anything about her new partner but she felt like she
already hated him, but that could be because he was from Chicago.
She had never liked change in her life unless it was on her own accord,
but life was full of surprises and they were only to get bigger as she
headed to the Windy City. Later that night as she was cleaning out her
desk, she was given a file by another agent. It was her first case in the
Chicago office. She got it early so she could start reviewing it.

3

It was a busy day at the Indianapolis Bank. It was Friday, the busiest banking day of the week. Franklin White didn't have time to deal with normal banking business that day, but there was one important thing he had to do that day ... he had been waiting twenty-seven years to complete this business. It was a surprise to say the least when he received the call from the Old Man, a nickname that was given to the man that was coming to see him. Franklin White was nervous, demonstrated by him checking his watch every five minutes. Finally, 11:00 came around and the Old Man and his associate were right on time. Punctuality was one of his good qualities.

Franklin White stopped what he was doing and had the Assistant Manager take over for him with the customer he had been talking to. He walked up to the Old Man as he came through the main door of the bank. "It's good to see you again," he said to the Old Man.

"It has been a long time, Franklin ... you're an old man now, just like me. "

"Twenty-seven years will do that to you."

"Yes it will. This is my associate, Mr. Smith ... we're here to empty the box."

"Of course, right this way."

Franklin led the two men into the safety deposit box vault. Two boxes were taken out and laid out onto the table in the middle of the room. The Old Man looked over at Franklin and said, "We will also do the transactions here. I'm sure the waiting period will not be a problem.

"I already took care of that with the paperwork. I want to get this done as soon possible, just like you."

"I wish we could have waited a few more years, but the time table has been moved up and we have to do this now. "

Franklin smiled. "At least I get to retire early now!"

The contents of the safety deposit boxes were emptied. Each document was counted and Franklin entered all the information from the document into the computer outside the vault. He was handed a piece of paper with two bank account numbers. The Old Man looked at Franklin and said:

"The second number is your bank account. It's completely set up … all you have to do is give them your ID to access it. You will not be able to access it for 30 days from today. That was our deal. After that you will never hear from us again and you can go and live your life in whatever luxury you see fit. "

Franklin White nodded. "I understand. Thank you."

"No, thank *you* Franklin … you've been loyal all these years and now you have been rewarded. Enjoy!"

The Old Man and Mr. Smith left the bank and Franklin filed the documents away after all transactions were done. The nervousness he had felt was replaced with happiness, something he had not felt in 27 years (when it came to safety deposit boxes he opened when he was a first-year New Accounts employee at the bank). It didn't last long, though.

When the day was done and it was time to leave, Franklin White walked to his car with a smile on his face. He was getting in his Honda Civic knowing that he was about to trade it in for the sports car he always wanted, a '68 Ford Shelby GT. With his back turned to the bank, he was about to get in his car when a hand went over his mouth. He then felt an object pierce his lower back, burning the skin with such intense heat that Franklin White passed out. One moment he saw the light outside and the next it went dark. Minutes later, the last breath escaped his body.

∞∞∞∞∞∞∞

By Saturday afternoon, Agent Main was packed and on a flight to Chicago. She was always restless when she flew, but she made the best of it by reading through the case file she was given right before she left Washington. It would be her first case with her new partner. It was a brutal murder in Indiana, the same MO as a serial killer from the Chicago area that had never been caught. It was the kind of case that, if solved, might get her back to Washington.

Agent Main also had an FBI dossier on her new partner, Gavin Donnelly. She wanted to know about him, at least as much as she could from an FBI file before meeting him. The dossier didn't tell her everything, but it gave her an idea of who he was and his background. Mainly she wanted to know if he was a good FBI agent in some capacity. She thought to herself, if he had some success solving cases at the FBI then he might be okay to work with, despite virtually being a rookie in the Violent Crimes division. She looked through the file and read.

Gavin Donnelly, born December 26, 1973 in Chicago, Illinois to a Chicago police officer, Michael Donnelly and Gabriela Rousseau, a teacher from New Orleans, Louisiana. He moved to New Orleans when he was two years old and lived there until the age of six, when his parents were murdered in the French Quarter. The case was never solved. Gavin Donnelly was raised by his father's brother, Liam Donnelly, and his aunt, Mary Donnelly. Liam Donnelly is a Chicago police captain and has been with the Chicago Police Department for thirty one years.

Gavin Donnelly graduated from DePaul University in 1995 with degrees in Economics and Political Science. He went to law school, graduated from the University of Chicago in 1997 with a law degree, and passed the Illinois Bar Exam that same year. Gavin Donnelly joined the FBI later that year and graduated from the FBI Academy at Quantico, Virginia in 1998, top five in his class. He requested transfer to the White Collar Crimes division in Chicago. He received his first commendation in 1999 as a member of the joint task force that brought down Stein & Roth, an investment firm that defrauded hundreds of investors in a 100-billion-dollar Ponzi scheme. In 2001, he worked in the antiterrorist unit investigating terrorist cells in Chicago after 9/11. Received his second commendation after discovering an al-Qaeda cell linked to the 9/11 plot through financial records linked to the Pakistani government. He received the Director's Award for Excellence in 2004 for running the Organized Crime Task Force that brought down Frank Salvo and the Salvo Family in Chicago on racketeering and murder charges.

Gavin Donnelly had a distinguished career so far with the FBI, according to the dossier. It looked as if he was being groomed for Section Chief or head of the Chicago Field Office. He could also have a great career in Washington, maybe even one day Director of the FBI. His career was promising and he certainly was a good FBI agent on paper, but the Violent Crimes division was another animal. It takes a certain kind of agent to be successful there, the best of the best, an agent that has a strong stomach for the most gruesome murders ever committed. And more importantly, an agent who can get inside a killer's head and still come out sane at the end of the day. For Agent Main, that was the biggest question regarding her new partner and, with the kind of case that they were assigned, she was about to find out if Agent Gavin Donnelly really was that good.

4

It was Monday, the beginning of Agent Main's first week in Chicago. She had barely gotten settled in the city before she had to be at The Chicago FBI field office. She was still staying at a hotel. It was first thing Monday and even though she arrived early, 7:00 a.m. to be exact, there was already a case she and her new partner had been assigned to. The case wasn't going to be easy and it looked as if they could be on the case for a long time. It was a murder, but not just any murder, a serial killing. There had not been one committed the same way as this serial killing in five years.

Agent Main had already drunk two cups of coffee and taken one more look at the case file before heading to Agent Donnelly's new office. He had opted to convert a huge storage room in the Violent Crimes division into an office and he made room for a partner, despite the fact that he would be paired with a partner he didn't particularly want. Of course he also knew that she probably wouldn't like him either … it wasn't going to be the easiest of partnerships because of the way it happened. Agent Main walked up to the office with the door wide open. Agent Donnelly was moving things around and trying to get organized. At the moment, he was hanging peg boards and setting up a large dry erase board. She knocked on the door and he didn't even bother to turn around.

"Come on in," he said. "You don't have to knock, the door is wide open, but if you're a real G-man then you should already know that. "

She shook her head, a little annoyed at the sarcasm. She replied, "Agent Donnelly." He turned around at the mention of his name. "I'm Agent Rachel Main. I've been assigned as your partner."

He smiled at her and reached out his hand to shake hers. "Ah, you're the one from Washington that they assigned to watch over me."

"Are you implying that I'm here to spy on you?"

"No, but I'm sure you're here to baby-sit me. I'm a rookie in this division and the powers that be have to make sure that I'm teamed with a real pro."

She finally smiled at his joke. She already knew that she would be annoyed at his sarcasm, but at least that comment was funny and she agreed with it. "If it's any consolation, I'm not here to be a babysitter, but you are being teamed with a pro. "

"Good, but I am curious about something. What did you do to get transferred here and get assigned with me? Must have ticked somebody off or screwed up pretty big to get teamed with me."

"Are you already telling me that you're not that good and I should be asking for another partner?"

He laughed. "We both know that the Bureau is keeping a very close eye on me and wants to see if I am really this good at solving violent crimes or just plain lucky. And you getting transferred here to be partners with me is like getting sent down to the Minors in baseball. I just wanted to know what happened. "

Agent Main had a stern look on her face and replied, "That's not what I am here to talk about because it's not relevant to the new case we have. Besides, I'm sure you can get the report on what happened to me transferred. And as for you being good in this division or just plain lucky, if I see that you're severely screwing up an investigation I will be the first to bench you and get you kicked out for good like Shoeless Joe."

Agent Donnelly laughed. "Fair enough, Agent Main … and hey, you're already getting the Chicago references down, but I have to warn you: around here, we're Cub fans, White Sox suck."

"Good to know. We have a case and I have the file right here. Do you want to go over it before we head out to the crime scene? "

Agent Donnelly put down the hammer he had in his hand and got his service weapon and suit jacket. Then he said, "I got a copy of it last night and had a chance to review before I came in so I am up to speed and I got the old case files already here. I was putting up peg boards so we can lay everything out. And someone will be bringing you a desk in with a phone while we're gone."

"You don't want to talk about this case for a few minutes before we go?"

"We can talk on the way."

"You don't have to impress me on the first day and act like you know everything that's going on. This is your first case in the division, too, and we can take some time."

Agent Donnelly stopped for a moment and said, "White Caucasian, 5'9", 55 years old and Manager of the Indianapolis Federal Bank in Indianapolis, Indiana. He disappeared after the bank closed, never made it home, was reported missing and killed 72 miles away in Richmond, Indiana -- close to the Ohio Border. All ten of his fingers were cut off, his eyes were cut out, and both ears had acid poured on and them to burn them shut and damage the ear drum. The way he was murdered suggests that it was a serial killing by a man never caught by the FBI: Albert Soranno, the only son of Chicago mob boss Mickey Soranno, who has not been seen or heard from in five years. And because the killing was done with the same MO as Albert Soranno that makes it a federal case and the FBI now has jurisdiction. Does that about sum it up?"

"Are you familiar with the old case?" Agent Main asked. "You read the old case files, right?"

"Agent Main, I know you're new here but I'll let you in on something. This isn't Washington, this is a kind of a small office, and I have been here for 12 years . Everybody around here is familiar with that case and we have all looked at those files at least once just to see if we could find something that another agent didn't. That case was an embarrassment for us because he got away and we've never been able to bring Mickey Soranno down either. I'm not some rookie who doesn't know about this case, so believe me, I'm up to speed on it."

"Okay then let's see if this office can get a victory and solve the case. I certainly don't want a loss on my first day here." Agent Donnelly smiled at her and adjusted his service weapon on his belt. She noticed and asked him, "Just out of curiosity, have you fired your gun lately? "

"It's been four years, " he replied. "I fired it in my last qualification test."

" You do know how to actually fire a gun, right?"

" Oh yeah ... the end with the hole is the dangerous end." He looked at her with a sarcastic look and patted her on the back. "Don't worry, if we have to use our weapons I've got your back."

Agent Main had a dissatisfied look on her face; she was not amused to say the least.

∞∞∞∞∞∞∞∞

By the time Agent Main and Agent Donnelly flew to Indiana, the body had already been moved to the Medical Examiner's office at the local FBI office in Indianapolis. The vehicle that the victim was transported in still had not been found. Agent Main and Agent Donnelly were going to examine the body and start looking for clues there.

The ME pulled the body out in the morgue for the agents to look at. Agent Main asked him for his initial report. The corpse had its

[24]

eyes and all 10 of its fingers removed, as well as multiple stab wounds in the chest with what the ME described as a hunting knife. Agent Main was looking at the body closely as Agent Donnelly stood behind listening to the report. She had seen close to a hundred dead bodies similar to this in her career and one thing that she was good at was not letting the gruesome scenes get to her. The ME looked at both agents and said that there was something weird about the body.

"I noticed some differences in the way this person was killed compared to how Albert Soranno used to kill his victims."

Agent Main responded, "Like what, doctor?"

"First of all, Albert Soranno was known to be left handed and the stab wounds were done by someone who was right handed. "

"He was ambidextrous, actually."

"Yes, but he favored his left hand and stabbed his victims with his left hand. This was done by someone using his right hand. "

Agent Main commented, "He could have been using his right hand this time to make it look different for the ME's."

"There's something else. Whoever did this was sloppy about the stabbing. You have two wounds at the top of his chest that were done by someone standing behind him and then the rest were done by someone standing over him. The markings where his fingers were cut off are very sloppy and it's the same with the eyes. This was done by someone who did not know what they were doing or at least were not that precise. "

"Albert Soranno hasn't killed anybody in five years and he may have been rushed when killing the victim. Couldn't that make somebody sloppy, doctor?"

"I suppose so, Agent Main. I just wanted to point out the differences from how Albert's victims were killed in the past."

Finally Agent Donnelly asked a question. "Doctor, is it possible that somebody else killed this man, perhaps a copycat who didn't know what he was doing? "

"I'm sure that's possible, too."

Agent Main looked at Agent Donnelly and said, "The exact details of how Albert Soranno killed his victims were never released to the public. To be this precise it would have to be a killer who has done it before or someone that had access to these files in Washington. You really think an FBI agent killed this victim? It had to be Albert Soranno."

Agent Donnelly dismissed the comments and walked over to a tray containing the victim's belongings that were found on the body. "Is this all the victim's stuff?"

The ME replied, "Yes, that's all that was found on him."

There was a wallet, a watch, car keys, an ID badge from the bank, 58 cents in pocket change, and a piece of paper with 4 digits on it. Agent Donnelly picked up the piece of paper – his eyes flashed and he saw a vision.

It was a man wearing a baseball cap and dark coat. He was asking the bank manager to give him access to his safety deposit box. There was another man standing next to him: slightly taller, wearing a suit, tinted glasses and had a white beard. The man who owned the safety deposit box asked the bank manager if he could make some transactions and transfer some money to an off shore account. The Manager said that he could and it would take about 30 minutes to complete.

Agent Main asked Agent Donnelly about the numbers on the paper. Agent Donnelly replied, "The numbers could be an alarm code, a PIN number, ID login." Agent Donnelly used his cell phone to call the bank where the victim worked at to see what the numbers might be. Agent Main told him that it probably didn't matter what the numbers were and had nothing to do with the murder, which is what they were investigating. Agent Donnelly ignored her and, after a five-minute conversation, got on the phone with the bank. He told her, "According to the manager on duty, the only thing he would have written down that contained four numbers is a PIN number or safety deposit box code …I'm betting it's the latter."

"He was probably helping a customer with a safety deposit box and wrote the numbers on a piece of paper," Agent Main said.

"The person on the phone said that he was and that the customer got out a large stack of bank documents and inquired about cashing out and making a money transfer."

"Like I said, normal banking duties."

"And then the bank manager who helped the customer is brutally killed hours later. You don't think that's odd?

"It's odd, but I don't think it has anything to do with this murder by a former serial killer. And besides, the Soranno family kept their money in Chicago and New York. There are no records of them keeping any kind of money or safety deposit box in a bank in Indiana."

"It's too much coincidence for me. I want to check out. "

"We have a body right here that we need to finish examining."

"And you can do that; you have more expertise than me. The Indianapolis Federal Bank is 10 minutes from here. Let me check out the lead at the bank then I'll be back."

"You're going to need a court order to find out what was inside. It's a waste of time."

Agent Donnelly was already halfway out the door when he replied, "All I need is a really scared bank manager to show me the records when he's threatened with obstruction of justice. He'll tell me what I need to know. Be back in an hour. "

Agent Main just gave the ME a dirty look, which was directed at her partner. She couldn't believe he just left without her say-so. The ME looked at her and replied, "You two must be new partners, haven't really fallen in sync with each other yet."

"I guess if I shot him he would listen to me more and we would be in sync." The ME laughed.

Agent Gavin Donnelly arrived at the Indianapolis Federal Bank 15 minutes later. He was directed to the acting bank manager. Agent Donnelly introduced himself to the bank manager, whose name was Jack. He pulled out the piece of paper with the four numbers on it that was found on the victim. He told Jack that he wanted to know about the customers that Franklin White had helped in the safety deposit vault and if he knew anything about the contents of the box with those four digits.

He asked, " Do you have a safety deposit box with these numbers on it?"

Jack looked at him and said. "Yes, those numbers correspond with one of our boxes. "

"Do you have a record of who owns it? "

"Yes, if you give me a minute we can look it up."

Jack went to one of the computers, logged in using his ID and looked up the name of the owner for the box. He told Agent Donnelly the owner was named Michael Harris.

Agent Donnelly asked Jack, "When was the box opened?"

"I can't tell you that," Jack responded. "I would need a court order to give you that information."

"Jack, do you know what obstruction of justice is? If you interfere with this investigation in any way, such as not giving me the information I request, you can be charged with that and it's a felony."

"Look, Agent Donnelly, I will help, but our policy is that we have to ask for a court order to give you that kind of information. I can tell you the name of the owner, but that's it. "

"I can have a court order here in an hour, but I need information now. Every minute counts in our investigation."

"I'm sorry agent, I can't do it. Our clients pay a lot of money for this kind of protection and privacy. "

"I understand and I'll get you the court order, but in the meantime I can call your boss and tell him that you're interfering with a criminal investigation. For someone that is looking for a promotion, that won't look well on you."

Jack stared at Agent Donnelly for a moment with disgust and then replied, "Fine, but I will need the court order here today for our files so I am protected. "

"I will take care of that for you, Jack," Agent Donnelly replied. "Now, when was the box opened?"

Jack looked it up. The box was opened in March of 1983. Michael Harris had the box for 27 years. Agent Donnelly also asked him how many times the box had been accessed. Jack looked that up and said that it had been accessed two times in twenty-seven years: the day it was opened, a week after that, and last Friday. Agent Donnelly had a look as if he had solved a puzzle. There was too much of a coincidence. Based on a hunch, he finally asked who opened the box for Michael Harris in 1983. It was the bank president, Franklin White. He was an Accounts Specialist banker back then. As Jack was looking at the records, he noticed that it was also Franklin White who helped Michael Harris on Friday with his safety deposit box; it was something a little unusual for a Bank President. Now Agent Donnelly was really curious about the connections between the Bank President, his murder, and the safety deposit box.

Agent Donnelly got to thinking. He had a theory about Franklin White; the man might have been involved, more than just helping a good customer. He asked Jack, "Did Franklin White have a safety deposit box here at the bank?" Jack looked that information up, and as it turned out, he did. Jack looked up the entire record of the box because he knew that Agent Donnelly would probably want it. Franklin White opened his box in 1983, a day after he opened the safety deposit box for Michael Harris and he had only accessed it once in 27 years … until Friday.

Agent Donnelly was stunned by the information. There was a connection between the two boxes and their owners. He finally asked Jack, "Has anybody come to open Franklin White's box since Friday, such as his wife? "

"No, and she wouldn't be able to get inside the box because she is not on the account. Mr. White was the only one on the account. Not until she had a death certificate and the property passed to her, but that can take months. "

"Really, I need to see inside of it now."

"Look Agent Donnelly, I've helped you about as much as I can. This is going too far. I need the court order here at the bank before I can do that."

Agent Donnelly gave Jack a stern look. He replied, "And that's the right thing to do in your situation, but I don't have to time to waste. Do you want me to catch his killer?"

"Of course, Frank was my friend."

"Then quit wasting my time and help me. There's a connection between these two boxes and I need to find it out quickly. Every minute counts here. "

Jack paused for a moment and then he finally led Agent Donnelly into the safety deposit box vault. He got Franklin White's box, put it on the table in the room and opened it up. What it contained was the biggest shocker so far. There was a transaction receipt for the cashing of 25 Bearer Bonds, and the date on the receipt was the same date that both safety deposit boxes were accessed. Agent Donnelly looked at the receipt more closely to see what they were worth. They had a value of $1,030,000 today -- over the course of 27 years they had matured into over a million dollars. Agent Donnelly made a quick call. He had a court order delivered to the bank within the next twenty minutes and requested that the receipt be logged into evidence. He asked Jack if anybody might have known about this. He shook his head no, but he did tell Agent Donnelly that Franklin White was looking up information for Michael Harris about how long it would take to cash out of something and have the money transferred to an offshore account. It was going to take two days to complete it. Jack was offering more information now than he was willing to give at first; he couldn't figure out why, but it had to do with being surprised about his friend. He didn't know if Franklin White was a really a victim or a criminal.

As Agent Donnelly was finishing up gathering his evidence, his cell phone started to ring. It was his partner. He answered the phone and she didn't even bother to say hi. She asked him in a stern voice, "Did you find anything useful there or do you want to come back and join the real investigation?"

Agent Donnelly chuckled and then answered, "I did find something; a big piece of the puzzle. "

"What did you find?"

"Franklin White had a safety deposit box there and he had bonds in it. "

"So? What's so surprising about that?" Agent Main asked.

"They were bearer bonds and have not been issued since 1983 by the Treasury Department, but that's not the weird part. He opened the box in 1983 and hadn't gotten into it until Friday -- except a week after it was opened. He got into the box the same day after a customer of his by the name of Michael Harris got into his box and cleared out the contents. Franklin White opened up Michael Harris's safety deposit box in 1983 when he was just an Accounts Specialist at the bank. Both boxes have been opened only twice in 27 years, both on the same day. "

Agent Main had a surprised look on her face while on the other end of the phone. She said to her partner, "Okay, now you have my attention. Why would a bank president have bearer bonds in a safety deposit box that he apparently put in there almost three decades ago and only accessed it the same day a customer (who he created the account for) he has not seen in that length of time accessed their box? "

"I don't know yet," Agent Donnelly replied. "But I bet you anything that what Michael Harris got out of his box last Thursday was the same thing. The new bank manager said that Mr. White was looking up information for this customer on how long it would take to cash something and transfer the money to an off shore account. "

"Sounds like money laundering to me."

"That's what it is, Bearer Bonds are a good way to clean to money. Plus the bonds in Mr. White's box are worth over a million dollars. Sounds like a payoff to me, a clean one. This is where I run a financial background check on Franklin to see what's in his past."

"He may be guilty of fraud, but does it mean he had something to with his murder by a known serial killer?"

"I don't know. There's someone that we need to question about that."

Agent Main paused for a moment and then said, "We can make time to question that person later. We're heading back to Chicago and we're going to question Mickey Soranno about his son's whereabouts."

"That's who I want to question, too. "

Agent Donnelly didn't forget his vision. He was sure that the person in the vision was at a bank somewhere trying to cash some bearer bond, but he didn't know where and it was too late to find out. His visions only showed what was happening 30 minutes in the future. He hoped that a clue would present itself while questioning Mickey Soranno, somebody that had a long history with his own family. It was a Chicago thing!

5

Two hours later, Agent Donnelly and Agent Main were back in Chicago, walking up to the Soranno home in downtown Chicago. Before they walked in, Agent Main needed to get something out in the open -- she wanted to make sure she and her new partner were on the same page before they started questioning a notorious mob boss. She stopped Agent Donnelly before they walked in and said to him:

" Look … before we walk in there, I want to make sure that you know that this is still a murder investigation and his son is the lead suspect. I know you may have a different theory, but the investigation of Franklin White's murder is still our number one priority. "

Agent Donnelly smiled at her. "I know that, Agent Main, and we'll solve this murder. But I doubt that it really was Albert Soranno and there's more to this case than just a murder."

"This is what I am talking about; we need to be on the same page before we walk in there. "

"You ask him questions about the murder and his son and I will ask him about the money conspiracy that we apparently have in this case. He might be able to shed some light on it. "

"Fine, but keep with the task at hand." She was more annoyed than ever because she felt he was undermining her authority. Agent Main was still the lead investigator.

The two agents knocked on the door and a butler of sorts answered the door, the kind that carried a .45. They showed their badges and asked to see Mickey Soranno. The goon who answered the door didn't want to let them in and that's when Gavin replied to him, "Don't let us in and I will have a team of agents here in an hour tearing this place apart. Ask your boss if he wants that. Besides, tell him Gavin Donnelly is here. " Agent Main gave Gavin a weird look, wanting know if his name alone would get them an audience with Mickey Soranno -- turned out, it did. Now she was really surprised. The two agents were led into the kitchen, where Mickey Soranno was cooking.

Mickey was wearing an apron and stirring what looked like marinara sauce. He turned around and said, "Gavin Donnelly, it's been awhile since I've seen you. I see your Uncle Liam a lot more at Church. In fact, we helped raise a lot of money at the Bishop's fall charity last month."

"The FBI keeps me pretty busy. It's not like I'm a police Captain like my uncle where I get a lot of time off," Gavin replied.

" He's earned it, though."

" That he has."

The two men shook hands and Mickey asked him what the visit was about. Gavin told him they had some questions they needed to ask. Mickey said he was glad to help unless they were investigating him. Gavin smiled and said they weren't.

Agent Main finally said something. "Mr. Soranno, we have to ask you about your son Albert. We had a brutal murder last Friday and it was done with his MO. Have you seen your son lately or do you know his whereabouts? "

Mickey got an angry look on his face and, before he answered the question, looked at Gavin and asked him, "Who is this?"

"She's my new partner," he replied. "And you need to answer her questions. I'm sorry we have to ask them … you know the routine."

Mickey gave her a cold look. "My son is gone and I haven't seen or heard from him in five years. Whatever he did back then, he hasn't since."

"How can you be sure of that if you haven't seen or talked to him in five years, Mr. Soranno?" Agent Main responded.

"A father knows. I can tell you don't have children. How do you know for sure that it was Albert who killed this person?"

Gavin spoke up. "We don't know for sure, but the way the murder was done points in his direction. It was done the same way as his victim's years ago. So we have to ask."

"I gave you my answer and until you show me proof that it was him, I won't believe it."

Agent Main asked Mickey another question. "Do you have any enemies that would be killed the same way your son murdered people in order to send you a message? Maybe someone working at the Indianapolis Federal Bank?"

"No, guys in my line of work don't that kind of thing. Two in the back of the head is all you need to send a message. Now I've answered your questions about my son. I won't talk about it anymore unless you bring me downtown and I have my lawyer present."

Agent Main had another question, but Gavin looked at her and shook his head no. She was going to ignore it, but he interrupted and started to ask Mickey a question of his own. Agent Main broke in and asked to step out of the room with her. She was really annoyed with him now. She looked at him sternly and said, "I don't know what you're doing, but I still have more questions about the 'murder' investigation we are conducting on his son. Don't cut me off until I'm done."

Agent Donnelly replied, "There aren't any more questions you can ask him. You are done."

"Now you're out of line."

"Maybe, but I'm not wrong."

"That's not the point. I'm still the lead agent here and I have more questions so I am going to ask them." She started to walk away and go back into the room they just came from when Gavin said to her:

"Agent Main … you think if you ask the same question 10 different ways that Mickey Soranno will finally crack and give you the answer you want? He's not going to give up his son to the FBI."

She turned around and said, "You don't know that. I'm not done questioning him. I can get it out of him."

"He's been drilled by the FBI over and over, and never once cracked under the pressure. I don't care how good you are, he's better. You may not want to hear that, but it's the truth. The bad cop routine won't work with him, trust me. "

She stared at Agent Donnelly with rage. She was madder than hell … mad that she was transferred to Chicago, mad that she had been partnered with a guy who did not belong in the Violent Crimes division, and mad that her ability as an interrogator was being called into question. After a brief pause, she finally responded, "Believe me when I tell you, Agent Donnelly, that I am not like anybody that he's dealt with; I can get him to talk. You're not dealing with some girl fresh from grad school or the Academy. I was the best in Washington and I guarantee you that I am the best here in Chicago."

"That may be true, but this isn't Washington. This is Chicago and you're dealing with the mob here. There are three ways of doing this: the right way, the wrong way, and the Chicago way. The only way to deal with Mickey Soranno is the Chicago way. "

"What is this, *The Untouchables*? We gonna put a gun in his mouth to make him talk?"

"Something like that, but we won't have to do it this time. " He winked at her and walked back into the kitchen.

She was still angry, but she was smart enough to know that Agent Donnelly was partially right. Washington's by-the-book ways would not work here, so she asked Gavin, "What do you want to do?"

"Let me ask him some questions about something besides his son's murders. He just might give up something that's useful to this investigation, the whole investigation. The murder and the bearer bonds are connected. "

She motioned for him to follow her back into the room and, as he was walking by her to take the lead, she said to him, "We'll try it your way, but don't step on my toes."

As they walked into the next room, Gavin apologized for the interruption and said he had some questions over some family history and finances. Mickey jokingly said that Gavin couldn't get him to admit to racketeering charges that easily. Because it was Gavin Donnelly and they all attended the same church, he could make those kinds of jokes. There were no illusions between the two; Gavin knew that Mickey Soranno was a criminal and Mickey didn't try to hide it. He knew that for Gavin to bring him down, he would first have to prove his criminal activities.

Agent Donnelly asked Mickey, "Have you ever invested in any kind of securities, such as bonds, stocks, or CDs?"

Mickey cracked a smile. "My accountants always try to get me to invest in those kinds of things, you know, to make my money the right way; then, I can be making more money with interest. But if I can't see the cash or if my banker can't show it to me then I don't really have it. Cash has no enemies in this world ... my father taught me that."

"So your father, Victor Soranno, never invested in those things before, either?"

"No way, my father was all cash. He didn't even like banks. Hated them more than me. Banks can rob you."

"Mickey, do you know what a bearer bond is?"

"Some kind of bond that I would never have!" Agent Main even cracked a smiled at that comment. It was amusing, even from a gangster.

"Fair enough. Did any of your father's associates ever have anything to do with any kind of money transactions, other than cash?"

Mickey smiled at the questions. "The FBI is constantly watching us. You should know that it's strictly a cash business. "

"I know that, but my partner is new and she's never dealt with the family before." Gavin turned to Agent Main and winked at her again. "The answer is for her benefit."

Agent Main was not amused as the comment, but Mickey laughed.

"No, Gavin, my boy, nothing but cash. And we only clean cash with cash. Anything else can get you robbed by the government and when the mob steals, it's only cash. I'm sure you know how it works with the rules and all. When you do it to another family then you take all the honor out among thieves -- just like they did with my father in 1983."

Gavin was surprised by the comment even though he knew Mickey liked to talk too much. He asked him about it. "What do you mean just like they did with your father?"

"I'm sure you're uncle Liam has told you the story about how my father was set up by the Balduchi family. They stole 20 million dollars in cash from him right before the FBI raided his warehouse. "

"I knew that five million was confiscated by the FBI during the raid, but I did not know about the 20 million that was stolen. "

Mickey chuckled. "Yeah, my father was so worried about his money being stolen by the feds if he put in the bank, or any other kind of what you call securities, that he held onto it all in cash -- only to have it stolen by another family who made a deal with the FBI to get my father. I guess I inherited the same fear. No matter what kind of war may go on with the families, you don't use the FBI to set someone up and then steal their money. No honor, and your grandfather knew that."

Agent Main finally spoke up about Mickey's comment; not about his family history, but about Agent Donnelly's grandfather. "What about his grandfather?"

Mickey looked at her with a mischievous smile. "Since you're new in town and don't know the history yet, let me tell about the Donnelly family tree. His grandfather, Jimmy Donnelly, the former Chicago cop, used to be a bootlegger during Prohibition. He made a small fortune with my father when they were both youngsters."

Agent Main looked at Gavin with a surprised look. "You're grandfather, a cop, was a bootlegger?"

"Yes he was," Gavin replied. "When Prohibition ended, he had to get an honest job and becoming a cop was the next best thing. At least, that's what he thought. "

As soon as Gavin got through saying that, Agent Main's phone rang. She looked at Gavin and told him what the call was about. There was another murder and it was time for them to go. They both thanked Mickey for his time and told him that they would be in touch if they had more questions. Mickey told Gavin to tell his uncle hello for him. Agent Main didn't like that one bit and the look on her face let Gavin know it. As they were walking to the car, she had to ask, "How did your grandfather, a known bootlegger who worked with the mob, become a Chicago police officer?" Gavin smiled and told her:

"He went to work for the guys that he had been paying off when he was running liquor. They were all Irish and from the same neighborhood. It was that easy."

"Is everything about this town corrupt?

"Just the politicians. But this is Chicago, where thieves can become cops and the cops can become thieves. They all go to the same church, pray to the same God, and protect the same neighborhoods … together."

"I guess that's the Chicago way, huh?"

"Yep. Welcome to the Windy City."

6

There was a crowd already surrounding the murder scene by the time Agent Main and Agent Donnelly arrived. People were gathering around the police, trying to get a look and satisfy their curiosity. Chicago PD was the first to arrive after an innocent bystander found the carved up body and they had everything roped off. They had been there two hours, starting their own murder investigation before the FBI was called about the body. The lead homicide detective looked up and saw Agent Donnelly and started shaking his head. It was just his luck that, when FBI was called, it was Gavin Donnelly who showed up. He looked at Agent Donnelly and said:

"Man, I get a murder that the FBI takes over and they send you. God's having a laugh at my expense. "

Agent Donnelly smiled. "They had to send someone smarter than you to solve this case."

"I guess that's why they made you bring a new partner. "

The two men shook hands and laughed. Agent Main was a little confused at first by the banter, but soon realized that they knew each other. Agent Donnelly looked at his new partner and introduced her to the detective, his cousin, Alex Donnelly. He shook her hand and told her jokingly that if Gavin got out of line, she should call him and he would kick his ass. She smiled for a moment and then went back to being serious; she asked him what they had. Alex looked at Gavin and said, "We got a brutal one for your first day on the new job." Alex filled them in on the rest.

The John Doe was found a little over two hours ago in the alley. He was killed early that morning. It was just like other murder in Indiana. The eyes were cut out and the midsection and chest were full of stab wounds and the ears were burned from acid. It was just as brutal as the last body. Agent Main looked at Gavin. "It's the same MO. It looks like the body was done in the same way as Franklin White." When the Chicago PD arrived, the only one that touched the body was a medical examiner who made an initial report about the murder. There was no wallet on the victim, so identifying him took a little time. Chicago PD took his prints and matching those in Chicago CID didn't take too long.

Alex Donnelly looked at his cousin and said in a serious tone, "He's a cop, or was a cop. His name is Michael McGregor; he was a homicide detective out of the 26th Precinct, retired in 1998." Alex went on to explain that after the ME entered her notes about the murder in the CID, which is also monitored by Federal Agencies, the case got flagged for an FBI investigation.

Gavin looked at his cousin. "We had a murder just like this in Indiana last Friday, a bank manager. We're investigating it for a possible serial killing."

Agent Main, while still bending down to look at the body, chimed in as well. "It's also consistent with an old serial killer's case, one who was never caught. "

Alex asked her who it was and she said, "Albert Soranno." His pleasant mood turned to anger and so did the tone of his voice. "This is one of Albert Soranno's victims? He's back, and killing cops?"

Gavin gave his cousin a stern look, knowing how Alex's temper could be. "We don't know that for sure. The murder has similarities, but we're not going to confirm that it's him yet."

"If he's back and killing cops then there's going to be a thousand trigger fingers pointing at the Soranno family. The next time the Feds investigate him, it will be his death. "

Agent Main turned around to face them after looking at the body and said, "There's no reason to sugarcoat what this is. The evidence points to Albert Soranno and Chicago PD has the right to know."

"Let's not try to scare the shit out of everybody here until we have more facts. Republicans around here already do enough of that!"

Gavin bent down to check the pockets of the body; he wanted to see if there was a clue on the body as there was with the bank manager. Sure enough, there was: a piece of paper with a note. It said, *CFB, 9:30 a.m.* It looked as if it was a note reminding the victim of an appointment. Agent Main asked him what he had found as he continued to check the other pockets of the victim. Before he could answer, Gavin saw a vision. *Two men walked into a bank and one of them nodded at a man wearing a long, dark coat, who was sitting down in the lobby and reading a magazine. It was a signal, but Gavin could not figure out for what. The two men walked up to a desk and one of them looked at the bank employee and said, "I am here to get into my box; here is my key and my ID." The men were escorted down the stairs of the main lobby to where the safety deposit boxes were located. Gavin could not make out any of the names on the name tags of the bank employees, but he did see one thing in his vision. The man sitting at a desk outside the safety deposit box vault took a sip out of a green coffee mug that appeared to have a yellow C or G on it. The two men went inside the vault with all the boxes and that was it. Gavin could not see* anymore and rubbed his head as if he were in pain after the vision was gone.

Agent Main asked him if he was okay. He replied, "It's nothing. I just have a headache."

"Did you find something?" she asked him again.

"A piece of paper with what appears to be a reminder on it."

She bent down and looked at it carefully. "What is CFB?" she asked out loud. "

Alex Donnelly and the other detectives who were standing around didn't have an answer. They looked confused by the initials. Gavin thought for a moment and then realized what it was: a connection with the other victim. "Chicago Federal Bank, that's what it stands for."

Alex Donnelly replied, "That's four blocks from here. I guess he stopped off at the bank or was supposed to before somebody killed him."

Gavin looked at his cousin. "You guys canvassed the area, right?"

"Yeah, they're finishing it up as we speak."

"Did anybody go down that far?"

"No. Why would they? It's four blocks away; we wouldn't go that far. "

Agent Main looked at Gavin as he was staring down the street in the direction of the bank. He had a feeling that it was what he saw in his vision earlier that morning. She asked her new partner to take a look at something on the body; there was a strange mark on the spot where the left kidney would be. Gavin turned around and responded, "Show me later. I want to go down to the bank and ask some questions."

"We can do that later. We have a dead body to examine."

"The body is not going anywhere, Agent Main, but the bank is going to close within the hour and I need the time to question employees." Gavin took out his phone, used it to take a picture of the victim's face, and then got in the agent's car and drove off. Agent Main yelled at him to stay, but Gavin had already left. She turned to Alex. "Is he always like this?"

"Like what, Agent Main?"

"A stubborn jackass who doesn't know how to listen."

Alex smiled. "Only when he can't let go of a hunch."

∞∞∞∞∞∞∞∞∞

Gavin walked into the bank. Employees were busy with the end of the day work. After seeing the visions, he didn't have to ask around if anybody had seen the victim. He knew that the person to talk to was the manager over the safety deposit boxes. Gavin walked up to him while he was talking to another employee. He carried his FBI badge in one hand and his phone with the picture of the victim in the other. The manager and the other employee looked surprised when they saw they badge, but it was the other employee who had the strangest look as if he knew he was in trouble. The bank manager responded when he saw the FBI badge.

"Can I help you with something, Agent …"

"Agent Donnelly. I need to know if you recognize this man."

The bank manager was startled by the photo. It was horrifying, even more so because the eyes were missing. He was sickened, but it was to be expected.

Agent Donnelly, why are you showing me this picture? It's disgusting."

"I know, but it's the only photo I have and I need to know if you recognize him. "

The bank manager looked away and didn't want to answer. He felt like throwing up. "I can't tell you anything. The image is too gruesome."

"I think you have seen this person before," Gavin replied in a stern tone. "I'll make you look at it again until you give me answer."

The bank manager was already taking a disliking to him. He replied to Gavin, "The man in the photo was here earlier with another man. They needed to get into a safety deposit box. Christ, was this man murdered?"

"Yes, he was. Did you get a good look at the man with him? I need a description of him. "

"The other man was older, in his sixties maybe. He wore glasses and was a little overweight. Maybe six feet tall. That's all I remember. "

"Did you see what they got out of the safety deposit box?"

"Even if I did, Agent Donnelly, I can't tell you. Our customers' privacy is very important. "

"Let me guess, I need a court order?"

"That's the official policy."

"Look, it's important that we know what was in that box. The victim was murdered right after he left the bank this morning ."

"I can't help you with that."

"Can you at least tell me when the box was opened?"

"Fine, I can do that for you." The manager looked up the information on the computer. "It was opened in 1983. Do you want to know when the other safety deposit box was opened?"

"What other safety deposit box?"

"The two men accessed two different boxes. Now, that's all I can tell you without a court order."

The bank manager was annoyed at all the questions and answers. He kept thinking that he had better things to do and a customer being murdered was never good for business. He finally excused himself and told Agent Donnelly that he had other customers to attend to. Gavin didn't make too much of a fuss about it. He wanted to talk to someone else anyway, someone that might have more information. Gavin waited until the bank manager was out of earshot, then he looked at the other employee and asked him:

"You know what was in the safety deposit boxes, don't you?"

"Agent Donnelly," said the employee. "I can't tell you without the court order. My manager was right about that."

"But you do know what was in there and what the two men came here for?"

"I ..."

"It's okay. You just gave yourself away, so you might as well answer my questions. "

"I don't want to get into trouble."

"Then help me out and I won't file obstruction of justice charges against you. You'd be really fucked then."

The employee gave Gavin a dirty look and said, "They took bearer bonds out of the boxes."

"You saw them take the bonds out of the boxes?"

"No, but the two men came to my department to inquire about cashing them and doing wire transfers."

"Did they cash the bonds and complete the wire transfers?"

"Not at all. We told them that, by federal law, we have to wait two days to verify everything before we cash them out. The older gentleman got mad and cursed at us."

"What did they do after that? Did they leave?"

"Not right away. The older gentleman showed me his badge, his FBI badge, and told us that we didn't have to wait two days for a federal agent. He had the authority to override the waiting period."

Gavin now had a look of shock. What was an FBI agent doing with a murder victim and bearer bonds? He didn't need to see a vision to know that there was something bigger to this case and it had nothing to do with Albert Soranno. With a surprised tone he asked:

"Are you sure it was an FBI badge?"

"Yes, sure, it said FBI on it."

"Did it look like this?" Gavin showed him his FBI badge. "Was it exactly like this?"

"Uh, no. His had a different design. And it didn't have the hologram-looking thing that yours does."

"I don't suppose you got a name?"

"He said his name was Michael Harris."

"Was his name on one of the boxes?"

"Yes."

"What was the name on the other box?"

The employee had to go back to his computer to look up the information. He told Agent Donnelly that the name on the box was Michael McGregor and that the box was opened in 1983 … the same day as the one for Michael Harris. Agent Donnelly, covering all his bases, asked him how many times the boxes had been accessed in the past 27 years. The employee answered:

"The boxes were accessed two times since the day they were opened: two weeks after they were opened and then today."

Agent Donnelly reached out to shake the bank employee's hand and thanked him for his help. Those were all the questions he needed to ask and he got more information than he expected. It was shocking news because now it sounded as if there was a conspiracy, but he was wise enough to not give into such thoughts and only rely on the facts. There were still too many questions, but there was a connection with the safety deposit boxes … the same owner for two of them, bearer bonds in the boxes, and two dead bodies with the same MO. He headed back to the crime scene. He had a favor to ask of his cousin, Alex.

When he got back to the crime scene, the body was already being loaded into an ambulance and on its way back to the morgue. Agent Main looked up and asked with an annoyed tone, "Did you find out anything?"

"Yes, the victim was at the bank this morning with another gentleman and they were accessing two safety deposit boxes."

"Did you find out what was in the boxes?"

"Bearer bonds, Agent Main. The men withdrew them and tried to cash them. One of the boxes was owned by Michael Harris and the other one was owned by our Michael McGregor. "

"Just like before."

"Yep. Now we have a connection and a very big question of why!"

Gavin walked over to his cousin and said, "I need a favor. Still have your buddy in IAD that gives you tips?"

Alex, looking surprised, responded, "Yeah. What do you need from IAD?"

"I need him to find out the names of any Chicago police officer that opened up a safety deposit box in 1983, in any city."

"You think that has something to do with the victim?"

"Yes, and I want to know if other Chicago PD officers are involved or if this really is Albert Soranno. If we can get a suspect list for his next murders, then we might be able to catch him … or whoever the real murderer is."

"You're FBI. Why can't you get that information?"

Gavin looked over his shoulder to see if his partner was listening; she wasn't. "The other gentleman with our victim showed the bank employees an FBI badge. It may have been a fake, but if it's not, and FBI agents are involved, then they'll be watching this case … including the information we access from our office. I have to do this quietly. Chicago IAD can get it without the FBI knowing about it. "

Alex looked stunned. "You think FBI is involved now? Shit, man, your job just got really hard."

"I hope I'm wrong. Can you call your friend and see if he can get me that information?"

"I'll call him. How do you want the information to get you if you're being watched?"

Gavin smiled. "Send flowers to my office."

∞∞∞∞∞∞

Agent Michael Harris and Larry Crane stood in the safety deposit box vault at the bank. Two safety deposit boxes were put on the table and opened. Inside were bearer bonds. Agent Harris spoke up. "Larry, it looks like you can now enjoy your retirement."

"Thank you. It's been worth the wait," Larry responded.

Agent Harris handed Larry Crane an envelope. "This is the information for your new Swiss bank account, where the deposit will be made. You will not be able to access it for 30 days until all of our transactions have been made and we have left the country."

"I've waited 27 years. Thirty more days won't be that big of a deal."

Agent Harris smiled at the comment. The two men emptied the boxes and handed over the bearer bonds to a bank employee so he could cash them and begin the wire transfer. This bank was a little more lenient on the two-day waiting period; a small bribe could take care of that. After about ten minutes, the transactions were done. Agent Harris and Larry Crane walked out of the bank together. A man in a black overcoat, who had been sitting in the lobby, followed behind them. As Agent Harris and Larry walked around the corner, the man in the black coat walked up behind them.

He grabbed Larry from behind and stuck a sharp, burning object into his kidney, causing him to lose his balance and fall forward. Larry shouted, "Why? I did what you asked of me!"

[43]

Agent Harris looked down at Larry and replied, "You did, and we thank you, but we cannot have any witnesses."

Before Larry could respond, he was stabbed from behind in the heart with a knife. Blood began to fall and form a small pool at his feet. He stared at it for a moment before everything went black. He wasn't quite dead, but that would come later.

7

It was Tuesday morning and the leads were thin. Theories were all Agent Main and Agent Donnelly had. Gavin got to work early, 6:00 a.m. to be exact. He finished setting up his new office, including laying everything out about the case they were working on, all the old files on Albert Soranno and the files on the new murders. He lined up everything in an order where he could try to establish the connections. At 7:30, Agent Main walked into the office to find Gavin sitting on the small table, facing the peg boards that held pictures of murder victims.

She asked, "How early did you get here?"

"6 o'clock."

"You didn't think you could solve the whole case before I got here, did you?"

"No, but I wanted to get a head start and have everything laid out before you came in so we could work."

"Good idea. We've got a lot to work on." She looked over and saw that she had a desk now, and a phone. She looked over at his desk, which was already setup. Not many personal items, but he did have a picture of Wrigley Field and a Chicago Cubs banner hanging up behind the desk. Agent Main smiled to herself. She had to ask, "I thought all you Irish lads were White Sox fans?"

Gavin looked at her and laughed. "Most are, being from the south side and all, but I became a Cubs fan as a kid. I always liked the underdog and the kids I didn't like growing up were Sox fans, so I wanted to get back at them. May not be good reasons, but there are my reasons for being a Cubs fan. "

Agent Main smiled again. It was a new day and she wasn't as annoyed at her new partner as the day before. "Well, let's get to work," she commented. "It's going to be a long one. "

Gavin took a sip of coffee. "Alright, let's get to it. Over here, I have the eight victims that we know Albert Soranno killed." He pointed to the peg board. And over here, our two latest victims with the same MO." He pointed to the dry erase board, which had a line connecting the victims and words describing the bank accounts and owners.

Agent Main looked at the board. "You didn't find a connection with the eight victims from five years ago. "

"And neither did the other agents who worked on this case."

"Because there wasn't a connection; they were chosen randomly. That much the other agents got right. "

"But how did he choose them? And if he committed these murders then how did he choose these two? That's the question."

"Then let's try to find the answer." Agent Main picked up the first file to the Albert Soranno case and started talking the about the case as if she were a professor of forensics.

"There were seven murders, all committed in a 10-month period between April 2004 and February 2005. Albert Soranno's first murder, the FBI figured was committed in 2000. The first murder was a simple stabbing: two stab blows, and very sloppy. It appeared that the first stabbing was done in a panic and wasn't planned. The other two stab wounds came from the rush of taking a man's life. That's when Albert got his first taste for killing. There was nothing spectacular about the murder; it was done by an amateur. Albert got better, though. The next murders were about developing his craft. His second victim, Mary Harris, was killed with two stab wounds and had multiple incisions on her chest, as if somebody had been operating on her."

"The third murder, Gerald Stevens, was stabbed once in the kidney and had multiple incisions on his chest. This time, they were sewn up. The next four murders were done with the current MO: multiple stab wounds and carvings on the chest, the eyes were cut out, and the ears were burned with acid. The unique thing about these four murders was that the carvings or incisions were more precise and could've been done with the hands of a talented surgeon. The last murder wasn't as elaborate as the previous. He was rushed because an eyewitness caught him at the church clinic where he would perform his murders. Albert Soranno didn't even have time to completely prepare for his ritual. There were prints and DNA at the scene and that's how Albert Soranno was identified as the killer of the previous murders. There was no connection between the victims. He disappeared and was never heard from again after that night. Now, we have two more murders done with the same MO, but sloppy and without the same precision as his old murders. And these two victims have a connection."

Agent Main took a moment and paused, staring at the board with an intense look. The wheels were turning in her head, but as good as she might be, even she couldn't solve this thing in just a few minutes. There were too many questions without answers. As Gavin stared at the ME's report on the original murders, Agent Main finally spoke up. "How does someone like this become a killer? What is it in his nature that makes him do such horrific acts?"

Gavin looked up at her. "Then let's take a look at the past and see if we can answer that question." Gavin started lecturing about Albert's past. "Albert Soranno, the only son of Mickey Soranno, born in 1979. Never took part in the family business, educated in private school, went away for college at Columbia University. Then, came back home and went to medical school at Northwestern University. He wanted to be a doctor ever since he was a young boy because of his love for helping people. He was at the top of his class in medical school, graduated in 2004. Albert Soranno grew up in the Catholic church, was an altar boy and deeply religious. The free clinic at his church that was started by the Soranno family was his idea and, before going to college and during medical school, he spent a lot of time there helping low income families that couldn't get medical attention anywhere else. This was a big part of his life until April of 2004 when he committed the first serial murder."

Agent Main responded, "But none of that explains what drove him to kill. He never had anything to do with the family business. He chose the career of saving lives." She paused for a moment and then asked a question. "What kind of doctor did he want to be? What kind of residency was he going to do?"

Gavin looked the file. "He wanted to be a surgeon; he got high marks when he did his rotation in surgery. But after graduating medical school, he never got a residency for surgery. No hospital in the Chicago Area would give him one. "

"Why, he had the marks?"

"There are no notes that give us a reason why he didn't get one."

Agent Main thought for a moment. "Was there anything that happened with the Soranno family in 2004. "

"Well, Mickey was indicted on conspiracy to commit murder in March of 2004 and went to trial for it that summer. He was never convicted. "

Agent main chuckled. "I bet you anything that he was denied a residency because of who his father was and what happened that year with the indictment."

"Makes sense, everything around here is political, even with the hospitals. No matter how good you are, if they just don't like you, you'll be shut out and denied."

"Now we have motive, a reason for him to kill."

"But if its revenge that he wants, wouldn't he exact that revenge on the people that wronged him or somebody close to him?"

"True, so we see if there is a connection to any of the doctor's head of surgery at various hospitals that would have denied his residency, or friends or relatives that would have wronged him. "

After about an hour of doing research among the different hospitals and running the names in the FBI database, Agent Main and Agent Donnelly came up with nothing. There were no connections. It was a worth a try. Agent Donnelly finally came back to a question he had about the ME's reports an hour before.

He poured himself another cup of coffee. "You know, there was something in the ME report from those seven murders that I was curious about. They ran toxicology reports on the victims and found high traces of a drug called Pancuronium, but dismissed it as not being important or related to cause of death. But it was in all the victims; that's not a coincidence. Do you know what the drug is?"

"Yeah, it's a neuroblocker, a common surgical drug. Doctors use it along with anesthesia for surgery. It dulls the nerves so the patient doesn't feel the pain. All the victims killed between 2004 and 2005 had the drug in their system; that should have never been dismissed. I can't believe the agents before didn't catch it. "

"Maybe because it was a common drug, it was dismissed."

"Sure, but there's another connection that was missed. If Pancuronium was found in their system then they had surgery … all the victims were patients!"

Gavin nodded his head and went back to his computer to start looking at hospital records for all the victims. After about ten minutes, he found what they all had in common. All the victims were surgical patients from Cook County Hospital in Chicago between April 2004 and February 2005.

Agent Main started shuffling through files on the conference table. "Cook County Hospital … I recognize that name from the records of the Soranno family."

"They funded a free health clinic through Cook County Hospital, started it ten years ago. After medical school, that's where Albert Soranno spent most of his time, along with the free health clinic at the church. He had access to the hospital and patient files. It was the closest he came to being a doctor at Cook County Hospital."

Agent Main had an astonished look on her face; she figured out the pattern, how Albert Soranno found his victims. She commented, "That's how he picked his victims. They were patients at Cook County; that's how they're all connected. They weren't just picked at random."

"Okay," Gavin replied. "But it still doesn't explain why he killed them. Why these people? Were they terminally ill? Were they special somehow?"

Agent Main paused and examined the board. She looked closely at the wounds, studying them, being drawn to the precision Albert Soranno mastered. She looked for the pattern. After a few moments she answered.

"Go with me on this theory. These victims were not picked because they have any special connection to each other. The only thing they have in common is that were patients at the same hospital that Albert Soranno volunteered at in the free clinic set up by his family. That gave him access to patient files. The work he did on these victims were of a surgical nature, as if he was practicing his craft. He got better at it with each victim. He didn't kill these people because he wanted them dead; they were just a tool for him to show off with. He wanted to show the world that he was a great surgeon. He wanted to show those that rejected him what he could do, and he selected patients from the hospital so he could send a message that surgical procedures he did were better than what they could do. This is the not the work of a psychopath, but the work of a sociopath showing off. He's trying to impress the medical community. "

Gavin nodded in agreement. "It's the best theory I've heard, but there are still too many questions that need answers. One, the ME report said that each victim had needle marks on the arms and it looked like the victims were drug addicts. But according to toxicology reports, there weren't any illegal drugs found in their systems; the only drug that was found was Pancuronium. Why needle marks if they weren't really drug addicts."

Agent Main thought for a moment. "He was the one injecting them with the neuroblocker, but why?"

Gavin smiled a strange thought. "He didn't want them to feel the pain as he killed them; he felt guilty about what he did. He still thought of himself as a professional surgeon, not a killer, even though he was."

"And the eyes were cut out so the victims didn't see what he was going to do, while the ears were burned so they didn't hear their own screams. I don't know for sure whether that's completely demented or brilliant."

"Probably both. No matter how much of a monster he may be, that deeply religious part of him always came out and made him feel guilty. Your analysis of this case is brilliant, but it doesn't explain these latest murders."

Agent Main sat down at the conference table and her look of satisfaction went away. She had more unanswered questions. After a moment's pause, she spoke up again. "Serial killers have been known to change their MOs to throw the authorities off their scent."

"Yeah, but doesn't changing the MO mean changing the way they kill people, not changing to victims that have a connection with each other?"

Agent Main sighed. "And that's what makes this hard to figure out. The latest victims were killed with more of a deliberate purpose, almost like they were … assassinated. Why these guys? Why did they have to die?"

Gavin walked to board and pointed to the bearer bond transfer receipt from the Indianapolis Federal Bank. "Because they knew too much. They knew the secret behind the bearer bonds and why they had been sitting in a safety deposit box for 27 years. They also got part of the money, which I bet they were never meant to have. Whoever is pulling the strings made sure they were going to die. I think this is an assassination."

"You think this is a copycat murder and Albert Soranno really isn't our guy?"

Gavin smiled at his partner. "The only thing I know for sure is that this doesn't make sense and we have too many unanswered questions. But one way we can be sure is to run a toxicology report on the latest victims. If this is a true copycat murder, then we should see Pancuronium or some other kind of neuroblocker in their systems."

"That, we both agree on." She picked up the phone and called the medical examiner's office at the Chicago Field office and ordered a toxicology examination on the latest victims. It would take the whole day to get back.

Agent Main gave Gavin a serious look. "If this a copycat murder, there's another way to help verify it. We have an expert at the FBI that we can talk to, right here in Chicago, in fact. If anybody will definitely know, it's him. He's an expert in killing. "

"Who is he?"

"Dr. Steven Larkin."

"I've heard of him. He's a forensics professor at the University of Illinois at Chicago. Why is he the expert?"

"Because he used to be a copycat serial killer and the best one we ever caught. His real name is Dr. Henry Lee Roark, or as everybody knows him, Dr. Death."

"I thought he was shot and killed."

"No, that was the story we put out to the public. He really came to work for us."

Gavin smiled and responded sarcastically, "The FBI budget is well spent."

As they grabbed their coats and started to walk out of the office, Agent Main replied in her sarcastic tone, "You've got to love the assets we have here at the FBI."

8

The University of Illinois at Chicago campus was busy. Students were hustling about, trying to get to class. It was two weeks into the spring semester. For both Agent Main and Agent Donnelly, it had a long time since they had been on a college campus, rushing to get to class. Things looked very different from their days in college, mainly the wide use of cell phones and text messaging. They walked into one of the science buildings and bumped into a student who was halfway out the door in a hurry. The student said he was sorry and Gavin politely told him to watch where he was going. He looked at his partner and commented, "I don't ever remember being in that much of a rush when I was in college."

She laughed. "You were a college kid. You were probably drunk."

A lecture was just ending in one of the lab classrooms when the agents walked in. There he was gathering his things, Dr. Steven Larkin, or as the world knew him, Dr. Death. Agent Main spoke up and said, "Dr. Larkin, I was wondering if we could get some help on a case."

Dr. Larkin looked up and smiled. He had always liked Agent Main, even though she was the one who caught him. He thought she was beautiful and that's why he flirted, perhaps a little too much. "Agent Rachel Main," he replied. "To what do I owe the pleasure?"

"We have a case and need your expertise."

"I get to see your beautiful smile and hear you flatter me. It must be my lucky day."

While flirtations like these might be annoying to some women, Agent Main just laughed it off. He may have been a killer at one time, but he was still charming, unlike the psychopaths she usually dealt with. She responded, "Cool off, doctor, this isn't a social call."

"Well, that is disappointing. I have hoped that one day you'll realize how magical we can be. After all, you were the only one to catch my eye."

"I'm sure the young girls on campus never grab your attention," she said sarcastically.

"I'd be lying if I said that wasn't my favorite perk of this job. So, who did you bring with you?"

"This is my new partner, Agent Gavin Donnelly."

"He's not from Washington; he's from here. You got transferred to Chicago."

"Yes, I did."

Dr. Larkin smiled. "Both of us in the same city… this is my lucky day!"

Gavin interrupted by reaching out his hand to shake Dr. Larkin's. "Dr. Larkin, I've heard a lot about you … a lot of surprising details."

Dr. Larkin shook Gavin's hand. "I'm glad that, with all your years in the FBI, they can still surprise you. Isn't it amazing how a guy like me can end up working for the Bureau?"

Agent Main spoke up. "We have a couple of serial killings. We think it's a guy that has never been caught, but it might be a copycat. We need you to take a look at some photos and tell us if it is."

Dr. Larkin was intrigued. He was on the run for years before he was caught. All killers competed to be the best, even if they didn't know they were competing. He didn't like to hear that there was another serial killer that had never been captured…somebody that was better than him. "Who's the guy that's never been caught?"

"Albert Soranno."

"It's been, what, five years since there was a murder done by him?"

"Until the other day. A bank manager in Indianapolis and a retired Chicago police officer right here in the city."

"Let me see the photos of the latest victims and from his old murders."

Agent Main pulled out a folder from her briefcase and handed it to Dr. Larkin. He spread the photos out on the lecture table at the front of the laboratory classroom and examined them carefully. He took a few minutes to really look at them and then he spoke.

"It's hard to tell. If this is Albert Soranno, then he's rusty when it comes to the cuts in the chest. Also, before it looked like he used a scalpel, just like a surgeon would. On the last two victims, he used a knife, a military grade knife called the Markarian. To the untrained eye, it might look the same, but it's not. The blows to these latest victims are more deliberate, have more force to them, and the cuts are deeper. They were killed differently."

Gavin responded, "Does that mean it wasn't Albert Soranno?"

"That's not what I am saying. It's hard to tell."

"Can you take a look at all the photos and give us a more definitive answer?"

Dr. Larkin looked again at the photos, even more carefully. He looked at the photo of Michael McGregor and, when he saw a small mark that looked burned where the kidney was, he paused and had a strange look on his face. Agent Main didn't catch it, but Gavin did. After a few more minutes he spoke.

"If this is a copycat kill, it's a very good one. The killer is somebody who definitely knows how to kill and probably had some training, military training, maybe. But there's an obvious question I'm sure you two have already asked. How would this killer know the exact details of Albert Soranno's murder without the case file … unless it is him? I'm pretty sure the FBI never released these kinds of details to the public."

Agent Main replied, "No, those details would never have been released. So, Dr. Larkin, do think this is Albert Soranno or a really good copycat killer?"

"Probably Albert Soranno. This is too good of copycat killing and it's more plausible that Albert just got better at killing people. The details of a killing change with the type of weapon you use. Besides, it doesn't have the flair that comes from a copycat killer."

Gavin asked the question before Agent Main could. "What flair?"

"Agent Donnelly, a copycat killer only murders for two reasons: to show off their skill, that they can recreate a murder by another killer and do it better. The other reason is to pay homage to a killer that they admire. By that reasoning, these latest two murders are neither of those."

Gavin was not happy by the answer, but he understood the logic behind it. However, he knew something that his partner and Dr. Larkin didn't know. He had seen more details about the crimes and had more facts than what was in those photos. Nothing so far in this case was what it seemed.

Agent Main asked the good doctor, "So, you think that we really are looking for Albert Soranno?"

"Based on those photos, you have a killer that has adapted and changed his ways. He has gotten meaner …more gruesome … more precise. I think you are looking for Albert Soranno, but he's not the same man he was five years ago. Of course, I don't know what the connections between the victims are, but the man who killed them was calculated about their suffering. He wanted the world to know how can cruel he could be. And I bet you anything this is just the beginning. "

"Why is that?"

"Because he has the taste again and it's too hard to get rid of. The only way to quell the urge is to get caught or to get killed."

Gavin spoke up. "But Albert Soranno was never caught. Does that still apply to him?"

"He was almost caught and went into hiding. That's a prison in itself for any serial killer that likes it. "

Agent Main asked the doctor, "Is there anything else you can tell us?"

Dr. Larkin replied, "Nothing else I can tell that you don't already know."

"Are you sure?" Gavin asked.

Dr. Larkin didn't even look at Gavin when he answered. "There's nothing else." That confirmed it for Agent Gavin Donnelly; it was a lie. He suspected the doctor of not telling them everything and now he knew it for sure. Agent Main gathered up the photos and shook Dr. Larkin's hand as she thanked him for his help. Gavin shook his hand as well and that's when he saw a vision involving Dr. Larkin. *The doctor was in his office. He reached back into the closet behind some boxes, where a safe was located. It had an alphanumeric keyboard. Dr. Larkin typed in a nine digit code to open it. Inside were a couple of passports, a gun, a stack of cash, and some thick files. He pulled a file folder out that had two words on it "The Ghost." He took it out and went back to his desk and started reading. That was all Gavin saw.*

As the two agents were about to leave, Agent Main got a phone call. There was another murder fitting the same MO as the previous two. She looked at her partner and said,

"There's been another one, this time in Milwaukee. We have to go to the field office there."

Gavin paused for moment,. He knew that another one was coming and now he felt sick to his stomach. He had seen another vision the day before, but knew now that he wasn't in time to save a life. He replied, "It's an hour away from here. I'll drive."

9

It was already late afternoon when Agent Donnelly and Agent Main arrived at the Milwaukee FBI field office to examine the body of Larry Crane, the latest murder victim with the Soranno MO. The body had been found the night before and was left to rot in an alley for most of the day. Gavin and Agent Main walked into the ME'S office. The ME was standing over the body, which was already laid out for the agents to examine.

The ME asked, "Are you the agents they called in to look at the body?"

Agent Main replied, "We are."

"Good, then can somebody tell me the reason for the urgency to get my report on the body? I have other cases that have been waiting a lot longer."

"Well, doctor … "

"Dr. Barnes."

"Well, Dr. Barnes, this one takes priority. It's the third serial killing in the last few days. We're not any closer to solving this case than we were this morning, so we need all the details you have ASAP."

The doctor's annoyance turned to sympathy; she felt bad for her abrupt tone before. Dr. Barnes began to tell them what she had found. The victim had carvings in the chest as if they were done by a surgeon and made with a military grade knife. The eyes were cut out and the ears were burned with acid.

Agent Main asked the doctor, "Do you have a time of death?"

"He was killed yesterday, morning probably. Been dead for at least 16 to 18 hours."

Gavin finally spoke up and asked the question that had been lingering on his mind since they got the call. "Did you run a toxicology exam on him yet?"

"Yes, and there was nothing unusual about it."

"Did you find a drug called Pancuronium, or any other kind of neuroblocker, in his system?"

Dr. Barnes gave him a strange look. It was not the kind of drug she would expect to find in a murder victim; that would be suspicious. She took another look at the toxicology report and her notes. "There were no traces of neuroblockers in the victim's system."

Gavin gave his partner a satisfied look. They found another big piece of the puzzle. Agent Main responded, "Call the ME's office in Chicago and see if they have the toxicology reports back on the other victim." Agent Main was a little annoyed. She was sure that her theory about the murders was correct, but then again, there were too many things unexplained. It led her doubting what she originally believed. As Gavin made the phone call, she walked over to the body to take a closer look. She was looking for something in particular, something she had seen on the other two bodies.

She asked the doctor for help to turn the body over. The doctor asked her what she was looking for. Agent Main told her that she was looking for a mark on the back around the kidneys. Sure it enough, it was there; a small piercing on the lower left part of the back. Agent Main said to the doctor, "Look at that mark. Does it look to you like that skin has been burned as it was being pierced?"

Dr. Barnes ran her hand over the mark and looked more closely. "Agent Main, you may be right. It feels like the skin was burned as something pierced it, some kind of hot metal object. It would be hard to notice with the amount of decomposition on the body … unless you knew what you were looking for. The object would have to be very thin and rounded. Plus, once you pull the object out, the wound will be burned shut."

"Something like an ice pick or soldering iron?"

"Yeah, that would probably work."

"Why use those particular objects?"

"To pierce the kidney or the nerves around the area and make the body go limp."

Agent Main paused for a moment and thought about what the doctor said. She commented, "If the body is limp or subdued, then it makes it easier to kill them, especially if they fall to the ground."

Dr. Barnes replied, "It's a clever way to kill someone: make them limp so they can't fight back."

Gavin walked back into the room and said to his partner, "The reports are in."

Agent Main replied, "Let me guess … "

Gavin interrupted before she could finish her sentence. "There were no traces of Pancuronium or any other neuroblockers in their systems. In fact, there were no traces of any kind of drug except blood pressure medication."

"Still doesn't mean that the murders weren't done by Albert Soranno. He still could have changed his MO."

"Sure, but it also means that it's not a true copycat killer."

"Maybe Dr. Larkin was right. This is Albert Soranno and he just got better ... killing with more purpose."

Gavin chuckled at the thought. "While that may be true, it doesn't answer the question: Why these latest men? They weren't picked at random." Agent Main gave her partner a disappointed look.

Gavin looked at Dr. Barnes and asked her, "Where was the body found?"

She answered, "It was found in an alley among some homeless people on Brewer Street."

Gavin pulled out his iPhone and started looking up information on the maps feature. He wanted to see what was around the area of Brewer Street. What he was looking for was five blocks away from where the body was dumped. He said to Agent Main, "The Milwaukee Federal Bank is five blocks from where the body was found. I'll bet you a pint of beer that he was at that bank yesterday morning before he was killed."

"Okay," she replied." That's too much coincidence for me."

"There's a connection to that bank and we need to question them."

"That's the second time I actually agree with you."

Agent Main looked at Dr. Barnes and told her that the body needed to be moved to the Chicago field office and her report needed to be sent there as well. The body was part of an ongoing investigation to which they had more questions than answers. Agent Donnelly and Agent Main left the ME's office for the federal bank to try to answer some of those questions. Before they left the office, Dr. Barnes spoke up.

"Do you want the report on the victim's prints? They were run through the FBI database and were flagged."

Agent Main replied, "Why were they flagged?"

"Larry Crane was a retired Chicago police officer. He got flagged because he used to be a cop."

Gavin and Agent Main gave each other a surprised look. This was the second former Chicago police officer killed this week. Gavin asked the doctor if that information had been released yet; she said no. He told his partner that they needed to keep it classified for as long as possible or it would cause unwanted shockwaves in the department. They would want to take justice into their own hands and it would impede their investigation. Agent Main agreed.

∞∞∞∞∞∞∞∞

It was late afternoon by the time Agent Donnelly and Agent Main arrived at the bank. They went straight to the safety deposit box area to find the manager. They found him by the desk of the vault employee. Gavin noticed something on the employee's desk: a green coffee mug with a yellow G. It was a Green Bay Packers coffee mug and Gavin had seen it in his vision. He felt sick to his stomach again. This was the bank he had seen the day before and now it was too late; another murder had occurred. Agent Main showed her badge to the manager and the employee, then introduced herself and Agent Donnelly. Jerry, the manager, was surprised to see the badge and asked her:

"Are you here about a bond transfer, too? Just like the other agent from yesterday?"   Agent Main gave him a shocked look. "What other agent?"

"He was here yesterday with the older man, cashing some bearer bonds and doing a money transfer. The two day waiting period was waived for him since he was a federal agent. You're here today, so I just thought that it was about the same thing."

Before Agent Main could say anything, Gavin responded, "Did he introduce himself as Agent Michael Harris?"

The manager replied, "Yeah. Is he from your department?"

"Did his badge look like this?" Gavin pulled out his badge and showed it to the manager. "

"No, it looked older and didn't have the hologram logo that yours does."

Agent Main was pissed and she didn't hide it on her face. Before she could say anything, Gavin pulled out a photo of the victim, Larry Crane, and showed it to the manager. "Was this man here yesterday with the agent?"

The manager cringed at the photo of the dead body, but he answered the question. "Yeah, that's him. Is this man dead?"

"Yes, he was murdered after leaving the bank."

The manager was shocked. They had never had a customer who was murdered right after leaving the bank, not even when they were robbed a few years ago. After a moment's pause, the manager replied, "Do you think it was the man in the black overcoat that followed them out of the bank when they were done?"

"What man in a black overcoat?"

"There was man wearing a black overcoat, sitting in the lobby, that followed them out of the bank. I didn't think anything of it until you said the guy in the photo was murdered."

"Did you see his face?"

"No."

Agent Main spoke up. "We're going to need your security tapes, and I don't want any hassles over court orders to see them. We're going to view them here." Then she looked at her partner and said in an angry tone, "I need to see you outside … now."

The agents walked outside and that's when she laid into him, angry as hell. "You lied to me! You knew yesterday about this Agent Michael Harris. Why did you keep that piece of information from me?"

Gavin looked at her with a sympathizing look, trying to get back on her good side. "Because I didn't have all the facts yet."

"Bullshit. You don't think that's a detail I should know for this investigation?"

"Would it have made any difference in you trying to solve the Albert Soranno case?

"What's that supposed to mean?"

Gavin stared at her for a moment to see if she could figure out that answer herself. Then he replied in a stern tone, "You've been so hell-bent on solving the Albert Soranno murders that you've missed some important facts ... the main one being that he may not be our guy and we're only meant to think he is."

"Well, I might be more inclined to entertain that idea if my partner wouldn't keep things from me."

Gavin paused for a moment and said to her, "I'm sorry for that, but I also had my reasons."

"Such as?"

"If this Agent Michael Harris really is an FBI agent … I ran his name last night in our database. "

"And what did you find out?"

"The only Agent Michael Harris that's ever been in the FBI was an agent from the 50's and 60's. He died in 1966, shot and killed in the line of duty."

"So this guy isn't real and is using a fake badge?"

Gavin raised his voice little bit. "Or he is a real agent, but using a different name."

"You think somebody in the FBI is involved?"

"Agent Main, I don't think you're ready for what I think."

She was livid. Her professionalism and intelligence were being questioned. She wanted to hit Agent Donnelly because he infuriated her to no end ... or maybe it was that she was in Chicago, but it was probably both. She took a deep breath and tried to calm herself. Then she responded, "Fine, let's say that's true. What better theory do you have?"

Gavin looked at her with a serious look and started talking. "Alright then, I don't think this has anything to do with Albert Soranno. He's not our guy, but we've been led to believe he is because of the MO with these murders. While it's not a perfect copycat killing, it's good enough to make us chase the wrong guy. Think about it; if we're looking for Albert Soranno, we won't be looking in the right direction and see what's really going on."

"Okay, it's the start of a good theory, but who do you think is really behind this?"

"It has to be someone with access to the FBI files on Albert Soranno. That's the only way to get enough details on the murders in order to do a copycat killing. That's why it could be a real agent using a different name."

"So what about the bearer bonds being stashed away for 27 years?"

"That I don't know, but it takes a long time for them to mature and be worth the kind of money that those transactions were for. They're worth more because of the type of bond they are. Bearer bonds haven't been issued since 1983. The victims who received bearer bonds and hid them in their own safety deposit boxes would earn at least a few million dollars after all these years. It's almost like a payoff for keeping a secret. But why are two former Chicago police officers involved? That's the bigger question. The bank manager, I can understand; if he was the one who opened up the box and cashed them out years later, they would bribe him for his silence."

Agent Main replied, "If this has something to do with Chicago PD, the easiest way to find any connection is to see what police officers opened up a safety deposit box the same year these were opened."

"I already did."

"When did you put the request in with the Bureau?"

"Yesterday, but I didn't make it through the Bureau. I made an unofficial request for that information with Chicago Internal Affairs."

"Why? We have better resources."

"Because of this so-called Agent Michael Harris. If someone in the FBI is involved, then they will be monitoring the information we request and that will tip them off that were closing in on them. I don't want to take that chance, so I called in a favor and did this unofficially."

"Don't you think it will be a little suspicious when Chicago IAD delivers that information to our office if we're being monitored?"

Gavin laughed. "It would be if it was coming that way, but here in Chicago we have another way to pass information to one another off the record. We send flowers." Agent Main gave him a funny look. Of course she would be confused by this since she was not from Chicago. Gavin replied, "Doyle's Flower Shop on the south side will send flowers with the information tucked inside. They delivered mine to our office 30 minutes ago."

Agent Main was really annoyed at this point. She turned away and cursed. Gavin asked her, "What are you so mad about? That I may be right?"

"Yeah, that does annoy me, but I'm pissed off at this case. It should be black and white, but you got me investigating some goddamn conspiracy involving the Chicago PD and money laundering and the passing of secret information. We're the FBI and not the CIA. Only in Chicago, goddamnit."

Gavin laughed at her again. "What can I say, we don't like our criminals to be boring. And although it's never easy in Chicago, we're professionals and we can handle it. Right?"

She turned to him and gave him half a smile. She replied, "Let's take a look at the security tapes and check if we can see the man in black's face. Then we'll be head back to the office and take a look at this information you got. "

Gavin and Agent Main walked back into the bank and, after about 20 minutes of watching security tapes, didn't get what they were looking for. The man in black knew where the cameras were and hid his face so it wouldn't be seen. The man in black was the biggest mystery so far, a shadowy figure with no identity who just might be the real killer they were looking for. The agents went back to Chicago hoping to find some answers among the bouquet of tulips sitting on Gavin's desk.

10

The hotel suite looking out over Lake Michigan was dark, too dark for the middle of the day, but the old man liked it that way. He was waiting on a phone call. The man in black knocked three times on the door to let the old man know that he was back and then walked into the hotel suite. As he walked in with a bag of food and liquor, the small prepaid flip cell phone lying on the desk in the suite rang. The old man answered and just kept saying "okay" every few seconds; the phone call for him was about getting information. Finally, he put down the phone as the man in black laid out two Italian beef sandwiches for lunch. The old man spoke.

"That was my contact in IAD. He said that some information was requested for Detective Alex Donnelly on Chicago police officers that opened safety deposit boxes in 1983. Something tells me he did that for his cousin, Agent Gavin Donnelly."

The man in black replied, "He's smart. He knew somebody might be monitoring the information he and his partner requested through the FBI, so he made an under the table request."

"Too bad that he doesn't know about my contact in IAD. But it's only a matter of time before he finds the connection. I never expected he and his partner to pick up on this so quickly. They never should have gone to the banks; there was no reason to. How did they know?"

"I told you that starting with the bank manager was a bad idea."

"Maybe, but there's nothing we can do about it now. This doesn't feel right. They know too much now."

"Requesting them to be partners wasn't a good idea, either."

The old man got angry in his tone. "Look here, your job is not to be a critic. We need a solution before this blows up in our faces. We have two cops and two banks left. What are your thoughts?"

The man in black looked at the old man dead in the eyes. "We can always kill them."

"You and I both know that we can't. We're not supposed to kill them, and besides, killing two FBI agents will bring more heat than we need."

"There's another solution."

The old man gave a curious look. "What solution?"

"A little confusion. We make them think they're being hunted by the Chicago PD."

"Won't that just draw attention to the cops who are involved with us?"

"Who cares? Even if they find out about all the cops involved, they'll be too busy investigating the cops trying to kill them. The disruption will give us enough time to complete the transactions."

The old man thought about it. "I don't know; it sounds too risky. Why don't we just give them another body with the same MO that has nothing to do with a bank? That should throw them off."

"One more murder isn't going to change the direction they're looking in now, any more than making them chase Albert Soranno for the murders. They already have the bank connection. Let me do it my way and we can complete our work over the next couple of days."

"Fine, but get it done quickly. We've got the next person on our list tomorrow and we can't have any more complications."

The man in black left quickly. He had a safe house in Chicago where he kept the necessary tools for his trade -- every kind of tool for any kind of situation. He needed to prepare a little surprise for the agents, something to get their attention. He had something worse than death planned … the fear of death.

∞∞∞∞∞∞∞

It was already dark outside when Agent Main and Agent Donnelly arrived back at the FBI office in Chicago. For most people, the working day was already done, but the FBI was always on call and agents only took a break. They walked into their office and the flowers Gavin ordered were sitting on his desk. He grabbed the envelope from the bouquet and pulled the piece of paper out so he and Agent Main could read it together. A minute went by while they looked at the names on the paper. Finally, Agent Main asked him, "Do you recognize any of the names on the list besides the last two victims?"

"Yeah … Hank Morgan. He's a family friend. He was a like another uncle to me growing up. He and his son used to go fishing with me, my Uncle Liam, and my cousin, Alex."

"It may not mean anything. There are fifteen cops on here that opened up safety deposit boxes in 1983. It doesn't mean he has anything to do with this."

"Sure, but nothing in this case has been coincidence. He opened it at a federal bank that can handle bond transactions, and I know for a fact that he's no Boy Scout!"

Before Agent Main could reply, Assistant Director Graham Foster, their supervisor, walked in. He looked at them both with a serious look and said, "I just got the report back on Larry Crane, the third murder victim and retired Chicago police officer. Please tell me you have answers on who's doing this."

Gavin replied, "We have some answers."

The AD asked, "What is that supposed to mean?"

Agent Main responded before Gavin could. "What he means, sir, is that we do have some answers, but we don't know for sure who the real killer is."

"Three murders and you don't have a theory yet?"

"We have a few theories."

"Is this or is this not the work of Albert Soranno?"

"It's his MO, but we're not really sure if he's the one doing this."

Gavin spoke up. "It could be a copycat killer, but there are a few things that are different between these victims and the ones from five years ago. "

AD Foster looked at him strangely. It was as if they were talking in riddles. Finally, Agent Main started to reveal her theory about Albert Soranno and everything they had learned up to this point. She described her analysis of Albert Soranno and why he killed. She explained to the AD the difference between the murders from five years ago and now, especially the injections of neuroblockers and the absence of them in the latest victims. Gavin took his turn and explained his theory regarding the bearer bond transactions and the connections to the banks.

AD Foster seemed stunned by what he had just heard. He responded, "Okay, so let me get this straight. We have a mobster's son turned serial killer whose MO popped up in three murders after he's been in hiding for the last five years … and all three of the victims had safety deposit boxes filled with bearer bonds that sat there for 27 years … and when they finally cashed them, they were murdered with the MO of a serial killer whose father happens to be one of the most notorious mobsters in Chicago? Are you two seriously questioning the connection here? The Soranno family has been linked to money laundering before and bearer bonds are a good way to do it. You don't think Mickey Soranno might be using his son, who he's hidden all these years, to kill off witnesses to his money laundering scheme?"

Gavin replied, "The mob doesn't wait 27 years to access money they've laundered. There's no profit in being that patient. Somebody else is behind this, somebody that can afford to wait that long. We've questioned employees at each of the banks where safety deposits containing bearer bonds were located. Two of them confirmed that the man who accompanied the victims was an FBI agent."

AD Foster had a look of shock; then, it turned to anger. "I'm sure the mob, in this technological age, can get a fake FBI badge that would be good enough to fool bank employees."

Agent Main responded, "Maybe, but why? To make us chase our own? We wouldn't even have the bank connection without Agent Donnelly going to the banks in the first place. I happen to agree with Agent Donnelly. Believe it or not, somebody is trying to make us look in the wrong direction. The local mob doesn't have the brains for this and, even if this really is Albert Soranno, it has nothing to do with his father, Mickey."

AD Foster gave her a stern look. "Fine then, but get answers. I want this case solved, and quickly. Having two former Chicago police officers murdered in the Windy City was bad … very bad. If the names are released and the murders are linked to Albert Soranno, then we're going to have a war on our hands in Chicago between the police and the Soranno family -- and I don't want the FBI playing referee. Whatever doors you have to knock through to get those answers, do it. And I don't care what sleep you lose. There are too many murders going on in my city. I want a full report by the end of the day tomorrow on your progress, unless you can solve this thing by then. Oh, and if you can't get the answers to solve this case, then I will assign it to someone else."

AD Foster walked out of the office. Agent Main looked at her partner and asked him, "So, how do we find out about the cops on the list since they might be watching here at the FBI … Chicago IAD?"

Gavin smiled at her. "No, I have someone better. He knows more about cops and their secrets in this city than IAD. You get to meet my Uncle Liam."

◌◌◌◌◌◌◌◌◌◌

It was half an hour later when Agent Main and Agent Donnelly drove up to Police Chief Liam Donnelly's house. It was Gavin's childhood home from the age of six until he was eighteen and left for college. Before they got out of the car, Agent Main had a question on her mind and decided to ask before they went in.

"How did you know about the banks? There was no evidence about them at first. Franklin White seemed to have the MO of a random victim by Albert Soranno."

Gavin smiled at her. "I played a hunch."

[66]

"But what led you to that hunch? I mean, there was no evidence about safety deposit boxes at the bank and what was hidden in them. Franklin White was the manager of the entire branch and didn't work with safety deposit boxes. Did you have some other information about his murder that led you to the bank?"

Gavin thought for a moment. He couldn't tell her how he really knew and she was too smart to be easily fooled. He just gave her answer and hoped she would believe it. "The numbers on the piece of a paper we found in his pocket -- I figured it was either a PIN or safety deposit box code and it made the bank he worked at worth checking into. Like I said, I played a hunch."

Agent Main nodded her head. Gavin couldn't tell if she really bought it, but it was the best plausible answer he could come up with. Agent Main simply replied, "Well, it was a good call!"

Gavin knocked on the front door a few times to let his aunt and uncle know that somebody was there, and then he went inside. Liam Donnelly walked up from the dining room to the front of the house and greeted Gavin. "Gavin, I didn't know you were coming by for dinner tonight. I'll tell Mary to set a place for you ... and your friend."

"Uncle Liam, I'm not here for dinner. I needed to get some information and I figured you were the best source." Gavin pointed in the direction of Agent Main. "This is my new partner, Agent Rachel Main."

Liam extended his hand to shake hers and replied jokingly, "Well, if you've been partnered with my nephew, then I better get you a shot of whiskey instead of dinner. You probably need that more."

She laughed at the comment. "I don't need it now, but wait until after our third day of working together and I may take you up on that."

Liam laughed. "At least she has a sense of humor. So, what kind of information did you need from me?"

Before Gavin could answer, his Aunt Mary came into the room. She walked up to Gavin, gave him a hug, and asked, "Am I setting two more places at the table?"

"No, Aunt Mary. We're just here for a few minutes to get some information from Uncle Liam. No need to set a couple of places. "

"Nonsense." She looked at Gavin and Liam. "You go into the study and ask your questions. I will bring you a bowl of Irish stew, all three of you. You know can't get out of my house without getting something to eat. "

Liam and Gavin knew not to argue and Agent Main just smiled. She was a little hungry anyway and wouldn't turn down the hospitality. They all went into Liam Donnelly's study. As Liam took a seat behind his desk, Gavin looked around the room. He always loved his uncle's study. In a lot of ways, it was a like a museum with old sports memorabilia; not just Chicago sports, but Irish rugby and Gaelic football. There were also a ton of old books because Liam was a history and mythology buff. As Gavin was looking around the room, he noticed something on his uncle's desk -- something he remembered his father used to keep in his desk. It was an hourglass and, in fact, there were two of them. Gavin asked his uncle about the hourglass. Liam told him, "One of them is mine and the other was your father's. I found it in a box the other day and planned on giving it to you the next time you were over for dinner."

"I remember him having one and I also remember seeing yours growing up. Is there any significance behind them?"

"Your grandfather gave them to us. These are set to 30 minutes instead of an hour. He always used to say that if we were having trouble solving a problem, take a 30-minute break from thinking about it and then come back to it. The answer will usually come to you by then if you clear your mind and think of something else. Your father and I used these hourglasses to help time ourselves from not thinking about whatever problem we were trying to solve. It's good for police work."

Gavin smiled. "That's a great technique."

"Take it. Your father would have wanted you to have it. It just might help you in solving a case. Now, what can I help you with?"

Gavin put the hourglass in his coat pocket and handed Liam a piece of paper. He started asking questions.

"We have a list here of 15 Chicago cops that opened safety deposit boxes in 1983. I wanted to know if you knew any of them and if there are any connections between them."

Liam gave Gavin a stern look. "You know I don't like it when you don't give me a heads-up when Chicago cops are involved in a case you're working on. What are you investigating cops for? I know one was murdered yesterday, but shouldn't you be out trying to find his killer instead of worrying about who opened up a safety deposit box back in the early 80's?"

"Uncle Liam, it's relevant to the case we're working on. We're trying to find out who might be another victim and what connection they have to each other. There's a connection to safety deposit boxes opened up in 1983."

"Well, how do you know that?"

"Because there was another murder yesterday of a former Chicago cop who opened up a safety deposit box in 1983. Both victims are on that list."

"I know Michael McGregor was murdered. Who was the other one?"

"Larry Crane. Did you know both of them?"

"Not well, but I did know them."

"Hank Morgan is also on that list."

"Is Hank in trouble? I mean, if someone is out to kill him then we need to warn him."

"We don't know that yet. I need you to take a look at the list and tell me who you know and if there is any connection between them -- besides being a Chicago police officer."

Liam Donnelly looked at the list carefully; he knew most of them. He came across six names that were very familiar. He paused and remembered a story about them; a Chicago crime story, to be exact. He spoke. "I know ten people on that list and there is no other connection between them except six men."

Gavin took a seat on the couch. He knew his uncle well enough to know that there was a story involved, a bit of a true crime history in Chicago. He asked, "Who are they and what's the connection?"

"I'm sure at the FBI it wouldn't take you too long to figure it out, but there's a history lesson involved with this; a mob story, if you will. The six men that I speak of are Hank Morgan, Michael McGregor, Larry Crane, Steve Johnson, Frank London, and Clint Watson. They were all on the same SWAT team in 1983 and assigned to the same Organized Crime Task Force that worked in conjunction with the FBI. They were part of the team that took down Victor Soranno in 1983."

Gavin had an astonished look on his face. He knew the story, but realized in that moment that he may not have known every detail. Agent Main spoke up and said, "I don't know this story. What happened back then?"

Liam began to speak, but was interrupted by Mary Donnelly bringing in three bowls of Irish stew and some Guinness beer. She handed each of them a bowl and a beer. Agent Main didn't open hers since she was still on duty, but Liam and Gavin did. She gave a Gavin a funny look, but also realized that he was Irish and that kind of thing didn't really matter to him. Agent Main took a sip of her Irish stew and commented to Mary, "It's good, very good. Thank you for dinner."

"I'm glad that you like it, dear," Mary replied. "You've probably never had Irish stew like that. We use Guinness Extra Stout in ours, unlike those English Protestants, and no offense if you are one." Agent Main laughed. "It's okay, ma'am, I'm Catholic."

Mary smiled at her and left the room so the three of them could continue talking.

Liam Donnelly began to tell the story of Victor Soranno and how he was taken down. "In the early to late seventies and early eighties, the two biggest mob families, the Sorannos and the Puccinis, were competing for control of not only the racketeering game in

Chicago, but the trafficking of a new popular drug, cocaine. There was a lot of money to be made in the sale of cocaine, but it was also considered dangerous because it brought on extra heat from the federal government. None of the families liked the idea of cocaine being sold in neighborhoods with children. That was the biggest complaint by Victor Soranno; selling drugs where children and teenagers could get a hold of it wasn't considered honorable. After four years of war, the two families decided to consolidate power and control the trafficking because there was more money in it. The Organized Crime Division of the Chicago FBI office, while in conjunction with Chicago PD, was investigating the two families. They were getting close to making arrests and getting them on RICO charges. It was the largest investigation of the mob in Chicago since the days of Al Capone."

"In August of 1983, a big deal between Victor Soranno and Fredo Puccini went down. They each threw in 25 million dollars to buy up all the cocaine trafficking in the Midwest and control it, but Victor Soranno was sold out by Fredo Puccini to the Feds. Fredo made a deal to sell out his rival and so-called new business partner to the Feds to get the charges dropped on the Puccini family for Racketeering. It was a good ploy. The day the deal went down, the FBI and a Chicago SWAT Team raided the warehouse where the deal was happening. They found the heads of two mob families, their lieutenants, and the biggest cocaine dealer in the Midwest with 200 keys. Of course, a gun battle occurred. Most of the mob guys and the drug dealers were killed when they opened fire on the Feds and the Chicago SWAT Team. Victor Soranno was shot and killed that day as well. According to the original report, he pulled a gun and opened fire, but that was false. Victor Soranno never carried a gun and had not fired one since he was in the Army during the Korean War."

"The Puccini family never brought money to the deal, so there was nothing to confiscate. But, for the Soranno family, only five million was actually logged into evidence. Supposedly, 20 million dollars went missing, although it was never confirmed. There were eyewitnesses that could testify to the 25 million Victor Soranno brought to the deal. As for the Chicago SWAT Team involved, the six cops I mentioned from the list were on that team. Some say that the money was stolen by the Puccini family and some say that the FBI stole it." Gavin chuckled at that comment. "The FBI and Chicago police were able to bring down one of the most powerful mob families in Chicago and reduce the power of another."

Agent Main asked, "Whatever happened to the Puccini family?"

Liam replied, "Once Victor died, Mickey came back to Chicago to take over the family business. He was 26 at the time, with a young wife and a four-year-old son. Five years later, he killed Fredo Puccini, his sons, and his mafia lieutenants. He and three of his associates went to the Puccini family home to pay tribute to the Don and seek permission to continue running their own business. He got revenge, mafia style, and then became the most powerful mobster in Chicago. No one dared to challenge Mickey for power after that."

Gavin was curious about something. He asked, "Who was the FBI agent in charge of the Organized Crime Task Force back then? Do you remember, Uncle Liam?"

"Jack … last name started with a D."

"Agent Jack Denton?"

"Yeah, that was it."

Agent Main chimed in. "I've heard that name. A highly decorated FBI agent, he made a name for himself in New York back in the eighties, bringing down mob families. He led the first investigations into the Gotti family that eventually brought John Gotti down."

Gavin replied, "He was notorious here in Chicago … the Eliot Ness of the 80's. He was here for two years investigating the mob. Jack Denton was a legend at the Bureau and it figures that he would be the head of the task force that brought down Victor Soranno."

Agent Main responded by asking a question that was on everybody's mind. "What if the 20 million was actually stolen and used to buy bearer bonds? Let it sit for nearly 30 years and it would be worth … how much?"

Gavin replied, "Over 200 million dollars. A small fortune turns into a very large fortune. Everybody involved becomes millionaires. Dirty money turns into clean money and, even today, 200 million dollars buys a lot. Brilliant plan, but it takes patience."

"And that makes everybody involved back then a suspect!"

Gavin and Agent Main looked at each other with satisfaction. They were working together now and starting to find the answers to their questions.

Liam spoke up. "Do you know how many people were involved in that raid from the FBI to the Chicago police? That's a lot of suspects."

"And they all became rich being a part of this," Gavin responded, "including six police officers who have nothing to look forward to when they retire except their pensions."

"Be very careful where you go with this," Liam said in a stern tone. "I've known Hank Morgan for more than 30 years and, while he's not perfect, being a part of a criminal conspiracy like this is something he wouldn't do."

"Are you sure about that, Uncle Liam?"

"Gavin, I will always help you in any investigation you may have, but you will not come into my home and shit on the names of good police officers. I won't stand for that. It's bad enough that you're secretly investigating Chicago cops."

"I'm not trying to insult you or other cops, but we both know that, in a case like this, everybody is a suspect. We have to look at everybody and I have to question Hank."

Liam wasn't pleased. He was a true cop and took care of his own, no matter what kind of dirt they played in, but he knew Gavin was right. He responded, "Fine, but don't do it at the precinct. Make the interview informal. You know what you should do? Buy him a pint and do it at the pub during his lunch hour. You'll get more out of him."

"That's a good idea. We can do it tomorrow."

Agent Main spoke up. "Here's what I am wondering about this whole thing. Is this really about money and getting rich? I mean, you said it yourself, Agent Donnelly: somebody has to have the patience to wait 27 years to collect this money. Who would really do that, and why?"

Gavin looked at her. "Do you think the money is being used for something, more than just getting rich?"

Agent Main gave him a look that said yes. Before anybody could say something, there was an explosion outside. Agent Main and Agent Donnelly drew their service weapons and ran outside with Liam Donnelly right behind them. He grabbed a shotgun from inside the closet in his study. Nobody was outside, but the FBI Ford Crown Victoria that the agents arrived in was on fire and in pieces. Now it was serious. Somebody was trying to kill them.

11

The Donnelly house was crawling with CSU cops and Chicago firefighters. A car bomb in a residential neighborhood could cause a big stir. Alex Donnelly was called to the scene to help with the attempt of murder investigation of two federal agents and work in conjunction with the FBI who also had extra agents there besides Agent Donnelly and Agent Main. Liam Donnelly's front lawn and street was crowded and it wasn't anything like the block parties his neighbors had in the summer time. Liam was madder than hell. Gavin had spent the last hours talking to the police and the other agents, giving his report about everything that had happened. Agent Main had spent the last hour on the phone doing some more research on the case. Finally, the head of the CSU team came over to Gavin and his uncle Liam who was sitting on the front stoop of his house. He said to them.

"Well, we found the cause of the bomb, it looks like whoever did this went old school. They soaked a cloth in kerosene and stuck it in the gas tank as a fuse and then lit it. We did find some traces of C4, but there was no trigger to light, it exploded when the car caught on fire to make a bigger explosion. "

Gavin asked him. "C4, wouldn't the gas tank exploding destroy the entire car, why the need for C4. "

"Just because the gas tank explodes doesn't mean the entire car will explode, you want to do it right, C4 will cause a bigger explosion and pretty much destroy the entire car. "

Liam spoke up. So who whoever did this was trying to make sure that everything was completely destroyed including anybody that might have been in the car. "

The CSU investigator replied. "And C4 is the best way to do it. "

Another CSU investigator walked up and handed his supervisor a piece of paper and told him it was sticking out of the mailbox. He read it and handed it to Gavin. It said

This is what happens when you
start looking into cops.
We take care of our own.

Gavin frowned and showed his uncle the note. Liam just replied. "I've told you before; this is what can happen when you start investigating cops."

"This is attempted murder on federal agents. " Gavin replied angrily. "If you think I am going to let this slide for doing my job, you're crazy. "

"You're going to start a war and I won't be able to help you. Have it your way."

Agent Main walked up as Liam finished saying what he just said. She asked, "What was that all about?"

Gavin handed her the note, she was just as mad as they were about it. "How did someone know that you got that list of cops unless someone talked…that means your cousin Alex is a suspect too"

"He wasn't the one who talked."

"Really…you're going to say that after you just gave that speech in your uncle's study about everybody being a suspect. "

"He's a lot of things, but he can keep a secret for me and IAD can gossip more than a beauty salon. However, you're right, somebody talked and now we have cops sending us a message, it's going to be very hard getting any cooperation from them now."

"Nothing we can do about it now I guess, the cat's out of the bag, they know former police officers are being investigated, but I am going to add another wrinkle to all this. Been on the phone for the past 45 minutes confirming it, but two more cops on that list that your uncle mentioned were a part of the same SWAT team are deceased…Steve Johnson and Clint Watson."

Gavin had a surprised look on his face. "How did they die?"

"Both of them died of heart attacks in their sleep."

"Both of them?"

"Yep and I was also able to get their medical records as well…neither one of them had a history of heart complications, but their deaths were ruled natural causes. Steve Johnson died a couple of years ago and Clint Watson died last year."

"I don't suppose you found out if their safety deposit boxes were accessed before they died?"

"Already looking into it…we'll get that information in the morning."

"Is it just me or is the death of these two former cops being exactly the same too much of a coincidence?"

Agent Main smiled. "I think coincidence is going to be our worst enemy…but we know one thing."

"What's that?"

"Albert Soranno didn't kill these two cops. We just might have a conspiracy? "

Gavin smiled. "And now the plot thickens."

"So what now, Agent Donnelly?"

"We question the last two cops alive and we do it first thing…hopefully we're not too late."

As soon as Gavin finished his statement he overheard his cousin Alex arguing with the other FBI agents investigating the explosion. He walked over and intervened. Alex responded to the Agent's threats. "Look, I don't give a shit over jurisdiction…we can keep our own house clean."

Agent Michaelson replied. "You guys are doing such a bang up job…no pun intended. I have a threatening note by Chicago cops and an FBI vehicle in pieces. We will be investigating you, your precinct, and anybody else that's been involved in our federal investigation."

"Let me tell you what you can do with your investigation…"

Gavin interrupted before his cousin could finish his statement. "Alex…don't even finish that statement, the bureau has to question you and your precinct because you were called to the scene of Michael McGregor's murder and now we have an attempt on our lives with a note from what appears to be Chicago cops….of course you and your precinct are suspects. But you don't have anything to worry about, just answer their questions truthfully."

Alex replied. "Fine, but this guy can still go to hell." He walked off.

Gavin said to Agent Michaelson. "I'm sorry; everybody is a little on edge."

"Agent Donnelly, I haven't gotten to how bad you screwed up…what the hell are you getting information from Chicago IAD when we you can use the bureau's resources. You're just as much to blame for this incident. "

"I did what we did because we have leaks at the bureau and we have a guy running around impersonating an FBI agent who's involved with these murders. Getting the information we did under the radar was the prudent thing to do at the time."

"Well it didn't work and now we have a threat against two of our agents by Chicago's finest. This is a nightmare and it doesn't look good for you and your new partner."

"Then I will accept the consequences for what I have done, but the information I got produced leads and we may be closer to solving this thing."

Agent Michaelson paused for a moment. "You have a day before OPR gets involved and we start investigating the Chicago Police department for this act of violence…I suggest you use the time wisely to solve your case."

He walked away and left Gavin standing there feeling alike a child in trouble. Agent Main walked over and asked. "So what do you want to do?"

"Do you have an address on Frank London?"

"Yeah, he lives in Elk Grove Village Illinois. You want to go wake him up?

"No, but we let's a put a car outside his house to make sure nothing happens to him. We'll go first thing in the morning to question him…maybe we can finally get a head in this case. "

Gavin walked off and tried to smooth things over with his family. They weren't exactly happy about what happened on their doorstep because of a federal investigation, they never liked the fact Gavin became an FBI agent and tonight was a good reason why.

∞∞∞∞∞∞

It was early in the morning; the sun hadn't even risen when Gavin woke up. He and Agent Main had gone home to get at least a few hours of sleep. Gavin kept an apartment not too far from his family in the Bridgeport neighborhood of Chicago. He may have been a federal agent, but he still lived in the Irish neighborhood that he grew up in, a neighborhood filled with just as many Chicago cops, thieves, and politicians. He made himself a cup of coffee and opened his front door to get the newspaper. Gavin was just like his uncle, he still liked the printed newspaper. He had a Chicago Tribune delivered every day.

He opened the newspaper and was shocked when he saw the headline and then shock turned to anger. There was a leak. The headline read.

ALBERT SORANNO LINKED
TO CHICAGO POLICE KILLING

Gavin grabbed his cell phone and called his cousin Alex. He picked up the phone and answered Gavin. "What the hell are you calling me so early, can't you let a working man sleep a little longer. "

"Is your fucking precinct high?"

"What the hell are you talking about?"

"Have you seen the Tribune this morning?"

"No, you just woke me up…it's too early for the FBI this morning anyway."

"Today's headline reads 'Albert Soranno linked to Chicago Police Killing.' Now who the fuck talked to the press, they mention Michael McGregor by name as Albert Soranno's victim."

"What…that name didn't get released by my department."

[76]

"Nobody fucking talks, until the bureau says so…that's the way it works."

"There's any number of people that could have gotten that name and said something to the press. "

"Well, that's unacceptable, this is going to blow my investigation and start a war between the Soranno family and Chicago PD. I'm not cleaning it up. I want that leak found today…they're in a world of shit now. "

"Gavin, I know you're mad, but we don't have time to find a leak in our precinct, we have cases to work on."

"Find him today Alex, and I swear to fucking Christ I will bring a hundred agents down there to tear you precinct apart if any attempt is made on Mickey Soranno until we're finished with this investigation. Gavin threw his cell phone against his couch in anger. He was lucky that he didn't break it. He showered and got dressed quickly, checked on the agents who were sitting in front of Frank London's house, and then left. Gavin went to the hotel his partner was staying at and picked her up.

Agent Donnelly knew she would be even angrier than he was once she found about the news story breaking. This case was supposed to be her ticket back to big leagues in Washington and now as close as they were to solving it more trouble seemed to be raining down upon them. He tried to soften the blow by getting her a cup of coffee. He even had a flask of whiskey just in case she needed something stronger.

He arrived outside the hotel in his Nissan Titan Truck right as she was walking out. They hadn't been issued a new car yet so they had to take his. Gavin got out and greeted her with the cup of coffee. He said. "I don't how you take it, but I have cream and sugar in my truck. "

She tried to crack a smile. "I'll take it black this morning…I need it after the call I just got from AD Foster, you're won't believe what happened?"

"I get the Chicago Tribune, I saw the headline."

"Did your cousin talk?"

"No, but they have a leak at his precinct and it's being looked into."

"By the same people that leaked the story?"

Gavin gave her an angry look. "It was only a matter of time before the story broke…I admit, it's bad and we're going to catch grief for it, but we still have an investigation to conduct and that's what we're going to do. "

"AD Foster wants us in his office first thing."

"That's going to have to wait; we need to question Frank London first. We can get yelled at later."

Agent Main gave her partner a stern look. "Frank London is not going anywhere, we have a car sitting on him, let's get to the office and deal with it and then we can question who we need to question. "

"Look Agent Main, we're in trouble whether we see our boss now or later, I'd rather have some more answers when we do see him. Now if you want to go to the office first, be my guest. I'm going to Elk Gove Village to question Frank London. If you don't want me doing it alone then hop in."

Agent Main was furious, she didn't come to Chicago to break the rules and piss off her superiors. Gavin got in his truck, while Agent Main just stared at it for a moment. Finally, she opened the passenger door and got in. She said. "If they threaten suspension for this, I'm turning you in to get off the hook. " Gavin knew she was half kidding and just smiled at the comment as they drove off.

It took forty minutes to reach Elk Grove Village, a suburb west of Chicago. The other FBI car was still there parked a few houses down from Frank London's place. By the time Agent Main and Agent Donnelly arrived Frank London was starting to pack up his SUV. Agent Donnelly drove up beside the other FBI car and asked the other agents. "When did he start packing his car?"

Agent Harper responded. "He started about 5 minutes ago. We were waiting to hear from you on whether we should stop him. Do you want us to detain him?"

"No Agent Harper, we'll take it from here, but stick around until you're relieved…we did get you some coffee though."

"You're a lifesaver."

Agent Main grabbed the to-go tray with two coffees from Agent Donnelly and passed them through the passenger window to the Agents. Her hand slightly brushed again his and it triggered a vision. *Agent Main was on the phone speaking to someone she obviously knew. She said. "Richard, it's me. Yes, everything is fine here in Chicago. I need a favor. I know were separated and I shouldn't call you anymore asking for favors with my job, but it's important." She laughed a little bit. "I know that I've used that one before, but I need your help pushing through protective custody paperwork and I need it immediately. Can you help me with that?" There was a pause in the conversation. "Thanks Richard."*

Gavin didn't think anything of it. Finally they drove up to the London house and Gavin parked his truck right behind the SUV as Frank was coming out of his house with two more bags. He was scared, it was only a matter of time before someone came for him, that he was sure of and had been for twenty seven years. Agent Donnelly and Agent Main got out of the car. Gavin showed his badge. "Frank London?"

"Maybe," He replied.

"I'm Agent Gavin Donnelly and this is Agent Main, we need to ask you a few questions about a case we're working on."

"I don't think there is anything I can help you with. I never worked any cases as a police officer that involved the FBI...I'm sure you know that if you looked me up at the FBI. "

Agent Main spoke up. "What about working on the SWAT team in conjunction with the FBI's organized task force in 1983 when Victor Soranno was taken down?"

Frank London had an angry look on his face. "Still can't help you, I have bouts of dementia, don't remember anything from back then."

"Sure you do," Gavin said sarcastically. "I bet you remember everything."

"Look here Agent Donnelly, I can't help you and unless you have a warrant then I am going to ask you to leave."

"Frank London...Steve Johnson, Clint Watson, Michael McGregor, and Larry Crane have all been murdered, how long do you think it will be before they come for you.

Frank didn't say anything for a moment. His face turned a white shade of pale. The fear he had at the moment was the most he'd ever had in his life. Four of them are dead he thought, there was no escaping this time. He replied. "Then it doesn't matter now, even If I tell you everything, you can't save me...not even the FBI can stop them. "

"Of course we can save you," Agent Main replied. "We're the FBI, we have the power to do it"

Frank shook his head at her. "It's doesn't matter."

"Why?" Gavin asked.

"Because they're the FBI too!"

Gavin and Agent Main gave each other a shocking look. Apparently there wasn't somebody pretending to be a FBI agent and now they had confirmation. It was a scary thought and a hint of fear struck Agent Donnelly and Agent Main. Gavin responded. "Let us help, running won't keep you safe."

"But it will give me a chance; now please leave and let me get out of here! "

Before Gavin could respond Alice London walked out the front door and said. "Frank, enough running and hiding, it's time to tell them the truth. We can't survive on our own." She was scared and the agents could see it in her eyes. "Frank London loved his wife of 40 years way too much to argue. He invited Agent Donnelly and Agent Main inside his house for a cup of coffee and to tell them what he knew even though it would probably get him killed.

The all took a seat in the living room while Frank's wife got them a cup of coffee. Frank was pacing, something he did when he was nervous or worried. Finally Gavin spoke. "We know about the SWAT team and we know that each of you had a safety deposit box opened in 1983 at a federal bank. We know that Michael McGregor and Larry Crane both had Bearer Bonds in their box, I assume your box contains that as well."

Frank turned around and looked at Gavin. "Yes it does."

"Tell me how you got them and why?"

Frank paused for a moment, thinking about whether he really should tell them the whole truth. His wife came in the room and handed everybody a cup of coffee and that's when Frank began to speak. "I'm sure you know the rumor that 20 million dollars from Victor Soranno went missing the day of the raid where he was gunned down, it's not a rumor. We took it or I should say that we helped take it. The deal was that if we helped them steal the money then we got a share. A safety deposit box was opened up in our name at different federal banks in the Midwest, the money was converted to Bearer Bonds and we each got some that over time would turn into over a million dollars. It was the price for our involvement and our silence. I didn't even want to do, but we all had to or they would kill us and our family…that's what Hank said."

"Hank Morgan?" Agent Main asked him.

"Yes, he was the head of our SWAT team back then and he made us all go along with it. We didn't have much of a choice."

Gavin continued his questions. "Whose idea was it to steal the money and clean it with Bearer Bonds…Hank Morgan's?"

"No, all of it was planned by the FBI guy in charge."

"Who was that?"

"Agent Jack Denton…he was the head of the organized crime task force, we took our orders from him." Gavin and Agent Main looked at each other again with satisfaction. Another theory turned out to be true.

"So he put the whole plan together?"

"In Chicago he did, he was the money guy here, but there was another couple of FBI agents involved…one from New York and one from Washington. They handled the cleaning of the money and arranged for the safety deposit boxes to be opened."

"Do you have names?"

"No, the rest of us in SWAT never got their names and we never met them. The only reason I know about them is Jack Denton mentioned to us once that there were two other agents helping us in New York and Washington to clean the money."

Agent Main asked Frank a question. "What was your overall plan, take the money and run?"

Frank laughed. "Something like that! We each got a safety deposit box and Swiss bank account. We would have to wait thirty years to cash out and the money would be transferred to that bank account and from there we could transfer it anywhere we wanted. Then we could disappear."

"If you had to wait thirty years; why are you cashing out now?"

"I don't know the reason Agent Main, I got a call the other day saying that the time table had been moved up and we had to do the transaction this week. I didn't ask why and I don't care. All I want is my money and for this to be over."

Gavin asked. "Who called you?

"Jack Denton."

"Do you know who Agent Michael Harris is?"

"No and I've never heard that name before."

"There was no other Agent by the name working with you guys in 1983."

"No Agent Donnelly."

"Did you and Hank Morgan and the other cops keep in touch or talk about what happened after you were reassigned from SWAT."

"We kept in touch socially, we were friends. But we never talked about what happened with the money. We were sworn to secrecy and part of the plan was that we would never keep in touch after we were able to cash our bonds…we were supposed to disappear and I guess forget that it ever happened."

Agent Main spoke up. "You know that's not going to happen, right. If you go through with this they will kill you. "

"Yeah."

"What does Albert Soranno have to do with this?

"Albert Soranno, you actually believe that lie."

"What lie?"

"What the paper said…Albert Soranno didn't murder those guys, you're only made to think he did so you will chase the wrong guy and harass his father Mickey. It's misdirection!"

Gavin stood up and looked at Frank London dead in the eyes. "You know who killed the others don't you…you know who he is?"

Frank turned even paler at the thought. "Yeah, I do, but I can't give you his name."

"Why not?"

"Nobody knows his real name; he has several because he's an assassin that contracts out not only to the Mob, but also the CIA. They hire him when they want it done right because he never misses and he can recreate any murder. "

"But he's known by some name, right?"

"He's usually referred to as The Ghost, mainly because he's been working for thirty years and no one knows anything about him, not even what he looks like….he's a true ghost in the crime world and has no loyalty to anyone. "

Agent Main asked. "How do you know for sure that the killer is this 'ghost' that you speak of?"

"They would never use Albert Soranno for this, why would he work for the people that killed his grandfather? When I read the article and saw the name Michael McGregor, I knew that they must have hired this guy to recreate a Soranno murder. "

"You said he's worked for the Mob and the CIA, isn't there anybody that won't use him?"

"Not really from what I understand, he's worked for just about every Mob family here in the states and worked for other governments, but that's just what I hear. Mickey Soranno has hired him before, Rumor has it, this guy helped Mickey kill Fredo Pucinni."

Gavin looked at Frank. "We need you to testify and we can put you into protective custody."

"No way, I testify then I'm a dead man."

"You try to run and you're a dead man."

"I'd rather take my chances. "

"This is the best deal you'll get. I can arrest you right now for accessory to murder because you knew that this was going to happen and didn't try to prevent it. "

"I didn't know they were going to kill us."

"And that won't matter because we can still get you for criminal conspiracy, money laundering and accessory to the murders. We can make it stick and we both know that you won't be safe in prison. They can easily get to you there. This is your only way out."

Frank didn't want to admit it, but he knew Agent Donnelly was right. He was scared and rightly so. Everything seemed to end in murder. He finally agreed at the behest of his wife, she was even more scared and Frank loved her too much to let anything happen to her. At this point, it was the best way to keep her safe.

Gavin looked at his partner. "We need to get this done quickly and hopefully quietly."

"I know someone at the DOJ that can help us," Agent Main replied. "He can keep it quiet too from anybody that might be monitoring." Gavin nodded in agreement.

Agent Main walked outside to make the call. She didn't notice the Blue SUV sitting across the street that was watching the house.

Inside were Agent Michael Harris and the man in black. The man in black said. "They're getting closer; we're going to have to let this one go."

"Frank London still has to die."

"And we'll get him, but he'll have to die without us going to the bank."

Agent Michael Harries replied. "It's time for another murder; they need to be thrown off the scent. Your little exercise last night didn't seem to work. "

"Don't be hasty, give it time. This day is just beginning."

The Blue SUV slowly drove off.

12

Alice and Frank London were put in an FBI car with their luggage and taken to an undisclosed location -- a safe house somewhere in Chicago that not even the agents would know about until later. Agent Main's contact at the DOJ was true to his word; the protective custody paperwork was pushed through in 20 minutes. As the FBI car drove off, Agent Main looked at her partner and asked, "What now? I'm still getting phone calls from AD Foster."

"He can wait," Gavin replied. "It's time to talk to Hank Morgan."

"You think he's the key to this?"

"At least with the SWAT Team, he is. I would never say this to my uncle, but I've always believed that Hank Morgan was a dirty cop. He may be a good cop, but dirty. This just proves my theory."

"Then I have a suggestion. Your instinct will be to interrogate him like a criminal … don't. If you're his friend and act like you're just trying to get information, it will be easier to catch him in a lie."

"Good point. We'll try it your way."

Agent Donnelly and Agent Main got back into Gavin's truck and drove back to the city. They were heading to the pub that the Donnelly's had grown up in; it was where Hank Morgan had lunch on most days. Paddy Murphy's, as it was called, was the truest of neighborhood pubs. Where pints of beer were tall and full of flavor, where good whiskey flowed like honey, and cops, thieves, and politicians could find common ground. Gavin thought to himself, it was the perfect place to face an enemy.

An hour later, they arrived at Paddy Murphy's. As they were getting out of the truck, Agent Main commented, "So, this is the neighborhood pub?"

Gavin smiled. "We call it a home away from home."

"You've got to love a place where crooks and cops hang out together."

"It's holy ground in an Irish pub, so what we do doesn't matter. We can all share a drink and not let our differences get the best of us."

"And you're about to question a crook, who's a family friend, that you will probably have to arrest when this is all said and done."

"All we have in Chicago are shades of grey."

Agent Main smiled at him as they walked inside the pub. Hank Morgan was sitting in a corner booth surrounded by timber wood walls, which gave the booth privacy for eating lunch and drinking a pint of Guinness. Patrick, the owner of the pub, was behind the bar and said hi to Gavin as he walked in. The agents walked over to where Hank was sitting. He looked up and said, "Gavin! To what do I owe the pleasure?"

"Hank, how are you doing?"

"Can't complain. Heard what happened last night. Sorry, but at least you're okay. This Albert Soranno business has gotten everybody on edge."

"No more than us at the Bureau. I have some questions that need answers and figured you could help."

"Anything I can do, you know I will. Take a seat."

"Before we get started, let me introduce you to my new partner, Agent Main."

Hank extended his hand to her and she shook it. Agent Main was still polite, even though she knew Hank Morgan couldn't be trusted and that she probably wouldn't like him. Patrick brought Gavin a pint of Guinness as they started talking. His partner gave him a funny look. "Really? You're going to have a beer on duty?" Hank and Gavin laughed and then Gavin replied, "I could give you a lot of excuses, but it's an Irish thing. Drinking a Guinness is like drinking a soda, only more healthy." She shook her head and gave him a funny look. There was a philosophy among the Irish: the proper time to drink Guinness is anytime.

Gavin took a sip of beer and asked Hank, "I understand that you and Michael McGregor served on the same SWAT Team in 1983 and were part of the task force with the FBI that took down Victor Soranno?"

"Yes, we were."

"What do you know about the supposed 20 million dollars that was stolen from the Soranno Family that day?"

"Only rumors. I think every cop has heard that story. I always heard that the agent in charge took the money. Don't remember his name, though."

"What if I told you that we found evidence that Michael McGregor and two other officers on SWAT, Steve Johnson and Clint Watson, took the money?"

Hank Morgan had look of shock. "Are you sure that you have your facts straight?"

"I wouldn't be accusing cops of something unless I was sure. Do you know anything about it?"

"Gavin, I was the head of SWAT. If my men really did steal that money, I would have known about it. They got their orders from me and I got my orders from the FBI. My guys didn't do anything without my say-so and they couldn't have done anything without me. Anyway, I was with them all the time while we were on duty. Where is this questioning going?"

Gavin took another sip of beer. "If these cops really stole the money and Albert Soranno did kill Michael McGregor, then he could be targeting the SWAT Team that helped take down his grandfather. You know what that means; you could be a target."

"Is that true? Am I really being targeted by a serial killer?"

"That's what we are trying to find out. We also know that the cops I just mentioned opened safety deposit boxes in 1983. Those boxes contained bearer bonds, which today would make them all millionaires. As you probably know, bonds are a good way to clean stolen money. Did you ever open a safety deposit box back then, or did anyone ever approach you about opening one and putting bonds in there?"

Hank was getting angry now and it was obvious in his tone. "Look, I don't appreciate your subtle tone that suggests I might have something to do with this."

Agent Main spoke up. "Chief Morgan, we have to cover our bases and ask the questions. We're not trying to treat you as a suspect."

Hank replied, "Even though you are!"

Gavin said, "She's right, Hank, and our questions just make it seem like you're a suspect. Sorry about that, but we have to ask them."

"No, I did not open up a safety deposit box in 1983. My wife and I did, in 1976, and that's the only one I've ever had."

"What happened to the team after that assignment?"

"We got commendations for our work and, a year later, everybody was reassigned. Most of the team became detectives."

"Did you guys stay in touch? Relive your glory days?"

Hank laughed. "We were all friends; of course we did."

"And, in that time, none of the other cops mentioned what they might have done in 1983?"

"You really think they did it, don't you?"

"Doesn't matter what I think. I let the facts lead me."

Hank gave Gavin a stern look. "Then check your facts. You're going in the wrong direction. I have to get back to work. If you want answers, track down the FBI agent who was in charge and ask him your questions."

"What was his name?"

"Jack Denton, if I recall. I'm sure you can find him in the Bureau's records." Agent Main looked at Hank surprisingly. Gavin noticed it, too. They caught him in a lie; actually, two lies. Hank got up and walked to bar, paid his bill, and left. The two agents looked at each other. She spoke first. "You got your lie."

"Yes, I did, but it doesn't make me feel any better."

"You feel betrayed?"

"No, I don't, by my Uncle Liam will. That's the tragedy of all this."

Agent Main looked over to see who had walked in the door, a habit she picked up being an FBI Agent. It was AD Foster with Agent Michaelson. They walked over to the booth where Agent Main and Agent Donnelly were sitting. AD Foster was not happy and the look on his face was proof of that.

AD Foster spoke first. "You two have a lot to answer for. When I tell you to be in my office first thing in the morning, it's not a joke." He looked down and saw the beer in front Agent Donnelly. "Really? Drinking while on duty?"

"I could give you many excuses, "Agent Donnelly replied, "but I'm Irish and we don't think drinking a beer is bad. Besides, my drinking should be the least of your worries."

"Agent Donnelly, you're in enough hot water; don't add to it. Now, is there a reason why you haven't made it into the office today? And why there is a protective custody order for a retired Chicago police officer?"

Agent Main responded, "We've been out following leads this morning and we're closer to solving this case."

"I hope that means you're investigating members of the Chicago Police Department, since they apparently tried to kill you last night."

"Sir, we're not dismissing what happened last night, but we had more pressing leads."

"Did you find out anything useful to this case? And who is this Frank London, anyway?" Agent Main explained what they found out that morning and the details of their conversation with Hank Morgan. AD Foster looked stunned and he then he asked Agent Donnelly, "What's your take on this?"

"I think there's too much coincidence in this case. It's very plausible that Agent Jack Denton could have put this together and gotten these former Chicago police officers involved in a money laundering scheme with stolen money from the raid."

AD Foster had an angry look on his face. "You're going to accuse a highly decorated FBI agent, a legend in the Bureau, of theft, conspiracy to commit murder, and money laundering?"

"The facts are pointing that way, but to be sure, we need to talk to him."

"That's going to be a problem. He died five years ago."

Agent Donnelly and Agent Main were shocked. It was another wrinkle in this case and, just as things were starting to make sense for the agents, the more mysterious it became. Agent Donnelly asked, "How did he die?"

"A boating accident. Gas tank on the fishing boat he was on exploded and incinerated him. The only way he was identified was through partial dental records."

"It doesn't change what the facts are."

"Maybe not, but I won't let you accuse one of our best agents of being a criminal without any proof ... and until you have it, you will not take this any further. Now tell me, how does Albert Soranno fit into all of this? Is he targeting former Chicago cops that had something to do with his grandfather's death?"

Agent Main responded to the question. "It's a possibility, but it's starting to look very unlikely."

"So you don't think he's the killer now?"

"We have a couple of theories and we are exploring all possibilities."

AD Foster handed her a file. "There was another murder an hour ago with the same MO. Somebody found this mother of two in an alley outside of a grocery store. Her body is being sent to our ME. This is our initial report; you can get the rest from the ME when you look at the body. I think you need to explore your theory about Albert Soranno again."

Agent Donnelly asked, "Are you telling us that's who we need to pursue, regardless of what we've found so far?"

AD Foster looked at the agents. "You have a meeting tomorrow at 10 a.m. with OPR. In light of this new development, they will ask you about your progress on the Albert Soranno case. You better have more answers by that time. While I can overlook you blowing me off this morning, OPR will not be as kind if you do it to them. Be there and be on time. You have less than 24 hours to come up with answers on how to catch this guy." That was the last thing he told them before he turned and walked out of the pub.

Agent Donnelly and Agent Main looked at the photos in the file. She said, "I can already tell that this murder is too messy and whoever did it was rushed."

"You don't think it was the same killer?" Agent Donnelly asked as he finished his beer.

"I don't know. The only way to know for sure is to examine the body."

It was the fourth ME's office that Agent Donnelly and Agent Main had visited this week. They never expected to be in another one, but then again, who does? The ME walked out of the cooler and smiled at Agent Donnelly -- not to be nice, but to flirt. Dr. Kenrick said, "Agent Donnelly, you still have that roguish FBI look that drive women crazy. To what do I owe the pleasure?"

"Dr. Kenrick, good to see you again. You're looking lovely as ever. I'm here with my new partner, Agent Main. It's about the body of the woman that just arrived."

"Oh, did you get transferred from White Collar Crimes?"

"Got transferred to Violent Crimes. This is my first week on the job."

She winked at him this time. "Catching real bad guys now … sexy." She was flirtatious and didn't care how it looked at the FBI. Dr. Kenrick didn't want to be a typical ME. She preferred to be bubbly because it made her job more fun, as much as it could be … being a Medical Examiner. Agent Main rolled her eyes at her partner. Gavin saw it and commented, "Yeah, we know each other."

"Apparently!"

Dr. Kenrick went to the freezer and pulled out the body. An autopsy hadn't been performed yet; everything was left as when the body was found. It did have a similar MO as the other murders, but just as Agent Main noticed in the photos, it looked like a rush job. The carvings in the chest were as not as precise; they were messy. The acid on the ears burned all the ears and part of the head. It looked as if the killer just threw acid over the ears and let it drop all over the victim's head. Those aspects were easy to spot, but that's not what Agent Main was looking for. She was searching for the kill mark, as she liked to call it. She and Dr. Kenrick put on latex gloves and turned the body over. There it was, but it was different this time.

As she ran her hand over the spot, Agent Main said to her partner, "Look at this. The mark is different; it's bigger."

Dr. Kenrick spoke up. "It looks like someone stabbed her in the kidney with a military grade knife, probably the same knife the killer used to carve up the chest."

Agent Donnelly asked, "Does this mean it's not the same person who killed the other three?"

"Probably not," Agent Main replied. "Chances are, it's the same person, but he changed his instruments. The killer didn't have time to prepare as before. It's almost like he didn't expect to kill another person. I mean, this is a rush job."

"Would Albert Soranno do that?"

"Not unless he was caught by a bystander, like he was with his last murder five years ago, but there were no witnesses. This is not him. He would have prepared before killing someone."

Gavin looked at Dr. Kenrick. "Have you run a toxicology report yet?"

"Honey, it will be ready for you in the morning. You should come by yourself to pick it up."

Agent Main rolled her eyes at the comment. Gavin just smiled and told her that he would try. There wasn't much else to check out until all the final reports were in. Agent Main already had her doubts and didn't feel that there was anything those reports would tell her that she didn't already know. She and Agent Donnelly left the FBI Medical Examiner's office. As they were walking out, Agent Donnelly said to his partner, "I'm hungry. What about you?"

"I can eat. Haven't had anything but coffee all day."

"Come on, I will buy you a real hot dog."

"You act like I haven't ever had a hot dog in my life."

"You haven't until you've had a traditional Chicago Dog. It's made with real Vienna beef."

Agent Main laughed. She really didn't care because, as far as she was concerned, a hot dog was just a hot dog. There was a Super Dog nearby and they went there to grab some food, but it also gave them a chance to talk about the case. They got a couple of Chicago dogs and ginger ales.

Gavin asked the question they were both thinking. "Why commit this murder, if it's some random murder, when all the other victims had a connection to one another? And why murder someone if you're going to rush your method?"

"To waste our time; to make us doubt what we've found so far. That's the only reason for this latest murder."

"Sure, that's obvious, but blowing up our car last night was about wasting our time."

"Maybe that was just to scare us and this was about wasting our time."

Gavin laughed. "Do you really believe that?"

"No. This murder happened too fast and it was careless. More importantly, it was unnecessary, unless you just have to kill. Whoever is doing this is not a serial killer who has a taste for it."

"Then it's about disrupting our day. Maybe we are closer than we think."

Agent Main took a bite of her Chicago Dog. She was actually enjoying it. Gavin was right. She said, "Maybe it's about Hank Morgan. He's the next person on the list after Frank London. They could be drawing our attention away from him."

Before he could say anything, Gavin's phone rang. It was Father Joseph from his church. Gavin was surprised by what Father Joseph told him and he replied, "No, it's okay. You were right to call me. We'll be there in about 20 minutes." Agent Main had a concerned look on her face. Gavin responded, "We've got to go. Some of Chicago's finest are trying to kill Mickey Soranno. He's hiding out in a church. We get to play referee."

13

Like most old neighborhoods in Chicago, this Catholic church was the epicenter of the neighborhood. It breathed life into those that crossed its threshold and gave refuge to those who needed help. The church made no distinction between criminals and cops; all were given kindness. St. Thomas Catholic Church, where Gavin Donnelly grew up, was like a cathedral -- with a long set of steps leading to the massive front doors. When he and his partner arrived, they passed a silver Crown Victoria about 100 yards down the street. Gavin immediately knew that it was Chicago police officers. They were waiting for Mickey Soranno to come out. Gavin parked his truck in front of the church and he and Agent Main walked up to the front door. Father Joseph was there to greet them and told them where Mickey was with his bodyguards.

Before they went inside, Gavin told his partner, "Agent Main, do me a favor. There's a side door that leads out to the alley alongside the church. It will keep you hidden from the street. Can you go out that way and come up behind the car that we just saw? Make sure they don't open fire on us when we walk Mickey out."

She gave him a surprised look and asked, "You don't want to walk him out the back?"

"No, there's probably another car back there. That's where they want Mickey to go ... so when they gun him down, it won't be in broad daylight where everybody can see. It will be better if we walk out the front."

She nodded in agreement. When they walked inside the church, she slipped out the side door. Gavin dipped his right index finger in the holy water at the back of the church and did the Signum Crucis. Even on duty, he still respected ceremony. He walked up to the front with Father Joseph to where Mickey was sitting and praying. Mickey said, "Somehow I knew the priest would call you. You may be the only friend from the authorities I have left."

Gavin laughed. "How do you know that I am not here to arrest you?"

"I wouldn't be surprised. Are you?"

"No. I'm a friend today, but I do have some more questions for you."

"About my son?"

"And other things."

Mickey, while still sitting, turned around to face Gavin. He took a seat in the pew next to Mickey.

"Agent Donnelly, I know the FBI is still looking for him, but do you really think my son killed that cop?"

"No, I don't. And while we have not said so publicly, we can prove it."

"Then what's the idea behind that new article?"

"It wasn't us; somebody jumped the gun on that. The truth is we think it's a copycat killer. Somebody knew enough about how Albert murdered his victims that he recreated them to throw us off from what's really happening."

"And what is that?"

Gavin smiled. "Mickey, you know I can't tell you that."

"So, I am left to my own demise at the hands of the Chicago Police Department?"

"Not necessarily. We can help you as long as you help us."

Mickey clutched his rosary and sighed. "What do you want?"

"Information. Tell me about The Ghost."

Mickey was surprised by the comment. He debated internally on whether or not to answer the question. He would be incriminating himself if he answered ... but then again, they were on holy ground, and it was always understood that whatever was said in the church could never be used against you. Finally, he answered.

"So you've heard about him. How?"

"His name has come up. Rumor has it that you've used his services before."

"Nobody knows his real name. I don't think anybody has ever seen his real face; he was always disguised when I dealt with him. Supposedly, he's been a contract killer for 30 years and has been used by the mob, CIA, corporations, and pretty much anybody that wants someone dead. He's the best and doesn't care who he works for."

Gavin pulled out his cell phone. "How do you get in touch with him?"

"There isn't a number I can call. I go to a website for sports tickets and make an order. Instead of getting tickets in the mail, I get a prepaid cell phone and a number to call. I can only call the number once and have one conversation. At the end of the conversation, I get a Swiss bank account number to wire his money. Everything is completely untraceable."

"When was the last time you saw him in person?"

"Twenty-two years ago. If you want to catch him, you can't simply use me to order a fake hit and expect to nab him when he shows up. He lives in the shadows. You will never get him."

Gavin thought about it for a moment. He replied, "Maybe not that way, but we can still get him."

Mickey shot Gavin an annoyed look. "Why do you want this guy so bad?"

"Because we think he's the real killer. He recreated your son's MO and now we have four murders. But there's something else: if we get him, then he leads us to the real mastermind behind this whole thing."

"I don't follow."

"Two of the victims were cops that were on the SWAT Team that helped take down your father ... and stole 20 million dollars of his money. They laundered it and became millionaires. I think this Ghost is the one killing them off."

"Then he's serving up justice. Why would I want to help you catch him?"

"Because they want you dead, too. That's why there are cops sitting outside and waiting to gun you down, Mickey." And at that moment, Gavin figured it out without any psychic vision. It wasn't someone in the Chicago Police Department that leaked the story; the killers did it to cause paranoia and to start a war between the police and the mob.

Mickey Soranno was angry about the news he just heard. He always suspected that cops were involved in stealing his father's money. Now he had confirmation. Of course, he always thought the FBI was involved, too. Despite all his theories, he never believed the final report that his father pulled a gun on the cops and the Feds that day, or that his father's money magically disappeared in all the chaos. He didn't feel sorry for the cops that were murdered. He just wished he had pulled the trigger himself.

Gavin looked at Mickey and asked, "If I get you out of here, safely, will you help the FBI catch the men behind these crimes?"

"What do I have to do?"

"Just a little acting. I'm going to march you out of here and put you in protective custody for a few days."

Mickey sighed. "If I go with you, I won't be getting a decent meal for a few days."

Gavin rolled his eyes. "Like we can't get you take-out from Santino's Italian Restaurant."

"Now you're talking."

Gavin and Mickey thanked Father Joseph and walked out of the church. As they headed down the steps outside, the silver Crown

Victoria pulled up closer to do a drive-by. Agent Main, who had been in the alley around the back of the church, saw the car move and pulled out her service weapon. As the car slowed down, she ran out of the alley and came up from behind, her weapon pointed at the driver. The cop in the driver's seat pointed his gun out the window. Agent Main grabbed the gun and pointed her weapon at his head. "Don't even think about it. You two make any sudden moves and I'll put you down."

"Who the fuck are you?" the cop asked.

With her other hand, she showed them her badge. "FBI. You're in a lot of trouble." Both cops cursed out loud but didn't make a move.

Gavin opened up the cab door to his truck and helped Mickey inside. He told the two bodyguards that he would call them when Mickey could be picked up. Gavin walked over to his partner and handed her the keys to his truck. "Thanks, I'll take it from here. Drive to the corner and I will be with you in a few minutes."

"What are you going to do?"

"Have a little chat with these guys."

Agent Main did what he asked. As she turned around, Gavin pulled his service weapon and pointed it at the cops before they could grab their guns. He said to them, "You guys ought to know better. Chicago PD is not in the revenge business."

Detective Doyle, who was sitting in the front seat, replied, "Gavin, if you guys are not going to do something about this, then we will. Nobody kills a cop in the this town and gets away with it. We take care of our own!"

"You know, that's just what the note said that was left for me and my partner after someone blew up our car last night. Do you know anything about that?"

He didn't say anything for a moment. "You know how it works around here."

"I don't give a shit how it works. This isn't going to happen and the news doesn't always get it right." Gavin looked out of the corner of his eye and saw another Crown Victoria pull up right behind the silver one. He knew it was the other cops that were sitting behind the church. Immediately, he reached behind his back and pulled out his other weapon that was tucked underneath his suit jacket. He pointed at the car and kept the gun on them as the other two cops, in plain clothes, got out of the car. They tried to go for their guns and all Gavin did was shake his head 'no' at them. They knew Gavin and knew they didn't have a chance on the draw; they would be dead before they got their guns out of the holster. The whole scene was like an old-fashioned standoff in a western movie.

Gavin saw that Detective Doyle was reaching for another gun in the car. He didn't know for sure if they would actually kill him, but he didn't take a chance. He shot Detective Doyle right above the left knee. While the detective screamed out in pain, Gavin shouted to the cops, "Go for your guns and I'll blow your fucking head off. Doyle, if I were you, I would put your papers in, collect your pension, and retire. If not, I'll haul you in for making an attempt on a Federal Agent's life. Now, I'm walking out of here and taking Mickey with me." Gavin slowly backed away and walked to where his partner parked his truck. He slid in the passenger side.

Agent Main looked surprised. "Was that a gunshot I just heard?"

"Yeah, don't worry about it. Ain't nothing but a family thing." She didn't understand since she wasn't from the neighborhood, but Mickey did. They drove away and headed to a safe house guarded by other agents to help protect the most notorious mobster in Chicago.

∞∞∞∞∞∞∞

A few hours later, Agent Main walked through the front door of the safe house where they were keeping Mickey Soranno. She had two files in her hand. Agent Donnelly was sorting the take-out boxes of food from Santino's Italian Restaurant for Mickey and the other two agents. For Mickey, this was the best part about being in protective custody. Agent Main motioned for her partner to come closer so she could tell him what she found. She told him:

"Your theory proved right about Clint Watson and Steve Johnson. Both of them accessed their safety deposit boxes the day they died and they each made a bond transfer to a Swiss bank account."

"Just like the other cops."

"Yep, just like the other ones. We have a pattern, but how do we catch these guys when everybody's ending up dead and one is in protective custody?"

"Hank Morgan is the key and he should lead us to the ones doing this -- if we haven't spooked him already."

"Do you have a plan?"

"The beginning of one."

She smiled. "Well, I also have the file on where Frank London is being held. So, does this plan of yours involve him?"

Gavin laughed a little bit. "He's a part of it, too."

She handed him the file and went to get a bit to eat. Gavin opened it up and that's when it happened. He saw a vision. *The lights went dark in the house. A man walked through the shadows and grabbed a woman from behind, piercing her kidney with a sharp object. As she went down, she screamed out a name; "Frank!"* That's all Gavin saw, but it was enough. He knew who was in danger, and this time, he had a chance to save a life. He looked at his partner as she was taking a bite of lasagna. "We have to go. I have a hunch that there's a problem at the other safe house."

"Well, call the other agents and let them know."

"I will, but we still need to get there. We need to take care of this one ourselves." That was all he wanted to tell her without giving her too much detail. Agent Main gave him a strange look, but she didn't argue. She took one more bite of pasta and followed her partner out the door.

They had a safe house in Oak Park, about 30 minutes away. It was night by the time Agent Donnelly and Agent Main arrived at the house. They tried to get in touch with the agents at the house protecting Frank London and his wife, but there was no answer on either of their cell phones. When they arrived, the house was dark; the power looked as if it had been cut. Agent Main commented, "This can't be good!"

As he put on his bulletproof vest that said 'FBI,' Gavin replied, "No. You take the front and I'll take the back."

She put on her vest and chambered a round into her service weapon. It was shoot to kill this time and it made her nervous. Her gun hand was shaking, but she hid that from her partner. They approached the house slowly. Agent Main entered the darkness at the front of the house and tripped over a body. It was one of the agents guarding the London's. She knelt down to check for a pulse. He was dead; the throat had been cut and the carpet was soaked with his blood. Gavin came in through the back door that entered into the kitchen. He too found a body: it was Alice London. She was alive, but barely. The killer apparently did not have time to finish the job.

He walked through the kitchen and tried to be quiet, but the floor was no help. The creaking sounds penetrated the room. Finally, Gavin heard a footstep and then a shout. It was his partner. The killer came out from the shadows and tried to stab Agent Main, but her vest protected her and gave her a chance to fight back. All he could do was knock her down and send the gun flying from her hands and across the room. Gavin ran into the room as the killer ran out the front door. He fired six shots towards the door and through the front window, but the killer was able to get away. By the time Gavin came outside, the man he was chasing was nowhere to be seen. He looked down and saw drops of blood on the front stoop.

Agent Main got back on her feet. She asked, "Did he get away?"

"Yeah," Gavin replied. "But I shot him at least once. Maybe we will get lucky and he will seek treatment in a hospital. We should monitor all GSU's in Chicago."

They found Agent Main's gun and started searching the house. They discovered Frank London unconscious in the back bedroom. He had been stabbed but was still alive. Agent Main called 911 to get an ambulance. Gavin told her to get two because Alice London was still alive. Unfortunately, the other agent wasn't. They found him dead in the bathroom; his throat was cut as well. Thirty minutes later, an FBI CSU was at the scene. It was bad; two agents were dead and the killer wasn't in custody. The meeting with OPR that Agent Main and Agent Donnelly had the next day was starting to look more like a disaster every minute. Gavin couldn't help but think that they definitely were up shit creek.

Frank and Alice were rushed to the hospital with what seemed like an army guarding them all the way. But at this point, the more the agents, the better. Agent Main looked at her partner and asked, "How did you know that this was going to happen?"

"Two of our agents are dead. I didn't know this was going to happen."

"You said you had a hunch. Where did it come from?"

"I just got a hunch; there's no mystery about it."

Agent Main had a disappointed look on her face. "You're not telling me something. What are you hiding?"

Gavin was angry. "What do you think I'm hiding?"

"Goddammit, I'm your partner! Don't fucking keep things from me about this case."

"Oh, like you've told me everything?"

"I'm not hiding anything from you."

Gavin gave her a stern look. "Like that your contact at the Department of Justice who pushed through the paperwork for protective custody is your husband. You failed to mention that little fact." She had a look of surprise. "Yeah, Agent Main, I checked who signed off on this."

"My personal life is none of your business. It doesn't matter whether he's my husband or not."

"It does when it affects this case. How did the killer know where the safe house was? We have a leak, remember? Maybe more than one."

She was mad and wanted to hit him for the insinuation. "My husband may be a lot of things, but he's not a rat."

"Maybe not, but we have someone monitoring what we do through the Bureau and DOJ. Trusting your husband was a mistake and now we have two agents dead because of it. Accuse me of whatever you want, but you're just as much to blame for what happened here."

Gavin walked off before she could respond, but a part of her knew he was right ... and that pissed her off even more. But she also knew her instincts were usually right. Agent Donnelly was hiding something and it made her wonder if she could trust him as a partner. It made her question whether or not they could solve this case together. How many lives would be lost if they couldn't work together? That was the scariest thought.

14

It was early in the morning and Agent Donnelly was already running around. He had been doing research since late last night and needed one more thing before he went into the office: the toxicology report on the latest victim. He already had a feeling what was on the report, but needed it for his meeting with OPR. He walked into the ME's office and, of course, she was there -- the vivacious Dr. Kenrick. She turned around and smiled. "Agent Donnelly, you're getting my morning off to a good start. What can I do for you?"

"I need to get the toxicology report on the female victim."

She grabbed a folder off her desk and walked over to him. "Are sure that's all you need?"

Gavin smiled and stared into her beautiful emerald eyes. He grabbed the folder from her and threw it on a metal cadaver table. With his other hand, he brought her in close and kissed her with intoxicating passion. She pushed him up against the wall, taking off his sport coat along the way and then started to undo his pants. His hands reached down and opened her blouse. Gavin kissed her all the way down until his soft lips reached her perfect breasts and moistened each one of her erect nipples. It her made moan. She loved to have her nipples sucked on just as much as she loved to have a popsicle traced around them.

Dr. Kenrick led him to one of the tables and took a seat on it while his hands moved her skirt up and found her panties. He slid them off carefully and found his way in between her legs. She reached down and pulled his boxers off. They weren't the easiest garment to remove, but she knew how to do it with ease. As she got the boxers off, she reached in and found something stiff and hard that gave her delight. The feel of her hands around it made Agent Donnelly moan. He was sensitive that way. She was moist and wanted to return the favor so she bent down and kissed what she was holding in her hands. That warm and wet embrace almost made him explode. After a minute of her kissing and sucking, he pulled her up and put her back on the table. With a light touch, he ran his hands up and over her legs until he reached what was in the middle, the Garden of Eden. He entered with one finger, tickling her and making her shiver with pleasure. Dr. Kenrick grabbed the swollen instrument she was handling before and guided Gavin inside, parting that Red Sea between her legs and making her really shake with excitement. It was cold in the ME's office before he got there, but together they raised the temperature to a comfortable degree.

For the next fifteen minutes, nothing else mattered in the world as they screwed each other until their bodies were too tired to move. It was the best they had felt in a long time … a great morning workout. When they were done, they smiled at each other again. Before walking out the door, he kissed her long and hard while running his hands down her back and squeezing her right butt cheek. She let out another moan. It wasn't the first time that this happened between them and they both knew that it wouldn't be the last.

∞∞∞∞∞∞

Any meeting with OPR had the same feel of gloom and doom. Nothing good ever seemed to come from those meetings; that's the way Agent Main felt. This would be her second one in less than a week and, for any FBI agent, that wasn't good. Her partner was running late and it made her even angrier than she was already. It made her feel that she was being left high and dry. AD Foster walked into the lobby and told her that it was time to start. Agent Main looked at the office entrance for her partner, hoping that he would come running in at the last minute … nothing.

Agent Main walked in the room and sat at the desk in front of the three-member panel. The man in the middle of the panel said, "Agent Main, I'm Agent Greg Taylor. Do you know why you're here?"

"I have a good idea," she replied.

"We've read the reports about the murder victims, the attempt on your life, and this latest incident with a former Chicago police officer in protective custody -- and no arrests have been made. You can see how big of a debacle this case has turned out to be. Do you have anything new to report about this case before we make a decision?"

Before she could say anything, Agent Donnelly walked in and responded, "I can probably answer that question. Sorry that I am late, but I've been doing some research."

"Agent Donnelly, being late doesn't look good or win you any favors with this panel," Agent Taylor replied.

"I understand that, but I'm still doing my job until you tell me otherwise."

"Fine. What do you have?"

"As you well know, we took Mickey Soranno into protective custody yesterday. We're ready to make an arrest for accessory to murder."

"An accessory to murder!"

"Yes, sir. We feel that the MO of the murders fits with Albert Soranno. We think that his father, Mickey, has been helping him to exact revenge on the former Chicago police officers who supposedly stole money from his father, Victor Soranno, in 1983." Agent Main looked shocked. It was the complete opposite of what they thought was going on behind the murders.

"That sounds like a conspiracy, Agent Donnelly."

"I know it does, but the evidence is pointing that way."

"How is Mickey Soranno helping in all this?"

Agent Donnelly laid it all out for them; the perfect plan of revenge by the Soranno family. Mickey had been hiding his son for five years until the right opportunity came along for him to use his son as an assassin. Agent Donnelly found a Customs report indicating that an agent thought he spotted Albert Soranno entering the country a few weeks ago under a different name. Agent Main was startled to hear that, as well. One by one, they found the cops and killed them so they could cash the bonds themselves and steal the money back.

Agent Taylor asked, "What about the incident last night?"

"Somehow, they found out where we were keeping Frank London and made an attempt on his life. It appears that we have a leak, either here or at the DOJ."

"That's a serious accusation. Any evidence to back it up?"

"Not that we can prove, but it's the only explanation we have."

Agent Taylor paused for a moment to consider what he just heard. Then he said, "Okay. This is a lot to take in, but I want to know about the attempt on your life the other night. We have an FBI car that was blown up and a note from what appears to be Chicago cops giving you a warning."

"I think we're dealing with some overzealous cops who were mad that one of their own was murdered and we hadn't caught the killer yet, If we arrest Mickey, I think that he will lead us to Albert Soranno ... and we'll solve this thing and calm the Chicago PD down."

"Are you investigating who did that? The FBI doesn't tolerate rogue police officers trying to kill federal agents."

"Sir, we will conduct an investigation, but we are pursuing all avenues to catch Albert Soranno first."

"Are you prepared to arrest Mickey Soranno now?"

"Yes, we are."

Agent Taylor looked at Agent Main and asked her if she agreed with this. She answered, "Yes, this is what the evidence is pointing to." She didn't really know what her partner was up to, but she wasn't going to hang him out to dry in front of OPR. The three-member panel talked for a few minutes and then Agent Taylor looked at Agent

Donnelly and Agent Main. "We're not suspending you today or removing you from this case, but you have 48 hours to solve this thing and make more than one arrest. After that, there will be disciplinary action. We have to close the book on this soon. Four murders with no arrests is bad for the FBI and even worse for you. That will be all, agents."

Agent Main and Agent Donnelly walked out of the room, but Agent Main couldn't stop giving her partner a strange look. "What was that song and dance?" she asked. "That's not our theory and we have never been on board with Albert Soranno being our guy."

"No, but OPR doesn't know that. They need to hear something good to get off our backs. Besides, you can't afford to be in trouble with OPR twice in one week. I saved you."

"I can take care of myself and my job."

"Look, what I just told OPR fits with my plan."

"What brilliant plan do you have?"

"It's time to flush the rats out. And before you ask, yes, Hank Morgan is the key. He's the last one that can lead us to the assassin and this rogue FBI agent."

"So, you're using Mickey Soranno as a decoy."

"We make his arrest public with a press conference. We'll say that Albert Soranno is the killer and his father is an accessory while hiding him the past few years. It might be just enough to convince them to continue their plan and go with Hank Morgan to the bank."

"And then we catch them in the act?"

"Might be our best shot!"

Agent Main sighed. "Unfortunately, you're probably right. Why were you late this morning?"

"I was picking up the toxicology report on the female victim."

Agent Main detected a scent and then gave him an angry look. "I can smell her perfume on you. Guess it took a little longer than usual to get that report."

Gavin chuckled. "What? She gave me a hug. Friends do that."

"What was on the report?"

"Just like the other victims, there were no traces of neuroblockers in the system."

Before she could ask what else he'd found, AD Foster came over to them. He had arranged with Media Relations to do a press conference about Mickey Soranno's arrest. He wanted to know when they were ready to make the formal arrest. Gavin told him that they could have him in cuffs and in front of the cameras within the hour. AD Foster gave him the go-ahead. Agent Main had to ask, "Does Mickey know he's about to be arrested?"

"All part of the plan!"

An hour later, an FBI van arrived in downtown Chicago and pulled up in front of the Department of Justice building. Local and national media swarmed around, waiting for the man of the hour … a criminal or a saint, depending on who you asked. Some were already calling it the arrest of the year. Agent Main and Agent Donnelly escorted Mickey Soranno out of the van in handcuffs and through the sea of photographers and journalists, all trying to a shot or word out of the accused. Mickey was all too happy to oblige.

He cursed the FBI, calling them fucking assholes and racists against Italians. But he didn't hide his face from the cameras; he wanted his close-up, just like a movie star. They walked him past everybody and into the building to begin processing while the press conference began. Mickey looked at Gavin and smiled. "How did I do?"

Gavin laughed. "If there were an Academy Award for criminals, I would give it to you."

The FBI Media Relations agent started to speak. "I'm Agent Daniels. I have a brief statement and then I will take a few questions. As of 10:00 a.m., Mickey Soranno has been arrested for accessory to murder for the brutal killings of two retired Chicago police officers, Michael McGregor and Larry Crane. Our prime suspect for the murders is his son, Albert Soranno. We believe Mickey Soranno has been hiding his son for the past five years and helped him commit these murders. Those are all of the details we have for you now."

The man from WGN asked the first question. "Is it true that you have suspected Albert Soranno all along in the murders?"

"He has been a suspect, but we waited for enough evidence to be sure," Agent Daniels replied.

"Do you think that, if the FBI had acted on those suspicions, you could have stopped the other murder?"

"I won't comment on that."

The woman from CNN asked a question. "We've heard that there have been more than two murders that Albert Soranno is a suspect for. Is that true?"

Agent Daniels sighed. "I won't comment on that. We are only announcing what the facts are."

"We've also heard that this is a conspiracy involving a revenge plot against the Chicago Police Department. Can you comment on that?"

"Ma'am, we don't act on conspiracy theories at the FBI; we rely on facts. That's all I have to say about this. No further questions."

It didn't stop reporters from trying to ask more questions, but Agent Daniels was done. He did what he was supposed to and gave the facts as they were. There were enough theories running around Chicago about the murders. The best the FBI could do was try to contain them. Only one story would fit with Agent Donnelly's plan.

∞∞∞∞∞∞

Thousands of citizens in Chicago saw the press conference. It couldn't stop the paranoia that gripped the city; their most famous serial killer was back. However, that was not Agent Main and Agent Donnelly's concern. They were hoping that two people in particular would be watching. They got their wish.

The Old Man walked into the other room of the hotel suite and asked the man in black, "Did you see the news on TV?"

The man in black was on his laptop. "I saw the news headline on WGN's site."

"It looks like the plan worked. They think Albert Soranno is the killer and that his father is helping him. We got two birds with one stone. This is good news."

"Don't get too excited. They did question Hank Morgan and I guarantee he aroused their suspicions."

"What are you saying?"

"It could be a trap."

"Then the FBI would have surveillance on him or any bank. If they do, we'll back off."

The man in black looked disappointed. "I wouldn't be doing my job if I didn't warn you."

"Your job is also to avoid those traps."

"True, but don't say that I didn't warn you. What do you want to do?"

"We're going to wait out the day to see if anybody starts watching Hank Morgan, and then we'll proceed."

"It might help to leak the story about the girl since you wanted to kill her."

The Old Man was curious. "Why didn't they say anything about her murder?"

"It doesn't matter. For the record, killing her wasn't a good idea, but we can still use that to help ensure that they're not looking for Hank Morgan."

"You want to create more panic?"

[105]

"That's just a bonus. I want to force the FBI's hand and make them look for ghosts in the dark. It might just give us enough time to complete our mission and get out of here."

The Old Man had questions about the plan. He asked, "What about Frank London?"

"He won't survive. The other one on the account will just have to access it for us."

"You know that, in a month, that will be a lot harder for him to do."

"Then you'll figure something out. But you're not getting to Frank London now."

"Fine. Carry on with your plan. A little help wouldn't hurt."

The man in black pulled out his phone, plugged it into his laptop, and opened some encryption software. He called the Chicago Tribune and asked for Haley O'Brian. She answered the phone and he said, "Miss O'Brian … it's your anonymous friend. I have another news tip for you."

15

Agent Main and Agent Donnelly went back to work. There was more to this case than just a money laundering scheme. They wanted to find the people behind it all. Sure, Hank Morgan was the key to finding the assassin and the rogue FBI agent, but there was somebody pulling the strings and that's who they wanted.

Just like before, the agents' office was filled with files on the victims. Several documents filled the peg board while the dry erase board had many lines drawn from one box to another -- they were trying to make the connections. Agent Main said, "This morning, you mentioned that you found more information. What did you find?"

Gavin smiled. "The first thing I discovered was that it wasn't a cop who leaked the story."

"How do you know? Did you call the reporter and get her to divulge her source?"

"That's what I tried first, but she wouldn't give me a name. She was willing to sit in a jail cell for obstruction of justice."

"You threatened her with that? Goddamn journalistic integrity! I ran a trace on her office phone. There was a Google Voice number that we couldn't track."

"What do you mean, you couldn't track it? Internet numbers should have another phone number to call in to that is easy to track."

"That's the thing; we did look for a number and we couldn't find one. The tech guys ran a trace and said that it wasn't a phone at all, but an IP number that bounced around all over the world. Somebody made sure that no one could find where he was calling from. It's very high-tech stuff. Cops don't have what it takes to make that happen."

"But the NSA does. They would have the power to make their call untraceable and to monitor what we do at the FBI."

Gavin smiled. "Be careful, Agent Main. That sounds like a conspiracy."

She laughed. "I'm just going to say theory; doesn't sound so bad. "

"Now, it brings up another question: why would the NSA be involved?"

"Let's put that aside for now. We're not writing a fiction novel here."

Gavin laughed at the comment. Agent Main wasn't prone to making jokes, but he thought it was funny. He reached for a file on his desk that contained information about the safety deposit boxes. He found another connection between all of them when he dug a little deeper.

He told Agent Main, "We found safety deposit boxes for all six cops and one for the bank manager, Franklin White. Every one of those banks also had a safety deposit box for a Michael Harris; we already know that connection. However, I found something else. There is a second name on all of the boxes, including the ones for Michael Harris -- and it's the same name."

"What name?"

"James Smith."

"It's a common enough name, I guess. Why keep two names on each box? So they have another person who can access it?"

"That's one reason. Also, if the other person dies, then it automatically gets willed to the second person on the account. Most of the time, it's a husband and wife that own a box; so, when one of them dies, ownership gets transferred to the other. It's no different when the second name is a person not related to you. "

Agent Main sat back in her chair and sighed. "Even if we keep Frank London in witness protection and keep him alive, they can still access the box and get the bonds. It's better if they can kill the cops involved and the bank manager so that there are no witnesses. "

"I guess that was the plan."

"But this James Smith still has to go inside the bank, get the bonds from the box, and then cash them. There's still a chance of being seen and getting caught."

Gavin laughed. "I thought about that, too, so I did some more checking. When you open a box at a federal bank, you get to set the rules of how it's accessed and what happens if one of the owners dies."

"Let me guess. The rules are outside the norm for these boxes?"

"Oh yeah. If the primary owner dies and this James Smith is the only one left, then he doesn't even have to go into the bank to access the box. There is a 10-digit password on the account. Once that's given and the signed request is made, the bank manager can go into the box and remove its contents. They can make any transactions the customer wants, including transferring the money to a Swiss bank account. The bank can also send the contents to the owner in a protected truck with armed guards. That service is paid for by the owners of the box."

"Even without Frank London, they can get the money and they don't have to risk being seen."

"Yeah. It's brilliant if you really think about it. "

"That also means they don't need Hank Morgan."

"But they can't leave him alive, either."

"What makes you think they won't kill him and avoid the bank altogether?"

Gavin sighed. He didn't want to think about it, but she had a point. "It's a risk, but what other choice do we have? It's the only chance we have of getting the bad guys."

"To be honest, if they wanted to kill Hank Morgan before going to the bank, he'd be dead by now."

Gavin laughed. "You're probably right."

"Did you run the name James Smith?"

"I did. The last James Smith to work for the FBI retired in 1994 and died in 2002. It's used many times as an alias by FBI agents; there are over 500 James Smiths in the military and government agencies. Do you want to know how many James Smiths are in the state of Illinois? Over ten thousand."

Agent Main laughed. "So, what you're saying is that it's a needle in a haystack. Just the way they wanted it to be."

"The only way they could have made it harder is if the name were John Smith."

"Regardless of the name, the cross-referencing and research on every James Smith, just working for the government, would take weeks!"

"They created the perfect ghost. Someone who would never come out from the shadows."

She leaned back in her chair and started thinking. "A 10-digit password is kind of extreme and even the best minds would have trouble remembering one. If they wrote it down, then there's a paper trail."

"Yeah. Where are you going with this?"

"Ten digits could be a code. Maybe the easiest way to remember it is to have numbers correspond with letters."

"So, a name could be a code. What about James Smith? That name has 10 digits. If it were turned into numbers, it could be the password."

Agent Main laughed. "It might be that easy."

They figured out the corresponding numbers to James Smith. They assigned only a single digit to the letters that had double-digit numbers. There could be two sets of numbers, depending on if you took the second number or the first number of the double digit. They both decided that most codes would avoid lots of zeroes, so they took the second number of a double digit. They finally came up with 0135993908. Gavin called one of the banks that he already spoke with. He asked if he could use the password to get information about the safety deposit boxes where James Smith was the second name on the account. It didn't work; the password was incorrect. Gavin replied:

"It was a worth a shot."

"That doesn't mean we're not correct. Maybe it's a different name we're looking for and rearranging the numbers will give us that name."

"You could be right, but the possibilities are still endless. I think it's something the cryptology guys at the Bureau can work on."

Agent Main stood up. "So, how do we keep track of Hank Morgan if we can't use FBI resources to watch him? Can we even stake out the bank?"

"Not with a full surveillance team, but I have been giving it some thought. There's a building across the street that you and I can use. The fewer agents around the bank, the better."

"Are we just going to watch the bank for the next couple of days until they show up?"

"No. He will probably call in and take the day off. That will be the sign that he's going to the bank. We can get some help from IAD to let us know when he's not at the station. He already knows that IAD is watching him and I'm sure the other two know that as well. If they keep an eye out for us, it won't be suspicious."

"What makes you think they'll do you another favor?"

"Because they want Hank Morgan even more than we do!"

AD Foster came by their office. He wasn't happy, but they knew he wouldn't be until this case was solved. He looked at the two agents and asked them, "Do you have something new to report, or a perhaps a plan to catch Albert Soranno?"

"We're working on it, sir," Gavin replied.

"Has Mickey given anything to you yet?"

"Nothing new to report."

"Well, get something fast. I'm tired of hearing about this in the news."

Agent Main asked, "What do you mean?"

"You haven't seen the wires. The online edition of the Tribune just came up. That reporter who broke the story on the second murder just released a story naming the female victim and how Albert Soranno is picking his victims at random again."

Agent Main and Agent Donnelly both looked at each other with shock and anger. AD Foster continued, "I don't know for sure how she's getting her information, but put a stop to it."

"We can't intimidate a journalist or violate their civil rights just because we don't like what they print, "Agent Main replied.

"We can if they're obstructing justice and impeding our investigation. Causing panic in a city with false accusations is a crime. I want this reporter dealt with."

Gavin spoke up. "Then let's bring her in for questioning. We can hold her for at least 48 hours."

Agent Main looked at her partner. "Are you serious? How does this help us?"

AD Foster interrupted. "It will help the Bureau. We don't need a reporter spreading lies in the media. Bring her in." He walked out of the office. Agent Main shot her a partner a dirty look.

"How will this help us?"

"It makes us look desperate and it will provide an added ruse for what we're doing."

Agent Main thought about it. "You know, it just might work."

"We can use all the help we can get."

∞∞∞∞∞∞∞

A black Crown Victoria drove up to the front of the Tribune Tower, home of the Chicago Tribune. Agent Donnelly and Agent Main had finally gotten a new car from the FBI. They didn't say anything to the employees at the front desk; they just flashed their badges and went up to the Tribune offices. They asked for Haley O'Brian and she was pointed out at a desk in what the Tribune called the bullpen. Haley looked up and could immediately tell that the agents were coming to talk to her. As they approached her desk, Haley put her phone down.

Agent Main flashed her badge and introduced herself and Agent Donnelly. Haley had an annoyed look on her face and said, "As I told your partner, Agent Main, I won't reveal sources and I haven't broken any laws."

Agent Donnelly replied, "Well, Miss O'Brian, that's where you're wrong! You can't base your facts on anonymous sources and publish a news story. You work at the Chicago Tribune, not some trashy tabloid."

"How do you know that they're anonymous sources? Are you tapping my phones?"

Gavin laughed at her. "No ... but you just told me the sources were anonymous."

[111]

She scowled at him. "Screw you."

"You didn't even get a name? Just accepted what some unknown man told you as the truth?"

"He was credible."

Agent Main replied, "You know that's bullshit, Miss O'Brian. The worst part is that it's now obstruction of justice."

"What am I obstructing?"

Gavin yelled at her. "You're screwing up our investigation and you're causing unnecessary panic! "Everybody in the bullpen could hear him and most of them stopped what they were doing. Haley was startled.

"I'm doing my job," Haley replied.

Agent Main pulled out her handcuffs. "Doing your job just got you into trouble. You're under arrest for obstruction of justice. You have the right to remain silent and you should do it."

Agent Donnelly and Agent Main helped Haley get out of her chair and then Agent Main handcuffed her hands behind her back. They grabbed her purse and then walked her out of the office. Agent Donnelly smiled at his partner. "You feel better?"

"Well, I did get to handcuff someone today. I guess that's something."

"And tomorrow, you may get to handcuff someone else." She smiled at him. It had been a long week and, as new partners, they didn't exactly get off on the right foot. Agent Main didn't know if she would like Agent Donnelly, but he was growing on her. His sense of humor was something that she did like and it was a start to a good partnership. But it would be tested again, even more than it was this past week. Death was still waiting to collect!

16

It was another early morning for Gavin Donnelly. The sun was not even up yet, but he got out of bed and made some coffee. For him and his partner, it was a waiting game to see when the other side would make its move -- if they would at all. Waiting was the worst part for Gavin and Agent Main. He started thinking about last night's conversation with Detective Riggs from Chicago IAD.

∞∞∞∞∞∞

It was midnight when Agent Donnelly and Detective Alex Donnelly drove up to the 'L' station on Adams Street. They were meeting with Alex's IAD guy, Detective Riggs, in the shadows underneath the 'L' train, where they would not be seen or heard. As the two cousins approached Detective Riggs, he said to Gavin, "Agent Donnelly, you're racking up the favors with us. How does the Bureau feel about that?"

"This is just for me. I can't involve them just yet."

"The last time I helped you or your cousin, it ended up in the paper. Now we have a panic in the city."

"That wasn't us; it was the guys we're trying to catch."

"What do you want now?"

"We need help tracking Chief Hank Morgan's movements."

"Why can't you put a surveillance team on him?"

"The same reason I couldn't get the information about the safety deposit boxes through the Bureau; we have a mole who's watching what we do. If we're going to catch the guys behind these murders, then we can't spook him. And I know you guys have been watching Hank."

Detective Riggs paused for a moment. "Of course we have; he's corrupt. Taking him down would be big and the mayor gets to look good on not tolerating police corruption. What do you want with him?"

"He's a suspect in our investigation and an accessory to the murder of four other retired police officers. He's going to lead us to the bigger fish involved."

"So, we help you and the feds get the collar. What do we get out of it?"

"You get to help take down a corrupt cop and that will be reflected in our reports."

"Helping the feds doesn't do us any favors. IAD needs to be the one to arrest him."

"I understand that, but if you help us, you can bring whatever charges you want against him and he can go down for that, too."

"The problem is, if we let the feds take him down, then it looks like we can't clean our own house. That really isn't a win for us."

Gavin extended his hand to shake Detective Riggs's hand. "You help us, we help you, and this fucker gets taken down. He's going down anyway, so you can be a part of it or not. It's the best deal you're going to get."

Detective Riggs thought about it for a moment and then reached out his hand to shake Agent Donnelly's. "Alright, what do you want from us?"

"Put a couple of patrol officers outside this bank." Gavin handed him a piece of paper with the name and address on it. "Let them get coffee at the shop next door and they can keep an eye on the bank and provide backup if needed."

"Is that all?"

"No. Give me call when Hank Morgan calls in and doesn't show up for work." Gavin handed him his card. "The number on the back is untraceable. Call that one when you have the information. That's it."

"I suppose you still get to make the arrest?"

"Yeah, but you get to question him and charge him when we're done. And the mayor -- well, he can do all the press conferences he wants and say he helped the feds take down a corrupt cop."

"He won't like that."

"Probably not, but it's the best deal we can offer."

Detective Riggs paused for a moment. He didn't show any emotion but agreed to the terms of the deal. Hank Morgan was going down and, at the end of the day, it was still win-win for everybody.

∞∞∞∞∞∞∞

It was 6 a.m. when the prepaid cell phone began to ring on Gavin's dining room table. He answered the phone. Detective Riggs was on the other line and said, "Agent Donnelly, we got the word from our man in the precinct: Hank Morgan called in to take a personal day. We will have a few squad cars at the coffee shop taking shifts and watching the bank. They'll act like they're on break. Call me when you make an arrest."

Gavin was a little excited, hoping that today was the day they would catch the killers. He finished his cup of coffee, called his partner, and told her to be ready in 30 minutes. He picked her up and they drove downtown to the Chicago City Federal Bank. There was an office building across the street with a Starbucks inside. Agent Donnelly and Agent Main grabbed a table near the window with a perfect view of the bank's front entrance. The location was perfectly hidden and the agents looked like a couple of business executives having a meeting. They brought a laptop so that they could watch the security cameras from inside the bank. The tech guys at the Bureau were gracious enough to set up the surveillance on the laptop and hack into the security feed at the bank … off the books. Gavin always thought it was funny that the FBI hired former computer hackers for tech positions. They were considered criminals, but they were also the best in the business, so it made sense. And there were still a few tech guys that liked to do things unofficially and feel like a hacker again.

Agent Donnelly and Agent Main had everything set up and now it was back to waiting. Gavin never was a fan of stakeouts. They were ready to go by the time the bank opened at 8:00 a.m. and could only hope the guys they were looking for wouldn't slip through the crowd. Agent Main took a sip of coffee and asked her partner, "So, how long do you think we'll have to be here?"

"If they follow their pattern, they should be here early in the morning."

"What about Hank Morgan? What if they use him as a hostage?"

"Personally, I don't care if they kill him. But, if we can get him alive, then that's the way to go. It's the other two that we really want and we need them alive."

"I agree. And if they don't show, do we keep coming back and staking this place out?"

"It's the best shot we have at catching them."

Two hours went by and nothing happened. After three cups of coffee each, the agents were getting bored. They hadn't talked about anything while watching the bank, so Agent Donnelly finally struck up a conversation. He asked Agent Main:

"Why did you want to become an FBI agent?"

"Really? You want to talk about that now? Isn't that something you do on the first day of working together?"

Gavin laughed. "Sure, but we've had a chaotic week. I'm asking after five days of working together."

She laughed at his comment. "First, why don't you tell me why you chose to become an FBI agent instead of a Chicago cop, like the rest of your family? Then, maybe I'll tell you why I became one."

Gavin smiled. "Alright, I'll go first. I'm sure that, from reading my file, you know that I went to law school. I never had any intention of becoming a cop. In my last year of law school, the White Collar Division was called in to help with a local fraud and money laundering case in my uncle's precinct. The business was an investment and loan company that offered cheap loans and investment opportunities to people who could use retirement funds to get started. The company basically stole the money and laundered it, swindling working class people out of their retirements and savings. They couldn't make a case because they couldn't find where the money went, and that was the evidence of financial fraud. Since I was studying financial law and also had an economics degree, my uncle asked me to take a look at the case and offer a theory. It turned out that the company laundered the money through stocks, bonds, and an investment in a dummy company with a fake IPO. They made the money people gave them disappear on paper or financial records. I helped find the money and take this company down. The money they stole was spread out in four different accounts in the Cayman Islands. All the people that did business with this company got their money back and won a settlement. In a way, they did make more money. After that, I was recruited by the FBI. I chose a career with the Bureau because it felt good to stop a company from cheating people out of their fortunes. I wanted to do that with a federal agency instead of being a lawyer."

"Do you regret your decision?"

"Not at all, Agent Main. Although, when this week is over, ask me again."

She laughed at the comment. Her partner was right. It had been the week from Hell and the type of week that could make anybody rethink his or her career choice. Gavin asked her again why she became an FBI agent. She was about to answer but instead said with excitement, "Hey look! Isn't that Hank Morgan?"

Gavin looked out the window and spotted him. "Yes, it is. He's with what appears to be an older man."

"Looks like you were right. They took the bait and decided to come to the bank today. But I only see two of them. Shouldn't there be a third man?"

"He's there somewhere; probably already in the bank. I don't want to take any chances, so get your vest."

Agent Donnelly and Agent Main reached underneath the table and grabbed the duffle bag that was sitting there. They pulled out two bulletproof vests and put them on. After packing their gear, they took it to their car around the corner. Agent Donnelly motioned to the two police offers who were sitting at the coffee shop to go around to the back entrance of the bank and cover the alley. The agents walked into the bank during rush hour. It was Friday and close to lunch time, so there were a lot of people doing their banking before the weekend. The crowd was a problem for the agents, but it was planned that way in case the authorities did show up.

They entered the bank slowly, looking for Hank Morgan and the older man he was with. Agent Main gave the security guards the descriptions and told them not to let the men leave without permission, but to keep it quiet. They didn't want to cause a panic. Agent Donnelly was looking around the front area of the bank for anybody that looked out of the ordinary. He was trying to find the assassin, even though he had no idea what he looked like. He really didn't know what he was looking for and was hoping for some kind of vision that might help him. The agents found the safety deposit box vault down the main hall of the bank. Sitting at the desk in front of it, talking to the manager, was Hank Morgan and the Old Man. The agents drew their weapons and approached slowly. The Old Man saw them out of the corner of his eye.

Agent Main shouted, "Hank Morgan and the gentleman sitting next to him: this is the FBI and you're under arrest. Put your hands in the air and slowly get down on the ground."

Agent Donnelly was right behind her, but still looking around for the third man. Hank Morgan and the Old Man were startled. They didn't say anything, but slowly raised their hands and got out of their chairs. The Old Man smiled and it tipped off Agent Donnelly. As he turned around, there was a security guard with a gun in his hand. He opened fire and his shots were precise. Agent Main was hit in the top of her right shoulder, where her vest didn't cover. The guard knew exactly where to hit her to send her falling to ground. Screams could be heard all over the bank and the silent alarm was tripped. Customers were trying to get out of the bank.

Agent Main yelled out in pain. Agent Donnelly dove around a corner while firing shots at the guard, hoping to hit him. The Old Man pulled out his weapon and shot the manager they were talking to while Hank dove to the ground to avoid getting shot. The Old Man grabbed Agent Main and helped her up as she was bleeding out. She was in shock and shaking, which prevented her from defending herself as she was taken hostage. Agent Donnelly was trapped and couldn't go after the Old Man. He had to make a split-second decision. He hoped that the police officers at the back entrance could trap the Old Man and give him time to get there to save his partner. The guard fired a few more rounds, keeping Agent Donnelly trapped around the corner. Finally, he drew his other weapon and started firing both guns in the guard's direction, giving him a chance to come out from the corner. He kept shooting and started moving toward the guard's direction. By the time he got there, he had emptied both clips but found no traces of the guard who fired at him. The security guard at the front entrance was dead. Agent Donnelly figured the assassin had disguised himself as a guard and escaped through the front door. He didn't go after him; he needed to save his partner.

He reloaded both guns and headed the other way. Hank Morgan was still on the ground, trying to take cover. Agent Donnelly threw his handcuffs at him and said, "Put those on and lock yourself to the desk. If you try to escape, I'll blow your fucking head off." Hank didn't say a thing; he was too scared, so he handcuffed himself to the desk.

He ran to the back entrance of the bank and found one officer dead. The other was shot in the shoulder and lying on the ground. He told Agent Donnelly what direction the Old Man headed. The Old Man took Agent Main into the abandoned building next door and was looking for a way out. Agent Donnelly was right on his tail. The Old Man was looking for another door to escape from in the abandoned building. He found one that was locked and that's when Agent Donnelly cornered him. He shouted:

"Put your gun down. There's no way out."

The Old Man, with Agent Main in his arms and blood-soaked from her wound, turned around to face him. "You put yours down, Agent Donnelly, or I'll kill your partner."

Agent Donnelly wasn't that surprised that the Old Man knew who he was. "So you have been monitoring us."

"Of course we have. Now, put your gun down and let me walk out of here. Let me get away and I'll let her live."

"You know that I can't do that."

"And you know that the rules of engagement prohibit you from taking action while there's a hostage, unless you have a sniper on me. Don't be like my brother and break the rules of engagement. You will only get people killed."

Agent Donnelly paused for a moment and then replied, "You kill her and you're dead a half-second later. It's time to give it up. There's no way out, Jack."

The Old Man started laughing. "Agent Jack Denton … haven't heard that in a while! You think if you catch me or even get me to testify then all of this stops? If I go with you or tell you anything then I'll be dead the same day."

"She needs an ambulance. Let her go and we'll talk about letting you get out of here."

The Old Man laughed again. "You can't do that. The FBI wouldn't let you." Agent Donnelly had his gun pointed right where he wanted in case he had to shoot to kill. The Old Man shook his head, looked down at Agent Main and then looked back up at Agent Donnelly. He raised his gun a little higher and shouted, "Fuck …"

Agent Donnelly fired one shot and hit the Old Man in the right part of his forehead, killing him instantly. As he fired, he finished, "You!"

It was an impossible shot for most people, but not for Agent Donnelly. He was that good of a shot and held records at the FBI Academy to prove it. The Old Man was right about the rules of engagement, but he didn't care. Agent Donnelly would kill anybody to save his partner's life. When the Old Man's body hit the ground, Agent Main fell, too. Still in shock, shaking and breathing heavily, she started to cry as she put pressure on her wound to keep it from bleeding. Agent Donnelly ran to her and grabbed her tightly, trying to comfort her and stop the bleeding, too. He got his cell phone out and called for an ambulance.

Agent Main kept mumbling, "I can't … I can't."

Agent Donnelly sat with her and kept holding her. He told her over and over, "I've got you … you're going to be okay … you're going to be okay." He held on to her until the ambulance arrived and he never let her go. It was the best way for him to let her know that she was not alone and he would do anything to keep her safe.

17

Thirty minutes later, the scene outside the bank was chaotic. Chicago PD had the building surrounded while FBI CSU were locking down the crime scene to start their investigation. Two ambulances arrived; one of them took the Old Man's dead body away and the other one brought Agent Main out. Paramedics stopped the bleeding and she was groggy from the morphine drip she had been given. Agent Donnelly helped walk her out of the office building next door and load her up in the ambulance. AD Foster finally arrived at the scene and the first person he wanted to talk to was Agent Donnelly.

He looked at him and said, "You certainly caused a shit storm this morning."

Agent Donnelly chuckled. "We didn't expect to be shot at today. It was supposed to be a simple arrest."

"Who fired at you?"

"It was the same man who murdered our victims. He was an assassin and disguised himself as a security guard."

"So, it wasn't Albert Soranno?"

"No, he was a copycat killer. We think he's a contract killer hired to make it look like an Albert Soranno murder."

"Did you know this before your meeting with OPR?"

"It was a theory."

AD Foster sighed. "I don't want to hear that you purposely lied to OPR. You're already on thin ice. Also, your killer got away."

"There won't be any more murders. This was the last bank they needed to visit and we just got one of them."

"You mean you killed one of them. Are you okay?"

"I'm fine."

"I know that this is the first time you've killed someone in the line of the duty. It can be a tough thing."

Agent Donnelly smiled. "Really, I'm fine. Besides, you already know that it's not the first time I've killed somebody."

AD Foster didn't respond to that, but the look on his face said he knew what Agent Donnelly was talking about. He did say, "It looks like Agent Main is going to be okay. The bullet went clean through. It must have been an amazing shot or just plain lucky."

"He was a professional, sir. He knew where to hit her. "

"What about this Hank Morgan?"

"We can charge him on conspiracy and accessory to murder. But we also need to sweat him a little bit. He can help lead us to the bigger fish."

"Didn't you just kill him?"

"I think there is more to this case than a former FBI agent and retired police officers laundering money. There are still too many unanswered questions."

"I told you before: we don't deal in conspiracy theories at the FBI. If there are more involved, then offer Hank Morgan a deal for his testimony -- just like Frank London."

Agent Donnelly looked disgusted. "Sir, I understand offering a deal to Frank London, but Hank lied to us and helped put this whole thing together. He should be prosecuted and spend the rest of his life in prison. "

"We're not worried about him; he was evidently a pawn. Let Chicago IAD have him."

Agent Donnelly motioned for AD Foster to come with him out of earshot of everyone else. He had more questions and was trying to satisfy his lingering curiosity about this case. It wasn't an open-and-shut case. He asked:

"Sir, did Jack Denton have a brother? His file at the Bureau didn't list one."

"That's strange, but yes, he did … Kenny Denton. He was a federal prosecutor at the DOJ in Chicago. Why? "

"Before I shot the Old Man, he made a reference about his brother at the FBI. I don't understand how that can be if his brother was a federal prosecutor. "

AD Foster had a surprised look. "Kenny and Jack were identical twins."

Agent Donnelly paused with shock. Then he said, "Twins! Then that means …"

"I know what you're going to say, and it's plausible. In fact, it makes sense since Jack is dead."

"But what does Kenny Denton have to do with any of this? Was he even in Chicago in 1983?"

"I can't answer that."

"Why would that information be omitted from Jack Denton's file at the FBI?"

"Look, there are any number of reasons, the most plausible being that some information got lost when the FBI started putting everything on computer over 25 years ago. You and I both know that some information on old agents went missing. It's probably just an error."

Agent Donnelly, in a serious tone, replied, "Maybe, but it doesn't answer the bigger question: who did I really kill?"

"Perhaps an autopsy can tell us. "

"But the DNA test won't be conclusive if we're dealing with identical twins. We need to exhume Jack Denton's remains and test them, as well."

AD Foster shook his head. "Hold on. Even if you put the request in and get a court order, it doesn't mean the Bureau will let you go through with it. The last thing they want is the embarrassment of a former agent involved in a murder and money laundering conspiracy. Having Kenny Denton as our guy is a good thing. He was corrupt and did two years in federal prison after being disbarred. You solved a good case."

"There's no definitive evidence that it's Kenny, and we need to be sure. Besides, there was something else he did before I shot him. He laughed and gave me a look as if he knew something important that I didn't … kind of like someone does during a poker game when they know they have the winning hand."

"It doesn't mean anything, Agent Donnelly. You got your man and put a stop to this scheme and that's what the report should say. Don't drum up conspiracy theories that you can't prove. And let me give you some career advice: any theory you come up with that makes it seem the FBI is wrong will get you kicked out. You've had a good career so far; don't tarnish it." AD Foster was done talking about this and walked away.

Agent Donnelly shouted as he was walking off, "I'm not done looking for the answers. The truth is out there and I'm going to find it."

AD Foster shouted back, "Don't say I didn't warn you."

Agent Donnelly was pissed. He felt like he was the only one that cared about the truth. He called a contact of his at the DOJ to see if he could get Kenny Denton's records. He needed a timeline for when Kenny might have been working in Chicago. As he was talking on the phone, he noticed that his Uncle Liam had showed up to the crime scene. Gavin had forgotten that his precinct was nearby. He walked over to say hi.

Liam looked at his nephew, who was still covered in blood from holding his partner. "Are you alright, Gavin? I heard what happened. Is it true that you had to kill someone?"

"I'm fine; this isn't my blood. And yes, I did have to kill someone."

"What does Hank really have to do with all this?"

"He got the SWAT team to steal Victor Soranno's money and, with a rogue FBI agent, they laundered the money through bearer bonds. The murders were made to look like Albert Soranno was behind them."

"Did he have anything to do with blowing up your car and trying to kill you?"

"Not directly."

Agents were bringing Hank Morgan out of the bank in handcuffs. Hank looked over at Liam and Gavin. He didn't want to look his old friend in the eye, but he would have to. Gavin and Liam walked over to where he was and Liam asked if he could get a minute alone with Hank. Gavin told the other agents that it was alright. Hank told Liam, "I don't have anything to say. We did what we did. Nothing more to say! "

Liam shook his head. "I do have something to say. I don't give two shits about what you did. I've always stuck up for you, always had your back. But if you really had something to do with the attempt on a member of my family, I'll be the last person you see right before a bullet goes through your head." Hank didn't have anything to say to that, but he understood it. There would be honor in Liam's vengeance.

∞∞∞∞∞∞∞

It was two hours later and Agent Donnelly was at the DOJ building. He finally got a chance to change his shirt. His partner, Agent Main, was rushed into surgery at Cook County Hospital to repair her shoulder. She was fortunate and she wouldn't be out for very long. The department decided to make a deal with Hank Morgan, despite Gavin's protest. But he at least got to deliver the news.

Hank Morgan was a put in a room by himself with no windows. Gavin walked into the room with a file. He still had an angry look for Hank Morgan. He said, "It turns out that today is your lucky day. You're not going to prison."

"Oh!" Hank replied.

"The Department of Justice has decided to cut you a deal in exchange for your testimony behind this conspiracy. You get witness protection if you do this. I've got to tell you, it's a hell of deal. A damn good deal for a piece of shit like you."

"Hold on there, boy. I did what your uncle or any other cop would have done in my place. You would do the same if the FBI came to you and said they needed your help stealing a mobster's money and that you would get to be a millionaire for helping."

[123]

"Now, *you* hold on. First, I haven't been a boy for a long time and my badge demands a little more respect from you. Second, don't drag my uncle into the mud with you. You had a choice, and whatever great plan you thought you had got six people killed and my partner shot. You dance with the devil and bad things happen. If it were up to me, you'd rot in prison for the rest of your miserable life. But this is the best deal you're going to get and you won't face any charges by IAD. They want you real bad and, if you don't take this deal, we won't have to do anything to you; they'll take you down."

Hank started shaking his head. "You think that if I testify and tell you everything you want to know, then I'll be safe? I'll be dead in a day."

"You're the second person who's told me that today. Who are these people? Help me stop them."

"You are naïve, just like a little boy. You can't bring them down. "

"Help me and I will personally get you out of here safely. "

"Not that Irish honor can help me."

Gavin closed the file and headed for the door. "You have until Monday to sign the agreement or you'll be released to Chicago IAD. Until then, you will be in solitary confinement. Make the right decision, Hank, before you screw something else up."

∞∞∞∞∞∞

The FBI decided to let Haley O'Brian go. There was no reason to hold her anyway, and the little ruse that she helped in worked. As Gavin saw it, she could one day be an asset. She probably wouldn't have a problem with that, considering she now had a great arrest story for protecting sources. The FBI just helped her career in a major way. Gavin personally escorted her out of holding. She commented, "You know, cruel and unusual punishment isn't the holding cell. It's not being able to take a shower. "

Gavin laughed. "Then you will understand if I stay a few feet away from you. "

She smiled at his joke. "I guess no charges are being brought against me?"

"No. We got what we needed from you. You were a decoy."

She looked surprised at first, but then figured it out. "I helped you draw the bad guys out."

"Yes, you did, and you played your part perfectly."

[124]

"Well, I will have some bragging to do back at the office. I heard there was a shootout today at a federal bank and your partner got hit."

Gavin sighed. "That's right."

"Is she going to be okay?"

"Agent Main will make it. She took a round in the shoulder."

"I'm sorry to hear that. "

Gavin walked Haley to the front door after she got her purse. He told her, "I will go ahead and let you know that Albert Soranno was not the killer. It was a contract killer or assassin hired to kill the victims. You write that in your next piece. "

"Can I quote you on that?"

"No names. You can use 'FBI sources' only."

She smiled at him. "Agent Donnelly, you're not as bad as your whole FBI act. We should get together sometime. I bet we could have some fun." She leaned in and gave him a little kiss on the lips. He didn't try to stop her. Gavin always liked when women flirted with him. He just told her, "Try not to get yourself into trouble."

"If they send you to come get me, I might have to." She winked at him and walked out of the building.

18

For the past year, Gavin Donnelly had a Friday ritual. He had dinner at Berghoff's with Dr. Robert Schuman. He met the doctor over a year before by accident. In fact, he saved the doctor from being shot by a mugger because Gavin saw a vision of it. Dr. Schuman was a medical doctor with degrees in two fields: psychology and neurology. He used to practice, but now dedicated himself to teaching and research. As he put it, he was told that practice, research and teaching fit better with his laid-back lifestyle, especially during baseball season. He was a huge Chicago Cubs fan and loved going to afternoon games.

The doctor was the only one who knew about Gavin's ability. He figured it out after Gavin saved his life. He agreed to help Gavin try to control it, to help him become better at seeing things. For Dr. Schuman, it was a chance to work with a real psychic while trying to answer those looming questions about how the human mind really worked. The human brain was a dark and deep trench of mystery and Dr. Shuman had spent two-thirds of his life trying to solve it. While Gavin turned out to be the perfect research subject, he ended up becoming a good friend in the process. They would have dinner together and talk. Gavin would tell him things he saw and the doctor helped him make sense of it the best he could.

Gavin entered the restaurant and found Dr. Schuman sitting at the table in the back corner of the restaurant. It was his usual place. As Gavin walked up to the table, the doctor spoke up. "I didn't know if you would make it today. I heard about the shootout at the bank; sounds like it was messy. "

"It wasn't pretty. I had to kill someone in the line of duty today. It was my first. "

"How do you feel?"

"I feel fine. Sometimes, it's just part of the job."

"You started in the Violent Crimes Division this week, right?"

"Yes, and I have a new partner. She's good. She's a profiler from Washington."

The waiter came over and Gavin ordered a drink and a swordfish sandwich. Dr. Schuman took a bite of his bratwurst. He sensed the worry surrounding Gavin. "You're afraid that she will figure out your gift?"

"She will eventually. In fact, she already suspects something."

"Can you trust her?"

"Not with something like this. Maybe one day that will change. "

Dr. Schuman took another bite of food. He smiled. "I hope, for your sake, that it does. Your situation is not something I would want to be in. So, what we will talk about today? "

Gavin laughed as his food arrived. He bit into it and smiled at how good the sandwich tasted. It was one of his favorite items at the restaurant. He replied, "I had more visions this week than I usually do in a single week."

"Well, I've told you before that stress can trigger them. Sounds like you've had a rough week."

"Oh yeah. There's a lot I can't tell you."

"I heard some things on the news."

"Don't believe everything you hear. Albert Soranno isn't back in Chicago killing people, but we do have a copycat killer. Four people are dead. "

Dr. Schuman looked at him curiously. "You feel responsible for the deaths?"

"If I could've figured out the clues in things that I saw, I might have prevented some of the murders."

"Might have, but you're not certain. "

"No."

"Even if you see everything, there are no guarantees that you can prevent what's happening. The clues just provide you a better opportunity."

"Then what's the point of having this so-called gift if I can't save lives?"

Dr. Schuman paused. "I can't answer that; only you can. But look at it this way: everything you do well, you had to learn to do and train to get better. You didn't wake up one day and magically have your talents. You got better through practice. "

"Are you trying to tell me that I have to practice more to get better at figuring out what I see?"

"Exactly!"

"That's a little hard when I don't know when I'll have visions.
"

"All the more reason to not waste your opportunities," Dr. Schuman replied with a teacher's tone. "Try this breathing exercise when you see something. Breathe in through your nose and release the breath out through your mouth. Do that a few times and it will help calm your body and mind. It's a meditation exercise and should help you see things more clearly, help you to see more clues in the vision. "

"A meditation exercise?!"

"I know. Buddhists have proven that it can work."

"I'm not a Buddhist."

"Neither am I, but Western medicine doesn't have all the answers. There are techniques from Eastern culture that do work and can benefit you. "

Gavin smiled and took another bite of his sandwich. "It wasn't a total loss this week. I did see one vision and we were able to get there in time to save at least one life. "

"See? You are getting better. Even though it's a cliché, it's true: it is one step at a time. Are you still seeing things about 30 minutes in the future?"

"Yes."

"I think that's the most fascinating part about you. Why only 30 minutes into the future?"

Gavin chuckled a bit. "My Uncle Liam told me something interesting this week. My grandfather gave him and my dad an hourglass that was set to only 30 minutes. When they had a problem that they could not solve, the timer would be set for 30 minutes and they would clear their minds and not think about it. Then, a solution would usually present itself."

Dr. Schuman paused in thought and smiled. "Interesting. Very interesting."

"What? You have a theory?"

"I've always been amazed about how much our environment affects our brain patterns -- or, to put it more simply, the way we think. You were taught to base problem solving on 30 minutes of time. Therefore, the prefrontal cortex of your brain and its parts breaks the completions of its functions down into that particular increment of time. "

"English, doctor?"

"Problem solving, planning, organization … those functions, which are controlled by the prefrontal cortex, use 30 minutes to complete tasks because you've been trained to associate those things with that time frame. It stands to reason that your ability to see the future would also be associated with that time frame."

Gavin smiled. "Then it's another variable of the puzzle that I will have to solve."

"That's true, but it's another mystery solved about how your brain is working. I have a feeling that, in your new job, you will start to see more visions."

"I still feel as if this is a curse."

"Or you can see it as a gift, which you can use to save lives and help those that need it. Like me!"

Gavin finished his sandwich. "I still have more questions than answers."

"The answers will come in time, but let me ask you: if you hadn't had a vision this week, would you have been able to solve your case?"

"Maybe eventually, but not as quickly as we did."

"Then it's a gift. So, I have a question for you."

"Ask away."

"Do you think the Cubs will have a shot this year?"

"Probably not, with their lack of power hitters and a weak bullpen. I don't need a vision to know that. "Dr. Schuman laughed. Gavin had to leave, so he shook the doctor's hand, left money on the table for his meal, and said goodbye. As usual, he learned one more thing about his condition and how to use it for his benefit.

∞∞∞∞∞∞∞∞

Gavin was walking to his car after leaving the restaurant when his cell phone rang. He answered it. "Gavin Donnelly!"

"Agent Donnelly, I'm so very glad that you made it out alive today. You must be the more gifted between you and your partner."

Gavin's face turned to shock. He may not have known his name, but he knew who it was on the other end of the phone. He switched the phone to speaker so he could find the application on his smart phone to record the conversation. "You're the killer. Not sure if I should take that as an insult or compliment from you!"

"Well, I would hate to see you dead when this little game of ours is just getting started. "

"This isn't a game. You killed four people this week. We can't let that go."

The killer laughed. "But you did save one. Oh, I must congratulate you; you're the only person that has ever shot me. "

"Why are you calling me? To brag about getting away?"

"No, to ask you a question, Agent Donnelly. How did you know when to go back to the safe house and stop me from killing Frank London?"

[129]

"We were heading back there anyway. Just got lucky."

"No, you weren't. Is it possible that you are more like your mother than you let on?"

Gavin was startled again. "How do you know about her?"

"She had the gift; the true gift of seeing the future. You do, as well. "

"HOW DO YOU KNOW ABOUT HER?" Gavin shouted.

"Because the same man, who changed the course of your life, changed mine. Your mother saw something that she was not supposed to and that's why she had to die along with your father."

Gavin was full of rage. "If I ever find you again, I will kill you. "

"I'm not the one you really want. I'm just a foot soldier in this game. You want the men who wanted your mother and father dead. The same men who put this whole money laundering scheme together. The same men who hired me. "

"Why are you telling me this? "

"Because I want them, too. One day, we may need each other's help and, when that day comes, I want to make sure that we're on the same side. When you start looking for answers, make sure you look in the right direction."

The killer hung up the phone. Gavin was too angry to try to trace the call. He knew that it was probably useless anyway. He checked the recording; it was almost perfect. Of course, he could try running it through voice recognition software at the Bureau -- but that, too, would probably be useless. The voice in the recording was a ghost and made a living out of not wanting to be found.

19

It was Saturday afternoon and Agent Main was being released from the hospital. After undergoing surgery to repair the gunshot wound in her shoulder, she had to stay overnight for observation. Agent Main lost a good amount of blood from being shot, so keeping her overnight was the best thing for her. She was still shaky from the day before; part of that was fear and it was hard to tell how she would respond to that in a few weeks. She looked over and saw a few different flower arrangements from coworkers. One of them was from her partner. He had been by to visit more than once since yesterday. Every time he stopped by, she was sleeping. She thought about calling him for a ride back to her hotel, but she didn't want to deal with anything from work until Monday. Agent Main knew enough that the case had been wrapped up and that there wasn't anything more to investigate.

She was packing up some things when AD Foster walked into her room. He said, "I heard you were being released today. Glad to see you're feeling better. "

"Thank you, sir. They give you really good drugs here. It helps with the pain."

AD Foster laughed. "Is Agent Donnelly coming to pick you up?"

"No, I didn't call him. It's the weekend, so I didn't want to bother him. Besides, I'm a big girl; I can get back to my hotel on my own. "

"Understandable, but I will give you a ride there. You should have someone take you home."

"I guess I really can't argue with my boss."

"I wouldn't."

AD Foster grabbed her bag since her right arm was in a sling. He asked, if she wanted to take the flowers with her. She said no, that they would die in a few days anyway. She did have a question for AD Foster.

"Sir, I was wondering about something. I don't want to get anybody in trouble, so this question is off the record. Why hasn't Agent Donnelly taken a weapon qualification test in the last few years?"

"We don't have to worry about Agent Donnelly."

"Why?"

"Because he's a doesn't have to. He's that good of a shot, but you already saw that."

"Yeah, but he also broke the rules of engagement. He took an impossible shot. I don't know how he was that lucky and didn't hit me in the process. "

AD Foster gave her a worried look. "Are you angry about it?"

She paused. "More scared than anything. "

"You're worried that he's reckless and wondering if you can trust him. I've seen it many times with new partners. "

"We have the rules of engagement to protect us and to keep us from acting like cowboys in the Wild West."

"Do you really think that? Even though you've broken them, too? The only difference is, it wasn't a mother and an unborn child that he was trying to save. It was his partner. "

"I don't know if I can work with someone who's careless like that. "

AD Foster laughed. "Gavin Donnelly is the least careless person with a gun. In fact, he's probably the best shot in the FBI. He holds all the shooting records at the Bureau."

"You mean the course record? He doesn't hold that one."

"I'm not talking about that record; I mean the real records. He also went through sniper training with the US Marine School at Quantico. The long-distance records with pistols and rifles; he has those records. Gavin Donnelly could shoot a gun before he could swing a bat or skate on ice. All the men in his family are great shots. As far as we're concerned, he can take that shot if he needs to. That's why he hasn't taken a qualification test in years. "

She looked surprised. "I didn't know."

"You've had a long week and you got shot. It can't be the easiest situation: coming to Chicago and being teamed up with Gavin Donnelly. He's a good agent, but still a rookie in Violent Crimes. If you want to put a request in for a new partner, then we'll discuss it. "

"I appreciate that."

AD Foster smiled. "Although, you should know, it was my idea to have you transferred here instead of getting suspended."

Agent Main looked surprised. "Why?"

"Because you're too good not to be in the game instead on the sidelines. You two need each other, even if you don't see it." That was all he said. It made her wonder if he might be right. She asked him

where she could find Gavin on a Saturday night. He said two words:
Paddy Murphy's.

∞∞∞∞∞∞

Mickey Soranno was being released from prison on Saturday
morning. There was no evidence to justify holding him. He had done
his part to fool the killers into thinking that the FBI was going after him
and his son, Albert Soranno. Gavin was there to greet him as he was
coming out. Some of Mickey's guys were there, as well. The prison
door opened into the waiting area and Mickey walked out with a
surprised look. He didn't expect Gavin to be there. He smiled and
asked him, "How was my performance? Did I help you fool
everyone?"

"You did great. You might have the makings of a good actor.
Maybe earn some honest money."

"Now that would be comical. So, what are you doing here?"

"I just wanted to say thank you for helping. We caught one of
them."

"I heard that you killed one of the men in a shootout at a bank.
It's the first time you've actually killed somebody in the line of duty,
isn't it?"

"Yeah."

Mickey laughed. "No need to thank me. My lawyer says I have
a pretty good case for suing the FBI for false prosecution. "

Gavin laughed. "I guess going from racketeering to frivolous
lawsuits isn't that much of a stretch."

"Probably not. By the way, I have some information for you.
In 1988, a letter was sent to me with no return address. It told me that a
safety deposit box was opened in my name and it contained the money
that was stolen from my father. They were bonds and, in 20 years, they
would be worth more than what was stolen. I checked on the box and,
sure enough, they were right. I never took the money."

"Why not?"

"'Cause fuck them, I won't be bought off for my father's death.
I'm not Judas. And after what you told me, and what I heard about the
murders, I knew it was a trap. It wasn't about paying me off."

"They want to kill you?"

"If you take someone's life and want to ensure that no revenge
comes upon you, then you have to kill all those that seek vengeance.
Especially the son. "

"You didn't want to try to find the guys that did it? Set a trap
for them and kill them?"

[133]

"Of course I did, but I know an FBI agent who would get the guys that did it. That's good enough for me."

Gavin looked at him strangely. Mickey smiled and said, "We always want to put the knife in the enemy ourselves, but if a man we respect does it for us, then there's no reason to complain. You know that I've always had respect for you and your family. And you have always shown that to me. Justice has been served, as you boys like to say. " Mickey smiled again, shook Gavin's hand, and left. There were reporters standing outside and he did have to make a few comments about the FBI, telling the media how they were pigs and that he would be suing them. Gavin had to laugh. Mickey would have made a great actor.

∞∞∞∞∞∞∞

In an Irish neighborhood, the place to be on Saturday night was the pub. It was filled with laughter and Irish folk music. Inside the pub, even strangers were family. Most residents of the neighborhood would come in for dinner and a pint or two after a long, hard week. As for the Donnelly family, they were usually there to play music. Gavin Donnelly played guitar in an Irish folk band for over 20 years. Just like learning how to shoot, he had learned how to play Irish music since he was kid. The band was called The Donnelly Rovers and consisted of Gavin on guitar, his cousin Alex on mandolin and banjo, his other cousin, Catherine, on violin and flute, and his Uncle Patrick on the other guitar. The band had been playing at the pub for almost two decades. They were there on most Saturday nights.

Agent Main wanted to talk to her partner, so she went to the pub that night. As she walked in, the pub was crowded with the usual patrons. Kids were running around and people were singing and dancing. She looked over at the stage and spotted Gavin singing with his family. He was the happiest she had ever seen him. The band was finishing their first set with the oldest known folk song, *Whiskey in the Jar*. Agent Main took a seat at the bar and waited for the band to finish playing. She smiled at the fact that Gavin could actually sing. He was pretty good, in her opinion. The song finished and the crowd started shouting, "Toast! Toast! Toast!" Gavin usually gave at least one Irish toast in the evening.

He laughed and responded, "You want a toast? Alright. I will toast this evening for us all." He held up a pint of Guinness and said:

"It is nine o'clock on a Saturday,
And you can hear Piano Man another day
I'm glad to be here with family and friends

[134]

For with whom I'll never have to make amends
Although our week has been tough
And making it in this city can be rough
We have streams of whiskey that flows
To get us through our highs and lows
If we should run out then at least we have beer
So this night can be full of good cheer."

The crowd erupted in laughter while raising a glass and cheering for his toast. Even Agent Main laughed a little bit. The band took a break and headed for the bar to get beer. Gavin smiled when he saw his partner sitting there. As he walked over to her, she said:

"Nice toast."

"Thank you. What are you doing here? I thought you'd call me when you were being released from the hospital. "

"It's okay. I didn't need any help."

"How are you feeling today?"

"Sore, but they gave me really good painkillers."

"I guess I shouldn't buy you a beer, then. "

"I can have one before I have to take another pill. Besides, I should probably buy you one, considering that you saved my life. "

"No thanks required."

Patrick, the bartender, came over to see if they needed anything. Gavin introduced him to his partner. She asked about him and Gavin told her that he was the original owner's grandson. She asked, "So Paddy Murphy was a real person?"

"Just like the song. "

Agent Main looked at him strangely.

"There's a song about a Paddy Murphy who died, and his friends and family had a wake for him. We like to tell everybody that he's the guy in the song, even though he's not. But our Paddy Murphy did die behind the bar 25 years ago. The wake here at the pub was a huge celebration. "

Patrick chimed in, "The best way to remember somebody is to drink to his memory. "

"Well said, Patrick."

Agent Main laughed as two Guinness beers were placed in front of the agents. She told her partner that she read his report on what he found after the shooting. "A twin brother. Uh, didn't see that one coming. I saw your request to exhume the body of Jack Denton. You think it will actually go through?"

"I don't want to know, but I think it's important that we know who we really killed."

"I agree, but they're not going to let you shit upon the memory of Jack Denton."

"You think we should just let it go and wrap up the case?"

"I didn't say that, but I think this part of the investigation is over and the bigger questions will have to be answered later."

"I can't let those questions go unanswered. Is that the reason you came here tonight? To tell me that?"

She chuckled. "No, I did want to talk to you. First, thank you for saving my life."

Gavin gave her a look that said he knew what she was going to say. "You don't think you can trust me?"

"I don't understand why you took that shot and disregarded the rules of engagement."

"Because my partner was in trouble and that guy was not going to negotiate with me. He wanted to kill you and I saw it in his eyes. I killed him to save your life."

She smiled. "You also didn't tell me everything this week, which means you don't trust me. "

"This was our first case together and, in every partnership, it's a rocky road to Dublin."

"What's that supposed to mean?"

"It's something my grandfather used to say. Dublin may be beautiful, but the road getting there is rocky. It's not going to be easy working together, but I do believe that it will eventually be great."

"You're right … but right now, I don't know if I can trust you. There's something you're not telling me."

"Just like there are things you're not telling me, but we'll get there. And know this: you're my partner, and I'd kill every man standing in this room to make sure you went home alive. That's a start."

"And if I request a new partner?"

"Then I will honor that."

A nerdy-looking kid came running by and bumped into Agent Main. He apologized to her and smiled at Gavin. He gave the kid a high-five. Gavin said to him, "Alright, McLovin, get out of here."

"McLovin?"

"It's a nickname. He's the awkward kid who gets all the ladies. His older brother heard it from some teenage movie."

"Well, he's cute. I can see why."

"He has a new girlfriend at school every day. Remember that age?"

She laughed. "I don't think I've been in a bar where kids are running around."

"Because you've never been in an Irish pub! Best family place after 10."

Gavin was being motioned back on stage for the second set. Father Joseph came over and said hi before Gavin went back to play. He looked at Agent Main. "My dear, I am so very glad that you are okay. When I heard what happened, I said a few prayers. God must have heard them."

"Thank you, Father," she replied. "That's very nice of you. I'm surprised to see you here."

"I'm like Jesus. To save sinners, you have to be among them."

Gavin laughed. "What kind of this place would this be if we did not have spiritual guidance?"

Agent Main drained her glass and said, "Well, I need to go. Thanks for the beer. I will see you on Monday."

"Do you need a ride?" Gavin asked.

"I'll take a taxi; it's no trouble."

Father Joseph spoke up. "Why don't you let me take you? I was on my way out, anyway. Have to get ready for tomorrow so I can provide spiritual counsel to all these heathens." Gavin laughed at the comment. He was a good priest and a true man of God. He never judged anyone for a little carousing, especially when he did it, too.

"Father, I appreciate it, but I can take a taxi."

"Please, let an old man do something nice for you."

Gavin told her that she couldn't win an argument with a priest about hospitality. She finally agreed and Gavin took the stage for the second set of music. As the Father and Agent Main were leaving, Gavin told the crowd that the next song was dedicated to a new friend. Agent Main and Father Joseph left the pub as the song *The Rocky Road to Dublin* was playing.

20

Monday morning came early for Agent Main. She looked over at the clock sitting on the night stand in her hotel room. The bright red numbers showed the time as 4:30 a.m. Her shoulder was sore, reminding her of how much she hated Monday mornings. There wasn't much point in sleeping any longer, so she got of bed and prepared for the day. During breakfast, she stared at two things on the table. One was a picture of her at age 14 with her grandmother, the last picture ever taken of them together. The other was a request form for a change of partner. She filled it out, but still hadn't signed it. Decisions needed to be made, but they weren't easy choices.

Agent Main was supposed to wear the shoulder sling for another few days, but she tossed it aside and put her service weapon on her belt before heading to the office. It was 7 a.m. when she got there and Agent Donnelly was already working. He looked as if he had been there for a while. He was on the phone when she walked in.

"Okay, that's your expert opinion?" Agent Donnelly asked the man on the phone. "No, I trust you, but I still want a full autopsy just to confirm. I'm sure they will find the same. Thanks for staying after your shift and calling me."

Agent Main asked, "What happened?"

"They found Hank Morgan dead a couple of hours ago. The doctor says he died of a heart attack, but there weren't any symptoms indicating that he had heart trouble. They're going to do an autopsy today and give us a full report."

She laughed. "Wish I could say I was surprised, the way this case has been."

"Likewise!"

"You really think it was natural causes?"

"Not at all, but I bet the autopsy will read that way. No witnesses, right?"

"At least we have Frank London."

"But how long can we really keep him safe? Hank Morgan's death isn't the only development since Friday."

Agent Main didn't look surprised. At this point, nothing seemed to shock her. Agent Donnelly continued, "My request to exhume Jack Denton's remains and conduct more DNA testing was denied, but not by this office. It was denied by the Assistant Director himself. And on top of that, all the information about Jack Denton and Kenny Denton has now been classified with top secret clearance -- so we can't get to it without a congressional order. I called a buddy of mine at the CIA and he can't even access it."

"Wow, they really don't want us to find something. I think it's safe to say this isn't some simple money laundering scheme with cops."

"No, and this is more than just embarrassing one of our own. They had too many secrets that no one was supposed to uncover at the FBI. Makes you wonder what all that money is being used for and what dark forces are pulling the strings in our government."

Agent Main smiled. "You're making it sound like an X-File."

"I think dealing with aliens on Earth would be a lot easier than what we're dealing with now. Speaking of money, I was able to track a few of the transfers to Swiss bank accounts. They all went to separate bank accounts for the cops and Michael Harris, who we know wasn't real. A day later, five transfers went into one account under the name Kane Gheshott."

"That's an unusual last name."

"It seemed Eastern European, but really it's two names with the letters jumbled up."

"The Ghost."

"Yep, our killer."

Agent Main sat back in her chair, shaking her head. "I know you think this is an unsolvable case, but you stumbled upon something that no one else did. We did save at least one person's life and one of the bad guys is dead. It may be a small victory, but it is a victory."

"We have gone as far as we can with this today, but it isn't over. The whole truth is out there and I, for one, won't stop looking." Agent Donnelly got up to get another cup of coffee and asked if she wanted one. She said yes. Before he walked out, she spoke up.

"On Friday, you asked me why I became an FBI agent. I never got a chance to tell you." Agent Donnelly was intrigued and smiled at her. Agent Main continued, "When I was 14 years old, my grandmother, who I was very close to -- closer than I was to my own mother -- was brutally murdered. It was a serial killer that was never caught. The FBI investigated for over a year and never found anything. They were baffled by all the murders. I joined because I never wanted another family to go through what I did, with a victim's killer never being caught. I know it may sound like a cliché ..."

Agent Donnelly interrupted. "But you've been looking for the killer ever since, and if you catch enough of them, it will somehow make you whole?"

"Yes."

"So what if it's a cliché -- doesn't make your reasons crazy or untrue. It's what drives you and makes you good at your job."

"I also wanted to be better than the agents who investigated my grandmother's murder. If I can be the best, then I can catch the killers that no one else can."

"I completely understand. You know that my parents were murdered and the killer was never caught. I would do anything to catch that killer and make him pay."

"It's one more thing we have in common, I guess."

"Hopefully, I can help you catch the killers that no one else can so that the victim's families won't have to suffer."

She smiled and thanked him. It was one more step to finding common ground. He walked out of the office to get the coffee. While Agent Donnelly was away, she pulled out the transfer request and tore it up. Chicago was home now.

∞∞∞∞∞∞

Gavin got home late. He took some files from his briefcase and sat them on the desk in his living room. He then unlocked a drawer and punched a six-digit security code into the keypad. The drawer was basically a safe. He reached inside and found a file on his parents' murder. It contained reports from the New Orleans Police Department, forensic evidence, and photos of the crime scene. Hanging in his living room was a full-size, framed movie poster of *Bullitt* with Steve McQueen. He took it down from the wall and turned it around. On the back, he started attaching photos from his parents' murder and the crime scene photos from this case. Where a photo of The Ghost should be, he placed a question mark. There was a spot for his mentor, the same killer who was hired to murder his parents. It had a question mark too? The middle of the frame had a giant outline of the box with question marks for the men behind everything. Every other box had lines drawn to the one box.

He mapped it out to find the connections between these cases and the overall conspiracy. It was his wall of conspiracy, his map to the truth. At the top of the board, he wrote out in Latin, "Verum est gradum propius" ... the truth is one step closer! On Saturday, he had gone to see Dr. Larkin and thought back to what he told him.

[140]

"You're right, I didn't tell you everything, but believe me, I can't," Dr. Larkin replied to Agent Donnelly.

"You can't or you won't?"

"If I tell you what you want to know, the man who you are looking for is the man they will send to end me. Then I would not be any good to you."

"Who are these people that scare even you?"

"Men who will stop at nothing, including killing the rest of your family, to hold on to the power they have. They have no honor and are the worst kind. The killer you seek is just a hired hand."

"But he can lead me to them."

"Maybe, but he's a ghost and nobody knows his complete story. Don't go looking for this truth; you won't like what you find. I have to go, Agent Donnelly, but here's a book you might find interesting." Dr. Larkin handed him a storybook of mythology tales. It was big enough to hide a file folder inside of it.

Gavin picked up a folder from the stack in his briefcase. This one was titled, "The Ghost." It was a collection of notes and maps. It was more information than anybody had on this mysterious person. Gavin started writing some notes around the box on his wall of conspiracy for The Ghost. It was a start, but he still had a long way to go.

∞∞∞∞∞∞

One month later…

The office wasn't lit very well. Morning was just beginning, but the man who now occupied that office was getting an early start. It was his first day. There were dozens of classified files from different agencies sitting on the desk. He would get to them all in due time, but there were two that needed his immediate attention. One was a folder on Agent Gavin Donnelly and Agent Rachel Main. He read over their first case together. He wasn't pleased at all. He signed an order for immediate surveillance. They needed to be watched.

The other file was for a federal judge in Chicago. The judge was a Boy Scout, in his opinion, and it was a shame that he could not be bought. He couldn't even be intimidated. Two of the man's colleagues were in federal prison when the cases should have been thrown out for lack of evidence. This made the man in the office angry and now it affected the judge's family. Everybody was going to have to

[141]

die. He ordered a surveillance team for the judge, but this was a different kind of surveillance team; they were lethal. The man gave the order on a hand-written memo. It was sent in a top-secret pouch for his colleague, Mr. Bran.

The man watched the sun come up and drank his coffee. He smiled at his good fortune. He worked hard for this position and did what he was told. Now, he had been rewarded. He finally had unlimited power.

30 MINUTES

GUILTY UNTIL PROVEN INNOCENT

BOOK 2

1

It was getting late as Jackie sat in the car waiting for the two children to get out of their music lessons. Night was coming faster now and the time change was only a week away. As the evening turned into night, her Friday was getting late. While most people would think of that as a shitty day, she never did. Jackie actually loved her job and the family that she worked for, especially the kids, who were six and nine years old now. Jackie Slater worked as a housekeeper and nanny for the family of a federal judge in Chicago, Judge Henry Colin Doyle. She had worked for them for five years and, whether she realized it or not, had become a trusted member of the family. She was so trusted that Judge Doyle gave her the key to retrieve his hidden file and instructions on what to do if he suddenly died.

The judge had reasons to keep secrets. He had reasons to seem paranoid and even bigger reasons to trust someone with those secrets. He was the President of the United States' choice for the U.S. Supreme Court and, although some might believe it was because he and the President were friends who went to college and law school together, Judge Henry Colin Doyle was well qualified for the job. But even great men don't get that far without making a lot of enemies along the way.

It was completely dark when Connor and Sarah Doyle came out of their school and found Jackie waiting for them. Jackie was going to pick up dinner for the family, take the kids home, and be done for the weekend. At least, that was the plan, but the strangeness of the night was just getting started. About 30 minutes later, Jackie pulled onto the street where the Doyle's lived. Normally, it was well-lit with street lights, but it appeared that a few of them were out. That was Jackie's first clue that something was wrong. She hadn't always been a suspicious person, but her past made her that way. All she had was suspicion now.

Jackie slowed the car down as she passed the house, but she didn't turn into the driveway. All the lights were turned off in the house, which was very unusual because she knew the judge and his wife were home. The kids in the backseat didn't seem to notice and Jackie thought to herself, *that's a good thing*; she didn't want them to get scared. Instead of pulling into the driveway, she took the kids down

[144]

the street to a neighbor's house, who happened to be friends of the Doyle's. Her excuse was that the power was out and she didn't want the kids to wait in a dark house for the power to come back on. The truth was that she needed to investigate the house alone. She knew by instinct that something was wrong.

Jackie walked back down to the Doyle's house and skulked around the back. She found the entrance to the basement and decided to enter the house that way in case somebody was in it. She was one of three people that had a key to the door. Jackie went in and started to climb the stairs, hoping they wouldn't creak or make too much noise. As she started to climb the steps, she heard voices. One of them said, "Let's finish this up. We've been here too long." Jackie hoped it was a simple burglary and they would be in and out, but she also feared the worst.

She opened the basement door and was able to get out and duck around the corner. As she went around the corner, she saw two men. One of them was holding a knife covered with blood. She peeked around the corner and saw the two bloody bodies lying on the floor. Although she could not see their faces, fear grabbed ahold of her… her stomach curled. She knew that it was Judge Henry Colin Doyle and his wife, Elizabeth. Jackie put her hand over her mouth to keep from making a sound, and she started crying. She wept for a minute and then found an inner strength she hadn't felt in 12 years. She snuck into the kitchen and grabbed the butcher knife the judge liked to use when he was cutting meat. Some might have just used it to defend themselves, but not her; she figured that she had one chance to get one of the murderers.

One of the men walked out of the house, leaving only the man holding the bloody knife inside. Jackie took a deep breath and tiptoed toward the living room, where the bodies were laid out on the floor. The man holding the knife didn't hear her; she was that quiet. She came up from behind him and, just as he turned around to see her, she cut off the hand that clutched the bloody knife. The man screamed in pain and tried to hit her with his other hand. She moved out of the way and swung the butcher knife in a slanted upward direction, cutting his throat deeply until blood came gushing out like a waterfall. The man tried to use his only attached hand to apply pressure and stop the flow, but it was no use. The blood just poured out of him, painting the carpet around the dead bodies with red. Outside the house, there were two men putting things away in a work van parked on the side of the street. They heard the scream and instinctively drew their guns with silencers. The man in charge said out loud, "What the hell was that?"

The two men with guns ran back into the house to see what happened. Jackie quickly took a look out of the window to see if the other men heard the screams. As they came running toward the house, Jackie headed out the back, trying to get away. By the back door, there were sets of keys on hooks and a home security keypad. She grabbed one of the sets of keys and hit the silent alarm on the keypad. The two men entered the house just in time to see her run out the back door. One of the men raised his gun to take a shot at her, but the man in charge grabbed his arm and said, "No, don't. We can't afford to leave extra forensics at the scene. She's gone anyway."

"But," the other man said, "she saw us."

"She can't ID us and, besides, she's going to be on the run."

"Why do you say that?"

The man in charge held up the butcher knife. "She left this; her prints are all over it. She'll be the one the cops look for. When they find her, we'll get to her then and shut her up for good."

"But who is she?"

"The maid."

"How do you know?"

"The maid is the only other person who had a key to this house and could get it in. And she tripped the silent alarm on the security system."

"How do you know that? We cut the alarm."

The man in charge held up his iPhone, which was monitoring police frequencies and alarm codes and showed it to the other guy. "An alarm went off; there must be a separate silent alarm or panic button on the system that still works even after the main line has been cut. We have seven minutes before the police show up. Help me get the body and the hand. We can't leave it here. We need the cops to think she did it."

The two men removed the dead man from the house and put the body in the work van, which they had moved to the driveway. They left the butcher knife by the bodies of Henry and Elizabeth Doyle so the police would find it with Jackie's prints on it. In the meantime, she ran to the neighbor's house in a panic. All she could think of was getting the kids to safety. She wasn't stupid; she knew the police would be looking for her and would figure out who she was, but more importantly, she knew that whoever killed the judge and his wife would want the kids, too. Jackie had to rescue them from the men who did this, and there were only a handful of people she knew who could hide them and keep them safe. None of those people were anything close to law enforcement.

When she got back to the neighbor's house, she was out of breath. Maggie Wilson, who was watching the kids, was a good friend of the Doyle's. She was a little scared by the way Jackie was acting and asked her, "What's wrong? Is there something more than just a power outage?"

"Yes, it's a family emergency. I need to take the kids somewhere else," Jackie replied.

"What happened?"

"Look, I don't have time to talk. I'll tell Elizabeth to call you and tell you what's going on. Just help me get their coats on."

Maggie was worried by Jackie's actions. She tried to say something else, but Jackie cut her off and rushed out the door with the kids, telling them that they needed to go and everything would be alright. She got the kids in the car and buckled up. Finally, she turned around and told Maggie, who was standing in the doorway of her house, "If anybody asks where we are, tell them I'm taking the kids to their Uncle Jack's house. He's Henry's brother."

Maggie looked confused, but replied, "Okay, but who would ask?"

Jackie was already driving off. Maggie decided to call Elizabeth, but the line went straight to voicemail. A few minutes later, four police cars descended on the street and parked in front of the judge's home, blocking the driveway. The work van was long gone by then. Police officers surrounded the house by going through the front door and the back door. The silent alarm was a panic alarm, which meant, "come right now; life in danger." The police didn't have to knock when that alarm was tripped. They were trained to go right through the door in order to save a life. That's when they found the bodies. Maggie heard the police cars down the street and, like a nosy neighbor, walked outside to see what was happening. She knew something was wrong as she walked down to the house. The cops had turned on the lights. Maggie got close enough to the front door to see the dead bodies before the police officers could stop her.

Maggie screamed in horror at what she saw. After they got her to calm down, the police started asking her questions. She told them how she knew the Doyle's and what had just happened with their maid. The police asked her for a name. Maggie replied while crying, "Jackie Slater … she killed Henry and Elizabeth and just kidnapped their kids!"

2

It was Friday night and the workday was done. Most people would go home to their families, but not Agent Gavin Donnelly. The only place Gavin wanted to be was the pub; good beer and good music. Gavin's band, The Donnelly Rovers, was playing at the pub that night. As he was getting a pint from the bar, a voiced shouted at him, "Gavin Donnelly, I told you this wouldn't be over. You owe me."

Gavin looked over to see Detective Mike Doyle standing at the other end of bar, leaning on a cane with a brace around his right knee. The last time he saw him was when he shot him above the kneecap outside the church a month ago. In the back of Gavin's mind, he knew that it wasn't the end. The neighborhood where they were all from was too small for that.

Gavin just stared at him for a minute and then replied, "You did deserve it."

"You shot me in the knee and I had to retire," Mike responded.

"And you were about to assassinate a mobster on the steps of a church. This isn't *The Godfather*."

"We thought his son was killing cops. You know that we take care of our own."

Gavin smirked at him. Mike spoke up again. "But I guess I can't be too mad. I heard you killed the guy who murdered those cops, so that settles it. And my wife thanks you for forcing me to retire; she likes having me around for some god-awful reason." Mike extended his hand to shake Gavin's. He shook Mike's hand and smiled at the comments. He replied,

"It's settled, then … but you're right, I do owe you something. I did shoot you in the knee. You get one hit."

Mike smiled. "I don't need to hit. We're cool!"

Liam Donnelly walked over to the bar after overhearing the conversation. He said, "Mike, I'd take him up on it. How often do you get a chance to hit a Federal Agent and not go to jail? It will feel good.

"Gavin turned around to give his uncle a dirty look. As he turned back around to face Mike, he was surprised by a right hook. It hit him hard and knocked him down. Mike responded, "You're right; that did feel good." Gavin picked himself up. "Damn. For someone who can't put his weight forward, you have a hell of right hook. "He had a cut above his left eye, which was bleeding. He was going to have a black eye, too. Patrick, the bartender, handed him a wrapped-up towel with ice to stop the bleeding. After that, the two men bought each other a beer and laughed about the whole situation. It was an Irish thing.

Alex Donnelly motioned toward Gavin to let him know that it was time to start playing again, so he walked up to the stage with an ice pack over his eye. He put it down and grabbed his guitar. The next song they started playing was *Come Out You Black and Tans*.

∞∞∞∞∞∞

While Gavin was at the pub that Friday night, Agent Rachel Main was still at the office finishing up some paperwork. She didn't have much of a life in Chicago yet, so she opted to work late. In addition, she also read through police reports that got uploaded to the FBI server from various cities. Agent Main was looking for things out of the ordinary: heinous crimes too serious to be left in the hands of local law enforcement. If she hadn't been at the office late that night, she might have missed the reported murder of Judge Henry Colin Doyle. Even though the investigation would have eventually ended up with the FBI, it would've been days before they got it … plenty of time for local police to mess it up. Fortunately, Agent Main did see the report and the photos of the crime scene. The photos were what made her jump into action.

Agent Main's first call was to AD Foster, to tell him what had happened and to get approval for the case. Technically, she was still on duty and the case would be hers anyway, but this was going to be a high-profile investigation and she needed to get permission. AD Foster asked Agent Main,

"How much do we know so far?"

"Just that the judge and his wife were killed and, from the looks of the photos, they were tortured. A neighbor told police that the maid took their kids and was the last person to see the Doyles."

"Alright then, tell local PD to sit on the crime scene until you get there. Call the ME on duty and tell him to get over there right away with a CSU team. I will call the precinct that's on the scene and try to stop any leaks to the press. Also, one more thing: do you know where your partner is?"

"No. I didn't ask him what he was doing tonight when he left for the day."

AD Foster laughed. "He's probably at the pub. You're going to have to go and get him; make sure he's sober before you two walk into a crime scene. This is a high-profile case and there's no room for error, so you both have to be at your best."

Agent Main scowled. "It's not that late. He can't be drunk yet, can he?"

"You probably shouldn't bet on that. The whiskey and music are flowing freely right about now at the pub."

"I'll make sure he's sober. I guess that's my other job as his partner."

Thirty minutes later, after putting together the file on Judge Doyle's murder, Agent Main arrived at Paddy Murphy's to get her partner. She walked in and Patrick, who was standing behind the bar, said hi to her and offered to get her a drink. She declined and told him that she was there for her partner. Gavin, who was still on stage with the band, saw his partner at the bar. She gave him a serious look and held up the file, signaling to him that she had a case. Gavin nodded to her and, when the song was done, he told the band that they needed to take a break.

Agent Main looked at her partner as he came walking up to her and said, "Sorry to break up the evening, but we have a case."

"Who was murdered?" Gavin asked.

"A federal judge."

"No shit! Who?"

"Judge Henry Colin Doyle."

Gavin looked shocked. "Who knows the identity?"

"Right now, only a dozen police officers from the 30th Precinct, one of our CSU teams, AD Foster, and you and me … but, by morning, the media will have the story."

"Is the body still at the scene?"

"Yes, and they're waiting on us." Agent Main gave him a funny look. "Agent Donnelly, are you drunk?"

"Define drunk!"

She shot him a dirty look. "We are about to walk into a crime scene. You need to get sober now. You have five minutes."

Gavin could tell she was annoyed, but he also knew she was right. He looked over at Patrick and said, "I need the hangover cure."

Patrick reached behind the bar, grabbed an unmarked bottle, and poured a shot. The liquid didn't smell good. He also set out a bottle of Extra Strength TYLENOL. Gavin took the shot and winced because of how bad it tasted. He grabbed the painkillers and went into the bathroom, but not before he told his partner that he would be sober in three minutes. Agent Main asked Patrick, "What the hell is in that bottle?"

He smiled at her. "You don't want to know. It's one of the worst-tasting things on earth!"

Gavin came out of the bathroom and, as he passed the bar, Patrick tossed him a roll of breath mints. Agent Main shook her head at the scene. Finally, she asked the question she thought of when she first saw her partner on stage. "What the hell happened to your eye?"

He laughed and pointed to where Detective Mike Doyle was standing at the other end of the bar. "He hit me."

Agent Main looked at the detective. "Isn't that the guy you shot in the knee for trying to kill Mickey Soranno?"

"Yep. I owed him at least one hit."

"But he tried ..." Gavin cut her off.

"Yes, he did, but I still owed him. It's an Irish thing."

They left the pub and drove to the crime scene. Agent Main drove so that Gavin could read the case file. He looked at the photos. He had never seen anything like that. The last case they worked was bad, but everybody in the FBI was used to the way Albert Soranno killed people. They had all read his case file so much that they were immune to the gruesome nature of the killings. This was different. Judge Doyle and his wife were severely tortured, and the execution method had not been seen in over 50 years. Gavin winced at the photos. He had a strong stomach, but this was a bit much.

Agent Main looked over at her partner. "Do you recognize anything about the way they were killed?"

"No."

"It's called the Ling Chi method, an ancient Chinese form of torture where the legs, arms, and throat are slowly cut so the victims bleed to death. Then, they will finally be stabbed in the heart as a final death blow. After they're dead, the head is cut off."

Gavin looked at her after hearing the name and it finally clicked. "It's a killing method for traitors of the Chinese government."

"That's part of the history, but I am not exactly clear on why the head is cut off after death. I think it's for show."

"It is for show, but as with most ancient cultures, the dead travel to an afterlife. If the head is removed, then they're forced to wander the afterlife without it, which is the worst fate you can have."

"So, it's a symbolic killing?"

"In more ways than one, but the question is ..."

"Who did he piss off so badly that he would be killed in this way?" Agent Main finished his sentence.

"Well, he was the President's nominee for the Supreme Court. You don't become that without gaining a few enemies."

"True, but a witness gave us a prime suspect: the maid. The neighbor down the street says the maid was the last person to see the Doyles alive. She had the kids with her and then drove off with them in a rush."

Gavin looked concerned. "We have a kidnapping, too?"

"Appears that way, and that's not even the real kicker."

"What do you mean?"

"A butcher knife was found at the crime scene near one of the bodies. It had the maid's prints on it."

"You mean one of the kitchen knives that she would have used in preparing meat?"

Agent Main chuckled at the sarcastic comment. "That's not being called into question. When Chicago PD ran the prints, an unusual name came up in the federal criminal database. Jackie Slater is not the maid's real name."

Gavin was surprised. "Then what's her real name?"

"Look on the next page in the file."

Gavin turned the page and saw the name along with a mug shot. His look of surprise turned to complete shock. He responded, "No fucking way!" Jackie Slater was born Brenda Mason. She was arrested for murdering her 3-year-old daughter in 1995 and spent three years in prison while on trial, only to be acquitted of the murder in 1998. The press took to calling her "The Mommy Child Killer," and that's what she became known as in America during the trial and in the days afterward. Brenda Mason was the most hated person in the country next to O.J. Simpson in the 90's and had to go into hiding when the trial was over. She would forever be known as a murderer, and it wasn't like anybody really thought she was innocent. Gavin couldn't believe it. He commented,

"Her name gets released to the public and everybody with a weapon will be looking to gun her down. We have to find her soon."

Agent Main looked disgusted when she told him the next part. "There's another wrinkle to this situation. A new law enacted a couple years ago states that, if a former prisoner convicted or even tried for a capital crime is suspected in a new capital crime, the U.S. Marshals Service has jurisdiction over bringing that person in."

"You mean we don't even get to try to find her?"

"Oh, we can assist in the search, but the U.S. Marshals will be leading it. We have about six, maybe seven hours before they get here and take over the manhunt for Brenda Mason."

Gavin had a very serious look on his face. "We have to find her first. She's the only one that will probably have answers to why the Doyle's were killed. The maid always has the inside scoop on the family and what they do. The U.S. Marshals won't care if they bring her in dead or alive."

"You don't think she killed the Doyle's?"

"I don't know for sure, but it doesn't make sense. Why use that method for killing someone when there are simpler ways of doing so? Unless you're making a statement and sending of some kind of warning. I want to know what her motive is."

Agent Main smiled. "I agree."

3

He was in his office working late, as usual, but he was also waiting on a phone call. It was the confirmation that the job was complete. Finally, the cheap cell phone on his desk rang. He answered, and on the other end was Mr. Bran. There was no chitchat, no small talk, just four words uttered by Mr. Bran. "We have a problem."

The man hidden in the shadows of the office replied, "I don't want to hear about problems. This was a simple job. What happened?"

"The maid came home and caught us just as we finished. She grabbed a butcher knife, cut Mac's hand off, and then cut his throat. He's dead."

"Did you leave any of that evidence at the scene?"

"Of course not."

"Then don't worry about it."

"But she saw us."

"And left DNA and probably prints at the scene. The FBI will have its prime suspect now."

Mr. Bran didn't completely understand, but he had to ask. "What makes you think they will pin it on her? She doesn't have motive and has been with the family for years."

He smiled and told his associate, Mr. Bran, "Trust me. Once they see who she really is, they will never be able to let go of the idea that she did it. This actually works out perfectly. But, she needs to be dead soon. You have to find her before they do. The maid always has secrets that don't need to get out. Get another team and find her."

He hung up the phone before Mr. Bran could ask any more questions. He was only in the need-to-know. Mr. Bran put his phone away and looked at the other team member. "We need to call the boys. We have work to do."

∞∞∞∞∞∞∞∞∞∞∞∞

Agent Main and Agent Donnelly arrived at the crime scene. The street was filled with police cars and CSU trucks gathering every piece of forensic evidence. The street looked as if some high-profile politician was visiting; everything was blocked off. Gavin thought to himself, with all the traffic on the street and people in and out of the crime scene, it would be a matter of hours before the story broke about the murder. There would be an Internet story soon and everything would be out of control from there. Hopefully, they could keep Brenda Mason's identity a secret for as long as possible.

They walked into the house and immediately saw the ME kneeling over the bodies, collecting evidence. The ME on the scene was Dr. Kenrick. She smiled at Agent Donnelly as he approached. It was more than just a smile; she was good at flirtation. Agent Main saw the smile, gave her partner a dirty look, and then started asking questions.

"Dr. Kenrick, what do you know so far?"

"Agent Main, good to see you," she replied. "As reported so far, both victims bled out from the cuts above the ankles and wrists. That's probably what killed them, and then the heads were cut off. But there was something else."

"What?"

"Multiple needle marks on the arms. They could have had drawn blood recently, but the marks are clumsy. It looks like whoever did it didn't know what they were doing. And there are no signs of drug use."

"You're going to run a toxicology report, aren't you?"

"Of course. I will get it back to you as soon as possible."

Gavin was looking at some of the evidence that had already been collected. He picked up a bag of small, white fragments. He looked over at the doctor and asked, "What's in this bag?"

"Bone fragments. We found them around one of the bodies."

"Did they come from the heads being cut off?"

"They don't appear to be from the spine, where a head would be severed, but we're not exactly sure where they came from. No other parts of the body or bones were cut. We are going to run a DNA analysis on the fragments and see what they match."

Agent Main was curious about the fragments; she had a theory, but needed to ask more questions to confirm. Her first thought was that Brenda Mason might be injured ... or had a limb cut off, such as a hand. She asked the neighbor if the maid appeared to be injured when she came back to pick the kids up from her house. The neighbor told her no. Agent Main couldn't seem to shake the thought. Somebody else was missing a limb, but only more testing could prove that.

Dr. Kenrick was handed a small monitor from a CSU tech. They had been collecting blood samples from the crime scene. Her face was filled with surprise. She walked over to Agent Main and Agent Donnelly and said, "We found something else that was peculiar.

There's a different blood in the blood spatters on the carpet than that of the two victims."

Agent Main asked, "It's not the same blood type of the victims?"

"No. The Doyles were both O positive; the second blood type is A positive. There was somebody else who lost a lot of blood here at the crime scene, but we don't have any other forensic evidence to indicate that there was someone here."

Gavin responded, "Do you really think a 5'5" woman, weighing 130 pounds, could have done this all by herself? Whoever did this had help."

"And then was killed somehow, with his blood being left at the scene," Agent Main said. "Why, though? To have one less witness to the crime?"

"It's plausible."

"It's a pretty sloppy job, though."

"If Brenda Mason really did this and was a smart killer, why did she leave a butcher knife at the scene with her prints on it? She would have known that we'd find them and eventually figure out who she really is."

Agent Main looked over at the doctor. "Can someone survive long with the amount of blood loss you found from the third victim?"

"Depends on how quickly he got to a hospital and then got a blood transfusion."

Agent Main looked over at one of the Chicago police officers and asked him to start checking hospitals and clinics to see if someone came in that night needing a blood transfusion. Maybe they would get lucky and find the third victim, which could give them more answers.

While Agent Main was examining the bodies for more clues and asking questions to the CSU team, Gavin decided to take a look around the house for anything that might be able to give him answers to a motive. Brenda Mason killing the family she worked for the past five years just didn't make sense. Finally, he ended up in the judge's study. He could tell that Judge Doyle was very organized and kept his study very neat; nothing seemed to be out of place. That's when he saw it: the scales of justice, with a statue of the blindfolded Lady Justice, sitting on the desk in an odd place. Usually, something like that was placed at the front of the desk, not near the back of it. It was strange, so he checked it out. The statue had red spray paint on the blindfold and was sitting over a red mark on the desk. He moved the statue and saw a skull-like design on the desk in red spray paint. He just stared at it for a moment, trying to figure out where he had seen the design before.

Gavin called for his partner. "Agent Main, you're going to want to come into the study … found something big."

She walked in and saw the shocked look on his face. She had never seen it before. She went over to the desk and saw the skull design. "Have you ever seen it before?"

"I have, but I can't place where. What about you, Agent Main?"

"It seems familiar, but also very different, if that make sense. I don't think I have ever seen a skull with eyes in it. What's the meaning behind that?"

"That death is watching us and can always see us."

She looked at him funny. "Well, it's definitely a sign. Someone is leaving a calling card."   There was a desk pad with a calendar that was covering up a big part of the back of the desk. As Agent Main turned around to call one of the photographers into the room, she bumped it. Gavin saw the writing underneath it in red permanent marker. He moved the pad out of the way and saw that the writing was in Latin. She stared at the writing curiously.

**Etsi qui sunt tradidit fac sentire maiestatis
acriter, tamen proditor stat in peius de vae**

"Do you know what it says?" Agent Main asked.

"Yes, I do. 'Those that are betrayed do feel the treason sharply, yet the traitor stands in worse case of woe.' I don't think my Latin is as good as it should be."

"Where have I heard that before?"

"It's Shakespeare, from the play Cymbeline."

"What do you think it means?"

"Somebody thinks he's a traitor … and has a sense of humor."

Before she could respond, one of the CSU techs came into the study and said that there was a U.S. marshal waiting for them at the scene. His name was Bryan Rogers. Even though Gavin had never met him, he knew who the marshal was. Their lives had crossed paths before, but that was not the reason Gavin despised him. He didn't care who Marshal Rogers really was; he didn't care that he was one of the best marshals in field or that they were lucky to have his assistance. Gavin viewed this guy as a traitor.

The marshal walked into the study and introduced himself to the agents. He told them that he was in Chicago when he got the call about finding Brenda Mason, and that his team would be here in the morning. Agent Main asked,

"You figured you'd get a head start?"

"I was here anyway, and this is a big fish. Besides, she's got a few hours head start and kidnapped two kids. We don't have time to waste." He asked the agents what they knew so far and they told him, but there wasn't any new information on Brenda Mason as of yet. He pulled out a piece of paper and handed it to Agent Main. "Actually, we do have something new on her. We were able to trace her cell phone and, apparently, she is traveling south; she'll be in Missouri within the hour. She made a phone call to a Texas number, a man named Rick Grimes. We figure that's where she's heading."

Agent Main recognized the name. "Rick Grimes, which was her fiancé when she murdered her child. He even testified against her. Why would she call him?"

Gavin asked for the piece of paper with the information about the trace. The marshal handed it to him and that's when he had a vision. *Brenda Mason was outside a McDonald's while the kids were in the back seat of her car. On the marquee it said, "Chicago Bulls McRib Special." She pulled out an old phone book and looked for a number. She called and a man answered on the other end. She said, "Hey, it's Brenda. I know you probably don't want to hear from me, but I think you're the only one I can trust." He stood there, shocked to get that phone call. "Brenda, you can always trust me, you know that, but I don't know what I can do to help. Are you in trouble?" She had tears in her eyes. "Yes, but the help is not for me, it's for two kids. Someone is trying to kill them and I need to get them to safety." He looked startled. "Why can't you call the police?" She replied, "You know what happens when they find out who I really am. I can't go to them for help. Can you help me?" He paused for a moment and finally said, "OK, but eventually the police will have to be involved. You know that." She smiled with tears still in her eyes. "I know, but not right now!"*

Gavin rubbed his head as if he had injured it. His partner looked at him and asked, "You alright?"

"Yes, it's just a headache." He looked at Deputy Marshal Rogers. "Are you sure that she still has her phone? She could have dumped it by now."

Rogers looked him strangely. "If she really dumped the phone so she could not be traced, then she wouldn't have made a call on it. She called someone in Texas, and the phone says she's heading south, so there's the obvious answer: she's heading to Texas. It doesn't take a lawyer to figure that out."

Agent Main spoke up before her partner could make a glib comment and get into it with the Marshal. "It doesn't explain why she would call a man who despises her now."

Rogers smiled. "I don't care. My job is to bring her in and we have a good lead. I am sending a team of marshals to intercept her. With any luck, we'll have her in custody by the end of business tomorrow." He left after that. There wasn't anything else he needed to know from the crime scene and there wasn't anything else Agent Main or Agent Donnelly could tell him that he felt like he needed to know. Mainly, he just wanted to meet the FBI agents who could either help him or get out of his way.

Agent Main couldn't let it go. It bothered her that Brenda Mason would call her former fiancé for help. She said to her partner, "We need to get her old case files and find every name that testified for her and against her. We need to know the names of all her friends and people that she could turn to for help."

"I agree. I don't buy that she really wanted help from that guy, but she might go somewhere else for help. But there's something else, too."

"What?"

"Motive. Why would she kill the judge, especially in that way? Could she murder somebody like that without help?"

"Not likely. Killing one person in that method is hard enough, but two … I don't think so."

Gavin looked back at the skull logo and the quote. "What's the real motive here? I think it has something to do with an old case and somebody was sent to kill the judge."

She laughed. "Now you think Brenda Mason is an assassin?"

"Or we are meant to think that!"

Agent Main smiled. "Well, it's not the first time we've seen that."

Gavin pulled out his phone and called a former colleague. She answered the phone. "Agent Janney, its Gavin."

She replied, "Why are you calling me so late on a Friday night?"

"We have a murder. I need your help, and you're the best researcher in the FBI."

"Who was murdered?"

"Judge Henry Colin Doyle. I need to get the case files for every case that has been in his court since becoming a federal judge. We are going to have to go through every one of them to find any connections to this murder."

"That's a lot of cases. It's going to be days before the Bureau can get everything."

"We need it tomorrow."

"You're not going to get everything by tomorrow."

Gavin laughed. "Sure I will. Call Michael Henry from the clerk's office. Tell him that he gets a case of scotch from me if he helps you tonight."

"You know, Gavin, I have plans tonight."

"Like what?"

"I was on a date."

Gavin laughed. "It couldn't have lasted that long if you answered my call. It's probably not going to work out with that guy, anyway."

She gave Gavin a dirty look, even though he couldn't see it. "OK, you may be right. I will help you get those case files and get a research team put together, but you owe me big time."

Gavin got off the phone and looked at his partner. "The answers we're looking for are needles in a haystack, but we have to start somewhere."

Agent Main smiled. "That's why I joined the FBI ... for the challenge."

4

Six a.m. on a Saturday was not that early for the White House. The President of the United States was usually up by then, ready to start his day, for the country never slept. That was what he always told himself when it came to working weekends and long hours. President Barrett Sunder had been in office for two years now. He made history when he became the first African-American president. He was smart, and one of the most eloquent speakers on the political stage, but he was relatively inexperienced. President Sunder had only been a one-term senator from Illinois and a two-term state legislator before that. The only other experience he had before politics was as a lawyer in Chicago and a community organizer.

The president was finishing breakfast when his Chief of Staff, David Rollins, came in. He had a somber look on his face. It had been a while since the president had seen that look from his chief of staff.

"David, what's the matter? You look like someone just died."

"Mr. President, I have some bad news. We just got a report from the FBI. Henry Colin Doyle was murdered last night."

"What?"

"We're just getting some of the details. We still don't know much yet, but he and his wife, Elizabeth, were found dead."

The president dropped his coffee cup while his chief of staff explained what he knew so far. The president was in shock now. Judge Doyle was a good friend. They were in college together, then law school, and were lawyers together in the DA's office before the president went into politics and Henry Colin Doyle became a judge. David picked up the cup from the floor and sat down.

"Mr. President, I know this is difficult to hear, but you need to listen to me now. The story will break within the hour and you're going to have to answer questions later today. Then, of course, we will have to pick a different nominee for the bench."

The president finally spoke. "How was he murdered?"

"It's gruesome. It looks like he and his wife were tortured and cut in many places."

"Who is handling the investigation? Local Chicago PD?"

"Actually, the FBI office in Chicago has the case. Agents from the Violent Crimes division were assigned to it last night; an FBI profiler by the name of Agent Rachel Main, who has a good record with the FBI, and her partner, Agent Gavin Donnelly."

The president gave him curious look. "I know who he is. He cleared my name three and a half years ago before the campaign, when I was accused of fraudulent investments with the Glendale Homes Company in Chicago. He was working in White Collar Crimes back then. If it weren't for him clearing my name, I might not have been able to run for president."

"Because of the severity of the crime, I'm sure our new FBI director will be assigning a special task force to catch the killer."

"You mean, there's only one killer?"

Mr. Rollins smiled slightly. "Actually, they already have a suspect, the maid … and you're not going to believe who she is."

"Who?"

"Brenda Mason."

"No shit! How … ?"

"Apparently, she changed her name and became a maid. She had been working for the judge's family for the past five years. But, there's also something else: she has the judge's kids."

"Fuck me. Are there any leads on where she is?"

"A U.S. Marshal task force is assisting the FBI in finding her. According to their report, she is heading south, toward Texas, and they should be able to apprehend her in the next few hours."

The president got up and started to pace. "I guess that's something. After they do, I want to make a statement. We need to make a strong one and show resolve that, although this is a tragedy, we will go on in finding a good nominee for the bench, and his killer will have swift justice. Keep me informed throughout the day, David. He was my friend, and I want to know everything that's going with this investigation until justice has been served."

David nodded in agreement and let the president finish his breakfast.

∞∞∞∞∞∞∞∞∞∞∞∞

Deputy Marshal Bryan Rogers took a plane to St. Louis to meet his team. The sun was starting to come up as they were about to land. He slept most of the way with a smile on his face, thinking to himself that today should be pretty easy. He was about to catch a fugitive who was, as he put it, dumb as shit. She didn't get rid of her cell phone; that was her first mistake. One of the other marshals on the flight went to the back of the plane to wake Marshal Rogers up. They would be landing in a few minutes.

The U.S. Marshals Command Center was at the little airport where they were landing; an easy place to transport the prisoner once they had her. One of the other marshals brought him up to speed on what they had so far on the search.

"The trace on Brenda Mason's phone is still heading south, toward St. Louis. We had a couple of marshal's trail the car and it looks like she is on a Greyhound bus, number 689."

Rogers smiled. "I guess she was smart enough to dump the car."

The other marshal asked, "Do you want the team in place to take her down at St. Louis Union Station?"

"No, it's too crowded. We need to take her in a less busy place so that it's harder for her to slip away. Plus, we don't want the attention. It's better if we do this quietly." He pulled out a map of the greater St. Louis area and put it on the table. He pointed to the town of Union, Missouri. "We will get her here."

"What makes you think she will be there? She could change buses in St. Louis."

"She's heading to Texas. That's where her former fiancé is, the one she made the phone call to. Interstate 44, the way into Texas, is where Union, Missouri is located. If she doesn't suspect that we're onto her, she won't change buses. And if I'm wrong, that's why we have a car following the bus. We'll get her somewhere else before breakfast, but I'm not wrong."

The other marshals laughed at the comment. In the next hour, the bus would be stopping in Union. The marshals got there 30 minutes before the bus arrived. They weren't going to wait for everybody to get off the bus; they needed Brenda Mason trapped on the bus so she couldn't escape. Just in case she managed to, marshals would be in the crowd. Finally, bus 689 pulled into the Greyhound station in Union. Rogers had the terminal dispatcher radio in to the driver and say that police were looking for a missing person and wanted people on the bus to look at the pictures of the missing victims. It was a lie, but a necessary one in order to not spook the passengers on the bus.

Two marshals stepped onto the bus and showed the pictures of Judge Doyle's kids. Mainly, they were on the bus to see if Brenda Mason was there. She was nowhere in sight, and there wasn't even a woman with two kids there. The passengers were finally allowed to leave. Rogers was pissed. He kept saying, "This can't be right. The trace says she was on the bus." The marshals held the bus at the station and searched. After 10 minutes, they found it. Brenda Mason's smartphone was in the bathroom of the bus, and it even had the navigation feature turned on, making the phone easier to trace. Rogers was not happy.

One of the other marshals spoke up. "So, what now?"

"We go to Texas and find the fiancé. She was obviously wise enough to dump the phone, but she is still heading that way. I want roadblocks along the way on every major road leading into Texas. Coordinate with local law enforcement. Maybe we'll get lucky."

The team dispersed and headed to Texas. One of the marshals, who had been in the car following the bus, pulled out his phone and dialed. The man on the other end answered the phone and asked what they found.

"Mr. Bran," the marshal replied. "She wasn't on the bus. We're heading to Texas, where her old fiancé lives. They're going put up road blocks now and try to find her."

"Okay, good work. Stay on them and call back when you have more."

∞∞∞∞∞∞∞∞∞∞

Brenda Mason had gotten a room at a Marriott Hotel, something with room service so they would not have to go out to get food; a chance of being seen. Besides, the hotel had cable and movies. The kids would like that. She had to make it seem like a vacation so that the children would not be worried. It was early in the morning and the kids were still asleep. Her pre-paid cell phone rang. It was her childhood friend, Rick Henry.

"Have you gotten any sleep?" He asked.

"Not much. I'm too nervous … too scared."

"I can imagine. You're the prime suspect again."

She had a few tears in her eyes. "I can't believe this is happening again. What can you do to help me?"

"I can help you get out of there, but I need to make arrangements first. My wife can't suspect anything and I sure as hell can't take my car."

"Can you make an excuse that you have to go out of town for business?"

"Probably, but that means I can't do anything until Monday. Can you sit tight until then?"

"I can't stay here for another day. It's best that I stay on the move."

"Then we will pick a different place to meet. Give me a few hours and I will call you back with more details."

Brenda started crying again. "Rick, I can't tell you how much I appreciate your help."

[164]

"I told you when we were young that I would always be your friend and be there when you need me."

They ended the call and, right about that time, Sarah Doyle was waking up. She was always the one that got up early. Connor was a typical boy and slept in late. Sarah immediately asked, "Are we going to see mommy and daddy today?"

"No dear, not today. You still get to have a vacation."

"I want to see them."

"Sarah, they took some time for themselves, but you will get to see them soon. Do you want to go to the movies today and eat candy and popcorn?"

"Yeah!"

"Well, that's what we are going to do." Brenda needed to keep the kids entertained and out of sight while waiting for an escape plan.

∞∞∞∞∞∞∞∞∞∞

Gavin was already at the office early Saturday morning. He got there before his partner did. Agent Main finally came into the office with a box of files. She had the court documents from the Brenda Mason trial from 12 years ago. Both of them had gone through this before: to understand a killer who got away, they had to go back into the old case. Agent Main told her partner the night before that there were clues in the old case, and it just took someone smart enough to find them and catch the killer. Gavin was reading at his desk when she walked in. She saw the book and jokingly commented to her partner:

"Shakespeare? Isn't it too early in the morning for that?"

He smiled. "I've been up for a while, so it's not too early. Besides, the quote is a message and I haven't read Cymbeline since college. If there's a message in there, I need to study it. Have you ever read it?"

She laughed. "Once, when I was in college. If I remember correctly, it wasn't very good."

"I wouldn't rush out to go see it on stage, but it's fascinating."

"If you would like a break, I have the case files to the Brenda Mason trial. There's interesting reading in there."

Gavin put the book of Shakespeare's completed works down and yawned. "I bet there is."

"Did you get any sleep last night?"

"I got a few hours."

"At home?"

"Well, partner," he laughed. "That may be getting too personal."

"We have a lot of work to do today, so don't fall asleep on me."

[165]

They started pulling out files from the box and putting them up on the board like before, laying everything out so they could see it. While they weren't necessarily trying to solve an old case (everybody thought she was guilty, anyway), they were looking for clues on how she could have gotten away with murder, who could have helped her, and what she might do to get away. Agent Main's phone rang. She got an update from the marshals about finding Brenda Mason. She gave her partner a surprised look.

"They didn't get her."

"She got away?"

"Not exactly. She wasn't on the greyhound bus they traced her phone to. You were right; she dumped the phone by putting it on the bus. Even had the navigation app running on the phone, making it easier to track."

Gavin smiled. "Told you she was smarter than the marshals gave her credit for."

"Are you happy?"

"That the marshals are stupid, no, but she's been on the run before. She knows how to stay hidden."

"Do you think she really went to Texas to get help from her old fiancé?"

"Not at all, but she might go to somebody for help. These files might provide some answers."

About the time Gavin and Agent Main finished laying out all the files, Agent Jannay came into their office. She smiled at Gavin. "You know, if you're going to get me up early on a Saturday and ruin Friday night, I should at least get you to buy me breakfast."

"Funny. What do you have for me this morning?"

"Some of Judge Doyle's old cases. More will be delivered today. Plus, I got you some researchers to help you go through them." She pointed to the five 20-somethings standing in the outer office.

Gavin asked, "Who are they? Where are the other agents that were going to help with this?"

"You don't get agents for this. There's not enough manpower to help you, but I got you law students."

"What?!"

"I couldn't get you any agents, so I called your old professor, Dr. Holland, at the University of Chicago. I asked for his five brightest students and got them cleared to help you with research. They're exactly who you need to go through these cases."

"They look young and inexperienced. Do they know anything?"

"Agent Donnelly, they're smart and, believe it or not, you were young and inexperienced once, too."

"There's no proof of that."

Agent Jannay smiled. "Where do you want this stuff?"

"Let's go to the conference room and get them set up."

Gavin introduced his partner to Agent Jannay as they walked out. On the way, he grabbed a donut for Agent Jannay and told her it was the breakfast he owed her. She laughed. Now, Gavin had to be the tough guy to the law students. They needed to be good; this was too important of a case for screw-ups. They laid out all the boxes of cases that had been in Judge Doyle's court, and then he looked at all of the students. "I want to thank all of you for coming in early this morning and helping the FBI. If Dr. Holland recommended you, then you must be good, but this isn't school. Today, you're in the real world. We can't afford any mistakes here. I need you to go through every one of the cases brought to you, read every detail, and find any connections between the cases."

One of the students asked, "Are we going to help solve a case for you?"

Gavin gave him a serious look. "Yes, the biggest that this office has ever seen."

5

The marshals arrived in Duncanville, Texas a couple of hours after their failed attempt in Union, Missouri. Their next plan was to try to apprehend Brenda Mason at her old fiancé's house. James Rollins moved to Texas after the trial in 1998 to get away from all the press. He needed a new life and, unfortunately, had become well-known as the fiancé of the child killer. He was on TV a few times, including when he testified against her, so everybody knew his face. Over the last 14 years, he had made a new life for himself; he got married and had kids while the world forgot about him. He was happy and had forgotten that part of his life until last night, when he got a phone call from Brenda Mason.

The call had startled him, but nothing like the knock on his door that Saturday morning. Rogers and a few of the other marshals went to his house. James wasn't even the one who answered the door; his wife did. When the badges were flashed, she got scared. She yelled for her husband when the marshals asked for him. He came to the door and asked,

"Can I help you? What are you doing here?"

"James Rollins, I'm Deputy Marshal Bryan Rogers. We need to ask you a few questions about Brenda Mason."

"I haven't talked to or seen her in 14 years. What can I possibly tell you about her?"

"Start with why she called you yesterday."

He was shocked; how could they know that? James looked over at his wife, who was glaring at him angrily. She couldn't believe that, after all these years, he would break his promise to her, the one he had made to never speak to Brenda again. He looked at his wife and said apologetically,

"Honey, I was going to tell you." She just continued to shoot him a furious look.

Rogers asked, "What did you tell her?"

"I told her to never call here again because I didn't want to speak to her. Then I hung up the phone."

"Why did she call you?"

"Before I hung up, she said that she needed my help that she was in trouble."

"But she didn't say why?"

"No. What is this about, anyway?"

"She's wanted for murder."

James was shocked again. "Again? Who did she kill?"

"A federal judge and she's on the run."

"So, you think she's on her way to see me?"

Rogers paused for a moment. "She called you for a reason; she might be heading this way. I am going to put a few marshals in cars on the street, just in case she shows up."

"You mean I'm going to be used as bait?"

"Yes, you are, and don't go anywhere. We may need to ask you more questions."

Rogers and the other two marshals walked back out to their black SUVs. Two of them were stationed on the street to keep watch for Brenda Mason, if she actually showed. James Rollins was not exactly happy about the whole thing, but he got the phone call from her. No matter how much he had tried to get away from that part of his life, he couldn't completely escape it. He would always be known as the Child Killer's Fiancé.

∞∞∞∞∞∞∞∞∞∞∞

By 5 p.m., Agent Donnelly and Agent Main had gotten nowhere. The law students hadn't come up with anything, either. It had been a long day of searching through piles of information, looking for connections, but nothing could be found. The agents went through the Brenda Mason trial documents, looking for anything that could help them. Agent Main was also trying to dissect the case to see where the prosecution and the investigators went wrong in not convicting her. Sure, it wasn't a cut-and-dry case, and part of the investigation was sloppy, but Brenda Mason was a killer; that much Agent Main was sure of.

The ME's office called and said that some of the initial reports were in. Agent Main got off the phone and looked at her partner. "Dr. Kenrick has something for us."

He laughed a bit. "Finally. I was hoping we would get something today. I don't like getting nowhere."

"You and me both!"

When they arrived at the ME's office, Dr. Kenrick still had the bodies laid out on the tables. She smiled when Agent Donnelly walked in and said in a flirty voice, "If it had just been you, Agent Donnelly, I would have put the bodies up and kept the tables free … but no use in cleaning up with both of you here."

Gavin laughed at the comment while his partner gave him a dirty look. She didn't know exactly what had happened, but she was smart enough to know that something went on. Agent Main asked, "Dr. Kenrick, are you ready to put down a cause of death?"

"Not exactly."

"You're saying the Doyle's didn't die from bleeding out?"

Dr. Kenrick looked up. "I can't say for sure. There was a something strange on the toxicology report."

Gavin asked, "Drugs or poison?"

"That's the thing," Dr. Kenrick replied. "It's not either of those things. We found an unknown substance that showed up in the bloodstreams of the victims. I don't know if it's actually a poison."

"Is there any way to identify it?"

"I am going to have to run more tests to find out what it is. Now, at first, we thought it might be drugs, because there are some slight needle marks on the arms. Both of the victims had them. There are not so many that it looks like they were heroin addicts, but enough to give the appearance that they both had a drug habit. However, there are no signs of drugs in their systems. They were injected with something."

"Couldn't they have just given blood? Would that account for the needle marks?"

"There are too many marks, and they're too fresh to have been caused by donating blood. They were injected with a substance, so we'll try to find out what it is."

Agent Main spoke up. "Do you think this unknown substance could have killed them?"

Dr. Kenrick looked at her. "I don't know for sure. It's a possibility, and that's why I haven't ruled a cause of death yet."

"But why inject them with something if this cutting and bleeding is going to do the job?"

"Well, if all you want to do is cut someone to let him bleed out, the best way of doing that is slitting the wrist or the throat. The Ling Chi method, like all forms of torture, is a show. You don't have to do it to kill someone, or even to make them feel pain."

Gavin asked, "How long will it take to determine what the substance is?"

"Most tests take a few days and some can take a week. I will get some help and we will try to get you guy's results sooner." Dr. Kenrick walked back over to the table where the bodies laid. "I have some other interesting details for you."

"Interesting?" Agent Main asked.

"Yes, ma'am. As you probably already figured out, the butcher knife we found at the scene with Brenda Mason's prints on it was not used to kill the victims. A longer and thinner blade was used, except for the heads. An ax was most likely used for those."

"Could a Butcher Knife cut the head off?"

"Probably, but the cuts would be sloppy and wouldn't be straight as we see on the bodies…an ax is better for that. Besides why use a Butcher knife at all? Let me show you something.

Dr. Kenrick picked up a petri dish containing very small fragments. "These are bone fragments found at the scene. At first, we thought they might have been from a spinal cord."

"They weren't?"

"No. The fragments are from a wrist."

Gavin asked, "Are saying the butcher knife cut a hand off?"

Dr. Kenrick replied, "Yes, but we didn't find anybody's hand at the scene. A DNA test confirmed that the bone fragments match the DNA from the second blood type at the scene. Apparently, there was a third victim and he lost a hand."

Gavin and Agent Main gave each other the same curious look. It said that there were more questions than answers, but they were heading in the right direction. Gavin asked the doctor if there was anything else. All she said was that, most likely, the cutting from the torture was what killed the victims, but until they identified that mysterious substance, she wasn't going to state a definitive cause of death. The agents walked out and headed back to the office.

Gavin and Agent Main were talking the case out as they walked back into their office. Agent Main was the one who asked the question that they were both thinking. "If you kill someone and cut his hand off, why get rid of it? Forensics is going to find the blood type and bone fragments, so it doesn't really matter if you leave another body; we're going to figure out that there was another victim…unless you don't want the third victim easily identified with fingerprints or dental records."

Gavin responded, "If Brenda Mason killed this other person, she could have been in a rush. The alarm was tripped, and the neighbor who watched the kids while Brenda went back to the house said that she was in a hurry when she came back to get the kids. If that's true, then she didn't have time to clean up the scene, so she just removed the body and the hand."

"Makes sense. Go with me on this. Brenda Mason kills the person helping her because she can't leave witnesses, but he or she struggles. So, in a fit of rage, she grabs a knife and cuts the hand off. Once that happens, it's much easier to kill someone, and then she has to hide what she did."

Gavin thought about it for a moment. "Okay, but it doesn't explain a few things. First, why leave the knife with your prints on it when you removed the person you just killed from the scene? And why are you leaving prints, anyway? They didn't find anybody else's but Brenda Mason's. And, of course, the most important question: Why? What's the motive?"

Agent Main thought for a moment. "It's a stretch, I admit, but the one thing about motive with sociopaths is there's not usually a reason why they kill."

"You think Brenda Mason really is a sociopath, out to kill anybody that bothers her?"

"Yeah, I do."

"You know the reason they never convicted her? They never could prove, without a shadow of doubt, that she actually killed her child and dumped the body. There was enough evidence pointed at the baby's father being the killer and possibly framing Brenda Mason. That's why the jury never convicted her."

"She had good defense attorneys."

"Maybe, but I still want to know why she killed the judge and his wife. I mean, if you are a disgruntled employee and want to get back at your boss, you sue him. Since the judge was the president's nominee for the bench, if he was being sued, the Senate would get to ask why during the confirmation hearings. You get revenge by embarrassing the guy on national TV; you don't kill him."

Agent Main nodded in agreement. "Maybe she was hired by someone because of her past. The motive wasn't hers; it was somebody else's."

"Again, who wanted the judge dead?"

"He was a Supreme Court nominee and a liberal. You don't think the other side would want him out of the way?"

Gavin laughed for a moment. "Hey, I like a good right-wing conspiracy as much as the next guy. I mean, for God's sake, they would eat their young just to win! But killing a federal judge is a stretch."

"Maybe, but it's Shakespearean and it sends a message."

Gavin laughed. "A numbered code is a message and not as dramatic as Shakespeare. There's no reason to use Shakespearean words to send a message, unless ..." He paused and appeared lost in thought. Agent Main asked him,

"What is it?"

He picked up the book of Shakespeare's complete works and turned to the page in Cymbeline where the quote was. Act 3, scene 4, line 87. He wrote that down and then went to his computer to Google something. He remembered reading about Shakespeare in the Park and, sure enough, he found the DePaul University Performing Arts website. This week was their annual Shakespeare in Grant Park festival. The university's drama department actually acted out all of Shakespeare's plays. It just so happened that the reconciliation plays were being performed that night, which Cymbeline was a part of. The

Tempest, The Winter's Tale, and Cymbeline were all being performed and the trio of plays had already started. Gavin figured that the numbers were a message. In any case, it was a lead, at least to him. He printed something out from the computer and, when he grabbed the piece of paper, a vision flashed in his mind. *He didn't see much. Seats were filling up outside the amphitheater in Grant Park. As he looked over the crowd, he could see one man sitting in a far-off section near the trees, away from the lights. He was hidden and Gavin couldn't make out his face. That's all he saw, but he knew that he had about 30 minutes before it would happen.*

Agent Main asked again, "What is it? Do you have something? Does the Shakespearean quote actually mean anything?"

"Maybe. I need to follow up on a lead. There's somebody I need to talk to and I have to go alone."

"Is this somebody from the Chicago underworld that you know? Someone that wouldn't like to see an FBI agent with you?"

He smiled. "Something like that! Try to find out more about the people in Brenda's past that she could turn to for help. And see if there is anything on Jackie Slater's past. There has got to be more on that name."

"You want me to call you if I find anything?"

"I'll be back in a couple of hours." Gavin put on his sport coat and started to head out.

Agent Main said to him half-jokingly, "You can at least bring back dinner for leaving me here." Gavin laughed at the comment. His partner was starting to develop a sense of humor. A laugh was something he needed since he was on his way to see a Shakespeare play, and he was not excited about it.

6

Agent Main was staring at the bulletin boards containing information about Brenda Mason's old murder case and information about the latest murders. She was looking for connections. Assistant Director Foster walked into the office, looking disgruntled. He asked her, "Have you seen the news yet?"

She was worried after a question like that. "No. What happened?"

He walked over to the small TV that was in the office and turned it on. The story had finally broken and the local CBS channel was the first to report it.

"In shocking news today, the president's nominee for the U.S. Supreme Court, Judge Henry Colin Doyle, was found murdered last night along with his wife. While the police are investigating all leads, fingerprints were found at the scene and they belong to the family's housekeeper of five years, Jackie Slater. Even more astonishing, that is not her real name. This news channel just found out that the housekeeper was none other than Brenda Mason, who was accused of murdering her three-year-old daughter and was acquitted of the murder 12 years ago. She is not in police custody and is suspected of kidnapping Mr. and Mrs. Doyle's two young children. If anybody knows her whereabouts or sees this person, then please call the number below."

They posted a picture of Brenda Mason and the two kids on the screen. They held the pictures on the screen for a minute and then cut to a reporter in the field, who gave more details about the murders. Agent Main was mad, but wasn't surprised. The story was going to break soon anyway, but the release of Brenda Mason's name, she thought, came too early. Everybody had hoped they could have kept that one quiet for at least a few days, but no such luck.

Agent Main yelled, "Goddamnit! How did this happen? Who leaked it?"

"What does it matter now? It's out there, but it may not be a bad thing."

"What do you mean?"

"The marshals haven't found Brenda Mason yet and they have no leads. Having her face out there can help us."

"I don't disagree with that, but we need her alive. The Child Killer has been accused of murder. You don't think someone is going to take a shot at her? You think people want her to be brought in alive?"

AD Foster paused for a moment. "I understand what you're saying, and I realize that she may have some answers you're looking for in finding a motive, but you have to find her first. Now, tell me what you have so far."

Agent Main looked angry. "We don't have much."

"Where's your partner?"

"Following up on a lead."

"Then what's the little information you do have?"

Agent Main told him what they had found out so far from the ME's office and the theories they were kicking around. She also let him know about the law students going through old case files to see if there was any motive. AD Foster shook his head with disappointment. "So, between you and the marshals, you have nothing and we have gotten absolutely nowhere in this case."

"Yeah!"

"Have something by tomorrow; the clock is running out. And to add a little incentive, the president will be flying in for the memorial service that is happening in four days. He's going to want a report from the FBI, and you don't want to fail in front of him."

Agent Main didn't have a smile in her; all she had was anger as AD Foster left. The pressure was on now to produce leads. She picked up her cell phone and sent a long text to her partner, telling him what happened with the news story breaking and the news that their boss just gave her.

∞∞∞∞∞∞∞∞∞∞

Gavin was walking through Grant Park when he got the text. He read it and yelled, "Fuck!" and a few people walking in his direction heard him. He didn't care. He also knew that he should head back to the office, but he had to follow this through. He had seen a vision and that made it critical. Each time he had one, it turned out to be important.

The amphitheater seating was broken up into three sections, with each of them having four sections of their own. Section 304 was in the very back of the far-right section, covered by trees and sort of hidden from everything. He walked toward it and saw a man sitting in a row all by himself. No one else was sitting in section 304. He was a middle-aged man wearing a dark suit and looking out of the ordinary, but still a stranger that no one would notice. Gavin walked up to his row. It was row eight, and he was sitting in seat seven. Gavin smiled at the hidden meaning in the numbers: Act 3, scene 4, line 87 (eight, seven). The man in the dark suit looked over at Gavin and said,

"Congratulations, Agent Donnelly, you figured it out. You're not as dumb as some of my colleague's think you are."

Gavin didn't really know what to say, but he started with a question. "Who are you?"

The man in the dark suit smiled. "Make up a name. You can call me whatever you want."

"Then let me rephrase the question. Who do you represent, and why am I talking to you?"

"I represent powerful people who don't want you to succeed, and you're talking to me because you're curious to see the truth."

Gavin nodded in agreement. The man in the dark seat politely told him to take a seat. He did and asked, "So, the message at the scene has nothing to do with the crime; it was meant for me, wasn't it?"

"Yes, and it was also my way of telling you that I know something personal about you. You're fluent in Latin and familiar with literature."

"Fine. You know something about me, but I don't know anything about you."

"It's more fun that way."

"But does it get me to stay and listen to you?"

The man in the dark suit smiled. "Very good, Agent Donnelly. Trying to make me need you more than you need me. Of course, we both know that isn't the case."

"Look, I still don't know who you are and why you wanted me to find you. No disrespect, but get to the fucking point. Who are you and what do you have for me?"

"I am here to warn you. Don't pursue this case any further than you have to. Let Brenda Mason take the fall for it. You go looking for answers beyond that and you won't like where you end up."

"Is that a threat?"

"Not by me. I'm trying to warn you what the consequences will be if you don't drop this. The people I represent won't tolerate another failure. You weren't supposed to solve your last case."

Gavin chuckled. "You just admitted that there's a conspiracy behind this, and that it's connected to my last case."

"But you already knew that. I'm not telling you anything new. So don't act surprised."

"Fine, but again: Who are these people?"

"Well, I won't help you figure that out, but let's just say that they have a controlling interest in making sure that Judge Doyle didn't interfere with their plans. Nothing angers them more than when somebody gets in their way."

"What do 'they' want?"

"What all men in power want: more power. This is not an original idea, but it's the honest-to-God truth."

"What did Judge Doyle do to anger these men?"

"I told you. He got in their way."

"But why kill him? He was the president's nominee for the bench. Couldn't you have just ruined him by not having him confirmed, by stripping away his power?"

"That's a good political move, but murder is the best way to make a statement."

"So, it was a warning for someone else." The man in the dark suit nodded. Gavin asked, "A warning for whom?"

"Somebody more important than you, and they won't stop until they've succeeded or until more blood runs in the streets. And that's why you should end this investigation. The woman is the perfect scapegoat for this crime. It will be easier for everybody."

Gavin thought about it for a moment and then replied, "You think I can just drop this? Let an innocent woman take the fall? My job is to find the people behind this crime and bring them to justice."

"Even if you found the men behind it all, they would never be brought to justice. Even if you exposed them, this would still be swept under the rug. They're not some local Chicago politicians that can be exposed and ruined. They not only have the power to kill you, but to make your life disappear as if it never happened. These are not the people you mess with. There's no protection against them, especially for an FBI agent. And besides, who says that Brenda Mason is actually innocent? If you're really smart then you will listen to this warning."

Gavin looked at the man in the dark suit dead in the eyes. "And if I don't leave this case alone, they'll just kill me?"

"They can, but that's too easy. They'll go after the ones that you care about the most. They will take everything away and make you watch. That's true suffering." The man in the dark suit got up from his seat. "While the message I left you is a simple Shakespearean quote about traitors, it doesn't make it less true."

"And you know the problem with traitors? They never get a say in the matter. One day, they're told they're a traitor and expected to pay the price. I'd say that's the worst part about being one, because you can't give a shit once you're dead."

The man in the dark suit laughed. "You're probably right, Agent Donnelly. Take the warning to heart." He walked away and headed for the trees behind section 304. He seemed to fade into the darkness surrounding them and disappear, just like a spook. Agent

Donnelly rarely got scared, but there was a little bit of fear in the air. He had already seen what these men in the shadows could do. Knowing that these men had connections to his parents' death made him a little fearful, but he wasn't going to stop. He was one step closer to the truth.

∞∞∞∞∞∞∞∞∞∞∞

Brenda had been at the movies most of the day with Connor and Sarah Doyle, trying to stay hidden. She was smart enough to know that the story of the judge's death would break soon and her real identity would probably be revealed. However, she was hoping that it would be a few days until that happened and that she could quietly get the kids where they needed to be right now. She also hoped she could escape quietly, too. Brenda had her prepaid smartphone on her at all times and she checked it constantly. She was looking for news headlines, any information that might help her, as well as messages from her friend. As she and the kids were leaving the movie theater, a notification from CNN popped up on her phone. The headline read:

President's Nominee for the
U.S. Supreme Court Murdered
Housekeeper Brenda Mason,
acquitted child killer, suspected in slaying

She was scared before, but now she was petrified. They had a picture of her. There was even a TV in the main lobby of the movie theater. FOX News was on and they were covering the news story, as well. Her picture was on the TV and it was only a matter of time before somebody recognized her. After all, there was a crowd around the TV.

Brenda held the kids' hands and quietly tried to make her way through the lobby of the theater, hoping that no one would recognize her. A woman accidently bumped into her and apologized. It took her a moment, but the woman did recognize her from the TV. Brenda could see the fear in her eyes as she walked away. That's when Brenda hurried the kids out of there. A police officer was moonlighting at the theater, and the woman who recognized Brenda Mason found him and told him what she had seen. The officer walked outside, looking for Brenda, and called into the radio attached to his shirt and asked for backup.

Brenda had always been good at observing her surroundings, especially since the first time she was on the run. She noticed the police officer outside the theater calling for backup and jerked the kids to move faster as they were trying to get to the car. Sarah dropped her

[178]

doll and started crying. Brenda tried to be nice, but she was also trying to get away quickly. She raised her voice at Sarah and told her to pick up the doll. Connor was scared now because he had never seen Brenda act that way. Brenda helped Sarah get her doll and managed to get them to the car. She didn't have time to buckle Sarah into the seat, so Connor had to do it. She was able to start driving out of the parking lot when two police cars were driving in.

Brenda was hoping that the police didn't see which car she got into. It was a calculated risk, but it was all she had. The movie theater was crowded and the parking lot was filled with people going in and out, so it was possible that she had slipped away through the crowds. One police car parked at the front of the theater while the other one drove around the parking lot. The lights weren't flashing, so he hadn't spotted the car. Brenda slowly headed for the exit. She was looking at the police and not paying attention when she hit the back end of another car that was backing out of a parking spot. That's when the police car's lights started flashing. The officer saw Brenda Mason's car, even if he thought he was just responding to an accident in the parking lot.

Brenda didn't know what to do. She was scared and rationale didn't play a part in her thinking. She backed up, drove around the car she hit, and sped up to get out of there. Sarah was crying hysterically and Connor was petrified, not knowing what to say. The police car in the parking lot was closing in on Brenda as she got through the exit and onto the main road. The officer had to dodge another car, which spun around to avoid hitting Brenda. The other car hit the police car coming through the exit, stopping him from pursuing Brenda's car. She had gotten away for now, but she couldn't go back to the hotel; it would be too dangerous. The kids knew something was wrong and it made them fearful of her now. That was the worst part of the situation, because she needed them to trust her if she was going to get them to safety and away from the people trying to kill her.

7

Gavin got back to the office late in the evening. Everybody had gone home, except for a few agents. Agent Main was in their office, going through paperwork and constantly looking up at the bulletin boards of information. Gavin noticed the empty conference room; the law students and Agent Janney had gone home, too. He walked into the office and asked his partner, "Where are the law students?"

She looked up and answered, "It was late, so I sent them home."

"Did they find anything?"

"No, and your friend said that it could take days just to find anything because there were so many cases that went through his court."

"We don't have days. Not anymore."

She chuckled. "You've got that right. I've still been trying to figure out who leaked the story to the press. I mean, the story of the judge's murder, I understand … but getting Brenda Mason's name out; it was too fast."

"I bet the marshals did it. Think about it. They spotted her, and now they're using the press to help them by getting her photo out there."

She looked disgusted. "You're probably right, but all they're going to do is cause pandemonium."

Gavin leaned on his desk and asked his partner, "So, have you found anything?"

"Nothing from her past that's helpful, but I did find something interesting."

"What?"

"Her change of identity. If we track everything about Brenda Mason, she seems to disappear and not exist after April 1998, a month after her murder trial ended. That same month is when Jackie Slater started to exist with a new social security number, driver's license, passport, and credit cards. Now the weird part is, she started with a social security card instead of a birth certificate, which you would need to get a social security card. I can't even find a birth certificate that matches any of her IDs. Plus, I can't find any form that was filled out to get a social security card. A number appears to have been created in April 1998 with a birth year of 1969."

Gavin thought about it for a moment. "So, no paperwork can be found on creating the social security card, and there's no record of a birth certificate. It's almost like somebody went into the social security administration's network and created the number that way. Once that happens, it's easy to have other IDs created."

Agent Main smiled. "And if you have all those IDs, then nobody needs a birth certificate; you've created an identity."

"You got it. It's genius, actually."

"But the real question is: who has the power to just go into the social security administration's network and create a number?"

"Somebody powerful!"

Agent Main walked over to the picture of the skull. "Now, the one thing I cannot find anything about is this skull. We don't have anything in our database about it, and the only thing on the Net that skulls refer to are crystal skulls and pirates, but nothing about a skull with eyes."

Gavin scratched his head. "I've been thinking about that, too. It's obviously a symbol of some kind, but I don't know anything about it, either. However, I know someone who could help us. A friend of mine is an anthropologist at DePaul University. He has written many books and is pretty renowned in the field."

"But can he help us tonight?"

"Yes, he can."

"You know where he's at on a Saturday night?"

"Of course. He's at the pub."

Agent Main looked at her partner. "Is every expert you know some drinking buddy at your pub?"

Gavin laughed. "Not all of them; just most of them! Come on, I'll buy you a pint."

"Is this just some excuse to go drinking because I interrupted you last night?"

He laughed again. "Sure, why not! But we're FBI agents. We can work and play at the same time."

They grabbed their coats and the picture of the red skull and headed out to Paddy Murphy's.

∞∞∞∞∞∞∞∞∞∞∞∞

The agents arrived at the pub about half an hour later. They walked in and, as per usual on a Saturday night, the regulars were there, including Gavin's family. Patrick, who was behind the bar, saw Gavin walk in and immediately handed him a Guinness beer. Agent

[181]

Main didn't really want to drink since they were still on the job, but Gavin gave her a hard time until she finally ordered a Guinness, too. She tried to hand Patrick her credit card to start a tab, but he wouldn't take it. He said that the beer was on the house. She didn't like that; a federal agent receiving a free gift, that's how corruption starts. Her partner pointed out that, sometimes, people are nice just for the sake of being nice.

Gavin said hi to a few people as he made his way to the table he was looking for. Dr. Henry McSwain always sat in a booth towards the back. He liked to keep to himself, but stay close enough to the music so that he could enjoy himself. He was a quiet Irishman, which seemed to be rare at Paddy Murphy's. He walked up to the booth.

"Dr. McSwain."

"Gavin, it's a pleasure to see you. I was sorry to see you rush out last night, but I saw the news a few hours ago, so I can understand why."

"It was unfortunate what happened to Judge Doyle. Doctor, I would like to introduce you to my partner, Agent Rachel Main."

Dr. McSwain and Agent Main shook hands. He said to Gavin, "If you don't mind me saying, you have the look of a man searching for answers and needing some advice. But I guess as an FBI agent, that's every day."

Gavin laughed. "These days, that's very true. We could actually use some help with something that was left at Judge Doyle's crime scene, and you may be the expert we need."

"Oh, what can I help with?" He directed the agents to take a seat. Gavin showed him the picture of the red skull.

Dr. McSwain stared at it for a moment. He had a look of concern on his face. Gavin asked if he recognized the symbol, and he nodded yes. Both agents perked up when he did that. Dr. McSwain looked at them both and said,

"I recognize something familiar about it. The skull having red eyes makes it unique, but I'm sure you've already picked up on that."

"We did," Gavin replied. "What's the history behind it?"

"This special design has shown up throughout history for a thousand years. There is an interesting etymology behind it."

"How so?"

"The earliest known assassins in history used something similar to this skull as a sign that they were responsible for the killing. Do you two know where the word assassin comes from and what is regarded as the first assassin group in history?"

The agents shook their heads no. Dr. McSwain laid the photo on the table and started to tell them the history. "The word assassin is often believed to derive from the word <u>Hashshashin</u> and shares its etymological roots with hashish. However, it has been strongly argued that this was a point made out of mistranslation, and that the origin of the term in Middle Eastern culture comes from the word Asasiyun, meaning those who follow the Asas; believers in the foundation of faith. It referred to a group that was part of the Nizari branch of the Shia, a denomination of Islam. Founded by Hassan-i Sabbah, the Assassins were active in the fortress of Alamut in Iran from the 8th to the 14th centuries, and also controlled the castle of Masyaf in Syria.

The group killed members of the Muslim Abbasid, <u>Seljuq</u>, andChristian Crusader elite for political and religious reasons. Saladin used this group a lot during The Third Crusade because he saw the advantage of a war behind enemy lines that could cause dysfunction and unrest. Crusade knights who were assassinated by this group would be marked with a skull that contained eyes, as if to say that death is always watching."

Agent Main looked at her partner and chuckled, remembering that he said that before, too. Dr. McSwain said to them, "Now, during The Third Crusade, the story gets interesting and the power of this red skull gets bigger. You know who the Knights Templar are, right?"

Agent Main replied, "You mean the order of knights from the Dan Brown novel whom the Catholic Church supposedly murdered?"

"Yes, and while his books contain a lot of fictional nonsense, the Knights Templar were real."

Dr. McSwain went on to explain. "After the First Crusade recaptured Jerusalem in 1099, many Christian pilgrims travelled to visit what they referred to as the holy places. However, though the city of Jerusalem was under relatively secure control, the surrounding area was not. Bandits abounded, and pilgrims were routinely slaughtered, sometimes by the hundreds, as they attempted to make the journey to The Holy Land. Around 1119, a French knight approached King Baldwin II of Jerusalem with the proposal of creating a monastic order for the protection of these pilgrims. King Baldwin agreed to the request, and granted space for a headquarters in a wing of the royal palace on the Temple Mount. The Temple Mount had a mystique because it was above what was believed to be the ruins of the Temple of Solomon. The Crusaders therefore referred to it as Solomon's Temple, and it was from this location that the new order took the name of *Poor Knights of Christ and the Temple of Solomon*, or "Templar" knights. The order, comprised of about nine knights, had few financial resources and relied on donations to survive.

But the Templars' impoverished status did not last long. They had a powerful advocate in Saint Bernard of Clairvaux, a leading Church figure and a nephew of André de Montbard, one of the founding knights. Bernard spoke and wrote persuasively on their behalf, and in 1129, the order was officially endorsed by the Church. With this formal blessing, the Templars became a favored charity throughout Christendom, receiving money, land, businesses, and noble-born sons from families who were eager to help with the fight in the Holy Land. Another major benefit came in 1139, when Pope Innocent II's papal bull *Omne Datum Optimum* exempted the order from obedience to local laws. This ruling meant that the Templars could pass freely through all borders, were not required to pay any taxes, and were exempt from all authority except that of the pope. Now, this is what history tells us, but what's not written in most history books is where legend and fact seem to mix. The real power of the Templars resided in their control over trade routes from the Middle East to Europe. A secret deal was made with the Nizari, the group of assassins used by Saladin, who also protected trade routes in the Middle East."

Both agents looked surprised, but it was Agent Main who said what they were both thinking. "What are you talking about? It sounds like a conspiracy theory."

"That's what most historians think, but there are facts that support this. It always comes down to what you're willing to believe, so I tell you what some might call a legend." He continued his story.

"Saladin wasn't stupid; he knew that, no matter how many lives were lost and how many times Jerusalem was captured and recaptured, the Church and European kings would always send Crusaders to the Holy Land. He figured that the best idea was to control the war from both sides and get rich doing it. He made a deal with the head of the Templar order and, while all the details of it aren't clear, one thing is certain: the Templar order had enough money or power to convince the Pope that they should have a high level of power."

Gavin asked, "Did they bribe the Pope?"

"Yes, actually, but not with the Holy Grail or any of that nonsense. They did it with money, access, and power. Like all wars, it was a cover for something more sinister; in this case, trade routes for resources that Europe didn't have but wanted. The Church was let in on the control of those trade routes and they didn't have to share with any kings."

"Wow, sounds just like The Mob," Agent Main said sarcastically.

"It's amazing how much a church can be like that, especially the Catholic Church."

Gavin gave him a dirty look. "You're Catholic, too, and despite all the bad things the Church has done, it has done a lot of good, as well."

"Bhagavad Gita said, 'Though they, blinded by greed, do not see evil in the destruction of the family, or sin in being treacherous to friends.' Nobody is perfect!"

"Very funny…using a Hindu saying to mock the church!"

Dr. McSwain smiled and continued. "The Templar order was given their power and riches because of the deal with the Church. As a result, pilgrims could travel safely to the Holy Land under the protection of the Templars. Saladin became rich beyond imagination, as well as the Church. And, of course, Jerusalem came back under the control of Saladin."

"Wasn't it just easier to do business instead of war?" Agent Main asked.

"Yeah, but war is business, and the Church would never just do open business with people who were considered heretics. It would be like the FBI doing open business with The Mob."

"But there were how many Crusades over the centuries?"

"Nine major Crusades and 12 minor Crusades between 1095 and 1303 A.D. And most of them were just a cover for commerce in the Middle East."

Gavin asked, "I thought the Crusades were in response to the Byzantine Empire needing help with the growing Muslim population?"

"Sure, that was part of it, but only when it came to business. Muslims were taking control of the commerce and they needed someone to help clear out the competition, and who better than the Church?"

Gavin sneered at the thought, but it wasn't entirely untrue, either. Agent Main asked Dr. McSwain what happened to the Templar order; they were obviously no longer around. He explained, in detail, what happened.

"In 1305, Pope Clement V sent letters to both the Templar Grand Master Jacques de Molay and the Hospitaller Grand Master Foulques de Villaret to discuss the possibility of merging the two orders. Neither was amenable to the idea, but Pope Clement persisted, and in 1306 he invited both Grand Masters to France to discuss the matter. De Molay arrived in early 1307, but de Villaret was delayed for several months. While waiting, de Molay and Clement discussed charges that had been made two years prior by an ousted Templar. It was generally agreed that the charges were false, but Clement sent King Philip IV of France a written request for assistance in the investigation. King Philip was already deeply in debt to the Templars from his war with the English and decided to seize upon the rumors for his own purposes. He began pressuring the Church to take action against the order as a way of freeing himself from his debts."

"In October 1307, Philip ordered de Molay and scores of other French Templars to be simultaneously arrested. The arrest warrant started with the phrase: "Dieu n'est pas content, nous avons des ennemis de la foi dans le Royaume" ["God is not pleased. We have enemies of the faith in the kingdom"]. The Templars were charged with numerous offenses, including idolatry, heresy, homosexuality, financial corruption, and secrecy. Many of the accused confessed to these charges under torture, and these confessions, even though obtained under duress, caused a scandal in Paris."

"After more bullying from Philip, Pope Clement then issued a papal bull in November 1307, which instructed all Christian monarchs in Europe to arrest all Templars and seize their assets. (A papal bull is a particular type of letters, patent, or charter issued by a Pope of the Catholic Church. It is named after the lead seal (bulla) that was appended to the end in order to authenticate it. Papal bulls were originally issued by the pope for many kinds of communication of a public nature, but by the thirteenth century, papal bulls were only used for the most formal or solemn of occasions). Clement called for papal hearings to determine the Templars' guilt or innocence, and once freed of the Inquisitors' torture, many Templars recanted their confessions. Some had sufficient legal experience to defend themselves in the trials. In 1310, Philip blocked these attempts, using the previously forced confessions to have dozens of Templars burned at the stake in Paris."

"With Philip threatening military action unless the pope complied with his wishes, Clement finally agreed to disband the order, citing the public scandal that had been generated by the confessions. In 1312, he issued a series of papal bulls, which officially dissolved the order and turned over most Templar assets to the Hospitallers. The Church, along with King Phillip, took control over their business, so to speak. With the Crusades finished and business commerce already set up with the Middle East, there was no need to use a Crusade to cover up the real actions of the Church. They had just eliminated the competition with the Templar order and taken over their territory like The Mob or a gang."

Agent Main asked, "So, what happened to the Nizari after its partners were destroyed?"

"The Nizari disappeared, too. There was no need for a secret order of assassins to fight against Crusaders, but their business interests didn't go away, either. They just reinvented themselves in the years to come and aligned themselves with European companies wanting to make a profit and have power."

"Reinvented themselves? How?"

"You've heard these names before: British East India Trading Company, The West India Trading Company, British Petroleum, and Halliburton just to name a few."

Gavin sneered. He didn't like crazy conspiracy theories involving governments. Dr. McSwain just told him that you can't deny history, and corporate thugs are worse than governments when it comes to corruption. Agent Main asked,

"So, what are you trying to say? That whoever left this skull at the crime scene is from some ancient group trying gain power again?"

Dr. McSwain smiled. "I can't tell you that for sure, but whoever left this knows his history. This is a warning to stay away. The Dutch used to put a similar symbol on their cargo from the Middle East as a warning to those who wanted to steal it."

Gavin asked the professor, "Can anybody get this information? I mean, it's on the Internet, right?"

"Most of it is, but some of what I just mentioned can only be found at universities: published papers from professors, research that can only be found in the restricted sections of university libraries. An ordinary person can't just access it."

Gavin started thinking. His partner was curious, too. Somebody did his research; somebody knew history well, and whether Brenda Mason was the true killer was getting to be less likely. The agents let the professor get back to his meal. They found another table and talked about the case, trying to answer the endless questions that Judge's Doyle's murder gave them.

8

Brenda was able to get onto Interstate 80 and get out of Moline, Illinois. She was racing to get another city and, more importantly, across the state line in Iowa. She tried not to speed and draw attention to herself, because she needed to get off the road and ditch the car. After an hour, she finally arrived in Iowa City. The kids didn't say a word the entire way there. They were still scared and Connor was starting to figure out that something was wrong. He feared that it might have to do with his parents.

Brenda found a hotel that was hidden from the main roads, a place where she could ditch the car without anybody really noticing. The hotel was big enough to stay hidden among the crowds, too. Brenda figured she had about a day before she would have to be on the move again. The local Moline police didn't have jurisdiction outside that city, and it would be at least a day before the FBI arrived; that's what she was assuming. She told Conner to watch his sister while she reserved a room. Being afraid of what was going on; he decided to try to get away from Brenda.

As she came out of the hotel office, she saw the kids missing from the car and immediately panicked. She looked all around for them but couldn't find them. Her worst fear was that they had been kidnapped. After all, the hotel wasn't the nicest of places. Brenda finally spotted the kids along the side of the main road, about a block from the hotel. Connor was trying to flag down a car, but there weren't any vehicles coming by. She ran to the kids and shouted, "What are you doing, Connor? You know you're not supposed to get in the cars of strangers!"

Sarah was crying again. She was still scared, but her brother was trying to be tough. He shouted back, "Get away from us! We're going back to mom and dad."

"Connor, honey, you can't go back to them."

"Why won't you let us see our mom and dad?"

Brenda Mason started crying a little. She couldn't fake it anymore. "Connor, I wish I could, but they're not here anymore. They died."

Connor was shocked to hear it. He didn't want to believe it, but Brenda had never lied to him. He was old enough to realize that, and so he started crying. "I don't believe you," he said, hoping deep down that what Brenda said wasn't true.

Still crying, she responded, "I'm sorry, Connor, but it's true. They died yesterday and the people that killed them are after you, too. I brought you with me to keep you safe."

She watched as Connor's face became pale. He was terrified and was shielding his sister from any kind of danger that could harm them, even from Brenda. Although he was mature for a nine-year-old, he still had a hard time trusting people, and Brenda had broken the trust he had for her. Brenda loved both Sarah and Connor as if they were her own children. She knew the only way to gain that trust back was to tell them everything, especially her plan for getting them to safety. She walked over and, despite the kids still being afraid; she hugged them and told them that, no matter what, she would not let anyone hurt them. Eventually, they went back to the hotel room and made plans to escape. Although the kids were still scared, they were also a little excited about getting to pretend to be other people just get away. It was like a game, and Brenda had always been good at making things fun. With some takeout food and the TV turned up loud enough so that no one could hear them, the three of them made plans and the kids learned to trust her again.

∞∞∞∞∞∞∞∞∞∞

Gavin and Agent Main both got another beer at the pub and continued talking about the case. Dr. McSwain had given them an interesting history lesson, but there were still plenty of parts that didn't make sense. Agent Main asked her partner,

"Do you think there really is some secret group that killed the judge and is now trying to scare you?"

"I don't know about a secret group, but I think it's obvious that someone is trying to scare us; and why not use something from history that has worked before? Isn't it common for killers to leave some kind of signature at the crime scene?"

"Yes. Killers, especially serial killers, like to sign their work, but it's unusual for them to leave something behind that's meant to scare the general public. The crime itself is the scary part."

"So, it's a political hit. But why? I still don't buy that it's because Judge Doyle was nominated for the Supreme Court."

[189]

Agent Main thought about it for a moment as she took a sip of beer. "What could he have done that's so bad that someone would torture and murder him and his wife? It has to be a powerful murderer. It could be a serial killer, but we would have more murders like this, and picking the judge is too high-profile. A killer would target someone ordinary who doesn't draw attention."

"So it is a political murder."

"Probably, but I wish we could figure out the real motive. Then maybe we could solve this thing."

Gavin took a sip of his beer and thought for a moment. "You know, there's one thing that we haven't mentioned as being a possible motive."

"What?"

"Money. Money is power and power is the one thing people kill for."

She frowned. "You think he had money problems and someone killed him over that?"

"No, but somebody might have. He was a federal judge that might have presided over a case involving money. He could've been the one blamed for it, depending on the ruling. Maybe that's what we should be looking for in his cases." He pulled out his phone and texted Agent Janney to have the law students cross-reference any case that involved financial crimes and China.

About the same time Gavin was texting his message, Agent Main received an alert on her phone. It was already being reported to the FBI by local authorities that Brenda Mason was sighted in Moline, Illinois a couple of hours before. She handed her phone to her partner so he could read the alert. As soon as he touched it, a vision flashed in his mind. *The kids were sitting on the bed nearest the TV, watching some program that they thought was boring, but it kept their minds off of everything. Brenda reached inside her purse, looking for her cell phone, but she didn't find it. She was frantic now because she always kept it in her purse. Brenda ran out to the car and tore through it, furiously looking for the phone, but again, she couldn't find it. That's when it dawned on her that she might have dropped it while trying to get away from the theater. While it was a prepaid phone, it was evidence left behind at another crime scene and that's what made her fearful. Brenda went to the front desk of the hotel to ask if there was a store nearby that sold cell phones. It turned out that there was a 24-hour Walgreens drugstore a mile up the road. Her perfect plan was starting to fall apart. There were too many bumps in the road and she was miles away from where she had to be.*

Gavin responded to the text message alert. "According to this she damaged the car… if the car is damaged; she probably didn't get very far. She'd have to get the car off the road. I bet she's within a 100-

mile radius, at a hotel somewhere, figuring out how to find different transportation."

Agent Main said, "We'll coordinate with the local FBI offices in Iowa and Wisconsin. They can get in touch with local law enforcement and put up road blocks, as well as conduct searches. Maybe we'll get lucky."

"If they find her, tell them to sit on her until we get there."

"Why?"

"We don't want her spooked, and we don't need the kids to be scared or harmed. If we take her quietly, then she might be more cooperative with us and give us answers about why the judge was really killed."

"And if she's the killer, you think she's just going to give it all up for us?"

"I don't know, but treating her like every other cop has, like she's the Child Killer, won't get us anywhere. If being nice doesn't work then we'll play a little bad cop with her."

She laughed. "You know, you just might make a good FBI agent in the Violent Crimes division yet."

Gavin laughed at the comment and then he smiled at something. "The marshals are really going to be pissed about this. They've been embarrassed more than once now."

Agent Main looked at him. "What is it about this Deputy Marshal Rogers you don't like? You're glad that he has been wrong?"

"I don't want the marshals stealing our thunder, that's all."

"No, there's something else about this guy. I thought you said you didn't know him, but you do know him."

Gavin didn't say anything, but it was written all over his face. He really didn't want to tell his partner the story, but he wasn't going to get away that easily. She wanted to know and wasn't going to let him off the hook. Gavin was leaving a tip on the bar, even though the drinks had been free, when his Uncle Liam came walking up to say goodbye. Agent Main asked Gavin again about the marshal and he tried to ignore her. Finally, Liam spoke up and explained how they knew the marshal.

Alex and Gavin Donnelly's best childhood friend was Jimmy McManus. They had all grown up together and, like most friends from the neighborhood, did everything together. Most Irishmen from the neighborhood followed in their father's footsteps, and Jimmy McManus was no different. Like his father and uncle, Jimmy became part of the Irish Mob and the IRA syndicate in Chicago. His uncle was Tommy McManus, head of the Irish Mob in Chicago, and he ran the neighborhood. They were involved in loan sharking, gun running, and, of course, any kind of property deal they could get their hands on.

While Alex and Gavin entered law enforcement to serve and protect their neighborhood with a badge, Jimmy did it another way: with fear and a gun. But no matter what, he always protected the people in his neighborhood from any outsider that would harm them.

A little over five years ago, Jimmy McManus was caught transporting illegal weapons in an attempt to make a deal with a drug cartel from Columbia. The ATF had a sting operation and gunfire was exchanged. One of the cartel members killed in the raid was the son of Hector Villa, the leader of the cartel. An ATF agent also got shot. While there was no way to prove who actually did it, Jimmy got 15 years in federal prison, including attempted murder of an ATF agent. They pinned it on him because he was the only one caught that was still alive after the raid, and the justice department needed to make a statement. He was sent to Welling maximum security prison in Colorado. A year later, the cartel put a hit on Jimmy's family. They were going to murder his wife, Maggie, and 6-year-old son, Peter. He found out about it in prison and figured he was the only one who could save them. Jimmy escaped by faking an injury that forced the staff to take him to the hospital outside the prison to have surgery. By the time he called his uncle and tried to get help for family, it was too late.

Three members of the cartel shot and killed his son when Maggie brought him home from school. They shot Maggie, but she was able to shoot one of the assassins and kill him. The other two ran away before they could finish the job. By the time Jimmy got to Chicago, his son was dead and his wife was in surgery from a gunshot wound. U.S. marshals were called in to find Jimmy, and he didn't really try to hide or get away. He went to the hospital to see his wife and find out about his son, and the marshals captured him there. The marshal who caught him was Deputy Marshal Rogers. He was hauled off by the marshals in front of his wife, who had just come out of surgery, and in front of his colleagues. He never even got to say goodbye to his son, who was lying in the morgue.

Agent Main looked sad and said, "I can see why he's not liked, but your friend did ..."

Gavin interrupted her. "... Break out of prison, yeah, he did. And he knew he was going back to prison for a long time, but it was worth it to try to save his family."

"I didn't mean to make it sound like he was the scum of the earth."

"That wasn't even the worst part of it. The day he was transported back to Colorado, they had his son's funeral. Even though Jimmy's lawyer put a request in for him to attend the funeral, the DOJ said they never got the request from the marshals, who were supposed to deliver it. So Jimmy didn't get to go to his son's funeral; he was transported back to Colorado."

"Was it some clerical mistake with the DOJ?"

"No. Rogers didn't send it."

"How do you know that?"

Gavin looked angry. "Because there was never any proof that he sent it. As far as I am concerned, a man who doesn't let a father bury his son can't be trusted."

Liam spoke up. "Every father, no matter his deeds, has the right to mourn and bury his child. This Marshal Rogers never even had the decency to allow Jimmy to go to the funeral. He could have driven him there for 30 minutes, just to say goodbye. He's just as good as a traitor around here."

Agent Main said, "I can understand that." She looked at Gavin. "Your animosity for him isn't going to get in the way of solving this case, is it?"

"I'm still a professional and will work with him if I have to, but he doesn't get any free handouts from me. He's still a bastard!"

Agent Main smiled. She knew that there was no way to change his mind on the matter. She just hoped that the marshal wouldn't piss her partner off too badly and cause an incident. They didn't need that to happen, for there were too many problems with this case as it was.

∞∞∞∞∞∞∞∞∞∞∞∞

He walked out to his patio and the cold air hit him like a bullet. He never got used to it, but he loved the freezing air; it had a way of making everything more real. He lit a cigarette and pulled out his cell phone. The number he needed was at the top of the most popular list.

The phone only rang once before the call was answered. "Mr. Bran, I shouldn't have to be making this call. You should already know what I am about to tell you. Brenda Mason is not going to Texas. She was spotted with the judge's kids in Moline, Illinois."

"Is it a confirmed sighting?"

"Of course it is; I wouldn't be calling you if it wasn't. Remember, you're the one that's supposed to be calling me with Intel reports."

"I just wanted to be sure before we move locations. We can be there in five hours."

He took a puff of his cigarette. "Stand by for further instructions. I am placing a man with the FBI task force that's going there in the morning. Keep with the marshals for now so you can intercept her while she's on the move."

"You don't think the FBI agents are going to find her?"

"I know they're not. We're going to make sure she stays on the run so you can grab her. We want to drive her into a trap."

"Okay, just tell us where you need us to be."

He took another drag from his cigarette while the cold wind was starting to pick up. "You need to be logged into the FBI current crimes database, too, so you can get constant updates. You need to know what's going on before I do. I will text you an untraceable access code."

" Yes, sir."

"Mr. Bran … we can't afford mistakes. She needs to be in a body bag soon."

9

Agent Main was waiting outside St. Thomas Catholic Church for her partner early on Sunday. Despite the fact that the agents had to get to Moline, Gavin insisted on going to Mass. He came out of the church at 8:30 and saw her standing next to the FBI's Crown Victoria. The last time she was sitting in front of the church was when some Chicago police officers were trying to kill Mickey Soranno. As Gavin was coming down the steps of the church, she said to him,

"You know, I think God can forgive you at least once if you don't go to Mass. I'm sure he knows that we have a murder to solve."

He smiled. "The way this case is going, I think we need God on our side. Doesn't hurt to have a little karma from him when it comes to this case. That's why I went to Mass."

"I guess I can't argue with that."

They drove to the office, where they would be taking a helicopter ride to Moline. They were meeting up with the FBI task force that was already there, setting up road blocks in a 200-mile radius around the Moline area. Agent Main drove to the FBI office so Gavin could read the latest intelligence report. She said, "If you look on the next page, you will find that somebody else reported seeing her at a Holiday Inn after the news story broke last night. Apparently, she had been there for a day, holed up in the room until she took the kids to the movies."

"Let me guess; nothing seemed suspicious until the news story broke and then they called local law enforcement instead of the FBI."

"Yeah."

"Did anybody see her go back to the hotel?"

"Not that we know of, but I doubt that she did if she was on the run. There's a CSU team there now."

About an hour later, the agents arrived in Moline. The first place they went to was the movie theater. It was still roped off and closed from the night before. Local law enforcement officers, along with FBI agents, were questioning staff and examining the wreckage from the traffic incident. It was a mess at the theater, chaotic and disorganized, but the FBI had to look like they were covering all the angles because of the crime and the fugitive they were after. Gavin finally asked his partner, "Do you really think they're going to find anything that we don't already know?"

"I know this is boring, but it's procedure … and you never know, there might be a witness here that can offer some clues." He gave her a sarcastic look. She responded, "Probably not!"

Gavin walked over to the manager of the theater as he was being questioned by the chief of police and another agent. They were in the middle of questioning him when Gavin walked up and said, "I just have two questions for you."

The chief of police replied, "We're not done. Wait your turn."

Gavin gave him a dirty look and said, "No. You're done."

"I beg your pardon! This is still my town and you can wait until I'm done talking to him."

Chief, I don't care if this is your town or not. This is a federal investigation and you haven't even asked the right questions yet. We don't need for you to finish asking all the wrong questions." Gavin looked at the manager and asked, "What's the children's or animated movie you have playing?"

The manager replied, "How to Train Your Dragon."

"Were there any cell phones found last night?"

"I have to check, but I think they found two. They're probably in the lost-and-found bin."

Gavin asked to be taken to the lost-and-found bin. Sure enough, there were three cell phones in there. As he looked at all of them, he found a prepaid android smartphone. He figured it might be the phone he was trying to find from his vision. He walked over to where Agent Main was standing and showed her the phone. She asked, "You found something?"

"A prepaid cell phone that was found in the theater of the movie they saw last night."

"How do you know that it's hers? It would be a lucky break for us, but it could be anybody's phone."

"Look at it. Only two numbers have been dialed: the activation number and a Wisconsin number that was called over five times. She also texted the number quite a bit and she never saved it, as if she didn't want anybody to know who she was contacting."

Agent Main nodded in agreement. She started looking through the phone to see what apps were on it. There were just a handful of apps downloaded. She said, "Check this out. Brenda Mason only had apps for local news stations, CNN, and a flight tracker. She used the news sites to check on news about herself … and the flight tracker, well, it looks like she's planning a trip or waiting for someone to get in."

"Could be both." Gavin wrote down the number she had called and texted. Then he called a friend at the local office. "Hey Jack, its Gavin. I have number for you that I need a trace on. Get me everything you can find about the person who owns the number. We'll be back later this afternoon." He motioned to another agent who appeared to be gathering evidence. The agent walked over to where Agent Donnelly and Agent Main were standing. Gavin asked the agent, who appeared to be younger than anybody else at the scene, "What's your name?"

"Agent Burke, sir."

"You're collecting evidence. Dust this phone and see if the prints on it match Brenda Mason's. Then bag it. We're taking it with us." Gavin grabbed the other phones out of the lost-and-found box and handed them to Agent Burke. "Take all of these phones and get them dusted for prints." Agent Burke gave him a funny look when he was handed all of the phones, but he hadn't been an FBI agent for very long, so he knew not to question a senior agent.

Agent Main looked at her partner. "We just got a big lead. How did you know to look for a cell phone?"

He smiled. "Just a good, old-fashioned hunch."

"Bullshit. You knew to look for it."

"I had a feeling that she might have lost it at the theater, that's all." He walked off to avoid having to answer more questions, but his partner suspected something. There were times that he was too lucky when it came to being right. She knew the feeling.

Eventually, the agents ended up at the Holiday Inn where Brenda Mason had been staying. A CSU team was in her room, working the scene and gathering evidence. Brenda didn't leave much at the hotel. She was always prepared to leave in a hurry, so she didn't leave any bags at the hotel; but she did leave clues. Agent Main asked if any bags had been left, but the CSU team told her no. She looked through the desk and found some maps and travel brochures for Europe and South America. Most people would have disregarded those items in a hotel room, but a wanted fugitive having them meant that they weren't just ordinary things.

She unfolded the map on the desk to see if Brenda had marked anything on it. Gavin walked over to the desk and asked if she had found something. She answered,

"It's a map of Illinois, Iowa, and Minnesota. On the back is a map of the United States." She looked at her partner. "So, if you have to escape quickly from Moline, what direction do you go? Do you stay on the road for very long with a wrecked car? Do you take side roads?"

Gavin looked at the map. "If you're on a highway, then you can travel faster and there's less risk of being pulled over by cops. The problem is there are major highways in every direction, so figuring out which one to take is the hard part. But at most, you can stay on one for about an hour before you have to get off and ditch the car."

"It's a good point. We should get with local law enforcement in every city within a two-hour radius and have them check hotels. We could get lucky. She also had travel brochures. Is she really trying to get out of the country, or is this just to fool us?"

"Might have been her original plan."

"To leave the country, she's got to get three fake passports. And that takes a lot of cash, especially for good ones, and traveling with children will get you noticed."

"Europe is where you can go to be hidden. South America has more non-extradition countries, but it's not the best place for kids. Where do you choose to go?"

Agent Main paused for a moment and then spoke up. "You know, maybe it's not about where she's going, but who she's trying to meet. Let's say that she's trying to get the kids to safety. Where could she go, and who can help her? Maybe that has something to do with the travel brochures."

"There's a passport for Jackie Slater, right?"

Agent Main smiled. "Yes, there is. We can see where she has gone and match it to this map and the brochures."

"But we also need to find any connections that her alias had overseas."

"I suppose you don't want to share this with the marshals."

"Hell no. They can get their own leads."

There was nothing else in the hotel room that seemed to help them. They didn't need to dust for fingerprints; they already knew she had been there. The hotel staff identified her because of the news. The media was working for them and making everybody look out for Brenda Mason, but she was still at large and everybody wanted her to be in custody by now. The agents folded up the map and the brochures to take with them. Gavin looked around for Agent Burke and, when he didn't see him, he asked the other agents in the room where he was. Nobody seemed to know. Finally, the ASAC (Assistant Special Agent in Charge) walked over and said, "Agent Donnelly, we don't have an Agent Burke on the task force. Did someone identify himself as Agent Burke?"

"Yeah. There was a young agent, about 5'10", sandy blond hair, looked like he was in his mid- to upper-20's, and he was collecting evidence."

"We don't have an agent matching that description."

Agent Main and Agent Donnelly looked at each other with the same expression of shock and anger. They didn't have to say it; there was a spy among them. Gavin got on a walkie-talkie and called down to the agents in the lobby. He gave them a description of this so-called Agent Burke and told them to stop the guy. Agent Main called back over to the movie theater to see if he was still over there. She looked over at Gavin and shook her head to let him know that the guy had come with everybody else to the hotel. They spread out and started covering the hotel to look for him. Chances were that he was already gone, but they had to search for him. Maybe they would get lucky and find him.

Twenty minutes went by and nobody had found him. Agent Main and Agent Donnelly met each the other in the lobby of the hotel. He asked first, "You didn't find anything?"

"No. You?"

"No. Where could he have gone?"

"It's not hard to blend in and sneak out as an agent. Hell, we don't know everybody here."

Gavin got back on the walkie-talkie and asked everybody to check in. Nobody had anything. Agent Main asked, "Are all the cars still here?"

"Let's check." They went to the parking garage and quietly entered. If he was there, they didn't want to spook him. They both had their service weapons drawn and ready to fire. Agent Main peeked around the corner and saw the guy sitting in one of the FBI cars. It looked like he was texting on his cell phone. They were about to sneak up on him when another car came into the parking garage. It slowed down and approached the FBI car that Agent Burke was sitting in. Agent Main, who was taking point, motioned for Gavin to stop so they didn't let the two men know they were there. Agent Main wanted both of the men in the same car so it would be easier to get them. All was quiet as Agent Burke started to get in the car, but Gavin's walkie-talkie went off as the ASAC was calling him. It was loud and the two men in the car heard the radio. They looked up and saw Agent Main. Instead of driving off, Agent Burke pulled his gun out and opened fire on the agents.

Bullets flew over the agents' heads. Agent Main was able to shoot Agent Burke and he fell to the ground, but he got another shot off. The bullet whizzed by Agent Main, scraping past her arm and cutting a hole in her suit jacket. She wasn't hit, but the bullet grazed her and caused her to fall down, panic, and shake. She was still a bit anxious when it came to bullets flying at her, not only from the gun fight at the bank a month before, but also from when she was shot a month before that trying to take down a serial killer. Gavin loudly spoke up, "Are you alright?"

She shouted back, "Get the other guy."

Gavin peeked out from the corner where he and his partner were hidden and shot at the car. He was trying to wound the driver through the windshield, but even as good as he was he couldn't get the shot. The windshield shattered and the car started to drive off, so Gavin took another shot. This time, he got the driver's-side back wheel. The car spun out of control, but the driver tried to control it and get away. He got about 20 yards before crashing into a couple of parked cars. Gavin couldn't tell if the guy was unconscious or not, so he approached the car slowly. He shouted, "Get out of the car with your hands in the air. Put your face on the pavement with your hands interlocked behind your head."

The man in the car didn't move. Gavin edged a little closer to the car. He waited about 30 seconds before repeating his order to the driver. As he started to speak again, the driver got out of the car with his Glock 19 and opened fire on Gavin. The shots were sporadic, and Gavin had a round hit him in his left arm. It was a deep wound that was gushing blood. Gavin ducked behind the side of a parked car and waited for a clear shot. The guy in the car finally emptied his clip. As he started looking for another one, Gavin shot him and killed him instantly. With his arm bleeding, he walked over to the body to make sure the man was dead. As he looked down at the body, two more gunshots startled him. When he turned around, he saw Agent Burke fall to the ground. Agent Main was standing about 12 feet behind him, pointing her gun toward him. She was shaking a little bit, but she aimed her shots well. She killed the guy who was impersonating an FBI agent and saved her partner's life.

He smiled at her and held his hand over his heart as if to say thank you. She nodded at him and then tried to catch her breath. It took a lot out of her to get those shots off. Gavin called for the ASAC and the CSU team to get down to the parking garage. They had two more dead bodies and needed to run their fingerprints to try to identify them. Gavin knew that it would probably be useless. They weren't going to get anything.

10

Brenda Mason was able to get rid of the car first thing on Sunday morning. There was always someone willing to pick up a scrap car for free, especially with no questions asked. That was the most important thing she had to do. Next was getting a new phone, since she lost the other one. She and the kids put on hats to help disguise themselves and went out to make their purchases. They had to be on the move. Iowa City was a small enough town where she could find a cheap car and pay cash. After getting a new phone and car, as well as new clothes and some wigs to help with disguises, they ended up back at the hotel so they could prepare to get on the road. Brenda had to make a call first.

She activated the new prepaid smartphone and called her friend, Rick. He answered, despite not recognizing the number. "Rick, it's me."

"Jesus Christ, where are you? It's been on the news since last night!"

"What are they saying?"

"That you're on the run and have kidnapped the two kids."

"Is there anything else?"

"They just reported this morning that you were spotted in Moline, Illinois at a movie theater and crashed into a car trying to get away."

Brenda sighed. "At least they got that part right."

"Shit, Bren," he said, calling her by the name he had for her since they were in grade school. "Where are you now? Did you get rid of the car? What's your next move?"

"Slow down, Rick. I have it all under control. I'm in Iowa City and I got rid of the car this morning. We got another one and we're going to be on the move today."

"Tell me where to meet you and I can probably get there tonight."

She smiled. It had been a while since she had a real friend help her out. Sure, the Doyle's were her friends, but they never knew who she really was. "I don't know where we are going to be yet, but I will call you later. Now, I need you to do something for me."

"What?"

"Get a passport photo today and bring it with you. You can get one quickly at a Walgreen's."

"Passport photo? Why?"

"We're going to get you a new ID."

"What? How can you even pay for fake IDs and new transportation?"

"Look, Rick. I won't tell you everything about my past, but I've been prepared to run for a long time and I've had money stashed away for this for a while. We're covered."

He chuckled. "Somehow, I'm not surprised. I'll take care of the photo today. Call me and let me know where to meet you." Brenda hung up the phone and sat down to eat breakfast with the kids, trying to forget, at least for a moment, what she was going to have to do.

∞∞∞∞∞∞∞∞∞∞∞∞

The President arrived back from Sunday church service to find his chief of staff, David Rollins, waiting for him in the oval office. The look on David's face let the president know that something was wrong. President Sunders asked,

"David, what is it?"

"I'm afraid I have some bad news on the manhunt for Brenda Mason. The marshals were wrong about where she was going. After the news story about her was aired last night, she was spotted in Moline, Illinois at a movie theater. Unfortunately, she got away."

The president was angry. He, like everybody else, expected her to be in custody by now. He asked, "Do they have leads on where she might be?"

"No, as of yet."

"How can one person get away, with the manhunt the FBI has out for her?"

"Right now, it's just one task force of U.S. marshals and the local Violent Crimes division from the FBI Chicago office. They may be stretched a little thin."

"What? My nominee for the bench has been murdered and his two children have been kidnapped. The FBI director has ordered a full-scale manhunt, yet … what the hell is going on over there?"

"David paused. "I think he felt that the local office and the marshals could get the job done. It's not some kind of terrorist threat, so there's no need to have thousands of agents being sent to Chicago."

The president got angry. "I don't care if it's protocol or if I am stepping on the toes of the director. This is a high-priority murder case and just as important as a terrorist threat. Their manhunt should be large enough that nobody mistakes the FBI's presence in trying to find my friend's murderer."

"Mr. President, I know you're angry and it's understandable, but you can't intervene with the FBI. You have to let them do their jobs. They can be impartial; you can't."

The president didn't say anything for a moment. "It's not about being impartial. Maybe others need to be just as pissed off about this as I am."

"Sir, we've talked about this before. Just because you have power doesn't mean you can go beyond the powers of this office, and calling the FBI director to tell him how to do his job is doing just that."

"The attorney general can do it, and he works for us. I want a huge task force in place by tonight, and that woman better be in custody in the next 24 hours. Make it happen, David."

His chief of staff replied, "I don't think this is a good idea. We should let the agents in charge of this case handle it for the time being."

"I'm not saying they can't be in charge for right now, but there needs to be more men helping them."

"Well, if you order a huge task force, then somebody from Washington is going to be put in charge. It will basically be taking the reins from the Chicago office ... which, if I can remind you, helped you out of that jam during the election by clearing your name during their investigation of Lambert Industries' Ponzi scheme."

"I haven't forgotten that, but this is bigger. We shouldn't have to worry about their feelings getting hurt. We're all professionals, damn it. Just get this done."

David Rollins said, "Yes, sir" and went back to his office to call the attorney general.

∞∞∞∞∞∞∞∞∞∞

By noon, the dust had settled from the gun fight in the parking garage. EMS was on the scene collecting the bodies and seeing to the victims. Medics were stitching up Gavin's left arm when Assistant Director Foster arrived. Nobody expected him to show up, but the day was already turning out to be a disaster and he had bad news to deliver. Gavin saw him and said, "Well it must be pretty bad if you're here."

AD Foster laughed. "Nobody expected a firefight at a hotel without Brenda Mason being in custody afterwards."

"We didn't expect to be fired on by somebody impersonating an FBI agent."

"Do you have any idea what he was doing?"

"Trying to steal our evidence. We found a prepaid cell phone that Brenda Mason was using, but we didn't find it on him after he was shot."

"If he dumped the phone, what did he do with the information on it?"

"We haven't figured that out yet."

AD Foster looked closely at Gavin's arm. "Are you going to be alright?"

"Oh yeah … just a scratch that needed some stitches. I will be ready to go here in a moment."

"Where's your partner?"

"She's getting checked out, too. A bullet grazed her during the firefight."

Before AD Foster could say anything, Agent Main walked up to the ambulance that Gavin was being treated at. She said, "Actually, I'm right here."

"You okay?" AD Foster asked.

"Yes."

"Good. I have some news for the both of you. I literally just got a call from the new FBI director 20 minutes ago. The president is pissed off that we still don't have Brenda Mason in custody and the judge's murderer hasn't been brought to justice. He called the attorney general, who then called the FBI director. A huge task force was ordered and it's going to be the largest manhunt the FBI has ever had. The task force will arrive in Chicago tonight. The investigation has just been taken out of your hands."

Gavin sighed. "I was surprised it took them this long."

Agent Main asked, "Who are they putting in charge?"

"Assistant Director Tom Gasper, out of the New York office," AD Foster replied. "He's done this kind of thing before."

Agent Main had a disappointed look on her face. Gavin saw it and asked what was wrong. She didn't want to say anything, but her partner asked again. She replied, "Out of all the people they could have gotten, they picked him. Not exactly the best choice."

"Agent Main, he's very qualified, and you'll be nice to him. You're a professional; remember that," AD Foster replied.

Gavin spoke up. "So what do we do now?"

"Follow up on any leads here and get back to Chicago. You will be briefed in the morning, along with everybody else."

Deputy Marshal Rogers and his task force arrived on the scene. It had taken them longer to get to Moline, but they also brought an update on Brenda Mason that nobody else had. Rogers walked up to where the agents were and said, "I heard about the excitement here. Sorry we missed it." Then he looked at Agent Donnelly and said in a dickhead type of tone, "Don't you know that you're supposed to shoot them first, before they shoot you?"

Gavin sarcastically replied, "Haven't you learned by now that just because we get a trace on a phone doesn't mean the owner still has it in her possession? Or did you have to scare the shit out of everybody on the bus before you figured it out?" There was a bit of a pissing contest between them, and they really didn't like the fact that they had to work with each other. Any chance they had to show their distaste for the situation, and each other, they took advantage of it.

AD Foster spoke. "Enough from you two. Marshal, what do you have?"

The marshal replied, "We got a hit off the car she was driving. She got rid of it for scrap. A tow truck carrying the car to the junkyard was spotted by police."

"Where?"

"Iowa City. According to the driver, he picked it up at a hotel a few hours ago."

Agent Main asked, "Do we know for sure if she is still there?"

"I sent marshals on ahead to stake out the place, and we called the local cops to set up roadblocks in the city."

Gavin replied, "We should get roadblocks around Des Moines. It's the next biggest city, and if she tries to get on an airplane, then she'll do it from there."

The marshal replied, "We don't have enough manpower to get that done, especially in this time frame."

"Then we should at least get men at the airports and the bus stations."

"Agent Donnelly, not to tell you how to do your job, but we'll get her where she was last spotted. She's not going anywhere."

"Really … okay, go with that if you want to be wrong again."

Rogers shot Agent Donnelly an angry look. "You know what, go solve your murder. The adults are going to bring her in. We're in charge, anyway."

Gavin was about to retort, but Agent Main stopped him. "Don't say anything. Come on, let's get out of here. There's something else we need to be doing, anyway." He was going to say something to her, but she shook her head "no" at him and then they walked off.

Gavin asked her, "What do we have to do?"

"We're going to the airport in Des Moines."

"You think I'm right."

She shot him a sarcastic glare. "Don't get full of yourself. There's a good chance she's going there, and we both know she couldn't have gotten another car. Let the marshal's act like idiots. Also, when I looked at her phone, she was tracking flights at the Des Moines airport. And you know what else?"

"What?"

"It's the only airport in the in the Midwest that has charter services where you don't have to register the name of your guests for the flight plan."

"Really? How is that legal?"

"Some ridiculous state law about privacy regarding passengers on charter flights."

"Nice. Live free or die!"

She smiled. "I bet you anything that's where she's going. A flight with no questions asked."

Gavin laughed. "You know, I have lived in the Midwest all my life and I didn't know that about Iowa."

"I only know because a killer slipped through our fingers a few years ago using that method."

"I love the FBI. I'm always learning something new."

The agents got in a car and headed for Des Moines. Agent Main texted AD Foster to let him know they were following up on a lead. They arrived at the airport 30 minutes later. They did notify airport security just in case, but they wanted to keep everything quiet so they didn't alarm Brenda Mason if she really showed up at the airport. While the agents were at the airport, the marshals arrived at the hotel where Brenda and the kids had been staying. She wasn't there; she had left an hour before. As always, she stayed on the move and escaped ahead of those trying to pursue her.

After they didn't find Brenda Mason at the hotel, Deputy Marshal Rogers got to thinking. Maybe Agent Donnelly was right about the airport. That's when they got a call. It was a tip; somebody had spotted Brenda Mason and the kids in Des Moines, getting lunch at a McDonald's. There was a high probability that she was going to the airport.

Agent Main and Agent Donnelly went to the private charter terminal and tried to blend in with the crowd. Security was standing by, but not with an overwhelming presence. Gavin started looking around and noticed something a little out of the ordinary, a few faces in the crowd that didn't belong. There was an older man wearing a fishing hat and reading US Weekly, a gossip magazine. There was a man dressed like a maintenance worker at the airport, who had a briefcase with him. And finally, there was a man who had been using a payphone but not really saying anything while staring at the front door. Gavin pointed the three men out to his partner. She said,

"You're right; they don't look like they belong. Let's go talk to them."

"No, let's see what they're here for. We don't need to let them know that we've spotted them."

She didn't do anything but her eyes stayed on the three men. Gavin watched the door and that's when he saw them: a woman and two children. He couldn't tell if it really was Brenda Mason; her hair color was different and the children were wearing hats and sunglasses, disguising their faces. They walked into the charter terminal, but Gavin didn't react right away. The little girl dropped her bag, which caused the three of them to stop. While Gavin remained still and kept watching the woman and two children, two of the men in the crowd did react. The one with the briefcase bent down and opened it up. Gavin couldn't see for sure if there was a weapon or not. Agent Main saw the men react to the woman and children, too. She took her gun out of the holster and started towards the men, but Gavin stopped her.

She asked, "Why are you stopping me?"

"Let's see what happens first."

"What?!"

Gavin pointed to the woman, who had started to look around. She noticed the men in the crowd and decided that the airport was not a safe place anymore. About the same time, both of the agents were getting text messages that the marshals had arrived at the airport. Gavin knew they would just get in the way, so he decided to create a little diversion. He walked over to the TSA agents at the security desk, quietly showed his badge, and told them that there were men coming the airport with guns and that they should be detained. He needed to see how it was going to play out with the woman and the kids.

While walking to the main ticket desk, she kept looking out of the corner of her eye at the men slowly approaching her. There was a line, but only a few people were ahead of her. She stood in line for a few moments as the men kept coming closer. That's when she knew they couldn't stay at the airport any longer, so she created a little diversion herself. She got to the front of the line and told the woman behind the desk that there were two men behind them, who were stalking her and the children and who might be carrying weapons. It worked. Security started approaching the men and they weren't going to come quietly. The men knew they had been compromised and made a break for it, even getting in a scuffle with security in order to get away. The fight with security was just enough of a diversion to get out of the terminal.

Even the agents had to intervene. They were able to get one of the men down, but the other two got out of the terminal. Brenda and the two kids got into a cab and drove off just as Gavin and Agent Main came out of the terminal. Agent Main was trying to get another cab so they could go after her, but Gavin stopped her and said, "No, I have a better way of getting to her."

"Letting her go is a big gamble. Just because we have one of those men in custody doesn't mean he's going to talk."

"Precisely why we need to let her keep being hunted by these men. We only have one of them; she could lead us to all of them."

"You better be right."

"You think I'm right about this?"

"Remains to be seen. If we get into a position to talk to her, maybe we can build a little trust with her if she knows we deliberately let her go."

Gavin smiled at that thought. The marshals came running into the terminal. Rogers saw Agent Donnelly and Agent Main standing outside and yelled, "Where is she? We were told that she was seen in this terminal."

Gavin replied, "She got away while we were detaining the other guy."

"You're not going after her?"

"Hey, that's your department, as you've told us so many times. If you'd gotten here quicker then she wouldn't have made you look like a jackass again."

Rogers took a swing at Agent Donnelly and yelled, "Fuck you."

Gavin was about to hit him when his partner stepped between the two men and stopped it from going any further. She yelled at the both of them, "Knock it off! This isn't the school yard." Then she glared at Marshal Rogers. "You stay the fuck out of our way, you glorified bounty hunter. If you want her so badly, then go get her."

He started to say something to Agent Main, but she spoke up first. "Don't say a fucking word or I'll be the one knocking the shit out of you." She grabbed her partner and left before anything else could be said.

As the agents walked away, Rogers got a call on his cell phone. It was a phone call he didn't want to get, but he knew it was coming.

∞∞∞∞∞∞∞∞∞∞∞∞

[208]

The man stood on his balcony, smoking a cigarette, when he made a call on his cell phone. He wasn't happy; there were too many bad reports coming in. The man on the other end of the line answered after two rings. He took a puff off a cigarette and said, "Deputy Marshal Rogers, you don't seem to be having a good day."

"No sir. Look, not to be rude, but I need to call you back."

"Is it because Brenda Mason got away again and you need to run after her?"

Rogers sighed. "I'm sorry, sir, but she escaped again and we are trying to find her. I guess you already know that."

"Yes, Deputy Marshal. I am well-informed. Since you can't seem to capture her in a timely manner, I am sending you some help. The Jackal will join you tomorrow."

"That's not necessary, sir."

"Maybe not yesterday, but after today, you need help."

"Sir, we can get her."

The man took another puff of his cigarette. "I don't like failure, especially when somebody owes me and can't seem to pay his debt. Remember that the next time you screw up." He hung up the phone and finished his cigarette. Then he called the man everybody referred to as the Jackal.

Agent Donnelly and Agent Main went back to Chicago along with the prison transport. The man who was caught at the airport never said a word from the time he was arrested. He had been trained well, Gavin thought to himself. Both agents knew that the usual interrogation techniques were not going to work with this guy; he was a pro. It was already evening when the agents arrived back in Chicago. After the man was processed, he was put into an interrogation room.

The agents were the first to get to talk to him. The marshals didn't really care about interviewing him; they were only after Brenda Mason. Before they went into the room, Agent Main asked her partner, "How do you want to handle this? Because I have a suggestion."

"What is it?"

"He's not going to talk unless we can truly make him afraid … not of us, but of the people he works for."

Gavin smiled. "I like it. Let's try that."

They walked into the room. The man handcuffed to the table sat there, breathing slowly and staring into space, while the bright lights of the room beat down on him with intensity. Agent Main laid a picture of Brenda Mason in front of him. "You know who this is; we already know that. We want to know why you were trying to kill her and who ordered you to do it."

The man didn't even look at the picture. Gavin spoke up. "We also know that you're not going to talk to us … yet. You're well-trained and you're probably a contract killer. We are not going to bother with all the usual interrogation stuff because it won't work on you." The man finally looked at Agent Donnelly. His expression didn't change, but he wasn't ignoring Gavin anymore. He continued, "We're going to leave you with a thought. All we have to do is tell the press that we have a man in custody and he gave us lots of details about the judge's murder. If your employers think you talked, then you're dead for sure. We know that they can get to you in here; somebody like The Ghost is that good! But if you help us, then we can let you slip away and you get a fighting chance to escape." The man nodded at Gavin as if he understood what he was saying, but he still didn't talk.

Agent Main reached into her pocket and pulled out a bullet and a handcuff key. She looked at the man dead in the eyes. "If you help us, then you get this." She put the handcuff key on the table, far enough away so he couldn't reach it. "If you don't help us, then this is what's waiting for you." She put the bullet in between his hands. The man looked down at the bullet and the expression on his face changed; there was a hint of fear. Gavin said to him, "We'll give you some time to think about it. When you're ready to talk, just ask for us." They walked out of the room and headed back to their office. Agent Main asked her partner, "How long do you think it will be before he talks?"

He jokingly replied, "If he's smart, before the night is over, and before the new head of this so-called task force wants to talk to him."

The agents were walking into their office when Gavin's phone rang. It was his buddy, Jack, who had traced the phone number. Gavin answered. "Hey Gavin, its Jack. You need to check your messages. I've been trying to get a hold of you for a while."

"Sorry. We had a shootout in Moline this morning and then we caught a suspect. It's been busy."

"I know what you mean, but I have a name to go with that number. His name is Rick Henry and he lives in Milwaukee, Wisconsin."

"Thanks, Jack."

Agent Main asked her partner, "Did we get a name from that number?"

"Yeah, Rick Henry … does that name sound familiar?"

"I don't recall anything from the Brenda Mason case file, but it doesn't mean it's not there. We just need to check and cross-reference the name."

In their office, files covered every surface and the marker board was filled with notes; the peg boards were completely covered with paper and pictures. After about 15 minutes of going through the original murder case file, they had come up with nothing. There appeared to be no connection between Brenda Mason and the name Rick Henry. Agent Main spoke up. "It could be an alias, somebody she met after her name was changed."

"Could be, but I have a feeling that it's not. I think it's somebody from her past … Brenda Mason's past."

They continued to look through the files but still didn't find anything. As they were looking, a few agents, including AD Tom Gasper, came into the office. He looked at Agent Main. "Rachel, good to see you again." He looked at Gavin. "We haven't had the pleasure. I'm Assistant Director Tom Gasper. I'm taking over this investigation."

Gavin frowned. "We already heard."

"I appreciate everything you have done so far. We're going to be moving everything you have here to the conference room so we can all go through it. And tomorrow morning, I will need a report from the both of you on what we have so far."

The other agents started packing up the case files and removing everything from the peg boards. They moved everything to the conference room. There was nothing Gavin or Agent Main could say; they weren't in charge anymore. As the other agents were packing up stuff, Agent Main saw something she thought was peculiar: Brenda Mason's old yearbook. She grabbed it and told the other agents that it was nothing, that she put it in one of the boxes by mistake.

After the agents left, Gavin asked her, "Why do you want to keep that?"

"I got to thinking: if this Rick Henry guy is from Brenda Mason's past, then maybe they went to school together." She opened the yearbook and flipped to the index. There was a Rick Henry in her class and, best of all; the yearbook had a photo of them together. Gavin smiled. "It's a connection, but still thin."

They spent the next ten minutes looking up information on Rick Henry, and it wasn't hard to find. He was a childhood friend of Brenda Mason. They actually grew up on the same street. After high school, she tried going to college and he joined the Navy. The reason he was never listed as character witnesses during the trial was because he was still in the military at the time. Rick Henry was only seen as a high school friend and not important enough to help Brenda Mason during her trial.

Agent Main spoke up. "Here's my theory. Rick Henry was her best friend, maybe even a childhood sweetheart, and he was always the one that she could count on … no matter what. We didn't find him because he never testified on her behalf; he was in the Navy. Basically, their association ended after high school, so that's why the name is overlooked. But a childhood friend will still do anything for you if you grew up together, especially if he thinks you're innocent."

Gavin chuckled to himself. "It would make sense, but why call him for help? What's her plan?"

"She went to an airport and had brochures about traveling to other countries. What if he is helping her to get out of the country? Think about it: we would be looking for a woman and two children, but not necessarily a woman and a man with their kids, or even a single mom and single dad traveling with a kid."

"You're saying that she needs another person to help her get past security unnoticed."

"Exactly."

"Again, it makes sense."

"So, what do you want to do?"

"We need to talk to Brenda and see if we can get her to trust us. If we just hunt her down and arrest her, she won't talk."

"You think we should do it through him?"

Gavin paused for a moment. "No, we'll trace his number to get her new cell number."

"And then we call her."

"Yeah, it's that simple."

"Except that, when we call her, she'll know that she and Rick's cell phones are compromised and then we're back to square one."

"Then we better do a great job of convincing her. It's our only shot."

Gavin walked out of the office to check on the law students. He hoped that they had found something; they needed a break. He walked into the conference room only to find all of them gone, and the boxes of case files had disappeared. He didn't have to ask what happened; he already knew. Gavin barged into the main conference room where AD Gasper and the task force were setting up shop. He asked, "What happened to the students and Judge Doyle's case files?"

AD Gasper replied, "We sent them home, Agent Donnelly. We don't use students at the FBI. We moved the case files into our war room."

"We were using them because they're lawyers-in-training and know what to look for."

"Look, I'm not going to argue with you. We have enough manpower to go through them. It was a good idea to get them here and see if there was any motive; it's not likely, but a good idea. Anyway, we have agents that will go through the files starting tomorrow."

Gavin shook his head in disbelief. Agent Main walked in to see what was going on. Gavin replied, "The students are two days ahead in going through the files. If time is of the essence, then using them is the smart move."

Gasper stared at Gavin. "Get this through your head. I'm in charge and we don't use students for help. Now get out of here and get some sleep. We all have a big day tomorrow."

Gavin was about to say something that could get him kicked off the case. Agent Main knew it and stopped him while leading him out of the room. As they left, she said, "It's not worth it. If you say what you're about to say, he will suspend you. And believe me when I tell you that nothing you say is going to change his mind. He only sees things in the simplest terms. He's never been able stretch the imagination and be a good investigator."

Gavin was going to reply when his phone rang. It was Agent Janney. She said,

"I'm sure you know by now that AD Gasper dismissed the law students and took all of the judge's case files."

"Yeah, I just had words with him."

"Well, I'm here with a couple of them at the University of Chicago Law Library. They found something before they were told to go home and called me about what to do next. You need to hear what they found."

"Where are you in the library?"

"In the basement study room."

"Good place for a secret meeting."

"Hey, not for nothing. They've been working hard for the past two days. Bring them some coffee … good coffee."

Gavin smiled at the comment. Agent Janney went to law school there, too, and he knew what she meant. The basement study room had always been a good place to drink while studying. It had an interesting history, for it had once been a speakeasy during Prohibition and law students carried on the tradition while studying for their degrees. There was a lot of irony when it came to the law in Chicago.

Gavin told his partner what was going on and they immediately went to the library. Along the way, he told her the history of the library and some funny stories from his law school days. They arrived at the library 30 minutes later and, sure enough, Gavin had coffee for everybody. It was Irish coffee, real Irish coffee. He drank a lot of it during his days studying at the library. Agent Main commented as they were walking down the stairs toward the basement, "Bring back memories?"

"Too many, and it seems like a lifetime ago. Guess I'm getting old."

When they entered the room, two students were sitting with Agent Janney. They were the only ones that stuck around when the others were sent home. They were also the ones that found a connection. Their names were David and Molly.

Gavin smiled and said to them, "This better be good. I brought you real Irish coffee; goes hand-in-hand with the room we're in."

David and Molly laughed. Gavin passed out the coffee to everyone as David started speaking.

"Agent Donnelly, you know how you had us start looking for connections to financial crimes or China? Well, we found two cases that were similar to each other. One was a case about two years ago involving a false rumor that made stock prices go down. There was a company called Wright Ship Industries, and they were developing a new seal for pipe fittings that would go on oil tankers to reduce the amount of spillage when oil is transferred onto the boat. It was supposed to be revolutionary because it's estimated that 1.5% of every gallon pumped into an oil tanker splashes out and is dumped into the environment. Add that up and that's a lot of oil that's being lost. This new seal would make it so that no oil would be lost. It was so revolutionary that government standards would require this seal to be outfitted on every oil tanker built in the U.S."

Agent Main spoke. "Wright Ship Industries would be a very rich company if that happened."

"And that's where it gets interesting. Three months before the seal was going to be released to the public, there was a rumor that the government was going to take the patent away from the company. Within two days of this rumor, the company's stock went from $30 a share to $8 a share, bankrupting the company. Then a Chinese company came in and bought them through a hostile takeover. The seal was released to the public and the new company made a fortune."

Gavin spoke up. "They devalued the stock on purpose so that another company could come in and buy all the stock at a cheap price. And even if we find out that the rumor isn't true, we can't do anything about it; a foreign company has already bought it because it's publicly traded."

Molly responded, "Two former board members came forward and testified that the rumor was false and done on purpose. The Justice Department started to investigate and the case ended up in Judge Doyle's court, but it was dismissed for lack of evidence. The board members who came forward both died, one from a heart attack and one from a car accident. The judge had no choice but to dismiss the case."

Gavin replied, "Maybe somebody at Wright Ship Industries would have enough motive to kill the judge, but we don't have any links to anybody that worked for them or owned the company."

"There was another company 6 months ago that had something similar happen to them," David replied. "P & M Electronics was developing a sensor that could be attached to oil pipelines. It's another revolutionary device because it could accurately measure the consistency, weight, and amount of oil that was being pumped through the pipeline. It would've given companies a more accurate reading of how much oil they were getting, and if there was anything wrong with it. But a false report said the sensor didn't work. P & M Electronics' stock prices fell, which bankrupted the company until they were bought out by a Chinese company."

"So, someone came forward from P & M?"

"The CEO did. He claimed that the report of the sensor not working was false, and he had evidence to prove it. The Justice Department investigated."

Agent Main spoke. "It went to Judge Doyle's court, and this time he didn't dismiss the case. Right?"

David smiled. "Yes ma'am."

Gavin responded, "And because the case is being investigated, it holds up the sale of P & M Electronics until a decision is made."

Molly replied, "You got it, Agent Donnelly. It looks like a financial crime." She handed Agent Donnelly folder of documents. "I know we weren't supposed to take these, but we wanted to give you something in case you didn't have access to the case files anymore."

Gavin shot her a dirty look. "You're right; you can go to jail for this, but good work on all of it. You found what we were looking for." It wasn't the whole story, but it was a start. Most importantly, things were starting to make sense in this case … at least, for now.

12

Monday was finally here and a shit storm was waiting for Agent Donnelly and Agent Main. They weren't in charge anymore and the man who was didn't want to listen to them about the case. Gavin already knew that they were about to get some crappy assignment, but he didn't care; they had a leg up on everybody. They finally had a real motive for the murder, but as he told himself, he and his partner were the only ones that could see it -- and maybe even solve it.

The task force was assembled at the Chicago office by 8 a.m. There were a hundred new agents crowded into the auditorium in the FBI office. Finally, AD Gasper walked in. He started speaking.

"Okay, let's get started. As you all know by now, we are here to solve the murder of Judge Henry Colin Doyle. Our prime suspect is Brenda Mason, who was working as a maid for the family under a different name. She disappeared two days ago with the judge's children. She is our top priority right now. Whether she was working alone or not, we start by capturing her. The U.S. Marshals will be assisting us in the manhunt, but we have agents from offices all over the country working with local law enforcement officials in major cities. We're not dicking around anymore. I want her in custody today. I have appointed different ASACs and all of you will report to them for your assignments. I spoke to the president yesterday, when I got to Chicago. He will be here at the end of the week to speak at the judge's memorial service. We will have this case solved and the killers in custody by then; make no mistake about that."

After he was done and agents were breaking into their groups, AD Gasper asked to see Gavin and his partner. He spoke to them in private.

"Look, I know we got off on the wrong foot yesterday, but I need you to understand what I have been sent here to do. This is an important case and we can't fail. I appreciate what you two have done so far. So what do you know that's not in your reports?"

Gavin didn't want to tell him anything, but he knew that they had to give him something. Agent Main spoke up and tried to answer the question. "The only thing we know that's not in our reports is there's a possible motive with one of his cases that's still pending."

"Okay … what?"

Gavin spoke up. "An electronics company developing sensors for oil pipelines had their stock devalued based on a false rumor that this new sensor didn't work. A Chinese company was trying to come in and buy them. The CEO had evidence about the false rumor that caused the stock go down. He went to the Justice Department and they filed a suit, which put the sale on hold."

"You think that's the Chinese connection to the way Judge Doyle was murdered?"

"Could be. We need to follow the lead."

"Is there any connection to Brenda Mason?"

"We don't know for sure."

AD Gasper paused for a moment to think about what he had just been told. "Okay, follow up and report back to me today about what you find."

As the agents turned around, AD Gasper said, "Hey, I heard you got a number off the cell phone that Brenda Mason lost. Did you trace it and find out who she was calling?"

Gavin gave him a simple answer. "It turned out to be a dead end."

"What was the number to?"

"A travel agency. That's also how she got the brochure for Europe."

That was all he asked and it looked as if he believed it; there wasn't any reason not to. When the agents got into the hallway, Agent Main said to her partner, "You know he's going to figure out that you lied to him."

"You want to go back and tell him so you don't get into trouble?"

"No, I wouldn't tell that stupid son of a bitch, either. He wouldn't use the information right, anyway. But this could backfire."

"Then let's tell the plan to our boss. He's more likely to go along with it."

"Unless he suspends us first. But, as you once told me, better the devil you know than the devil you don't know."

Gavin smiled. "See, now you're getting it. Now, let's go talk to the U.S. attorneys that are working on the case. "

ထထထထထထထထ

For the last couple of years, Gavin always had an uneasy feeling when he visited the DOJ building in Chicago. That's where his life changed two years before. Every time he walked across the old bricks in the courtyard that stretched out in front of the building, he could still see the gunman coming out from the shadows and firing his weapon. It almost made Gavin sick to his stomach. Agent Main could see the anxious look in his eyes and asked if he was okay. Gavin replied, "I'm alright. I just hate coming to this building."

"This is where you were shot two years ago, right?"

"Yeah. I don't really remember anything from that night, but sometimes, I can still see it plain as day, like it was a dream." Maybe it was his gift for seeing the future or some kind of pain hidden in his subconscious, but he could see what happened … not the events before or after, but the exact moment of the shooting.

It was still early in the morning, so there was a good chance they could catch the attorneys in their offices before they had to go to court. The agents didn't call ahead to let the attorneys know they were coming. Normally, they would have, but Gavin didn't know who might be listening in and didn't want to tip their hands. He and his partner needed answers and they needed to get them without alerting the wrong kind of people.

The lead attorney on the DOJ's case was Gary Sanders. He was next in line to become the U.S. Attorney in the Northern District of Illinois, which covered the city of Chicago. The agents arrived at his office and showed their badges to his assistant. He had to be in court soon, but it would have to wait.

The assistant led the agents into Gary Sanders' office. He looked at them and said, "Good morning. I hope this doesn't take long; I have to be in court in half an hour."

Agent Main spoke up first. "We don't mean to keep you, but this is about Judge Doyle and one of his cases. You might want to see if you can be late."

The attorney looked shocked. "You know, I keep hearing all this stuff about Brenda Mason being the killer, but I was wondering when someone would wise up at the FBI and start asking questions about his cases."

Gavin asked, "You were expecting us to question you?"

"Agent Donnelly, I have at least three cases that were in his court that could provide enough motives for his murder. There's one that, if I were a betting man, I'd wager it could be the one that got him killed."

The agents looked at each other; it seemed that all three of them were on the same page. Gavin asked, "Would it be the case on P & M Electronics?"

Sanders, stunned by the question, only had a one-word answer. "Yes."

"Well, that's what we're here to talk about."

"How did you figure it out?"

"One of our researchers found a connection between that case and another case that was in Judge Doyle's court a couple of years ago. It was a case involving purposely devaluing stock so that another company could come in and buy the company whose stock was devalued. We have a lot of questions, Gary, so we could be here for a while."

Sanders called his assistant and told her to inform the court that he was held up talking to the FBI about Judge Doyle's murder. He knew that, by saying that, he would get an automatic continuance on the latest case he was working on. Sanders offered the agents coffee. While Gavin was putting cream and sugar in his cup, he asked the attorney to start from beginning.

Sanders started talking. "About 6 months ago, Stephen Walsh, the CEO of P & M Electronics, came to us. He had evidence that board members were purposely starting false rumors to devalue the stock of the company so they could be bought out by another one. The rumors were that the new sensor for oil pipelines didn't really work and that the company was knowingly selling faulty equipment to oil companies. The rumor was based on a coding error in the software. It kept giving false readings that were lower than what was accurate, such as the amount of oil that would actually flow through a pipeline."

Agent Main asked Sanders, "Could the coding error be fixed?"

"Yes, and in fact, part of the evidence we have is a report from the head of R&D (Research and Development) at the company saying that they did fix it."

"Gavin asked, "Did the stock rumors start before or after the report said that the problem had been fixed?"

"After. A report was emailed to the board members, which was deleted off the company's server, according to the CEO. But at least one board member claimed to have seen the email."

"What happened to him?"

"Died in a car accident. Convenient, huh?"

"Yeah. What's the other evidence?"

"The same report was faxed to the CEO and we have a copy of it."

Agent Main asked, "What does the head of R&D have to say about this?"

"He's denying everything, and the only copy of the report that we can find is the faxed report."

"Do you know who sent the report?"

"We're not sure, but we think it was the assistant director of R&D."

Gavin asked, "What makes you think that?"

"While we were investigating, we interviewed him about the sensor. He was very helpful. He told us flat-out that the coding could be put in the form of an application which, with the push of a button, could manipulate the readings from the sensor. We didn't ask him about that, he just offered up the information as if he were trying to help us make a case against the company."

"You think he's a potential whistleblower?"

"Actually, I do. Two days after we talked to the guy, an anonymous report was faxed to my office about a new fail-safe device for the sensor that R&D was developing. Whoever sent this report said that he recognized the coding in the device as being the same as the coding in the sensor software."

Gavin grinned as if a light bulb was going off in his head. "So, it has to be somebody working in R&D that has a background in software engineering, someone that was working on the sensor and the fail-safe device."

"That's what we think, but if it is him, then we're screwed."

Agent Main asked, "Why?"

"He has a confidentiality agreement with the company."

Gavin responded, "If he testifies in court, it's inadmissible because he broke his confidentiality agreement and is subject to criminal action."

"Yes, but the reports we got were detailed about the software coding and application processes on this sensor."

"That's all well and good, but you don't know who sent them and if it is someone in R & D then they still break their confidentiality agreement by sending those reports. So, walk me through this: you have a CEO who is willing to testify about fraudulent stock information, and you have a couple of faxed reports about software problems in their new sensor and, of course, evidence that they might be making a device that manipulates the sensor readings. But you can't get anybody in R&D to testify because of their confidentiality agreements."

"Yes, but the reports are detailed."

"P & M's lawyers filed to get the case dismissed, right?"

"It was the first thing they did."

"And Judge Doyle ruled that there was enough evidence to go to trial, even though there really wasn't."

Sanders took a sip of coffee. "We were kind of surprised by it, too, but the Justice Department has been taking these kinds of cases more seriously ever since the financial crisis in 2008."

Agent Main spoke up. "There was another case similar to this one two years ago, involving a company called Wright Ship Industries. Did you know that?"

"Actually, we did. We investigated to see if there was a connection to this case. It's similar, but the companies are different."

"What do you mean?"

"Wright Ship Industries was bought by a company called Mao Tech two years ago. It has never done business with Ming Industries as far as we can tell, but there is no Mao Tech anymore. It became another business under the Churchill Group."

Gavin was surprised even though he shouldn't have been. He knew the name, the Churchill Group, and had investigated the group before, when he was in the White Collar Crimes division. Agent Main asked, "The Churchill Group … what is that? I've never heard of it before."

"It's a European company of sorts, a very old company. They have business dealings in pretty much any industry all over the world, and they specialize in buying out companies."

Gavin had heard of Ming industries before too so he asked. "Is Ming Industries connected to the Churchill group?"

"We don't know. Our investigation hasn't turned up anything."

"Okay… what's next in your case now that …"

"… Now that it won't be in Judge Doyle's court? We'll get a new judge. The other side will get to file a new motion to have the case dismissed, because it's a new judge. And this time, they will probably get it, because all we have are two faxed reports that we probably can't use."

"What about the CEO's testimony?"

Sanders had a disappointed look on his face. "We don't know where he is. He's been missing for two weeks."

"Didn't you put him in witness protection?"

"Of course we did, but … and this is embarrassing … he went missing and we don't have any leads on finding him."

"You think he could have been kidnapped?"

"I'm sure it's possible. But I will tell you this, Agent Donnelly: if you find any evidence that P & M Electronics is connected to the murder of Judge Doyle, I will go after them with the full weight of the U.S. Attorney's office."

Gavin didn't say anything, but Agent Main spoke up. "We're trying to find out who really did this. Of course, the company does have motive, as well as Ming Industries. But how far we will get with all this, we don't know."

Sanders was going to say something but noticed the press conference on the TV. He kept the news on all day to keep up with what was going on in the world. Assistant Director Gasper was holding a press conference. It didn't take him long to let the world know he was in charge. Sanders turned up the volume so everybody in his office could hear.

AD Gasper made a statement to local and national news outlets. "I'm Assistant Director Tom Gasper with the FBI. I will not be taking any questions today, only reading a statement. I want everybody to know that we will not stop or rest to bring Judge Henry Colin Doyle's murderer to justice. As you may already know, our prime suspect is Brenda Mason, who had been working as a maid for the Doyle's under a different name for the past five years. We do not know her motive, but she will be caught and she will be brought to justice. This kind of crime will not be tolerated in the United States, and we will never let murderers go free again."

Gavin called him a fucking asshole under his breath. FBI agents were not allowed to have opinions; they were just supposed to get facts.

AD Gasper continued, "We will be conducting the largest manhunt this country has ever seen for Brenda Mason. She will be caught soon; you have my word on that. The FBI will be working with local law enforcement in major cities throughout the country to help find her. So, we are asking citizens who have any information on Brenda Mason to call the FBI tip line here in Chicago. Your news outlets will give out the number. We have a killer, we will find her, and justice will be served."

Sanders asked the agents, "Did you know this was happening?"

Gavin answered his question. "No, we didn't. Believe me, she is not our only suspect."

"Then why is your boss going on TV saying that Brenda Mason is the top suspect?"

Agent Main responded, "Because he's an idiot and wants to fuck up this investigation!" She didn't curse a lot, but when she did, you knew she was livid.

13

Brenda Mason saw the news conference from her hotel room. She knew what it meant; it was going to be harder to get away, even with disguises. She and the kids made it to Lincoln, Nebraska during the night and found another hotel room to hide in. Brenda had to put her plan into action a little early. Her friend, Rick, was going to have to come to Lincoln to meet her. While the kids were eating breakfast, she called her friend.

Rick was on his way to the airport after having just told his wife that he would be gone for a week on business in Dallas, Texas. She seemed to believe him, but then again, he could never tell whether or not she knew if he was lying. When he answered the phone, he knew immediately who it was.

"Brenda, you just caught me on the way out. You have interesting timing, as always."

"How did you know it was me?"

"There's nobody else who would be calling me this morning."

Brenda laughed. "Fair enough. Did you see the news conference this morning?"

"Of course I did. Since talking with you again, I've been watching the news every day just to see if I could get tidbits of information about you."

"Well, I barely escaped yesterday and it wasn't even that big of a manhunt. The real one starts today, so we have to change our plan. I need you to come to Lincoln, Nebraska."

"Is that where you are now?"

"Yes. We are going to have to travel by car for a little while just to get where we are supposed to be. A family of four on vacation is a good disguise."

He paused for a moment and then replied, "I hate that you have to do this, but I'm glad to be doing this with you."

Her eyes welled up with tears. Rick had always been her best friend. She knew he had loved her and she never cared enough, always taking advantage of him with the worst kind of selfish attitude. She couldn't help but feel that she was doing it again, but this time, she truly appreciated his friendship.

Gavin and Agent Main were leaving the DOJ building. Gavin spotted a hot dog cart. He knew the owner. He looked at his partner and smiled. "Come on, let's grab lunch."

"It's not even noon yet."

"Yeah, but it's not too early for the best hot dog in the world, a Chicago Dog."

"You know they're better in New York."

"I'll pretend you didn't say that, and you can still get the best hog dog in the world … on me." They walked over to the cart and Gavin spoke up. "Hey, Ramone. How's business?"

Ramone smiled. "Can't complain, but it can always be better. You federal guys need to start eating more and keep me in business."

Gavin smiled and ordered two traditional Chicago Dogs, and then he told his partner, "Ramone here is the eyes and ears of the streets. He knows more about what's going on than most of the cops in this town."

"Like when the Bulls can win without Derrick Rose. Tell your cousin, Alex, that he owes me $20.00."

"He owes me a few pints and still hasn't paid up. I'll tell him that he will have to give you extra tips."

Ramone smiled at the comment. Gavin introduced him to his new partner and then he and Agent Main walked off to eat their hot dogs. Since becoming partners, they were getting into a routine of talking out the case they were working on. They were starting to fall into sync, and so she asked, "Do you really think P & M had something to do with this?"

"I think they have the biggest motive. If Sanders is right and they can use that sensor to falsify oil readings, they could control the oil industry … create demand, even though there's plenty of supply."

"But no one has made any money from this. In fact, P & M has lost money to the point of bankruptcy."

"It's not about the money they've lost; it's about the money they can make under a new company."

Agent Main finished her hot dog. "Even if that's true, where's the evidence of murder? And how does Brenda Mason fit into all this? I mean, the only physical evidence we have at the crime scene to indicate she's a possible killer is her fingerprints."

Gavin thought for a moment. "I guess that's the million-dollar question."

Agent Main spoke up. "Okay, we have a few possibilities. One: Brenda Mason acted alone, which we really don't think is plausible because there's no motive. Two: Brenda Mason walked in and killed one of the murderers, thus leaving her fingerprints. Three: P & M is behind this and they hired or blackmailed Brenda Mason into killing the judge."

Gavin pondered the theories for a moment. "Why use her, especially when it comes to that kind of killing method?"

"Because she's a killer who got away with it! Maybe they found out who she really was and blackmailed her into doing it, but she needed help, and they had someone assist her. Then they set her up because they knew she's the only person we'd look at."

Gavin smiled. "I like it. It's a good theory, but it still doesn't explain what she's doing with the kids."

"Maybe we answer that by finding out where she's taking them. In the meantime, we need to question P & M about the murder."

"You know the board members aren't going to talk to us while this trial is still pending."

Agent Main chuckled. "I don't care about talking with them. I want to talk to the assistant director of R & D, the one who sent those reports to Sanders."

As they were walking to the car, Gavin's phone rang. It was his friend at the Bureau, Jack, who had been running the trace on Rick Henry's phone. He had good news. Gavin answered. "What's up, Jack?"

"You know that call you've been waiting for us to trace? We got it."

"Really? That didn't take long."

"It's a prepaid cell phone on the AT&T network. You want us to keep the trace on so we can track it?"

"Won't do any good; the phone will be dumped by the end of the day. Where is it located?"

"Lincoln, Nebraska."

Gavin started thinking about geography. "Jack, I need a favor. Can you misplace the paperwork on this trace for a few days?"

"Yeah. What's going on?"

"I need to keep a few people in the dark. Can you help?"

"Sure, but you're going to owe me big. I'll text you the number we got; you can do what you want with it."

Gavin received the text message. It was Brenda Mason's new prepaid cell phone number. It was the biggest lead they had so far, and a chance to bring her in safely. Gavin told his partner, "We have Brenda Mason's new number. Time to see if we can convince her that she needs to trust us."

"Hope you know what you're doing. If this doesn't work, you may not have a job."

"Do you have a better idea? One that might actually work?"

"Not really."

Gavin smiled at her as they got into their car and drove away. They still had more questions than answers, but they were closer to catching Brenda Mason than anybody else was. The tragedy of it was they might have to let her go just to get the answers they were looking for.

∞∞∞∞∞∞∞∞∞∞∞

The agents went to P & M Electronics to see if they could get some information. They started with the R & D department. It was useless to start with the board members; in a case like this, they would have all been instructed not to talk. Business was still going on at P & M, so R & D would still be working. Gavin and Agent Main started with the head of R & D and, of course, he invoked his confidentiality agreement and wouldn't talk to them. In fact, nobody would. The assistant director came into the office the agents were in with the head of the department. He was surprised to see them and, of course, he wouldn't answer their questions, either. As he was leaving the office, he accidently bumped into Agent Main.

The agents figured this was a dead end, so they decided to leave. As they were walking out, Agent Main reached inside her coat pocket and found a wadded-up piece of paper. She didn't put it there, and it finally dawned on her where it came from. She pulled it out and unfolded it.

"Agent Donnelly, check this out. I think the assistant director put this in my pocket when he bumped into me."

"What does it say?"

"Parking garage – 10 minutes."

Gavin smiled. "I guess he does have something to say to us."

The agents went back to their car and waited. Ten minutes later, the assistant director came into the parking garage and saw the FBI car. He walked up to it, got into the back seat, and said, "There's a park about a mile from here. If you take me there, I will answer your questions."

Agent Main asked, "They're not going to be suspicious of you leaving?"

"I'm on my lunch break, so we have an hour."

They went to the park he was talking about. It was quite beautiful, with reflections of the surrounding trees bouncing off the lake. They went to a park bench so they wouldn't have to be cooped up in the car. Also, he didn't trust the FBI car; it could have recording devices.

As they sat down, Gavin asked, "Do you have a name?"

[227]

"Dr. Paul Stiles. Please understand that I do take my confidentiality agreement seriously, so I can't give too many details about the technology we develop."

"We're not asking how everything works. Now, it was you who faxed those reports to the U.S. Attorney's Office and to the CEO that started this whole thing?"

"Yes."

"Does anybody else know about the reports?"

"I showed the first one, about the coding problem, to my boss -- the head of our department – and, of course, to the CEO. The second report, about the application we were designing, I only showed to the U.S. Attorney's Office."

"What was the reaction to the first report?"

"They said it would be fixed and we all thought it was."

"How did you figure it out?"

"Agent Donnelly, I developed the sensor and wrote most of the coding, so I would recognize it in other applications."

Agent Main asked, "What went wrong with the coding in the software? Just curious."

"Without using too much technobabble, it was a scripting problem. I wrote a script wrong and didn't realize it until we were testing the sensor. You remember ten years ago, during the presidential election, when there were complaints about electronic voting machines processing a different candidate than who people voted for?"

Both agents answered yes.

"It's the same kind of problem. Part of the scripting was off, and you can use that same script for an application that manually changes results."

Gavin asked, "Has anybody been threatened over this? I mean, besides prosecution for breaking a confidentiality agreement?"

"You mean, has anyone been threatened with his life?"

"Yes."

"Nobody in our department, but from what I understand, whistleblowers usually don't get warned before they're dead."

Agent Main spoke up. "What do you mean? Have there been incidents in the past with this company?"

Paul paused for a moment. "I used to play chess once a week with one of the board members, Harold Miller. One day, he told me something about a whistleblower in the company that ended up dead -- and it was actually planned by a few board members of the company. He said that he was in a meeting where they half-jokingly discussed killing the whistleblower. When this guy ended up dead, he knew that the board members really did it."

"Did he ever lie to you before?"

"No, and I have no reason to believe he would have lied to me. If you want to know if there's a history of murder in this company, you might want to talk to him. I can give you his phone number if you want."

He pulled out his phone and gave the number to Agent Main.

Gavin asked, "Do you think people in this company are capable of murder?"

"While I have never seen any evidence of it myself, and I don't know for sure if they really had anything to do with the judge's murder, I've also learned not to put anything past these bastards."

"Why did you send the reports? You could have ignored them."

"Agent Donnelly, not to inflate my own ego, but I'm very smart and I'm good at what I do. Using this coding to manipulate results will change an industry for all the wrong reasons; it would bankrupt the world while rich oil guys keep getting richer. I don't want to be a part of that. That's not what I do."

"If we go after this company for conspiracy to commit murder, you're gonna have to testify. If that happens, whoever did this will come after you. Let us take you into protective custody."

"No way, man. If they find out I had anything to do with this, I will never be able to work for another company again because I couldn't be trusted. I can point you in the right direction, but that's it."

"We can't keep you safe unless you cooperate."

"I'll take my chances. Maybe Harold Miller will be in a better position to help you. Talk to him."

The agents took Paul Stiles back to work. Then they got an address for the phone number they were given for Harold Miller. More and more, it was starting to look like a conspiracy to commit murder, but they needed more proof; they needed more testimony. Harold Miller lived in in the Lincoln Park area of Chicago; it was one of the upscale areas of the city. They arrived at the house to find several people going in and out of it. The house was busy for the middle of the day. Agent Main commented, "This doesn't look good. Are we sure this is the right house."

Gavin had a curious look on his face. "According to the FBI, it is!"

They walked into the house and were greeted by his daughter. They both flashed their badges and it was Gavin who asked if they could speak to Harold Miller. The daughter looked horrified, but she answered, "My father died on Saturday. I guess you haven't heard yet?"

Agent Main and Agent Donnelly looked at each other, shocked. Agent Main asked, "How did he die?"

The daughter, crying, replied, "He was shot in the head. They're ruling it a suicide."

Gavin, as insensitive as it might've been, had to ask. "Was your father suicidal?"

Harold Miller's daughter was still crying. "No … he would never do that. I don't care what they say. He would never kill himself."

<h1>14</h1>

The marshals were still working out of the FBI office in Des Moines, Iowa. They set up a makeshift command center there, trying to find any leads they could about where Brenda Mason was going. They figured out that she had doubled back from her taxi ride and was about to get out of the city for good. Rogers figured she slipped through because the roadblocks weren't that good. He stood in the conference room they were working and just stared at the map of the United States on the wall. There were thumb tacks marking the places she had been spotted. While he was looking at the map, the new marshal walked in. Rogers was expecting him.

The new marshal spoke up. "Deputy Marshal Rogers. A mutual friend of ours called and said I would be arriving."

Rogers turned around and felt a twinge a fear. "Yes, sir. What do you need from me?"

"You'll introduce me as Marshal Sanchez to everybody else, and then stay out of my way."

"I can't just let you go rogue without explaining why."

Sanchez smiled and replied, "Tell them I'm a sniper."

"Really?"

"My job is to get rid of Brenda Mason because you boys can't seem to catch her. If we get into position -- and I can do that from a hundred yards away -- then I'll do it. That's all you need to know."

Rogers didn't say anything as Sanchez started to walk away, but he turned around before walking out. "Oh, and marshal ... anybody that gets in my way or screws up will be put down, too. That's not a warning; it's a promise."

∞∞∞∞∞∞∞∞∞∞

Assistant Director Foster walked into Paddy Murphy's to find two of his agents sitting in a booth, waiting for him. He wasn't exactly in control of the FBI office in Chicago these days, since the task force in charge of finding Brenda Mason set up shop there. It was strange to get a call from two agents that didn't report to him anymore, but he was the only person that Agent Donnelly and Agent Main could turn to.

He walked up to the agents and saw Agent Donnelly drinking a Guinness. He spoke. "Normally, I would frown on my agents drinking during the day. But in your case, it probably helps." Gavin laughed at the comment. "Agents, why have I been called down here?"

"We found new evidence that Brenda Mason may not have committed the murders. Also, we have the number to the prepaid cell phone she's been using."

"How did you manage that?"

"She's been calling her best friend from childhood to ask for help. We didn't know about him because he never testified during her trial 12 years ago. We traced his number and got hers."

AD Foster looked shocked. "That's good work, but why are you telling me? Gasper is the one you need to talk to about this."

Agent Main spoke up. "Sir, he can't be trusted. There's more to this case than Brenda Mason and we need to find out what it is. Gasper's only concerned with getting her and pinning the murder on her."

"Be careful where you go with that, Agent Main. Don't throw out blameless accusations just because you have beef with him."

Gavin responded, "She's not wrong, sir. It seems like everybody just wants to capture her and not ask the bigger questions."

"Fine. What are the bigger questions?"

"What would be a bigger reason to kill the judge? A financial motive!"

AD Foster's blank stare turned to curiosity. "Ok, what do you know that nobody else does?"

Gavin started telling him what they'd found out so far. He explained the connection with the two companies, the false rumors that devalued their stock so they could be taken over by Chinese companies, and how the cases ended up in Judge Doyle's court. Gavin also told him about P & M Electronics' assistant director of R & D and how he secretly faxed reports to the U.S. Attorney's Office about the new oil sensor software problems. Finally, Gavin told him about the dead board member who had information on assassination plots against whistleblowers.

AD Foster was shocked. "Well, it's an interesting theory. It's still thin, though. How did Harold Miller die?"

Agent Main answered, "He died on Saturday of an apparent self-inflicted gunshot wound. However, we found out that he never owned a gun, and his family said that he hadn't even fired one before in his life."

"Agent Main, it's not hard to get a gun in Chicago and figure out how to shoot yourself in the head."

Gavin replied before she could. "But it's very suspicious that a man who never used a gun would shoot himself, especially when there are better ways to commit suicide. Plus, it happened the day after the judge was killed. I don't buy it."

"Ok, Agent Donnelly … it's suspicious, but still flimsy. There's still more evidence connecting Brenda Mason to the murder than anybody else. So, I'm confused; are you trying to clear her name for some reason?"

"Sir, we want to find the real killers, not a scapegoat."

"And what if you're wrong?"

"Then we'll be wrong. But we need to find out for sure."

AD Foster chuckled. "Then what's your plan?"

"We'll call her and try to convince her to come in quietly. She can probably shed more light on all of this."

"What makes you think that?"

Agent Main replied, "Because she's not running from *us*; she's trying to get away from the men who did it. She saw what happened and we think she's trying to get the kids safely out of the country."

AD Foster smirked. "Is there evidence of that?"

"The second blood type at the crime scene; somebody else was there and the body was removed. If she killed the Doyle's and also somebody else, then why remove just one of the bodies? Plus, the kids are alive. If she really were a cold-blooded killer, then they'd be dead by now."

Gavin said, "Sir, we have to bring her in alive. If we can get her to trust us, then she may be more inclined to talk."

"What makes you think she will trust you?"

Gavin took a sip of beer. "Because she wants to trust somebody, especially someone who can keep her alive."

"It's a big risk. Go ahead, but if you call her, then you need to trace the call so you know where she's located. No loose ends!"

Agent Main responded, "We need a favor from you."

"This can't be good."

She laughed. "We need you to give us an assignment and date it a couple of days ago so we can meet her somewhere."

"And, I suppose, lose the paperwork so a clerical mistake can give you an excuse to disobey orders?"

Gavin laughed. "Something like that."

AD Foster chuckled. "Tell me something, both of you. Are you sure about your theory? I mean, if you're wrong, your asses are on the line and I can't protect you from any kind of punishment."

Gavin replied, "One hundred percent, sir."

Agent Main responded, "As sure as I am of anything else."

AD Foster smiled. "Okay, see if it works, but remember: you are on your own when it comes to this." He got up and started to walk out, but turned back around and said, "Just out of curiosity: why did you guys call me? Why didn't you just do all of this on your own?"

Agent Main replied, "You're our boss, and we have to trust someone."

AD Foster looked over at Gavin as he answered the question. "She's right, sir. Besides, you always turn to the ones that have your back."

AD Foster smiled. At the FBI, it was hard to trust people. There were too many politics involved, too many people willing to screw you over just to get ahead. It was comforting to have the agents underneath you feel like they could trust you, and to know that you can trust them. But the big question among these agents would always be: how far would that trust go?

After AD Foster left, Gavin got to thinking. They needed another element of trust when it came to Brenda Mason, something they could show her so she would know that they could be relied on. Gavin suggested the idea. Agent Main asked, "What do you have in mind?"

"If Tom Gasper is going to use the media to scare the shit out of everybody and look for Brenda Mason, then let's use the media to our advantage."

Agent Main smiled. "You mean, let them know that we have another suspect in custody? Maybe turn public opinion?"

"Absolutely. And maybe give them a few hints about the investigation into one of the judge's cases that has motive to kill him."

"It just might work. But who do we go to?"

Gavin smiled. "I have just the reporter who could get this story out and won't give up any sources."

"Who?"

Gavin kept smiling and then Agent Main finally figured out. She said, "No … the Chicago Tribune reporter!"

"No one better."

"You can't find someone that's not a pretty face in a short skirt?"

Gavin laughed. "Sure, but that part is just a bonus." Agent Main chuckled. Gavin called the Chicago Tribune to make sure Haley O'Brian was still there, and then the agents headed over to the Tribune building. Last time they went there, it was to arrest her. This time, they needed her help.

They arrived at the Tribune building about 30 minutes later. The day was almost done, but good journalists never left at 5:00. As they arrived on the right floor, it wasn't hard to figure out that they were feds. Haley O'Brian saw them as they walked toward her cubicle, and the look on her face turned from serious to surprise. Before the agents said anything, she spoke up. "Holy shit, are you here to arrest me again?"

Gavin chuckled. "No, but have you done something worthy of being arrested for?"

"There's no telling with you guys."

Agent Main responded, "I'm sure that we'll have to arrest you again sometime, but it's not today. We actually have a story for you."

"A story? What kind of story?"

Gavin smiled. "What if I told you that everything our office has been saying about Judge Doyle's murder is only half the story, and that we actually have another suspect in custody?"

Haley's look turned to curiosity. "Is that true, or are you just trying to tell me what I want to hear because you need something from me?"

"We need something from you, but we're not lying to you. Do you have some place we can talk? I'd rather not do it in a newsroom."

Haley grabbed her coat and led them down to the main floor. They all got some coffee from the local Starbucks in the lobby, and then went across the street to a branch of the Chicago Public Library. A secluded study room was a good place to talk in private.

As they sat down at the conference table, Haley asked, "So, what do you have for me that I can write about?"

Gavin said, "First, whatever we tell you, you can only quote us as 'FBI sources.' We're in trouble enough just talking with you. We need you to put a story out in the morning with the actual facts."

"And what are those?"

"Do you believe everything you hear on the news these days? Do you think Brenda Mason is the sole killer of Judge Doyle and his wife?"

Haley thought about it for a moment. "No, it doesn't sound plausible, even if it's Brenda the Child Killer. I heard the victims were tortured with an unusual style of killing."

"That's true, too, and the Chicago beat cops need to learn to keep their mouths shut. We have evidence that someone else might have done it; she was set up."

"Okay, then. If I do this story and help you out, then I'm going to need something from you."

Agent Main responded, "Giving you a story that no one else has isn't good enough?"

Haley looked at her. "No offense, Agent Main, but you two are coming to me. You want the story out more than I need to write about it. "

"What do you want?"

"I want an exclusive story on this case when it's solved, and I want to know what's going on before it's announced to the press."

Agent Main was about to say something when Gavin spoke up. "Fine. We'll give you a heads-up before things get announced to the media and an exclusive story when it's all said and done. Now, get out your notepad and start writing."

They didn't tell her everything, just what she needed to know. They told her about the man they captured at the airport who tried to kill Brenda Mason. They also told her about the possible motive of P & M Electronics, who was going to be bought out by Ming Industries, without telling her any confidential details about the sensor. They gave her enough information to paint Brenda Mason as someone who might be innocent. When the agents were done, Haley asked them,

"What's your plan for Brenda Mason, if you catch her?"

"We can't tell you that, Haley," Gavin replied.

"Does she have proof of what you just told me?"

"We have to catch her to find out. But that's all I can tell you. When will this be out?"

Haley put her notepad away. "Probably first thing in the morning, but I'm sure I can get it in the online addition in about five hours."

Gavin smiled at her. "Thanks, Haley. We owe you one!"

"No, thank you for the story."

Agent Donnelly and Agent Main left. As they were walking out of the library branch, Agent Main asked, "What about Paul Stiles? As soon as this story breaks, his life will be in danger. We need to get him into protective custody now, but we can't do it with the FBI. If we take him, then P & M will know he talked and the evidence he provided would be useless in a court of law. Plus, it would ruin his career."

Gavin was about to respond when his head started aching, and a vision flashed through his mind. *Paul Stiles was leaving work a little late. He got into his car and left the parking garage. It started raining, so he went a little slower than usual. He drove a mile before he stopped at the first traffic light. All of a sudden, a black SUV came speeding up from behind and slammed into his car, pushing it into oncoming traffic. A city bus appeared from the left side of the road and hit Paul Stiles' car, crushing it into another vehicle. He was impacted on both sides and was killed instantly. The black SUV drove off.*

Agent Main asked if he was alright, since he was rubbing his head. He replied, "I'm fine. We'll get somebody in Chicago PD to pick him up on some fake warrant for his arrest. Then we can take him from there. That way, nobody suspects him of being a whistleblower. Hopefully, they'll get there in time."

Agent Main replied, "What do you mean, get there in time?"

He smiled, trying to hide what he saw. "All I meant was, before the story comes out."

15

A taxi drove up to a hotel in Lincoln, Nebraska. A man got out of the car looking a little lost, but this is where he was told to go. He found the room number he was texted. He was a little nervous; he had never done this before. Brenda Mason answered the door and smiled. "You made it."

"My flight was delayed and my wife asked too many questions, but I'm here."

As Brenda hugged him, she held on for a moment longer. Rick was the only friend she still had in the world. Even after 20 years, she could still count on him. The kids were watching TV in the room. Brenda introduced them to Rick and explained that he was a friend of hers who was going to help them.

While the kids continued to watch TV, Brenda and Rick went out to the balcony to talk.

Rick smiled at her. "You know, Brenda, you still look good after all these years."

All she could do was smile while a few tears came to her eyes. "Thanks. You always knew what to say to make me feel better. And, if I might add, the years haven't been too badly to you."

"I could stand to lose about 20 pounds."

"Couldn't we all?"

Rick finally asked, "What's your plan?"

Brenda thought about it for a moment. "I have to get these kids out of the country. It's the only chance they have of staying alive."

"You mean to tell me that whoever killed their parents will stop at nothing to kill them, too? It sounds drastic."

"You don't know these people. They will do anything to stop those that get in their way."

"How do you know about them?"

More tears came to her eyes. "I wish I could say that I've always been good since the trial, but I've had to do some pretty despicable things to stay alive."

Rick was about to ask her what she had done, but Brenda stopped him. She said, "Don't ask, Rick. I don't want to talk about it.

I've already involved you too much in my ugly life; no need to go any further."

Rick nodded at her. "I just care about you, that's all."

"I know, and I've always loved you … maybe not enough to have a life with you, but I never forgot how much of a friend you've been to me and the fact that you never gave up on me."

Rick walked over to her and put his hand on the side of her face. He leaned in and kissed her, and she didn't stop him. While they never dated before, they had slept together a few times. If things had not turned out the way they did, Rick and Brenda would've probably ended up together by now. After the kissing stopped, Brenda grabbed a couple of beers and told him the plan. The next part was heading to San Francisco and getting the fake IDs they needed to get out of the country.

∞∞∞∞∞∞∞∞∞∞

Gavin and Agent Main went back to his apartment in order to get things set up for the call to Brenda Mason. Gavin's friend, Jack, would meet them there with his computer equipment. While there was a lot of trust going into this call, as FBI agents, they still had to trace the call to find out where she was hiding now. Agent Main laughed at the apartment. It definitely belonged to a man; even though it was a little bit neater than what she was used to, it still lacked a woman's touch. She commented, "I can tell you've never been married."

"You mean, I have a typical guy's apartment."

"That's one way of putting it." She looked at the Chicago Cubs memorabilia on wall. He had Ernie Banks', Ron Santo's, Billy Williams', and Ryne Sandberg's jerseys framed and hanging on his walls. "I guess I should tell you that I am a New York Mets fan. My father still celebrates 1969 as the greatest year in Mets history."

Gavin laughed. "Well, I won't hold that against you or your father. I'm a Cubs fan, so I'm used to disappointment." He grabbed a couple of beers out of the fridge and offered one to his partner. She looked at him. "Do you always have to get a beer? We could drink just water, you know."

"And you know that this is better for you than half the shit that's out there. It saved mankind during the Middle Ages. Besides, we've both been tense all day; it will relax us better than a cigarette."

Agent Main smiled. "Okay. You probably don't have bottled water, anyway, because this is your version of bottled water."

Gavin laughed at the comment and then he got serious. "Look, you don't have to do this. I know you're trying to keep your record clean while you're in Chicago. I can keep you out of this in order to do that."

"I appreciate it, but we're partners. If you go down, then I go down! Besides, I think this is the right play for us. Let's do it and see if it works."

Jack finally arrived and set up his laptop on Gavin's kitchen table. He was still going to have to log in to the FBI's server to complete a trace, so there would be a record of it. The agents knew that, but it was a risk they had to take. Hopefully, if anybody found out their plan with Brenda Mason, it would already be happening and would be too late to stop it. After setting everything up, Jack said to Gavin, "For us to get an accurate location on a pre-paid cell phone, you have to keep her on the line for 60 seconds. If she hangs up and shuts the phone off, that's all she wrote. We can try to trace Rick Henry's number and we might get a hit, but ..."

Agent Main spoke up and finished the sentence. "... If they're smart, they've already gotten rid of the phone."

Jack scowled. "Yeah."

Gavin said, "Then we better get this right." He looked at his partner. "Anything you think I should say to her? We can treat it like a hostage negotiation when we talk to her."

"That might work, but I think she'll know what we're trying to do. Just sympathize with her; see where that gets you."

Gavin took a sip of beer and nodded toward Jack to get ready. He picked up his home phone and dialed the number.

∞∞∞∞∞∞∞∞∞∞

Brenda and Rick were still talking on the balcony when her phone rang. It startled her because she wasn't used to getting calls on that number. She looked at the caller ID and it said "Gavin Donnelly." She didn't know who that person was, so she just let the phone go to voicemail. The phone rang again. Rick told her that she should just answer the phone call and tell the person that it was the wrong number. She ignored it for a second time, but the phone rang yet again. After the second ring, she decided to answer it.

"Hello?"

Gavin had a look of excitement when she finally answered. He thought for a moment that she would never answer and this would all be for nothing. He said to her, "Brenda, please don't hang up until you hear what I have to tell you."

Brenda was shocked and stood up out of her chair, but she didn't say anything. She also didn't hang the phone. Gavin continued. "I'm Agent Gavin Donnelly with the FBI. We know you didn't kill

[240]

Judge Doyle, but I think you know who did." She still didn't say anything. Gavin waited for her to talk, but when she didn't, he continued. "I'm calling you to see if you will turn yourself in willingly and help us catch the men who really did this. You can trust me and my partner."

She finally spoke. "How do I know that?"

"Because you're not in handcuffs right now. We let you slip away at the airport in Des Moines while we caught one of the guys trying to kill you."

"Bullshit."

"It's true. And we're not descending upon your location right now trying to capture you. You already know that we're tracing the call when I said I was an FBI agent, and you didn't hang up. I think you want to trust somebody other than your friend Rick Henry. Yes, we know about him."

Brenda was surprised that he knew so much, but Gavin was right: she was looking for someone to trust. "You know a lot, agent, but it's still not good enough."

"What if I told you that, tomorrow morning, there will be a story in the Chicago Tribune that says we have another suspect for the judge's murder? I'm sure you've watched the news and know what they're saying; you're the only suspect. The story will be done by Haley O'Brian. You will see it online in a few hours and it will be national news by the morning. We gave her the story. Does that buy me a little trust?"

Jack signaled to Gavin that the trace was complete. They had a location for Brenda Mason. Brenda responded, "I won't let the kids be harmed by anyone. How do I know that you can guarantee their safety?"

"Is that why you took them? To get them somewhere safe, out of the country? Tell me, who's after them?"

"I'm not ready to answer your questions yet."

"What do we need to do to gain your trust?"

Brenda thought about it for a moment. "Alright, you get a riddle. If you can solve it, then we'll talk again. I will keep this phone until 8:00 a.m. tomorrow. I will turn it back on for only five minutes to wait for your call. If you have the answer, we'll go from there."

"What's the riddle?"

"Where balance and scales reside, find Urban's decree, for what is behind sword and shield will not lie. There, you will be set free!" Brenda Mason hung up after that.

Rick asked her, "Why would you even talk to him?"

"Because we may need a little help and I want to see if I can really trust this FBI agent."

After the phone call ended, Jack showed the agents the map on his computer. It was pointing to Lincoln, Nebraska. He told them that it was the best he could do on the trace. He couldn't get an exact address, but there were only so many hotels Brenda could be staying at. Jack had also recorded the conversation, so they were able to go back and listen to the riddle. Agent Main spoke up. "It's good that we got a trace, but a riddle? What the hell are we supposed to do with that? We only have 12 hours to figure it out."

Gavin finished his beer. "Come on, Agent Main; we're smart people. We can figure it out, and 12 hours is plenty of time."

"Alright, then. Let's start with the first clue. Any ideas?"

"'Where balance and scales reside' is an obvious reference to the law, to justice. I think there are three places that would fit the criteria for Judge Doyle. They would be: the law library where he studied, which is at the University of Chicago; his court; or his office, because there was a weight and scales statue on his desk."

Agent Main thought about it for a moment and then realized something. "She wants us to find something of his, something that he's keeping hidden."

"Then let's start at the crime scene. Maybe he was keeping something in his study that he wanted us to find."

The agents grabbed their coats and left Gavin's apartment. Jack stayed behind and used his computer to cross-reference words in the riddle. Gavin and Agent Main arrived back at the crime scene and started looking around the study for any clues. They couldn't find anything, not even a hidden safe or secret compartment in his desk. After a half an hour of searching, they decided this location was the wrong one. Agent Main asked Gavin about the library at the University of Chicago, and if there was any place that the judge would hide something. He said he couldn't think of any, so they decided to check out Judge Doyle's court.

When they arrived, the only people there were night security and cleaning crews. As they walked in, Agent Main asked her partner, "Is there anything in a courtroom that would reference a sword and shield? Any murals, paintings, or other designs?"

"Not in a federal court."

"Is there anything in this building that would reference a sword and shield or urban?"

"Not that I know of, but maybe urban is a reference to the fact that we are in a public place."

"Of course. If that is a clue, then out of the three places you mentioned earlier, this is the most urban place."

Gavin thought for a moment. "Let's start in his office."

They walked past a security guard and showed their badges. He waved them through. The judge's office was cluttered, just like his study at home, making it hard to find anything. One of the things that Judge Doyle liked was art. He had lots of paintings from different periods. They were recreations of the originals, but they made the office look nice. Agent Main finally noticed something: a medieval painting hanging over a small shelf. The only reason she paid attention to it was because of the history lesson Dr. McSwain had given them. She said to her partner, "Look at the painting! It's of the Crusades, right?"

Gavin looked at it. "Yes, those are Templar Knights in the painting."

"And there's a sword and shield in it. Move the painting."

"What?"

She walked over to the painting and moved it, but nothing happened. Gavin asked, "What are you looking for?"

"A safe. I thought there might be one behind the painting." She tried to put the painting back in place but accidentally knocked it down. As soon as it came off the hook, a trap door opened at the bottom of the wall, near the baseboards.

The agents looked down and saw a safe with a digital keypad. Agent Main said, "If you need to hide your secrets, you always keep a safe. But the problem with this one is that it will take some time to crack the code. We'll need an electronics expert. Can Jack do this?"

"Probably. I'll call him." Gavin pulled out his phone and, while looking at the safe, started thinking. He muttered a part of the riddle: *find urban's decree.* After a few moments, an answer came to him. He said, "Urban's Decree is not a public place. It's Pope Urban II. He gave a speech in 1095 with a decree to retake the Holy Land, thus beginning the First Crusade. Urban's Decree is the four-digit password. Try 1095."

Agent Main typed it in and it worked. The safe door opened and inside was a documents pouch. Inside the pouch was information on a Swiss bank account that was opened up three months ago. The electronic key to the account was in there, along with transparent fingertip pads. They both were confused and it was Agent Main who asked, "What are these pads for?" Gavin had seen something like this before. "They're fingerprints. You can put these pads on the tips of your fingers, and whoever's fingerprints are on the pads become your own. I think it's one of the keys to getting into this Swiss bank account."

"But there are two sets. Does that mean it takes two people to access the account?"

"That's what I'd bet."

"What is in that bank account that he couldn't keep in here?"

"Perhaps something so damaging that he couldn't keep in the United States. I bet if there's an answer to why the judge was murdered, it's in that bank account."

16

AD Gasper and his task force started early the next day. They still didn't have any leads on Brenda Mason. One of the agents brought a report to Gasper and told him it was a trace on a man named Rick Henry, ordered by Gavin Donnelly. After checking the name, they found the connection to Brenda Mason.

Gasper asked, "How did we miss Rick Henry, her childhood friend?"

"The name didn't show up in the court documents," the agent replied.

"Did Agent Donnelly report this trace to anyone?"

"Not that I know of, sir."

"Alright, I'll deal with him later. For now, let's get tabs on Rick Henry. Find out where he is by tracking his phone."

"You think Brenda Mason might be getting help from an old friend?"

Gasper thought about it. "I don't know for sure, but Agent Donnelly may think so; that's why he was running the trace. I want to know what he knows."

It didn't take them long to figure out what Agent Donnelly and Agent Main were doing. But the bigger question was, how long could they get away with it in order to find the real killers?

∞∞∞∞∞∞∞∞∞∞

Agent Main arrived back at Gavin's apartment with coffee. It was nearly 8:00 a.m. and she had the sneaking suspicion that the next couple of days were going to be the longest of her career. She knocked on the door and Gavin told to her to come in. He smiled when he saw the coffee. "You read my mind. I think we're going to need a lot of this today." She laughed at the comment and responded,

"I've been thinking about the Swiss bank account. If we think in terms of an intelligence operative, you hide what you need to escape and to survive in hiding. We have government agents that have boxes in Switzerland because it's a neutral point in Europe."

"Okay, I'm with you so far."

"What if Judge Doyle was hiding information that had to be in a neutral place because it concerned illegal activities not in the U.S., but in other parts of the world? Switzerland is the one place that nobody will go and try to steal it."

"Because it's neutral for everybody, thus making it the perfect safe haven. If that's true, then it has to be really damaging."

Agent Main nodded in agreement. It was time to call Brenda Mason again.

She was waiting outside some country restaurant in Nebraska. Gavin took a sip of coffee and made the call. She let it ring once and then answered. "Good morning, Agent Donnelly. Do you have the answer I am looking for?"

Gavin laughed. "The riddle was good, but we did find the safe."

"Just because you found the safe doesn't mean you were able to get inside it."

"We found the envelope with the information on the Swiss bank account."

"Very good."

"Does that mean you will turn yourself in to us?"

Brenda paused. "You've proven yourself, but if I turn myself in to you, then I do it on my terms."

"And what are your terms?"

"You only get me, not the kids. I will make sure they are safe and out of the country before I turn myself in."

"Okay, then where do we do this?"

"San Francisco International Airport, 9 a.m. United Flight 1292 to Barcelona. I turn myself in only to you. If I see any other agents or U.S. marshals, then I walk."

Gavin was curious. There weren't enough details in the plan that she was giving. "We just meet you at the gate and you'll turn yourself in?"

"No. Wait for a diversion and I will come quietly with you."

"What diversion?"

"You'll know it when you see it."

She hung up after that and immediately smashed her phone. Brenda had already gotten two new phones for herself and Rick. She walked back into the restaurant and told Rick that everything was set, and then finished breakfast with the kids.

Agent Main asked, "So, we're just supposed to show up at the airport and she'll just turn herself in? I don't buy it."

Gavin replied, "I don't think we have much of a choice. She talked to us, and that's trust. Maybe we should trust her, too."

"Okay. What's your plan?"

Before he could say anything, Gavin's phone rang. It was AD Foster. Gavin answered.

"This is Agent Donnelly."

"Agent Donnelly, did your plan work?"

"Yes, sir. She agreed to turn herself in to us at the San Francisco airport, on a few conditions."

"What are they?"

"The main one is that we have to let her get the kids out of the country safely."

"Who is she giving them to?"

"We don't know, but we're going to find out."

AD Foster changed the subject. "The reason I called is to tell you that your little game is up."

"What do you mean?"

"The call you traced … there's a record of it on the FBI server and an agent found it. He showed it Gasper, and now he knows you've been hiding something."

Gavin put his phone on speaker. "How much trouble are we in?"

"You have about 10 minutes before agents from Gasper's task force come to get you and bring you in for questioning."

"Is he removing us from the case?"

"You'll be in lockdown until this thing is solved. I can't stop it, but I can warn you. He'll also notify all FBI offices to hold you, so you can be brought in if you contact them. If you're going to try to bring Brenda Mason in, then get to San Francisco before they do. Work with local law enforcement if you need help."

"Thanks for the warning."

AD Foster had a worried tone. "Agent Donnelly, Agent Main: you two better be right about this or you probably won't have jobs next week." He hung up the phone.

Agent Main replied, "I guess we're going to San Francisco today."

"We won't have time to go by your place and get stuff."

"That's alright. I always have an overnight bag in my car. I never know where I'm going to be. I'd say you have about three minutes to get packed so we can get out of here."

Gavin rushed around his apartment and packed a suitcase with another suit. Anything else, he would just have to buy later. They left in a rush. On the way out, Agent Main spoke up. "You know, we could create a little diversion of our own to help us get out of the city."

"What do you have in mind?"

"Call in an anonymous tip that Brenda Mason has been sighted in the city. Gasper would probably respond to it himself, but more importantly, the team that's coming to get us would have to re-route themselves to the call."

Gavin smiled. He got out his phone and called his cousin, Alex. His cousin answered. "Hey Alex, does your partner still have her hair dyed blond?"

"Yeah. You looking for a date?"

"Ha ha. No, I need a favor. Can you grab coffee at that diner on Rush? The one that has the really good pastries we like."

"Sure, I guess."

"I need to get out of the city. I'll explain why later, but I need a diversion from the rest of the Bureau. We're going to call in a tip that Brenda Mason was seen at the diner."

"So, my partner is the decoy and this whole thing is just a sideshow."

Gavin smiled. "You got it. Can you help?"

"Sure. It'll be fun to piss off some of the feds."

"Great! Make sure you're there in five minutes." Gavin pulled out a pre-paid cell phone he always kept on him that the FBI didn't know about. He called the tip line and said that he saw Brenda Mason at the diner. The plan worked. AD Gasper pulled the team of agents that were sent to get Agent Donnelly and Agent Main off their assignment, and sent them to the diner to check out the lead. No matter how ridiculous the lead might have been, the FBI had to check out all leads. It would take at least 30 minutes to sort things out, which was plenty of time for the agents to get to the airport.

On their way to O'Hare International Airport, Agent Main asked, "Are we going to get any help at the airport, or is it just going to be you and me? We know part of her plan is to flush whoever is chasing her out. We can't do this alone."

"No, you're right. We're going to need spotters at the airport and we can't use FBI agents. I have a contact in the San Francisco Police Department. He can probably help us." The agents booked tickets on the first flight out of the city and were on a plane to San Francisco within the hour.

Mr. Bran and his team, minus one man, had stayed in Des Moines to monitor the U.S. marshals' team and all of their leads. He was eating a sandwich and monitoring the marshals radio frequencies and phone calls when his own phone rang. It was the boss.

"Mr. Bran, you need to go to San Francisco. Brenda Mason will be turning herself in to a couple of FBI agent's tomorrow morning at the airport. You need to be there and make sure that happens."

"Is that confirmed?"

"Mr. Bran, I would not be calling you if this was a false report. We have a very reliable source. She is putting the kids on United Flight 1292 to Barcelona, and she has help."

"What do you want me to do with the kids and whoever is helping her?"

"Mr. Bran, we don't want witnesses." That was all he said, and then he hung up the phone. Mr. Bran looked at his associate. "Pack up. We're going to San Francisco."

∞∞∞∞∞∞∞∞∞∞

The U.S. Marshal who had infiltrated Marshal Rogers' team was getting a phone call while going over surveillance tapes. He answered his phone; it was Mr. Bran. He said to the marshal, "Johnson, treat this like a tip. Brenda Mason will be getting on a flight to Barcelona at the San Francisco airport tomorrow morning. Tell the boss that."

"Has my mission changed at all?"

"No, you still have one job. The Jackal is the primary shooter, but make sure that all witnesses are erased."

"What about the FBI agents?"

He smiled. "It would be a good thing if they were shot in the linc of duty during the chaos." That was all he said, and then he ended the call. Johnson went to tell Marshal Rogers that he just got a tip: somebody matching Brenda Mason's description had just purchased four tickets to Barcelona, United Flight 1292, departing the San Francisco airport at 9 a.m. Rogers finally got excited. It was the break he had been looking for over the last day or so. He told his team to get prepared. They were heading to San Francisco.

∞∞∞∞∞∞∞∞∞∞

Gavin and Agent Main finally arrived in San Francisco later that afternoon. They got a hotel room and, while Agent Main stayed behind to do some research, Gavin went to find his contact with SFPD. He needed to work out the details with his contact. He was a detective who had helped Gavin on a case a few years back. Any time either one of them needed a favor; the price was glass of scotch, the detectives' drink of choice. By the time Gavin got back to the hotel room,

[249]

everything had been worked out with the police. His contact, Detective Mike Ryan, had gotten about five other detectives to help as spotters at the airport. For the detectives, it was a chance to be heroes while helping the FBI take down Judge Doyle's murderers.

Agent Main had been researching a hunch while her partner was away. Her hunch proved right; she found something big. That's what she told Gavin as he came walking into the room. He asked her what she found.

Agent Main replied, "It's been bugging me who Brenda Mason would give the kids to in order to keep them safe, so I did some checking. In the event that Henry and Elizabeth Doyle die, her older sister gets custody of the kids. Do you know who she's married to?"

"Somebody important, right?"

"The Greek ambassador to the United States."

"No shit."

Agent Main smiled. "Yeah. Her sister studied abroad and met him while in college. They fell in love and got married. Been married for 23 years and have three kids. Their 21-year-old son, who just graduated from Stanford, works on his father's staff. Josephine, Elizabeth's sister, has dual citizenship. And the best part is ..."

Gavin smiled. "... They're here in the States."

"And they have diplomatic immunity, which creates all sorts of possibilities."

Gavin thought for a moment. "They have easy access to the airport, and they have a private flight that we can't search and can't get access to."

"I checked where the ambassador is right now. He's in Washington, but Josephine is here in San Francisco with a security team."

"That's Brenda's plan. She's not really going to Barcelona. Whatever the diversion is helps her and the kids get on that flight with the ambassador's wife, so we can't touch them."

"So, you don't think she's really going to turn herself in, do you?"

"Maybe not. Or, she will turn herself in, and Rick Henry is the one that'll make the exchange with Josephine. Either way, it's a good plan."

"If she gets on that plane, then we're really screwed. Any information she has goes with her, and we can't kill her."

"I know. We still have to take her alive. I guess we have no choice but to trust her."

Agent Main frowned. "I hate gambling this big. This is why I hate playing poker."

The airport was crowded, especially for international flights. Gavin and Agent Main were there early, helping his contact and the other detectives get into place. The gate that United Flight 1292 was leaving from was very crowded, and the layout was very open. There were exits everywhere and it was hard to tell who was who in the crowd. Security agents could easily hide in the crowd. Gavin had three of the detectives hide there, as well. The agents stood by a food kiosk, just waiting. Gavin had received a text message early that morning from another cell phone number. It said that they needed to be standing by the food kiosk and, after the diversion, a woman with black hair would approach them and it would be Brenda Mason. They still didn't know what the diversion was.

As 9:00 a.m. was approaching, the agents got a surprise. Deputy Marshal Rogers and his team showed up at the airport. The agents were caught off-guard. As the marshals approached, Gavin said out loud, "Holy shit! How did they find out about this?"

Agent Main replied, "Nothing we can do about it now. Let's see if we can get them out of the way so Brenda will turn herself over to us."

Rogers walked up to the agents and said. "I don't know what you're doing here, but is there any sign of her?"

Gavin responded, "Look, I don't have time to give you the details, but Brenda has agreed to turn herself in to us, and only us. I don't know how you found out what's happening here today, but you need to get out of sight so we can handle this."

"No way, Agent Donnelly. I'm here to arrest her."

"Look, I don't have time to argue. You'll get credit for helping us bring her in. Hell, you can put the handcuffs on her, but she won't turn herself in if you're standing here. Please hide your team in the crowd so we don't spook her."

Rogers thought about it for a moment. "Fine, but we'll move in as soon as we see her. This is still our capture." The marshals disappeared into the crowd. Agent Main said, "This complicates things."

Gavin replied, "Yeah, but we'll still play this out. The marshals may be able to help us, which I hate to admit."

All of sudden, there was a commotion at the ticket counter. A woman started yelling at the girls behind the ticket counter. Everybody noticed it and, just like a fight, everyone was watching. Gavin spoke up. "Is that the diversion?" Both he and Agent Main were looking for a woman with black hair. No one approached, and then they heard it. The entire gate heard it. Two gunshots rang out.

17

It was pandemonium at the gate after the gunshots were fired. There were so many people in the area that it was hard to tell anyone apart. The agents couldn't find the detectives in the crowd and, to add more craziness to the situation, the marshals ran into the crowd to look for the shooters. Agent Main was the first to say it as she and Gavin dove to the ground: "Where did those shots come from?"

"I don't know." They waited a moment to see if there were going to be more. "There was spacing between the shots. I think it was a sniper rifle."

"Are you sure?"

"Ninety-five percent sure."

Rogers and the other marshals came running toward the agents. Rogers shouted, "Is anybody hurt?"

"We're fine," Gavin replied.

"Where's Brenda Mason?"

"For fuck's sake, Rogers, don't worry about that right now. We just had a sniper fire into the crowd. Use your men to find him."

People were still running around, trying to get out of the gate; some were getting trampled. The detectives were doing the best they could on crowd control. Finally, a woman started screaming at the top of her lungs in the back corner of the gate, near a security exit. Gavin, Agent Main, and the marshals all turned in that direction to see what was going on. At the same time, when nobody was looking, Deputy Marshal Johnson fired at Rogers. He was bumped by somebody running by, so his aim was off. The bullet grazed Rogers' left arm and he fell down. Gavin was the first to turn around and see it.

Marshal Johnson was aiming again. Gavin pointed his service weapon at Johnson, firing two shots and killing the marshal instantly. Rogers looked at him with surprise and Gavin just replied, "You can thank me later." Then he yelled at the other marshals to find the shooter while one of them stayed behind to help Rogers. He looked at his partner. "Come on, we need to find Brenda Mason."

Agent Main asked, "Where do we start?"

"With the person, who, I think, just got shot."

The agents walked over to where the woman was screaming. Airport security was there, standing over a body. It was man in a baseball cap; he had been shot in the head. Agent Main rolled him over to see who it was. She asked, "Is this him?"

Gavin replied, "Yeah, it's Rick Henry." That's when Gavin started to look around. The crowd was still scattering and it was hard to see anybody, but he was looking for a woman with black hair. The woman screaming didn't have black hair, so it wasn't Brenda Mason. He said to his partner, "Spread out. I think Brenda is still here somewhere." They started looking around for a woman with black or blond hair. They both had stared at Brenda Mason's picture so many times that they could recognize her face blindfolded, despite the hair color. Agent Main asked,

"How do you know she's still here?"

"Because she set this whole thing up to help flush out whoever is trying to kill her. She wants us to catch them, and they haven't revealed themselves yet."

Agent Main nodded in his direction. She figured he was right. They searched frantically for her, but Gavin was also looking for something else. He was trying to spot anybody in the crowd that had a gun aimed at a woman. Finally, Agent Main walked over to Gavin and pointed to a woman in the crowd. They couldn't see her face because she had her back turned to them. "See that woman? She's not trying to get out of the way; she's surveying the crowd. I think that's her."

Both of them walked over to her and each agent grabbed an arm. The woman struggled to get free, and it was Agent Main who put her on the ground. Gavin said, "Brenda, it's me, Agent Donnelly. This is my partner, Agent Main. We're not here to harm you."

Brenda was panicking. "Who fired those shots? Did you catch the shooter? What about Rick?"

"Slow down, Brenda. We're looking for the shooter."

"What about Rick? Is he okay? I dashed when I heard the shots."

Agent Main replied, "He was shot. He's dead."

Brenda started crying and shouted, "Noooo!"

Gavin responded, "Brenda, listen to me. You can't do anything for him right now, but you are still in danger. What did you do with the kids?"

She answered, "They're in safe hands now."

"Who did you give them to? Josephine and her diplomatic security?" Brenda was shocked that he knew the answer. Gavin continued, "It wasn't hard to figure out who you could give them to, and they would be safe under diplomatic immunity. It was a good idea."

Brenda paused for a moment and then she answered. "I made the exchange with the security detail about a minute before the shots fired."

"Where are they now?"

"It doesn't matter; they're safe. Nobody can touch them."

"Brenda, the men who are after you can still kill the security detail and harm the kids. Where did they go?"

Panic came back to her face. "They went through the security door. There's a private jet at gate 52. It's for government planes."

Gavin looked at his partner. "Get her out of here and make sure she's safe." Gavin radioed Detective Mike Ryan and told him to escort his partner and Brenda Mason to a safe location. Agent Main asked, "Where are you going?"

"To make sure that the kids get on that jet safely and out of this country!" Gavin charged through the security door and down the hallway.

While Gavin was heading to gate 52, The Jackal was taking apart his sniper rifle and putting it back into its case. He had to get out of there before security figured out his position and apprehended him. Airport security was all over the place. As he was coming down the stairs from the top level, he was confronted by airport security. They told him to stop and informed him that they were going to search him. The area he was in was restricted. The Jackal slowly put down the case and reached for the gun tucked into the back of his pants. It had a silencer on it, so no one could hear him shoot the two guards. He muttered, "I fucking hate rent-a-cops."

He got out of there as quickly as he could. His phone started ringing. Before he could answer it, he needed to clear the text message on the screen.

"*B. Mason, SF airport, United Flight 1292, 9 a.m. She will be traveling with a male friend. Take them both out.*" He didn't answer the phone call, but he texted his boss to let him know that he only got one of them, and that team two was en route to intercept the others.

∞∞∞∞∞∞∞∞∞∞

Gavin was approaching the door at the end of corridor when he heard multiple gunshots. He turned the corner and went through the

[254]

door with his gun drawn. There was no one in sight, but he did see the ambassador's plane outside the gate. He dashed through the door to the outside, where the plane was. There was a guard down at the bottom of the stairs that led into the plane. Gavin went up the stairs and inside the plane. He found three bodyguards and the pilots; all were shot dead. Then he heard a woman's scream. It was Josephine. She was screaming at the sight of another man with a gun. She was shot in her right shoulder. He looked at her and said, "I'm FBI. You can stop screaming. I'm here." The next thing he did was radio to his partner and the detectives, telling them that he needed to get an ambulance at the plane outside gate 52. He found some towels and put them on her shoulder, and grabbed her left hand to apply pressure to the wound.

"Josephine, keep your hand on the cloth and press hard. Keep pressure on the shoulder. Paramedics will be here soon."

She anxiously replied, "Okay."

"I need to know who did this."

"Two men dressed as airport maintenance workers came in and started shooting."

"Did they take the kids?"

"Yes."

Gavin told her to stay put and went outside to see if he could see anything. He figured the two men had a vehicle stashed somewhere nearby and were taking the kids there. Outside of the gate were open fields and roads connected to the runways. He could not see anything in the way of a vehicle, but he did notice a maintenance hangar where vehicles could be stored. All of sudden, a Land Rover came speeding out of the hangar, coming toward him. It had two men in it, and Gavin could see the kids inside, as well. Gavin raised his gun and fired two bullets into the front window. He hit the driver with both shots and the Land Rover swerved uncontrollably.

It veered off the road and into one of the fields, and it was luck that the Land Rover didn't flip over. Gavin slowly approached the vehicle. The man in the backseat rolled down the window. It was Mr. Bran, and he was holding the children. He said to Gavin, "Agent Donnelly, you may be a good shot, but if you don't put that gun down then I will kill the kids right here."

Gavin was surprised that the guy knew his name. He replied, "How do I know that you won't just kill them later?"

"You don't!"

Gavin fired one shot and hit Mr. Bran in the head, killing him instantly. He said, "That's what I thought."

The kids were shaken up. Sarah was crying when Gavin walked up to the Land Rover. Conner asked him, "Who are you?"

"Gavin Donnelly, FBI. You must be Connor." Gavin reached out his hand so Connor could shake it. He wanted to treat Connor like a grownup and bond with him. After the past few days, it would be hard for Connor to trust anyone. Sarah was still hysterical, so Gavin reached inside, unbuckled her seat belt, and helped her out of the Land Rover. She was so scared that she hugged Gavin and wouldn't let go. He held her, rubbed her back, and told her that it was going to be okay, that it was all over now.

She didn't let go as they walked back to the gate, and Conner stayed at his side. They were greeted by Agent Main and a slew of FBI agents. Paramedics were there, too, attending to Josephine. Gavin spoke up as they got inside. "I see you brought the Calvary."

Agent Main laughed. "I didn't call them. They were alerted to the airport when the first shots were fired. I see you made some friends."

"There are two bodies in a Land Rover over by the maintenance hangar. I'm pretty sure they were also at the Des Moines airport, trying to get Brenda Mason."

"Maybe one of these days, we'll work a case where you don't have to kill somebody."

Gavin laughed at the comment. Agent Main took Sarah from her partner's arms and told her that she didn't have to worry, that they were going to take good care of her, and that she could see her Aunt Josephine in a few minutes. Connor started to go with her, but Gavin stopped him for a moment. "Connor, there are two things you should know. First, you did great job helping your sister. As an FBI agent, I'm proud." Connor smiled; he needed to hear that. "Second, you will hear a lot of things about Brenda … I mean, Jackie, but you only need to know one thing about her: she loves you and helped save your life. Remember that." Conner said okay and then he and his sister were taken away.

Part of the FBI task force that was at the gate was an old friend of Gavin's, Agent Ben Waters. He looked at Gavin and said, "I don't seem to remember you causing so much trouble in San Francisco when you were in White Collar Crimes."

Gavin laughed. "Violent Crimes means more mischief."

"It's good seeing you again."

"You too."

"I hate to tell you this, but we got a call from Chicago. AD Gasper ordered us to escort you back to Chicago since you broke protocol."

Gavin frowned at the thought, but he also wasn't surprised. "Yeah, that bastard doesn't care if we solve this case."

"Sorry that we have to do this."

"We may as well all go together. We need to get Brenda Mason back to Chicago, anyway."

"The first flight out is in an hour and we'll all be on it, which also means I can't let you out of my sight."

Gavin had to laugh. "Fine with me, but I still have questions for some people. You're not going to stop me from completing my investigation."

Agent Waters smiled. "It's not like I could stop you if I tried."

Gavin went over to where Josephine was being treated by the paramedics. He asked if she was going to be alright. Paramedics told him that she would be fine; the bullet went clear through. Josephine said to Gavin, "Agent Donnelly, I want to thank you for saving me and getting my niece and nephew back."

"You're welcome. Ma'am, I have some questions for you."

"Okay, I'll try to help in any way I can."

"When were you first contacted by Brenda about getting the kids out of the country?"

"She called us on Friday night, but the plan you speak of was made long before that."

Gavin was surprised. "What do you mean?"

"About three months ago, when my husband and I were visiting Henry and Elizabeth, he told us that he had stumbled upon some illegal activities based on cases coming through his court. He had started investigating them, but it was dangerous. He said that if anything should happen to him or my sister, then Jackie would get the kids to us so they could be safe under our diplomatic immunity."

"Did he give you any details on what these activities were?"

"No. All he said was that it was getting dangerous and that he might die, but he wasn't going to back down."

"A month ago, he was nominated for the Supreme Court. This plan didn't change because of that?"

Josephine smiled. "The one thing you may not know about Henry is that he didn't scare easily. He wouldn't back down; it's the Irishman in him. He wasn't going to be scared off from accepting the nomination from his old friend, the president."

"Was he threatened with his life if he went to the Supreme Court?"

Josephine glared at Gavin with intensity. "What do you think, Agent Donnelly?"

18

Everybody was loading up on the FBI flight back to Chicago. Deputy Marshal Rogers and his team were heading back, too. Rogers was pissed off at Gavin; he even tried to punch him before they got on the plane. Rogers wasn't convinced that his deputy was dirty and was trying to kill him. He wanted to investigate Agent Donnelly, but that was just the anger talking. Everyone else knew what really happened. Brenda Mason was going to have to be taken back in handcuffs since she was still a person of interest. The agents apologized for that, but she didn't mind. Agent Main had been on the phone with the Washington DOJ and the DOJ office in Chicago. She was trying to get them to accept a witness protection deal. She got off the phone and told her partner,

"Agent Donnelly, it looks like they're going for it. The U.S. Attorney's Office in Chicago really wants to get her testimony. Apparently, they're running out of witnesses."

"What do you mean?"

"They were going to get Dr. Paul Stiles' deposition, but he died in a car crash a few days ago. The police you sent to pick him up got there too late. According to witnesses, an SUV rammed him from behind and pushed his car into traffic."

"Somebody got to him."

"Whether that's the case or not, they need Brenda's testimony now."

"We still get to talk to her too, right?"

"I don't know; you and I are in trouble. But we have a long flight, so I would get started on those questions now."

Agent Waters came walking up right when Agent Main said that. He overheard it and said to Gavin, "She's right. I have orders to take you to AD Gasper as soon as we land, so if you have questions, get them asked on the plane. You can use the private cabin to question her. No one will bother you."

Gavin asked, "Are we being arrested on Gasper's orders?"

"No, just detained, which might as well be the same thing. You really pissed this guy off. I can't say that I'm surprised."

"He's just mad that we were right and that my partner and I are smarter than he is."

Agent Main rolled her eyes, even though she knew he was right. Agent Waters just laughed. "You think you got the nickname 'Superagent' because you're good, when really it's just because you're a pain in the ass."

They all got on the plane and it took off back to Chicago. It would be a three-hour flight, which gave the agents plenty of time to question Brenda. About 20 minutes into the flight, the agents took Brenda Mason into the private cabin. Agent Main took the cuffs off of her. Brenda asked, "I don't have to be handcuffed anymore?"

"No, at least not during the flight," Agent Main replied. "We don't think you're going to escape from the plane."

Brenda Mason smiled and then asked a hard question. "So, has it been confirmed? Is Rick dead?"

"The sniper at the airport shot him in the head. He died instantly."

Brenda started crying again. "It's my fault! I got him into this, knowing that there were trained killers after me. How does anybody explain that to his wife?"

Gavin spoke up. "It's not your fault, Brenda. It's their fault, the men who really killed the judge. We need to ask you some questions. What can you tell me about these men?"

Brenda told them about the night she walked in on the murder and what she saw. Gavin showed her pictures of the guys he shot. She confirmed that they were the ones who committed the murder. She also told the agents about the other man, the one whose hand she cut off before slitting his throat. At least there was one witness who put the murderers at the crime scene.

Gavin asked, "According to Josephine, this whole plan of yours was put together months ago. Is that true?"

"Yes, although I knew about it before the Ambassador and his wife did."

"How so?"

"About six months ago, Henry started seeing a pattern of companies devaluing their own stock so they could be bought cheap by foreign companies. What tipped him off was a case that came before his court."

Agent Main asked, "P & M Electronics, right?"

"Yes. He saw the ties to a Chinese company and remembered another case that came before his court that was very similar. A company called Wright Ship industries."

Gavin and Agent Main smiled at each other. Their theory was confirmed. Gavin asked,

"Did he pick up on the connection before he decided not to dismiss the case with P & M? Is that why he didn't throw out the case?"

"Yes."

"How did you know about all this?"

"Because, after he made the decision to let the case be tried, he knew that it could be dangerous. He even received a few death threats through e-mail. Both Henry and his wife confided in me. So a plan was put together in case anything happened to them. According to their will, the kids were supposed to go to her sister and the ambassador. My job was to get them there."

Agent Main asked, "Did they know who you really are?"

"Yes. I told them about six months ago."

"What was their reaction?"

Brenda frowned. "Elizabeth was mad at first. She gave me a day off so they could decide what to do with me. It was Henry who was more sympathetic; I guess it was the judge in him. He told her that I hadn't done anything to lose their trust, and that I wasn't guilty of the crime … there were still too many questions about my old case." Agent Main rolled her eyes at that statement. There was a part of her that still thought Brenda Mason had something to do with killing her child. Brenda continued, "Anyway, they still kept me on. Elizabeth and I had a heart-to-heart talk about it, and she even admitted that her anger was more over the fact that I had waited over four years to tell them. But once we got all of that out of the way, Henry started to confide in me more about what was going on with the case."

Agent Main asked, "How did you change your name? We did some checking and there was no record of any legal name change."

"When you're a criminal, Agent Main, you learn who to go to for the perfect fake ID. I only needed one in order to get more IDs and then start a new life. Once you develop a history with an ID, nobody asks questions."

"You paid for them."

"Yes, a lot of money. That's all I will say on that matter."

Gavin spoke up. "Tell me about the file we found in the safe."

"It's just information on how to access a bank account in Zurich, Switzerland. You need two sets of fingerprints to access it; that's why there are the transparent pads that you can put on your fingertips. The account is protected by a high level of security."

"What's in the account?"

"I can't tell you everything that's in there because I honestly don't know. I do know that he was doing research on companies that did the same thing as P & M Electronics, and he found out a lot. He found a conspiracy. He put the research in the safety deposit box at the Swiss bank."

"Why?"

"Two reasons. First, it's not safe to keep things here in the U.S. Second, he knew that the president was probably going to put him on the Supreme Court. And if you're going to be vetted by the Senate ..."

Gavin finished the sentence. "... You can't have research on conspiracy theories laying around. But nobody will ask questions if the research is hidden in Switzerland."

Brenda had questions, too. "What's going to happen to me?"

"You're going to give a deposition to the U.S. Attorney's Office on the murder of Henry and Elizabeth Doyle, and give information about the case with P & M Electronics. Then you will be put into witness protection."

"I'm not going to be tried for the murder?"

"No. There's enough forensic evidence to prove you didn't do it, especially the knife with your prints on it; it wasn't the knife that killed the Doyle's. Also, I have been meaning to ask you about something. We found a second blood type from the body that was removed. When you killed that man at the scene, did you know that we would find his blood and ask questions?"

Brenda smiled. "I thought it was a good plan."

"It got our attention."

"You know, in the three years I spent inside prison while awaiting trial, I got a college degree. It was in criminology, with an emphasis on forensics. It's amazing what you can learn in prison."

Both agents smiled at that. She also asked, "I'm not ever going to see the kids again, am I?"

Agent Main answered, "Unfortunately, no. Once you're done with your depositions, you will be transported to your new home. We won't even know where that is."

Gavin replied, "Brenda, they know what you did. They know you saved their lives." Tears came to her eyes. She loved the kids as if they were her own and it hurt to know that she would never see them grow up or be a part of their lives.

Those were all the questions that the agents had for her. Gavin recorded the conversation on his phone for his own private records. A couple of hours later, the plane landed and Brenda was immediately transferred to the FBI building. Gavin and Agent Main stayed with her until they arrived at the building. Agent Waters stayed with the agents to make sure they got back to the building and reported to AD Gasper. Most of the FBI agents applauded Agent Donnelly and Agent Main as they brought in Brenda Mason. Most thought she was still guilty. After she was taken into custody by the U.S. Attorney's Office and was prepped to do her deposition, the agents were escorted to AD Gasper's office.

Gasper was furious and he let everybody in the room know this, including AD Foster. As soon as the agents walked in, he tore into them. "First, I don't give a shit if everybody thinks you're heroes. You broke protocol and then you embarrassed this office with that phony anonymous tip about Brenda Mason being sighted in Chicago … which turned out to be your cousin, Detective Alex Donnelly, and his partner."

Gavin replied, "If it was an anonymous tip, then how do you know it was us?" Agent Main and AD Foster smirked.

"Can it, Donnelly. Tomorrow, you two will go before OPR. I want your badges and your service weapons, now."

"Sir, by law, they can't be taken by an outside Assistant Director to whom the agents are not directly assigned to with an OPR review."

"Bullshit. I want them now!"

AD Foster spoke up. "He's right. They're directly assigned to me, so it's my call."

"Then take their badges and guns away."

"I'm not going to do that. Yes, they broke protocol and should have to go before OPR, but they did crack this case and they were the ones that caught Brenda Mason. It's uncalled for to ask for their badges and service weapons."

"That's horseshit. Fine. You two are on restrictive duty pending the outcome of the OPR meeting."

As the agents left the office, Gavin's phone rang. It was Dr. Kenrick. She had some news for the agents, big news. Gavin told his partner that the doctor had isolated the substance in the Doyle's bloodstreams and she needed to talk to them. The agents arrived at the morgue where Dr. Kenrick worked. When they walked through the door, she said to them, "I heard you two caught Brenda Mason and someone else that was involved in the murder. Congratulations."

Gavin smiled. "Thanks. What do you have that is so urgent?"

"I wouldn't rule her out as a suspect yet. The unknown substance we found is called Polonium-210. It's …"

Agent Main cut in, "It's radioactive material." Gavin looked at his partner with surprise. He asked her, "How did you know that?"

"I've seen it before in a victim. He was poisoned with it."

Dr. Kenrick said, "You got that right. Plus, it's also what killed Yasser Arafat."

Gavin asked, "How did you find it?"

"Because it's radioactive, it doesn't show up on any toxicology report. That's why we couldn't find it right off the bat. So I did some other tests, and one of them happened to be an ionization test … and bingo, we found it. It looks like it's been in their bloodstreams for over six months."

"How long did they have before they would have died from the poison?"

"Maybe a year."

Agent Main asked, "How did they come into contact with the material? Were they injected?"

Dr. Kenrick walked over to a table and picked up a tube of toothpaste. "No, it was in their toothpaste. We gathered things from the house and tested them, and this is what we found. The toothpaste had the radioactive material in it. With each brushing, they were poisoning themselves."

Gavin replied, "That's pretty ingenious. Is that the only toothpaste in the house that was poisoned?"

"You want to know if the toothpaste the kids used was poisoned, right? No, it wasn't, but that doesn't mean kids don't sometimes use their parents' toothpaste."

Agent Main look shocked. "You mean they could be poisoned?"

Dr. Kenrick looked at her. "We'd have to test them. If they are, they will probably need a lifetime of treatment to survive." Agent Main was horrified by the answer. The first thought in her mind was that it was Brenda Mason who did it. The maid usually buys groceries for the family she works for.

Agent Main walked out of the morgue. Gavin saw that she was upset and knew they had to question Brenda Mason again. He looked at Dr. Kenrick. "Thanks for the report."

"I'm sorry for the bad news. Nothing is what it seems in this case."

"Have you ever seen this kind of poisoning before?"

"No. This is a new kind of assassination method and we don't have a way to fight against it. There's no cure for it."

Gavin went outside to find his partner. He saw her leaning against the wall. He walked over to her and she said, "If she was the one poisoning them, including the kids, then I'm the one that's going to put a bullet in her."

∞∞∞∞∞∞∞∞∞∞∞∞

Later in the day, Brenda Mason was finally done with her depositions and was about to be transported away with the witness protection crew. The agents didn't have access to her anymore, but Gavin was able to convince the agents watching her to let them have five minutes with her in the holding room. Agent Main said to her accusingly, "Why were the Doyle's being poisoned? Were you poisoning the kids, too?"

Brenda had a frightened look on her face. "What are you talking about?"

Gavin spoke up. "We know you're not telling us everything. The toothpaste the Doyle's used had Polonium-210 in it."

Brenda's face went pale. "I didn't know that the toothpaste was poisoned."

"What do you mean, you didn't know? How did you get the toothpaste?"

"I can't tell you everything. They will kill me."

"If you don't tell us, then we can't protect you."

"You can't protect me from them, anyway."

Agent Main grabbed her and shoved her up against the wall. "Tell us what you know! Who gave you the toothpaste?"

"Fine, I'll tell you. Twelve years ago, I didn't have anything after I was acquitted. I couldn't get a job and trying to change my name was proving to be difficult. A man approached me and said he could get me a new ID, a new life, and plenty of money, along with a new job. All I had to do was give him information about my employers."

Gavin replied, "You became a spy."

"Yes, of sorts, but I didn't give detailed information. I didn't go through financials or anything like that. It was just information like where they were going on vacation, what charities they were donating to, and if they were getting along. I worked for a congressman before Judge Doyle."

"Who are the people you work for?"

"They don't have a name. All I was ever told is that it was a group of people trying to make sure that my employers weren't doing criminal things."

Agent Main asked, "Did they give you the toothpaste?"

"Yes."

"Did you know what was in it?"

"No."

"You never asked why they were giving you toothpaste?"

"These are not the kind of people that you ask questions to."

"Did you let the kids use the same toothpaste?"

"I didn't, but I can't say for sure that they never used their parents' toothpaste."

Agent Main slapped her. "You bitch! You poisoned those kids, didn't you? Just like you killed your own child!"

"I didn't harm those kids! I never would. I love them and I didn't kill my own child. Only a mother who actually had a child would understand that."

"What are you fucking talking about?"

"Come on, Agent Main, it's written all over your face. When you did you lose your child? That's why you hate me so much right now."

Agent Main was infuriated at the statement and tried to hit Brenda again, but her partner stopped her. He yelled, "Out of the room, Agent Main."

"No!" she screamed back.

"Get out of the room, now. You're not helping." She finally left and slammed the door on her way out.

Gavin looked back at Brenda. "Tell me who your handler is."

"I called him Red, but it's probably not his real name."

"How do I stop him?"

AD Gasper came bursting into the holding room with two other agents. He shouted, "Donnelly, you're not permitted to talk to her. Get the hell out of here before you lose your job."

Gavin was still looking at Brenda and not even paying attention to the other agents. "Tell me, Brenda. How do I stop them?"

Finally, the two other agents grabbed him and started to haul him out of the room. Brenda shouted to Gavin, "I can't tell you everything, but the truth you want is out there. For you, it starts with Zurich." Gavin was pulled out of the room after that. He and his partner were told to go home. The next time they were allowed to show back up would be for their OPR review.

19

Both agents had been here before, and not very long ago. Agent Donnelly and Agent Main were earning a reputation for getting into trouble. Agent Donnelly had the bigger reputation for it. They sat before a panel of agents at the OPR. Agent Greg Taylor was doing the review, just like last time. After spending a few minutes reviewing the reports given by the agents and AD Gasper, he spoke. "Well, I'm sorry to see you two back here. It's becoming a bad habit. After reviewing the report you submitted and the one AD Gasper submitted, all I can say is that this is a mess. So, you two believe that P & M Electronics has the strongest motive for murder and hired someone to do it?"

Gavin answered, "Yes, sir."

"The two men you shot, Agent Donnelly, still cannot be identified. There's no connection to P & M Electronics. All we know is they were trying to kill Brenda Mason and kidnap the Doyle kids. Are you sure it's P & M Electronics that committed the murders?"

"Sir, I don't think we can be absolutely sure. But the evidence we found proves that Brenda Mason did not kill the Doyles and that somebody else did, so we looked at a motive."

"Your report sounds more like a conspiracy."

Gavin smiled. "We didn't create one; we're just reporting what we found."

"Why did you break protocol and ignore the orders of AD Gasper?"

"Because he wouldn't let us follow up on the leads we needed to. For him, it was a manhunt for Brenda Mason only; there were still too many questions that needed to be answered. We were following up on the investigation we'd started since the murder."

"But you realize that there is a chain of command and, like the military, we don't function without it."

Gavin looked Agent Taylor straight in the eye. "I do, sir, and knowing that, I was willing to accept the consequences of my actions."

Agent Taylor looked over at Agent Main. "What about you, Agent Main? You purposely broke the chain of command. Are you willing to accept the consequences?"

"Yes, sir," she answered with confidence.

"I thought so. Both of you have done a good job, but we can't ignore the disobeying of order. Despite the recommendation of AD Gasper that you be dismissed from your jobs, our punishment will not be that extreme." AD Gasper became angry and shouted, "What?! This is an outrage!" Taylor looked over at the Assistant Director. "Control yourself!" he sternly commanded. "The only reason you want them dismissed is because your pride was ruined. That's the least of our concern at the FBI." He looked at the two agents. "Now, as I was saying, you two will be suspended for 30 days without pay. And I should add that part of the reason you're not dismissed is both of you received a presidential commendation for your work in solving the Doyles' murders. He signed them this morning before he left to attend Judge Doyle's memorial service. If I were you, I would take the time to reflect on how you should act as an FBI agent regarding the chain of command. That will be all. Please turn in your badges and service weapons to your Assistant Director."

The agents stood up and gave their badges and service weapons to AD Foster. They were lucky. AD Gasper was furious, but there was nothing he could do about it. Both agents headed to their office to collect their things. AD Gasper stopped Agent Main as she was walking down the hall. He said, "You know, this doesn't change anything. Eventually, you'll screw up so badly that they'll have no choice but to dismiss you."

Agent Main smiled. "I can't figure out what pisses you off more: the fact that I was always a better agent than you or, no matter how much dick you suck to get to the top, you'll never sit in that director's chair."

She walked away before he could reply. It wasn't worth arguing about and she loved getting the last word, anyway. When she got back to her and Gavin's office, she found her husband, Richard, waiting for her outside. She was surprised. "What are you doing here?"

He smiled. "I came in early this morning to take care of the witness protection agreement with Brenda Mason."

"You could have done all that from Washington."

"Sure, but this is an important witness. I wanted to make sure it got done right ... and I wanted to see you. How are you?"

"I've had better days."

"I heard you got suspended, but also got a presidential commendation."

"Yeah. It's a cruel irony."

"Well, I'm proud of you. You should know that you have a lot of colleagues who are behind you. You'll get past this."

"Thank you."

He put his hands on her shoulders to comfort her. He knew when she was in a bad mood. "Is there any chance you'll be coming home, since you're suspended?"

"Richard, I know we need to have a serious talk about our marriage, but I just can't do it today. I will call you while I have some time off and maybe I'll come back to Washington for a little bit. That's the best I can give you right now." He smiled and said okay. She walked into the office. Gavin said to her, "So that's your husband, huh?"

"I guess you met."

"Briefly. He seems nice."

"He is, but I think he and I are going to have to finally admit that it's over. Besides, I have a life here -- at least, while I still have a job with the FBI."

"I'm sorry for your marriage ending and for getting you into trouble."

"You can't do anything about my marriage. And about the other thing: I made the choice to go with you because I thought you were right."

Gavin smiled at her. "What happened yesterday with Brenda Mason? What did she mean …?"

Agent Main stopped him from finishing the sentence. "I'm not ready to talk about that yet, but she did hit a nerve and I'll get over it in my own time."

"Ok, but just know that I am here if you need to talk."

She smiled. "Thank you. So where are you off to?"

"I'm going to the memorial service and then the wake. Paddy Murphy's is using one of the empty buildings next to it for extra room to host the wake. I'm going to pay my respects. And of course, I've been asked to play."

Agent Main laughed. "I wouldn't expect anything less from an Irishman."

"You know you should come to the service and the wake; find out what kind of man Judge Doyle really was, from a community that knew him best."

"How about I meet you at the service?" Gavin smiled, told her he would see her there, and then walked out.

Gavin walked down the street from the FBI building. He stopped at a newsstand to pick up a copy of the Chicago Tribune. He wanted to see what Haley O'Brian wrote about the capture of Brenda Mason. She had done her job perfectly a few days ago when she wrote the story saying that Brenda wasn't the only suspect. He was reading her latest article when a man walked up behind him and spoke. "Agent

Donnelly, you did a good job this week, but you should have taken my advice."

As Gavin turned around, he saw the man from Grant Park, the one who warned him not to take the case. "You knew I wouldn't back down. Why did you warn me?"

"Because of what happens next."

"What do you mean?"

The man smiled. "You don't think the men behind this will just let it go, do you? You stopped them from making a lot of money and having a controlling interest in a new technology. People end up dead for that sort of thing, as you may have noticed."

Gavin had a stern look on his face. "Are you trying to tell me that I'm next?"

"It's not my job to tell you if you're going to die, but you will only get one more warning … the same one Judge Doyle got."

"How will I know what it is?"

"You're an FBI agent; you'll figure it out. Besides, the clues are in what Brenda told you. I hope you got all the information you needed from her because you'll never have another chance."

Gavin looked shocked. "Have you done something with her?"

"She's already gone, and there will be somebody waiting to take her place."

"I don't understand."

"Did you really think she was the first? The first to be set up so they could make her look like a killer, and have nowhere else to turn, so that she's willing to spy for them?"

"You mean, 15 years ago, she was set up so they could make her work for them?"

"All you need to know is that they've done it before and they'll do it again."

"Why can't you give me a straight answer?"

The man smiled. "That would be too easy." Then he turned around and walked away.

Gavin's head started aching. *Brenda Mason was being transported to the airport by FBI agents. When they arrived, she was handed to new agents who were waiting by the FBI Gulfstream V plane. She was escorted into the plane by a man that she thought she recognized. She had a strange feeling; something wasn't right. It was too quiet. She finally figured out who the agent was a few minutes after the plane took off. She asked, "I know you, don't I?" He didn't say anything. She spoke up again. "You're the one they call The Ghost. You're only sent in to make sure the job us done right, so I guess we're not going to North Carolina."*

Finally, he spoke. "Very good. I was told to give you a message. 'The only outcome for traitors is death.' She was mad and yelled out, "Fuck you and fuck them!" He took out his gun, which had a silencer on it, and shot her twice. Her body fell out of the chair she was sitting in and rolled onto the floor of the airplane. Two other men dressed as FBI agents put her lifeless form in a body bag.

Gavin quickly pulled his phone out and called the supervising agent in the Witness Protection office. The agent answered and Gavin, in a panic, said, "Agent Burns, this is Gavin Donnelly. Where's Brenda Mason right now?"

"Gavin, you just can't stop working, can you? Brenda Mason is still here. She's not scheduled to leave until tonight …. wait a minute; this isn't right."

"What?"

"I have two sets of paperwork on her. One says they changed the time of her departure. It looks like she was sent out of here 30 minutes ago."

"Burns, can you call and tell them to hold her before she gets on the airplane?"

"Wish that I could, but the plane is already in the air. You want me to have them hold her when they land in Charlotte?"

Gavin sighed. "Don't bother; she won't be on that flight." He hung up. There was nothing he could do now.

∞∞∞∞∞∞∞∞∞∞∞∞

AD Foster was walking to his car in the parking garage when a man approached him. It was the same man that gave Gavin the warning not to take the case. He said to AD Foster, "You didn't do a very good job this time around of keeping Agent Donnelly and Agent Main off this case."

"Sending in AD Gasper to run things was supposed to have done that. Remember?"

"Why did you assign the case to Agent Main in the first place?"

"Because she and Agent Donnelly are the best agents in the Violent Crimes Division. I can't very well not assign them a case like this without looking suspicious. Besides, I warned you what would happen if they were put together. You underestimated Agent Donnelly, and you underestimated what he and Agent Main could accomplish by working together."

The man smiled. "I'm just giving you a reminder of the agreement you made. You have to do a better job the next time they're assigned a case that gets in the way of the bigger agenda."

[270]

AD Foster gave the man a serious look. "I don't need to be reminded of what I agreed to do, but you need to understand what you're getting with the both of them."

"Part of the equation can easily be removed, and that goes for everybody." AD Foster didn't reply to the empty threat as the man walked away. He just cursed under his breath, knowing that the storm was coming and that he would have to add to the destruction it brought.

∞∞∞∞∞∞∞∞∞∞

Both agents went to the memorial at St. Thomas. The church was packed. Although the body had not been officially released to the family, that wasn't going to delay a memorial service for one of the pillars of the community. Judge Henry Colin Doyle was well-respected in Chicago, not only by the law enforcement community, but even by the crooks that he fought to put away -- because he was fair. The President of the United States was there in Chicago to speak at the service. Henry Doyle was his friend and the right man, in his eyes, for the Supreme Court. Despite the tragedy, his life was celebrated. As the president spoke, he told the crowd about a man who was fair, tough, and would never back down from a fight, especially when it was morally right.

The service was great, even though ordinary citizens would never know how true it was when the president said Judge Doyle would never back down and stood up for what was right. Agent Donnelly and Agent Main knew the truth. The judge stood up to criminals and paid for it with his life, but the fight would not be in vain if Agent Donnelly had anything to say about it.

Later that evening, both agents ended up at Paddy Murphy's. Gavin was playing with his family. An Irish wake is party; that is all that can be said of it, except that death should never be mourned and life should always be celebrated. Paddy Murphy's was packed. One of the things Agent Main commented on was that Mickey Sorrano was there, and she wondered why. Gavin said to her,

"Even members of the mob pay their respects. Judge Doyle was liked on both sides of the law."

"Who is he talking to? That man looks familiar."

Gavin smiled. "That's Tommy McManus, head of the Irish Mob and connection to the IRA here in Chicago."

"The Italian mob and Irish mob are getting along?"

"Actually, they're friends. While the Irish and Italian mobs have not always gotten along in Chicago, those two men made a deal

[271]

many years ago when they took over their families. They both realized that they could each have a piece of Chicago and make money, and that bloodshed disrupted business. Besides, they all go to the same church. It's bad business to have a civil war in your church."

Agent Main laughed. Gavin led the way over to introduce her. It was strange that an FBI agent would be introduced to the mob as if they were old friends, but this was Chicago; strange went with the territory.

Tommy shook her hand and said, "I heard that Gavin got a new partner, but nobody mentioned that you were so pretty."

She smiled. "I doubt those were the real words Mickey used to tell you about me."

"Love, he did use those words … after he said you were a scary bitch."

Agent Main laughed. "Now that sounds more like it." Mickey shot Tommy a dirty look, but it was still funny. Agent Main considered it a compliment that she could scare a notorious Chicago mobster.

Tommy said to her before walking away, "Well, Agent Main, keep our boy here safe. Lord knows we don't need another dead Irishman."

"I'll do the best I can, but we all know how much trouble he is."

Tommy laughed. "That he is. It was nice meeting you, Agent Main. Hopefully we'll never have to meet under professional circumstances."

As the two mob figures left, Agent Main got a phone call. She had a contact in witness protection. The phone call was not good and the look on her face showed that. When she got off the phone, she looked at her partner. "That was my contact in WITSEC. They were taking Brenda Mason to North Carolina, but the plane never got there."

"Did the plane go down?"

"No, it went to Seattle instead, and Brenda Mason never checked in. She's missing."

Gavin now knew that what he saw was true. He replied, "I think she's probably dead."

"What makes you think so?"

"Because, in any conspiracy, you don't leave witnesses … and too many have ended up dead in this case."

Agent Main sighed. "Something else is weird, too. There were two sets of paperwork on Brenda Mason. The second set was delivered early this morning, causing confusion about what to do with her."

"Let me guess; only a handful of people knew where she was going and when she was leaving, and had the authority to change that?"

"Yes, this also means that the DOJ or WITSEC has a leak. Who are these people?"

"People who think they're above the law and can get away with anything."

She didn't say anything for a while. "We need to know what Judge Doyle has in Switzerland, but it would be too suspicious if we both went. Find someone you trust who can pretend to be your wife. Go there and find out what he had on these people."

Gavin, with a serious look, replied, "I think you're right. There are more answers that we don't have yet, and Switzerland may be our starting point."

She smiled and said, "Good night, Agent Donnelly."

"You know you can call me Gavin, right?"

She paused and then smiled again. "Alright then. I guess if you're nice enough, I will let you call me Rachel." Gavin smiled and watched her walk away. They were becoming friends.

∞∞∞∞∞∞∞∞∞∞∞

The wake went on for hours. There was lots of singing, drinking, and, of course, laughing. Gavin and the band were finishing up a song when he looked over at the door and saw Deputy Marshal Rogers walk into Paddy Murphy's. The pub was filled with cops Irish mob members, and IRA members. Everybody, for the most part, stopped what they were doing when he walked in. They all knew who he was, and saying he wasn't welcome there was an understatement.

As the band finished playing the song, Patrick, the bartender, reached underneath the bar and grabbed his 9 mm Beretta and cocked the hammer. He was preparing for trouble. Tommy McManus looked over at the marshal and then motioned to a couple of his guys to get their guns ready. Gavin noticed what was going on in the room. He quickly put his guitar down and walked over to the marshal. He didn't raise his voice, but he sternly told him, "Roger, you have a lot of nerve coming into this pub. You shouldn't be here."

Rogers was taken aback by the statement. He didn't think it was that big of a deal to come in and talk to Gavin. He replied, "Look, I don't want any trouble. I just came by to thank you for saving my life and to apologize for trying to hit you yesterday. I was angry and shouldn't have done that."

Gavin just gave him an angry look. "That's fine, Rogers, but you still need to leave before someone shoots you." Gavin saw

[273]

McManus' men coming toward the door where they were standing, drawing their guns. He held his hand up to them so they would stop, and told them, "No, don't. I have this."

Rogers asked Gavin, "I come here to apologize and I get a hostile welcome. What the fuck is with you people?" Gavin saw Patrick bring his gun up toward the marshal and he said to him, "Patrick, put the gun away. The marshal will be leaving; we don't need an incident." Then he turned back around and said to the marshal, "You're a traitor. What you did to Jimmy Flynn will get you killed around here."

"The man was a fugitive and I did my job. I caught him and took him back to prison."

"Jimmy only broke out to save his family from being murdered. When his son was killed, you didn't even have the decency to let him see the body or go to the funeral so he could mourn his dead son. Even our enemies are allowed to bury their dead."

"Criminals don't get that right."

"And that's why you're a traitor who deserves to be shot, and we would still let your loved ones mourn your death. Take this as the only warning you're going to get. If you ever come here again, you're going out feet first."

Rogers gave Gavin a dirty look. "You'd kill a federal marshal?"

Gavin smiled. "No, I wouldn't, but I would look the other way if they did it." He looked around the room as he finished the sentence. Every man there would've loved the chance to put the marshal down.

"You took an oath as a federal agent. This isn't very patriotic."

"Want to see how patriotic we are around here? Watch this." Gavin got back on stage, grabbed his guitar, and told the rest of the band what he was about to play. He said to the audience, "This is for the man who thinks we're not very patriotic." He started singing *God Bless Ireland*, the Republic of Ireland's first national anthem. Rogers stood there angrily while the entire pub sang loud and proud. After the first few verses and passes through the chorus, Gavin walked back over to Rogers and said, "Now get the fuck out of our pub!"

"If you want me dead, why did you save my life?"

"Professional courtesy. Besides, you don't deserve to die in the line of duty. Now get the fuck out of here."

Deputy Marshal Rogers walked out of the pub and could hear them singing from the street. He cursed the Irish in Chicago under his breath. Maggie Flynn walked over to Gavin and pulled him into the storage area by the door. She kissed him on the lips and then said to him, "Jimmy would have liked what you did, despite not wanting to talk to you."

"At least I can show him some respect."

She kissed him again. "I know you're not supposed to sleep with a prisoner's wife and that it's disrespectful, but I don't care. I still love you."

"And I never stopped loving you, but it's still stabbing him in the back. He has every right to hate me."

Maggie smiled. "I know. Am I still seeing you tonight?"

Gavin leaned in and kissed her. He replied, "Of course. The bed has been a little cold without you. I need something to warm it up."

She put her hand on his crotch and rubbed his dick through his pants. "I have just the remedy for that."

20

The room was dark and windowless, so no one could see what these men were doing. Stephen was sitting at the end of the conference table, waiting to be questioned by his colleagues. The murder of Judge Doyle had been his operation and, while it was a success, the very people who were set up to fail had been given too much information and had started to find the connections to the group. Finally, one of the men spoke up. "Stephen, you're here today because we have questions. First, how much did Brenda Mason tell the agents?"

Stephen took a sip of water. "We're still trying to find out. But she has been eliminated."

"She gave a deposition linking us to the murders. This is very, very bad."

"I realize that, but our plan is still intact. The new judge who will be assigned to this case will dismiss it like he's supposed to, and the deposition will disappear."

"That doesn't mean Agent Donnelly and Agent Main will stop looking."

"And what are they going to find? There are no more witnesses and no paper trail."

"But they will ask questions and keep searching until they find something."

Stephen smiled. "Let them ask questions. Their time is short, anyway. It won't matter in the months to come."

The other man had a curious look on his face. "What do you mean?"

"It means that we will clean up the situation and all traces will be gone. You have nothing to worry about."

"Stephen, we put you in the position you're in because we thought you could get results. Don't make us regret it, because we can easily find another that will protect the group better."

Stephen chuckled. "You don't have to remind me. We've had setbacks before and they've been taken care of; this one will be, too. My plan is already in the works."

"Good, because the last thing we need is this stubborn Irishman to find the connection to his parents' murders and seek revenge."

"You won't have to worry about that much longer."

∞∞∞∞∞∞∞∞∞∞∞

The next day, Agent Main decided to stop by St. Thomas Church. She was looking for Father Joseph. It was in between services, so there was no one in the church. She saw Father Joseph picking things off the pews and walked over. He smiled when he saw her. She said to him, "You told me, the night when you drove me back to my hotel, that when I was ready to talk, you would listen. I'm ready to tell you about my tragedy."

Father Joseph smiled. "You've come to the right place for forgiveness, but it only works if you're ready to forgive yourself. Take a seat and tell me what happened."

"This week, a suspect asked me about losing a child. Normally, I can block out what suspects and criminals say, but not this time."

"Why did it affect you so much?"

"It was Brenda Mason who told me this."

"And it bothered you that a woman known as a child killer would say this to you?"

Agent Main's eyes started to well up and she shed a few tears. "It bothered me because I did lose a child a few years ago ... it was a miscarriage. I was told that, if I had not been on the job, the stress wouldn't have caused me to miscarry. I feel like my job killed my baby."

Father Joseph put his hand on her shoulder and said, "Your job didn't do that, and it wasn't your fault."

"Are you going to tell me that it was God's plan?"

"No. I don't pretend to know what God's plan is for us. I just know that he loves us and that we're never given anything so hard that we cannot handle it or get past it."

"My marriage was ruined because of it."

"Maybe God has someone better for you, somebody that will love you through any tragedy. Did you ever think about that?"

Agent Main smiled. "Do you always look on the bright side?"

"It's my job."

"Maybe that's why I feel like I can talk to you and no one else ... not even my partner."

Father Joseph prayed with her and continued to talk to her about the burden in her heart. It's hard to lose a child, especially when you feel like it was completely your fault. It's never easy to love

[277]

through a tragedy and find strength to keep on living. Rachel Main was strong and intelligent, but she was far from perfect and could still feel pain and guilt. She was human.

∞∞∞∞∞∞∞∞

Dr. Schuman and Gavin didn't get a chance to meet during their regular time on Friday, so they decided to get a drink at the pub while Gavin waited for Haley O'Brian. They did the usual chitchat that people do when they haven't seen each other for a while. Finally, Gavin told him, "Something new happened to me this week."

Dr. Schuman looked curious. "Oh, what happened?"

"Normally, I don't see anything unless I touch something related to what I see. But twice now, all I had to do was hear a name and I saw what was happening to them."

"It means your other senses are coming along. Touch is usually the most sensitive of all the senses; that's why you used that one first when it comes to your gift. It was only a matter of time before you used another sense to see things."

Gavin smiled. "Does it mean anything if what I saw was focused on one person?"

"Who was it?"

"Brenda Mason."

"Your last case was a hard one, filled with lots of emotions. Emotion can heighten the senses. Perhaps your focus on her pushed you beyond your normal limits for seeing the future."

"If what you're saying is true, then any kind of emotion can trip a flash."

Dr. Schuman smiled. "It also means that, through emotions focused on something or someone, you might be able to control it; and eventually, all the senses will trip a flash."

Gavin laughed. "I guess this is the part where I get to think happy thoughts and hope that I can control what I see."

Smiling, Dr. Schuman said, "Actually, yes. The happier and calmer we are, the easier it is to focus. If your emotions are good, then you may just be able to control it. Anyway, it's something we should work on."

Haley O'Brian arrived at the pub to find Gavin Donnelly sitting in a booth with Dr. Shuman. Gavin saw her and told the doctor that they would have to cut this meeting short; he had other business. She smiled when she saw him; she had a bit of a crush on him. The doctor left and said hello to her on his way out. Haley asked, with that journalist's curiosity, "Who was that?"

[278]

Gavin replied, "Oh, just a friend. It's my neighborhood pub, so I know everybody."

"I got your email. What is this story of a lifetime that I can't turn down?"

He laughed and showed her the file folder that he and his partner had gotten from Judge Doyle's office, and a picture of his wall of conspiracy. "I can't give you any more information on the Doyle case. I've been suspended, so technically I can't even talk to you about the case. But I have something else for you: a bigger story and one that you will get to keep writing. You might even win a Pulitzer for it."

She was intrigued. "What is all this?" "The picture is something I've been working on, my wall of conspiracy; and also, stuff from my first case with Agent Main. The other is information from Judge Doyle on a Swiss bank account where he put secret information."

"What kind of information?"

"I think he was researching a conspiracy of sorts, and he had information on who really killed him. Whatever it is, it was the kind of information that can get you murdered and could not stay in the United States. I need your help to get it."

"What can I do?"

He showed her the transparent fingerprints and the passports. The passports didn't have photos, but had the judge's and his wife's names in them. "We have to be the Doyle's. It will take both of us to get into the safety deposit box. You get to be my pretend wife."

"So, you're taking me to Switzerland?"

"Do you want to find out what the judge was researching?"
She smiled. "Absolutely!"

"I have to warn you that it might be dangerous. People have ended up dead because of what they found out."

"I didn't get into this business to play it safe."

Gavin smiled. "Good girl. We leave on Monday."

Three days later, both of them were in Zurich, masquerading as a married couple. Every FBI agent who had been undercover at one point had an alias, and the IDs to go with that alias. Gavin's was David Bennett. He was able to get a fake passport for Haley; her alias was Sara Bennett. They used those names to get into the country. At the bank, they would be Henry and Elizabeth Doyle. They each had the transparent pads on their fingertips for the fingerprint identification at the bank. They walked into the bank and the service was great. They had access to gourmet coffee and good scotch. As customers, they were treated like royalty.

When they first arrived at the bank, Gavin and Haley showed the passports that identified them as the Doyle's. Next, they were led to a private room, where they had to give their fingerprint IDs. The last step was typing in a 12-digit password. Gavin had found a piece of paper with different dates on it in the folder that Judge Doyle put in his safe. The note Henry Doyle wrote looked like a piece of scratch paper with years scribbled on it, as if it were done by a historian. Gavin knew that it was a passcode made up of important dates from the research Judge Doyle had been doing. Haley was a little confused. He told her, "The passcode is the dates. You have to put them in order."

"How do you know?"

"My partner and I had a history lesson a few days ago; I recognize them from that. I think I know what order they are supposed to be in."

Gavin held out the piece of paper and typed into the computer: 1095 1119 1307. It worked; the password was authenticated. A large safety deposit box was brought out to them. Haley was excited. She had never been on an assignment like this before. Inside the box were numerous thick file folders; there was a great deal of research. There were government documents, pictures, writings, and lots of other information. Gavin knew that it would take days to go through and even longer to figure everything out. They started thumbing through the folders. Gavin spoke up. "This is amazing. The judge has research on companies connected to the Churchill Group and information on politicians. He's got historical information going back hundreds of years; it looks like he started digging really deep. This makes my wall of conspiracy look like a children's book."

"Do you recognize anything?"

"Some things, but I don't know where to begin. I mean, this information makes the judge look like a conspiracy nut; no wonder he couldn't keep it in the States. He may not have been confirmed for the bench if they knew about this. But I think there are answers in here. It's just a matter of finding them."

Haley pulled out a picture of the red skull with eyes. "Have you ever seen anything like this before?"

"Yes. Something like it was left at the crime scene. I think it's a threat."

Haley read the quote on the picture. "You can never escape, for death is always watching."

Gavin looked at her. "Sounds like a warning, doesn't it?"

"A very scary warning."

Gavin started pulling the files out of the box and putting them in the backpack he brought. "Come on, let's get out of here. We have a lot of reading to do."

"Are we going to take any breaks?"

Gavin smiled and then leaned in to kiss Haley. That got her excited. He told her, "Of course. Just because you're a pretend wife doesn't mean everything has to be pretend. You won't even need underwear during our breaks." Haley kissed him passionately, making the sensitive parts of their bodies shiver.

While that was happening in Zurich, Switzerland, a mysterious stranger walked down the hall toward Gavin Donnelly's apartment. It was after midnight and dark in the hallway. The stranger was trying to avoid being noticed. He had a delivery for Gavin. It was a black postcard displaying a red skull with eyes. He slid it underneath the door face up, so Gavin would see it when he first walked in the door. It was a message for Agent Gavin Donnelly. You can never escape, for death is always watching.

30 MINUTES

A SOLDIER'S SONG

BOOK 3

1

John O'Kelly had never liked flying. Maybe it had something to do with being a fisherman's son. He grew up to the feel of the sea off Galway Bay, working on the boat alongside his father and trying to make a living the only way O'Kelly's knew how. He definitely liked the feel of the sea. Plane rides just made him feel like shit, yet he took at least a dozen flights a year to the United States. Normally, a few glasses of whiskey could make John feel at ease while flying across the Atlantic, but this trip was probably the most important he would have to make this year.

As the Deputy Chief of Staff to the President of Sinn Fein, the Irish political group, he was the contact between the political party and the Army Council of the IRA. He was also the liaison between Sinn Fein and the Irish Mob in the U.S., which still raised money for Irish Relief and weren't just petty criminals. When he came to the United States, it usually meant that he had important news to deliver and reports to receive on the state of things in America. But this trip was different; this was a secret meeting, the kind he didn't want the FBI, Interpol, or ATF to know about. John O'Kelly knew that the authorities kept tabs on him and he usually didn't keep it a secret that he was meeting with those that the government considered criminals or terrorists. This meeting had to be kept under the radar because he was carrying a secret letter from the Prime Minister of Great Britain. If the authorities (or anybody, for that matter) found out he had it and where it was going, then the whole plan would be ruined; and there was too much at stake to let that happen.

John O'Kelly flew from London under his alias, George Stewart. He disguised himself as an investment banker; a perfect fit for New York City, which is where he was heading. He knew nobody would ask questions with that particular alias, especially if he had a driver, and Customs never questioned anything. The driver, however, was a member of Real IRA and the car came fully-loaded; it had everything you would need to hold off a small army. It was already nighttime when O'Kelly got to New York, and he didn't make any stops before arriving at a warehouse behind O'Malley's Irish Pub on the Lower East Side of New York. He was meeting with the heads of the Irish Mob from around the country; they were the real Irish Mob, also known as the IRA Commission. These men may have been criminals, but they weren't two-bit, petty criminals who had loyalty just to themselves. They were loyal to the cause; they were loyal to Ireland. One of the members at that meeting was Tommy McManus, head of the Irish Mob in Chicago.

John O'Kelly was escorted into the warehouse by his driver, who also acted as his bodyguard. There was a long conference table in the middle of the room where all the heads of the Irish Mob sat, drinking whiskey and beer. O'Kelly said hi to everybody, making the usual cordial greetings for these kinds of meetings. When he shook Tommy McManus's hand, Tommy was the one to ask him the question that was on everyone's mind.

"While it's good to see you, and I'm sure everybody in the room feels the same, why have we been called to a meeting that has to be kept secret? And why the urgency of the meeting?"

John looked around the room and saw the same expression on everyone's face: the look of suspicious curiosity. His smile turned serious. "We have an offer from the British government to return Northern Ireland to the Republic of Ireland."

The rest of the room was stunned at the news. Nobody said anything for a few moments. Michael Delaney, who was head of the Irish Mob in New Jersey, spoke up. "How serious is this? We have had these kinds of offers before."

John looked at him. "This offer is as serious as it gets." He pulled out a letter that was folded shut with an official seal. He put it in the middle of the table so everybody could see the seal. It was Tommy McManus who spoke up and commented on it. "It's the official seal of the prime minister! Where did you get this?"

"From the man himself," John said, looking at Tommy sternly. "There was a secret meeting last week with the prime minister, other heads of the British government, President of the Republic and the President of Sinn Fein. The prime minister offered his terms. In fact, he was the one that called that meeting." John O'Kelly told them that last part to drive the point home about how serious this offer was. The room was taken aback by the news. Tommy opened the letter and read it, and then passed it around so everybody could see how real this was.

John O'Kelly got right down to it when it came to the stipulations. "The prime minister feels very strongly that this can happen, but there are conditions. The most important is that the illegal sale of guns and military-grade weapons has to be stopped in all of the United Kingdom, which also means that any sale in the U.S. cannot enter the Republic of Ireland." The room filled with rage; there wasn't a man in the room that wasn't angry about what the prime minister wanted. It was basically telling the army that they could not have weapons or even try to get weapons. He was basically demanding that Ireland disarm. Finally, somebody in the room asked, "And what about the British? Will they just pack up and leave?"

John said, "Yes, that's what they're proposing."

"Bullshit! It's the British; they can't be trusted," Michael Delaney responded.

"I know," John replied. "But this is the closest we've ever come to getting Ireland back, and the only British entity that will remain is an embassy. So everything is on the table when it comes to this deal."

Tommy replied, "They want us to throw down our guns and we're supposed to just trust that they will leave?"

"Yes."

"That's a big leap of faith, even if we have a signed letter from the prime minister. What else do they want?"

"Mostly minor details, but there is one other major stipulation. A new energy company wants to be able to drill for oil and natural gas in Northern Ireland. They are based in London, but they will hire mostly Irish workers. They just want to be allowed to come into Ireland."

A voice yelled from the back of the room, "Fuck the British! All they want is another way to rape our land and take advantage of our people." Most of the people in the room seemed to agree with him.

John O'Kelly replied, "Yes, it seems like the same old tricks played by the British government, but how long have we fought for an all-free Ireland? We have to ask ourselves, what are we willing to do to get it? Violent revolution didn't work, and the peace accord isn't really that much of a peace is it?"

Tommy asked, "How do the others feel about this?"

"Both the President of the Republic and Sinn Fein are prepared to move on this, but they won't do it without a vote from the Commission. That's why I am here."

Finally, Conner O'Malley, the head of the New York Irish Mob, spoke up. "We will need a day to discuss this. Half our business will be gone once we give up gun distribution in Ireland. This is a serious matter."

John O'Kelly looked at Conner. "I will be here for a couple of days, but all of you have to vote by tomorrow and no one can abstain. The party and the Army Council have to give their responses to the prime minister by week's end." The letter was left in the room so the men could read it more closely as they discussed the matter. O'Kelly went inside the pub to get a beer.

The Commission debated the issue for hours and tried to come to some sort of consensus, but by midnight there was still no answer. O'Kelly decided to head back to his hotel; he was tired. He couldn't find his driver, but one of the New York boss's lieutenants offered to give him a ride. O'Kelly was too tired and drunk to say no. He was helped into the town car and driven a few blocks before the car turned into an alley and stopped. O'Kelly asked the driver, "Why have we stopped? Is everything okay?"

The driver turned around to face O'Kelly, who was sitting in the backseat. "Everything will be." Then he used a mini blow dart gun and shot O'Kelly with a poisonous dart. As O'Kelly started to pass out, he uttered, "Why?" The driver replied, as O'Kelly fell face down in the backseat of the car, "Because you want peace." O'Kelly was out cold and slowly dying. The driver got out of the car and pulled the body out of it, laying it down among the trash along the building walls. He emptied O'Kelly's pockets and then he pulled out a knife. He still had more work to do before disappearing into the night. After a few minutes, when he was done, he pulled a pre-paid cell phone from his pocket and made a call.

∞∞∞∞∞∞∞∞∞∞∞∞

Stephen was sitting at the round table, impatiently waiting. He kept looking at his phone, expecting it to ring any minute. He was nervous but he didn't let it show in front of the other men that were sitting in the room. There was a lot riding on this deal. Finally, the phone rang and Stephen nearly jumped out of his seat.. The person on the other end said to him, "It's done, sir."

Stephen smiled. "Good. Did you find it?"

"It's with the others. He let them look at it. I will have a better chance of getting it after their meeting is over."

"Make sure you get it … then destroy it. The existence of that document can't happen."

"Understood. It will be taken care of."

[286]

Stephen hung up the phone and turned to the other men in the room. "Step one is complete."

One of the men in the room replied, "You really think this is going to work?"

Stephen smirked at him. "If you want the FBI agent out of the way without using murder, then we have to do it this way."

"But how many people do we have to kill to accomplish that?"

"Don't tell me that you're getting remorseful all of a sudden!"

"More dead bodies lead to more investigations, which can expose us."

Stephen smiled confidently. "That's why you have me to take care of details like that."

An older man with silver hair turned his chair around and responded, "Enough with the chit-chat, ladies. The only thing we want to know is, will you succeed this time? I personally don't have any more patience when it comes to your failures. You can always be replaced."

Stephen gave the old man a serious look. "Remember, I didn't get to this position because of my failures. The agent will be dealt with … accordingly."

2

It was early in the morning for Gavin. You would think that, with being on suspension, he would sleep in late and take a vacation, but he still had plenty of work to keep him busy. He was shuffling through files on his coffee table while sipping on a cup of coffee. Haley O'Brien came out of his bedroom wearing his button-down shirt. She had missed him in bed, but she understood that, as pretty as she might be, he was more curious about those files. They were Judge Henry Colin Doyle's secret files and there was a lot of information to go through. Most of it didn't make any sense. Haley poured herself a cup of coffee and then walked over to the couch where Gavin was sitting and kissed him good morning. "Have you made any headway in deciphering these files?"

Gavin laughed. "Very little, but I did find this." He showed her a list of companies with numbers written beside them. "I think these companies are somehow connected to Wright Ship Industries and P & M Electronics, the other companies the judge was investigating before his murder."

"What makes you think so?"

"He made a list of these companies and wrote these numbers next to them."

"Do you know what they mean?"

"They're case numbers. These companies must have lawsuits pending, and the only way the judge would be interested is if they were similar to ones he was already investigating."

"Good point. Or maybe they're just similar in nature without actually being connected to Wright Ship Industries or P & M."

Gavin smiled. "Interesting. We have to find the connection between all of these companies. What makes them special?"

"I guess that's a good place to start this investigation of ours."

"As good a place as any!"

Haley was looking at the files and saw one marked 'Ireland.' She was curious and asked Gavin about it. He picked it up and opened the file. Inside were a map and a memo from a company called H & M Mining. Haley asked, "Do you know what this is a map of?"

"It's somewhere in Northern Ireland from what I can tell… but this H & M Mining, I've never heard of that company before. As soon as I get back to the FBI from suspension, I can do a background check on the company and see if there is anything suspicious about it."

Before Haley could respond, Gavin's cell phone rang. It was his Uncle Liam. He listened to what he had to say, and the surprised look on his face told Haley that it must be important. When the phone call was done, Gavin looked at her and said, "We'll have to discuss all of this later. I have to go."

She looked concerned. "What is it? Is everything okay?"

"I hope, but probably not. I have just been asked to sit down with the Irish Mob."

That was all he said to her. He took a quick shower and left for Paddy Murphy's Irish Pub.

He arrived about 20 minutes later to find Liam Donnelly, in his police captain's uniform, sitting next to Tommy McManus, head of the Irish Mob in Chicago. Both of them were drinking a Guinness. Both men had drunk a beer with each other before. Some might even say that they were friends, but Gavin had never seen his uncle sit down with a member of the mob for a friendly visit while in uniform. This made the meeting more official and, somehow, Gavin knew that this meeting didn't have anything to do with illegal activities in Chicago. He walked over to the table where they were sitting. "Normally, I would say this is a conspicuous meeting: a cop in uniform and a mobster having a beer together… but this is Chicago!" Both men laughed at the comment. "So, why do you want to see me?"

Liam spoke up. "Tommy called me to see if you could help find out something through FBI resources. It's an Irish matter." That really piqued Gavin's interest. Usually, when he heard the phrase "an Irish matter," it meant something political that could cause a lot of tension in the Irish community; not only in Chicago, but also across the sea.

Gavin took a seat at the table in front of the Guinness beer that was waiting for him. "Okay, what do I need to find out?"

Tommy spoke up. "We need to know what the FBI knows about the assassination of John O'Kelly. It happened the other night in New York City." Gavin looked surprised. "He was found dead in New York?"

"Found stabbed to death in an alley, two blocks from O'Malley's Pub."

"Did he have all of his belongings on him?"

Tommy winced at the question. "No."

"Sounds like a robbery-homicide more than an assassination. I'm assuming he was in the States to meet with the Commission?"

Tommy didn't like to talk about the Commission in front of law enforcement, especially an FBI agent, even though the Commission wasn't really a secret. He replied, "Yes, but he didn't come to the States under his real name. Because of the nature of the meeting, we have reason to believe it's an assassination. He has a second passport, a second identity for when he needs to come here in secret and hide from the eyes of the FBI."

Gavin smiled at the last part. "Okay, if this was a secret meeting, with what I can only guess had the highest importance, was there anybody there that you don't trust? Someone who would have benefited from killing John O'Kelly?"

Tommy paused for a moment. "We think we might have a traitor."

"His driver ... he did have a driver, right?"

"Yes, he had a driver, but the driver didn't take him anywhere from the pub. Somebody else was driving."

"Do you know who?"

Tommy frowned. "Unfortunately, no. Nobody saw who drove him."

"So, whoever drove him is most likely the traitor you're talking about. Just out of curiosity, why was O'Kelly here?"

McManus paused for a moment. "He was meeting the Commission. I'm assuming you know what that is?"

Gavin chuckled. "Yes, I know what it is. The FBI still keeps tabs on you." McManus laughed and then Gavin asked, "Just out of curiosity, what was the meeting with the Commission about?"

Tommy McManus didn't want to answer, but Gavin wouldn't let it go. He asked the question again. Finally, McManus replied, "Is it relevant?"

"Only if you're the traitor, Tommy."

McManus didn't know what to say to that, but he still didn't want to answer the question. Liam spoke up. "Tommy, you have to trust him if he's going to trust you. He has a right to know."

Tommy McManus started to talk. "He came to New York with a secret letter from the Prime Minister of Great Britain. We know it was real because it had the PM's official seal and signature. He wants to negotiate a new peace accord where Northern Ireland is returned to the Republic of Ireland. Before he can officially announce it, he secretly reached out to Sinn Fein, to the Army Council, and to the Commission to see where everyone came down on the issue. Before a decision can be made on negotiating a new peace agreement, the Commission and the Army Council have to vote on whether or not to accept the offer. O'Kelly was here to get a decision from the Commission."

Gavin was astonished by what he was being told. He responded, "England wants to return Northern Ireland to the Republic? Is this a serious offer?"

"Apparently it is."

"I can't believe it! After all these years, it's the Brits who are offering it first. Now I can see why you think O'Kelly's murder is more than a robbery gone bad."

McManus took a sip of beer. "This is why we need to know if the feds have any leads on who killed him or if they're just going to sweep it under the rug."

"How do you know the FBI has the body?"

"We tried to get the body from the NYPD so we could send it back to Ireland, but within hours of the police getting it from the crime scene, the FBI claimed it. Of course, we can't find out anything from the feds."

Gavin took a big sip of beer. "I'm curious: how did you vote?"

That was another thing Tommy McManus didn't want to answer, but he did. "I voted yes."

"And what are you guys having to give up for Northern Ireland to be free?"

McManus paused. "We have to give up illegal arms sales in the United Kingdom."

"And you still voted yes?"

McManus smiled. "I may be a two-bit mafia hood, but I'm a patriot first. I'll die to see an all-free Ireland."

Gavin smiled and finished his beer. "Please understand that I can't get in the middle of another agent's investigation, especially while I'm suspended, but I can make some inquiries."

"We appreciate it."

"Also, remember: I won't tell you what the FBI has on all of you. I won't violate my oath, but I will help in any way I can to see this peace agreement go through from your end, without interference from those who don't want it."

McManus was about to say something snide or even remind Gavin how they helped him in his first year as an agent when he made the worst mistake of his career, but Liam stopped him. He said, "Don't. He's not wrong. I take my oath as a police officer seriously, too. Don't forget any of that just because we're all sitting here having a beer together." McManus didn't finish his sentence. Instead, he removed two first-class plane tickets from his sport coat. He gave Gavin a serious look. "I have two plane tickets here for you and your partner, heading for New York City tomorrow. Please find out what you can. Now you know how serious this is."

Gavin smiled. "I don't know if I can accept those tickets from somebody like you. If I get suspended again, I'll be out of the FBI. But under the circumstances that may be the least of my worries." He grabbed the tickets, shook hands with the two men and left. He had to visit his partner earlier than he'd planned after they got suspended.

∞∞∞∞∞∞∞∞∞∞∞

Rachel Main finished moving the last of her boxes into her new apartment, but she was far from being completely moved. She hadn't put anything on the walls yet. She hadn't even unpacked any dishes and there were still a few empty boxes of takeout food sitting on her kitchen counter. Her new home wasn't really a home at all, but she was getting settled in Chicago and not living in a hotel anymore. That was a big step for her. Suddenly, there was a knock at the door. It was little surprising, considering no one really knew she was in the new apartment. She answered the door and found her partner on the other side. She was a bit shocked to see him and it showed in her tone of voice.

"Hi. What are you doing here? I thought we weren't going to see each other until our suspension was over."

Gavin laughed. "I know we agreed to that, but I have a favor to ask."

Rachel let him inside her new apartment. "Okay, but if I have to do you a favor, then you have to move the heavy boxes in my apartment." Gavin smiled and nodded in agreement. Rachel spoke up again. "So, how did you find out where I moved to?"

"I'm an FBI agent, remember? I can figure these things out."

"You called the office and got my new address, didn't you?"

Gavin looked as if he had just been caught with his hands in the cookie jar. "Okay, I might have done that, too. Besides, I needed to get a police report from the FBI database."

"Does this have to do with the favor you're about to ask me?"

"Yes. Do you know who John O'Kelly is?"

Rachel thought about it for a moment as she was getting a Guinness for her partner. "The name sounds familiar." Gavin smiled at the fact that his partner knew him that well and automatically gave him a beer. He replied, "Thank you."

[292]

"You always seem to think better during an investigation when you have one, and I can already tell that you've got a new investigation going on in your head. So, remind me who John O'Kelly is."

"He's the Special Assistant and Chief of Staff to James McAdams, the president of Sinn Fein, and also the point of contact between the Irish Commission and the IRA. He was found murdered in New York City a couple of days ago after a meeting with the Commission." Rachel was interested, so she asked Gavin to give her the details. Gavin told her what he knew so far. When he was done, Rachel said the same thing he did when Tommy McManus told him about the O'Kelly's murder.

"Gavin, I'm sure you already know that it sounds like a typical robbery-homicide and that there's no reason to ask any more questions about this."

"That's what I said when I was first told. You know what?"

"What?"

"A guy like this always has a bodyguard and someone always knows where he is. Nobody saw him leave and his regular driver wasn't the one who took him from the pub."

Rachel sighed. "Okay, that is odd, but what if he was drunk and stumbled out of the pub and then got robbed?"

"I'm not saying that it's not a possibility, and of course that's what the NYPD report said, but trust me; they wouldn't have let him leave on his own, wandering through New York City drunk out of his mind."

Rachel finished the beer she was drinking. "That's a good point. So, what do you need from me?"

"Come to New York with me so we can use some of your old contacts at the Bureau to find out what they know about O'Kelly's murder."

"We're almost off suspension and you want to get in the middle of another agent's investigation. Are you out of your mind?"

"I'm not trying to solve their case for them. I just want to ask a few questions based on how it pertains to my case, and that's how I'll put it."

"What case? It's the same case."

"Not exactly. I haven't told you why O'Kelly was in town. This is really going to shock you … it did me."

Rachel asked why. Gavin replied, "The Prime Minister of Great Britain sent a letter to the party and the Army Council about his intention to give Northern Ireland back to the Republic Ireland. O'Kelly came to the States to deliver that letter to the Irish Mob Commission. Before the party can negotiate a peace accord for the return of Northern Ireland, the Commission has to approve it, along with the Army Council and the party."

Rachel was a little shocked. "Are you serious? That's a very big deal for the Irish."

"It's what we fight for, and it's just as important as America's own revolution."

"Why does the Commission have to approve any kind of peace accord?"

"Because of gun business and IRA funds that get raised here in America."

Rachel never knew that; in fact, most FBI agents didn't. It was a highly-guarded secret outside the Irish community. Gavin said to her, "You see why this is important?"

"I can see that. Did the Commission vote?"

"Yes, they did. The majority of them voted in favor of the new peace accord, where Northern Ireland would be returned."

Rachel gave her partner a serious look. "I guess if this turns out to be something other than a normal robbery-homicide, it would be bad."

"Very bad, and I wouldn't ask for your help if it wasn't important."

Rachel smiled. "I know, and I didn't join the FBI to play it safe with my career. You're right to be suspicious about this, so let's go find out if there's more to it."

"Thanks."

"When do you want to leave?"

Gavin pulled out the plane tickets and showed them to his partner. She smiled. "First class. How did you get these tickets? We're FBI agents, so I know you can't afford them. Do I want to know where you got them?"

Gavin laughed. "It's better not to ask."

"Okay then. I will put a call in to a friend of mine there and see if we can get some time with him."

Gavin reached out and took her hand. "Thank you."

∞∞∞∞∞∞∞∞∞∞∞∞

Tom O'Casey was sitting at his desk in the office of Sinn Fein, going through the mail, when he spotted a package that had been sent overnight to the president. He opened the FedEx package and found another package marked, "For your eyes only." He put everything down and immediately took the package to James McAdams. With it being marked the way it was, he knew it was very important. The president was in his office, sipping tea and reading some reports.

O'Casey walked in and said, "Sir, you have something from America. It's urgent."

McAdams looked a little startled when he was handed the package. He opened it up and found two pieces of paper. One was the NYPD police report on the murder of John O'Kelly. The report said it was a robbery-homicide, but McAdams had a deep suspicion that there was more to it. The other piece of paper had the results of the vote from the Commission. He wanted to be happy about that, but his good friend had been murdered and he knew better than to think it was just an accident. He handed the pieces of paper to O'Casey so he could see what they said and then said, "Assemble the Army Council. This is real now and we have work to do. Get a reply written and sent out to the prime minister."

He wanted to shed a tear for his friend, or at least raise a glass of whiskey in his name, but he knew that now wasn't the time. They had a chance at peace, real peace in Ireland, but there were too many out there that didn't want it to happen; they had already made the first move.

3

Gavin Donnelly never realized how busy O'Hare International Airport was. He could always avoid the line by flashing his FBI badge; but this time, he and his partner were just regular passengers. They had to endure the long lines and uncomfortable pat-downs by the TSA. Now they both understood why so many people complained about the security at airports and the U.S. government slowly taking away the rights of citizens. However, they got through the security checkpoints and boarded a plane headed for New York City. Gavin tried to recall if he had ever flown first-class before. The government would never spring for something like that, even for a decorated FBI agent.

Agent Donnelly and Agent Main got settled, masquerading as a rich married couple going on vacation, so no one would be the wiser. After the plane took off, Gavin finally asked, "Did you hear back from your friend in the New York office?"

Rachel answered, "I did, but he didn't say much… only that they won't have the body for much longer. Homeland Security is taking it."

"Why?"

"He didn't say."

"Did you get any other information from him?"

"Not really, which is kind of strange."

"Why is that?"

Rachel chuckled. "He's always been too chatty, giving more details about things than he really should. If this murder really was a routine robbery-homicide, then why wouldn't he tell me everything over the phone?"

"So you're saying that he's not telling you everything on purpose."

She smiled at Gavin. "Exactly!" Gavin didn't respond to that. He just pondered what she said because it confirmed what he already knew: nothing was what it seemed with this murder. Rachel changed the subject. She was going to ask about Switzerland when they got back from suspension, but now was as good a time as ever. "I was wondering, did you find anything in Switzerland?"

Gavin smiled. "As a matter of fact, we did."

"We?"

"I took Haley O'Brian with me as my cover wife. I figured, with her research skills and her being a friend in the media, she could be useful."

Rachel laughed. "Was that the only way she could be useful?"

Gavin smiled. "I plead the fifth on that. But we did find a lot of material that Judge Doyle had been collecting and we're still trying to make sense of it. I'm sure it will be useful if we can figure it out."

"Did you find any answers about our last case?"

"Only a list of other companies, like P & M Electronics and Wright Ship Industries that went under because of stock fraud. The judge must have found similar companies, but stock fraud is the only link between them."

Rachel looked at her partner and said, "When we get back, we can take a look at it together and see if we can find any other link between them. After all, we do have another week before we're back at work; might as well get some work done on our little side investigation."

"If you're going to help, there are other things I should probably tell you."

"Save it for another time."

A few hours later, the agents arrived at the New York office. They were going to meet Rachel's friend at the Bureau, Agent Nick Caster. They worked together for a few years when Agent Main was in New York. Rachel always thought he was a good agent, but she was obviously better and that's why she got promoted to the Washington office, becoming one of the FBI's rising stars. Sure, they had a competitive rivalry when they worked together, but they remained friends as well as colleagues that could be counted on when needed.

As they were walking into the building, Rachel said to her partner, "I know you have a ton of questions, but please, let me take the lead here. He's not going to like you."

"Why do you say that?"

"Because you can be kind of overbearing when you have questions about a case, especially when your instincts are right."

"Are you saying that he's going to be threatened by me?"

"He won't like somebody that's smarter than he is. He hated me for the longest time when we worked together. And keep in mind, this is a courtesy; no agent likes another agent questioning his judgment or trying to poach his case."

"Do I get to ask any questions?"

"Sure, but let me start."

Gavin shook his head in disapproval, but he also knew she was right… something he would not admit out loud. The agents walked through security and had to get visitor passes, since they were still on suspension. But they easily got through security and found Agent Caster on the fourth floor. He smiled when he saw Rachel. "Agent Main, I was wondering if you would ever come back and visit the old stomping ground."

She laughed. "Well, I had to get suspended to get the time to come out for a visit."

"Yeah, I heard about that, but you caught the bad guys and that's what counts. So, how's Chicago?"

"I'm still trying to get used to it, but it's not as bad I thought it would be. Agent Caster, this is my partner, Agent Gavin Donnelly." Gavin reached out and shook Agent Caster's hand, telling him that it was nice to meet him. After the small talk was done, Agent Caster went back to his desk and pulled out the file on John O'Kelly and led his visitors into the conference room so they could discuss everything. Rachel told him as they were walking into the conference room, "Thank you for doing this. We really appreciate it."

Agent Caster replied, "No problem, but I don't know what else you can find in this case. It seems pretty straightforward; just a typical robbery-homicide." He pulled out the photos of the body and laid them out on the table. Gavin picked a few of them up and took a long look. He was trying to find a pattern in the stab wounds, but he couldn't see anything. While he was looking at the photos, Rachel spoke up. "Agent Caster, the police report said that O'Kelly was found two blocks away from O'Malley's Pub. Did you guys question anybody from the pub to see who he might have left with?"

"A couple of us went down there to ask more questions after the police did. They didn't talk to either of us."

"You think they knew who he left with and just weren't talking to the Feds?"

"If they did, they're not talking and that's as good as not seeing anything, so it's a dead end. But there isn't anything for us to know, anyway! We have no leads and Homeland Security is taking over."

"So, that's the extent of your investigation?"

"Like I said, it's a routine robbery-homicide."

Gavin finally said something. "I don't think so, Agent Caster."

Caster looked at Gavin. "What makes you think so?"

"The police report said the muggers took everything off the body, right?"

"Yeah, so?"

"Well, look at the photo." Gavin showed Agent Caster and his partner one of the photos. "They didn't take his cross."

"It's not worth anything, so why would they take it?"

"Actually, it is worth something. It has gold and silver in it; to any mugger or junkie looking to get a few bucks, it's worth taking. The cross was left on purpose."

Rachel spoke up before Agent Caster could say anything. "Why would they leave only that?"

"I think the man who killed O'Kelly is deeply religious and views the cross as a sacred artifact, something that O'Kelly would take with him to the afterlife."

Agent Caster replied, "I guess what you're going to say is, it's a clue."

Gavin was sarcastic. "What would you call it? Of course it's a clue! This wasn't some random robbery-homicide."

"That so-called clue doesn't prove anything."

"Then why is Homeland Security claiming the body?"

"Because he was a terrorist who was murdered on American soil."

Gavin shot Agent Caster a dirty look. "Be very careful who you label a terrorist. This man has never killed anybody, built a bomb to kill anybody, raged war on the innocent, and certainly hasn't taken up arms against the United States. He has fought for Irish freedom, through peace and through the political system, against a country that has occupied his nation for hundreds of years. Just because one of our allies labels him a terrorist doesn't mean the United States has to have the same moronic opinion. Besides, the historical record will always show that the British only label people terrorists who come from the countries they've invaded… illegally."

Agent Caster angrily started, "How dare you, you son of a bitch…"

Rachel cut him off before he could finish the sentence. "Alright, you two, this isn't a dick-measuring contest. You have different views on the matter; just leave it at that."

Gavin and Agent Caster didn't say anything to each other after that. They just stared at one another with angry looks as if they were trying to see who would blink first. Rachel diffused the tension by asking Agent Caster if they could see the body before it was taken by Homeland Security. He was angry, but agreed to the request. He called down to the morgue to let them know that they would have two visitors, but he didn't go down with Gavin and Rachel. Agent Caster didn't like Gavin, especially after his judgment was questioned.

As the agents got on the elevator that led to the basement, Rachel looked at her partner with disgust. "You didn't have to slam the breaks on him so hard. I know he's not the best of agents and not as smart as you, but he did us a favor today."

Gavin shook his head. "I wasn't mad because he was wrong. It pisses me off when narrow-minded assholes like him label Irishmen terrorists."

"Ok, I get that, but can you try to hold your temper? We're not even supposed to be here asking about this case, remember?"

Gavin apologized and then the elevators opened up. They were in the morgue. Gavin noticed that the New York office had better facilities, but the doctor on duty wasn't nearly as good-looking as Dr. Kenrick back in Chicago. The doctor in the morgue looked up, saw the agents, and then walked over to introduce himself. "Hello, I'm Dr. Morris. I was told you two would be coming down. You're from the Chicago office?"

Gavin replied, "Yes, we are."

"Ah, you must know Dr. Kenrick. She worked here right after graduating from the Academy. Brilliant student."

Rachel responded as she looked at her partner sarcastically, "My partner knows her better than I do. He has better insight about how gifted she can be." Gavin shot her a dirty look, but she wasn't wrong. Gavin asked the first question. "So, doc, what can you tell us about the body?"

He led the agents over to the freezers and pulled out the body. He looked at the agents and said, "There's not much to tell. He was stabbed multiple times, but there's no pattern to the marks. I can tell you that whoever did this was right-handed and he wasn't sloppy."

Rachel asked, "What do you mean?"

"His hands were steady, Agent Main. He's done this before and has good control, much like a surgeon. I would also say that he probably is an older man or woman and is not squeamish about blood or death. Mainly, he has the control of an older man."

Gavin asked, "Do you think he or she is a surgeon, or has some kind of medical training?"

The doctor responded, "I would say the killer has some medical knowledge, but if he were a surgeon, then the cuts wouldn't be so random like this. He would know where to cut or stab to kill somebody."

"He could have done what he did just to cover up his surgical knowledge, so it's still possible that it could be a surgeon."

The doctor smiled, chuckling at the questioning. "Anything is possible, Agent Donnelly, but here is the astonishing thing: the stab wounds didn't kill him, so you may have a good point."

Rachel asked, "What killed him?"

"He was poisoned. We ran a toxicology test and found an LSD-like substance. Enough was injected into his body to make him overdose."

Gavin and Rachel were surprised by the news. The doctor continued, "We found a puncture mark in the neck that was put there with some force, and then it was opened more when the killer put a second needle into the wound."

Rachel said to her partner, "We've seen that kind of killing before, haven't we?" Gavin nodded in agreement while he remembered the first case they worked on together and the assassin they came across.

The doctor spoke up again. "I guess the killer could be a surgeon or a doctor, but I don't think you're looking for Jack the Ripper."

Gavin asked, "Why do you say that?"

"Agent Donnelly, we're doctors with egos. If we have surgical talent, we want to show it off, and the killer did the opposite of that. He or she may have medical training, but he's no Jack the Ripper. You two deal with the behavior of the killer… wouldn't you agree?"

Rachel smiled. "You have a point, doctor." Gavin walked over to a table and found a tray with the victim's Gaelic cross. He picked it up and that's when he flashed. It had been a while since that happened.

The young man, dressed in a leather coat and half-shaven, walked up to a hot dog stand. There were old, run-down buildings all around the area. There was another man standing there, eating a hot dog. He was the first thing Gavin recognized in the vision. It was the man in black who warned him to stay away from the last case, the man in the park who used Shakespeare as a hidden code for Gavin to find. The young man in the leather coat walked to the man and handed him a letter. The letter was folded, so he couldn't see what it was. The man in black handed the young man an envelope with what Gavin could only assume was a case. The man in black said, "Thank you for bringing me the letter so fast. I can't let this fall into the wrong hands.

Before Gavin could finish, the sound of two people coming out of the elevator brought him back to the current moment. He and his partner were surprised by the visitors, but as it turned out, they were Homeland Security agents. Gavin quickly stashed the cross into his pocket before anybody could see. One of the Homeland Security agents spoke up. "Okay, you two are done here. This is a Homeland Security matter now. You're not authorized to be here." Gavin wanted to say something, but Rachel saw that he was about to speak up and she just shook her head at him. He followed the advice and didn't say anything. They thanked the doctor for his time and walked out of the morgue.

4

The President of the United States was sitting in the Oval Office sipping his second cup of coffee when David, his Chief of Staff, came into the room. He had a serious expression on his face when the president looked up. He asked his Chief of Staff,

"David, what's wrong? You look like somebody just died. Is everything okay?"

He finally smiled and replied to the president, "Actually, this may be a bit of good news." He walked over to the president, who was sitting behind his desk, and handed him a folder. "Sir, we got a secret cable from the Prime Minister of Great Britain. They are in negotiations with the Irish Prime Minister and Sinn Fein for the return of Northern Ireland back to the Republic."

The president got excited. "Really, is this true? It's been confirmed?"

"Yes, Mr. President. The cable and the authentication report from the CIA are in the folder." The president looked over everything and then asked, "What do they want from us?"

"They haven't said much up to this point, but according to the Prime Minister, they are looking at neutral sites and New York is one of them. They figure they can get better security here in the States."

"Are there places in Europe that they're considering?"

"Zurich is one of them, and I think Paris is on the list." The president rolled his eyes at the mention of Paris. David continued, "One thing's for sure, and the Prime Minister is right: they can't guarantee safety in London or Dublin."

The president nodded in agreement and then he asked, "Are they asking for our help?"

"Not yet, but they will. Helping with this will be a big win for you, Mr. President."

He smiled. "Let's not get ahead of ourselves. This is the English and the Irish; it's never easy. And I doubt this will be a peaceful transition."

David told his boss that he would keep him apprised of the situation and then left the room.

∞∞∞∞∞∞∞∞∞

Gavin and Rachel were walking back to their rental car when she spoke up and asked, "So, do you still think this is an assassination?"

Gavin replied, "More than ever now; isn't it obvious?"

"Not as much as you might think. I know Homeland Security taking over is suspicious, but I think they did that because what they consider a known terrorist is dead on American soil, and he didn't use his real passport to enter the country. That's something they would investigate. And, of course, the killer having remorse."

"What do you mean?"

"It's true that some killers have remorse about what they do, but they do it because killing is a compulsion and remorse can't make them stop. True-blue assassins, they don't have remorse; they're trained to ignore it."

Gavin thought for a moment. "Maybe it's an assassin who's trying to tell us something… give us a sign of some sort."

"What kind of sign?"

Gavin smiled. "That's what I can't figure out."

Rachel paused for a moment. "I hate to even ask, but a fellow Irishmen would leave the cross, right?"

"Probably."

"Who among the Irish would benefit the most by killing O'Kelly?"

Gavin thought about it for a moment. "Probably the person who would lose the most illegal gun business if this deal went through: Peter O'Malley, head of the Irish mob!"

"Do you think he would have hired one of his men to kill O'Kelly?"

"Anything is possible, which means we need to ask them questions."

"Then let's drive over to his pub."

Gavin gave her a serious look. "Better let me do this one alone. They're not going to want to talk to the FBI."

"Did you suddenly forget you're an FBI agent?"

"Yeah, but…"

Rachel cut him off. "You're Irish."

"I may have a better shot at getting that information."

[303]

"Just out of curiosity, now that we know what we know, what's the end game?"

"What do you mean?"

"Is this going to be an official case for us, or a side investigation like the judge's files? I'm not looking to get busted for something I wasn't supposed to be investigating."

Gavin paused for a moment. "I know that, but I can't answer that question right now. Maybe I can after I talk to the mob."

Rachel looked at her partner sternly. "If it's a side investigation, then you're on your own. I'm not going to let it hurt my career."

Gavin smiled at her and then hailed a cab to take him to O'Malley's Pub, the heart of the Irish Mob in New York.

∞∞∞∞∞∞∞∞∞∞

The reckless cab driver pulled up outside of O'Malley's about 40 minutes later. Gavin gave him a dirty look as he handed over the money for the fare. The cab driver just looked at him and said, "What? Get out of my cab. The ride is done."

Gavin replied in a snarky tone, "You know, there's two things you should learn when you come to this country: how to speak English and how to drive."

The cab driver started going off on Gavin in a different language, one he couldn't understand or even try to guess what part of the world it came from. Unlike most Irish pubs, this one made him a little nervous; he was Irish, so that was saying something. Being an FBI agent would make just about anybody nervous, but not the guys inside the pub. They would not have any problem shooting him and burying his body out back. They wouldn't even blink before they did it.

He walked in and immediately felt that he didn't belong. The man behind the bar knew it, too, and quietly reached for the gun underneath the bar. He didn't bring it out; he just wanted his hand on the gun. There were a couple of men sitting at a table, playing cards, who reached underneath the table to put their hands on their guns. Gavin walked up to the bartender and asked, "I'm looking for Peter O'Malley."

The bartender replied, still touching the gun, "And can I ask who you might be?"

"You can ask, but if you want an answer then you have to take your hand of the gun." Gavin pointed at the two guys playing cards. "I think the two guys sitting over there have you covered."

[304]

The bartender pulled a Glock 19 out from behind the bar and set it on the counter in front of Gavin. "If I have to ask again, I'll put a bullet in you."

Gavin was about to say something when he heard a voice shout, "Don't do that, Danny. He's an FBI agent." Gavin looked over to his right and saw Peter O'Malley standing there with a smirk on his face, like he knew everything. Peter O'Malley spoke up again. "It's okay, Danny, put the gun away. He's not here to arrest us."

Gavin walked over and asked, "How do you know I'm with the FBI?"

"You look like an agent, Gavin Donnelly."

Gavin smiled. "You know who I am?"

Peter smiled back. "Of course I do. I know your Uncle Liam and I knew your father. You look just like him."

Gavin was shocked to hear that, but he also knew that there was a great deal about his father that he didn't know before he became a police officer. Peter responded before Gavin could ask. "I'm sure you have lots of questions about how I knew your father, but that's not what you're really here for, is it?"

"No. Tommy McManus asked me to look into John O'Kelly's death."

Peter frowned. "Terrible tragedy and, believe me, the NYPD doesn't know what they're talking about."

"So you agree with Tommy that he was assassinated?"

"It's the only logical conclusion."

"You think so? Did anybody see O'Kelly leave?"

"Somebody drove him back to his hotel."

"Who?"

"I can't say for sure."

Gavin chuckled. "You can't or you won't?"

Peter looked directly into Gavin's eyes. "A bit of both. You're still an FBI agent. I can't tell you everything, despite the fact that my friend, Tommy, sent you."

Gavin nodded as if he understood. "Was he drunk when he left, since he didn't know where he was and he had to be helped to the car?"

"That, I don't know."

"He had a driver who picked him up from the airport, right?"

"Yes."

"Was he the one who drove O'Kelly that night?"

Peter thought for a minute, trying to decide if he should answer the question. Finally, he responded, "No, he wasn't."

"But you do know who drove him, don't you?"

Peter didn't say anything for a moment. "I can't say for sure."

"Okay, play it that way if you want."

"Did you find anything, Agent Donnelly?"

"I did, but I can't tell you."

Peter smiled. "How much did Tommy tell you about that night?"

"He told me about the letter from the Prime Minister of Great Britain and he told me about the vote from the Commission."

Peter looked at Gavin curiously. "The Commission? What is that?"

"Stop it. You think the FBI doesn't know about it? And let's not forget, I am Irish."

Peter smiled. "I can't admit to anything; I never know who's listening. So, if you know all of that, then you know why we think what happened to O'Kelly wasn't an accident."

"I can tell you one thing: whoever tried to make it look like a robbery-homicide left his cross on the body. Whoever killed him is religious; I think he's Irish."

"Why would a fellow Irishmen kill him?"

"You tell me, Peter. Not all of you voted 'yes.' There are some of you that don't really want peace because the of the gun business you would lose."

Peter shot Gavin a dirty look. "I voted 'no,' so does that make me the killer?"

"Are you trying to confess? Why did you vote 'no?' You don't want peace?"

"Of course I do, but my grandfather was one those Irishmen hung by the British in 1916, after they were promised peace. Like the Greeks, I don't trust them when they bring gifts. The only way we get Northern Ireland back is if we do it right, if we take it back by force. I voted 'no' because this is not the way to do it, but it doesn't make me a killer. I would cut off my hands before I betrayed a fellow Irishman."

Gavin nodded in agreement. "I believe you, but you still have a mole. Somebody around here killed him."

"And I guess you've been sent here to find that man."

Gavin sat back in his chair and thought about what Peter O'Malley said. "I guess I have."

Peter got up and walked over to the bar. The bartender handed him a bottle of Jameson Irish Whiskey and two glasses. Peter sat back down at the table and poured whiskey into both glasses. "Then let me send you on your journey properly." Peter handed a glass to Gavin and they both took a shot. "I hope you find the traitor, despite what happens with this deal for Northern Ireland. Having a traitor in our organization would be a worse thing."

Gavin agreed, but then he felt a sense of guilt, like he was about to do something wrong. Maybe it had something to do with the fact that he was working for the mob while trying to find a killer. Of course, he never claimed to be a saint; that part ran in the family. He got a text message on his cell phone, so he excused himself and walked to the corner of the bar to read it and respond. He noticed the TV behind the bar. Soccer had been on when he walked in, but now there was a breaking news story on BBC. He asked the bartender if he could turn the volume up so they could all hear it.

There had been an explosion on a supply ship in the Irish Sea, off the coast of Liverpool. Not many details had come out yet, but there was one thing significant about the news report. The BBC was claiming that it was an attack by the IRA. The whole bar heard that part and it left a deafening silence in the room. It seemed that, when tragedy struck that part of the world, the IRA was always accused. Gavin got on his smartphone and started checking other news sites. CNN, MSNBC, and even FOX News were reporting the event, but they weren't claiming the IRA had anything to do with it. It appeared only the BBC was doing that. Gavin thought that was the strangest part of the story. Somehow, he had a feeling that the news story wasn't right. He couldn't see the future on this one, but good, old-fashioned instinct told him something was wrong. He called his partner.

"Hey, did you see the news?"

Rachel replied, "I got a news alert on my phone. You think this has something to do with our investigation?"

"Right now, the BBC is the only one saying that it's an IRA attack. Whether it is or not, I think that someone wants us to believe it. "

"Why? To derail the peace process?"

"Maybe. I mean, that's the obvious answer."

"But you don't want the obvious answer, do you?"

Gavin laughed. "I just want the truth. I'm done here, so I'm heading back now."

∞∞∞∞∞∞∞∞∞∞

The Prime Minister of Great Britain, George Mallory, was sitting in his armchair when his Chief Assistant came into the office with a panicked look. He said to the Prime Minister, "Sir, there's been an explosion in the Irish Sea, off the coast of Liverpool. Early reports say that it's an IRA attack."

[307]

The Prime Minister's eyes filled with anger. "How many are dead?"

"They don't know yet."

"Goddamnit! Nothing has been announced yet, so how did they know?"

His assistant sighed. "The Irish. The secret letter you sent was supposed to remain a secret; they obviously talked."

"But why? Don't they want peace? Why do something to hurt people?"

"It doesn't matter why, sir. I think it's clear now that this isn't going to work."

"We knew violence would happen."

"You can't have this kind of violence and get a peace accord through. I told you this wouldn't work."

The Prime Minister slammed a folder on the table. "I'm not giving this up. We can still bring peace to the United Kingdom."

"Why do you want this so much?"

The Prime Minister smiled. "Because we can have real peace in the United Kingdom and create economic stability among all nations with everybody working together, thus ending the cycle of violence we've had for hundreds of years. That's real peace. That's a legacy."

His assistant smiled. "So, this is about your legacy."

"Part of it is. The other part is, I grew up watching Maggie Thatcher and the Tories destroy our country and exacerbate the violence with the Irish. Not to be cruel, but I always wondered what would have happened with Northern Ireland if the IRA had gotten her in '84 with that explosion."

"If this explosion isn't going to detour you, then we're going to have to get some help with the peace accord. We are going to need a neutral site for the peace agreement."

The Prime Minister was glad to hear that from his assistant. He didn't want to debate the issue, and he certainly didn't want his assistant telling him, "I told you so." He replied, "Let's call the American president. Perhaps he can help us with neutral locations in the States."

5

Agent Caster walked into the liquor store near his apartment. He was out of scotch and, today, he wanted to drink. Not only was he made to look like a fool by another agent (and one that didn't even have as much experience as he did when it came to investigating murder), but he was just screwed over by Homeland Security. He had been trying to get a transfer to the agency and was told that, if he helped more than he was supposed to on the John O'Kelly murder, he could get that transfer. But that was then and this was now; it didn't quite happen that way. Tonight, he needed some drinks. He walked in and it didn't take too long to find what he was looking for. Agent Caster walked out with two bottles of 15-year-old Macallan scotch.

As he turned to the right to start walking down the street, something hit his neck. It felt like a bee sting. He started to get a little woozy and then stumbled. He caught his balance, then stumbled a second time. He hit the ground, dropping the bottles of scotch as he fell. They shattered on the ground like raindrops. A few pieces of glass flew towards Agent Caster's face, cutting him, but he never felt it. He was so numb that he couldn't feel anything. Suddenly, through his blurred vision, he saw a stranger trying to help him; and then he felt it. A cold, sharp metal object pierced his stomach. He didn't really feel the pain; he just knew something was wrong when he saw the blood. The stranger grabbed Agent Caster's wallet and gun, then shouted, "Time to die, you fucking pig!" The stranger ran off and Agent Caster blacked out. He was dead a few minutes later, lying in a pool of his own blood. An ambulance arrived at the scene ten minutes later to find a crowd of people around the body, but it was too late.

∞∞∞∞∞∞∞∞∞∞

It was a busy day at the White House, but the most important meeting the president had that day was a teleconference call with the Prime Minister of Great Britain and the Prime Minister of Ireland. It was the first of what he knew would be a lot of meetings with the two leaders. David Kenny, the Prime Minister of Ireland, had been the leader of Ireland for over ten years and he was known as a hard-liner when it came to the British. He would never make a move or an agreement with the British without the backing of Sinn Fein or the Army Council. They rarely all agreed, but because they did on this issue, here he was, sitting down with the Prime Minister of Great Britain to negotiate the return of Northern Ireland. But he knew better than anyone that the road to real peace with the British was a long and twisted one. His great-grandfather helped negotiate peace in 1916 and it eventually cost him his life.

The president walked into the Situation Room with his Chief of Staff, David. Both prime ministers were already onscreen when the president arrived. He looked at both large monitors in the room and said, "Good morning, gentlemen I'm glad that you both agreed to this teleconference. I suspect that, if the leaders of both of your countries could've had this technology the last time we were talking about Northern Ireland, then there would've been a lot less casualties. I know how the Irish and the British don't like to be in the same room with one another when it comes to this issue." It was crass, but the president took a gamble with it to help lighten the mood. Fortunately for him, both prime ministers had a sense of humor and laughed. They both agreed to the statement.

George Mallory spoke first. "Mr. President, thank you for talking with the both of us. I think it's important that we all agree on a neutral site to discuss this new peace accord, especially after yesterday's tragedy in the Irish Sea. We can't let terrorists deter us from peace."

David Kenney replied with a sharp tone, "Let's watch the terrorist talk. The Irish haven't spent centuries raping and pillaging another country. Just because the BBC says the IRA did it doesn't make it true. They had nothing to do with that."

George Mallory gave David Kenney a dirty look, even though he knew he was right… but he still had to make his snide remarks like a pretentious ass. The president responded, "Alright, enough. I'm not here to play referee between you two."

Both prime ministers apologized. The president spoke up again. "Gentlemen, we have five cities that could work for this peace accord: New York City, Boston, Baltimore, Washington, D.C. and Chicago. We would be able to provide the best security in all of them."

"Can you guarantee everyone's safety in all of these cities?" George Mallory asked. I mean, really guarantee the safety of everyone. There's a strong Irish presence in all of these cities."

David Kenney snapped back, "And all of them have a lot of English sympathizers, too."

The president replied, "Gentleman, we'll have three U.S. agencies providing security and they will be able to stop any violent sympathizers. If you want my suggestion, I think Washington, D.C. is the best choice. It's the safest city in the country." He smiled, trying to lighten the tense mood again. "They do have a very important guy in the city that requires a lot of security." It wasn't a great joke, but it made the prime ministers laugh and change the angry atmosphere that filled the room.

George Mallory responded, "It's among our considerations, but we still want to look at European cities as well." Before the president could reply, his chief of staff, who had been on the phone and then received a file from a White House aide, walked over and handed the file to the president. He looked at its contents and frowned. He looked up at the two prime ministers. "Gentlemen, I have some disturbing news. The FBI agent who was investigating John O'Kelly's murder with the Bureau was murdered last night. Now, it looks like he was mugged and murdered in the process. While it may not be related to this investigation, I don't want to take any chances. I think we should cross New York City off the list."

David Kenney replied, "Do you really think safety is an issue? No offense about the murder, but people get killed in New York all the time and it's usually not for political reasons."

"I understand that, David, but do you really want to take that chance?" the president asked.

"We'll consider it, Mr. President, but we have a lot of strong Irish support in New York and that's very important to us when it comes to picking a city for these negotiations."

The president smiled. "Please take a day, gentlemen, and get back to us so we can start prepping security."

Both prime ministers agreed and that ended the teleconference. The president walked out of the room with his chief of staff and they began to talk. David asked the president, "So, is New York officially off the list?"

"It should be, but just in case, get the local FBI office and Secret Service to work together on a security plan."

"Do you want the same for every American city on your list?"

"Of course." The president paused for moment; he had an idea. "Speaking of Chicago, I have a suggestion for the head of the FBI's security team. They've helped me out before and I think they would be perfect for this. Put a call in to the local office there and make that happen."

∞∞∞∞∞∞∞∞∞∞∞∞

Agent Rachel Main was at JFK airport waiting for her and her partner's flight back to Chicago when her phone rang. It was their boss, Assistant Director Foster. She answered, "Hello, sir. What can I do for you?"

AD Foster, on the other end of the phone in his office, replied, "Agent Main, what you and Agent Donnelly can do is get back from New York City and come into the office... both of you."

"How did you know that we were in New York?"

AD Foster smiled. "This is the FBI. Since Hoover died, there aren't many secrets anymore."

"Are we in trouble?"

"You should be, but not this time. I have something to talk to you and Agent Donnelly about and it's important. Please be in my office tomorrow at 9:00 a.m." He didn't even say goodbye; he just hung up the phone. Rachel couldn't help but be worried. From the tone of his voice, it sounded as if they were in trouble. Gavin had just gotten through security after being uncomfortably groped by the TSA when he found his partner sitting at the airport bar across from their gate. She ordered him a Guinness because, somehow, she knew that he would need it. He smiled when she put it in front of him.

She said to him, "I just got a call from AD Foster. He wants us in his office tomorrow at 9:00 a.m."

"Did he say why?"

"No, but he knows we came to New York to investigate O'Kelly's death."

"You think we're in trouble?"

"We could be...we did do a no, no with the FBI."

Gavin kind of chuckled at her statement. "It's a good bet we're in trouble, but look on the bright side: if we were being fired, he would have said so on the phone."

She gave him a dirty look. "I'm not worried about being fired, but if I get another suspension, then my career is pretty much over and I may not get out of Chicago."

Gavin laughed. "It sounds like you've been sentenced to Hell on earth."

[312]

Rachel smiled. "Since I became your partner, it sure seems that way."

Gavin was going to say something, but then his phone rang. The caller ID said "Unknown number."

He felt suspicious of the call; call it gut instinct, but he knew to be suspicious of it. He answered the phone anyway. "This Agent Gavin Donnelly."

"Agent Donnelly," said the mysterious voice on the other end of the phone. Gavin recognized the voice immediately. He replied, "You're the man from the park."

"Very good. Now listen up, Agent Donnelly. What I have to tell you is very important."

Gavin walked away from the bar. "Can you give me just a minute?"

"Agent Donnelly, don't bother trying to trace the call. The FBI tracing software on your smartphone won't even come close."

Gavin smiled. "I guess you know our tactics, just like a former FBI agent would."

The mystery man smiled. "You would like to think, but I won't give you any information that reveals my identity. Besides, you should already know that, to remain a ghost, I have to know all there is to know when it comes to counter-intelligence and espionage."

Gavin smirked. "Okay, then, you see my hand. Now that all the cards are on the table, what do you want to tell me?"

"This is your last chance to turn back and stop your investigation."

"What investigation?"

"Don't be coy. You have two investigations going on that are not for the FBI."

Gavin paused for a moment. He was annoyed that this guy knew so much, but he really wasn't surprised. "Okay, you know everything, but if I am going to have this conversation with you then I want to know your name."

"Even if it's not my real name?"

"Sure."

"Then what do you want me to call myself... Deep Throat?"

Gavin smiled. "Let's try not to be cliché."

"Fine. Call me Byers."

"Okay, Byers, what do you want from me?"

"Agent Donnelly, stop your investigation. It's not worth your life."

Gavin was mad now. "Are you threatening my life now?"

"I'm not, but the people I work for will."

Gavin paused again and then asked, "How dangerous am I to them?"

Byers replied sternly, "Dangerous enough that they will kill an FBI agent and won't think twice about it."

"You think I'm afraid of death?"

Byers smiled at his confidence. "No, I reckon you're not, but they won't stop with your death. They'll kill the people you love the most. That is what you should be afraid of."

Gavin thought about it for a moment. "Threats are not going to stop me. I'll keep searching for the truth and, if it's out there, I will find it."

Byers smiled again. "There won't be another warning."

"I wouldn't expect it."

"Then let the games begin," Byers replied before he hung up the phone.

Gavin didn't know how to respond to that, even if he had gotten the chance to. He looked at his partner and she asked him if everything was okay. He just smiled and replied, "Everything is fine. Let's go home."

6

Byers was waiting outside the conference room when a man in a dark suit came out and told him that he could go in now. The conference room was dark and a bit creepy; at least, that's always what he'd thought. It had a very cold feeling about it, but it was perfect for the men who used it. As he walked inside, he saw his boss, Stephen, sitting down with the other men, waiting for his update. It had the feel of a disciplinary hearing, but it was far from it. Byers had done his job and the first part of Stephen's plan was working.

Stephen was the first to say something. "Do you have it?"

Byers walked over and handed him the letter. Stephen looked over at the man sitting to his right that everybody called Damian. He replied, "See, I told you everything would go according to plan." He then flicked his lighter and started to burn the letter. It was the secret letter from the Prime Minister of Great Britain to the Irish Mob, Sinn Fein, and the IRA. The man that everybody called Jonah shot him a dirty look and then turned his attention to Byers. Jonah asked, "What about the dead FBI agent? Does anybody suspect anything yet?"

Byers replied, "No sir, not yet, but I would give it no more than 48 hours before a couple of agents start investigating the murder."

"Why do you say that? The murder was perfect, wasn't it? It looked like he was robbed and then killed, right?"

"Yes, but one of the agents is very curious. He wants the truth and he won't stop until he gets it."

Jonah looked at Stephen. "Which has been part of the problem, but will his curiosity help us this time?"

Stephen didn't answer the question, but Byers did. He replied, "It will, sir, and you should get the city you want for the peace summit."

"And you can guarantee that?"

"Guarantee, no, there is no such thing, but I can tell you for sure that he will do what we want him to do."

"Why is that?"

"Because I know that man. He will do anything for the truth, especially what we want him to do."

Jonah smiled at the answer. It was the kind of answer they all wanted to hear. Jonah replied, "The curiosity will be the most dangerous thing for them. Let's see how this plays out."

∞∞∞∞∞∞∞∞∞∞

Agent Donnelly and Agent Main arrived back in Chicago late in the afternoon. While Agent Main went home, Agent Donnelly had other plans. He needed to see Tommy McManus before the day ended. He had information for him, but he couldn't decide if he wanted to tell him everything or not. He was still an FBI agent and wasn't supposed to trust the mob, even if they were Irish. However, there were times when he didn't have a choice, especially in Chicago.

It was close to 6 p.m. on a Tuesday, so he knew that Tommy McManus would be playing cards at Paddy Murphy's. He also knew that his Uncle Liam would be there, since he had the first shift that day and would be getting off early. Gavin didn't go straight home like his partner; he went to the pub instead.

When he arrived at the pub, he nodded a greeting to Patrick, who was behind the bar. Patrick poured him a Guinness, as he always did when Gavin came into the pub. Both Tommy and Liam saw Gavin as he walked in with a solemn look on his face, the kind of look one usually has when he's about to deliver bad news. Liam got up to greet Gavin and he was the one to say it out loud. "Glad to see you back, but from the looks of it, you didn't bring me good news."

Gavin smiled at the comment. "I guess I don't have a very good poker face." He looked at Tommy and asked, "Can we talk in private?"

Tommy grabbed his drink and walked to the back room of the pub, which was a makeshift conference room. They had to walk through a metal door that would take a lot of effort to knock down or blow up. Whoever used that room didn't want people who did not belong there to get in, especially an FBI agent. Gavin had only been in there once before.

Tommy McManus asked, "What did you find out?"

Gavin, with a stern look, replied, "You were right. There was something suspicious about John O'Kelly's death. He was murdered."

"I knew it! Did you find out who did it?"

[316]

Gavin chuckled. "Therein lies the mystery! The FBI doesn't have any evidence on who might have done it… just theories."

"And what are those theories?"

Gavin paused for a moment and shook his head no. "I can't tell you everything, Tommy."

"Then what's the point of telling me you think he was murdered? I already knew that. I wanted you to find something I didn't know."

"I can tell you this: the Commission has a mole."

Tommy was shocked by what he heard. "What are you talking about?"

"Whoever killed John O'Kelly was among all of you the night he brought the letter, which means somebody let the killer in. Ask yourself, who in the Commission doesn't want peace? Who would be willing to kill O'Kelly in an effort to stop the peace process?"

Tommy begrudgingly thought about it. "Yeah, there are a few who voted against it."

"Would they hire someone to kill another Irishman?"

"If you're trying to get me to admit that we've murdered people before, I'm done answering questions."

Gavin gave him a dirty look. "I already know that all of you kill people, but that's not what I'm asking. Who would hire someone to kill one of your own?"

Tommy still wouldn't say anything, so Gavin spoke again. "Somebody in the Commission brought someone that would be trusted enough to be in the room that night. Was there anybody that you didn't recognize?"

Tommy finally answered. "I don't know every person that works for the other men in the Commission, especially new people that may have been hired."

"If you want to figure out who the killer is, then that's where you start."

Tommy smirked at Gavin. "But you're the FBI. You solve it."

"It's not my case. I looked into it for you as a favor, but that's as far as I go."

"An Irishman was murdered by someone trying to stop the peace process. That concerns you, too."

Gavin gave him a harsh look. "I know, but I can't steal another agent's case or I won't be an FBI agent anymore. Then what good would I be to you?"

"That's not good enough."

"I don't care if you think it is or not. Besides, there's not anything I can do about it now. Homeland Security took over. They have his body because they think he was a terrorist."

Tommy was shocked to hear that. "What are we supposed to do now?"

"Continue the peace process and try to find the mole, the best way you know how."

Tommy didn't respond; he just shook Gavin's hand as a way of saying thank you for what he did. Gavin walked out of the back room and saw his uncle at the bar, getting another beer. He walked over to the bar and said hello. Liam smiled and asked, just like a cop would, "So, did you tell him everything you found out?"

Gavin laughed. "Of course not."

"You found out something important, didn't you?"

"All of you were right to be suspicious. It was murder." Gavin told his uncle what he told Tommy McManus, but then he said something that was even more shocking. "There's something else. Whoever killed O'Kelly was Catholic; probably Irish, too."

Liam was shocked to hear that and asked, "What makes you say that?"

"You know that whoever killed him tried to make it look like it was a robbery-homicide."

"Yeah."

"Everything was taken like he was robbed, except his Gaelic cross. There's no reason to leave that unless you're deeply religious."

"Or they're leaving a sign."

Gavin thought about that for a moment. "That's true; maybe the killer was sending a message by leaving the cross. That would actually make sense, considering O'Kelly didn't die from the stab wounds."

Liam was surprised again. "What do you mean?"

"I didn't tell Tommy this, but O'Kelly was poisoned. He was injected before he was stabbed."

"You've seen that before, haven't you?"

"Yes, my partner and I have."

"Well, what does that tell you about the murder?"

Gavin smiled as if he had just figured out the answer. "It was a sympathetic murder. They don't have the taste for it, at least to the point where they can't stop killing. Yeah, there's a message with the murder."

Liam smiled. "You have good instincts, Gavin. You always have. Don't ignore them."

"Thank you. There's another wrinkle to this whole thing, as well. The FBI agent who was investigating the murder was killed last night in a robbery outside a liquor store."

Liam asked, "Does that seem normal?"

"Not at all. It could be a coincidence, but I don't believe in those anymore. I haven't seen the file on his murder, but I'll bet you anything it isn't typical."

"What does this all mean for a supposed peace summit?"

Gavin frowned. "It means a storm's coming. I have a feeling there will be more killing."

"I guess we're all about to find out how serious both sides are for peace."

Gavin smiled and nodded in agreement while he finished his beer.

∞∞∞∞∞∞∞∞∞∞∞

Agent Donnelly and Agent Main sat outside Assistant Director Foster's office the next morning as if they were being sent to the principal's office. At least, that's the way it felt. Both of them knew they would have to answer for going to New York, but how much trouble they would be in remained to be seen. Finally, their boss came out of his office and said, "Alright, you two. Come on, we have a lot to talk about."

Gavin was the first to speak. "Sir, how much trouble are we in?"

AD Foster chuckled a bit. "Don't want to have any small talk first?"

"If we're going to be in trouble, we might as well hear about it first and get the lecture over with."

AD Foster shook his head. "Smartass. Can't you keep your mouth shut for once? You're not in trouble, although we are going to talk about your trip to New York."

Gavin was going to say something sarcastic, but Rachel cut him off and asked, "If we're not in trouble, then why did you want to see us? We still have another month of suspension."

AD Foster replied, "That's what I want to talk to you about." He opened his drawer and pulled out Gavin and Rachel's FBI badges and service weapons. "Your suspension is over."

Both of the agents were surprised, and they hesitated to pick up their weapons and badges. Rachel asked the question that was on both of their minds. "Why is the suspension over so soon?"

AD Foster replied, "You have a new assignment. You were asked for specifically by President Sunders."

Gavin asked, "Why does he want us?"

"Did you know that there is a proposed peace summit for the return of Northern Ireland to the Republic of Ireland?" The agents didn't say anything. "The president has convinced the prime ministers of both Great Britain and Ireland to consider having it here in the States, so there are three cities that are on the table: Chicago, New York, and Boston. The president has asked the local FBI offices in those cities to work with Secret Service on a security plan for the summit in case one of the cities is chosen. You two will be head of the FBI security team in Chicago."

Both agents were shocked at the news. While it may have seemed like a dull assignment, it was a promotion of sorts. It was considered an honor to be asked by the president himself. But they weren't that excited, especially Rachel. She believed this assignment was beneath her. She thought of herself as too good of an agent to run a security team for a peace summit. She wanted to be out there catching serial killers. AD Foster spoke up. "You two should be thrilled. You get to come back to work early."

Gavin replied, "That's great, but we're doing security detail. It's not exactly a glamorous job."

"This is the FBI. We're not here to give you something glamorous. The President of the United States asked for you personally; that's about as glamorous as you're going to get."

"So, when do we start?"

AD Foster pulled out a couple of folders with security plan and contact information for the Secret Service agent in charge. "Start going through that and get in touch with Agent Carter of the Secret Service. As of now, you're back on the job."

Rachel thanked him, but Gavin had a question. "Are we allowed to investigate any murders that have to do with the peace summit and could cause problems with security in Chicago?"

AD Foster chuckled. "Yeah, let's talk about your visit to New York. You're lucky that the president asked for you, because you should be suspended a lot longer for what you did. We don't investigate other agent's cases, especially in other cities, without permission."

"I know, sir, but do you see why I am asking?"

"Look, Agent Donnelly, I get why John O'Kelly's murder causes concern when it comes to this peace summit. After reading the report, I agree that it's suspicious, but Homeland Security took over and there's nothing you can do about it."

"What if something like that happens again, especially here in Chicago?"

AD Foster had a smirk on his face. "If I told you not to investigate murders that you thought were suspicious and stick to the security plan, would you actually do it?"

Both Gavin and Rachel laughed at the question. Gavin replied, "I don't have a problem following orders."

"Use your best judgment on this. The first priority is the security plan, unless Chicago is not the chosen city and you get reassigned."

Rachel asked their boss, "Is there anything else you need from us?"

AD Foster replied, "No. Get settled back in and go to work."

As they were about to walk out of the office, AD Foster said to Gavin, "Agent Donnelly, can I get a quick word with you in private?" He stayed behind as his partner walked out and went to their office. Gavin asked, "What can I do for you?"

"I'm curious, who asked you to go to New York to look into John O'Kelly's death? Was it Tommy McManus or your Uncle Liam?"

"What makes you think somebody asked me to go?"

AD Foster gave Gavin a dirty look. "Stop it. You think I don't know your relationship to McManus and the Irish Mob? You know more than most FBI agents what goes on with them and their ties to the IRA."

"I haven't done anything illegal."

"I'm not saying you have. There was a secret letter from the Prime Minister of Great Britain to the IRA and the Irish Mob Commission, telling them of his plans to return Northern Ireland. John O'Kelly came to the States to deliver that letter, but I think you already knew that. Is that true?"

Gavin chuckled. "My uncle told me once that, if you want to be good at your job as a police officer or a federal agent, then never tell the boss everything."

AD Foster smiled. "And how does he feel about that now that he's a police captain?"

"Probably the same way you're feeling now."

"Keep this in mind, Agent Donnelly. This whole thing is deeply rooted in politics on both sides of the ocean, and religious politics at that. It's a powder keg waiting to blow. Don't be the guy that lights it and takes his partner down with him because he forgot where his loyalty lies."

"I'm the last person you need to tell that to. I may be Irish, but I'm still an FBI agent who took an oath. I take that seriously."

AD Foster smiled again and then said something strange. "Don't go chasing ghosts because that search doesn't end well." Gavin didn't know what to make of the comment, but he didn't dwell on it too much as he walked out of the office.

7

Clifford Rollins had been the North Shore Harbor Master for the past five years. It was the largest harbor in Chicago and had the most sea traffic in the Midwest. He had been a seaman all his life: first, in the Navy, and then working on transport ships. After being away from his family for most of his children's lives, he took a job at the harbor, only to become the man in charge. He was strict about details, along with the rules of the sea and ships in port, but he was far from perfect. Like most men, his integrity could be bought and sold. He was reviewing manifest and cargo lists for ships that were scheduled to dock the next day and entering them into the computer. He was still old-school; while his computer contained all those lists, he still kept hard copies of the list on a clipboard and made sure they matched what was in the computer.

Suddenly, he was startled by a man dressed in black coming into his office. He didn't know what to say because nobody he didn't know ever came into his office. He was annoyed and it showed in his voice when he asked, "Who are you and why are you in my office?"

The man in black smiled and took out two photos from the envelope he was carrying. He placed them on the desk in front of Clifford. The photos were shocking to Clifford. They were pictures of his daughters and a stranger. Seeing them put a little fear into the pit of his stomach. Clifford responded, "How did you get those?"

"That's not the right question, Clifford. What you need to be asking is what I will do to them if you don't do what I need you to do?"

"What do you want from me?"

The man in black smiled and then did something very odd. He placed both of his hands on Clifford's face and replied, "It's going to be so easy that you won't even remember this day." Clifford felt strange; he didn't know if it was fear or if he just felt grossed out because another man put his hands on his face in a flirtatious way. The man in black took out another envelope and reached inside to pull out the paperwork. "You need to replace a manifest list with this one."

"What's the name of the ship and when is it coming in?"

"The Ocean Wanderer out of Galloway Bay. It comes in tomorrow."

Clifford looked on his clipboard and found the manifest list for the Ocean Wanderer. "Okay, so you know about a boat coming in tomorrow, but there's more to it than just handing me a new list. I have to put it in the computer and make the changes on our server. I can make changes on our computer, but not the server. I don't have access to that."

The man in black smiled again and leaned in, like he was going to kiss Clifford. "Do you really think I didn't have that figured out? I'm a bad guy. We always have the details figured out." He pulled a USB flash drive out of his sport coat pocket. "Put that in your computer, run the program on the drive, and you will be able to get into the server to change the manifest there as well."

Clifford hesitated for a moment. The man in black said to him in a more serious tone, "Tick tock, Clifford. Get this done so your girls can say 'I love you, daddy' one more time." Clifford took the flash drive and did what he was supposed to do. It took about four minutes to change everything. He removed the paper manifest list from the clipboard and the man in black took it from his hands and put it in the envelope that carried the other one. Clifford asked, "So, nothing will happen to my daughters?"

"Not by me." He put a hand on Clifford's face again. "But I can't guarantee that somebody else isn't taking advantage of them right now." Clifford was horrified to hear that. The man in black laughed. "Don't worry. I'm sure it's some college guy fucking them inside-out and making them scream when they stick their little pricks in your daughter's dirty little assholes." As Clifford sat there looking worried, the man in black pulled out a flask from his other pocket and told him to take a sip. The whiskey was supposed to calm him down and help take away his fear. It did do that, but only when the poison in the whiskey started to make Clifford choke and finally stopped his heart. That's when the man in black went to work on the body.

∞∞∞∞∞∞∞∞∞

Agent Main went right to work on a security plan for Chicago, in case there was a peace summit with the president attending. As she was reviewing the file on a security plan that was given to her and her partner, Agent Donnelly was looking up a file on the FBI server. He was trying to find the crime report on Agent Nick Caster's death. He had a hunch about it, that it wasn't ordinary. When an FBI agent died from a crime, the report was always in the FBI database and access was available to everybody. However, there was a lockdown on the report; Gavin and Rachel didn't have access to it. In fact, the only people in the FBI that did have access to the report were the director of the FBI and just a few assistant directors. Homeland Security also had access to the report, which Gavin thought was very strange.

Normally, he would ask his boss why he couldn't see it, but this little investigation had to be under the radar. He decided to visit a friend of his in the Chicago office who could help him get around the encryption and access the report. He looked at Rachel and said, "Hey, let me know what you find in there. I will be back in about 30 minutes."

"Where are you going? We have work to do."

"I know, but I have to take care of something first. This has to do with what we're working on."

Rachel didn't believe him. "You're probably lying to me, but you can at least bring me a latte when you come back to make up for it."

Gavin smiled and then went down to Cyber Crimes. He went to see Agent Dan Moore, a longtime friend of his that had been in Cyber Crimes with the Bureau for 15 years. The FBI liked to think that they had the best computer hackers in the world, but in one particular case, that was true; it was Agent Moore. Dan was stuck on something on his computer that consumed all of his attention when Gavin walked up behind him and startled him.

"Geez, Gavin, you're going to give me a heart attack," Dan replied.

"Sorry, buddy, but you never know what's going on around you when you're on the computer."

Dan smiled at the comment. "True. What can I do for you?"

"I need help getting access to something."

"Something you're not supposed to see, I'm assuming?"

[324]

Gavin chuckled. "Yeah, something like that." He handed Dan a piece of paper with Agent Caster's name and badge number. "Can you look this person up and see why his file is encrypted?"

Dan took the piece of paper and typed the name in his computer. He saw whatever other agents would see on the server, but he also ran a diagnostics test on the encryption, mainly to see if he could get past it. It took a few minutes of running different tests, and he was shaking his head in frustration while doing it. Finally, he replied, "Wow, this is the most sophisticated encryption I've ever seen. It's not the FBI's."

"Then why is it on our server?"

"Somebody in the Bureau doesn't want anybody to see this file, not even the higher-ups."

"Would another agency use this on us?"

"They wouldn't be able to do it without us knowing about it. We do constant security sweeps on our system to see if any outside agency or government has put something like this on our system."

"Can you find out who put it on here and when they did it?"

Dan went back to work on his computer, trying to find the source and the date of the encryption. Finally, with even more frustration, he replied, "Whoever did it didn't leave a digital footprint. I can't find the source or the date of the encryption."

"Can you get past the encryption?"

Dan thought about it for a moment. "I can, but I'm going to need some help."

"Who can you go to for help that can be trusted?"

Dan chuckled. "You probably won't like it."

Gavin was trying to figure out who he was talking about, somebody he obviously knew. Finally, it dawned on him. He responded with disappointment, "No, you're not suggesting Janie Myers."

"She's the best hacker we've ever busted and she's the only one that I can use as an asset that won't get both of us in trouble."

"Her hacker name is fingerbangedUSA. She really can't be trusted that much; I don't know any anarchist that can."

"That may be true, but she's still the best."

Gavin didn't like to hear that, but he knew his friend was right. "Fine, but if I find this information on some anarchist website, I am going to arrest her and violate her parole."

Dan laughed at that. "That's fair, but you and I both know that if she wanted to do that, she would do it and disappear and we would never find her. Trust me, friend, she's the devil we know and it's better to work with her than try to stop her."

"Alright, get her to help."

"When you take your lunch break, go to Morelli's Diner three blocks away. We'll meet you there with the information. Also, you owe me big-time for this."

Gavin smiled. "I'll get you a couple of Bulls tickets."

"Something close to the floor!"

"Like I would get you cheap Chicago Bulls tickets."

Both men laughed at that, then shook hands to solidify their agreement. Gavin went back to his office to work on a security plan with his partner. Dan went to see his friend, who he did have a bit of a crush on. It was one of the reasons he wanted to get her help on this computer hack. If relationships work because the people involved have common interests, then this would certainly qualify… even if it was a strange common interest. This was the thought running through Agent Moore's mind as he left the FBI office.

A few hours later, Gavin went to the diner and waited for Agent Moore and Janie Myers. He sat there for about ten minutes, drinking a cup of coffee, when he saw a strange-looking woman enter the diner carrying a laptop. She looked as if she was trying to not be recognized. The woman walked up and sat down across from Gavin. She said in a hushed tone, "Agent Donnelly?"

"Maybe."

"Don't be coy, G-Man, I already know who you are. Danny had to get back to the office, so you only get me."

"You're Janie?" The woman nodded yes. "You look different from your mug shots."

"Sorry to disappointment you, G-Man, but I prefer not to be recognizable to the Feds."

Gavin smiled. "Don't trust us, huh?"

"Maybe one or two of you, but the system… fuck no."

Gavin shook his head in disbelief. "What did you find?"

Janie opened up the laptop and clicked on the file folder that was saved to the desktop. It was the crime report on Agent Caster's murder, as well as some additional information. An autopsy had been performed and they did a toxicology test as well. Gavin read the report thoroughly and, while there was something shocking in it, he wasn't surprised by what he found. The report confirmed his theory about the murder. Agent Caster was poisoned before he was stabbed, the same way as John O'Kelly. Janie saw the frustrated look on his face and asked, "Are you not happy with what you found?"

"It's just bad news, but I knew it was coming."

"There is some pretty interesting reading in those files."

"You looked through everything?"

"Of course, but you need to know something about those files and how they were encrypted. They weren't done by a government agency."

"You're saying a hacker did this?"

She smiled at him. "There are maybe four people in the world that can make something that intricate. One of them is me, one of them is in jail, one of them is dead, and the other one is rumored to be dead."

Gavin chuckled. "I suppose you recognize the work?"

"Sure. We each have our own style, our own signature."

"You talk as if hacking is like creating a work of art."

"Because it is, G-Man." Janie didn't use formal titles when it came to the Feds. It annoyed him, but he also knew that it was just her way of being rebellious. She continued, "A work of art doesn't have to be a painting, or even something you write. It's something unique that you create, and if there is any truth to that, then hacking certainly counts."

Gavin smiled. "So, out of the four you just mentioned, who do you think made this encryption?"

"That's not the question you should be asking. It's not important who made it, but who he made it for."

"Can you tell me that?"

"There are nameless faces, men who live in the shadows. Maybe they are government spooks, but one thing is for certain about them: they live outside the law, not because they are anarchists seeking the world's destruction, but because they want absolute power."

"That's the only reason to make something like this and hide this kind of information... to hold on to whatever power they have, the kind of power that can run the motor of the world."

Janie smiled. "Now you're getting it."

"But if I wanted to find the person who made this encryption, where would I look?"

"I can't help you there, but his hacker name is worlddomination."

"That's kind of generic for an anarchist."

"That's the point, G-Man. There's something else. The encryption did leave a kind of digital footprint, a symbol if you will. I rendered it out as best as I could in the form of an image. It's in the file."

"Have you seen the image before?"

She didn't really answer the question, but she gave Gavin a look that told him she had seen it before and it was bad news. That's when she got up to leave. Gavin scrambled to get a flash drive so he could copy the file from the laptop, but she stopped him. "No need to do that; you can keep the laptop. It's not mine, anyway."

"Is it stolen?"

"Borrowed… from somebody who didn't pay very much attention to it at a Starbucks."

Gavin gave her a dirty look, but she just smiled and kissed him on the cheek to try to make him feel better about not getting the answers he wanted. Then she walked out of the diner. Gavin started to go through the files more thoroughly. He did find the image she was talking about and he had seen it before. It was the skull symbol that was found at Judge Doyle's crime scene. He touched the computer screen and traced the outline of the symbol, and that's when he flashed.

Byers walked into a morgue and started talking with two men. One of them was in a suit and one of them was wearing medical scrubs. He looked at the man in the suit and asked him, "Is the body ready for transport?"

"Yes, it is," the man in the suit replied, "but I don't understand. I thought another autopsy had been ordered and then the body was going to be cremated."

"Change of plans, Agent Banning. This body is to be moved. It's to be put in my vehicle and escorted to an undisclosed location."

"With all due respect, we can't just release this body without authorization."

Byers handed him a piece of paper. It was an authorization to move the body, but Gavin couldn't see where it came from. The other agent wasn't exactly satisfied with it, but he didn't argue. They loaded the body into the vehicle. Gavin could see the name on the label of the coffin-like box that the body was being carried in. It was John O'Kelly. Byers started to text someone on his phone but Gavin couldn't see the number. It didn't take long to load the body, and the vehicle drove away.

8

Frankie O'Brian had controlled the Boston Harbor for the past 20 years. The last three harbor masters were in his pocket and, of course, he was the unofficial employment agency for the harbor. You couldn't work on the docks unless you went through him. He was the Irish mob in Boston, but he was also an Irishman and true to the cause. That's why he voted 'yes' for Northern Ireland to be returned to the Republic of Ireland, even though his business would take a hit. However, he was still human and wanted lots of money, so it was natural that he questioned his decision. It became apparent when the alderman from his district showed up to collect his weekly payoff from the Irish mob boss.

The alderman arrived at the harbor, all smiles as usual. He was a cocky son of a bitch, and it showed. He walked into the office with his driver and had a big smile on his face. "Frankie, it's a beautiful day. What are doing cooped up in here? You should be out on the water."

Frankie smiled. "The problem with old age is that it's easier to get seasick. Besides, I wouldn't leave a regular employee to meet with you; only the boss should be here."

The alderman laughed at that. He looked up and saw a new kid in the office working for Frankie. "That's a good call from one of my constituents. And it seems like you always have a new guy working for you."

"It's hard to find good help. Maybe one of my new boys will work out and be with me for a while." Frankie looked at the new guy standing by a shelf with bottles of liquor. He told him to pour everybody a drink. Then, he reached into his desk drawer and pulled out an envelope filled with cash. He handed it to the alderman, and that's when he asked Frankie an unsettling question.

"So, I heard an interesting rumor regarding a peace summit between England and Ireland. Northern Ireland gets returned, but the IRA and the mob have to give up gun running?"

"This is Boston; it's filled with rumors, more rumors than truth."

"Is this a rumor or is it truth?"

Frankie smiled. "Don't worry, alderman. Whether it's true or not, our business won't take such a hit to where we can't contribute to your campaign."

"That's what I like to hear."

Frankie's new employee handed everybody a glass of scotch. The alderman was the first to take a drink. He started making small talk about the Boston Red Sox, since they were all baseball fans. It wasn't important conversation, but something to talk about while they all drank their scotch. Suddenly, the alderman started feeling sick. He was sweating profusely and then the double vision set in. He yelled out, "What the fuck, Frankie?! What did you do to me?"

Frankie had the same symptoms and replied in anger, "What are you talking about? I'm feeling like shit, too." Even the alderman's driver was feeling the symptoms; he was seeing three glasses of scotch in his hand. His first instinct was to reach for his gun and shoot the man who was trying to harm his boss, but he was having a hard time getting his gun out of the holster. His reflexes were shot. But Frankie's employee didn't feel anything and he was able to pull his gun out before anybody else could. He shot the alderman first, then his driver, and then he finally shot Frankie in the head. He went around the room and checked each body to make sure they were dead.

As he was checking the bodies, his phone rang. It was Byers on the other end and he only had one question. "Is it done yet?"

Frankie's employee replied, "Yes, they're all dead."

"Good. Make it look like the mob boss started the shooting and then make the call."

He put the gun in Frankie's hand after wiping his fingerprints clean. He whispered, "Sorry, boss… you were good, but they pay better." Next, he dialed 911 on his phone and reported that he heard gunfire at the harbor.

Gavin was frantic when he left the diner. He knew he only had about 30 minutes before O'Kelly's body disappeared for good. There wasn't much an FBI agent could do with Homeland Security. The two agencies didn't play well together, but he did have one card up his sleeve. He knew someone that could probably help; not exactly a friend, but somebody he could do business with, so to speak. He called Agent Michelle Harper, who worked in the Chicago Homeland Security office. Gavin had actually known her from his first days as an FBI agent when she was still with the FBI. Harper was one of the first federal agents to transfer to the newly formed Homeland Security Agency. And, like most federal agents that Gavin knew, there was a little bad blood between them. It probably had something to do with Gavin showing her up on a case when he was a rookie agent. He had proven Agent Harper wrong and he knew she didn't like that too much.

Gavin had her private cell number because of their history together. As Gavin found her number in the contacts on his phone, their history crossed his mind. She probably wasn't going to like him calling her. The phone rang and she answered. "This is Agent Michelle Harper."

"Hey, Michelle. It's Gavin Donnelly."

She was already annoyed by the call and it showed in the tone of her voice. "Oh, now you call me. Thank you for proving that you're an asshole."

Gavin laughed. "Okay, I deserve that."

"What do you need?"

"I need a favor."

"Wow, your balls did get bigger since the last time I saw you."

Gavin laughed again. "No, not really. I'm just a little desperate right now. I need to locate a body with Homeland Security."

"What for?"

"It's part of a murder investigation... a possible serial killer or assassin and trying to stop a summit."

Michelle thought about it for a moment. No matter what her feelings were toward Gavin, she was still a patriot, and her job came first. "Alright, what's the name?"

"John O'Kelly."

"The Irish political official who was found dead in New York?"

"Yeah, and you have about 25 minutes before the body disappears."

"What are you talking about? How do you know that?"

"It doesn't matter how I know; I just do."

Michelle shook her head in disbelief. "That's a big name. I can't turn the body over to you without approval... you know that."

"I know. I just need you to hold the body. Say it's part of another investigation so no one can confiscate it."

"What makes you think that?"

"Again, I just know. Somebody is trying to get rid of the body for good."

"Is this really important? Be honest, because I'm not going help you if this is some routine case you're working on."

"Michelle, I wouldn't have called if it wasn't very important."

"Twenty-five minutes is not a long time to get this done."

Gavin chuckled. "If this was easy, I wouldn't call you."

"Flattery isn't your style."

"It's all I got right now."

"Will you tell me what this is all about if I help you?"

Gavin smiled. "Yes, and I'll even let your agency get partial credit, which is really what you want."

Michelle laughed at the comment. "You still know me well. If someone is going to transport the body, I will see if I can get it stopped. Meet me at our usual deli in 45 minutes."

There was an old deli near Daley Plaza that had been around for over 80 years. It had the best Reuben sandwiches in the city, according to Agent Donnelly and Agent Harper. They ate there a lot many years ago, so it was fitting that they would meet there again. Forty-five minutes passed by quickly; it felt like all Gavin had to do was blink and it was time to meet Agent Harper. The look on her face told Gavin that it wasn't good news. She had a large manila envelope with her and, as she walked up, she didn't even say hi. Michelle said in a sarcastic tone, "Wow, I have to hand it to you, Gavin. You sure know how to pick them."

"That bad?"

"Yes. I couldn't stop the body from being moved. It was transported to another facility, which I can't even find a record of."

"You couldn't get anybody to stop it?"

"No, even outside of the usual channels, which I thought was strange… so I did some checking."

She pulled a piece of paper out of the envelope. It was a Homeland Security transfer order. Gavin was shocked to see it because he wasn't supposed to, but he was even more surprised when she pointed to the name on the order. Michelle said, "The only way to make sure the transfer went through, so no other agent could stop it based on another investigation, is to have the order signed by one of the directors. The deputy director signed this order."

Gavin asked with surprise, "Why would he do that? A deputy director wouldn't get involved with something like this, would he?"

"No, not at all, this makes it even stranger. The only other explanation is as a cover-up."

"A cover-up?"

"The deputy director is trying to hide something… and if you're hiding something, then it's usually part of a cover-up." Gavin chuckled at the statement. He knew that her paranoid attitude was correct. She asked, "So what is this all about?"

"You've heard the rumors about a possible peace summit between the British and Irish governments?"

"Yeah, something about Northern Ireland being returned to the Irish government."

Gavin smiled. "It turns out, they're true. John O'Kelly was here in the States to get the okay from the Irish Mob Commission to negotiate the terms, because one of the stipulations is that they have to give up running guns."

Michelle was shocked. "Geez, that's a big deal. Big enough to have a cover-up."

"That's what I was thinking!"

She put her hand on his shoulder, like a mother comforting her child. "I can't tell you what to do, but whatever you're investigating is the kind of thing that can ruin your career. Don't ask questions that they don't want you to know the answers to." She left the transfer report with Gavin and walked out.

Gavin finally got back to the office. His partner was a little annoyed that he was out for so long and left her with all the work. As he walked into the office, she spoke up. "Where have you been? We have a lot to go over."

"I wanted to find out about Agent Caster's murder."

Rachel shot him an angry look. "It's not our job to look into it. Besides, we don't have the clearance in the FBI database to look at his file."

"So you tried, huh?"

"I will admit that I was curious, but if we can't look at it then it's time to move on."

Gavin smiled and pulled out the laptop that he got from Janie Myers. "Actually, we can look at it."

"Where did you get that laptop? It's not yours, is it?"

"Not exactly. I'm pretty sure it's stolen."

"You didn't..."

"No, but a hacker friend of mine was able to get help from someone who got past the encryption on the FBI database. I have Agent Caster's file here."

Rachel was angry. She was trying to do things by the book now that they were back from suspension, and her partner seemed intent on breaking the rules again. She had that deep, disturbing feeling that he could very well bring her down and ruin her career, just like she had been warned. She said to him, "We can't afford to be doing this kind of stuff. If we're not supposed to see this file, then it's best to leave it alone."

"You said yourself that you were curious. Why not take a look at it? What's the harm in that?"

"If our superiors find out that we have it…"

"They're not. And if they do, I will keep your name out of it." Rachel didn't say anything as her partner opened the laptop and turned it on. She couldn't deny that she wanted to see the file, so she looked through everything and was stunned by what she saw. Gavin spoke up. "Same kind of murder as John O'Kelly; poisoned and then stabbed, in order to hide the real cause of death. Why do that?"

"It's a pattern, I will give you that, but it's not enough."

"You mean, not enough to investigate this?"

"Look, Gavin, this is not a case that we're assigned to. We can't go to Foster with just two murders, while having to explain how you got Agent Caster's file, and ask to be assigned to this case. This isn't enough."

"But we can investigate something that's related to the security plan we're supposed to be putting together."

She frowned. "This is still too thin, and I won't keep investigating this unless we're assigned to it."

"Don't you want to know the truth?"

"Not if it's going to cost me my job."

Gavin couldn't say anything to that. He knew how she really felt about going against protocol. She still hoped to get back to the Washington office. He did respond with this: "I'm not going to stop looking into this, despite what our job is now."

She smiled at him. "I get that, but I can't help this time. You're on your own."

He nodded in agreement and then walked out of the office. He called Agent Moore. "Hey. I have another favor to ask."

9

The crime scene at the harbor was chaotic. There was an unusual amount of cops and crime scene investigators there… that was the first thought running through Detective Denny Kilgore's mind as he walked onto the gruesome scene. He had been working organized crime with the Boston Police Department for 20 years and, although he had seen a lot of mafia murders, this one was by far the worst. It was a borderline massacre. He walked into the harbor office and shouted, "Fuck me!"

"All three men were shot with a 9-millimeter at close range, all by the same gun… found here in Frankie O'Brian's hand. Then, he shot himself in the head."

"That's strange. I never took Frankie for one to feel guilty and kill himself after murdering someone."

"And that's not even the weird part. Whoever shot the alderman and his driver was left-handed. The gun was found in Frankie's right hand."

"So?"

"Frankie was right-handed."

"He could have switched hands."

"Do you really think that's what happened?"

Detective Kilgore smiled. "Not likely, just like he's not the type to kill himself."

"It was a staged killing. Plus, we have a witness who says a man left the office after the shots were fired, but the witness didn't give a very good description of him."

Another crime scene investigator walked over and said, "We found something else." He held up a bottle of whiskey. "It was poisoned, and it looks like it's the whiskey that everybody was drinking." Kilgore picked up the glass of whiskey sitting on the desk in front of Frankie's body and smelled it. He replied, "He's right. There's something funky in the drink."

The first crime scene investigator responded, "Whoever did this poisoned everybody first and then shot them. Why?"

"Like you said, it was staged. I guess it's some kind of sign."

"Then I guess that explains why he took everybody's wallets, jewelry, and guns, making it look like a robbery gone bad."

Kilgore responded, "I hate the weird ones. Homicide is going to have some fun with this one." He looked over at Frankie's body and saw his rosary sticking out of his pocket. He reached down and took it out. "If you're going to take everything to make it look like a robbery, then why leave this?"

The other investigators shook their heads. Detective Kilgore responded, "Whoever did this knew Frankie well. He knew that he was deeply religious and left it out of respect. What is he trying to tell us?" Another detective walked into the office. "Hey, Kilgore, you're going to love this: there's an FBI alert on murders with this kind of MO. It looks like the Feds will be taking over this case."

Detective Kilgore was pissed and it showed when he kicked the desk. He shouted in anger, "When are the goddamn Feds going to learn that we can take care of our own in Boston?" He glared at the other detective, even though his anger wasn't directed at him personally, and said, "You let me know when they get here. I want a word with them first, before they fuck up my world." Everybody in the room laughed at the comment.

∞∞∞∞∞∞∞∞∞∞∞∞

It was a late night for David Kenny, the Prime Minister of Ireland, and James McAdams, the president of Sinn Fein. For the two of them, that meant an extra glass of whiskey. They were going over reports and discussing the possible peace summit. Both of them were unsure about the whole thing, whether or not it could actually happen, but mostly because they still didn't trust the British. As they were drinking their whiskey, Tom O'Casey walked into the prime minister's private study with a folder of reports. James asked Tom, "What new information do you have?"

"It's not good, sir." He handed each of the men a folder.

David Kenney was the first to say something. "Fucking hell, is this for real?" He was looking at crime scene photos of Frankie O'Brian and the alderman's murder.

James asked, "Does this have anything to do with us?"

"We don't know yet, but we are going to reach out and see if we can get some answers."

[336]

"I thought everything was okay with Frankie's arrangement with the alderman. They had been doing business together for the past 15 years."

Tom shrugged. "There's no indication that there was anything wrong between them, and I think Frankie would have let the Commission know if there was."

David spoke up. "So, this must be a setup of some kind, or retaliation against us."

"If that's true, then it makes the death of the FBI agent who was originally investigating O'Kelly's murder suspicious."

James asked, "Do you have information on that one, too?"

"Apparently, it's highly classified information, even to the FBI. Our sources can't get to the information."

David finished his whiskey. "So, let me get this straight: we have a dead FBI agent who was investigating our man's death... and a member of the mob Commission, along with an alderman who was sympathetic to our cause in New York City and Boston. Are there any other strange deaths in other cities that could be linked to the Irish?"

"No, sir, not that we have found."

"This doesn't make my job any easier. I have to admit, I am at a loss here on what to do."

James responded, "We knew there would be backlash, and these deaths do cause concern, but it has to be asked: is this peace worth it?"

David Kenney paused for a moment and then smiled. "I would give my life for this peace. I would give my life for Ireland, but it's my life to give. I can't ask innocent people to give their lives for this."

"Maybe it's not your right to ask. Perhaps it is Ireland herself that asks each of us if we're willing to give up our lives for freedom."

"She has been asking that of each of us since the first empire invaded our country."

James nodded in agreement. "Do the needs of the few really outweigh the needs of the many?"

"That should be an easy answer, but there are never easy answers when you're an Irishman. I know that we have to keep pursuing this and that we have to let some lives be lost, but I wanted to contemplate the moral issue before us at least once."

"And that is why you will keep your humanity in these dark times."

David poured himself another glass of whiskey. "What other options do we have for this peace summit?"

"The other American city on the president's list is Chicago. Right now, it looks like it's the safest city we have as an option."

"Who can the Army Council work with there?"

"Sir, it's Tommy McManus' territory. Plus, he has an ally in the local FBI office there."

David was intrigued by that statement and asked, "Who is that?"

"An Agent Gavin Donnelly. He's been a friend to the Irish community there and his uncle is a police captain in Chicago."

David paused out of curiosity. "Donnelly… why does that name sound familiar?"

Tom O'Casey responded to that question, since part of his job was researching and keeping up with important names. "Gavin Donnelly's father was Michael Donnelly. He was one of the Callan Raiders."

David responded, "He was at the Callan River incident? Wait a minute; he was the American that fought with the IRA back then!"

"Yes, sir."

The Callan Raid was a famous IRA attack and rescue mission on Christmas Day in 1972, along the Callan River in Northern Ireland. It was during the era known as The Troubles in Northern Ireland. The IRA had accidently discovered an internment camp set up by the British Army. They locked up people who they considered political prisoners, not all of whom were Irish. The IRA made a daring raid and liberated the camp in the early morning hours on Christmas Day. It was considered a high military target and the raid turned out to be a great success. The raid happened in a shift change during the holidays, when the camp had fewer guards, so fewer lives were lost. Ten IRA soldiers carried out the raid and none of them were killed or even wounded. The Callan Raiders, as they would be called, liberated 87 prisoners, 31 of whom were women. Since the camp was hidden in a gully along the Callan River, and there was not any access out of the camp except by the main road, the soldiers were forced to get people out through the back fence and get them across the river. Their plan worked with the help of six large fishing boats. While this was one of the most successful missions of the IRA during The Troubles, it was never found in history books. In fact, all the information on it was classified by MI-6. It was considered classified by the IRA, but the story got out, becoming a legendary triumph in the quest for freedom. There were some, who did not believe the story was true, but most Irish believed the legend, and only the top Irish political officials knew the real facts.

David Kenney drank his whiskey with a sense of pride. He considered the son of Michael Donnelly being a friend to their cause a good omen. He said to the others, "It must be fate. Chicago must be the place for us."

James replied, "We should reach out to Tommy McManus and see how they can help us make the city safer for this peace summit. They can keep an eye out for certain people we don't want there."

David nodded in agreement.

∞∞∞∞∞∞∞∞∞∞

It didn't take too long for Gavin to get a phone call from the Boston PD about the murder at the harbor matching his FBI bulletin. He didn't waste time getting on a plane to Boston to check it out. The only thing is, he was alone. These days, his partner wouldn't have believed in his theory; not enough to investigate, anyway, so Gavin was on his own. He didn't even check into a hotel when he arrived in Boston. He went straight to the 24th Police Precinct in Boston to find the investigating officers on the Frankie O'Brian murders. As he walked into the police station, he showed his badge to the officer at the front desk and asked for whoever he needed to talk to. The officer pointed to Detective Kilgore's desk.

Gavin walked over and said, "Hi, I'm Agent Gavin Donnelly. I was told you're the officer in charge of the Frankie O'Brian murder."

Kilgore glanced up from his desk with a disappointed look. "Oh, you're the Fed asshole who's here to take my case away, aren't you?"

Gavin laughed. "I don't know about the asshole part, but the rest is true. I am going to need some help, though."

"I thought you FBI guys traveled in pairs?"

"We do, but it's just me this time."

"Lucky you, but why would I help the Feds, who just swoop in whenever they want and fuck with our world?"

Gavin laughed again. He didn't want to let the detective get underneath his skin; punching him in his own police station would not be professional. "That's funny. My cousin back in Chicago is always telling me the same thing. He's a homicide detective. And I'm not here to fuck up your world, but the murder is part of an ongoing investigation in my office. We're trying to catch a killer, or killers."

"You're not sure which?"

"That's why we're investigating this murder: to see if the pattern can tell us how to catch this killer. That's why I could use your help. You were investigating Frankie O'Brian, weren't you?"

"Yeah, I was."

"Come on, detective. Let me buy you a beer and you can take me to the crime scene."

[339]

The men were gathered around the table in the darkened conference room, waiting on the latest report. Each of them had a glass of whiskey or some kind of bourbon. One of the men looked over at Stephen and asked, "Do you really think your man can get this done?"

"Are you questioning me about the men I use?"

"Since being in your position, you haven't exactly had success."

"You worry about your own men and I will worry about mine. Everything is going according to plan."

The other man was going to reply, but somebody else entered the room to give his report. He was a man in his mid-forties, looking eager for a promotion. He was intense, but proficient. The man in charge sitting at the table asked, "Mr. Chambers, what do you have to report?"

Mr. Chambers passed out file folders to the men sitting around the conference table. "I was able to sign off on the transfer order for John O'Kelly's body. Nobody can hold it for any further investigation. The body has completely disappeared."

"Good to hear, Mr. Chambers. I guess being Deputy Secretary of Homeland Security does have its privileges."

Mr. Chambers nodded in approval. "I also have an update on the package. Our man has been contacted and the package is en route."

"Good to hear. Since we still don't have a destination yet, once the package reaches the first point of contact, it can be put on standby until the destination is certain. It looks like everything is proceeding as planned."

The group was about get up and leave when Mr. Chambers interrupted. "Sir, I don't mean to press the issue, but when is the changing of the guard supposed to happen at Homeland Security?"

The older man smiled. "Soon. I think your office is about to be embarrassed, and the president will have no choice but to make a change. I think we both know you're the best choice for the job."

10

Detective Kilgore and Agent Donnelly walked into the Boston Harbor office that used to be occupied by Frankie O'Brian. The place was still roped off by the police and covered in blood stains. Agent Donnelly looked around the room a few times, trying to see if there was anything out of the ordinary besides a triple murder. Detective Kilgore started telling him what they found; basically, giving him a rundown of his police notes. Finally, he paused and kind of chuckled at this particular thought. "Then, here's the strange part…"

Agent Donnelly replied, "This case wasn't already strange to begin with?"

"That's funny… we found the gun that killed everybody in Frankie's right hand. The person who shot everybody was left-handed and the head wound was on the left side. Frankie couldn't have killed everybody, especially himself."

Gavin let out a small laugh. "Because you can't kill yourself with your left hand and then place the gun in your right hand."

"We figured the killer was trying to stage it and make it look like a robbery."

"That's exactly what he was doing, but it was done poorly. Why make it obvious?"

"Maybe this was his first kill; he didn't know how to do it right."

Gavin thought for a moment. "Could be, or the killer is trying to tell us something."

Detective Kilgore pulled out some autopsy photos and showed them to Gavin. "Speaking of trying to tell us something, here is something interesting. The Catholic cross found on the alderman's body was not his. It was put there by the killer…they removed his Star of David and put the cross on his body."

"What makes you say that?"

"According to the coroner, he was Jewish. He was uncircumcised."

Gavin was shocked. "Now, that is particular. Yes, the killer is definitely trying to tell us something."

"What?"

"The killer is deeply religious. He or she is Catholic and thinks every other religion is crap, hence putting a Catholic cross on a Jewish victim. Plus, he sees the religious icon as an important tool for the victim's trip to the afterlife. The religious icon is a symbol. He has no problem killing, but respects the journey we take to the afterlife. He or she is probably of Irish, Italian, or French descent."

"You got all that from a Catholic cross?"

Gavin smiled. "It's just the beginning of a profile. My partner could make the profile better." Gavin continued to look around. He fanned through the files in the filing cabinet. He looked at the detective and asked, "What were you investigating Frankie O'Brian for?"

"Racketeering, smuggling, and bribery... general organized crime stuff."

"Smuggling, huh. That explains why he ran the harbor! Did you ever find out what he was smuggling?"

"Not really, but it could be any number of things. There's tons of illegal stuff that comes through this place: drugs, weapons, black market stuff from China, and even people. But there was not any concrete proof."

"Frankie sat on the Irish Mob Commission. He smuggled for fun, that's for certain."

Detective Kilgore was a little stunned. "Irish Mob Commission... that's a real thing? I thought it was just a rumor."

"Oh, it's real."

"How do you know that? The FBI has proof of that?"

"Not exactly. I know about it because I personally know people on the Commission."

"Like who?"

"The same person that asked me to look into these cases: Tommy McManus."

Detective Kilgore was even more stunned. "Don't take this personally, Agent Donnelly, but are you being bribed by the mob?"

Gavin laughed a little bit. "No, I don't take that personally, but it is a legitimate question. I'll tell you about it over a beer; I'm done here, anyway. I would like to request the files in this room to be sent to Chicago, including anything you might have on your investigation into Frankie."

Detective Kilgore was annoyed at the request, but he didn't argue. He put a call in to the station to get the request expedited and then suggested a place to grab a beer. This was a story he wanted to hear.

Thirty minutes later, they were at a pub called the Galway Bay, a true Irish pub in Boston. It was the best place to be when the Red Sox or the Bruins won a championship and it also reminded Gavin of Paddy Murphy's back home. For the most part, it was a cop bar in Boston, but according to Detective Kilgore, it was the best place to get a Guinness in the city. Gavin started to explain the relationship between the mob and the police in Chicago, and how they learned to co-exist there. Sure, the mob had their illegal businesses such as gambling, prostitution, and maybe a little marijuana distribution, but these were all considered harmless vices. Most of the mob had ancestors who were bootleggers in Chicago, something no one ever considered illegal there. Plus, the mob had learned to police their own neighborhoods and didn't let hoodlums sell drugs to schoolchildren. They didn't let child prostitution happen and, if it did, they would take care of their own. The police would tolerate the harmless stuff and crack down hard on the most dangerous activities. And then, of course, the peace agreement came between Mickey Sorrano and Tommy McManus after a bloody mob war 20 years earlier. Both of these men saw that peace and learning to live with one another was more profitable than trying to kill each other.

Detective Kilgore shook his head. "You act like there's some kind of perfect harmony in Chicago where criminals and cops can live together."

"I'm not saying that it's perfect. It is the way it is. Besides, we have a different definition of criminal."

"They break the law. Isn't that the definition?"

Gavin laughed. "If you assume that the definition is strictly black and white. My grandfather was a bootlegger before he became a cop, but that never changed the fact that he was a good man in both careers."

"You're right, I don't see it the way you do."

"Oh, that's alright. We don't have to agree to be good at our jobs. Hell, we don't have to agree in order to be civil with one another and have a beer together."

Detective Kilgore smiled. "I'm curious. You said Tommy McManus asked you to look into this case. Why you? I'm sure they have someone on their payroll that could have gotten information on these murders."

"Well, in answer to your question from earlier: I'm not on their payroll, but I'm sure someone is. And yes, they could have gotten the information from someone else, but they asked someone who they consider a friend to their cause."

"What cause is that?"

"What this whole thing is about: Irish independence. The British Prime Minister is trying to make a deal to return Northern Ireland back to the Republic of Ireland. Before that can happen, all Irish political parties, the IRA Council, and the Irish Mob Commission have to approve the peace summit so that war, or what they call The Troubles, doesn't break out again."

Detective Kilgore was a little shocked by what he heard. He had never heard anything like this before, not even as a rumor. Gavin proceeded to give him a little history behind everything. Much like the Italian mob, the Irish formed a commission among all the main families in major cities throughout America. The purpose of the Commission was to keep control over all illegal activities and make sure they were just the harmless vices that Gavin talked about earlier. And the most important part of the Commission was to raise money for the cause: Irish independence from the British government. The Commission was set up in 1984, after the IRA bombing that nearly killed Margaret Thatcher. It was a response to the British government's attacks on the Irish. Their intention was to be better organized and raise more money for the war effort. They also wanted to make sure nobody was acting outside the cause, since one of the main purposes of the Irish mob was to raise money for it. Of course, they could have their own illegal businesses within reason, but the cause was always more important. No one who did not believe in the cause would be a part of the Commission. One of the main sources of income was running guns. That would always be profitable because the world would never be without a war somewhere. And, if the Irish were to continue the war effort, then they would need weapons. As Gavin explained, the Commission wasn't just about making mobsters rich. Gavin also told him about the secret meeting and the condition of giving up illegal gun running from the British.

Detective Kilgore replied, "Wow. If that's true, then it sounds like the Brits are trying to end the Commission, too."

"It's possible. So, if the Commission voted 'yes' to a peace summit, then you know how serious they really are about Irish independence. They are willing to give up their main source of income and a peaceful existence among the families for Ireland."

Detective Kilgore shook his head in disbelief. "I never realized their real purpose."

"Most people don't, but then again, most freedom fighters or rebels always get labeled as criminals or even terrorists."

"That, coming from an FBI agent, is a strange thing to say."

Gavin laughed. "Yeah, it's probably not the thing to say in my job! However, it's not strictly black and white on who the good guys and bad guys are. You have to make that judgment yourself."

"Do you support their cause?"

"I am an FBI agent and I take my oath seriously, but I'm also an Irishman whose family has been persecuted by the Brits going back many generations. So yes, I support the cause. I don't support everything about it, but I want peace. And if you're wondering if I will violate my oath for that cause, well, that's a question I ask myself every day." Gavin got up and pulled out some cash from his pocket so he could pay for the beers. "Thanks for your help, detective, but I have to get back to Chicago. The beers are on me."

"Thanks for the beer."

Gavin was about to leave, but he had another question. "Earlier, you were asking me if I had a partner. How come you don't? Cops don't usually work alone."

"I do these days. I haven't had a partner stick around long enough to make it a permanent thing since my old one left three years ago. She was the best partner I ever had, the kind that always had my back and that I could trust my life with. They don't come along very often, but she wanted more and left."

"You mean, she fell in love with you and you couldn't love her back?"

"The thing is, I was in love with her, but I wanted her on the job with me and not being a cop's wife. I couldn't protect her as a wife… at least, at the time, I thought I couldn't, and so she left. She moved to Buffalo and got married. She had her first child a few months ago."

"I can see why it's hard to find another partner."

Detective Kilgore smiled. "What about you? Do you have a good relationship with your partner?"

"We haven't been together that long, but she is a good one."

"Take it from me: if you find a good one, don't let her go. It's a bitch being alone in our kind of work." Gavin smiled, shook his hand, and said goodbye.

∞∞∞∞∞∞∞∞∞∞∞∞

It was a busy day at the White House, but the most important meeting the president had that day was another conference call with the prime ministers of Great Britain and the Republic of Ireland. The peace summit was important to the president, as much as it was to the prime ministers, but what was more important to him was the location of the peace summit. He wanted it in Chicago for a number of reasons.

[345]

Sure, he was from the city and having a home field advantage was always good, but politics played into it, as well. This would bring Chicago onto the international stage, making it outshine places like New York and Boston. This was a big deal for the president. His chief of staff, David, followed him into the Situation Room, where the teleconference with the prime ministers was already set up.

The president took a seat and didn't even start with small talk. He simply asked, "Okay, gentlemen, do we have a consensus on where this peace summit should take place?"

George Mallory, the British prime minister, spoke. "I think we have, Mr. President. Prime Minister Kenney and I have been speaking about it for the past day or so."

David Kenney responded, "Mr. President, we believe that Chicago is the best choice, giving the recent events in Boston."

The president hadn't said anything about the murders in Boston. He had only seen the intelligence report on it that morning, but he also knew that the Irish and the English had their own intelligence sources. There was no use trying to hide anything. He replied, "Yes, I saw the report on the mob boss and the alderman's murder in Boston this morning. It was a tragic thing, but I am glad that you made Chicago your choice. We can definitely provide better security there and, of course, better accommodations."

George Mallory replied, "Thank you, Mr. President. We also have some requests regarding those accommodations… things that will make life a little easier on both the Irish and British governments when it comes to this controversial summit."

The president smiled. "I figured you would, but the logistics can be worked out with my staff. I do have one more question. What date did you want to have this summit?"

David Kenney replied, "One week from today. Does that work for you, Mr. President?"

He nodded in agreement and replied, "One week from today will be perfect."

∞∞∞∞∞∞∞∞∞∞∞

Gavin had gotten back the night before and was dead tired. For the first time in years, he overslept and was late to the office. His partner noticed and gave him hell for it when he walked into their office. He laughed and said, "Well, I did bring you coffee."

She gave him a half smile and replied, "It almost makes up for it. At least, it's a start. How was your trip to Boston? Did you get any answers?"

"You knew about that?"

"Of course; I'm FBI. What did you go for?"

"A triple murder with the same MO as our killer. I am having all the files sent here."

"Who died?"

"Frankie O'Brian, head of the Boston Irish Mob, plus an alderman who was being paid off by him."

Rachel was a little stunned to hear that and replied, "What was his territory in Boston?"

"He mainly ran the harbor. From what I can gather, he did most of the smuggling in Boston."

"It sounds like a strategic kill."

"That's what I think, too. I could use some help looking at everything."

She smiled. "Three murders with the same MO. There is a pattern and it's worth looking over, especially if this is linked to the peace summit."

"You think it is?"

"I'm not saying that, just that's its worth looking into. You have a different theory?"

"I think there are too many coincidences with these murders and the proposed peace summit. I think somebody is trying to derail the peace process."

"Gavin, I know you're in favor of this peace agreement, but don't go looking for conspiracies. Don't take this personally."

Gavin was going to respond, but the phone in their office rang. It was Assistant Director Foster and he needed to see them right away. They rushed to his office and took a seat. He had a serious look on his face when he delivered the news. "Agents, I just got a phone call from the White House. The peace summit is coming to Chicago in one week."

Gavin and Rachel were a little shocked by the news, but then Gavin started thinking about something. He added another piece to his theory, but he wasn't ready to share it with his partner yet. He still had some more investigating to do on his own. Both of them were handed some file folders with instructions. They were the logistics that the FBI had to work out. As they were leaving, AD Foster asked Gavin to stick around for a moment. "Agent Donnelly, I got a request to get files on a Boston murder. Do you know what that's about?"

"Yes, I do. It has to do with a murder I investigated yesterday."

"You're supposed to be working on a security plan."

"I know, sir, but you also said I can check into anything that could disrupt that plan. I have three murders that have the same MO and could be linked to all of this."

AD Foster was annoyed, but he didn't say anything. He just asked a question. "Is there anything you need to tell me?"

Gavin smiled. "Not yet. It may be nothing, but I still want to check it out."

"Okay, but don't let it get in the way of this peace summit. This is a big one for our office. Screw-ups won't be tolerated. Those are the stakes."

Gavin just nodded in agreement and then walked out. He knew the stakes, but the stakes could be even higher if he ignored the possible threat... whatever the threat could be. He still couldn't figure that part out.

11

Roger Jackson had been working as a security guard at the Citibank building in Daley Plaza for the past three years. He didn't mind the work, but it wasn't the dream job he always wanted. He needed the job because of his gambling habit and what he liked to call his recreational drug use. Roger didn't know if he could hide his problems anymore. He was sure that he would be fired any day now and that just made the stress worse. So, he would do the only thing he knew how to do; he would get a fix.

He left after working the early shift and took a 30-minute train ride to the south side of Chicago to find his dealer. The neighborhood he went to was near the train stop, so he didn't have to walk too far. He went into a rundown apartment building and proceeded to the second floor. No one bothered him. He wasn't really out of place, considering he was a regular there. He knocked on the door of apartment 25D, but didn't find his regular dealer answering the door. He was startled, but he didn't walk away, either. Roger asked, "Who are you?"

"I'm Sal. I'm covering for Mr. Smith. What can I get you?"

Roger didn't say anything for a moment. "I think I will come back another day."

"Don't be stupid. You rode the train a while to get here and I have the stuff you need."

"You're not a cop, are you? If you are, you have to tell me."

Sal laughed. "That's a good one. No, I'm not a cop. Come in and I will get you what you need. "

Roger was still hesitant, but he needed a fix badly, so he decided to buy something from a guy he had never met. He walked in ahead of Sal, who was holding the door open for him. Roger was looking around the room when, all of a sudden, he felt a hand go over his mouth and a needle go into his neck. It was a matter of seconds before he fell to the ground, dead. Sal checked his pockets and found Roger's electronic security badge. Sal pulled out his cell phone and made a call. When the person on the other end answered, he replied, "He's dead. I need you come and get the body."

∞∞∞∞∞∞∞∞∞∞

The next day, Gavin and Rachel were at the office early, going over the security plan. Since announcing the peace summit would be in Chicago, it was decided immediately after that the Richard J. Daley Center would be the best place to have the summit, considering it was used for the Chicago city government and would have plenty of security. There was lots of office space at the top of the building to hold meetings, and the entire area around the building would be easy to block off for security. While all of that sounded nice, the Daley Plaza still presented problems when it came to security. The agents were not exactly happy about the location. That sentiment was shared by the Secret Service, who was having to do their own security plan for the president's visit to the summit.

There was a press conference that morning from the White House about the peace summit. Up to this point, the whole thing had been a secret; not even the media had gotten wind of the event, but that was about to change. And once it hit the airwaves, the work for the FBI would triple. There were not a lot people that would be happy with the peace agreement, and that meant the possibility of violence. There would be a lot of calls and threats that the FBI would have to check out in the next week.

The press conference from the president was what they expected it to be: a great speech about peace, making amends among nations, and that, despite the coming protest, the president and the prime ministers were committed to peace. When it was done, Rachel looked at Gavin and said, "Well, now it begins. This office will have at least 20 phone calls with threats of violence and we'll have to check them all out." Gavin chuckled a little bit at the notion and led his partner over to one of the peg boards in the office.

"Before that starts happening, take a look at this and lend me your expertise." He had crime scene photos of John O'Kelly, Agent Caster, Frankie O'Brian and the murdered alderman hanging up. "Ok, four dead bodies, all done the same way. Poisoned first, which is the cause of death. Then, they were stabbed and personal belongings taken to make it look like a mugging, but there's one thing left… one little sign."

Rachel replied, "A Catholic cross was left on each body."

"Except for one…the alderman…a catholic cross was put on his body…he was Jewish."

[350]

"So, we know that the crosses are a sign, but is it a message for us directly? Is it a warning?"

"Could be that he just feels guilty for killing. We've seen that before."

Rachel smiled. "True, but poisoning somebody still causes pain, and the killer didn't mind that. Albert Sorrano used neuroblockers to dull the pain so they wouldn't feel anything when he killed them. This killer might be deeply religious, but he doesn't feel guilty for what he's doing." She stared closely at the pictures while Gavin asked what may have seemed like an obvious question.

"Okay, you say it's a message, but to whom? The FBI... the Irish?"

She didn't say anything for a moment. She just continued to stare intently at the picture. Then, as if a light turned on in her brain, she figured something out. "The message is for you!"

Gavin was stunned by the comment. "What? Why do you say that?"

"Think about it. Who asked you to look into these murders? Who stands to lose something big if this peace agreement happens? And you said it yourself: there is a mole in the Commission."

"You're talking about Tommy McManus. He voted 'yes' for peace, so why would he have anything to do with this?"

Rachel smiled. "If he wants to hide his real intent, then of course he will vote with the majority. And, before you give me some excuse that he couldn't possibly do this, take a cold, hard look and see if that's really true."

Gavin laughed. "I'm not saying that it's not possible. I mean, he's no saint, and not above double-crossing someone to get what he wants, but I think Peter O'Malley would be a better candidate as the mole."

"If that's true, then what's he trying to tell you with these murders? That's the big question, isn't it?"

Gavin paused for a moment. "The only thing I can figure is that peace is not supposed to happen, or that they don't really want it to happen."

Rachel laughed. "You know that's too easy of an answer, right?"

"Yes, I do, and that's what bothers me. Here's another question: are the murders supposed to stop the peace summit altogether or make sure that it happens in a certain location?"

"You're suggesting that somebody is forcing the peace summit to be here in Chicago?"

"Maybe!"

"If that's true, then the murders are just a prelude to something else."

Gavin was about to reply when the phone in their office rang. It was a call reporting a bomb threat and they had to check it out. These kinds of calls would not be uncommon in the next week. As soon as he was about to hang up, his head started to hurt. All of a sudden, he flashed. *The older man led the two younger men to a back alley where there was a dark blue van waiting for them. It was designed as a plumber's van and even had lettering on the side that said 'Grimes Plumbing.' The younger man was stunned to see his name on the van, but he understood why. The older man looked at him and said, "Robert, I told you we had everything taken care of. You'll find everything you need in the back and no one will bother you. If anybody checks on the plumbing company, they will not find anything out of the ordinary. It's a legitimate company. All the documents are in a file folder within the briefcase I gave you."*

Robert replied, "Do you really believe in our cause?"

The older man smiled. "Does it really matter? The only thing that matters is that you believe, and we have the tools to help you make a statement." Robert was expressionless, but he did shake the old man's hand and took the keys to the van.

∞∞∞∞∞∞∞∞∞∞∞

Robert Grimes had been a radical most of his life; at least, that's how he was labeled. There was always something for him to protest. He hated the government, pretty much all religions, the United Nations, the World Bank, and any organization that exerted too much control over people. Some questioned why he would even go to college, but when asked, he simply replied, "If they're trying to control me and put me into debt, I might as well get an education for it." He graduated with honors from Northwestern University with degrees in Political Science and Sociology. While that may sound interesting, the most fascinating part about his college career was the political organization he started. Its purpose was to protest any organization he thought had too much control… think Nader's Raiders, but more violent. He called his organization the United Front. It was supposed to be non-profit, but they did a lot of things to make money for the cause. Most people who joined did not have the same passion or commitment to the cause as Robert did and would leave after they graduated college, but about 20 percent who joined were truly dedicated.

A few hours after the media announced the peace summit between the British and Irish governments to return Northern Ireland, he wrote on the United Front's website about government intervention and how the U.S. was always getting involved in something they shouldn't. He had a lot of fan e-mails and comments praising him for his words, but there was only one person who called him and said he could help. The mysterious gentleman asked Robert to meet him at an English pub in the Lincoln Park area... not exactly the kind of area you would expect criminal activities to happen. Robert was promised a $10,000 donation to the organization if he showed up to listen to what the man had to offer him.

Robert was suspicious, but he wasn't about to turn down $10,000. He arrived an hour after the call and brought his friend, Sam, who was in the organization, too. Robert walked into the English pub and found the man who called him sitting at a table in the corner. A man who appeared to be a bodyguard was standing off to the side. The man looked up and said, "Thank you for coming. I've made this offer before and they never show. You seem to have more courage than the others."

Robert didn't know how to respond, but he did ask the obvious question. "How can you help me?"

"By giving you what you want, Robert...more than just money."

"And what is that?"

"A chance to make a real difference, a chance to make them listen, and I have just the tools to do it." The man was a little bit older than everybody else, but his age didn't slow him down. He quickly reached for a briefcase that contained multiple file folders. Robert opened it and started looking through the files. There were plans for bomb-making, suggested targets, and false IDs in case they needed to get away in a hurry, along with escape routes in the city of Chicago. Robert was amazed, to say the least, but he had to ask. "How do I know that this isn't some kind of setup?" It was a legitimate question.

The old man simply replied, "Why would someone go through such an elaborate scheme, with all the details we included, just to set you up? If we wanted you out of the way, then all we have to do is pin something on you and call the cops."

Robert wasn't sure if he was truly convinced. "That may be true, but my organization has never done anything violent before."

"But you want to. You just didn't have the tools until now. I know you have been searching for a way to get the things you need. I have them for you."

Everything inside Robert was telling him not to trust the old man, but he was too easily persuaded by money and gifts. Robert nodded in agreement and shook the old man's hand. They walked to the back of the pub and out into the alley. There was a dark blue van parked there with the name 'Grimes Plumbing' on it. The old man proceeded to tell Robert Grimes about the rest of the gifts he had to offer and his suggested plan.

∞∞∞∞∞∞∞∞∞∞∞

It had been a long day for Agent Donnelly and Agent Main. They checked out three bomb threats that turned out to be false. It was already dark when Gavin finally got home. As he was about to unlock his apartment door, he heard the TV on in his apartment; it was the Chicago Blackhawks game. He pulled out his weapon and quietly unlocked the door. He tried the best he could to sneak in and not alarm the person who might be inside. As he darted around the entrance corner, weapon aimed with the safety off, he found Haley O'Brian sitting at his kitchen table. She was drinking a beer and looking through the judge's files. She was somewhat startled, but then smiled and offered Gavin a beer. He had a dumbfounded look on his face and she responded, "You did say to just let myself in."

He smiled. "I know. I guess I forgot. It's been a long week so far, but I'm glad that you took me up on the invitation."

"She smiled. "Me, too! By the way, the Blackhawks are up 1-0 in the second period."

Gavin grabbed a beer. "So, I guess you heard the press conference today?"

"Yeah. I'm one of the reporters covering the peace summit next week. I wanted to get some of our research done now before I get swamped with that."

"Did you find anything?"

"As a matter of fact, I did. First, the list of companies like P & M Electronics is a no-go for us. For every one of them, their case is pending review by the Justice Department. That was all the information I could get. To be honest, I don't even know what that really means. I don't know what the Justice Department review is."

"It means that the cases will eventually be dropped. It's the nice way of saying that the Justice Department doesn't think there's enough evidence to go to trial, but they will allow them to be reviewed anyway."

Haley gave him a frown. "I had a suspicion that would be your answer. I also found something else. Have you heard much about some of the representatives that will be at this peace summit?"

[354]

"We haven't gotten an official list yet. Should by tomorrow, though. Why do you ask?"

Haley got a file from the table and handed it to Gavin. "Apparently, there are reps from HM Mining coming to this thing. From what I can gather, part of the deal is a joint cooperation between the Irish and British governments for mining operations in a region of Northern Ireland."

"I've heard reports, and it wouldn't be unusual for their reps to be at the summit."

"I get that, but I did some digging on HM Mining. I can't find any evidence of them mining anything. There are no records of geological surveys or using mining equipment. It looks like the only mining part of this company is in the name."

"Did you find profit reports and tax records?"

"Of course, and it shows that it's a profitable company, but I can't see how that money is coming from mining operations."

Gavin paused for a moment. "Are you saying this company is a front for something else?"

"That's the way it appears. Look inside the folder. Judge Doyle was investigating it, too."

Gavin was thumbing through the folder and found the map of Northern Ireland. There was a big red circle on it marked 'HM Mining' and it was along the Callan River. "So, this is where the mining company is supposed to have its operation in Ireland."

"Supposedly, but underneath it is a photo of men called the Callan Raiders. There's a name that you might be interested in. His real name is in parentheses."

Gavin looked at the photo that was underneath the map. John O'Neil's name was crossed out and had 'Michael Donnelly' written underneath it. Haley asked, "Do you know who that man is?"

"Yes. It's my father, but I've never seen this picture before."

Haley stood up and walked over to Gavin." I asked around about the Callan Raid and the men in the photo. There's no record of it, but it was an IRA military operation where they liberated a research facility, disguised as prisoners, about 40 years ago along the Callan River. That's what I have been told, at least. But here is the strange thing: the name of the facility was called the Benburb Research Facility. Of course, it's been closed down and ownership has changed hands, but the company is now called…"

Gavin interrupted. "It's called HM Mining now."

"Yes."

"What did the research facility do?"

"That's the bigger mystery. Did you know about the Callan Raid?"

"I've never heard of it before, but I've never heard much about my father's time in Ireland."

Haley grabbed Gavin's hand and looked deeply into his eyes. "I think you are tied more to all of this than you realize. Your family history is right in the middle of this story."

"Story?"

"There's a story behind all of this and it's dark. Maybe the question for you is what your role is."

Gavin smiled. "There are a lot of questions I have for my uncle."

"There are a lot more questions than answers right now, but they can wait." She leaned in and kissed him. It was a pleasant distraction and Gavin took full advantage of it. He grabbed her, propped her on the table, and then started unbuttoning her blouse. She loved it and quickly went for his belt, unbuckling as fast as she could to get to the prize inside. Haley found what she was looking for and grabbed ahold of it while Gavin let out a small moan. He loved her touch and she loved his soft lips on her breasts. They didn't make it to his bed. They got as far as the couch and collapsed into each other's arms as the Blackhawks scored another goal on the TV.

12

Byers was standing next to a hot dog cart in Daley Plaza, eating a good, old-fashioned Chicago dog. He had to admit to himself that a good hot dog was his favorite food in the world. While he was eating, he received a blocked phone call. Most of the time, he knew who was calling him, but this call was going to be a surprise. He answered, and the man on the other end said to Byers in a very serious tone, "I have been getting some disturbing reports about this peace summit in Chicago. How is your plan progressing?"

"It's progressing fine, sir. Everything we anticipated is working out."

"What about this FBI agent you've told me about? I heard that he snuck into Switzerland with some reporter, under a false identity, and got the judge's research."

"I heard that, too."

"That could be a problem. He may not be ready for the truth."

Byers had to laugh at the paranoia, but it was a legitimate concern. "I don't think it's a problem, sir. He needs to ask the questions in his own time. The truth can't be forced upon him if he isn't ready. Let him find out on his own and then he will be a true believer."

"Are you sure about that?"

"It's how I came to be a believer."

"I hope you're right, because I know the judge had information on his father... and the secrets about a father can be a very dangerous thing."

"And once he learns about him, it will open his eyes."

"Do you have any information on the Gang of Eight and how they may be involved?"

"The only thing I know for sure is there is a playmaker involved, but I have no other details."

The man on the other end of the phone sighed. "I had feeling that might happen. This thing is too big for them not to be involved. Will it be a problem with this FBI agent you're fond of?"

Byers smiled. "He's following the clue. He will figure it out in time." The other man didn't say anything else. That was all he needed to hear and so the conversation was over.

∞∞∞∞∞∞∞∞∞

One of Gavin's duties over the next week was to brief the Chicago PD about security procedures for the peace summit. It turned out he was going to be working with the 23rd precinct, the one his cousin Alex Donnelly was stationed at. He had to admit, when he got to work with his cousin, it was always one of the best parts of his job. However, this time, he needed to ask Alex some very serious questions. He walked into the precinct and didn't have to show his badge. Everybody there knew who he was and even considered Gavin a part of their family, despite being a federal agent. After all, he was Captain Liam Donnelly's nephew and, while tensions always ran high among the PD and the Feds, Gavin always had a good working relationship with the precinct.

Alex was busy, as always. He was trying to find stuff on his computer, which he still didn't know how to use very well. Gavin walked up. "So, is the computer getting the best of you again?"

Alex shot him a dirty look. "Not funny, but yes, it is. The new police server is driving me nuts. Can't find a fucking thing on it "

"Shouldn't it have to be that hard in order to be a good cop?"

"That's true. By the way, we did get the security packet from you guys and we are going over it in about an hour, if you want to stick around."

I might just do that, but before we talk about that, I have a couple of questions for you. It's about the family."

Alex stopped what he was doing. He could tell that this was serious. "What's going on? What do you need to know?"

"Has your father ever told you about what mine was really doing in Ireland in the 70s? Like, maybe his connection to the IRA?"

Alex gave him a strange look. "No. Why would he tell me anything about your father, and not you? I know he has secrets, but I wouldn't know anything more about your father than you would. Why would you ask that?"

[358]

"Maybe he wouldn't tell me anything 'because he thinks he's protecting me from something, but he may have mentioned something to you."

"I can't see Liam doing that."

Gavin paused for a moment before he asked his next question. He wanted to see his cousin's reaction to gauge the truth in his answer. "Have you ever heard of the Callan Raid in Northern Ireland?"

Alex didn't say anything for a moment. "I've heard the name, but I don't know what it is. You should ask my father about it; he will probably know more. What does this have to do with your father?"

Gavin could see that Alex wasn't telling him everything, but also realized that Alex was trying to get him to talk his uncle instead. Liam would have more answers. This led Gavin to believe that there were a lot of things his Uncle Liam had never told him, but why? He was going to ask another question, but Alex interrupted. "I meant to call you, but since you're here, we have a new detective that got ahold of a case matching your FBI bulletin."

"She found a murder matching my description?"

"Apparently so. I will call her over here so you can take a look at the case file."

A young detective walked over to Alex's desk. She looked like she had just graduated college. At least, that's what Gavin thought. Her name was Sara Reilly. She had just made detective, one of just a handful of female detectives in the city of Chicago. It was a big deal getting her detective badge, especially for her. Sara Reilly had also been the first in her family to graduate college. She hadn't been a detective for very long and was still very green. The men in her precinct let her know that every day, too. Gavin stuck out his hand and introduced himself. "Hello, I'm Agent Donnelly."

"I'm Detective Sara Reilly."

"My cousin here tells me that you have something for me."

"Yes, sir. Clifford Rollins, the North Shore Harbor Master, was found dead a few days ago. The ME was going to rule it a suicide at first, until I found some strange things about him… the most important being that he fit your profile from the FBI bulletin."

"How so, detective?"

"First, I think he was murdered, and whoever did it poisoned him. They tried to make it look like he overdosed on heroin, which would explain the needle marks on his left arm, but that's not the substance that was found in his system."

Gavin smiled. "Let me guess: some kind of poison that can't be isolated in the lab and, therefore, doesn't have a name?"

"That's right, Agent Donnelly."

"Why did you assume he wasn't a drug addict?"

"I was right, and you're questioning my investigative skills?"

"On the contrary. I'm just curious about how you came to your conclusion."

She gave him a confident smile. "He never had any history with drugs. Clifford Rollins was a gambling addict and he was into his bookie for eight grand. I found that out from his oldest daughter. She was still pissed at him for gambling away her college money. If some guys were leaning on him for money, they would have beat on him, leaving marks on his body. Plus, if they wanted to kill him and make it look like a suicide, his gun was in his desk drawer. They could have used that; it's simple and clean. No reason to go through all the theatrics, unless whoever killed him wanted to hide something."

"There's one other thing you're leaving out about the guys trying to collect money for his gambling debts…"

Sara interrupted. "A bookie's body men wouldn't make a death look like a suicide. They would want to send a message, so that everybody knows who did it."

"Exactly, detective. Good work. It probably was a murder, and it does fit the MO. But there's a bigger question here: why kill Clifford Rollins when it has nothing to do with a gambling debt?"

Sara shook her head. "That's the part I can't figure out. There was nothing important about this man except the fact that he ran the North Shore Harbor." The last part stuck out with Gavin, but before he could say anything, Alex got a call about a death threat and handed Gavin a piece of paper with the address of the threat. That's when Gavin flashed.

The two men were looking intently at the bomb instructions. This was the first time they had done anything like this, and to say they were nervous would be an understatement. They were both dressed as plumbers, looking very much the part in their disguises. They were in the basement of the building, trying to set the bomb around the hot water heater. In case anybody came into the storage room, it would look like they were just doing their job. Sam looked at his friend. "Robert, are you sure you want to do this? If we set this bomb off, there is no going back."

Robert smiled at this friend. "I've already thought of that and made peace with it. I'm not sure I want to go back. If you don't want to do this, then leave now."

Sam thought about it for a moment. "I've always stood by you and this is no different. Let's do this."

"Thank you, my friend." They finished hooking up the bomb, which was a hot water heater. They were still nervous and rushed out of the building, hoping they would not be seen. They were clumsy in trying to get away, but they got away.

Gavin shook his head from the pain he always felt when he flashed. His cousin looked at him with concern and asked if he was okay. He said yes and immediately called his partner. She answered, and he said, "We have a possible bomb threat. It just came through my cousin's precinct."

"What's the address?"

"It's the Sharon building on State Street. It's mostly office space, and I think we have about 30 or 40 minutes before the bomb goes off."

"How do you know that?"

"Call it a hunch."

Agent Main smiled. "It's one of those, is it?"

"We don't have much time to get the building evacuated, but we're on it." She hung up the phone and Gavin told his cousin to get every available man in the station. They had work to do.

∞∞∞∞∞∞∞∞∞∞

It was a busy day at the Sharon building. Not exactly the perfect day to evacuate the building based on a bomb threat, but when is it ever? The FBI and Chicago PD arrived on the scene in ten minutes. Security had already been working on getting the building evacuated. The FBI bomb squad started its search. Gavin was able to let slip that they should start in the basement of the building, without revealing how he knew that. The street in front of the Sharon building was blocked off. The police were moving people into buildings across the street, away from the potential blast site, in case a bomb did go off. The FBI didn't waste time checking everything in the building. It took about 40 minutes to go through and double-check it. They didn't find anything. Agent Donnelly and Agent Main were shocked and frustrated. Finally, Agent Main spoke up.

"Look, we have been getting false threats over the past couple of days. Why should this one be any different?"

Agent Donnelly replied, "This feels different. I don't believe the threat to be false."

"They've checked and double-checked the building. If there's not a bomb in here, then where is it?"

Agent Donnelly didn't have an answer as he stared out of the windows in the lobby of the Sharon building. He noticed something... he noticed the buildings across the street and the police escorting people inside. He noticed an English-style pub called Big Ben. He thought for a moment about the vision he saw and what the basement looked like inside the building. As he turned around to say something to his partner, there was an explosion inside the English pub. It was so intense that the blast shook the ground all the way across the street, causing the glass in the lobby of the Sharon building to shatter and the people standing there to fall backwards onto the ground. Agent Donnelly got hit with glass and could feel the blood dripping from his forehead. He looked over and saw his partner lying on the ground, covered in glass, with blood trickling from her face.

13

It was chaos. The bomb blast was so big that it caused debris to hit people in the street. Police were scrambling around, trying to get people to safety, while checking on the people that were hurt from the explosion. Gavin was the first to get up from the floor of the lobby, covered in glass. He was hurt, but not as badly as it may have looked. He stumbled to where his partner was lying. Believe it or not, she was okay, too, despite the blood coming from her forehead. He looked at her with concern. "Are you alright?"

"I think so," Rachel replied. "You're bleeding..."

He felt his forehead and saw the blood on his hands. "It's just a flesh wound."

She chuckled at the Monty Python joke. "Really, that's the comment you're going to make?"

"Well, at least you still have your sense of humor. Come on, let's check on everybody else." He helped her up and gave her his tie to put pressure on her forehead. There had been about ten people standing in the lobby of the Sharon building when the bomb went off. All of them were blown to the ground when the blast happened. As Gavin and Rachel checked everyone, they found that most of them were okay, but two other agents had been hit with flying debris so severely that they died on impact. Gavin and Rachel helped the other agents out of the shattered lobby, only to find panic on the street outside.

It took about an hour to quiet the street in front of the explosion and get the wounded treated. The street looked an army field hospital. The bomb crew went through the rubble to find parts of the explosive device and make a determination of the kind of bomb that was used. The head of the bomb squad reported to the command post that had been set up in a nearby office building. Gavin and Rachel were treated and had bandages on their foreheads. They both had minor cuts on their faces from flying glass. Gavin looked at the bomb tech. "What do you have?"

"We found what looks like a hot water heater that was filled with C4."

"Was it hooked up to the building?"

"Doesn't appear so, Agent Donnelly. It looks like it was standing next to the other hot water heater and had a timer on it."

Rachel responded, "So, somebody brought in another hot water heater, made it look like they were going to hook it up, and left it as a bomb? It's a good disguise."

Gavin asked the bomb tech, "Any word on the number of casualties from the pub?"

"They are still pulling bodies out of the rubble, but we estimate that there were over 200 people inside. Most likely, they're all dead."

It was not the news that he wanted to hear, but he appreciated the honesty. He looked at his partner and asked, "What do you make of this?"

She chuckled. "We have a smart enemy. He called in the bomb threat at a building that would take a long time to search, knowing that we would evacuate people to the other buildings, including the one that had the bomb. This wasn't just about blowing something up; it was strategically planned."

Gavin paused for a moment to ponder what she said. "Big Ben is an English pub. Are there are any British companies in the Sharon building?"

Another FBI agent was pulling up the building directory in his laptop. He found what they were looking for. "Agent Donnelly, there are two British companies that have offices here: BP Oil and HM Mining Surveys."

Gavin responded, "There it is. They targeted a place where British employees would frequent, and I bet that whoever did this is trying to make it look like an IRA attack."

Rachel replied, "The first part is a logical guess, but the second part is a bit of a leap. Are you sure you are being objective?"

"Maybe not, but with what's coming to Chicago this week, it's a safe bet."

Rachel didn't argue. She asked one of the other agents, who was in charge of taking statements from survivors in the buildings next the English pub, what he had found. That agent replied, "Not much. One person said there was a plumbing van in the alley behind the pub."

"Did he see a name on the van?"

"Yes, ma'am. Grimes Plumbing."

Rachel turned to the agent on the computer and told him to start looking up information on a Grimes Plumbing company. After a few minutes, he found the public records on the company. Rachel looked them over and then asked her partner to examine them. "It looks like the company was set up to be a fake."

Gavin replied, "What about this Robert Grimes, the owner? Can we find a photo of him? I'm sure there are many Robert Grimes' in the Chicago area."

Rachel asked, "What are you looking   for, exactly?"

"Something out of the ordinary… somebody who doesn't look like a plumber or a criminal." The agent on the computer started finding photos of different Robert Grimes' in the greater Chicago area. The agents looked through them like mug shots. As they were scrolling through pictures, Gavin saw something that stuck out. He spoke up, "Stop right there. The second one from the left. I've seen that face before."

The agent on the computer clicked on the picture and enlarged it. Rachel asked, "What is it about this guy?"

"He's on an FBI watch list."

"Who is he?"

"This Robert Grimes is a radical, always protesting something about the government. He's a borderline anarchist, if you ask me."

Rachel looked at the screen. "Twenty-nine-year-old male, graduated with honors at Northwestern with degrees in Political Science and Sociology. He's been arrested half a dozen times for protesting. He is the leader of a political activism group called the United Front, but they have never committed violence before. It looks like he just protests and writes blogs. Are you sure this is our guy?"

"Radicals always turn violent."

Rachel gave him a look as if she was unsure. She told the agent at the computer, "Check the address of the plumbing company and compare it to Grimes's home address." The agent did just that. Rachel looked at the addresses on the computer screen. "Look, here's the company address. It's a P.O. Box located at a post office two miles away. Perhaps this is our guy, but…"

"But what?"

"Why would he all of sudden decide to bomb a building and kill people? And why this target?"

Gavin paused. "I don't know, but let's go ask him." He looked at the agent on the computer. "Call AD Foster and tell him we have a suspect. Let him know that we need a warrant pushed through. We're about to make a house call."

∞∞∞∞∞∞∞∞∞∞∞

Robert Grimes lived on the third floor of the Lincolnshire Apartment Complex. It was one of the few apartment buildings that had adjoining doors between apartments. The FBI didn't know that when they started to surround the place. They covered all exits, including the fire escape, to try to stop the suspects from escaping. As Gavin and Rachel pulled up in front of the apartment building in their unmarked car, Rachel spoke up. "If he's smart, he won't be here."

Gavin smiled. "I'm counting on him thinking we're stupid and can't figure out that he's a suspect."

"That's a big gamble. What if you're wrong? We need to put an APB on Robert Grimes now and get him cornered, before he has a chance to escape the city."

"I know we should have done that beforehand, but I want the element of surprise with this guy. Plus, we don't need to be causing panic around the city. We need to do this quietly."

She looked at his watch. "If we don't have him in custody in ten minutes, I'm calling the APB, even if it causes panic." They got out of the car, checked their weapons, and put their bulletproof vests on. The head of the FBI Swat Team came over and told the agents that they were in position and ready to go. Gavin replied, "Okay, he's in apartment 3G. Let's go knock the door down."

The agents went through the lobby of the apartment building and climbed the stairs to the third floor. Two sets of agents stood on either side of the apartment door. The agent with the battering ram waited for the go-ahead. Gavin nodded 'yes' to him. In one swift movement, the door was batted down and explosions rang out. Gavin and Rachel were behind the first six agents when it all happened. The explosions were loud and filled the room with smoke. Rachel was the first to yell out. "Stand your ground! They are only flash bombs."

Gavin was going to say something, but gunshots rang out in the room. Nobody could see anything because of the smoke. They all started to scramble to avoid being hit by bullets. Gavin saw the door on his left that connected to the next apartment. He shot the doorknob to unlock it and kicked the door open. Then, he grabbed his partner and pulled her inside to avoid the bullets. Both of them hit the ground. Finally, the gunshots stopped as the second FBI Swat Team entered the first apartment, shooting and killing the guy with the gun. Unfortunately, before he was shot by the FBI, the man with the gun shot and killed two agents. As Gavin was trying to get up and go back into the other room, he felt the bottom of a gun hit him in his face. Someone pushed him down. Out of instinct, he winced and held his hand over his face to try to soften the pain, but then he heard a scream. He could tell it was his partner.

Gavin looked up and saw Rachel being held at gunpoint. It was Robert Grimes. He was nervous, but he was still strong enough to hold onto her from behind and put a gun to her head. Robert shouted, "Get back, man! Call your FBI men off, or I'll put a bullet in her." Gavin held up his hands to show Robert that he wasn't trying to hurt him. He didn't even draw his weapon to aim at the guy holding Rachel at gunpoint. Gavin replied, "Take it easy. No one is trying to hurt you. We're all one big, happy family." The FBI Swat Team from the other apartment was trying to enter the room, but Gavin motioned with his hand to tell them 'no.' "Stay back, guys. I have this under control."

Robert shouted, "That's right, you fucking pigs, keep back or I'll blow her head off!"

Gavin calmly responded, "Robert, let's talk about this. This place is surrounded. There is no escape."

"There is when I have a gun to her head."

"You're right, but I don't think you really want to kill her."

"You don't know that, FBI man."

"Sure, I do. If you wanted to kill her, then you would have done it already. Now, let's talk about how we can all walk out of here alive."

"That only happens if you let me walk out of here with her. When I'm safe, I'll let her go."

Gavin smiled. "It's not that simple. You know I can't let you walk out of here."

"Then your fucking partner is dead!"

Rachel yelled out, "Gavin, just shoot him already!" That made Robert mad and he hit her in the head with his gun. Then he yelled at her, "Shut up, bitch."

Gavin responded, "Be cool, Robert. This is not helping. Let me tell you what your only options are and, believe me, you don't have many. You kill her and you're dead a second later. You let her go, Robert, and then you and your friend in the bathroom will be escorted out safely and you won't have to die."

Robert was a little shocked, but asked the question anyway. "What guy in the bathroom?"

"Come on Robert. I'm not stupid. Your friend is standing behind the door with a gun, waiting to shoot this place up."

"I don't know what you're talking about."

That made Gavin angry and he didn't have any more patience. He grabbed his gun and fired four shots into the bathroom door. Everybody in the room heard the scream and then the sound of a body falling onto the floor. Gavin quickly turned around and pointed his weapon at Robert Grimes. Robert was shaken by what he just saw; he couldn't believe an FBI agent would do that. He lowered his gun a little and Rachel saw an opening. She used her free hand to push Robert's gun out of the way. Then, she made a fist and punched him in the nose, breaking it. She wrestled the gun out of his hand while the other agents rushed into the room and handcuffed Robert.

Rachel looked down at Robert while blood was running down his nose. "See what happens when you mistreat a lady?"

Gavin walked over and made a comment, too. "You're lucky, Robert, because I would have just shot you."

"Fuck you both. This is a total violation of my civil rights!"

Rachel bent down and looked at him. "We didn't kill you. That means you still have some rights." She looked at the other agents. "Get him out of here and don't make anything comfortable until he's ready to start talking." Gavin smiled at what she said. She told him, "Thanks for saving my life again. I guess I owe you… again."

"I'm sure you're going to have to save mine before this is all said and done."

She laughed. They both started looking around and found a file folder with some bomb instructions in it. Rachel said to her partner, "Hey, look at this. You know what this means?"

Gavin looked concerned and replied, "It means that this isn't over. Something tells me Robert wanted to get caught."

"Why do you say that?"

"He came home and left the bomb instructions lying around. Either he's completely stupid or he has a different agenda."

"You don't think he's stupid, do you?"

"Not at all!"

14

The Chicago PD and Chicago rescue crews were still cleaning up the streets and treating the injured at the bomb site when Gavin and Rachel got back to FBI headquarters with the suspect. Gavin was on the phone with his cousin, giving him an update on the situation. Alex was injured during the blast, too, but only had minor cuts and bruises. As soon as Gavin got off the phone, his partner asked, "How many are confirmed dead?"

"Alex said there are 238 confirmed dead so far, but they're still pulling out bodies from the buildings next door, too. The blast wasn't just confined to the pub; it carried over to the other buildings."

"Jesus, this is bad. You know what they're going to be saying? 'FBI fails again; they couldn't keep the city safe.'"

Gavin laughed. "Never mind, we just caught the guy, right?"

"Seems to be the way it goes: the media trashes us when we fail and never congratulates us when we succeed."

The both laughed at the comment. For the most part, it was true. Gavin replied, "Let's get this guy into a room and see if we can score some more points in this so-called victory."

Robert Grimes was put into an interrogation room and given a glass of water. They didn't even give him a new towel to help stop the bleeding from his broken nose. He had the same bloody towel and it annoyed him to the point that he hated the FBI even more. AD Foster met them outside of the interrogation rooms and said to Gavin and Rachel, "You two did good work today, despite the bombing. Getting a guy in custody an hour after the attack is impressive."

Gavin nodded in agreement. "It's not open-and-shut yet. Based on the plans we found in this guy's apartment, they were planning more than one attack. There can still be more than one bomb out there."

AD Foster looked concerned. "Then you guys better get it out of him. The president and the prime ministers are going to be here in two days and we can't have the city in chaos."

Rachel spoke up. "Speaking of chaos, has a press release been sent out yet?"

AD Foster replied, "Yes, it has, but we haven't released a name yet… just that we got a suspect. Hopefully, it will calm the storm that's been brewing since the bombing."

Gavin responded, "Sir, can we make sure nothing gets out about the bombing being an IRA attack? I don't want misleading information getting out that could cause the peace summit to be called off in Chicago."

"I understand, agent. I have already put a ban on words that can be used with the press, like 'IRA,' 'revolution,' and 'terrorists.' But keep in mind, there's no guarantee that it won't happen."

"That's not very comforting."

"If I find out that anybody from this office used my banned words with the press, I'm going to cut his nutsack off. Does that make you feel better?"

Both Gavin and Rachel laughed. Gavin replied, "It makes me feel a little bit better. You know how to inspire the troops, sir."

AD Foster gave him a dirty look for the sarcasm. "Get in there and find out what we need to know."

Gavin and Rachel walked into the interrogation room. Robert Grimes was stoic. He was trying to be tough, but he couldn't deny that he was a little scared. This was his first time in an interrogation room. Rachel let her partner take the lead. He started off by saying, "Well, Robert, you have caused quite a mess today. So far, 238 people are dead because of your stunt. That gets you the death penalty."

Nobody said anything for a moment. Gavin finally spoke up. "No, nothing? You don't care about human life, do you? That doesn't make you revolutionary; it makes you a sociopath."

"Fuck you," Robert Grimes said out of anger. "Sociopaths kill for no reason. That is not me. I do care about human life, even the enemies of freedom."

"Is that what these people were? Enemies of freedom? Because you killed a lot of innocent people, too. Tell me… why did you pick this target?"

"The target is not important."

"So you're saying it was a random target?"

"It's about the people that would have been in that building."

"And who are they?"

Robert smiled. "Come on, Agent Donnelly. I can't do your entire job for you."

Rachel chimed in and asked a question. "Why is the United Front interested in blowing things up? Your organization had never committed violence. You'd never even threatened anyone before. What made you escalate to this?"

Robert smiled at her. "Isn't this the next evolutionary step for a political group?"

"Sure, if you're a sociopath. But you're not, are you? You knew exactly what you were doing!"

Robert didn't say anything. Gavin said, "You think you can still be this tough when they strap you down to a table and stick you with a needle to kill you? I hear it burns like a motherfucker. Not exactly a painless death."

Robert replied, "I'm not afraid of death."

"You will be."

"If you're trying to scare me, your tactics need work."

"Robert, I don't have to scare you to get what I want from you. You've never spent more than a night in jail. This time, you're going to a federal prison as a terrorist. After two nights, you're going to be begging me to let you out. You know what we do to terrorists? They're pretty much the only people we are allowed to torture, and no amount of protesting is going to stop the pain that you have coming. So… let's talk about who helped you with this."

There was a little bit of shock in Robert's eyes. He knew Gavin wasn't bluffing. Robert had always been good at reading people. "What are you getting at?"

"Robert, you wouldn't even know where to get the bomb-making materials that were found at the site. They were too sophisticated and you can't find them at a local store. You have no military background, no training of any kind to wage war against anybody. You're not the IRA. I think someone else wanted this done, and got you to do it for them. In fact, I am going to make a deal with you!"

"What kind of deal, agent?"

Gavin knocked on the window in the room to signal one of the agents, standing outside, to bring in the box. The box was set on the table in the room. It contained some wires, switches, and C4. "If you can actually put a bomb together with the materials in this box, which is all you need for a standard time bomb, then I will let you go."

Rachel was shocked to hear that. She didn't know what her partner was going to do, but was starting to get an idea. Gavin asked, "Come on, Robert, show us how to make a bomb!"

Robert Grimes stared at the box for a few moments. He didn't know what to say, but finally, something came to mind… something that could thwart Gavin's mind games. "Why would I show you my hand? And how can I trust that you will do what you say you're going to do?"

"Very good, Robert, you called my bluff. But what you may not realize is you just told me a very important detail about yourself. You don't really care about freedom, which means you either expected to get caught or you wanted to get caught. You still showed your hand, Robert!"

Robert was annoyed. "Fine, Agent Donnelly. I don't know how to build a bomb, and neither did Sam."

"Who's Sam?"

"The man you shot and killed through the bathroom door."

"Don't forget, he was still pointing a gun at me. Now, please continue."

"Fuck you."

Gavin chuckled. "That's the second time you've said that to us. You don't want to do it a third time."

"Fuck you!"

Rachel was the one to lean over the desk and hit Robert's broken nose. It started gushing blood and Robert screamed in pain. She yelled at him, "My partner warned you! Now, be nice." She threw him a fresh towel to help stop the bleeding.

Gavin laughed at the incident. "See what happens when you piss us off? Now, tell us the rest."

Robert's voice was a little muffled through the towel. "Some old guy gave my organization $10,000. He had the plumbing van, with all the documentation for my cover business and instruction on the targets. The bomb stuff was already made up."

Gavin was stunned. "You did all of this for $10,000?"

Robert smiled at him. "No, sir, I did it for two reasons. First, so that people will be afraid of the United Front. Second, so I can deliver a message to you and the FBI."

Rachel was the one to ask. "And what's the message?"

Robert had a stern look on his face and directed it at both of the agents. "This is only the beginning. There will be more bombs, there will be more deaths, and you will not be able to stop it. There will be no peace. And this part is especially for you: you cannot escape death, for death is always watching."

Gavin was taken aback by the last part. He simply asked, "Where are the other bombs?"

Robert smiled at him. "Not even I know that. I wasn't supposed to know everything. That was my role to play. Now, here is the part where I ask for my lawyer and use my right to remain silent."

There wasn't anything more the agents could ask. He'd asked for his lawyer and, as much as they hated it, Robert Grimes did have rights. Gavin and Rachel left the room. AD Foster was the first to ask the question. "What was all of that about? Is this some kind of setup for the FBI?"

Gavin replied, "I think this much is clear: he wanted to get caught. He's not the man who planned this and what's about to come. He's a pawn or a patsy in the plan."

"Why?"

Rachel answered, "To cause chaos. To get us stretched so thin that security wouldn't be that good. They know we don't have the manpower to search every building in Chicago or find every member of the United Front."

AD Foster replied, "We still have to try to find those bombs and known associates of the United Front. I can put a call in and see if we can get extra Secret Service men to help track down members of the United Front."

Gavin responded, "For the buildings we have to search, we'll start inside the perimeter of the peace summit and do a security check of every employee that works in every one those buildings. If there is going to be a bombing, it's most likely going to be there. Next, we'll start checking every Irish and English business in Chicago. We know that the Big Ben pub was targeted because of the employees from BP Oil and HM Mining who went in there, and the fact that those companies' offices are across the street. We'll work the MO of the bombers. This will help narrow down the search."

Rachel nodded in agreement and AD Foster replied, "Good idea, Agent Donnelly. And I am going to try to get the president and the prime ministers to limit their public appearances while in Chicago."

Gavin had to ask. "They're still coming to Chicago, right?"

"As of right now, they are, but that can change. However, it doesn't matter. We may have more bombs in our city and our main priority is to find them and to save lives. This city will not turn into Belfast."

Gavin and Rachel walked back to their office. Rachel could sense her partner had another theory. "So, what is it? Why do you really think this is happening?"

"I think this is connected to the murders we have so far. There's an assassin out there somewhere that we also need to catch. What if this is a diversion to keep us from looking for the killer?"

Rachel shook her head. "While I still think you are taking all of this personally, you have a good point. But if the killer is going after either one of the prime ministers or even the president, then he has to get close to do it. The closest people to these men are the Secret Service."

Gavin chuckled. "Are you suggesting we do background checks on the Secret Service?"

"First, we probably won't even get a chance to. That kind of cooperation doesn't exist among federal agencies. Second, if we even suggest that, we may not even have a job at the end of the week. Accusing the president's detail or any Secret Service agent of being a spy, without proof, and then investigating them without congressional approval, is a felony for us."

Gavin smiled. "It doesn't mean we shouldn't do it. I might have a way of doing it without there being a record of it."

Rachel was not happy to hear that. "Is this going to get me into trouble?"

"Maybe, but I can keep you out of it."

"What are you going to do?"

Gavin smiled. "You probably shouldn't know if you want to keep out of it."

15

The parking garage was not very crowded in the middle of the night. In fact, a car hadn't driven through the garage for the past hour. These were the things Mr. Chambers noticed as he sat in the car, waiting for the old man. The parking garage was the only place they could meet without being noticed. Finally, a black Cadillac sedan drove up and parked next to him. The old man got out of the car and walked around to the passenger's side of Mr. Chambers' car. He looked at the old man and said, "It looks like things went well. I have seen the reports of the bombing. Nearly 300 hundred people are dead; that's more than expected."

The old man smiled. "It worked perfectly. Nobody saw it coming, and it looks like your Homeland Security boys weren't smart enough to check for bombs in the other buildings. You were right about that."

"My boss is as stupid as he is predictable when it comes to security. Now, I have some questions about this Robert Grimes and his United Front organization. Why did you choose this guy? He's actually a believer, a crusader."

"That's exactly what you need. He was willing to be a martyr for his cause, and all for the price of $10,000."

"That doesn't sound like a crusader to me. They usually can't be bought, and that's bad for us."

The old man smiled. "You're missing the point, Mr. Chambers. The money wasn't for him; it was for his organization. His true cause is for them, and having a group like the United Front cause disarray in society is good for you."

"How?"

"Radicals turned violent; homegrown terrorism that can't be contained. This is the perfect organization to make it look like your boss is not doing his job. And the best part is, this organization will create fear among the populace."

"What good is a little fear going to do for me?"

The old man looked at Mr. Chambers sternly. "In the beginning, it may not seem like much. But in the end, this kind of terrorism will create so much fear that the people will willingly give up their rights in order to stay safe. A useful tool for you and your friends, especially when you become the head of the agency."

"What good is this group if it only has a few members? If they're going to make an impact, then they need more people."

"Recruiting won't be hard. All you need to do is find people who are fed up with the system… or, at least, make them think they are."

Mr. Chambers laughed. "You make it sound so easy. How could it possibly work?"

"It worked for the Tea Party. It's a hysterical and paranoid political group that's on the verge of revolution because they think they're fed up with the system. Their membership keeps rising every day. And, of course, the best part is, they want to limit the freedom of people they don't like, while still fighting for liberty. We've created political hypocrisy in the name of freedom. This can be done again. The easiest thing to do is make people go against their true nature for a made-up ideal!"

"Jesus. This sounds worse than just shooting someone for no reason. But how can this be used to effectively get rid of a pesky FBI agent without killing him and turning his investigation into a crusade?"

The old man smiled. "That plan, my friend, has already been set into motion."

∞∞∞∞∞∞∞∞∞∞∞

Gavin met his friend, Dan, at their favorite diner. Dan didn't know what the meeting was about. He knew he was probably going to be asked to do something under the radar of the FBI, or even illegal, because the other person that was invited was Janie Myers. Dan arrived first and got a cup of coffee. A couple of minutes later, Janie walked in dressed up in some kind of Goth outfit. She looked very different and Gavin thought to himself that it must have been some kind of disguise. However, there were still people in the diner looking at her. After all, she was very out of place there. Dan was the first to ask the obvious question.

"So, Agent Donnelly, why are we here?"

[376]

Gavin looked at both of them. "I need a couple of hackers to go through the profiles of every Secret Service agent that will be here in Chicago for the peace summit. I can't go through proper channels to do it. There's isn't time. Plus, the Secret Service…"

Dan interrupted. "The Secret Service isn't going to cooperate with the FBI, especially when they think we're investigating them." Gavin nodded. Dan asked, "That's what you're doing, isn't it?"

"Yes."

"Why?"

"Because there may be an assassin among them. We have a lead that an assassin may be trying to stop the peace summit, and he or she could be among the Secret Service."

Janie smiled. "Why is it just the Secret Service? Why can't the FBI have a mole?"

Gavin responded. "Yes, I am not denying that. If you want to do background checks on everybody in our office, then go ahead. But I don't have to give you permission; you'll probably just do it, anyway."

Janie laughed. "If it makes you feel more powerful, then give me permission."

Gavin smiled at her, but it was Dan who responded. "If that's all you need, then why is Janie here?" She gave Dan a strange look. Gavin replied, "It's not because I don't think you can do it yourself. But if you're caught, then it should look like a hacker was doing it." He looked at Janie. "No offense, Janie."

"Only if you don't take offense that you're too stupid to catch me."

Gavin laughed. "See, Dan, this is also a reason I asked her to be a part of this. You need this kind of foreplay in your life, and I thought you might enjoy working together." Dan just gave him a dirty look, but there was truth in the statement. He did have a bit of a crush on Janie. Gavin got up from the table and put some money down to pay for everybody's coffee. He handed Dan a business card with a different cell phone number on the back. "Call me on this number if you find anything. It's a line nobody knows about and I would like to keep it that way." Both Janie and Dan nodded in agreement with the arrangement.

∞∞∞∞∞∞∞∞∞∞

Gavin had just gotten off the phone with his partner, who wasn't exactly happy that she was stuck doing both of their jobs, when he arrived at the University of Illinois at Chicago. He walked up to the classroom of Dr. Steven Larkin, better known as Henry Lee Roark, or

[377]

Dr. Death. Rachel wasn't happy that Gavin was still conducting his own investigation. While Gavin was under time constraints to solve this little mystery, he didn't want to disturb the class until it was completely over, so he waited. Finally, students started coming out of the classroom. Most of them were nice and said hi to Gavin. He walked into the classroom and said, "Dr. Larkin. Or should I call you Henry?"

"Ah, Agent Donnelly. Why don't we keep up the farce? Doctor has a better ring to it."

"As you wish, doctor!"

"I didn't smell her perfume, so I take it Agent Main is not here."

Gavin smiled. "Very good, doc. You just get me today, but if you're a big help, then I'll get her to visit you."

Dr. Larkin had to laugh at the comment. "What can I do for you, Agent Donnelly?"

"I need your expertise in a series of murders."

Dr. Larkin smiled and asked to see the files. Gavin laid the files out on the conference table at the front of the classroom and told the doctor what they had figured out so far. Gavin told him his theory, too. The former serial killer looked them over carefully and then finally took a step back and had a small smile of pride on his face.

Gavin asked, "What is it, doctor? You see something, don't you? You know who did this?"

Dr. Larkin nodded. "I can't give you a name, but I can give you some insight into this… but not here. This place has ears. Walk with me."

They walked out of the building and started going down one of the walking paths in the middle of campus. It was in-between classes, so the walking paths were crowded. It provided some cover from anyone that might be listening. Gavin had to remember that the doctor was heavily monitored. As they were walking down the path, the wind was blowing a little bit. It was still a beautiful day… not the kind of day one should get bad news. Dr. Larkin spoke up. "You're right to think these murders are connected and done by the same person, but this isn't a true serial killer. He doesn't have the nature of a serial killer. This is the work of an assassin."

"Why do you say that?"

"Because a serial killer wants to show off his work. And like you said, Agent Donnelly, this killer is hiding something… maybe, for instance, the way he's truly killing them."

"We already know that all of the victims were poisoned."

Dr. Larkin smiled. "That's not what I am talking about. Did you find out what the poison was?"

Gavin looked stunned. "No, we didn't. We couldn't isolate it."

They finally stopped at a park bench in the middle of campus and took a seat. Dr. Larkin looked around to see if anybody might be watching. Gavin asked, "Are you paranoid?"

"Just a little. The FBI agents are not the only ones who watch me."

"Who else would be watching you?"

Dr. Larkin laughed. "The men who have set all of this in motion. Yes, Agent Donnelly, I know about some of the men who are behind all of this, which makes what I am about to tell you very dangerous. You could die just for having the information. Do you understand that?"

Gavin paused for a moment. "Yes, I do."

Dr. Larkin patted him on the shoulder. "Good. Have you ever heard of the Gang of Eight?"

"You mean the security council that the president has to report to when he's about to do something covert or assassinate someone?"

Dr. Larkin laughed. "No, not exactly! The term refers to a group of the eight most elite assassins in the world."

Gavin laughed. "Surely, you're joking."

"I wouldn't joke about something like this. Each member of this gang has one special talent when it comes to killing. Even though they can all kill in many different ways, that special talent is their calling card. That also goes for making a murder look like someone else did it. Using an untraceable poison is one of those unique signatures. He makes the poison himself… grows it, cultivates it, and only he alone knows the true recipe so that it can never be traced. Now, that's a true talent and makes him an elite assassin."

"How do you know so much about this?"

Dr. Larkin didn't say anything for a moment, but then he looked Gavin dead in the eye and replied, "Because I used to be one!"

Gavin jolted up from the park bench in shock. "What are you talking about? How come the FBI didn't know about this?"

"Because they think Henry Roark is my real name, and that all the documents leading to that name couldn't possibly be fake."

"What is your real name?"

"I wish I could remember. I've used so many names over the years that I don't know anymore."

"How do I know that you're not still part of the Gang of Eight?"

Dr. Larkin pulled up his pants leg and showed the ankle bracelet. "Do you really think I can be an assassin these days? I am monitored every second of every day."

Gavin smiled. "Good point. Tell me about this group." Dr. Larkin nodded and began to tell the story. In 1913, a group of men who controlled the banking practices and monetary policies of the world knew that the only way to succeed was to kill anybody who stood in their way. So, they formed a group of killers, or a gang. They would be the best in the world and have no real identities. They would be myths spoken about only with fear. They would be the shadows behind the powerful men who wanted to control the world. Each assassin would have one special talent in the way they executed people, and they would be able to do it with no traces of how they killed. While these murderers would be independent of one another and true contract killers, all contracts for kills would come from the same group of powerful men. Assassins like these had been used to get rid of those who stood in the way of these powerful men ever since the Middle Ages, and especially during the Crusades, but never had a group like this been created. There was one simple rule: each assassin would have an apprentice, someone he would teach and mentor into the perfect killer, who would replace him in the Gang of Eight when the assassin's services were no longer required. There would always be a master assassin and an apprentice.

Gavin was shaking his head in disbelief. "Why are you telling me this?"

"Because you want the truth. And, also because the question of *why* is more important to you than any other answer."

"Won't they kill you for telling me all of this?"

"Probably, but I'm an old man now and death is more inevitable than it used to be."

Gavin chuckled. "What happened to you? Why were you kicked out?"

"Because I had one weakness: I enjoyed killing way too much. My nature became that of a serial killer instead of an assassin. And when you go off the reservation, Agent Donnelly, they replace you."

"It seems to me that replacement for someone like that means death."

Dr. Larkin smiled. "Sometimes it is, unless they can find another use for you. It wasn't an accident that I was caught by FBI agents and came to work for them."

"What do you mean?"

"I am no longer an assassin, but my role hasn't changed."

Gavin stared at him for a moment. Then, it finally dawned on him. "Disinformation. You help us without really helping us."

"Exactly!"

"So, how do I know that what you're telling me now is true?"

Dr. Larkin laughed. "The better question is, can you afford not to trust what I'm saying right now? Death is coming soon. These murders have two purposes: one is diversion and the other is a message."

"A diversion for what?"

"Sometimes, assassins work in pairs. With the event that's about to happen in Chicago… well, like I said, death is coming soon."

"You said there's a message behind these murders. What is it?"

"I believe the message is meant for you and you alone. It is for you to figure out." Gavin didn't say anything for a moment. He was trying to process everything. He couldn't figure out if his thoughts were more of shock or disbelief. He finally asked, "The first time we met and you helped with the murders that looked like those of Albert Sorrano, did you lie to me and my partner?"

"I can't answer that. But the information I gave you about the real assassin that night , the one they call the Ghost… the reason I knew who he was is because I trained him, so I recognized his style." Gavin was shocked by the statement, and then he remembered something: the phone call he received from the Ghost after his and Rachel's first case. It was the call letting Gavin know that he knew his secret, but he also remembered what else the Ghost said. Gavin told Dr. Larkin, "I have to ask you something based on the call I got from the Ghost after that first case, about something he said to me. 'The same man who changed the course of your life, changed mine.' Were you ordered to kill my parents?"

Dr. Larkin looked off into the distance. "I will not answer that. You already know." Gavin started to pull his service weapon from the holster. The doctor spoke up again. "If revenge is more important to you than the bigger truth, then so be it. But you will never answer the question *why*. This is bigger than your own personal demons."

Gavin put his weapon back. "Who are these men behind all of this?"

"The way is always nameless, for that is its true power. They are men of belief, and having a name would only diminish their power and lessen the fear you should have of them. But you will figure it out."

"I don't need any philosophy from Lao Tzu. Just give me a straight answer."

Dr. Larkin smiled. "You know your philosophy, and this is a straight answer. You want to know the truth behind these men? Then understand the philosophy. That means the way is forever nameless, for that is its true power."

Gavin was full of anger, but he began to understand how big all of this truly was. He shot the doctor an angry look. "The only reason

I won't kill you right now is because of the information you gave me. I may need more before it's all said and done. But know this: one day I will come back and kill you."

"Chances are, your revenge will come too late. My death is sooner than you think. Take the information I've given you and save lives. That's the only way you can win."

Gavin didn't bother to shake Dr. Larkin's hand. He put the file folders in his briefcase and started to walk away. He was still too angry to be respectful of the doctor. There was still a chance that he would kill the doctor right then and there, but he did what was in his best interest and walked away. As he started walking, he flashed.

Two men went inside the harbor office with a huge duffel bag. They looked like maintenance workers, but it was strange that they would be carrying a duffel bag. They went inside Clifford Rollins's old office and pulled out what looked like a timer. Then, they pulled out some binders that looked overstuffed with paper, but the paper was gray. That was all Gavin could see as the two men put the binders in different places in the office. He was trying to see more, but the phone started ringing.

He answered the phone and said, "Detective Reilly, thank you for calling me back. I need you to walk me through the crime scene at the harbor. Can you do it tonight?

Detective Reilly replied, "Yes, that's fine. Can you swing by the station and pick me up?"

Gavin smiled. "Sure thing, detective. See you tonight."

16

It was a media circus in Chicago when the President of the United States arrived. Even though it was late in the day, it didn't stop people from coming out to see the president. He arrived with the Prime Ministers of England and Ireland. The peace summit would begin the next day with the first of the negotiations between both prime ministers. But first, there would be a press conference in Daley Plaza, announcing the details of the peace summit. Security was tight. The Chicago PD was like an army, having the square of the plaza center roped off. There was extra Secret Service agents surrounding the area that pretty much built a wall around the president and the prime ministers while they were standing at the microphones, talking with the reporters. There were also a lot of FBI agents in the crowd, disguised as ordinary citizens and looking for suspicious behavior. Gavin and Rachel were in the security office of the Daley Center, looking at TV screens that showed every camera angle in the plaza. As head of the local security team in Chicago, they were looking for anything out the ordinary, which, in the last week, could have meant just about anything.

There had been numerous bomb threats in the last few days and they had to check out every one, but that did not stop the peace summit from happening. President Sunders spoke about the tragedy that happened in Chicago, but the most important thing he said during his speech was that he and the prime ministers would not be deterred by terrorists. Even David Kenny, the Prime Minister of England, said during the press conference that Ireland and England could put their bombs and guns aside for the prospect of peace. Unfortunately, all these great leaders knew that it would not be that easy, the evidence being the tragedy, which had just happened a few days ago.

Rachel spoke into the headset. "Team two, check in. What do you have for me?"

The agent on the other end replied, "Agent Main, we haven't found anything. We're on our second sweep."

"Okay, do a third sweep." She told all the bomb detection teams to do the same. Gavin chuckled. "You're not making friends today."

She smiled. "I'm not here to be their friend. Besides, we can't take any chances."

"I don't disagree." That's when Gavin saw something on one of the monitors. "Look at this guy in the crowd with balloons. He's out of place; I want him out of there." Gavin spoke to one of the agents in the crowd through his headset and told him to detain the man and get him away from the crowd. Gavin figured it might be nothing, but he was being extra careful.

The FBI teams made their third sweeps and then checked in. There was a small sigh of relief from Gavin and Rachel, but it was short-lived. There were noises in the crowd that sounded like gunfire. Secret Service agents collapsed their security wall around the president and the prime ministers, ushering them inside the Daley Center. Chicago PD and the FBI agents in the crowd found the guy who made the sounds. It was another man in the crowd with balloons; he popped them, which made the sound of gunshots. The FBI agents reported what happened, but Gavin and Rachel were not amused. Gavin shouted through the headset, "Arrest them both! We'll deal with them later."

The press conference was over at that point, and the President of the United States was furious. What happened didn't make him look like a strong leader, and he had gotten plenty of insults from Republicans to that effect. AD Foster received a call from the president's chief of staff. He got off the phone and looked at Gavin and Rachel. "Well, the president is pissed as hell. He wants to see you two for a security briefing."

Gavin laughed and replied, "Ask him if he'll still be pissed when we save his life."

AD Foster smiled. "You can ask him that yourself. He's not mad at me, and I'm trying to keep it that way."

Twenty minutes later, they were in a conference room in the Daley Center with the president and the prime ministers. Agent Brice, the head of the president's Secret Service detail, was there as well. Having to deal with him all week long about the security for the peace summit and the president's visit had been complicated, to say the least. They didn't agree on the parameters for security or what should be considered a priority. President Sunders was mad because he only saw the political ramifications of what just happened. He looked at Gavin and Rachel and asked, "What the hell happened out there? I thought the FBI had everything under control. That's what you said after the bombing."

Gavin and Rachel looked at each other, trying to figure out what the other should say. Gavin spoke up first. "Mr. President, I'm sorry for what happened today, but we're taking every precaution to ensure everybody's safety. If being a little paranoid over balloons is a way to do that, then we'll do it again. It's better to keep you and the prime ministers safe and suffer a little embarrassment rather than risk your lives."

"Easy for you to say, Agent Donnelly. Your job is not an elected position. Were those men part of the same group that did the bombing?"

"We don't know yet. By all appearances, they look like innocent bystanders, but we will question them and run background checks."

George Mallory, the Prime Minister of Great Britain, spoke up. "Does this group have any ties to the IRA?"

David Kenney, the Prime Minister of Ireland, sarcastically replied, "Why do you always assume any bombing that involves you is an IRA bomb? There are plenty of other people in the world that want to kill the English. You did invade more than one country and claim it as your own."

George Mallory gave him a dirty look. He was about to respond when Gavin said, "Before you start a fight over something that isn't true, let me tell you that there were no IRA ties to the bombing."

The president interrupted the prime ministers before anything else derogatory could be said. He asked Gavin, "What are you going to do to make sure everything is okay with this peace summit? What assurances do we have that we will all be safe?"

Gavin replied, "We will continue our bomb sweeps. We're going to make sure there is no one in the crowd with potentially dangerous objects. We will do more background checks on everybody that has access to the buildings, and we will make sure that nobody who has the potential to kill you and the prime ministers will get close enough. No matter who those people may be, they will not get close to you."

"And what else?" the president replied.

Rachel responded, "Sir, if you're looking for a guarantee that we can keep you safe, then the only way that happens is if you don't put yourself in harm's way."

At first, the president looked angry for what he thought was a glib answer from Rachel, but then he laughed. "Agent Main, that's very true. But when you're supposed to be a symbol of hope, then you're constantly in harm's way."

Gavin responded, "Mr. President, I urge you not to hold any more press conferences outside. We have a better chance of keeping you and the prime ministers safe if you stay indoors."

"I know you don't care about politics, Agent Donnelly, but doing this outside shows the world that we can create peace and that terrorists will not deter us. The symbol of that is greater than all of our lives."

"I agree, Mr. President, but my job is to keep you and the prime ministers safe, so I had to advise you. I do have one request."

"What is that?"

"A little interagency cooperation. Allow someone to do background checks on the FBI, Chicago PD, and the Secret Service agents that are assigned to this peace summit. We need to make sure that everybody who's here should be here."

Agent Brice of the Secret Service angrily replied, "Oh, come on. You think fake Secret Service agents would be allowed to work this detail? We perform extensive background checks on everyone. If someone was a mole, then we would find it."

Gavin replied, "An independent security team needs to check everybody out to make sure nothing slipped through. Agent Brice, you can't honestly tell me that you know every Secret Service agent on this detail and have seen their background checks."

Agent Brice retorted, "Look here, I won't have the FBI tell us how to do our jobs. What you're proposing is bullshit..."

The president cut him off and said, "Enough. Agent Donnelly, get it done. This summit should take about three days. Run checks on everybody and see if there's anything out of the ordinary." He looked Agent Brice. "Brice, every one of your guys will cooperate or they will be suspended." Then he looked at Gavin again. "Agent Donnelly, get this done. I need daily security briefings and a final security plan the day before the peace signings." Normally, one of the parties in the peace summit would have something to add, but both prime ministers agreed with the president. Gavin replied, "Yes, sir. We will get that done."

Everybody was dismissed. As the agents were walking out, Rachel turned to her partner and said, "That was fun. It's not every day you get to brief the president and try to calm him down at the same time."

Gavin laughed. "Well, you wanted back in the big leagues. Here you go!"

"That's true. Now, who are we going to get to run these background checks?"

"Actually, I already have someone doing that now. I just wanted it to be a legitimate assignment."

She shook her head at him. "That's the thing you said I shouldn't know about?"

"Yes, and now you won't get into trouble for this assignment."

She smiled at him. Gavin said, "Look, I hate to ask this of you, but I need a favor."

"Let me guess… you need to go and check something out, and I get to work on the security plan?"

He laughed. "Yes. A Chicago detective found a murder that fits our MO."

"Go get it done, but you owe me big time."

He smiled back at her and nodded. He headed to the parking garage to get his car.

∞∞∞∞∞∞∞∞∞∞

It had been an hour since Gavin left the Daley Center and picked up Detective Reilly at the 23rd Precinct. His cousin, Alex, volunteered to go with them, but Gavin declined. His instincts told him to leave his cousin behind. The main office of the harbor building was closed. Everybody who worked the day shift was already gone for the day. Other offices in the harbor were still operating. Since Clifford Rollins, the victim, was the head of the harbor for the past ten years, he got to work the day shift. This was the perfect time to check the crime scene in his office.

They drove up to the harbor security officers and showed their badges. There wasn't any fuss about FBI agents coming through. Feds were always in and out of the harbor, checking on things. Detective Reilly said, "I thought these harbor guys hated the Feds. I didn't think it would be so easy to get through."

Gavin smiled. "They do hate us. But when the president is in town, Secret Service is all over the place, checking for any potential threats, especially at the harbor and airports. Ever since 9/11, this has been a big part of the Secret Service's job when a president visits a big city. Feds have been coming and going from here for the past week, so they're used to seeing us."

"Ah, that makes sense."

They parked and walked into the office. Detective Reilly carried the case folder. She asked, "So, what are we looking for?"

"Detective, we are looking for anything that can tell us why he was murdered, and why someone wanted to cover it up."

The crime scene was still roped off and nothing had been disturbed in the office. They did what any detective should do first:

[387]

they started going through the drawers to find any files that didn't look like normal business for a harbor. There was nothing out of the ordinary in the drawers, just typical stuff you would find, including lots of scattered office supplies. Gavin found the clipboard of manifest lists. He thumbed through it, not really understanding everything on the lists. He noticed something. All of the pieces of paper had coffee stains on them, except one. He pointed it out to Detective Reilly. She said, "It looks like somebody replaced the original."

"Exactly! I wonder what they were hiding on the list." Gavin went to the computer to see if there was another copy of the list in the computer. He looked around the desk to see if Clifford kept his username and password written down. As it turned out, he did. They were able to get into the computer and compare the manifest lists. All the lists matched, but Gavin wasn't convinced. He looked at Detective Reilly. "Detective, can you get the crime scene bag out of my car? I want to dust for fingerprints again and see if we can pull anything."

"Agent Donnelly, we already did that. We didn't find anything."

"I know, but I want to do it again. Maybe we will get lucky."

She was a little stubborn, and the angry look she gave Gavin showed it. She didn't say anything. Gavin said, "Detective, I promise you, I'm not questioning the Chicago PD or trying to make you do busy work. I would appreciate it if you went and got the bag." She still thought it was busy work, but she did it anyway. Meanwhile, Gavin used his other cell phone to call Agent Dan Moore. He needed some computer assistance. Dan answered the phone and Gavin responded, "Hey, Dan. I need some help. If I give you an IP address, can you get into a computer and see if any information has been erased?"

Dan replied, "Yeah. What exactly are you looking for?"

"I am at the North Shore Harbor. I think someone altered a manifest list and I want to see what was changed."

Dan did his thing from the Chicago FBI office. It didn't take long to see what happened and find the code that had been run to delete the original information. It wasn't completely deleted, just covered up with code. Dan laughed. "Whoever made this program was not very good. I found what you are looking for." Gavin clicked and found the missing list. He looked over the list and found a missing name. It was a like a light switched on in his head. He saw what they were planning, and now it made sense why the harbor master was killed. All of a sudden, Gavin was startled by a custodian in the hallway who was starting to mop. He didn't expect to see anyone in the office. He just shook his head, but he knew he couldn't do anything about it.

Detective Reilly was having a hard time finding the crime scene bag. She was about to call Agent Donnelly when she was shaken by an explosion. It pushed her back into the car and, when she was finally able to look up; she saw the harbor office on fire. Her first instinct was to try to get back inside and find Agent Donnelly. Before she could move, there was another explosion, and it blew her backwards onto the ground. Detective Reilly cut her head when she hit the ground. When she got back up, she didn't even notice the blood, but she did feel the panic of the situation going through her body.

Detective Reilly didn't know who to call first, so she called Alex Donnelly. She was almost in tears trying to tell him what happened. An hour later, a Chicago PD Crime Scene Unit was at the harbor, and they pulled a body from the ruins. Alex was there at the scene. One of the investigators found a badge and brought it to him; it was Agent Donnelly's badge. He was in tears at this point. One of the hardest things he had to do was put the burnt badge in an evidence bag.

∞∞∞∞∞∞∞∞∞

Rachel was still working late in her and her partner's office when AD Foster came by with another agent. She thought it was peculiar, and then she saw the look on his face and knew something was wrong. Before he could say anything, she asked, "Sir, what's wrong? Was there another bombing?"

With a sad expression, he replied, "Yes, and Agent Donnelly was in the explosion. Your partner is dead. They just pulled his body out."

Rachel couldn't say anything. Tears started falling down her cheeks. Then, in a fit of anger, she knocked everything off his desk. That's when she also realized that the second agent was there because of protocol. The protocol is for when a death is reported to family members or a fellow agent if that agent happens to be the victim's partner. She had never lost a partner before, especially one that she cared about and who annoyed her all at the same time.

[389]

17

It was the second day of the peace summit and Agent Rachel Main, in order to avoid agonizing over her partner's death, was knee-deep in work. She would go over and over the security plan while making the FBI bomb squads do three times as many sweeps as they usually did. If there was a bomb threat called in, she would take the call personally. Rachel just wanted to stay busy. It was easier to forget that way.

She finally decided to clear Gavin's personal things out of his desk and put them in a box. She figured his Uncle Liam and Aunt Mary would like them. It would also give her the excuse to pay them a visit, which she had been avoiding. It still hurt too much, and would only remind her of the tragedy that just happened. She could handle the most brutal murders the FBI had ever seen, but this death got to her. Finally, an Agent Green came into her office.

He spoke up. "Agent Main, I'm Agent Green. I have been assigned to your security team."

She looked up while still putting things into the box. "Ah, yes. I was told they were going to add someone."

"I'm glad to be working with you, despite the circumstances. Sorry to hear about your partner."

"Me, too."

He handed her the latest report on the bomb threats and security sweeps. There was nothing out of the ordinary. There was also nothing on the two men with balloons that they arrested in the crowd. They were still being held for the maximum time possible without being charged: 48 hours. All in all, there was nothing to be concerned about, which was a good thing, Rachel thought to herself. But there was still one report she was waiting on: the forensics report of the harbor bombing. Nobody knew for sure what had happened. In most circumstances, this might seem like an accident, but not this week. There was no such thing as coincidences.

Rachel finally got a call about the forensics report. It was going to AD Foster's office, since it was one of his agents who died in the explosion. They all wanted to look at it together. She arrived at AD Foster's office and was handed a folder with the reports in it. The thing that stood out the most was the C4 description in the report, so she asked the question. "What is a C4 page? I've never heard of that before."

Dr. Cassidy, the forensics expert, replied, "From what we can tell, the bombs were encased in notebook binders. There were pages in there coated with C4. Bomb makers love to come up with new techniques to hide the bombs. A small wire was connected to the electrical wiring in the walls and to a plug-in timer that went into a light socket. It looks ordinary in an office and hides the bomb well."

Rachel replied, "So, they put multiple binders with C4 pages in the office and used the wiring or electrical flow to set the timer. Correct?"

"Yes."

"That's pretty elaborate for a bomb, right?"

"Correct. Most bomb makers don't try to hide the bomb itself. They want people to see it so they can scare them."

"Hiding a bomb only means you want to hide something big at the target, something we're not going to look for."

AD Foster asked, "Did Agent Donnelly call you and tell you he found something before the bomb went off?"

"No, but according to the detective, they were comparing manifest lists on a clipboard to what was in the computer."

"Why was he there in the first place?"

"The harbor master was killed, and it fit the MO of the other murders we had been looking into."

"He was murdered the same way as John O'Kelly. That can't be a coincidence."

"That's what I was thinking." She paused for a moment, remembering someone that might have helped Gavin. "Sir, there is someone that Agent Donnelly might have gotten help from. Maybe he can give us answers about the harbor. Do I have your permission to investigate?"

AD Foster didn't hesitate in his answer. "Find out what you can, and quickly. A bombing at the harbor of the city the president is visiting is definitely not a good thing."

Byers was running late to the meeting with the council, but the report he had would make up for it. As he entered the darkened conference room, everybody skipped the pleasantries. It was the most senior man on the council that asked the question. "What do you have for us?"

Byers passed around his report and replied, "The bombing was a success. The FBI agent that's been causing us problems is now dead. His body was found in the explosion."

Stephen spoke up. "Then it looks like we have a victory. We won't be having any more problems from the FBI." Stephen had been advocating that the FBI agent be killed in the line of duty. A lot less questions would be asked compared to him being suspended or fired from the Bureau. Besides, whatever crusade he was on would be gone if he died.

The senior man asked another question. "What about the evidence? Are we sure that it's completely gone, and that there's no way to find what was really there?"

Byers replied, "Sir, everything was destroyed. The FBI or even Homeland Security won't be able to reconstruct anything. All the hard drives are completely gone."

"And what about our timetable?"

"The playmaker is moving into position now. The Secret Service transfer orders just went through, so everybody will be in position tomorrow."

The senior man smiled. "Good. The last thing we need is a complication."

Mr. Chambers asked a question. "What about the Boston Harbor? Is that being taken care of, too?"

Byers smiled. "Yes, sir. They will discover that accidents happen all the time. And that should make Detective Kilgore's case disappear."

"What about this United Front leader? Do we leave him in prison or get him out?"

Mr. Chambers answered that question. "Right now, while he's being viewed as a terrorist, he will also be seen as a martyr for a good cause, a hero to some. This will spark a revolution that will help us in the long run. I suggest we leave him there for now. When the time is right, we will fake his death, making him an icon, like Chavez, to those fed up with the system."

"Okay, then. As the future Director of Homeland Security, I'm sure you can handle that." Stephen didn't like hearing that. He disagreed with that plan, but they all had their particular assignments in this power game He didn't say anything. After the meeting was done, Stephen caught up with Byers and said, "No matter what happens, you report to me first. I'm still not convinced that this overall plan is really going to work."

Byers nodded in agreement. Even though he reported to the council, he was brought in by Stephen, which was as good as saying that he was given his promotion by Stephen. He was loyal to him first.

∞∞∞∞∞∞∞∞∞∞

Rachel walked into the Cyber Division and found Agent Dan Moore doing background checks on Secret Service agents. He saw her walk in and immediately got up from his seat. He had been too busy to see her since Agent Donnelly's death, so he hadn't expressed his condolences yet. He had to admit, he was surprised to see her, since it was Gavin who was investigating these murders. He said, "Agent Main, I was going to come see you today. I was sorry to hear about Agent Donnelly."

"Thank you. Did you talk to him right before the explosion?"

"Yes ma'am, I did."

"What did you talk about?"

Dan went to one of his computers and brought up a report. "Let me show you. He was looking at manifest lists and found a discrepancy."

"What do you mean?

"Apparently, a ship came into the harbor a few days ago with an extra man. Some kind of program was run on the computer to change the information on the list within the harbor server."

Rachel was stunned by the information. "Did Clifford Rollins do that before he was murdered?"

"Not likely. Before the explosion happened, Gavin called me to log into the computer through the IP address. So, I dug around and then found the coding for the program. It was pretty sophisticated, but it wasn't downloaded from the Web. Judging by the activity on the computer, Clifford Rollins wasn't that computer savvy. He never did any routine maintenance on his computer, and the only two programs he used were Microsoft Outlook and a program to check the manifest lists on the server."

"What about internet activity?"

"The only three sites he checked were WGN, ESPN, and The Weather Channel. The program was probably run using a flash drive, so it's more likely that whoever did it was the one who murdered Clifford Rollins."

[393]

"What's the name of the extra man or woman on the list?"

"Joseph Smith."

Rachel laughed. "You mean, the leader of the Mormon church?"

"Yes. When doing a background check, that's what we usually get, so we know it's a fake."

"Unless you're a Mormon and really believe he's the son of God."

Dan laughed. "Well, if that's true, then why would the son of God hide himself on a boat coming into Chicago?"

"So, we have a missing man in Chicago while the president is here with two prime ministers, and the harbor was just blown up. Okay, now I am officially worried."

Dan asked with a concerned tone, "If a person is being smuggled into Chicago, then for what purpose?"

Rachel looked scared. "To kill the president or one of the prime ministers. Somebody smuggled in an assassin, but how are they going to get close enough to do it? And with what? They have to get close somehow and, even if it's a bomb, they know we're going to be looking for that." She looked over and saw what Dan had been working on. "You're the one running the background checks on Secret Service agents, right?"

"Yeah."

"Find anything?"

"Not so far, but there's a lot to get through and even more coming in. There was a transfer order for a few more agents that will be coming in tonight and stationed at the signing tomorrow."

Rachel was suspicious of that. "Check them next. Maybe a fake Secret Service agent is how they're going to do it." That's when she remembered something. Frankie O'Brian, one of their victims, ran the harbor in Boston. That couldn't be a coincidence, either. She asked Dan to print out a report of what he had done for Gavin. Rachel had more investigating to do.

∞∞∞∞∞∞∞∞∞∞∞∞

The negotiations between Ireland and England had been going well for a day and a half. While most, including the president, thought there would be a lot of fighting between the prime ministers on all the issues, there actually wasn't. Unlike with the Anglo-Irish Treaty of 1922, Ireland was well on its way to becoming a true country of its own… all of it. Part of the agreement would be that Northern Ireland would still have a British embassy and multiple military bases for the British and other allied countries. There would be no illegal gun

[394]

manufacturing or gun sales in Ireland and all British countries. They would also be subject to sanctions by the United Nations. The most important issue was that Northern Ireland would return to the Republic of Ireland. Both David Kenney and George Mallory agreed on almost everything, but there was still one issue that needed to be settled. It was an economic dispute.

Since Northern Ireland was rich in gas deposits and minerals, the British government still wanted everything, or at least a portion of it. So, the British had a company that wanted to go in and drill for those resources. That made tensions during the negotiations run high. George Mallory, the Prime Minister of the United Kingdom, spoke first.

"We have come to an agreement on every issue, except one: mining rights in Northern Ireland. David, I understand that you have reservations."

David Kenny, the Prime Minister of Ireland, replied, "Yes, I do. Most of the issues at hand, I can go along with. Military bases with British soldiers and Irish Soldiers, I can agree with, despite that a lot of citizens want to see all British soldiers go home. But this mining issue... where a British company is going to come in and drill in Northern Ireland and, as a country, we have to give up 40 percent of what is found to the British government. No, sir, I have a big problem with that."

"It's a fair deal."

"For who? If this is the price of peace in Northern Ireland... well, I think there was a saying about Greeks and gifts that can apply here!"

"Is there anything that you do like about this proposal?"

"Why does it have to be a British company?"

"Is there an Irish mining company that can do an operation like this?"

"Maybe not, but we should have the right to contract our own company and sell whatever portions of what we find to whoever we want. I understand that Great Britain needs those resources, but 40 percent is a high number, and we don't know what's beneath the ground."

The representative from H M Mining, who was present, replied, "We have already conducted studies and know that there is a considerable amount of minerals and gas deposits down there."

David looked at him. "Sir, I don't know you. Why should I trust your study? In cases like this, isn't it protocol to perform independent studies outside of the company that wants to drill? We have not seen those."

George smiled. "I understand your point, but why waste money on another study that will tell us what we already know?"

"Because it's an independent study and, frankly, you may be wrong. Also, the country where the minerals and gas deposits are found has ownership of them. The rights to them should not be dictated by another country."

"David, we don't have to give Northern Ireland up, and we can keep everything we find there. As much as this peace agreement will add to my legacy and make my approval rating go up, I can walk away from this and claim that the Irish refused to work with us and still be seen as a hero for trying."

"Always the same with the British, dictating their own version of peace!"

George shook his head in disbelief. He honestly thought that he could work with this prime minister. "De Valera walked away from negotiations 90 years ago, during the treaty talks, which caused a civil war in your country and 75 years of violence. Don't make the same mistake, David."

David was angry and it showed on his face. "I would cut off my right arm or put a dagger through my own heart before I betrayed my country! I won't let the British government dictate mining operations that could jeopardize the economic stability of my country."

"Then perhaps peace cannot be reached, and the British government will have total control over the natural resources found in Northern Ireland."

"Do you want another war, Mr. Mallory? Because that's what you're going to get if you continue this way."

George Mallory was going to respond but the president interrupted. He was there as a mediator and, for the most part, he hadn't needed to intervene. This was different, though. He responded, "Enough of this. Let's find a compromise." He looked at David. "If an independent study is conducted within six months, and the region is found to be viable, then will you agree to let H M Mining do the work?"

David replied, "I can agree to that, Mr. President." George Mallory consented, as well. The representative from H M Mining responded, "I have to object to this. We have done more than one study and that should be good enough."

David responded, "I don't care if you object or not. I'm in the business of running a country, and making sure your company is happy is not part of that business. You should be grateful that I'm even considering your company for mining operations in Ireland." The representative didn't reply; he just gave the prime minister a dirty look.

David said to the President of the United States, "I have a problem with 40 percent of Ireland's resources going back to Great Britain. The number is too high."

The president replied, "What if it was for the first two years only? After that, the amount could be decreased by 5 percent every two years until you are only giving them 25 percent of Ireland's natural resources."

David Kenney agreed to that and so did George Mallory. But there was one more issue they needed to agree on: the number of Irishmen that would be employed by H M Mining compared to British employees. George Mallory wanted 60 percent British employees and 40 percent Irish employees, but after another compromise, they agreed on a 50/50 split. There were minor details that still needed to be worked out about the mining operations, but they did come to a great compromise and the peace agreement was finalized in negotiations. It would become final the next day at the signing. All three leaders shook hands on the deal and celebrated with good Irish whiskey.

∞∞∞∞∞∞∞∞∞∞

It was already late in the evening when Agent Rachel Main arrived at Liam and Mary Donnelly's home. She had only been there once, and it was over bad news, as well. She had been so busy that she had not been able to express her condolences in person. Rachel rang the doorbell and it was Mary who answered. She recognized Rachel immediately and gave her a hug after seeing the tears in Rachel's eyes. Rachel didn't know what to say, but she finally managed some words. "I thought I should bring Gavin's things to you personally." Mary smiled and hugged her again.

Rachel stayed for about half an hour. When she was done with her visit, it was Liam who walked her to the door. Rachel never knew what to say in these situations, but she had to compliment Gavin to the police chief. "I wanted to tell you that Gavin was the best partner I ever had, even though he was a pain in the ass sometimes."

Liam laughed. "He gets his stubbornness from my side of the family. I think he was glad to have you as a partner, someone that could keep him on his toes."

She smiled at that. "He certainly will be missed. My job has been harder without him around."

"The best way you can honor him is to do your job well. Keep the president and the prime ministers safe so this peace agreement can succeed."

"I will."

As Liam walked back inside, he said goodbye, and then mentioned something else. "If this peace accord succeeds, then Gavin will never truly be dead." Rachel thought the comment was strange.

After thinking about it for a moment, she just thought that, as an
Irishman, he was trying to be poetic about death.

18

Janie Myers was enjoying her first cup of coffee of the day back at her place. She was busy looking at the multiple computer monitors that were hooked to more than one computer and several servers. She was a hacker, so of course she would have one of the most state-of-the-art computer systems. She had built much of it herself, and it was even better than the ones at the FBI. She was helping with the background checks on Secret Service agents, something she actually enjoyed because she got to snoop into the lives of federal agents. She loved secrets, and she loved exposing those secrets even more. As she finished her coffee, she got a hit on one of the new transfer agents that arrived yesterday from Washington, D.C. She smiled at the fact that she was about to expose a corrupt government agent. Janie did a little more digging to see where the fake identity originated and then printed out a report to take to Agent Moore.

∞∞∞∞∞∞∞∞∞∞∞

Rachel knew that it was going to be a busy day, so she got a head start. It was still dark when she arrived at the office. She looked at the current security reports and then went straight to the board in the office. Rachel still didn't have a clear answer on why those particular murders were committed. Clifford Rollins was easy at this point, because of the explosion at the harbor and the smuggling of a person they couldn't find. But she couldn't see the strategic value of the other murders, except for the fact that some people just wanted them dead. And, of course, there was the question of Agent Caster's murder; she couldn't read the report because it was highly classified now. She remembered her partner saying that it was a message But what kind of message? She knew killers liked to put hidden messages into their murders, and the message was always to answer the question of why they killed. AD Foster came by her office. He said, "I like when my agents get an early start. Have you found anything today?"

She frowned. "Unfortunately not. There's something about these murders that I am just not seeing."

"I saw your report about the manifest list at the harbor. Do you think the answer to whoever is trying to kill the president and the prime ministers is in these murders?"

"Yes. Agent Donnelly said there was a message behind these murders, and that's what linked them."

"Okay. If that's true, besides the way they were killed, what else do they have in common?"

Rachel was going to say something but then paused for a moment. She looked at the photos again and centered her vision on one thing: the Catholic crosses. She responded with excitement, "It's the crosses! The man who dies must wear a Catholic cross. The man they're going to kill will be wearing one. The target is the Irish Prime Minister; he's the only one that's Catholic."

AD Foster nodded in agreement. "It still doesn't tell us who the killer is, though."

"Maybe we don't get that answer until we flush him out." Rachel got a phone call from Agent Moore about the Secret Service agent. When she got off the phone, she told her boss, "They found a fake Secret Service agent, one of the new transfers that came in last night. The background on her was fake."

"Her?"

"Apparently, whoever is pulling the strings on this whole thing doesn't have a double standard when it comes to their spies or assassins."

AD Foster laughed. "Okay, let's go pick her up."

Thirty minutes later, she had a warrant and arrived with other FBI agents at the Daley Center. That's where Agent Josephine Smith was stationed, at the Secret Service office, among the agents on the president's detail. She walked into the room at a hurried pace. Rachel flashed her badge, along with the warrant, to Agent Brice, head of the Secret Service detail. He looked angry and surprised. "What is the meaning of this?"

Rachel answered, "I'm here for one of your agents."

By the time she was done saying that, Agent Smith had already pulled her service weapon and badge to give to Agent Brice. She walked over, handed them to him, and then put her hands out to be handcuffed. She smiled at Agent Main. "I've been waiting for you. What took you so long?"

Rachel was shocked by the statement. Again, Agent Brice demanded to know what was going on. Rachel replied, "She's not a

Secret Service agent. At least, that's not what her deep background check showed. See, this is why we do them."

Agent Brice was not amused. "This is such bullshit! If she wasn't a real agent, then we would have found out. I have her file on my computer."

"Yeah, I'm going to need that. In fact, I'm just going to take your computer for harboring a fraudulent federal agent."

"You have no authority to do that!"

"Should we ask your boss, the President of the United States?"

Agent Brice shot her a dirty look, but he didn't argue. He handed her his laptop and she left with Josephine Smith in handcuffs.

Agent Brice was going over security briefs with the president about an hour and a half before the signing. While he didn't always tell the president every little detail of things they were investigating, on important days like this, he did disclose the important details to his boss. A Secret Service agent being arrested by the FBI was one of those things he had to tell the president. The president was shocked to hear that, and it did cause concern, but he would not be deterred from having the peace signing outside.

Agent Brice said, "Sir, I know you don't like wearing bulletproof vests, but I have to insist that you wear one today. In fact, we want the prime ministers to do the same."

The president replied, "Tell you what; I will make a deal. I'll do it, and I will get the prime ministers to do it, as well, if you don't try to get me to have the signing inside."

Agent Brice laughed. He was always amazed at how well the president could find the best compromise in any situation, to where nobody could disagree with it. He replied, "It's a deal, Mr. President. But the situation with the Secret Service agent doesn't make you want hold the signing inside, where you might be safer?"

"No, because I'm not worried about anybody trying to kill me."

"Really? You should be."

The president chuckled. "Agent Brice, in my job, somebody is always trying to kill me. That's why you get to do what you do. Hope and peace always come with a price."

∞∞∞∞∞∞∞∞∞∞∞

Josephine Smith was sitting in an interrogation room with a smile on her face. She wasn't going to let the FBI break her. That was not the role she had to play. Rachel and another agent brought Robert Grimes down the hallway in handcuffs and legcuffs. They put him in

the same room with Josephine and just left them there for a while. AD
Foster asked Rachel, "Why do you want them in the same room
together?"

She smiled. "I want to see how they interact with each other. I
want to see if they know each other. Give them some time and let's see
what they do." After 20 minutes, Robert was the only one nervous. He
asked her a few times who she was, but she never answered. After a
while, Robert started to breathe a little heavier from getting nervous.
Josephine finally spoke. "Robert, calm down. Everything is going to be
okay. Your new friends are going to help you." Robert was shocked to
hear that; Rachel could see it on his face through the one-way glass.

Rachel spoke up. "Okay, it's time to move Robert Grimes." She
and another agent walked into the room and moved Robert to another
interrogation room. Then she walked back into the room with
Josephine and said, "Thank you."

Josephine replied, "For what?"

"For telling me what I need to know."

"And what's that?"

"You two don't know each other. Robert Grimes is just being
used and made to be your martyr."

"You must be the smart FBI agent."

Rachel smiled. "Yes, I am. So smart that we figured out that
you're not a real Secret Service agent and that your name is fake. Now,
you will make it a lot easier on yourself if you tell me why you did all
of this, just to be close to three world leaders, and who sent you."

Josephine started laughing. "Really? You're not even going to
ask me if I intended to kill someone, or all of three of them?"

"You're a fake Secret Service agent. It's pretty much evident
that you're trying to kill them."

"That's a narrow-minded view of things."

"It's an obvious fact. Now, who hired you? The same people
that are using Robert Grimes?"

"And there's the million dollar question: who pulls the strings?
Who wants them dead?"

Rachel paused for a moment. She knew that Josephine was just
trying to play games. "You see, I don't think you want all three of them
dead... just the Irish Prime Minister, David Kenny. Why do you want to
kill him?"

Josephine nodded her head then she had a small look of
surprise. "Why target one when we can get all three?"

"No, the look on your face gave you away. I'm right, aren't I?
This is about David Kenny."

"And what if it is?"

"Tell me why. You can make it easier on yourself and save us some time. If you do, life for you will be easier in prison. Or you can be labeled a terrorist and charged with conspiracy to commit murder against the president."

"You think I'm afraid of prison? I just allowed myself to get caught. I'm here because I want to be."

While most agents would've been surprised these comments Agent Main wasn't so she asked the obvious questions. "You wanted me to catch you, why? Why is it important that get arrested. "

"I think I've wasted enough of your time here. Agent Main, we all have a role in this game and mine was to get caught. Your role is to try to figure out why. I'm not just going to give you the answer…you have to work for it."

"So, you're not the one who was smuggled onto the boat?"

"No, Agent Main. But just because you found one potential killer doesn't mean we don't have more."

"Is that true?"

"We are the United Front and death is coming soon!"

That got Rachel's attention. There was no use in asking any more questions. This whole thing had been a setup from the very beginning with Josephine Smith. Rachel gave her a sarcastic smile and left the room. AD Foster was trying to ask her a question, but she hurried into the other interrogation room where Robert Grimes was sitting. She looked at him angrily. "Enough dicking around, Robert. You're going to start helping us catch a killer, right now, or I'll just shoot you for trying to escape." She pulled out her service weapon, loaded the chamber, and placed it on the table. Robert was starting to get nervous again.

Rachel asked, "How many bomb targets were there? Was the harbor a target?"

"Yes, the harbor was a target. I don't know why. It was just on the list I was given, but I wasn't supposed to do that one."

"What about the peace signing tomorrow?"

"Yes, there is a target. Two, actually, but they're diversions, nothing else."

"The United Front is not using a bomb to assassinate anyone?"

"No, but beyond that, I don't know what they're planning. I was given bomb supplies and a list of targets, but some of them were diversions. That's all I know."

Rachel believed him and it helped her form a theory. She asked Robert, "If I put you with a sketch artist, can you tell me what the old man who gave you the bomb materials looks like?"

"Probably."

She smiled and started to get up and leave. "By the way, why are you being honest? Why now?"

"Because it doesn't matter what I tell you at this point. You won't be able to stop what's about to happen, and telling you the truth won't get me out of prison." Rachel nodded at him and walked out. AD Foster finally got to ask his question. "What the hell is going on with these two? Why put them together?"

"To find out that she knew who he was... but Robert didn't know who she was. And to get the truth out of them!"

"Which is what ?"

"They're both decoys, especially her. They're just here to waste our time. Plus, she basically pointed out that there may be more than one kind of assassination attempt today."

"Why would they tell us that?"

"Ego... so they could waste our time, to stretch us thin so we can't possibly stop what's happening. That's what the bomb threats were all about this past week."

AD Foster looked confused. "You don't think there's going to be a bomb?"

"There may be, but I also think we have a shooter somewhere."

"If that's true, then how will he get past all of our security? We aren't allowing windows open in buildings, and we have snipers on the roofs of every building." Rachel shook her head, as if she didn't know the answer, and then she thought for a moment. "How would one get into a building past our security? They would have to have access somehow." Her face lit up with the answer. "We need to check to see if anybody is missing a security badge, or has been killed but still has a security badge that can get someone into a building. All of these buildings have security. Employees will have an ID card that grants them access."

One of the other agents replied, "There are over a thousand people to check and we only have 30 minutes until peace signing." Rachel frowned. She knew the guy was right; it wouldn't be enough time to check everybody. Rachel replied, "Start with security guards. They'll know more about security badges missing. Most likely, a shooter would disguise himself as a security guard to get in. Plus, it will be quicker. Get started. We only have 30 minutes to figure this out."

AD Foster said to Rachel, "I know that I put you charge of the security team for the FBI, but I have to ask: do you think all of this is the best use of our time?"

"I don't know for sure. We don't know if there really is a shooter, but this is the best way to find out if there's a security breach to begin with. Checking every room in every building would take too long."

"Ok, but double up on the bomb sweeps, especially around where they are doing the signing."

"Yes, sir. I was going to do that anyway."

The FBI agents were in panic mode, trying to work as fast as they could. It took about twenty minutes to get through the security checks with the buildings in Daley Plaza. An FBI agent working on the security team came running down the hall and caught up with Agent Main as she was getting in her FBI car. "Agent Main, we found a breach. The Citibank building across from the Daley Building had a security guard murdered last week. His badge was used to get into the building the morning after his death. A security guard by the name of Raymond Gomez had to get his security badge replaced yesterday, after he claimed it was lost or stolen."

"Is this Raymond Gomez working today at the building?"

"No, but his badge was swiped so someone could get in the building."

Rachel chuckled. "Wow, they a killed security guard and stole his badge to get into the building, just to steal someone else's badge. It's harder to trace and they knew that a dead man's badge would be deactivated quickly. Very clever."

"But how do we find this guy?"

"Get Secret Service and Chicago PD to detain every security guard in that building. We'll sort them out later. We just have to prevent him from taking a shot."

∞∞∞∞∞∞∞∞∞

The signing was exactly at noon on a beautiful Chicago Friday. Agent Rachel Main and her security team raced to Daley Plaza. Security guards in the Citibank building were being detained by Secret Service agents while they looked for Raymond Gomez. They couldn't get the president to delay the signing, so they were under serious time constraints. Chicago PD had snipers on all the buildings and more moving into position. One of the snipers moving into position didn't go to his assigned location. He moved a little bit higher on top of the Daley building to get a better line of sight. He was out of place, but nobody said anything because he was a dressed as a Chicago SWAT Team sniper. He checked his scope and looked down at the table where the president and the prime ministers would be sitting. The three world leaders came out of the Daley Center, surrounded by Secret Service. They all waved to the crowds of people that were there to watch the signing, as well as the press media. There were tons of TV cameras from all around the world since this was a huge international event.

The sniper checked his scope and his line of sight. He had a clear shot at the back of the president and the prime ministers. Then he did something strange. He pulled a different scope out of his bag, one with infrared reading capability for heat signatures behind walls and for nighttime vision. He checked his watch; it was two minutes until the signing started. The president and the prime ministers were seated and each had a pen in his hand, ready to get started. The president would be signing the treaty as a witness, since the United States, England, and Ireland were all part of the United Nations. The sniper turned on the infrared part of the scope and started looking through his lens at the Citibank building. All the windows were closed from what he could tell, but the infrared sensor would be able to distinguish between glass windows and fake windows. A fake window might have reflective capabilities to make it seem like it was real, or could have a hole in it where the barrel of a rifle could be placed. He scanned all of the windows on every story of the building, starting from the top and going down. Finally, on the twentieth floor, he saw it: a different color signature on a window. It was small and didn't fill the entire window, but the infrared sensor picked it up. The sniper had his target. He looked at his watch and saw the time ticking down. When it was two seconds to noon, he fired one shot at the window. It was loud and most people on the ground could hear it. Secret Service agents surrounding the three world leaders looked up and saw glass shattering. Before they could do anything, a bomb went off. It was a microphone exploding that caused a very loud sound and a lot of smoke. Agent Brice, who sprang into action with other Secret Service agents to shield the president, yelled out, "It's only a flash bomb!" Suddenly, another shot was fired, but it missed and grazed George Mallory's arm, causing it to bleed.

Security still surrounded the president and the prime ministers until everything calmed down. Everybody was looking for the person who fired the second shot. One of the agents put pressure on Mallory's arm to help stop the bleeding. After the bomb went off, the sniper fired two more shots at the window. The infrared sensor was switched off, so he was looking through a normal scope, and that's when he saw a body fall to the ground next to a rifle. Agent Rachel Main and other FBI agents were already in the Citibank building when the shots were fired. She heard one of the Chicago PD snipers shout into everybody's radio, "There's a shootout on the twentieth floor... front of the building, facing the Daley Center. Everything is clear. The shooter is down."

Rachel, along with the other agents, raced to the twentieth floor and found the dead body of the shooter lying next to his rifle. He was dressed as a maintenance worker. Rachel looked on his belt and saw an ID badge attached. It was Raymond Gomez's missing badge. Her phone started ringing; it was a blocked number. She answered, "This is Agent Main."

The voice on the other end asked, "Did I get him? Is the shooter dead?"

She recognized the voice. A smile appeared, along with a tear that ran down her cheek. "Yes, Gavin… you got him. You killed the assassin."

"Good. Now I don't have to be dead anymore."

Rachel started laughing. She radioed in that the shooter was dead; they found the missing ID badge, and that it was Agent Donnelly who shot him.

The scene at Daley Plaza was chaotic. The police were trying to disperse the crowds. The president was okay, but it was the British Prime Minister who was being tended to by EMTs. His wound was not serious, but he was still bleeding. Details were still sketchy about what had really just happened. The only certainty was that a flash bomb went off and a gunman, who fired one shot, was shot and killed by a Chicago SWAT Team sniper. The peace signing would be delayed because of this, until everything could be sorted out. George Mallory, the British Prime Minister, was being treated in an office in the Daley Center when his National Security Adviser came into the room. His name was Stewart Granger. George Mallory was not exactly happy to see him, but he needed to talk to him, so he asked everybody else to leave the room. He said to Stewart, "This is bollocks. What the hell happened? Why is David Kenney still alive?"

Stewart frowned. "This FBI guy, Agent Donnelly, faked his death and figured out that there was an assassin waiting to kill one of the leaders at the peace summit."

"How did you not see this?"

"The coroner's report on the dead body said it was him. It must have been a fake, too. He was the one who found our guy and shot him."

"Well, this seriously fucks up our plan. What excuse can I use now to give up this peace agreement and send British forces into Ireland to reclaim it for the Empire?"

Stewart smiled. "This plan can still work; we just have to change the story a bit." He pulled out some papers and handed them to the prime minister. "Sir, we have a report from MI6 saying that the gunman was an IRA assassin, working in conjunction with the United Front."

"No one will believe this."

"Sure they will. You have an excuse to call off the peace summit now. In the coming months, you can increase the amount of British troops in Northern Ireland and start working on invasion plans of the Free State, because of their links to terrorism; much like the U.S. did with Iraq."

The prime minister replied, "But their leader is supposed to be dead and they were supposed to attack me."

Stewart smiled. "Sir, they did just attack you, according to this report. This still works out in our favor and we can move on to other countries. Just because David Kenney is still alive doesn't mean he can stop what's coming... and who's to say that the IRA won't retaliate for real?"

"Okay, let's say this does work. Our friends are still not going to be happy about this FBI agent. We were supposed to kill him. I assured Stephen that he would be dead."

"Don't worry about it. Mr. Chambers has just informed me that he will be dealt with, that he will be forced to go away."

"Do I want to know what that means?"

Stewart smiled again. "No. On some things, you want plausible deniability. Show this report to Mr. Kenney and the president and bow out of the summit gracefully. We've done enough here in Chicago."

∞∞∞∞∞∞∞∞∞∞∞∞∞

The FBI and the Secret Service were still sorting things out in Daley Plaza when Gavin finally appeared back from the dead. He was still in the Chicago SWAT uniform when his partner finally saw him. She was happy and pissed off at him, all at the same time. Gavin smiled at her and she responded, "You're a son of bitch, you know that?"

"I can be."

She pushed him in the chest out of anger and said, "Don't ever fucking do that to me again!" Then she hugged him because, even though she would not admit it out loud, Rachel had missed her partner. "Why didn't you tell me what you were up to?"

"We were being watched, and the only way to do it was to be dead to the world. Our cell phones were tapped. If you knew that I was alive, then you might have accidently given me away."

"How did you know about the shooter?"

"I found the original manifest list of the ship he came in on. It also listed fishing rods in tall boxes as part of the cargo. If I were a sniper smuggling a rifle, that's how I would do it. So I took a chance

[409]

that that there would be a shooter in the building across from the Daley
Center. The only way to get him was as a sniper."

"Then why the flash bomb, besides it being a diversion?"

"Everybody knew that the signing was going to happen
directly at noon, and the bomb was probably set for that, too. The
sound of the bomb would have masked the sound of the gunfire, and
the Secret Service's reaction would have been too late. The shot I fired
first got their attention and shattered the window in front of the
shooter to help make his shot more difficult. That's why he never hit
his original target."

Rachel looked surprised. "You figured out who the original
target was?"

"It was David Kenny."

She smiled. "I figured that out, too. The crosses on the bodies
were a message that a Catholic was going to be assassinated, and the
only one of the world leaders who was Catholic was the Irish PM."

Gavin chuckled. "Thank God you figured that out. I didn't
know if you would do it. But, I also have some other evidence on why
he was the target."

"What are you talking about?"

Gavin pulled out some pieces of paper from the cargo pocket
on his pants. "I found something about the Solomon Islands in the
judge's files. I didn't think anything about it at first, but then I did
some research about a week ago. Since it's a commonwealth of Great
Britain, the same kind of offer was made to their government, ten
months ago, by the prime minister. They would be completely free
from British rule. They planned a peace summit and then an
assassination attempt was made. One member of the royal family was
killed. The Brits saw it as an act of war and sent in Special Forces to kill
who they thought was behind it. Then, they tightened control over the
government in the islands."

"Why? What strategic value does it have?"

"I don't know, but H M Mining does have operations in the
Solomon Islands."

Rachel was stunned to hear this. "So, let me get this straight.
The British PM proposed a peace summit to return Northern Ireland.
They planned an assassination, which would force the IRA to strike
back. Then, the British government would see it as an act of war and
invade the Republic of Ireland. You're saying that they did this to have
an excuse to reclaim the country, while looking innocent as proponents
of peace?"

Gavin smiled. "You got it. I'm pretty sure that was their plan."

"But what do they do now? David Kenny is still alive."

"I think there's a card yet to be played here. But for now, who's behind this is between you and me. We don't exactly have enough proof yet."

Rachel nodded in agreement. "By the way, how did you fake your death? They found a body in the rubble."

Gavin was saddened. "It was a maintenance worker and I regret what happened, but he helped us save lives. I snuck out the back and stayed underground for two days. Alex snuck me into the SWAT Team so I could get positioned as a sniper."

"What about the death record?"

"I had Dr. Kenrick falsify that for a couple of days, just in case anyone was monitoring."

Rachel smiled. "Clever, Agent Donnelly, very clever."

AD Foster finally arrived on the scene to find Agent Donnelly alive and well. He was pissed that he was not in the loop on this little plan, but proud of the job he did. "Agent Donnelly, back from the dead, I see. Congratulations on getting the assassin, but in light of the situation, you should expect a meeting with OPR."

Gavin smiled. "I always do."

AD Foster pulled out an electronic tablet and showed some pictures of the assassin. "We already pulled his fingerprints and came up with nothing. Not even DNA could tell us who he was. There's nothing in our databases."

Rachel looked at the photos and recognized something. "This guy looks familiar." She pointed that out to her partner. Gavin replied, "You're right. He was with the U.S. Marshals on our last case. He was one of the guys tracking Brenda Mason."

AD Foster asked, "Are you saying the U.S. Marshals had an assassin among them?"

Rachel answered, "He obviously isn't a U.S. Marshal or we would have found him in a database. I think it stands to reason that this guy infiltrated our federal agencies and was able to get into position to kill one or all three of our political leaders."

"But who hired him, Agent Main? That's what I want to know."

"We don't know, sir, but we need to investigate and find out."

AD Foster responded, "We'll address this at a later date. Right now, you two have to do a security briefing for the president."

Gavin didn't get a chance to change before they headed to a conference room in the Daley Center to brief the president. Rachel handed him his spare FBI badge. Gavin smiled at that. "Thanks, Rachel. It will be good to have this back. I felt kind of naked without it."

Inside the conference room, the president was mad as hell, trying to figure what had just happened. The Secret Service didn't even have the full details. Everybody was waiting on the report from the FBI. Gavin and Rachel walked into the room and it was a great surprise to everybody there to see Gavin. The president was the first to speak. "Agent Donnelly, you're looking good for a dead man. Care to explain?"

"I apologize that you were not briefed on this plan. It was a deep undercover mission, but we had to flush the shooter out."

"He still got a shot off. You call that a success?"

"Yes, sir. No offense, but he's dead and you're still alive, while Mr. Mallory only received a flesh wound. I consider that a huge success."

The president laughed. "I suppose you're right." He asked Gavin and Rachel for a security briefing. Gavin told them about the plot to disrupt the peace summit with an assassination attempt, and how the shooter was smuggled into the States on a ship that docked in the North Shore Harbor and came through the Boston Harbor, as well. That's why Frankie O'Brian was killed in Boston. He told them about how the bombings were used as diversions to keep them busy and not see what the true endgame was. Rachel told the president about the connection between the four murders and the Catholic cross, and how the president was not the target. That's when the president asked, "Well, who was the intended target?"

Gavin pointed to David Kenney and replied, "He was." The president was surprised, as well as David Kenny, but Gavin wasn't looking at them. He wanted to see the expression on George Mallory's face. The British PM was shocked that the FBI figured that out.

The president asked, "Why was Mr. Kenney the target?"

"Sir, there are some people that don't want this peace agreement. By having Mr. Kenney murdered, it would spark retaliation by the IRA and a whole new war in Northern Ireland."

"But who is behind this? The United Front group?"

"Sir, we still don't know who's really behind this. The United Front was just being used to cause panic and fear in the city. It's still a terrorist group, but not the true villain behind this plot."

George Mallory finally spoke. "Mr. President, my national security advisor received a report from MI6. This assassin has links to the IRA. It appears that Mr. Kenney may not have been the target, and that it is Irish militants that tried the assassination." He handed the report to the president.

David Kenney replied, "This is nothing but a lie. How did MI6 get this information so fast? And, if they knew of a plot, why was nothing done to stop it, except by the FBI?"

Mallory didn't say anything for a moment. "I don't run MI6. I can only act based on the reports and when I get them. I just received this about 20 minutes ago."

Gavin responded, "Mr. Kenney makes a good point about this report."

The president replied, "Are you saying that I should ignore this report, Agent Donnelly?"

"Not necessarily, sir, but I think U.S. intelligence agencies should also investigate this and confirm the report before any action is taken. After all, the last time an American president based his decision on a report from MI6 while ignoring reports from the U.S. intelligence community, we went to war with another country based on a lie."

The president was surprised by the remark, but he didn't disagree with it, either. George Mallory said, "Regardless of what anyone else does, as the British Prime Minister, I cannot continue this peace summit. We must rethink our course of action in light this new information."

David Kenney responded, "I guess you never were serious about peace. I guess that, even after all these years, we could never trust the Brits."

"Mr. Kenny, this could be considered an act of war. I would be very careful about what you say." George got up, said his goodbyes, and told the other two world leaders that he and Great Britain were done with the peace summit. Gavin was going to say something to him about what he discovered, but Rachel gently grabbed his arm. "Hey, partner, don't do it. This is not the time or place. Plus, we don't want to tip our hand and let them know that we know the truth." Gavin knew she was right and that he should swallow his pride. There would be a perfect chance to let the truth come to light another day. The president thanked both of them for their service and asked that they keep investigating to see who was behind this. Gavin was a little relieved by that. It now meant that his investigation was made official by the president.

∞∞∞∞∞∞∞∞∞∞∞∞

Dr. Larkin was watching the news in his classroom after he finished a lecture. The president was doing a press conference about the peace signing. It had been delayed now, as the delegates for Great Britain were leaving Chicago. The president was trying to be reassuring by telling the world that he and the Irish Prime Minister

[413]

were still fighting for peace, and that they would keep talking to the British about another peace summit. He wanted the world to know that terrorists and assassins would not deter them. Dr. Larkin thought to himself that it was a good speech, full of hope and inspiration, even though there would probably never be another peace summit and Northern Ireland would remain under British control. He knew somebody was behind him. Before he turned around, he said, "I knew they would probably send you." He turned around and saw The Ghost.

The Ghost replied, "How did you know I was here? You've been out of the field for a long time."

"I can smell your aftershave. You still use the same kind."

The Ghost smiled. "Your senses are still alive and kicking. That's good. I hope mine are when I'm your age."

Dr. Larkin smiled. "It is good to see you, despite the circumstances. I'm sorry that you have to be here."

"Are you really? Why did you tell the FBI agent the truth?"

"Because I am tired of playing by their rules. I'm tired of not having a choice anymore."

"You made your own choice when you decided to go off the reservation and kill all those people for sport."

"You're right, I did, but I'm an old man now. I want the choice to live my life my way, and to die my way. You'll understand when you get to be my age."

The Ghost smiled. "I am curious, though. Why did you decide this now? You were the one that truly believed in the code. You drilled it into me."

Dr. Larkin paused for a moment. "Haven't you ever questioned why we did what we did? Why they get to set the rules for our lives, as if there aren't any other options for us?"

"It's not my job to ask questions."

Dr. Larkin smiled. "Do they still know about your wife and daughter?"

The Ghost didn't say anything, but the look on his face told Dr. Larkin that the answer was yes. "If you want a choice, then you can choose how you die today."

"Thank you. I'm sorry you're having to do it. Two shots in the back of the head will make it quick and easy."

The Ghost put a silencer on his Glock 19 and told Dr. Larkin to turn around. The doctor did it and closed his eyes, waiting for the end. The Ghost said to him, "Thank you for being my friend when I didn't have one 30 years ago." Then he put two bullets in the back of Dr. Larkin's head.

Byers entered the conference room and found everybody sitting down. He brought the latest report and gave it to the old man sitting at the head of the table. He read the report and was disappointed, but also pleased at the same time. He looked over at Stephen. "It appears that your plan did not work; the FBI agent is still alive. Apparently, he faked his death. I guess bombing the harbor was a mistake."

Stephen was angry. "Sir, we can still find a way to kill him in the line of duty."

"No, I think that time had passed."

"Then let him be suspended indefinitely from the FBI and make him go away."

"We can't do that, either. He just saved the president's life. There wouldn't be a good way to do it. We tried it your way and failed, so let's try something else." He looked at Mr. Chambers. "You had an idea to neutralize this Agent Donnelly. What is it?"

Mr. Chambers looked at Stephen first and smiled with pride. Then he replied to the old man, "The plan has already been set into motion. We are going to take away everything he holds most dear. We are going to give him the best reason to walk away. It will not happen overnight. It will take time. In the end, the brave, heroic FBI agent will be nothing but a poor, wretched soul, begging for a new beginning and a new life away from government work."

The old man smiled. "Good. When does it start?"

"Tonight, sir."

"Good. Now that this peace summit is over, let us talk about our new plan of action."

20

Every professor at the University of Chicago had their favorite spot on campus. For Dr. Robert Schuman, it was a bench in front of a pond with a custom-made water fountain. The pond was surrounded by trees, and many birds made the area their home. Dr. Schuman loved birds and, when it was warm, enjoyed eating his lunch out there. His day had been busy, so he was having a later lunch there when Gavin showed up for their weekly meeting. He was a little early for the meeting, but the doctor was glad to have company. He smiled when he saw Gavin. "I didn't know if I'd be seeing you today. It sounds like you've been busy."

"It was a busy day, but good. I came back from the dead."

Dr. Schuman looked surprised. "Am I supposed to know what that means?"

"No. Just another case that didn't go by the book, but I did have some surprising things happen."

"Like what?"

Gavin sat down. "I hadn't seen anything for a while until I started investigating some murders."

"You've investigated murders and other crimes before and you didn't have any flashes. What made these murders so different?"

"They hit close to home. I'm sure you saw the news about the failed peace summit in Ireland. The murders had to do with this."

"This case was a little more stressful, wasn't it?"

"I suppose."

Dr. Schuman smiled. "I think stress has a lot to do with triggering these flashes, or maybe when things are more intense in your life. You seem to only have them when it's related to your job or when you help people."

"Are you suggesting they only come at a certain time, and therefore I can control them?"

"Well, that's what we've been working toward. Perhaps we should look at the timing of your flashes when talking about how to control them."

Gavin nodded. "I did have something strange happen. I touched a computer screen and had a flash."

"But you've touched things before and had a flash."

"Sure, but they were always items touched by the person I'm seeing, or somehow directly connected to them. The computer screen I touched was neither one of those things."

"Interesting! The power of touch within your senses is stretching beyond direct contact. It's extending through electromagnetic impulses."

"What's that in English, doctor?"

Dr. Schuman smiled. "It means you can touch something and still see something. You can touch a picture of someone on a computer screen and see them in the future. Your sense of touch just got a hell of a lot stronger."

Gavin was fascinated by this, even though the science was way above his head. "Well, that sounds good, but how do I control that?"

Dr. Schuman thought for a moment. "Try this: when it comes to something you want to see in the future, think of it as life-threatening. I think it's your stress levels that make you see things. The stress pushes your adrenaline up and that triggers a flash. If I'm right, then this should work, but it will be very hard to learn to control that because human beings were never meant to. Try this until the next time we meet."

Gavin laughed. "Sounds like you want me to become some kind of Superman."

Dr. Schuman smiled. "You may just have to. Besides, the word normal doesn't apply to you anymore."

Gavin smiled back and shook the doctor's hand. Then he said goodbye.

∞∞∞∞∞∞∞∞∞∞

Gavin was on his way to Paddy Murphy's. There was an event that night. It was supposed to be a celebration for the peace signing, but now it just turned into a fundraiser for the fight for peace. It was going to be a good Irish celebration and there was still plenty to be happy about. However, he had to make a stop first. He walked into the morgue to find Dr. Kenrick finishing her reports. She saw him walk in and smiled. "Best dead man I've ever seen."

[417]

Gavin laughed. "All because of you."

"I'm pretty sure you get your good looks from the Donnelly's."

"I also hear that my mother was very beautiful, so some of those looks probably came from her. I wanted to come by and thank you for fixing the report and helping me stay dead."

She walked up to him and smiled. "Any time, Agent Donnelly."

"I have to warn you: you will probably have to go before OPR. You can get into trouble for this."

"I'm not worried about it. I'm too qualified for them to fire me and, even if they did, I could get a job in the private sector very quickly and make five times as much as I do now. Like I said, I'm not worried." She put her arms around him and kissed him deeply and slowly. It was a sensual, passionate kiss, her favorite kind. Gavin liked it, too, and he pulled her in close, grabbing her ass, right before he lifted up her skirt. She smiled at the feeling, but stopped him. "Sorry, honey. Not today. I actually have a date tonight and you have an event to go to."

Gavin laughed. "I could just say that I won't make us late."

"Then what's the fun in that? I promise, I will make it up to you some other time. It's great to have you back." She kissed him goodbye and he thanked her again for her help.

Gavin was walking out of the FBI building when he bumped into a familiar face. Byers was waiting outside for him. Byers asked him to come with him. Normally, he would decline, but he had questions. They walked about a block and turned into an alleyway. Byers spoke. "It's good that you're alive, but you've made a lot of people angry."

"I don't know who these people are."

"You should, because what's coming next is worse than you dying."

"Why are you telling me this? Do you really want to help me?"

"I have been and I will continue to from time to time."

"Why?"

"Because I want to see if you have what it takes to find the truth, to go the full distance. The game you're playing is the most dangerous one you'll ever play and more serious than any case you'll ever work."

"You talk about this as if there is some major conspiracy that can destroy the world."

"A conspiracy that can destroy the world as you know it. It will be a world without choice…a world with slaves…slaves to a dark and brutal system. That's what I want you to understand."

Gavin didn't know what to make of what he just heard. It was puzzling. "You were the one who put a message within the murders... the message that was meant for me."

"Yes, and you figured it out brilliantly."

"That also means you committed these murders."

"Not all of them, but I'm not the killer you're looking for."

Gavin pulled out his service weapon and held Byers at gunpoint. "You're under arrest for the murders..."

Byers interrupted. "Really? How long do you think I will be in jail before someone gets me out? Besides, putting me in jail won't give you answers, and that's more important to you than this arrest. And we already know that you're willing to let a man die for your own cause."

Gavin was pissed. "What can you possibly tell me that would keep me from arresting you?"

"How about where your father really met your mother, and the facility he really rescued her from, as one of the Callan Raiders? You found a picture of him with the other raiders under a different name, so you have plenty of questions."

Gavin loaded the chamber of his gun. Byers said, "You're not going to kill me because you still have too many questions, and I have answers. You won't even shoot me."

"How can you continue to help me?"

"By warning you. While an attempt on your life will not happen again, the people you love most are in danger. If you continue to search for the truth, they will be taken from you one by one."

"What can I do to save them if what you say is true?"

Byers smiled. "You have to figure that out on your own. It starts with asking the question: how far are you willing to go? You saved a life today, but you didn't stop the overall plan; you didn't even put a dent into it. The people behind this can be stopped, but you will need my help to do it."

"What's in it for you?"

"I have my own reasons for that."

Gavin started to lower his gun. Byers gave him an arrogant smile. Gavin shot him in the right shoulder. The bullet didn't hit anything important, but he was bleeding and the gunshot hurt like hell. Byers was a bit surprised as he put pressure on his shoulder. Gavin glared at him. "Okay then, let's get something straight. I will take your help for now, but don't think I'm not willing to shoot you. The next time I do it, I will kill you. Does this answer your question about what I am prepared to do?"

Byers laughed. "Good for you, Agent Donnelly. Now I'm impressed."

Gavin walked away and went back to his truck. Byers used his tie to make a sling for his right arm. He then made a phone call. As soon as the voice on the other end answered, Byers told him, "I think he'll be a good one, but he's not ready to be a true believer yet. However, the potential is there. He wants the truth and he's willing to shoot someone for it."

∞∞∞∞∞∞∞∞∞∞

Gavin arrived at the pub about 30 minutes later. It was already crowded. The Prime Minister of Ireland, David Kenny, had decided to go to the pub. It was a big deal in the Irish community. Gavin walked in and saw his family. Alex may have helped him play dead, but it was really his Uncle Liam who allowed him to secretly infiltrate the SWAT Team as a sniper. Being a police captain had its advantages. His partner, Rachel, was there as well. Gavin was surprised to see her. She smiled when she spotted him.

He walked up and asked her, "What are you doing here? I figured you'd want to go home and finally get some sleep."

She laughed. "Trust me, I will be home early tonight and I think I'll probably sleep for a month, but I needed a drink, too. Plus, I had some news for you about this case."

"What happened now?"

"First, our fake Secret Service agent, Josephine Smith, is missing."

"How is she missing from federal prison?"

"That's the mystery; nobody can figure that out. I can't even find a transfer order. It's like she just walked out."

"Or someone just let her out."

Rachel chuckled. "That's probably more likely. Here's the other bad news: Dr. Steven Larkin was found murdered a couple of hours ago." She showed him a case file with pictures of the crime scene. "He was shot in the back of the head twice, like it was a contract killing."

"It probably was."

"What I don't understand is why he was killed. You went to see him a few days ago. Did he tell you anything?"

Gavin frowned. "Not anything useful."

"I was wondering if he was killed because of what he might have said to you."

"He wasn't able to help with the case. Maybe somebody just didn't like the fact that he was working for the FBI now."

"It doesn't look like a revenge killing. There's no DNA evidence and nothing on the security cameras at the school that can tell us who might have killed him. Whoever did it was a pro. I mean, the slugs in his head couldn't even be identified or matched to anything.

[420]

Sounds like a very good assassin who knows how to cover up the evidence…. something we've seen before."

"You're probably right, but it's something we should talk about on Monday." Gavin was being evasive, and Rachel didn't press it. It had already been a long day and there was nothing they could do about this tonight. There was no evidence linking anyone to Dr. Larkin's murder. Father Joseph was at the pub that night and he saw Rachel talking with her partner, so he decided to come over and say hi. It was a nice interruption and he wanted to check on Rachel, anyway. It had been a while since they last talked. Gavin took the opportunity to see some other people in the pub that he needed to talk to.

David Kenny was talking to various people, but at his side was Tommy McManus and Peter O'Malley, head of the New York City Irish Mob. On any normal day, it might be considered suspicious. But with the events of the last few days and the way this case had turned out, it wasn't. Gavin walked up to the men and looked at the prime minister. "Mr. Kenny, I have some information for you, something I did not include in my security briefing today. It's about the real suspect behind the assassination attempt."

David was very curious about this. "Do you want to talk to me alone?"

"I know how things are reported between the political party, the Army Council, and the Commission. If you don't mind them knowing what I have to tell you, then I don't mind telling you in front of them." David nodded that it was okay. He handed the prime minister a file folder and then told him what he and Rachel found out: the connection with the British Prime Minister and the Solomon Islands, as well as the link to H M Mining. The prime minister was shocked at what he heard. It sounded like some mystery novel. The prime minister asked,

"Are you guys going to do anything about this?"

"It's just circumstantial evidence right now. We don't have anything that directly links George Mallory to this plot, and we can't get him back to the States to question him, unless he comes voluntarily. The FBI can keep investigating, but that's all."

David Kenny frowned. "Why are you telling me this?"

"Because you deserve to know the truth, and I'm hoping you will do the right thing."

"And what is that?"

"Don't retaliate with violence; don't start a war. That's exactly what they want you to do."

"My life was threatened and they're making up lies about it. Decisive response is needed."

"Maybe, but if the IRA kills anyone, then you will start a war. That's all they'll need as an excuse to reclaim Ireland. All of it."

"You think this is about conquering our county?"

"I think someone wants to reclaim it for the British Empire. Maybe not Mallory himself, but the people behind all of this, the people pulling his strings. Don't give them an excuse."

"What makes you think I can control every aspect of the Army Council and what they do?"

"You're the head of Ireland, the head of the party and, technically, the head of the council. Do the best you can, even if it means not telling them everything I just told you."

David smiled. "You're asking a lot."

"I know, but the real fight for peace is not murder as a weapon. There's never a good war or a bad peace."

David laughed. "Isn't that a quote by Ben Franklin?"

"It is, but I thought it was appropriate in this situation."

David Kenney reached out and shook Gavin's hand. "Thank you for the information. If you find out anything else then I would greatly appreciate if you could let me know. I will do the best I can to stop any violence that might happen, but we can't completely ignore this. The tensions are going to run high with this one." He walked off to say hello to someone and left Peter O'Malley and Tommy McManus standing there. Both men were shocked by the news, as well. Gavin could tell that revenge was a better solution in their minds than peaceful actions. Gavin changed the subject by handing Tommy McManus a file folder. He looked at the two men seriously. "I have something for both of you. In our investigations, we found the man who hired John O'Kelly's killer so he could get close. He was also an informant for Homeland Security."

Tommy opened up the folder with Peter O'Malley looking over his shoulder. The name in the file popped out at them. Tommy spoke up. "Michael Delany, head of the New Jersey outfit. Are you sure about this?"

"Yes. I have a contact at Homeland Security who helped me track down where John O'Kelly's body went. A few days later, she found this for me. She hates my guts, so she has no reason to lie to me. He was your mole." Tommy and Peter were angry and it showed on their faces. Gavin responded, "Now we have enough evidence tying him to the murder. We can arrest him and put him away for life."

Tommy replied, "No, we will deal with him our way. No need to concern yourself with this."

"Okay, I just wanted to offer." He looked at Peter. "I owe you an apology. I thought you were the mole, so I looked into you. I'm sorry."

Peter smiled. "Ah, that's okay. The FBI is always investigating me."

"I did it because I didn't like you very much."

Peter laughed. "It's okay. Your father didn't like me much, either, but we respected each other and that's all I cared about."

"Everybody seems to know more about my father than I do. Maybe you can tell me something about him. Who were the Callan Raiders? I found a picture of them and my father was one of them, but he used a different name."

Both Tommy and Peter looked concerned. Gavin could tell they knew something about his father's involvement. Peter replied, "It's not my place to tell. That right is reserved for your Uncle Liam. He should be the one to tell you."

"Was my father doing something illegal?"

"No, although the British government would say differently. He wasn't doing anything illegal, not by morality standards. However, if you want to know more, then you need to ask your Uncle Liam." Peter walked away after that and, for Gavin, there was nothing more to ask these men. Peter was right; the answers would have to come from his Uncle Liam. Gavin went to the bar to find his uncle and ask him some questions. It turned out, he wasn't feeling that well because he was a little drunk. Alex was with him, trying to get him to drink some coffee. It was a bit humorous because he hadn't seen his uncle drunk in a long time. Liam said, "I'm fine. I don't need any coffee."

Alex replied, "Dad, you're drunk. You may not want to admit it, but you're drunk and it's time to sober up or go home."

Gavin chimed in. "Alex is right. You also shouldn't be driving. Let's get a squad car to take you home."

"Knock it off, you two. I'm fine!"

Gavin laughed. "Hey, what's the use in being the police chief if you can't get a free ride home from your patrolmen?"

Liam was going to say something, but Alex just told him to quit arguing. Alex and Gavin had a nice laugh over the matter. Alex helped his dad to one of the police cars outside and got a patrolman to drive him home. He called his mother to let her know, so she wouldn't be worried.

The music had been stopped as the Prime Minister, David Kenney, was asked to give a speech. It was appropriate after the day's events. He walked onstage with a pint of Guinness and looked out at the faces in the crowd. He began to speak.

"Friends and fellow Irishmen, thank you for allowing me to speak tonight in this fine establishment. Today was a tragedy, with all the years that we have been fighting for Northern Ireland, but the fight still continues. Peace is still possible and we'll still fight for it, no matter how long it may take. I was reminded a little while ago what the American Ben Franklin once said: 'there is no such thing as a good war or a bad peace.' But I do think there are wars that have to be fought in order to maintain peace. We shall not forget the Irish struggle, or those that have given their lives in the fight for peace. We do not forget the heroes of 1916; we do not forget the men behind the wire. As the Irish president in America once said, 'A man may die, nations may rise and fall, but an idea lives on.' That idea is a whole nation once again and peace throughout Ireland. So, raise your glasses and let's cheer for a nation once again." The crowd in the bar started clapping and cheering. Gavin, along with Alex, was asked to come up to the stage and lead the pub in song. He was happy to do that. Gavin led the pub in a rousing chorus of "A Nation Once Again" and then they all sang the Irish national anthem, "A Soldier's Song." It was a night of celebration... a celebration for those who had lived today, and the prospect of peace, despite the cold, dark storm that was about to hit Chicago.

∞∞∞∞∞∞∞∞∞∞

While Paddy Murphy's was in the midst of song, Officer Kyle Newman drove Liam Donnelly home. Liam was half-awake in the front seat of the car. He was drunk, and this time, he knew it. Suddenly, someone ran out into the road in front of the police car and made the car stop. They weren't going that fast, so it wasn't hard to stop. They avoided hitting the person who ran into the road. Officer Newman got out of the car to see what was going on. It looked as if the person on the road was hurt, so Officer Newman didn't bother to put his hand on his gun when he got out of the squad car. He asked the person with the hood pulled over his head, "Hey, are you alright?"

The man wearing the hood didn't answer at first. The officer asked again as he approached the man. "Sir, are you alright?"

"I am now." The man raised the gun in his right hand and shot Officer Newman twice, killing him instantly. Liam was awakened by the gunshots. Out of instinct, he grabbed his unholstered gun and loaded the chamber, so he was ready to shoot. He got out of the car and was greeted by the man in the hood. Liam told him to freeze and put the gun down, but the man in the hood walked closer to him. That's when Liam recognized him and said, "You. I know you. You were kicked off the force. What the hell are you doing shooting a police officer?"

The man in the hood responded, "I'm doing what I was destined to do. The struggle lives on, and I am the United Front." Liam gave him a strange look and then the man in the hood knocked the gun out of his hand. Liam tried to go for it, but he was shot twice and fell

[424]

to the ground in a pool of his own blood. He immediately fell
unconscious. The man in the hood said, "You can thank Gavin
Donnelly for this." Then he placed a card on Liam's unconscious body.
It read:

30 MINUTES

A BADGE OF HONOR

BOOK 4

1

The rain was coming down hard. It had been a beautiful day earlier, and then, all of a sudden, the skies darkened and let the rain fall like a feisty waterfall. Detective Charlie Finch hated the rain and this just made his day worse. It had turned out to be an all-around shitty day. Most people would get a drink after a bad day, but Detective Finch had his own routine. He always stopped by Molly's Diner on Adams Street to get two of their bacon, egg, cheese, and tomato sandwiches. They were a delicacy to him when to most people, they were just ordinary breakfast fare. It was a family diner, and everybody knew everybody. Ashley, the girl working behind the counter, smiled at the detective when he walked in. All she had to ask was how many sandwiches he needed.

Detective Finch smiled. They knew him well at the diner. He told her, "Miss Ashley, I will need two sandwiches tonight."

She laughed. "Looks like you've had a bad day, Detective."

"It's been a son of a bitch, I'll tell you that."

She smiled again. "Well then, I'll throw in a slice of pie for you. Just had an apple pie come out of the oven."

Apple pie was his favorite and his smile towards her lingered a little longer as a way of saying 'thank you.' While he waited for his order, he took a seat at the counter and watched the Cubs game on TV. There was another man sitting two seats down, watching the game, too, who looked like he was coming off a bender. He was scruffy and hadn't shaved for days. During the next play the Cubs made an error, leading to a run scored by the opposing team. Some of the people in the diner voiced their disappointment. The man sitting two seats down from Detective Finch said out loud, making sure the detective could hear him, "Somebody didn't say his prayers before the game. What a shame."

Finch said, "I don't think prayers could have saved him from making that error."

"I see, detective, that you're not a religious man."

"Oh, I am, just not when it comes to baseball. Especially Cubs baseball."

The man two seats down laughed. "I can understand that, but let me ask you another question, detective. Do you believe that every man must pay for their sins despite a lifetime of good deeds?"

Finch never minded small talk with strangers, but he felt uncomfortable with the question. He didn't respond for a moment and, luckily, the awkwardness hanging in the air was interrupted by his order being completed. He did say to the man two seats down from him, "That kind of question is best answered during mass." Then he said goodbye and walked out of the diner. The other man waited a few seconds, took a sip of coffee, and then followed after the detective. The unmarked police cruiser was parked around the corner so Finch didn't see the man walk up towards him before it was too late.

"Detective," the man from the diner shouted, startling Finch as he was trying to get into his car. "You forgot something." He pulled out a gun and aimed it at Finch.

"What the fuck do you want?" Detective Finch shouted back.

"You didn't answer my question, so let me give you the correct answer. Every man must pay for his sins."

Finch didn't know how to react to that because he didn't know what the man with the gun was talking about. It sounded like crazy talk, but he replied with this: "I don't give a shit about your religious epiphany, but if you gun down a cop, you're going to have every cop in the city looking to put you in a body bag."

The man with the gun smiled. "I may be there soon, but not before you and your friends pay for your sins."

"What are you talking about?"

He shot Finch in the arm and the detective screamed in pain. "You motherfucker, you're going down for this."

The man with the gun smiled. "Not today, but before I kill you, you should know the reason why."

"Why do you want to kill me?"

As Finch was sitting on the ground next to his car, holding his arm to try and stop the bleeding, the man with the gun bent down and looked him straight in the eye. "1989, detective."

"What?"

"1989. Detective." Finch now had a look of fear in his eyes, finally realizing what the man with the gun was referring to. He continued to look at the detective. "Every sinner must pay for his sins, and today is your day of reckoning." Before Finch could say anything, he was shot three more times and fell over dead. The man with the gun walked back onto Adams Street and looked up at a street camera and just smiled.

∞∞∞∞∞∞∞∞∞

Gavin was working late, but not on anything official. Every night after work, he would stare at the same Chicago police file. Looking at it over and over, he was trying to find something in the file he didn't already know. Still, there were no answers, just more questions. Agent Dan Moore stopped by his office with a CD. He said, "Agent Donnelly, I see you're burning the midnight oil."

Gavin smiled. "Yeah. Just catching up on paperwork."

"On the same file you've been staring at for the past few weeks?" Gavin laughed at that. "What's the latest on your uncle?" Agent Moore asked.

"He's alive, but still in a coma. I guess that's a good thing."

"It is a good thing because he's alive and stable."

"But what if he never wakes up? Then he might as well be dead."

Agent Moore didn't have anything to say to that, but he had something else to tell Gavin. "Since this whole United Front debacle, the cyber guys have been doing surveillance throughout Chicago using the street and webcams as well as picking up any kind of chatter we can through the satellites."

"You mean, you're doing what the NSA does."

Agent Moore laughed. "Yes, but we're going it legally." Gavin didn't quite believe that, but wasn't going to argue with it. Agent Moore continued. "I was examining camera footage from the night your uncle was shot and I was able to pick up some sound. We have a recording of the shooter."

Gavin was surprised. "You know what he said that night?"

"Yes, we do, and you're not going to like it. " Agent Moore played the CD recording for Gavin. He listened to the whole thing, including the part where the shooter said, "You can thank Gavin Donnelly for this." Gavin's look turned to utter shock. He couldn't believe it and responded in kind to his friend. "This is my fault. He was shot because of me."

Agent Moore put his hand on Gavin's shoulder to try and comfort him. "First, this is not your fault. Second, why would they try to kill your uncle because of you?"

Gavin thought of an answer to that question and all he came up with was, "That's the million-dollar question, isn't it?" Agent Moore

[429]

smiled. Gavin asked him another question: "Has this been shown to Chicago PD yet?"

"No, and it's not going to unless they get a congressional order for us to do so. Investigating the United Front is a federal matter, and the information we gather is classified as far as they are concerned."

"Good. I don't need my cousin and the rest of the Chicago PD knowing about this yet, at least until I get some answers."

Agent Moore was curious. "I thought you weren't assigned to this case."

"Not yet, but I will be eventually."

"You know, AD Foster won't do that for personal reasons, even if you are a hero."

Gavin smiled. "What's the use of getting a commendation if I can't use it to get what I want?"

Agent Moore had to laugh. "Good luck with that. I'm anxious to see how that turns out."

∞∞∞∞∞∞∞∞∞

Agent Rachel Main was sitting quietly in the conference room at the Baker and Stern law offices in New York City. It was the last meeting with the lawyers and her husband to finalize their divorce. She didn't like being there, even though the divorce had been easy-going for the most part. There were no knockdown, drag-out fights like in most divorces. They pretty much split everything down the middle, but Rachel still had a sick feeling. She had never really failed at anything in her life, and here she was with a failed marriage.

Rachel and Richard Main didn't talk. They had their lawyers do that for them. After about an hour, everything was wrapped up, and all they had to do was sign the papers. Richard was a little sad that this was happening. He had always loved Rachel ever since they met during her first case right out of the FBI Academy and he was first assigned to the Justice Department in Washington. They had hit it off instantly, but it didn't last as long as a great love affair should have. He knew that the marriage was probably over after they lost the baby a few years before and stopped talking. It was a regret he'd always had.

The lawyers asked if they had anything to discuss, and both Richard and Rachel said no. A copy of the divorce papers was passed to each one of them. Richard signed the papers as if he was in a hurry, and Rachel signed her copy with a heavy reluctance. Even though she didn't really love Richard anymore, she still felt a deep sadness that the marriage was finally over, but she still signed the papers. The lawyers packed everything up and told both their clients that there was nothing more they needed to do. The marriage was over.

[430]

Rachel was just going to leave, but Richard stopped her. He still wanted to try to smooth things over and end this as friends. He told her, "I still have some of your stuff. Do you want to come by and get it in the morning?"

Rachel tried to be nice, even though she was hurting. "It's okay. I'll arrange for a delivery truck and they can bring it back to Chicago. It will be easier that way."

"Some of the stuff is from your grandmother."

Rachel sighed. "It's fine. Let the delivery guys take care of it. Besides, I'm on a flight back to Chicago tonight."

Richard smiled. "Oh, didn't want to stay that long?"

"I have a lot of work to catch up on back in Chicago."

"Rachel, I'm sorry for how everything turned out. It shouldn't have been this way."

"Did you just now come to that realization, or did it happen before you walked out after we lost the baby?"

"We never talked about it, and that's partly my fault. But you never opened up about it, either. You always kept things inside too much."

Rachel gave him a dirty look. "Maybe, but it's too late to talk about this now. Our marriage is over, and we each have our own lives to live."

"Look, Rachel, I don't want this to end badly."

"Losing a baby, getting divorced … tell me how this ends well? The only way this ends is badly."

Richard put his hand on her shoulder and tried to comfort her like he used to. She shrugged it off. "Rachel, I'm sorry, truly sorry."

"It doesn't mean much anymore, Richard, but I do appreciate it. " She started to walk away and Richard said to her, "You can always call me for a favor if you need to. I'm still your friend at the end of the day."

She stopped and smiled. "And I'm yours, but we probably shouldn't talk to each other for a while." Richard nodded at her. There was still too much hurt to get over. As Rachel was leaving the office, tears filled up in her eyes.

∞∞∞∞∞∞∞∞∞∞

Mr. Chambers was escorted into the Old Man's office. He didn't have anything to report, but he was called to a private meeting with the Old Man not really knowing if it was something good or if he was in trouble. As he walked into the darkened room, he handed a glass of thirty year old bourbon, straight up. Mr. Chambers tasted the

[431]

vintage and smiled at the fact that he liked it, considering he did not drink bourbon. The Old Man said to him:

"Thank you for coming by so late. Instead of asking for a report, I have something to talk to you about."

Mr. Chambers looked concerned. "Is everything okay, sir?"

"It will be, but everything has not gone according to plan. The Irish Prime Minister is supposed to be dead and, with him still being alive, it leaves too many questions. Our plans have changed."

"Just let me know what I can do to help."

"I know you were expecting to be moved up at Homeland Security last week, but unfortunately the peace summit didn't make the President lose faith in the Director. However, that will change soon."

"I'm not too worried about it, sir, but I do have a question."

The Old Man poured himself another drink and replied, "I figured you might. You want to know about this Agent Donnelly, right?"

Mr. Chambers smiled. "Yes, sir. What are we going to do about him?"

"Well, I agree with most of the group. We can't have him killed … too many questions would be asked. We will be using your political friend's plan, with a few changes."

"I only suggested sending a message to Agent Donnelly with the first shooting."

"It's time for doing more than just sending a message. He's been warned before and it hasn't stopped his curiosity."

Mr. Chambers nodded in agreement. "What do you have in mind?"

The Old Man handed him a file folder that had the word "classified" stamped in red on it. "You've heard of Operation Paper Clip, correct?"

"Yes, sir. It was a program used to recruit the scientists of Nazi Germany for employment by the United States in the aftermath of World War II and to keep scientific advancements away from the Russians. They did a lot of inhumane experiments, all in the name of science, and all on the U.S. government's dime."

"Yes, that was part of it, but there are many programs that extended off of Operation Paper Clip that only a select few know about. One of them is Operation Morning Sun. The details are in this folder. In our group, you will be the 17th person to know about it."

Mr. Chambers looked in the folder. He was a little shocked by what he read. "What does this have to do with Agent Donnelly?"

"Nothing directly, but while this is still an ongoing operation, some of our plans are going to have to change. The project is being moved, and let's just say that when some things are discovered, Agent

Donnelly will share in the blame when it comes to one of the biggest tragedies in American history. I'm sure his career will be quite finished when all of this is over."

Mr. Chambers didn't quite understand what he meant. The Old Man could be cryptic sometimes. However, the Old Man poured Mr. Chambers, another drink and explained what was about to happen in more detail.

2

There was already a huge crowd surrounding the murder scene outside Molly's Diner when Detective Alex Donnelly arrived on the scene. A cop getting killed always drew more of a crowd and created more chaos. Uniformed cops had everything roped off and were trying to keep the crowd at bay. Alex got out of his car and walked up to the detectives that were already there. One of them was Detective Sara Reilly. Alex looked at her and said, "Detective, I would ask how your evening is going, but I already know the answer."

"You're funny, detective," she replied.

"What do we have?"

She walked him over to the body. "We have a dead police officer. Detective Charles Finch was shot four times at close range, 9mm casings. Witnesses in the diner said Finch came in tonight and got a to-go order. They said he was chatting with some guy at the counter and, when he left, the guy followed him out. It looks like he followed him around the corner and shot Detective Finch in the alley over there, and then moved the body onto the sidewalk so everybody could see it."

Alex was a little surprised to hear that. "Why move the body? The killer must have known that people would have heard the shots and would've wanted to get away from here. Plus, why did he want to kill Detective Finch, anyway? Were the two men arguing in the diner?"

Sara replied, "According to witnesses, no, they weren't. But I might have the answer to why he moved the body. We were able get some fingerprints off Detective Finch's jacket. The killer must have grabbed it when he moved the body. You're not going to like it."

Alex's look immediately turned to anger. "Don't tell me. Bobby McClain."

"Yes, sir, Detective. It looks like he has his second victim now. And there's something else that you're not going to like."

"We haven't reached our limit on bad news yet?"

"No, sir. We were able to get a photo of him from the street cam." She showed him the picture on an Android tablet. Alex responded angrily,

"The son of a bitch is smiling about what he did! He wanted us to see it … to see the crime. Goddamnit, he's laughing at us!"

"What do you want us to do now?"

"First, I don't want Bobby McClain's name released to the press; I don't give a shit what kind of pressure we get from the media. Second, get Detective Finch's file, and pull my father's file, too."

"Your father's file?"

"Yes, Detective. We need to start looking for connections between the two victims. I want to know why he targeted the both of them. We need to find the connections so we know who he might target next."

"You don't think this is over?"

"No, I don't. Shooting a cop that you might have had a beef with is one thing, but shooting two cops is not a coincidence. They were targeted for a reason, and I want to know why."

Alex walked off to go make a phone call while Detective Reilly called their precinct to get what Alex had requested.

∞∞∞∞∞∞∞∞∞∞

Rachel's flight was uneventful, or if it wasn't, she didn't notice. She had a window seat and spent the flight staring out into the dark abyss of the night sky, just replaying her failed marriage over and over. She even cried a little bit, but she did the best she could to keep the tears hidden from the other passengers. The small bottle of scotch she had during the flight helped. When she arrived back in Chicago she didn't want to go straight home. Home was cold and lonely. This was the kind of night that she needed a friend, and she really only had one in Chicago.

It was a little late, but Rachel knew her partner would still be up. She arrived at his apartment, and before she knocked, she took a deep breath. She knew that she would be crossing a line that she swore she would never cross, but it didn't matter tonight. Rachel needed an escape. She needed to take the pain away. After a moment's pause, she finally knocked on the door.

Gavin was actually in bed and was startled by the knock. He rolled over and kissed Maggie, who was lying next to him. He said as he smiled at her, "Don't go anywhere. I'll be back."

Maggie smiled back. "You better be. I don't want any more broken promises."

Gavin laughed as he put on some gym shorts and a T-shirt. He walked into the main room of his apartment and answered the door. Gavin was surprised to see his partner on his doorstep, but it was a welcome surprise. "Hi, I didn't expect to see you back until Monday. Come on in. What's up?"

Rachel smiled. "Sorry to land on your doorstep tonight, but I needed to talk to someone and you're pretty much the only friend I have in this town."

"Is everything all right?"

"For the most part."

"You want a beer?"

Rachel smiled. "Sure, but I may need something stronger later."

"Gavin laughed. "I'm sure I can help you with that. Did everything go all right in New York?"

"It went all right. No surprises. It was about what I expected."

Gavin handed her a beer. "I know divorce is never easy, but you've got a clean slate now and nothing holding you to New York or D.C. "

She laughed. "Is that your way of telling me that Chicago's officially my home now?"

"I'm just saying that you have a new slate here in Chicago and you just might meet a nice fella. There's a few around, unlike the ones we usually deal with."

Rachel walked closer to Gavin and raised her bottle to clink it against his. "Cheers. Here's to possibilities in Chicago!"

Gavin just smiled at her. "Sláinte." She just looked him and let her gaze linger for a moment. Gavin was going to say something, but then she did something that really surprised him. She set her beer down and kissed him right on the lips. It was a passionate kiss, and it was the most intimate kiss she had given a man a long time. Gavin didn't stop her. He passionately kissed her back, even though he knew he probably shouldn't. However, his conscience usually stopped him from crossing the boundaries he shouldn't cross. But those thoughts never entered his mind as he set his beer down and brought her in close while his mouth sensuously brushed against her soft lips.

They kissed for about a minute until they were interrupted by Maggie, who had come out of the bedroom wearing only Gavin's dress shirt. Rachel was startled and quickly backed away. She said, "I'm sorry. I didn't know you had company. I'm so sorry for interrupting your evening."

She bolted for the door as Gavin replied, "it's okay, Rachel. You can stay if you want and talk if you need to."

As she opened the door, she said, "I don't think I should now. You have company and I would just be in the way. I'll see you on Monday. Have a good night."

Gavin was going to say something, but she left in a hurry and lightly slammed the door behind her. Gavin turned to Maggie and said, "I'm sorry for that."

Maggie smiled. "You think I'm mad about you kissing your partner?"

"I really don't know. I never know when a woman is mad at me or not unless something is being thrown at my head."

She laughed. "Gavin, honey, I'm the last person to get mad at you for kissing another woman or to even judge you. Remember, I'm a married woman sleeping with my husband's best friend while he's in prison. I'm doing the one thing a prisoner's wife should never do."

Gavin smiled. "I still don't want to hurt your feelings."

"It's not mine, you should worry about. She's pissed at you."

"For what? Having another woman here?"

Maggie laughed. "No, dear. Kissing her for real and then having to stop."

Gavin looked a little dumbfounded. "What do you mean?"

"She wasn't here just to get laid, and she didn't kiss you just to make out. She was here to be with someone that she has a connection with, someone that she cares about. Your kiss was intimate, something with feeling and care. You don't kiss me like that anymore."

"I don't know if that's true."

"Trust me, Gavin; a woman always knows the truth behind a kiss." She grabbed herself a beer out of the refrigerator. "Don't worry. I'm not mad, and it isn't going to stop me from sleeping with you again, especially in the next five minutes."

Gavin didn't know for sure if she was right, but he knew that she had never lied to him since they were childhood sweethearts. He had to wonder if there was some truth to what she was saying.

∞∞∞∞∞∞∞∞∞∞∞∞

It was yard time at the Thompson Correctional Facility, one of Illinois' newest and most secure federal prisons. Jimmy McManus had finally gotten a transfer there a couple years before, so his family could be closer to him. Yard time was his favorite part of the day. Not that he did a whole lot of physical activity, but he loved being outside. He mostly loved to read outside, and it never mattered what the temperature was. Today there was a chill in the air, and the wind kept blowing the pages of his book. But he didn't seem to mind that, only the interruption that came during his yard time.

Another fellow inmate walked up to Jimmy as he was sitting on a bench near the basketball court, and he brought a newspaper with him. Jimmy asked, "What is it, Rocco? You know I don't like to be disturbed while I'm reading."

"I know, Jimmy. Everybody knows that, but I have something important for you. Some information from the newspaper that you should see." Jimmy was curious enough to stop reading his book. He had worked with Rocco for many years before they got pinched and sent to prison, and he always knew Rocco to have solid information.

"What information?" Jimmy was handed the newspaper. There were two stories circled in it. The first was about a missing U.S. congressman in Illinois and the second was about a Chicago police detective from the 9th Precinct who had been shot and killed.

Jimmy looked angry. He had a sick feeling in his stomach. "Do you have the name of the detective? The paper doesn't give one."

"I called one of my guys who got the name from the precinct. It's Charles Finch."

"Fuck, that's what I was afraid of. Liam Donnelly got shot three weeks ago, Detective Finch is now dead, and the congressman is missing. This is no coincidence. This is fucking bad."

"Your congressman is dead?"

Jimmy frowned. "Not yet, but I think he's trying to run."

"What do you think this is all about?"

"It's obvious they're trying to tie up loose ends, which means operations are moving."

Rocco looked surprised. "I thought the whole thing was just supposed to be delayed for a while."

"It was, but I'm assuming that after the attack in Chicago a few weeks ago the operation has to shut down and they don't want loose ends."

"There's a lot of loose ends in Chicago, going back many years."

Jimmy sat back and paused for a moment. "This is just the beginning. A lot more people are going to die, which means you need to make a call."

"Who am I calling?"

Jimmy smiled. "You have to call the Hound. We need to buy more protection."

∞∞∞∞∞∞∞∞∞∞∞

Detective Alex Donnelly had been running behind all morning, and it showed as he rushed into his precinct. He was rarely late to work and wished he could get back the 10 minutes that had made him late. When we he got to his desk, he found his cousin, Gavin, sitting there looking at files on the cop killer in Chicago that had shot Liam Donnelly. Alex, somewhat annoyed, shook his head and said, "The feds have no respect for anything, especially privacy."

Gavin laughed. "Yeah, Homeland Security can be real dicks." He set aside a cup of coffee and a chocolate glazed donut with sprinkles on it for Alex. "Here, this is for the intrusion."

Alex took a bite of the donut. "I guess this is an official visit by the FBI, which means you're not taking over the case."

"No. I have sent three requests in and they keep denying them."

"No offense, but I'm glad. It's bullshit when you guys take over and think we can't do our jobs."

"Well, I'm not here to take over, just to offer a helping hand. You know I have resources that can help."

Alex didn't really want the help, but like most cops, he wanted to catch a known cop killer more than anything. But Gavin was right. The FBI had resources that he didn't. Alex replied. "Fine. I'm sure you've seen the files on Detective Finch, our latest victim."

Gavin nodded. "Yes, I did. It looks like the shooter left his famous calling card again."

Alex chuckled. "It's a sick joke, if you ask me.

Gavin Laughed. "Couldn't agree more cousin."

Alex continued to voice his opinion. "I already hated this United Front group, but influencing a cop killer just fucking pisses me off."

Gavin gave him a sympathetic look and replied. "Right there with you." But there was something else on Gavin's mind so he had to ask. "I saw a file on your desk that says 'Chief Liam Donnelly,' I guess you pulled his service jacket, have you found any connection between the two? I assume that's why you pulled it."

[439]

"That's right."

"How did you get the old man's file? I thought only internal affairs could get it."

Alex smiled. "I called in a favor. Besides, we need to find connections, don't we?"

Gavin nodded yes. "Did you find anything?"

"Not a thing, but I have to tell you, his file makes for some interesting reading, and there's a lot blacked out."

Gavin laughed. "I bet there is. He's one of the last old-timers that truly knows where all the bodies are buried and whose career is more secrets than commendations."

"You know the strange thing about these shootings is Bobby McClain. It's like he's got nothing to lose and wants to show off. Don't you think true revenge would be to kill everybody and disappear, knowing that you've won?"

"Not unless you want to be a martyr and make a statement. Maybe that's what he's trying to achieve."

Alex started shaking his head. "What I don't get is why the FBI or Homeland Security can't shut down this United Front group. They shut down this group, we get our cop killer."

"It's not that easy. We can only arrest those that commit violence. Until members do that, then they have the right to believe their bullshit and spew any hateful nonsense they want. Besides, we don't know if there is a real connection with Bobby McClain and this group."

"What are you talking about? He left one of their cards on the victims."

"Doesn't mean he's really connected to them? I mean, think about it. Is there any evidence of him ever being part of a political or an anarchist group? If we were to build a profile of this guy, would there be anything to suggest he would join a group like this? According to his profile, he's never been political, never registered with a political party or even registered to vote."

"Doesn't mean he couldn't have joined this group recently or become political."

"Maybe, but this guy had no allegiance to anything except money. He just used the badge to further his criminal activities. The United Front is supposed to be against that."

Alex took another sip of coffee. "I'll admit, it's kind of strange, but it seems to be the only lead anybody has."

"Nothing from any known associate?"

"Yeah, we're not that lucky. Anybody that worked with him is either dead or in jail. His ex-wife was all too eager to turn him in if she ever saw him again so there's no chance that he's going there.

Anybody that would have helped him hasn't had any contact with him for years. He's completely changed his M.O."

"So who would be helping him?"

Alex and Gavin both took a sip a coffee trying to come up with an answer, but they were at a loss. Finally, Gavin spoke up. "There may be somebody I can ask … somebody who always seems to know what's going on."

"Can you trust this person?"

"Probably not, but we're running out of possibilities."

It was early Monday morning, and Agent Donnelly and Agent Main were being called into the boss' office. They hadn't done much since the assassination attempt in Chicago a few weeks before, but AD Foster had a new case for them. Both of the agents couldn't wait to get back to work … real work! Rachel was already at the office when Gavin arrived. He brought her a cup of coffee, hoping that it wouldn't be too awkward that morning, but he wasn't that lucky. She didn't really look at him when she thanked him for the coffee. He asked her, "Are feeling better?"

"Yeah, I'm fine. Thanks for asking."

"Do you want to talk about it?"

She finally looked at him. "No. We don't ever need to talk about it. Let's just get to work."

"OK. It's up to you."

"She smiled. "Besides, it will be nice to get a real case. It's boring around here."

Gavin laughed at her comment, and he couldn't disagree with her. Without any real work to do, all he had been thinking about was his uncle's shooting. Both of the agents went to AD Foster's office, and as they sat down, he handed them each a file folder. Gavin and Rachel both had a strange look after seeing what was in the folders. Rachel was the first to ask, "Is this supposed to be our next case?"

AD Foster replied, "Yes, and you should be grateful for this one. It's an important case."

"It's a missing person's case. This is Violent Crimes, so why are we getting it?"

Gavin finally spoke up. "We were asked to look into Congressman McMahon's disappearance, weren't we?"

AD Foster replied, "Yes, this one came through the Director's office. The thing about being heroes is you get important cases like this. I know both of you think this is a waste of your time, but a missing U.S. congressman is no small matter."

Gavin responded, "Do we suspect foul play?"

"We're not sure. He's been missing for five days, and we have no clue to what might have happened. He vanished mysteriously from a fundraiser. There were no witnesses, and he didn't have his cell phone on him that we could track. His car and driver were left at the event."

Rachel replied, "It says here one of his bodyguards is missing, too. I'm assuming he's a suspect."

"Possibly, Agent Main, but we don't know where he is. And we haven't found a body, so it just leaves us with even more questions."

"Is there any motive for kidnapping or murder?"

"That's what you are going to find out because, at this point, everybody is at a loss on why he's missing."

Gavin responded, "Not to be delicate, but are we sure he didn't run off with a mistress or anything of that nature? It's been known to happen."

AD Foster gave him a dirty look. "You mean, not to be indelicate?"

"Yeah, that's exactly what I meant." Rachel laughed at the sarcastic comment her partner had made.

"Agent Donnelly, all sarcasm aside, we know running off with a mistress is not what happened. He has three mistresses, and they're all accounted for. Two of them, he hasn't been with in over a month, but the other one, Polly White, might know something. The police haven't questioned her yet, so you get to do it. You two are going to fly down to Springfield and start your investigation there."

"Gavin replied, "Despite the fact that we were asked to look into this case, don't you think our time would be better spent with more important cases in the department?"

"Agent Donnelly, this is an important case. I am aware of the fact that you two don't want a missing person's case, but you don't get to pick and choose what you're assigned from the Director's office. This doesn't have anything to do with your requests for the FBI to take over the investigation of your uncle's shooting, does it?"

Gavin paused for a moment. "It's a lot more important than a missing congressman, especially when there are ties to a terrorist group."

"I told you before, don't make this personal. Now, you can work the case we assign you or you can resign. The FBI won't be used for personal vendettas. Now go work this case and if Chicago PD needs our help, they'll call us. Besides, it's not like you haven't been helping your cousin, Alex, on this case, anyway."

Gavin smiled. "I guess I can't fool you, huh?"

"Take your sarcasm and shove it. Of course I know what

you're up to. You're as predictable as some of the criminals we arrest.
Now get out of here and go find the congressman."

The agents walked out the office, and Rachel asked her partner
where he wanted to start first. He replied, "Let's get background
checks on all of his bodyguards and see if there's something unusual.
Then we can head down to Springfield, where his family lives. It's the
best place to start."

∞∞∞∞∞∞∞∞∞∞

Agent Donnelly and Agent Main were in Springfield a couple
of hours later. They interviewed the congressman's wife and his staff
all over again, even though the police had done it a few days before,
just to see if they could get anything new. Unfortunately, they didn't
learn anything that they didn't already know. As they were walking
back to their car after visiting the congressman's office, Gavin finally
spoke up. "Well, I'm not surprised that we didn't learn anything new
from these interviews."

Rachel replied, "Why do you say that?"

"Because mistresses always know more. We're asking the
wrong questions to the wrong people, all for the sake of protocol."

She laughed. "That's a good point, and why we need to talk to
his mistress, Polly."

They got in their car and headed to her apartment. It was quiet
during the car ride, so Rachel broke the silence with a question.
"Why?"

Gavin was a little startled by the question. "Why what?"

"Why do you do it, Gavin? Why do you sleep around like that,
especially with a married woman?"

"I thought you didn't want to talk about what happened."

"I'm not asking about you and me, I just want to know why
you sleep around."

Gavin tried to smile. "I do it because I like sex and it keeps me
entertained. As for Maggie, that's just a sad and complicated story, and
it doesn't get any easier each time I sleep with her."

"Then why do it?"

"Because I still love her. It's strange, but I never heard
anybody say that love wasn't fucked up!"

"Wasn't she your childhood sweetheart?"

"Yes, she was."

"And her husband, your best friend from childhood, is in
prison, right?"

Gavin laughed. "Like I said, it's complicated."

[444]

"When I kissed you, did I complicate things even more for you?"

Gavin smiled. "Surprisingly, no, but I would like to know why you did it."

Rachel paused for a moment. "Not today, but maybe some other time." The agents didn't say anything to each other for the rest of the car ride. After 20 minutes, they finally arrived at Polly White's home. When they knocked on her door and she answered, Polly wasn't surprised to see them and wasn't nervous when they flashed their badges. She let them into her apartment and offered them some coffee. Gavin was the first to say something. "Mrs. White, do you know why we're here?"

She tried to smile. "Yes, Agent Donnelly, I know why. Your investigating Congressman McMahon's disappearance, but I don't have anything more to tell you that I haven't already told the police."

"So you were questioned by the police. I thought, as somebody in your position, they wouldn't know about you."

"Just because I'm a mistress doesn't mean that my relationship with the congressman is a secret. Of course I would be questioned by the police."

Rachel asked her, "How many people know about your relationship with him?"

Polly gave her a full smile. "His staff knows about me. He doesn't exactly keep his affairs a secret. Plus, I'm pretty sure his wife knows about me, too."

"Do you know of anybody that would want to hurt the congressman, like his wife?"

"No. His wife doesn't really care about what he does. It's not like she doesn't sleep around, too. They have a political marriage, and the only thing she likes about him is his money."

Gavin asked, "Are you saying that his wife isn't capable of harming him out of revenge?"

"I'm sure she is, but I don't see her harming him. Like I said, she likes her lifestyle too much."

"If the staff knows you and you've been seen with him for a while, have you noticed anything out of the ordinary? Something you couldn't explain, that might be the reason for his disappearance?"

Polly shook her head. "It's been business as usual with him. I still see him on our regular days. If I go to Washington with him, then it's for the same kind of events with the same kind of people who all know me."

"What about his bodyguards? They know you, right? They help sneak you into places, right?"

"Yes."

"Can you tell me about them? Are they completely loyal to the congressman? I mean, he hasn't done anything to upset them to where they might betray him?"

She laughed. "No, they've been with him for years, and he's treated them very well. They're loyal, but one of them retired a few months ago, so he hired a new bodyguard for his security team."

Rachel nodded at her partner as if to tell him they had found a big clue. Gavin asked her, "Was there anything unusual about him?"

"No, he was very nice. He seemed to do a good job."

"Were you with the congressman the night he disappeared?"

"I saw him earlier that day, but I didn't go to the function with him."

"Was his new bodyguard with him that night?"

"Yes, he was." Gavin looked at his partner and nodded, letting her know that their clue was a big one. The agents thanked Polly for her time and told her that they would be in touch.

As they were walking out, Rachel was the first to say something. "I don't get this. The congressman disappears, but there's no evidence as to why. If he was kidnapped, then why are there no ransom demands? If he's dead, then why hasn't a body been found? And then again, if he's been murdered, why hide the body unless it's a random act and you don't want to get caught?"

Gavin was listening, but his head started to hurt. He was about to have a flash.

Polly's cell phone started to ring. She looked at the caller ID and knew exactly who it was. When she answered the phone, she immediately said, "Somehow, I knew you would be calling me."

The voice on the other end of the phone asked, "Did the two FBI agents come by and talk to you?"

Polly answered, "Yes, they did, just like you said they would."

Before Gavin could hear the voice on the phone reply back to Polly, he felt Rachel lightly tapping him on the shoulder, trying to get him to pay attention to what she was saying.

Rachel said to her partner, "Are you listening to me? You look like you're daydreaming."

Gavin looked at her slightly and laughed. "I heard you. You don't think this is random."

"Not to inflate my own ego, but people like us don't get called to investigate something random. And besides, if it's truly a random murder, then the killer wouldn't be able to hide it that well. And then the bodyguard can't be found, as well. There's no trace of him. If he's the killer, then it's not random."

"But it doesn't explain why somebody would want to get rid of him, Rachel."

She paused for a moment. "What if he's not dead, but running from something? Maybe his bodyguard is helping him to run!"

"Something he's working on in Congress?"

"No, you don't have to make a congressman disappear to get him to stop investigating something or for him to change his vote. Blackmail or buying them off usually works just fine. He used to be a cop, right?"

"Yeah, he spent 20 years with the Chicago PD."

"How long can a beef last between cops and crooks, or cops with other cops?"

Gavin laughed. "They can last a lifetime."

"Then maybe this has something to do with his past. Getting his congressional records won't be a problem, but how hard will it be to get his police records?"

"You have to get a subpoena for Internal Affairs. They are the only ones who can pull a service jacket, and they won't do it for a federal agent without the subpoena."

"Well, let's go find a district judge. There has to be one in Springfield who will give us one."

Gavin started shaking his head. "You may be right with your theory, but there's not a judge, even in Springfield, who will give you a subpoena to look into a former police officer's service jacket based on a theory ... especially when it might embarrass a congressman. Judges and politicians don't interfere with cops in Chicago. They take that seriously."

Rachel was a little shocked to hear that. "You're joking, right? This has to do with finding a missing congressman. They would be stupid not to let us follow up on this lead."

"It doesn't matter. He's still a former cop and there's shit in his file that can probably embarrass him, but I'll go with you if you want to try."

She smiled. "Oh yeah, I want to try. I want to see what's in that file."

The agents tried three judges in the city of Springfield before the fourth one finally agreed to see them. The other three were not going to be seen talking to them about a subpoena on a former cop's service jacket with an election year coming up. Rachel never truly understood how politics worked in this state. Unions wielded a lot of politics, not only in Chicago, but the whole state, especially police unions. Even district judges in the southern part of Illinois couldn't win an election without their help. Police unions had that much reach and smart judges didn't interfere. It makes you think who really had the most power in Illinois.

The fourth was a first term district judge and was at least willing to hear Agent Main's evidence for the subpoena. She asked Gavin to help argue for it, too, but he declined, knowing that it would be a waste of time. All he did was sit outside the judge's office, checking for news alerts on his phone. After about five minutes of waiting, Rachel came out of the office, cursing under her breath. She walked past her partner angrily, and he just laughed. He was going to say 'I told you so' but was afraid she would hit him. As they were walking down the outside steps of the courthouse, she finally said to him, "The fucking asshole wouldn't listen to reason and even had the balls to tell me that cops shouldn't rely on theories. For God's sake, we have to have a theory before we know what evidence to look for."

"I know you think they can't see reason, but there is a balance here. If judges fuck with cops, they wouldn't ever get re-elected, and you don't get cops on your side by letting others look into their pasts. It may not make sense in the real world, but it makes perfect sense in Chicago."

She gave him a dirty look. "Then we're screwed when it comes to finding the congressman. If we can't follow up on a lead, then what's the point of investigating this?"

Gavin smiled. "I know a way we can get his service jacket and take a look at it."

"Is it illegal?"

He laughed. "Not for us. All we are going to do is look at it. Somebody else will get it."

Rachel shook her head and started laughing, but she didn't tell him not to do it. She wanted to know at that very moment, more than anything, what was hidden in the congressman's service jacket.

4

For as long as anyone could remember, Jake's Bar and Club on Chicago's southeast side had always been a cop bar. Eighty percent of its patrons were current and retired cops. Even though it was in what some might consider a dangerous part of Chicago, nobody was stupid enough to fuck with Jake's. Every Thursday night there was a poker game in the back of the club, where many vices took place other than just illegal gambling. They were always done by retired cops who, at one time, swore to uphold the law but had no problem breaking it in their twilight years. It was a chance for them to gamble away part of their pensions and relive their glory days on the beat. Sometimes they allowed current cops to play with them just so they could take their money. Two of these retired cops who played their weekly had been lifelong friends and had served most of their careers together on the force. It wasn't surprising that Harry Stanton and Dick Burns would spend most of their retired lives in each other's company.

That night, they had been playing cards for quite a while and were already a few drinks in when a tall stranger came walking into the club and asked if he could join them. He flashed his detective's badge to let them know he was a cop and to make sure that they would let him play cards. Harry and Dick didn't recognize him even though they knew pretty much everybody who came into Jake's, but it didn't matter. They reveled in the idea of taking someone else's money. Harry was the first to introduce himself.

"Detective, pull up a seat. We've never met, but that's not going to stop me from taking your money."

The detective laughed. "Just because you're retired doesn't mean I'm going to make it easy on you. I'm Detective Sam Ross. It's a pleasure to meet you. I've heard about this game for quite a while now and thought I might take a shot at winning some big money. " Harry laughed at the comment and replied, "As the ranking old timers here, think of us as the house. You know the house always wins." The detective couldn't help but laugh at the comment and thought to himself that it was nice to meet retired cops with a sense of humor. Most of the retired cops he met were just pricks. Harry introduced him to his friend Dick and the other retired cop sitting at the table. As they were dealing him in, Harry asked him, "So, what precinct are you out of?"

"I'm at the 29th precinct now."

"Oh, that's kind of far from here."

"Yeah, but I grew up in these neighborhoods and still live around the area."

Dick smiled. "Ah, you must be a true cop. You still live in your old neighborhood and work somewhere else."

Sam laughed as he folded. "You can't leave your old neighborhood, no matter where the force sends you."

Harry smiled. "Very true. Dick and I have been friends since we were kids and still live in the neighborhood we grew up in. No thugs or gangs are going to run us out."

Sam asked, "Did you guys work at the same precinct together?"

Harry replied, "A few times we did during our careers. I did a stint at the 29th, too."

"What was your favorite precinct?"

Both men thought about it for a moment and answered almost at the same time. "The 12th."

Dick responded, "We had a great captain there and never had to deal with budget cuts that could affect our jobs."

Sam laughed. "I know that's right. Hate when I have to deal with the politics of being a cop. You know, I've heard that the 9th is the best precinct to work at. What do you guys think about that?"

Harry and Dick had serious looks on their faces when Sam mentioned the 9th precinct. The comment changed the mood in the room, but both men tried to keep their poker faces on. Harry commented first. "It's a pretty good place to work. I seem to remember my time there being enjoyable."

Sam gave him an uncomfortable stare and after a brief pause responded, "Don't you mean profitable?"

Harry and Dick didn't say anything for a moment, but they gave each other a slight look. Dick was the one to ask the obvious question, "Why do you say that?"

"It's what I've heard."

"You want to know a lot about this precinct. Why? You looking for a transfer?"

Sam smiled. "Not exactly!" He just stared at the two men while Dick reached around his chair into his coat pocket looking for a gun he always carried with him. The two men were spooked by the questions, which led to Dick reaching for the gun, but he wasn't fast enough. Sam quickly grabbed his service weapon and pointed it at the two former cops. "Don't even try it!"

Harry asked, "Who the fuck are you and what do you want?"

"It doesn't matter who I am, but what I want is you dead."

"Why?"

Sam smiled. "You should already know the answer." Then he put three bullets into each of them and shot the other man sitting at the table. The bartender heard the gunshots and grabbed his gun from behind the bar and started to head towards the back room to catch the shooter. He was stopped in his tracks by Sam coming out of the room, holding some kind of electronic device. The bartender yelled, "Freeze, you son of a bitch! You're not getting away that easily."

Sam was amused. "Oh, I think I am going to walk out just fine. One press of the button and the bombs I've placed go off."

"You'd kill yourself, too."

"I'm ready to go. Are you?"

The bartender shook his head and replied, "No way. You won't do it."

Sam smiled and pressed the button. There was an explosion, but not in the bar. It happened in the convenience store next door, but it shook the bar enough to knock the bartender over. Sam shot him and another cop sitting at the bar, and then he simply walked out through the chaos of people on the sidewalk as they were fleeing from the store that had just exploded. He walked past people who were bloody and covered in dust from the explosion. Unlike other people who were trying to help the wounded, Sam ignored the scene and safely walked away.

∞∞∞∞∞∞∞∞∞∞∞

Agent Donnelly and Agent Main returned to Chicago, and instead of going back to the office, they went to Morelli's Diner. They needed to meet with Agent Moore and his computer hacker girlfriend, Janie Myers. Gavin didn't know if they were really an item, but the way they acted around one another made it seem as if they were. Besides, Gavin always thought Agent Moore needed someone special in his life, and as weird as it might have sounded, Janie was a perfect fit for him.

Agent Main was tapping her hand on the dinner table

[451]

impatiently while they waited for Agent Moore, but it wasn't him who walked through the door in a rush and came to their table. Gavin was surprised to see Janie Myers. She never seemed like the kind of person to meet with law enforcement twice. Janie stared at the agents with disapproval, but commented, "I just thought it was going to be one of you."

Agent Main replied, "Who are you?" She looked at her partner. "Who is this?"

Gavin smiled. "Rachel, this is Janie Myers, better known as FingerbangedUSA."

"She's the hacker?"

"Yes, and who we use as an asset from time to time."

Janie asked, "Can she be trusted?"

Rachel responded sharply, "I'm his partner. I wouldn't be here if I couldn't be trusted."

"That doesn't answer my question."

Rachel was going to say something sarcastic, but Gavin stopped her and replied to Janie, "If I couldn't trust her, she wouldn't be here. You can trust her, too." Janie gave him a dirty look. Gavin responded, "You can trust her, for a Fed."

"We'll see, G-Man." She handed Gavin a laptop. "Internal Affairs files on Chicago cops are interesting. Not the most interesting things I've hacked, but interesting nonetheless. The cops in this town have a lot of secrets they want hidden."

Gavin opened up the laptop. Congressman McMahon's police service jacket was already opened up on the screen, but there wasn't much to see. A lot of it was blacked out. Rachel and Gavin gave each other strange looks. Gavin asked the obvious question, "What the hell is this? Most of the information is blacked out."

Agent Moore walked into the diner. Gavin asked the question again and the agent replied, "That was all we found in the Internal Affairs system. They started putting their files in the system five years ago."

Gavin responded, "It still doesn't explain why this file is blacked out."

"They wouldn't have put it in their computer system like that unless the original was blacked out."

Rachel asked why they would do that. Gavin said, "I suspect they did it when he became a congressman. Too many secrets from when he was a cop that they didn't want coming out."

"Is that something Internal Affairs would do?"

Gavin shook his head. "Not normally. Somebody there would have to be paid off to do that and then make it part of the official record."

Rachel looked at Janie and Agent Moore. "Was there anything in the congressman's service jacket that could tell us about his career?"

Agent Moore replied, "Not much. His academy records and the precincts he was stationed at during his career, but there's nothing about the cases he worked on."

Gavin was still looking through everything on the laptop and came across something peculiar. Any time Gavin was looking into Chicago police officers he always wanted to know if they had served with any of his family. He was looking for some kind of personal connection because he was Irish and everybody in his community knew each other. It always seemed to be that way among cops, too. What he found peculiar was that the congressman had served at the 16th precinct at the same time as his Uncle Liam. His uncle told him once that he had never served with the congressman when he was a cop. Gavin explained that fact to everyone at the table and how his uncle had been caught in a lie.

Agent Moore had a curious look after Gavin said that, but it was Rachel who asked, "Why would your uncle lie to you about something like that? Wouldn't it be a privilege to have served with the congressman?"

"You would think, but the only reason to lie is if you're hiding something. I know my uncle would never tell me everything about his time on the force, but I've never known him to blatantly lie to me, either."

"If you're looking for a connection, maybe it's the same reason why the congressman's file is blacked out. I'm not trying to accuse your uncle of anything, but you have to consider it if you look at everything objectively."

Gavin sighed. He didn't want to think about it, but he knew his partner was right. He couldn't think about this case objectively without considering the possibility that, if there was any dirt on the congressman, and there probably was, then that might extend to his Uncle Liam if they had served together. Gavin replied, "I have considered that, but there's another question bothering me. If these files were blacked out when they were put into the system, then there has to be a hard copy somewhere, a copy that isn't blacked out."

Rachel responded, "If that's true, then what makes you think the originals weren't destroyed?"

Janie Myers had to laugh at the notion. Rachel asked her what was so funny. She replied, "Insurance, Agent Main!"

"What are you talking about?"

"These cops aren't going to destroy anything they can hold over another cop or blackmail someone with. It's a safety net. In fact, there is a hidden place in Chicago that contains secret police files."

Gavin asked, "And you know this how?"

She smiled sarcastically at Gavin. "You know the answer to that. But you don't know what this place is referred to. It's called The Basement."

"Not exactly a stylish name, but I guess it doesn't have to be to get the job done. Do you know where this place is?"

"No, but I'm sure there's somebody in Internal Affairs that can tell you." Gavin hated to admit it to himself, but she was right. It was a card he didn't want to burn with Internal Affairs, considering they hated the FBI. However, he knew who to call to get the answers he and his partner needed.

Agent Moore pulled out a file and gave it to Gavin. "I have the background information you wanted on McMahon's security agent. You were right about him."

Gavin smiled. "His identity was false."

"You got it. It was the type of false identity that we would have created if you were going undercover. Looks like his identity was created about two years ago. What he's trying to hide, I don't know."

"Sounds like he was planted with McMahon's security detail. We've seen something like that before. The logical assumption is that he was spying for someone and then kidnapped the congressman, possibly killing him."

Rachel responded, "Still doesn't explain who wants him dead, but it does give us a clue."

Gavin looked at her curiously. Agent Moore was the one who asked, "What clue?"

"Somebody, without being government, has access to all national databases to create the kind of background that could get someone on a congressman's security detail. How many people could pull this off?" Rachel looked at Janie Myers and finished her sentence. "How many hackers in the world could do something like this? I bet the field is pretty small. That's where we start looking."

Janie replied, "To answer your question, there are four hackers in the world, including me, that can do this."

"Will you give us their names?"

"No, but I will give you their hacker names. You can find them from there -- if you can find them."

Gavin was about to say something when he started to flash. *He winced as his head started to hurt while his latest vision became clear as day. It was his cousin walking into a crime scene. His new partner, Detective Reilly, was the first to walk up and tell him what had happened. She said, "Somebody posing as a detective walked into the bar, pretended to play poker in the game in the back room, and then killed the two retired cops who apparently ran the game, according to a couple of eyewitnesses." She showed*

Alex the names of the dead cops and Alex shot her an angry look. "Great. Now we have retired cops being targeted."

"You think it's our guy who did this?"

"I hope so. I don't want to be dealing with another cop killer."

"If it is, then he's changing his M.O. He's using explosives. Apparently, he blew up the convenience store next door. You think that's an accident?"

Alex smiled. "Not even close. The store launders money – dirty cops' and mob money. I think he blew it up on purpose."

That was all Gavin saw in his vision. Everybody at the table were concerned by the way he was wincing, but he blew it off as usual, telling them that it was no big deal and that he had gotten something in his eye. He looked down at his phone as if he had just gotten a text message and then told his partner, "There's been another cop shooting. I am going to see if I can find out some more details. I will meet you back at the office."

Rachel gave him a bit of a dirty look, letting him know that she didn't like it, but she also knew he wasn't going to listen to her when it might involve the man who shot his uncle. It wasn't their case, but it was personal for Gavin, and he was going to solve it anyway.

5

It was raining outside the facility, hard enough that God might've been destroying the Earth again and leaving the building to be a modern-day ark. That was the thought running through Stephen's mind as he stepped out of his car and walked to the front door of the large facility. It was posing as a hospital, but its true purpose was far more sinister. It was a prison, completely state-of-the-art. It was nothing like any other prison site in the world, not even a government black site. Stephen showed his ID card to the security team at the front, who quickly led him past the front desk. He proceeded into an elevator that seemed bigger than normal, even for a freight elevator. It could fit a platoon of men, if needed.

The elevator took him and his security guards 10 stories beneath the surface. Once they arrived at the main level, Stephen was greeted by another man who simply said, "He's been uncooperative, sir." Stephen was not happy to hear that.

"Then I guess I will have to remind him why he's here."

Stephen was escorted to a locked room. It didn't look like a prison cell, more like a studio apartment with a few furnishings to add some comfort. After all, their guest was not there to be tortured and, even if he were, there were plenty of other rooms where the security guards could do that. The man in the holding room was simply a guest who couldn't leave. A security guard unlocked the door and let Stephen inside. The guest was sitting in a chair, reading a book and listening to music on his iPod. He looked up from his book and took the earphones out of his ears.

"Of course they would call you," said the guest. "And, just like a bored beat cop who's eaten too many donuts, you come running to interfere with something that doesn't concern you."

"That's where you're wrong. I'm the one in charge of this operation now. You are my concern."

The guest was surprised to hear that. "I thought the other guy was in charge."

"He was, and then he failed."

"Because of me?"

"That's one reason. Now comes the part where I remind you of the agreement you made and of the consequences that will occur if you break that agreement."

The guest shot Stephen a murderous glare. "You think I'm afraid of being tortured?"

Stephen laughed. "You really think I have to do that to get what I want? I don't make empty threats anymore. I'll just kill you."

"And then you won't get what you want."

Stephen laughed again. "I love how you think this is a renegotiation; it's amusing. But there's a sad truth that you'd better realize. You are not irreplaceable and you never were."

The guest was shocked. "No, you're lying. Nobody can do what I can do."

Stephen laid a handgun down on the stool in the front of the room. The guest nervously glanced at it while Stephen calmly looked at him. "If it makes you feel better to think that, then go ahead. But know this: there's an open grave out there for you. I suggest you finish what you were hired to do."

"And if do, our original deal is still in place?"

Stephen nodded. "We don't break our deals. If you don't finish your job by the deadline, we'll make you disappear forever. There will be no trace, especially in a database."

The guest nodded in agreement. He didn't want to admit it, but he was scared of Stephen and, more importantly, he knew he should be. With the other boss, he thought he could get away with his little rebellion, but Stephen was not as weak as the other one. He would actually pull the trigger himself, and that was the main reason their guest went back to work.

∞∞∞∞∞∞∞∞∞∞∞∞∞

While the Chicago CSU team was working the crime scene at Jake's Bar and Grill , a police officer brought Alex a piece of evidence found at the crime scene. It was a black card marked with a red skull and the phrase, "We are the United Front; Death is coming soon!" Alex muttered, "Fucking terrorists!" under his breath. Detective Sara Reilly walked up to Alex after another look at the crime scene. She was still considered a new detective and knew that she didn't have enough experience to gain the other officers' respect. This caused her to talk a crime scene out loud. She said to Alex,

"Okay, here is what I don't get. If your objective is to randomly kill cops and ex-cops, then why come in here and go to the back to kill someone when you can just walk in and have easy access to the door for an escape? If you start at the back, then you're trapped with all the other cops sitting in the place where they can easily gun you down. And besides, if you want to blow up the place next door, you can still do it from the front of the bar. It doesn't make sense."

Alex was about to respond when Gavin walked through the front door of the bar. He replied, "That's because it's probably not random. Your shooter was targeting these cops."

Alex shook his head, not because his cousin was wrong, but because he hated the notion that this wasn't random, and that they had no idea what the killer's motive might be. He responded, "Detective Reilly, he's right. This can't be random, and Bobby McClain was never stupid. He was corrupt, but not stupid. I think he's got a plan."

Gavin replied, "No offense, but that's an understatement. He had a plan before he started this."

"Is that the FBI's official position? Why are you even here? I mean, we appreciate the help, but until the FBI officially takes over, then we can handle this case."

Gavin gave him a hostile look. "You know what? Until you actually catch the guy, why don't you take all the help you can get."

Alex was going to respond, but Sara interrupted. "Look, while you two argue, let's start to ask the obvious questions. Why these cops? Did he know them or serve with them?"

Gavin and Alex both laughed at her for being like a little sister, trying to break up a fight. Alex spoke up. "The victims in the back room knew each other, but only served with each other once. There's no evidence that victims three and four knew the second victim or served with him. And, while I'm sure my father knew victims three and four, there's no evidence that they served together. Right now, there's nothing that ties the victims together except the fact that they're cops."

Gavin replied, "That's all we know right now, but there's got to be a connection."

"Look, Gavin. I'm sure there is and we will find it, but we're going to have to get everyone's service jackets and start going over everything, every detail. Unlike the FBI, it's going to take us time to get everything. We don't have access to everything at a click of a button."

"We'll start with your father's file and go from there until you can get everything."

"Why, because he always seems to know everybody?"

"No, because he's ground zero. He was the first to get shot and there's a reason for that."

"Why?"

"I don't know." It wasn't completely untrue. Gavin knew it had something to do with him personally; he just didn't know why. He wanted to catch Bobby McClain as much as everybody else did, but for Gavin, the bigger mystery was what it had to do with him.

Detective Reilly spoke up. "Why does he show his face to the victims he kills? He could kill them just as easily while disguised."

Alex held up the card with the red skull. "Maybe it has something to do with this. I think he wants to taunt us with his new political agenda."

Gavin replied, "Unless it's just a diversion."

"Then we should talk to their leader. I know an FBI agent that can make that happen."

Gavin looked at him fiercely. "That's a tall order, but if I can make it happen, then I need a favor. I need to talk to your guy in Internal Affairs."

"Does this have something to do with the missing congressman?"

Gavin laughed. "Yeah. I want his police record. What do they have on him?"

"Now that's asking a lot…you might as well ask for the winning lottery numbers, those will be easier get."

"Then I guess you and I are going to have to help each other out."

Detective Reilly rolled her eyes as if a fight were about to break out between the two Donnellys. It was humorous and it was better to leave it that way at the crime scene.

∞∞∞∞∞∞∞∞∞∞

The driver pulled the car up to a bar on a darkened street. It was out of the way and looked like the kind of place that upstanding citizens wouldn't go to. It was perfect for the meeting that was about to take place. The driver stopped and opened the car door for his boss while the other bodyguard got out of the car. They looked around to see if anybody was walking by that could identify them. After the area

[459]

was clear, they walked into the bar to find a man sitting at a table, surrounded by his own bodyguards.

The man sitting at the table stood up and said, "Simon O'Conner, thank you for coming. It's finally time that we met."

O'Conner replied, "So, you're the new man in charge of this operation."

"I am. The reason we're finally meeting in person is because a big part of this operation is coming to an end. Our plans needed to be discussed face-to-face."

"What do I call you?"

"Mr. Chambers is fine. Do you want something to drink?"

O'Conner walked up to the table and shook Mr. Chambers's hand. Even though he may not have trusted him, he at least respected him enough to sit down and hear the new plan. "I will take a Jameson's, neat."

One of Mr. Chambers's bodyguards went behind the bar and poured a round of drinks for everyone. Mr. Chambers handed O'Conner a file. "Things are changing and the operation is being reassigned to a new destination."

"I'd heard the rumors, but I can't believe it. Why are things changing, if you don't mind me asking?"

"Everything comes to an end eventually."

"It's been good for over 40 years here in Chicago. Business has been booming for 20 years with no signs of slowing down. I should know; I've been running it for the past two decades."

Mr. Chambers laughed. "Business is always good here in the Windy City, but there have been complications."

O'Conner's expression became serious. "Whatever they are, I can take care of them."

"We don't doubt your abilities. You've done a good job for the past 20 years, but some things are out of your control. Circumstances from the last few months dictate that it's time to move our operation. Details are in the file."

O'Conner looked through it. "I guess a move could be good for me and my boys. But there are a lot of loose ends that need to be taken care of."

Mr. Chambers finished his scotch. "Some of them have already been taken care of, but I need to know that you can take care of the last two."

O'Conner flipped to the last pages of the file and looked at them more closely. "Consider it done."

"Really? As an Irishman, I figured it would be hard."

O'Conner smirked. "It shouldn't be personal when it comes to lots of money. If you want to make it personal, then become a priest and not a killer."
Mr. Chambers smiled darkly. "I'm a better killer than I am a priest."

6

Gavin arrived back at the FBI office sometime in the late afternoon. He didn't really know what time it was because he had other things on his mind. But he knew he was late and would hear about it from his partner. He walked into his office with two cups of coffee for himself and Rachel, but saw that he should have brought three. AD Foster was waiting for him. He told Gavin when he came through the door,

"Agent Donnelly, glad you could finally make it back today."

"Sorry I'm late."

"I guess one of those coffees isn't for me."

Gavin laughed. "No, sir. I didn't think you'd be here."

"I've been waiting 20 minutes for my report on the missing congressman."

Gavin glanced at his partner. She responded, "Don't look at me. He was waiting on you so that we could both give the report."

Gavin handed Rachel her coffee, took a sip of his and then started explaining to their boss what they had. "This case is a dead-end for the most part. I'm sure you've already seen the report about tracking him down with the navigation on his cell phone and how the signal went cold."

AD Foster nodded. Gavin continued, "No one saw him after the fundraiser. His mistress, the one named Polly, said she was with him during the day, but hasn't heard from him since. So basically, it's like looking for a needle in a haystack, but we do have one lead. One of his bodyguards is using a false identity."

That piqued AD Foster's curiosity. "For what end, to kidnap the man?"

Rachel spoke up. "We don't think so because, after six days, there are still no ransom demands."

"Then is he an assassin, infiltrating the security detail so that he could kill the congressman?"

Gavin responded, "It's a possibility ... but if you murdered a congressman, wouldn't you want to show off and make a statement with the crime? Why haven't we heard anything yet?"

"I am assuming you have the bodyguard's real identity."

Rachel answered, "We do. His real name is Danny Spitzer. He has some known associates right here in Chicago, so that's where our trail starts."

"Have you found a motive yet? I mean, if this isn't a true kidnapping with ransom demands, then why take him or kill him?"

"That's what we can't figure out, sir. It doesn't appear to have anything to do with his congressional duties. From what we can tell, it's related to his work as a cop in Chicago. His police file ..." Before she could finish the sentence, Gavin cleared his throat and shook his head at her in order to get her to stop talking. She picked up on the signal. AD Foster asked Rachel, "What about his police file?"

"It's something that we need to get in order to find a possible motive."

Gavin responded, "It may be a long shot, but if nothing else, Internal Affairs should have plenty of information. We want to follow up on the false identity lead first."

"Then get to it. Each day the congressman is missing makes this more embarrassing for us. And Agent Donnelly, we don't care about needles in haystacks around here; just find the congressman. I want more updates in the morning." As he was leaving, AD Foster told Gavin to escort him back to his office. As they were walking, Foster spoke up.

"Agent Donnelly, I don't think I should have to tell you that you can't run to a Chicago PD crime scene if you're not working the case, especially on company time."

Gavin chuckled. "You think that's what I was doing?"

"I know that's what you were doing. I heard about the cop shootings at Jake's Bar and Grill. That's where you were, right?"

"Yeah."

"I guess they still can't find the shooter?"

"No, sir, but I can help them."

"I've already told you, Agent Donnelly: it's not your case, and any request you have for the FBI to take over will be denied."

Gavin looked at his boss contemptuously. "Look, I understand your position, but there's a connection to the police shootings because of the United Front situation."

AD Foster was out of patience. "You know that Homeland Security gets the case now. Just because you busted him doesn't mean you get to keep him. Just find the congressman and then we can get you a case that you might actually like." AD Foster walked off and left Gavin a little irritated.

∞∞∞∞∞∞∞∞∞∞

Twenty minutes later, Agent Donnelly and Agent Main drove up to a store front. They were checking out the only lead they had in the congressman's case. As they pulled up, Gavin asked his partner, "Where the hell are we?"

Rachel laughed at the fact that he had already forgotten where they were going, but she knew his mind was on other things. "It's a hardware store called Pappy's."

Gavin looked at the building. It appeared to be abandoned and had boards covering the windows. "I guess it used to be a hardware store. Why are we here?"

"Tom Felton, which is his real name, used to work here. According to the alarm company, he had a key and the passcode to the alarm. We don't know a place of residence for him, so we'll start here."

They got out of the car and Gavin asked, "How the hell are we going to be able to find out anything about this guy if no one's here?"

Rachel laughed. "Hey, it beats the office. If we don't find anything, then we can go home early ... or for you, the pub." Gavin had a nice chuckle at her comment.

Since most of the windows and the door were boarded up, the agents peeked through the only open window to see if anybody was in the building. As it turned out, there were a few guys inside who looked like movers. Rachel knocked on the window to get their attention. The men inside were a little startled; they weren't expecting visitors. One of the men quickly walked up to the front door to talk to Gavin and Rachel, hoping to distract them so that the other men could load the crates that were stacked in the back to a moving truck.

Rachel took the lead as the man opened the door. He was a younger guy that reeked of inexperience and Rachel could immediately detect the nervousness in his voice when he asked them who they were.

Rachel held up her badge. "Good morning, sir. I'm Agent Main and this is Agent Donnelly of the FBI. We need to ask you a few questions."

The young man looked at them strangely. "What about?"

Rachel held up a photo. "We are looking for Danny Spitzer. Do you know him?"

The young man tried to hide his shock, but he wasn't very successful. "Uh ... no, ma'am ... I don't know who that is."

[464]

"Are you sure? It seems like you recognize him."

"I don't."

"Can I ask your name, sir?"

The young man thought for a moment whether or not he should answer the question. This was his first time working with the crew in the back and he didn't really know how much he should tell law enforcement in this situation. He knew that he would look even more suspicious if he didn't say anything. He nervously replied, "My name is Joe."

"Joe what?"

"Ah … Wilson. Joe Wilson."

"Are you sure about that? You seem really nervous."

Gavin was peering through the open window and spotted something peculiar in the back. He saw two men take something out of one of the crates. They were about 30 yards away from the window and it was hard to tell what they were messing with. Gavin immediately became suspicious because they were clearly trying to hide whatever they were taking out of the box. Finally, he saw a gun magazine being attached to something and that's when he knew it was an assault rifle they were loading. He took out his service weapon and rushed into the building, pushing his way past Rachel. He yelled, "Freeze! FBI! Drop the weapons and come toward me slowly with your hands in the air." Rachel finally saw the two men in the back with the guns and drew her service weapon. The young man, who was still standing at the door, reached behind him and grabbed his gun.

Gavin didn't have a chance to turn around and stop the young man because the two men in the back opened fire with their AR-15 rifles. Rachel shot the young man in the shoulder, which caused him to drop his gun. He took off running. She was going to go after him, but bullets were flying everywhere. Gavin ducked, grabbed her, and they both dove behind the front counter. The two men were a little too trigger-happy and kept spraying bullets, hoping they would hit someone. Rachel looked at her partner and said, "And I bet you thought this was a lead not worth following." He smiled at her. "Let's get out of this alive and then you can tell me how I was wrong."

One of the men in the back stopped shooting long enough to shout, "Fuck you, FBI! You're not taking us alive!"

Gavin whipped his head and gun around the corner of the counter and shot the man in the head. The other man yelled, "You motherfucker!" and started firing again. Gavin looked at his partner. "I am going to lay down some cover fire and get around his flank." She nodded in agreement and they put their plan into action. She darted around a corner and snuck around an aisle to try to surprise the gunmen in the back of the store. Another man with a gun came around another corner and Rachel saw him immediately. She shot him in the leg to get him down. As she kicked his gun away, she asked him, "How many men are in here?"

The man didn't want to answer, so Rachel put a gun to his head and snarled, "Tell me now or I'll blow your head off." The man was surprised by the threat because he thought that an FBI agent wouldn't say that. "There are five of us."

"Good. You stay here. If I have to come after you, I'll shoot you dead." Rachel yelled above all the gunfire to her partner. "There are five men in here! Three down, two to go." As she was yelling, the man with the assault rifle heard the distraction and started firing in that direction. Rachel found cover as bullets were peppering the shelves. Gavin saw his opportunity and charged in the direction of the man with the rifle. Before the man could turn around and fire again, Gavin the shot the rifle out of his hand and yelled, "Don't move or I'll kill you!"

The fifth man appeared from around another corner and pointed a gun at Gavin. "Drop your weapon, FBI man, or you're dead." Gavin held out his gun and slowly lowered his weapon, but then he and the gunman were surprised by a voice. Rachel was holding a gun to the back of the man's head and saying, "You drop your weapon or I'll blow your head off, scumbag." Gavin smiled and pulled out his handcuffs. He bound the two gunmen together and told them not to move. Rachel asked about the guy who answered the door. Gavin replied that he must have run off, but he was bleeding and wouldn't be able to get away that easily. After looking around in the back, they realized what was going on in the building. It was being used to smuggle guns. Gavin couldn't believe what they had stumbled upon and commented on that to his partner. All Rachel said while shaking her head at the situation was, "We have to call this in and notify ATF." Gavin didn't like that; he hated the ATF. He considered them mall cops when it came to law enforcement, but he knew that they had to follow protocol and call them.

Thirty minutes later, there was a big crowd at the old hardware store. ATF was there, along with local police. Of course, with two FBI agents in a shootout over a lead in a missing congressman's case, AD Foster showed up at the scene. There were still a lot of unanswered questions and the shootout added another layer of mystery to the congressman's disappearance. The remaining three guys from the store were lined up after they had received medical attention. Despite ATF's objections, Gavin and Rachel were allowed to question the men first. Gavin held up a picture of the congressman's bodyguard and said, "Alright, here's the deal. The first one of you to tell me about Danny Spitzer gets a deal and a shorter prison sentence."

One of the men shouted back, "Go fuck yourself, FBI man!"

Rachel responded before Gavin could say anything. "You can curse us all you want, but you're looking at 25 years in prison. One of you might be able to do that, but I know some of you can't. This is the best deal you're going to get. After we walk away, the deal is off the table."

Gavin smiled at the guys. "Take a hard look at us. Does it look like we're bluffing? All we want is information about this guy that can help us with our investigation."

The same guy told the agents to fuck themselves again. He was trying to be tough, but really, he was just being stupid; that's how the younger of the men saw it. This was his first job with the crew and he wasn't going to prison in the prime of his life. He spoke up. "Danny Spitzer is a junior. He's the son of the owner of this building."

The man who had cursed the agents told the younger man, "Shut your fucking mouth! You don't have to tell them anything. They don't have anything on us. It was an illegal search, so they can't pin anything on us."

The young man replied, "No. Fuck you, dude! I'm not going to prison for you. You said it was easy money and no one would get hurt."

Gavin laughed as he pointed to the younger man. "Okay, you come with us. This is the smartest thing you've done all day." He looked back at the other men. "Dumbass, I'm licensed to practice law in this state, so let me explain how search and seizure really works. If you open the door to us and we can see illegal guns in plain sight, then I don't need a search warrant. But the biggest mistake you committed today was firing on two federal agents. At that point, search and seizure really doesn't matter. Attempted murder on a federal agent gets you to the big time where we can charge you with terrorist activities. That's hardcore prison time. So, good luck with that." The man told Gavin to fuck himself again as he walked away.

AD Foster walked with the two agents away from the crime scene so they could discuss what they knew about the case. Gavin was the first to say something.

"Okay, this case just gets stranger by the minute. The guy over there gave up his crew and told us who Danny Spitzer really is. Apparently, he used a fake name to get close to the congressman in order to blackmail him. The father, who owns this hardware store as a front to run guns, wanted to blackmail the congressman about some gun business."

AD Foster asked, "How is the congressman even connected to their illegal gun operation?"

"He didn't know. It looks like the father and son had some information on the congressman, but they didn't share it with the rest of the crew."

"Was kidnapping part of the plan?"

"According to them, no. They were supposed to be contacted by Danny Spitzer 54 days ago but haven't heard from him. But there's something really strange about this whole thing."

"What's that, Agent Donnelly?"

"This is a simple blackmail scheme. Whoever built Spitzer's cover identity was a real pro. I mean, it's the kind of stuff we do, but they seemed to make it easy for us to find this place. It's almost like they wanted us to find it. If this is not a kidnapping with ransom demands, and just a bunch of petty criminals blackmailing a government official, then why make a fake identity so extensive and give us the one clue that would lead us here?"

AD Foster looked curious. "You think it's misdirection, don't you?"

"It doesn't add up for me."

Rachel spoke. "If that's true, then there's somebody else behind his disappearance. I think the bigger question is why he's missing. We've ruled out that it has anything to do with his work as a congressman. This has to be something from his days as either a cop or an alderman in Chicago."

AD Foster looked at Gavin. "Do you agree?"

"I think she's right, and that's why we need to see what Internal Affairs has on him."

AD Foster nodded in agreement. "Okay, we'll get a subpoena for his files. Do what you can to find a connection. I don't like getting calls about an FBI shootout. ATF is pretty pissed at you for intervening with one of their cases. They've been watching these guys for a while."

Rachel shook her head. "Next time we're being shot at, we'll stop defending ourselves and take the time to call the ATF."

AD Foster gave her a dirty look for her sarcasm. "Just find me a connection, Agent Main."

Gavin and Rachel nodded, but they weren't really any closer to finding the congressman. While they had found some answers in this case, there were still too many unanswered questions. Finding the real truth about the congressman was proving to be a daunting task. For Gavin, it was time to get some help from an unlikely source. He took out his cell phone and found a contact marked 'Shakespeare.' He texted the phrase, '*Do you have any Shakespeare in the Park tickets?*'

7

Making your own bullets was considered an art form – at least for the kind of men who enjoyed killing, who got a huge rush from inflicting excruciating pain on their victims. While the man sitting in the darkened room of his apartment did not personally enjoy killing, he had what some might call a sick fetish for making instruments of death that would cause the maximum amount of pain. Bullets were one of his specialties. He was currently making a case of 9mm bullets for a customer when his cell phone beeped. The incoming text message read, "Inventory low, need more product … need to pick up ASAP!" The man smiled as he pulled the lever down on the machine that cased the bullet. This was a special order, which meant more money, but it was also a little bit dangerous. However, the money was worth the risk.

He responded to the text message, saying that the order would be ready in two hours. He wanted to get the order done to receive the money quickly. His daughter's birthday was in a couple of days and he wanted to get her something nice. He had a few more bullets to make, but he was running out of the liquid that he was putting in the bullet to completely case it. Fortunately for him, he had just enough to finish the remaining bullets. The liquid was highly toxic and it contained a special additive to make the bullets more lethal. Only a few people asked for this special bullet; they were true killers, devoid of any kind of emotion or conscience. The man who made the bullets always found it fascinating that it was possible for men to be like this. Then again, if it weren't possible, he'd probably be out of business. Irony was always more interesting than a dull reality for the man that everybody only knew as Nathan.

[469]

It was peaceful on the hilltop in Grant Park that overlooked the amphitheater. There was nothing going on in the park that night, so it was even quieter than usual. It was the perfect place to meet someone who you didn't want to be seen with. Gavin had been waiting for about five minutes, playing Scrabble on his phone, when Byers finally showed up. Gavin frowned when he saw that Byers was still wearing a sling. He asked,"How's the shoulder?"

Byers laughed. "Still sore, but I'll live, thanks to the best pain medication on the market."

"Good to hear. I'd hate for it to be permanent."

"That's nice of you, considering you made your point with me. Which brings me to my first question: why did you decide to call me for help?"

Gavin sighed. "I'm still trying to decide if I really want your help. I'm at an impasse with my current case, and I figure if there's anybody that would have information, it would be you."

Byers smiled. "Tell me what you're working on and I'll decide if I want to give you information."

"I thought you said that you were willing to help me."

"I am, but that doesn't mean that I will tell you everything you want to know. I can point you in the right direction, but you still have to do the investigating yourself."

"Fair enough!"

"What case are you working on?"

"I'm looking for a missing congressman. Can you help me?"

Byers smiled. "So you're the FBI agent who caught the case. I bet all you have right now are dead ends, hence why you called me. Tell me what you know so far." Gavin gave Byers the rundown. While he didn't tell him every detail, he gave Byers enough information about the case so he could get the gist. When Gavin was done, he simply replied, "You're right about one thing; it's not a ransom demand. The congressman was taken because of something he knows."

Gavin nodded. "That's what we thought, but I don't think it has anything to do with his work as a congressman. I think it has something to do with the old days, when he was a cop."

Byers laughed. "You're probably right, but he's smarter than most corrupt cops and politicians. There won't be a paper trail."

"What about the hard files from Internal Affairs? The ones that are blacked out."

"Sure, you might find information in there, if you can get to them. If you try to get a subpoena, then all you'll get are digital files, the ones that are blacked out. But the problem with the hard files is they only tell part of the story. Not even the Internal Affairs Division would have everything on him."

"But there are clues in those files that can help me find the people who took him."

Byers chuckled. "Still thinking like an FBI agent. You have to look at this from the point of view of a crook. It's not important who took him, but why they took him. If you figure out the why, then you'll find who."

Gavin gave him a somber look. "You know who took him and I think you know why."

"Agent Donnelly, I know a lot of things about many people. I can't tell you everybody who wants the congressman, well, let's just say, out of the way. You don't become a man in his position without having enemies."

"That may be true, but I need a place to start, especially if the IAD files aren't going to tell me everything I need."

Byers let out a mischievous laugh. "Don't discount those files, if you can get them. They will be enlightening. But if you're looking for a tip, then go to Hill & Myer Research Labs here in Chicago. The congressman was a member of their advisor board. He lobbied for them. It would be interesting to find out why."

"Should I be investigating this company?"

"That's for you to decide. I should point out that, like with most companies where a local congressman lobbied for them, you will find a lot of dirty secrets that nobody in this city wants to uncover."

Gavin was a bit amused. "That seems to be the way it goes with politics and business in Chicago."

Byers chuckled. "You know, Carl Sandberg once said that Chicago is the city of broad shoulders, but he never said what was underneath those broad shoulders."

"And what's that?"

"Secrets, Agent Donnelly! And you should be careful about what you go looking for. You're probably not going to like what you find in this case."

Gavin didn't know what to say to that. He had one more question for Byers. "Is the congressman still alive?"

"If you don't find a body, then it's still possible that he could be."

"That's not really an answer."

Byers grinned. "No, but I don't do spoilers, either. You still have to find the answer on your own." The comment pretty much confirmed for Gavin that Byers was not telling him everything. He clearly knew more than he was letting on. But he couldn't expect anything else from him. Everything seemed to be a game, and the only way Byers could tell him anything was through riddles and hidden messages. A man who lives his life through secrets can never give a straight answer, for that is his tragic flaw. Byers walked off into the night.

∞∞∞∞∞∞∞∞∞∞∞

Detective Alex Donnelly was working late, trying to understand the latest leads they had on the Chicago Cop Killer. That was the name given to Bobby McClain by the media. Unfortunately, all he had were dead ends. Alex had been trying to figure out a pattern with the victims, but it was still a puzzle he couldn't solve. As he stared at the files of the dead cops, Detective Sara Reilly walked up and put a folder on his desk. She said, "You're never going to believe what ballistics found on the bullets that killed our victims."

Alex was curious. "Something good?"

"More like something strange. The bullets had some unidentifiable chemical on them, something lead-based."

"You mean, like a poison?"

"Well, they're not sure. A lab tech found it by accident when he touched one of the casings with his bare hand. It burned him, but after running some tests, it doesn't look like it's fatal."

"So, it's not a poison?"

"Again, we don't know. Some poisons can take a long time to kill someone. We don't know what the substance is, so it's hard to classify whether it's a poison or not."

Alex gave her an impatient look. "Can we stop with the vague answers? Is it a poison or not?"

Sara laughed. "Don't you see? It probably isn't ... just something to make us think that it is. The real question is, why use this substance at all if you're just going to shoot these men?"

"Good point. But here is another way of looking at it: maybe using the bullets was a way to cover up the substance."

"Then why put the substance on the bullets? There's got to be a better way to inject it into the victims' bodies. Doesn't make much sense!"

"Again, good point. Well, detective, you're starting to build a profile. Good job. Now, what's the rest of your theory? I know you have one."

[472]

Sarah smiled. "There are only a handful of people that would put some kind of poison or other substance on their bullets. Bobby McClain would know the local guys, being a former cop, and I bet he wouldn't do that to his own bullets. So, he would go to someone outside of Chicago for these special bullets. I bet that list is small, too."

Alex grinned. "You're thinking that, if we can find the man who makes those bullets, then we can find Bobby McClain."

"You got it."

"It's a good plan, but we're going to have to get some federal help on this."

"Maybe that's not such a bad idea."

Alex sighed. "You haven't been on the job as a detective that long. You don't understand the politics behind this case. Asking the Feds to come and help us solve our case is bad and it embarrasses the department."

Sara nodded. "I get it, but I don't care. At the end of the day, it's about catching a killer. It doesn't matter how we do it or who gives us help. We're in the business of saving lives and catching bad guys, right?"

"It's never that easy in this city. Remember that when you're the lead detective. But it's a good theory. Nice police work." Alex sat back in his chair. "I'll ask my cousin and see if he can help. Besides, a little federal help wouldn't be so bad. I would like to get some answers in this case instead of just more questions."

The meeting with the group was short and to the point. Most of their meetings these days were brief because plans were already in motion and things were happening fast. That left very little time for anything else. After the meeting, the Old Man asked Stephen into his office. He had been conducting private conferences with the heads of their organization as they got ready for their transition.

The Old Man poured Stephen and himself a drink right before they both sat down to discuss matters. The Old Man was always serious and, more importantly, he was patient, especially with his words. He leered at Stephen for a moment and then said, "You haven't succeeded in this position as much as we were expecting you to. Do I have the right man for the job?"

Stephen didn't like the question, but he knew that it had to be asked. He replied, "It's true that I have made mistakes and some unexpected issues have come up."

"Yes, that does complicate matters, but you didn't answer my question. Do I have the right man for the job?"

"Yes, sir, you do! A few mistakes shouldn't diminish my years of good service and loyalty to this organization."

The Old Man nodded. "Good. I need confidence in the people that sit at that table out there. And yes, in case you're wondering, I am testing you a little bit."

"I understand, sir."

The Old Man took a sip of his whiskey. "I think we need to have a serious conversation about this FBI agent in Chicago. He ruined a lot of things a few weeks ago. While the peace signing didn't happen, it exposed us too much. Perhaps it's time for him to die. That we have a clear consensus on, instead of little schemes that happen in spite of our vote."

Stephen frowned. "I regret my decision on that matter, but I don't think we should just outright kill him anymore."

"Oh, why have you changed your mind?"

"Unfortunately, I have to admit that he and his partner are smarter than we anticipated. Because of their success, somebody curious will start asking questions if he dies, and that leads to exposure that we can't afford."

The Old Man paused for a moment. "It's an interesting point, Stephen. So, what is your plan?"

Stephen looked confident. "To take away the things he loves the most. To break him, to destroy his own cause. We don't have to kill him; we just have to kill his sense of purpose."

The Old Man paused for a moment. "It's diabolical. I like it. So, when do you start?"

Stephen smiled. "I already have." The Old Man nodded. While he didn't know the exact details, he had a pretty good idea what the first part of the plan was. He couldn't help but think to himself that there was a touch of genius to it. He poured himself another drink and grabbed a file for Stephen. He handed it to him and said,

"We have another assignment for you. This is your part in our next big move and it's a key element. There is no room for error."

Stephen looked inside the file and scanned the contents. An expression of pride spread across his face. As he read over everything, the importance of his assignment seemed to leap off the pages. It was an honor to be given this assignment, but he also knew that, if he failed, it could mean his life.

8

There was a chill in the air and it was the kind that could pierce a man's bones. It was sharp and crisp and mad the skin tingle when the wind blew. Bobby McClain never likes being outside when it was cold too many broken bones over the years made him feel the harshness of the cold more than most people. But tonight he was having to put up with it because he couldn't meet anybody in doors where somebody might recognize him. He stood in a vacant park that most people would never go to at night and waited for the man that he was supposed to meet.

Bobby could see his breath in the air as he got another cigarette and lit it up. He was a little nervous, even though he was alone because he was the most wanted man in Chicago and at any moment he could be recognized. All of sudden a man in a dark suit came walking up and extended his hand to shake Bobby McClain's hand. Bobby spoke up.

"You're late."

The man in the dark suit smiled. "Normally I would apologize, but I don't need to give you an explanation…you're working for us, remember!"

Bobby nodded. "You don't have to remind me."

The man in dark suit handed him two file folders. Bobby looked inside the folders to see if he recognized anyone and then he asked. "How many more…you said I would only have to do a few."

"You have a two more Bobby…maybe more. We can't guarantee that there won't be more witnesses that need to be taken care of."

Bobby was pissed and it showed in his tone of voice. "This bullshit. You can't keep changing the rules…you promised only a few cops if you can use my name."

The man in the dark suit laughed. "Of course we can keep changing the rules and you have no choice to work with us because you know what the alternative is…you're in your own as a cop killer in Chicago….just see if you get out alive."

Bobby just stared at him for a moment. "I can't do this much longer…the cops will eventually catch me and then I won't be able to do finish the job. "

"If we wanted the cops to catch you then you wouldn't be standing here… you would already be in cuffs. I told you when we hired you that we would make sure you don't get caught.

"When will the money and new ID be ready."

"When we decide you're done."

Bobby lit another cigarette to take the edge off. The man in the dark suit smiled at the action and then took the pack of cigarettes from Bobby. He took one out for himself and lit it. After a few puffs he spoke up again. "I almost forgot, here are two more cards to put over the bodies." He handed Bobby two cards with the Red Skull and the slogan, "We are the United Front, Death is coming soon."

Bobby chuckled. "More scare tactics?"

"Political movements always are!"

"I'm curious about the red skull, I've seen the symbol before, what does it mean?"

The man in the dark suit smiled. "It's a warning…it means don't fuck with us."

"Obvious, but where does it come from?"

"It's an ancient symbol, it's been around for over 1,000 years and although different groups have used throughout the years, they've used with the same goal in mind…to rule and change the world."

"Don't you mean to rule or change the world?"

The man in the dark suit smiled. "No… ruling the world and changing the world are usually the same thing." He started to walk off and flicked his cigarette away. Then he commented. "You should quit smoking, those things will kill you."

Gavin was getting an early start the next day and arrived at the office at 6:30am thinking that he would get there first before his partner did. As he walked into their office, he found Rachel going through files on the congressmen trying to find something resembling a lead. He laughed at the fact that he never beat his partner into the office no matter how early it was. He said to her. "Have you found anything useful in those files?"

She looked up and gave him a dirty look. "Not much…nothing that can really help up us."

He laughed as he showed her the file folder in his hand. "You can stop looking through those files…I have the best lead we've had so far, right here."

"What do you have?"

"Somebody with a real motive to get rid of the congressman."

"What kind if motive?"

"About a billion dollars' worth!"

Her eyes lit up with good news. She hated being stuck when it came to solving a case and the fact of the matter was they didn't have any real leads…they were nowhere with this case. Gavin handed the file to her and as he started reading through it he started telling her what he had found out about the Congressman.

About three years ago, Congressman McMahon joined the advisory board of the Hill and Meyer Research Labs in Chicago. They're a research facility doing cutting edge research on incurable diseases. At the time it was said that they were close to a drug that for all intense and purposes, could cure cancer. 10 months later they had a breakthrough with their new drug during the drug trials…first and second stage cancer patients went into remission. One of them was the Congressman's first wife. Rachel was surprised by the statement and had to ask.

"The wife we met wasn't his first wife?"

"No. The one we met was actually his mistress and then she became his wife."

She smirked. "Gotta love politics in this state. What happened to his first wife?"

"That's where this story takes a dark turn."

The congressman's first wife was in remission for about 6 months until she had a brain hemorrhage and died. She was complaining about a headache over dinner and as she was getting up from the table, she fell to the ground shaking and was dead in an instant. She wasn't the only one that died from the drug trials…there was one more death just like it. While the autopsy revealed that the cause of death wasn't directly related to the drug, some didn't see it that way especially Congressman McMahon.

The new drug was in the middle of getting FDA approved and the congressman was supposed to help speed that along, part of the reason he was on the advisory board. "

Rachel had to ask. "The congressman's involvement with this research facility, isn't that a conflict of interest?"

"Gavin laughed. "It is, but I guess he thought it didn't matter since his wife was dying of cancer. And yes, the politics in this state are screwed up." Gavin continued with what he knew.

After the death of his wife, the congressman intervened with FDA approval. The drug was denied and Hill and Meyer lost out on potential billions of dollars. The estimate if the drug had worked and been FDA approved was that Hill and Meyer would have made in the range of two hundred billion dollars. Now the company was facing bankruptcy because they couldn't get funding for research. At the end of the day the congressman had completely reversed his position when it came to the Hill and Meyer Research Labs and they lost billions of dollars."

Rachel let out a small laugh. "You weren't kidding about motive. How did you find out about this?"

"I got a tip."

"From who?"

"That's a little hard to explain, but it doesn't matter, we have a lead."

Rachel gave him a dirty look. "It does matter Gavin. Whoever gave you this tip could be jerking your chain and we don't know how much of this is true."

Gavin sarcastically replied. "Then guess what we're doing this morning. We go talk to the director of the facility who served on the advisory board with the congressman. We find out who stood to lose the biggest fortune there and stupid enough to do something to congressman."

They grabbed some breakfast first and then headed to the facility so they could talk to the director when he first arrived. Gavin wanted to be the first people he saw in his office, to catch him off guard and gain an advantage when they questioned him. Sure enough, it worked. David Graystone, the director of Hill and Meyer Research Labs, was greeted by Agent Donnelly and Agent Main when he walked into his office. He gave his secretary a dirty look when he saw them as she tried to explain to her boss that she had no choice, they were the FBI. He didn't like the answer, but couldn't do anything about it…he was going to have to talk to them and they weren't going to leave until they did.

Gavin pulled out his badge and showed it to the doctor. "Dr. Graystone…I'm Agent Donnelly and this Agent Main. We'd like to ask you some questions about Congress McMahon."

Dr. Graystone was startled by the question. "What would you like to know about him…it's a terrible thing what happened to him?"

Gavin laughed a little at the response. He felt it was little rehearse and that the doctor was trying to cover up something. "Doctor Graystone, when was the last time you saw the congressman."

"I saw him at his fundraiser over a week ago."

"You were there?"

"Of course I was Agent Donnelly… this facility is a major contributor to his campaigns… it would be odd if I didn't go there."

Gavin smiled. "Isn't it more odd to go to the event when you've had a falling out with the congressman."

Dr. Graystone was even more startled by the next question. "What…what are you talking about?"

Rachel finally spoke up. "Doctor, we already know about the falling out you had with the congressman over his wife's death. We know that she was in your cancer drug trial, we know that he was part of the advisory board and was supposed to help you get the drug FDA approved and then didn't when his wife died from complications with the drug."

The doctor was irritated now. It seemed that the agents had done their homework and that were more interested in making accusations than asking questions. The doctor asked. "Agent Main, are you accusing me of something am I a suspect in his disappearance. I mean, as far I know, a crime hasn't been committed yet…he's just missing."

Gavin replied. "That's true, but at this point we are suspecting foul play with the congressman…missing a few days is not that big of a deal, but over a week…that's suspicious."

"Maybe so, but that doesn't mean I had anything to do with it."

Rachel replied. "But you have a motive to see the congressman harmed. "

Dr. Graystone, laughed. "What kind of motive would I have?"

"How much money would this company have made if the drug had been approved and gone public…millions of dollars."

The doctor sighed for a moment and then angrily replied. "More like billions, Agent Main…we have the drug that can cure cancer…that's worth billions of dollars."

"And you're smart enough to know that this is a pretty big motive to kidnap the Congressman."

"Yes, Agent Main, I understand that, just like I understand that you have to question me about this, but there's a lot facts that you don't know.

"Such as."

Dr. Graystone set up his office coffee maker and started to make a fresh pot of coffee. He offered some to Gavin and Rachel…it was his way of trying to break the tension and be polite all the same. He responded to the Rachel's question. "Let me first say, that I don't wish the congressman harm in any way, no matter how mad he is in me and this company. And it wouldn't be smart to commit a felony when we have a chance to resubmit our phase 2 cancer drug for FDA approval. We have a good chance of getting this approved even without the congressman lobbying for us. I won't jeopardize that by being part of a crime. After all, this is what you really want to know… did I have something to do with his disappearance and why?"

Gavin replied. "Yes Dr. Graystone, this is what we are trying to figure out. And yes, you're smart, we're smart, and we can do this dance all day long, so let me ask you some direct questions."

The doctor gave a sarcastic reply. "You mean, you haven't been direct so far?"

"Dr. Graystone, when was the last time you spoke to the congressman, was it at the fundraiser?"

"No, I was at the fundraiser, but I haven't spoken to him for about a year… in fact, it was when he resigned from the advisor board."

"Was it a polite conversation?"

The doctor laughed. "No, not at all. I think he blamed me personally for his wife's death, even though I didn't make the drug myself."

Rachel asked. "What really happened…was it a bad reaction to the drug."

"No, Agent Main, although it's hard to prove that without doing an autopsy, which the congressman refused to let happen. There were a lot of factors with her death, one of them being, she was on other medication that we didn't know about and can't know for sure if mixing the drugs caused her death…this is why we get a complete medical history especially medications the patients are on. We can't do anything if the patient's lie to us. "

"Is that true for the other patient that died during the drug trial?"

"Not exactly, she had other complications and unfortunately she died."

Gavin asked another question. "How do you expect to get FDA approved without Congressman McMahon's help?"

"Agent Donnelly, I don't need his help to get our new drug FDA approved. All I have to do is donate enough money to some other congressman's campaigns and I'll get the influence I need. That's the beauty of our political system…it's not illegal buy a politician's influence."

Gavin had to laugh at that. There was a lot of truth in the comment. The agents didn't really have any more questions. Rachel handed her hard to Dr. Graystone and asked that have been heard from congressmen and please give them a call. While he was still considered a suspect, they were hoping that he could help them find as the congressman.

As I got back to their car, Rachel asked her partner. "So what you think, we have a suspect?"

"Oh yeah, he's not telling us the entire truth. Now, whether he had something directly to do with the congressman's disappearance that remains in the same, but he knows what happened. "

She smiled. "Glad to hear you say that. Just want to make sure that your head is in the right place despite the fact that the man who shot your uncle is still out there."

He smiled at his partner. "Don't worry partner, my eye is still on the ball. Now let's get a warrant for full surveillance on this guy and see if he leads us to the congressman. "He started the car and she made the call to get the warrant processed. Agent Rachel Main was always happiest when she and her partner were in sync with one another on a case.

∞∞∞∞∞∞∞∞∞∞

Jimmy and his cellmate Rocco were on laundry duty. It was quiet and easy work and the kind of work that Jimmy had to pay a lot of money for. The best part of his prison job was that nobody fucked with him and his cellmate who continually served as his bodyguard in the joint. He and Rocco was folding sheets when three inmates who didn't belong in the laundry room caught Jimmy and Rocco by surprise. Jimmy had his back turned to the door so he didn't see the men come in, he didn't hear them either because they barely made a sound. They weren't there to chat with Jimmy and Rocco. The first man pulled his shank too early as he was trying to stab Jimmy in the kidneys. Rocco saw him pull the weapon before he could get into position to harm his cell mate and with blind instinct he threw s pile of sheets in the inmates face to distract him from stabbing Jimmy.

Rocco rushed the three inmates and proceeded to take them all on at the same time. He hit each of them a few times before one them pulled his shank out and stabbed Rocco from behind in the kidney. He tried to ignore the pain and turn around to get the guy who stabbed, but he was too slow, the inmate cut his throat and finally killed him. Jimmy was looking for a way out when the guards came rushing in. It

[481]

was perfect timing and he was saved by the guards from the prison assassins before they could finish the job. Jimmy was taken to the prison hospital to be checked out as a precaution. He didn't care about that…his protection was dead and it was only a matter of time before somebody killed him. He was going to have to call in a favor and found the perfect way to do it when visitation was announced and his wife Maggie came to see him.

9

Simon O'Conner was trying to light his cigarette as a gust of wind blow his lighter out. It took Simon three times to light his cigarette, but that's how it could be around the harbors of Chicago. He and his partner were waiting for their police contacts. They always met at the North Shore Harbor by the maintenance building… it was out of sight and away from the traffic of the Harbor. Simon checked his watch…the cops were late. That bothered him, but there was too much at stake to be completely mad. Finally an unmarked police car drove up. There were two detectives inside the car. One of them Simon knew, the other one he didn't. He walked to the car after it stopped in front of the building.

"Detective Banner," he replied, "It's a good to see you again."

The Detective smiled. "And you too Mr. O' Conner."

"Who is your friend…you were supposed to come alone."

"I thought you should meet my replacement at the precinct."

Simon had a curious look. "Replacement?"

"I'm retiring in three weeks, so it's been decided that Detective Fisher, here will take over my duties."

"Can this man be trusted?"

Detective Fisher replied to the question. "I can be trusted or else I wouldn't have been chosen as the replacement police contact."

Simon stared at Detective Fisher for a while, giving him a disapproving look that seemed to penetrate his soul and make him feel uncomfortable. Finally he spoke in a scolding tone, "I wasn't talking to you… I don't know you yet.

Detective Banner was amused by the back and the forth. He replied. "Simon it's okay…I can vouch for him and I brought him along so you could get to know him."

Simon Paused for a moment and then handed a bag full of money to Detective Banner. The bag was larger than normal, it was a triple payment. Simon explained that the police were receiving a larger payment because they only had one last job to do and it was going to be a double shipment.

Detective Banner was not exactly happy to hear that. What it meant for him, was there would not be any residual income in his retirement and he felt that he risked too much to be denied that. Detective Banner responded.

"The partners are not going to happy about that…while it's nice to get extra money, I can't guarantee that you will receive the protection you paid for on the next shipment…you could have the attention you pay to avoid."

Simon smiled. "Detective Banner, flex your muscle all you want, but if we have unwanted visitors then a terrible accident will happen to the ones you love at 2241 Kenner Drive including your 19 year old daughter who just moved back there and is pregnant with your third grandchild."

Detective Banner was startled by the response. Simon continued. "We do our homework Detective…we know everything about you, especially where to hurt you the most so you do your best to make your partners understand that we will do one more shipment and it will go smoothly as usual." He looked at Detective Fisher and said to him. "If you are going to be his replacement its best you remember that too….we always know how to hurt you, how to make you suffer if you get in our way. You get paid well and that should be the end of this conversation. "

The detectives understood Simon's tone…they both knew that this was not an empty threat by the Irishman. They didn't say anything, they took the money and drove off.

∞∞∞∞∞∞∞∞∞∞

Gavin walked into his apartment to find Maggie drinking a beer and preparing dinner. She had been staying over a lot more lately and it gave her a good excuse to cook like she used to do for her family. Maggie enjoyed cooking for people…she loved to give dinners, but never really had an opportunity to do over the past few years with her son now gone and her husband in prison. Gavin smiled when he saw her. He had always imagined what it would be like if they had gotten married, started a family, and he could come home to a beautiful woman who loved to cook. This situation wasn't picture perfect, but it did make him happy even if it was considered wrong by everybody in their neighborhood. He didn't care though…he still loved her and if this was the closest they could come to playing house, he would take it.

He kissed her as she was cooking their dinner and she asked him how his day was. They made small talk for a few minutes and then she told him something that caught him off guard for a moment. "You know I went to see Jimmy today."

"How is he?"

"Not that good. Somebody tried to kill him, they didn't succeed, but his bodyguard Rocco was killed."

Gavin frowned. "I'm sorry to hear that and Rocco too. Rocco was always a nice guy despite being a thug and enforcer."

She laughed at the comment. "Yeah, he was, but Jimmy thinks somebody hired some prisoners to assassinate him…that it wasn't some routine turf war in prison."

Gavin took a sip of beer from the bottle that he just pulled out of his refrigerator. "He could be right, there are plenty of people that want him dead. Did he ask for my help?"

She gave him a dirty look. "You know he would never do that, but he did ask about you, which he hasn't done in a long time."

"It's nice to be asked about."

"You know, you could visit him every once in a while."

Gavin chuckled. "I'm pretty sure he doesn't want that…the last time we spoke, he didn't have any kind words for me."

"Well, he did want me to tell you something…he told me to tell you, don't look back in anger, which sounded strange."

Gavin was surprised and asked her. "Is that exactly how he said it?"

"Yeah, that's exactly how he said it, why?"

He smiled. "It's a coded message, we used to use them when we were young…to warn each other if the other was in danger or that one needed to see other ASAP!"

"So he's giving you a message."

"Yeah, he used you to signal me that he needs to talk and it's important. Wow, he hasn't done that in about 20 years."

Maggie walked over to him and put her arms around Gavin. "Is everything going to be okay, does this message it's an emergency?"

"I won't lie to you…it could be. I guess I'm going to see him."

"It must be really important."

He hugged and kissed her. "That's basically what the message says."

They held each for a few moments. Maggie was curious about something and asked a question out loud. "I always figured Jimmy never asked about you because he knew about us. If he's reaching out now then his life must be in real danger unlike the kind you normally see being in prison every day…I don't think he's lying.

"You got a point, but what makes you think he really knows about us."

She smiled. "I'm his wife, its intuition, but it doesn't really matter…he's not going to stop me from living my life."

Gavin interrupted. "Or fooling around with me?"

"No, because I never stopped him from stepping outside our marriage."

"If I've caused more trouble between you two, then maybe we should stop."

"You're getting a conscious now…do you really want to stop?"

Gavin paused for a moment before answering the question. The truth was, they had been in love with each other since they were kids. Maggie was his first love… his one, true, but it had always been complicated as love often is. His rational thoughts were usually thrown out the door when it came to her and he never minded that. She never minded it either. However, the lives they chose to make it hard to truly be with each other so in the end all they had was their affair, but in that affair they were happy. It had always occurred to Gavin that this, very well may be, the only way they could find happiness and he couldn't let that go because no matter he would always love her.

He smiled. "No, I don't because I'm still in love with you and I like being with you."

She kissed him. "Well, I don't want to stop either… I've never stopped loving you, despite how complicated, we've made things over the last twenty years. "

"And I know that's mostly my fault. Also, I know how this looks, sleeping with a prisoner's wife, but I don't regret it and there's a part of me that wishes things could've have been different. "

Maggie smiled. "Ok, then let me ask a serious question and I don't want you to ignore it or change the subject…I want you to answer honestly. If I were free, would you be with me for real…would we get married?"

Gavin was surprised by the question, but he wouldn't ignore it.

"How would you be free…if he dies?"

"That would be one way, but I don't want to see him dead…he should be able to go on and live his life. I'm talking about, if we were allowed to divorce. Jimmy and I have talked about it before and agreed to let me go and divorce me years ago if I asked for it."

Gavin frowned. "As much as I would like to see that, I can't be the cause of that. It shouldn't be about me."

"I wouldn't be doing only for you. It's not like my marriage is a happy one or an ideal marriage considering he's not getting out of prison for the next 15 years. But if I were free, would be together."

Gavin paused and before he could answer the question his phone rang. It was his partner letting him know that the meeting with Robert Grimes in Prison was set. She had pulled a few strings to get them and his cousin Alex a visit with the so called terrorist when they weren't on the case. They couldn't just walk into the prison and demand to speak with him…they had to get permission and he had to agree to see them without a lawyer present. It wasn't an easy thing to accomplish. After he got off the phone with Rachel, he called Alex to let him know what time to meet him and his partner. With the distractions and dinner being ready Maggie and Gavin didn't finish their conversation and just left it open for another time while they enjoyed their evening together.

The next morning Gavin was up early. He was the first one up so he made coffee and woke Maggie up with a cup. She had been staying over most nights now and since he tended to get it up first and wake her up with a cup of coffee before he left for work. She always loved the way he woke her up. She sat up in his bed and the sheet fell off her naked breasts. Gavin smiled. " I wish I had time to be lured back into bed, but I got to go."

She laughed and shook her tits a little bit. "You mean my breasts are good enough to get you back in bed."

"Oh, they are my dear, but time is not on my side this morning."

"I guess, I'll have to be here waiting for you when you get back."

He smiled. "I never answered your question yesterday and I don't want you to think I'm ignoring it. If you were free, whether it would be divorce or his death, I'd marry you in a heartbeat."

She kissed him, happy to hear him say that. He also said to her. "But, I think you also have to ask…could you be married to an FBI agent, know what my schedule is and the cases I have to solve."

She laughed. "Women from our neighborhood never really marry men with 9 to 5 jobs…we tend to marry cops or crooks. All I would ask is that you love me with all of your heart and don't bring your work home with you."

He kissed her passionately a moment, trying to make it last forever, but it couldn't. He had to go to work and he told her as he go up from his bed. "I wish I could stay, but I love you, always have and always will, no matter how this love affair goes. All I ever wanted is to be with you in some capacity." That was all he needed to say and that was all she needed to hear.

∞∞∞∞∞∞∞∞∞∞

Detective Alex Donnelly was waiting outside the FBI building for Gavin with coffee. It was the least he could do since he was getting a chance to talk to Robert Grimes. Gavin smiled when he saw the so -

[487]

called olive branch. He replied. "I'd prefer a beer, but I guess coffee would do since we're both on the job."

"I'm sure you have a flask in your office…you can make the coffee better if you want." Alex smelled something familiar. It was a perfume. With a strange look on his face, he said. "I know that perfume, I've smelled it before…who were you with last night."

Gavin shook his head. "It doesn't matter who I was with last night"

Alex gave him a curious look. "You were with Maggie last night, if not, you would have bragged about it."

"So what if I was. I don't care what people thing or might say."

"I know you don't, but if it was just a little bit of fooling around then it probably wouldn't be that big of a deal, but you've been seeing her for a while now…you're getting serious with her."

Gavin sighed. "Look, I'm not going to tell you every detail of my love life. And so what if I've seen her for a while, at least it's not some insignificant affair."

"You've never stopped loving her, have you?"

"No and I should have married her 14 years ago. If I had the chance to do it again…I'd marry her in a second. And that's all I'm telling you."

Alex laughed. "You know, I thought my life was complicated, but I have it pretty easy compared to you. Somehow I think you and Maggie always liked it to be complicated, made it more fun for you two."

Gavin smiled. "You're probably right. I guess I never liked it easy when it came to love."

Both of them went inside and met up with Rachel. An hour later they were at the Thompson Correctional Facility to meet with Robert Grimes. When they got there Robert Grimes was already in a visiting room hand handcuffed to the desk. Before they went in Gavin looked at his cousin and said. "It's better if I start the questioning, but I will let you ask some too. You're not really supposed to be here anyway." Gavin smiled at Alex. "We're probably going to ask the same questions anyway."

Robert Grimes wasn't surprised to see Agent Donnelly or Agent Main. He had a sneaking suspicion that they would have to question him again…he didn't expect it to be so soon. He smiled when they walked in. "Agent Donnelly and Agent Main, nice to see you again…can't get enough of me, can you?" He winked at Agent Main. "Especially you…honey."

Rachel shook her head. "Save the pillow talk for whoever is going to make you their bitch. "

Robert had to laugh at. Gavin started the questioning. "You've been busy since being locked up. You psychotic movement has taken off and we can't seem to shut you down… first amendments and stuff like."

"Agent Donnelly, it's not my doing…people want the truth and they will whatever they can to get it. "

Gavin chuckled. "Does that include killing cops?"

"Only if they're guilty of crimes against humanity."

"I'm sure you're aware that there's a cop killer in Chicago and he seems to be a movement…did you put him up to it?"

Robert smiled. "If you're talking about this Bobby McClain I keep hearing, then I can't help you there… I've never met him and don't know anything about him except what I hear from prison rumors. "

"So you know his name, we haven't released that yet, how did you find out."

"The name is not that big of a secret. You hear things in Prison."

Gavin pulled out the cards that had been left on the dead bodies. "He's been leaving these on the bodies, how did he get them and more importantly, despite your coy attitude, you still keep up with the members of the United Front so I'm betting you do know him, tell us what you know and we can get some of your privileges back for you."

Robert Laughed. "The answer to your first question is a printer. It's not hard to make these cards. And the second answer…I can't tell you what I don't know. While I get some information in here…I don't know every little thing about the United Front including new members."

Rachel responded. "We know you're still the leader of the movement and get daily briefings. Also, Bobby McClain signed up for your newsletter last year before you were super famous and this movement took off. You would recognize a name on the newsletter list from a year ago considering you had less than 50 people at the time"

Robert smiled. "So you've done your homework! Good for you. I never met him, he was just a name on a list, but he did email us a few times. He said that he had information on corrupt cops in Chicago, but when we asked for more information, he never really gave us anything, just a lot of vague answers and that was it."

Alex finally asked a question. "What exactly did he say about these corrupt cops?"

"And who are you."

"I'm Detective Alex Donnelly."

Robert had a curious smile and pointed at Alex and Gavin. "You two must be related. And I believe I heard that a Captain Donnelly was shot by Bobby McClain a few weeks ago. Are you two related to him?"

Alex got angry "He's my father and Agent Donnelly's Uncle…now answer the fucking question."

"So this personal, my sympathies, but if a member of the United Front is killing cops then trust me they have it coming because they're corrupt and prey upon the innocent. "

Alex reached across the desk in anger, trying to hit Robert Grimes. Gavin and Rachel had to restrain him. Robert just laughed. Gavin told his cousin. "Calm down, this doesn't help us get the answers we need. " Robert kept laughing and Gavin was going to let that go so he punched Robert in the nose and broke it. Robert cursed and Gavin told him. "Just because I won't let my cousin hit you doesn't mean I won't…if you want help to stop the bleeding then continue talking. " Rachel gave her partner a dirty look, but she didn't disagree with him either.

Robert was trying to stop the bleeding. "I don't know any more about this guy."

"But you would know if he's still receiving emails or talking with other people in the group. If he's in contact…you would know that, wouldn't you?"

"I don't know every detail of the organization…it's a lot bigger and in case you haven't noticed, I don't have access to the internet or a computer so getting information is hard. "

Gavin walked over and put his fist close to Robert's face. "Don't dodge the question…you can find out. If I hand you my cell phone, you could make a call and find out, couldn't you."

Robert didn't want to say, but after the dirty look he got from Gavin." Yes, I could make one phone call and find out for you."

Gavin handed him his phone. "Good…get it done, please."

Robert dialed a number and one of his associates answered the phone. He was happy to hear from Robert, but before could ask his associate to look up some information an older man came into the room. Robert recognized him immediately, but was completely surprised to see him walk in. The old man gave Robert a stern look. "Mr Grimes, put that phone down…I'm Benjamin Greer, your new lawyer, and you're not talking to these people anymore. " He looked at the rest of the people in the room, handed each of them his card and said. "Two FBI agents and a Chicago Detective questioning this man without a lawyer present…you three should know better and don't think I won't have you brought up on charges for it. This interview is over." Alex wanted to say something, but the lawyer in Gavin stopped him. He knew there was nothing they could do…they had to stop talking to him or they could lose their jobs, which meant on a bigger scale, they wouldn't be able to solve this case. The three of them left the room.

Robert was still shocked to see the old man. "You're a lawyer…I thought you were…"

Benjamin Greer. "You thought, I was just man with the money for your little movement. No Mr. Grimes…I'm your lawyer, your protector, your money line, and the fucking pope to you. You exist because I allow you to exist and you don't do anything without talking to me first. Next time feds walk in here and want to talk to you… you keep your mouth shut and I'm your first call."

"Why are you helping me Mr. Greer?"

"Because you're important Mr. Grimes…your organization and you being in prison are part of a bigger plan."

10

Gavin, Rachel, and Alex were walking towards the car after leaving the inside of the prison when Gavin noticed something familiar. He noticed one of the prisoners in the main yard of the prison, the prisoner was among a group having their yard time. Gavin told the others to hold on for a few minutes…he wanted to talk to one of the prisoners. Alex looked up and said. "Hey is that Jimmy McManus over there."

Gavin nodded. "Yeah, I need to talk to him for a moment…alone."

Rachel was about to say something, but Alex spoke up. "I wouldn't get in the middle of that…it's between them."

"I'm sure I don't know what you're talking about, but there's protocol when talking to federal prisoners."

"I know that Agent Main, but their history is more important than your protocol."

Rachel didn't necessarily agree with Alex, but she understood what he meant and didn't press the issue. Gavin walked over and saw Jimmy standing by the fence in the yard. He noticed the bruises on Jimmy's faces and had to comment.

"Jimmy…I'd ask how prison was treating you, but I can see it all over your face."

Jimmy laughed. "Good observation. This last week hasn't exactly been the best week in here."

"Maggie delivered your coded message, why did you send it through it her? "

"Because I knew she was the best person to deliver it to you and that you would see her sooner than later."

Gavin was startled by the comment. He couldn't tell for sure if Jimmy knew about him and Maggie, but that's not what his friend wanted to discuss. That much knew. He didn't want small talk so he just asked the direct question.

"So what's so urgent that you had to send a coded message?"

Jimmy gave him a serious look. "You have to help get me out of here!"

"You mean like a prison break…afraid, I can't help you there."

"Shit man, even I know, you won't do that. No, I need you to help me get a transfer."

"On what basis?"

"I have information that can help the FBI."

"After all these years in prison, now you're going to name names? You know who to call for that and it's not me."

Jimmy raised his voice. "Look man, I'm not talking to that cocksucker, Agent Simms…he and rest of the FBI organized crime division can go fuck themselves."

"Well, I can't help you…I don't have anything to do with your case."

"The information I have has nothing to do with my case…it has to do with yours. " I know what happened to the congressman…the one you've been looking for. "

Gavin was shocked. Jimmy was the least likely person to know anything about a missing congressman, at least that's what Gavin thought.

"What do you know about it?"

"Get me here out of here and I'll tell you."

"You know it doesn't work that way…the FBI doesn't know if I'm lying.

"I've never lied to you when asked a direct question. Why would I start now?"

Jimmy shook his head. "You may not be lying, but how I can trust you and this information. Coming from a desperate convict, information like that usually isn't that reliable. Give me something better and I'll consider helping you. Take care Jimmy."

Gavin started to walk away. Jimmy shouted to get to attention. "Mr. Greer, the lawyer for Robert Grimes…you just had a run in with him, right?"

Gavin stopped and walked back towards the fence. "And you know this Mr. Greer, how?"

"Because he also represents the Congressman McMahon…he's been doing business with the Congressman for 15 years. There's more, but that's all I can tell you until you can get me out of here. "

Gavin was surprised, he couldn't deny it. There was a connection even if it was not that unusual for lawyers to represent different kinds of clients, but there was something strange about a lawyer representing a terrorist and a congressman who couldn't be found. The problem for Gavin was always Jimmy…how much did he really know…how far down the rabbit hole did he want to go with his former best friend who could just as well be trying to con him.

While he was mulling everything over Gavin's head started to hurt. He knew he was about to flash. *Mr. Greer answered his cell phone and found Dr. Graystone on the other line. He was not happy to get a frantic phone call from the Doctor, but he had to humor him or the good doctor would be inclined to do something stupid. The doctor started talking. "Mr. Greer, we have a problem. Jimmy McManus is still alive."*

Mr. Greer showed frustration in his tone. "I know that and I also warned you that it was stupid to do what you did and that I would handle it."

"You were talking to too long. Jimmy McManus should have died before the congressman disappeared."

"You do not handle operations, Doctor, I told you that we had a plan and you now because of your failure, Jimmy is still alive and has talked to the FEDS.

Dr. Graystone cursed underneath his breath. "I made the move because there are too many connections to me and I have too much to lose."

"Look Doctor, I'm your lawyer and you should trust me the connections are being sorted out and within the year, you are going to be a very rich man. But if you keep interfering with our plans, then you will be sorted out as well."

Gavin was even more surprised by what he just saw. He turned back around to look at Jimmy and had a horrified look on his face. It was hard to face the fact that Jimmy was connected to this case in a big way – that the information he had could really provide the answers he needed. Gavin never wanted Jimmy's help even when they were young because he always had a habit of making things worse. Now he might be forced to take it.

∞∞∞∞∞∞∞∞∞∞∞∞

Detective Tom Buckner stepped off the elevator into the parking garage. He was tired, but he still noticed the little things. There were a few lights out in the garage and the lack of light caused more shadows than usual. Detective Buckner had always had good instincts and they were telling him to be cautious. As he walked to his car he noticed a man changing a flat tire. He could have ignored the man, but he was too nice for that. The cautious part of himself put his hand on the grip of his service weapon while he called out. "Are you okay, sir, do you need a hand?"

The man changing the flat tire smiled when he answered the question. "Thank You for asking… I could use help holding a flashlight, it's dark in the garage and I can't change the tire and hold the light at the same time."

Detective Buckner approached the man slowly, never releasing his hand from the grip of his service weapon. When he was about 5 feet away, the man changing the tire spun around quickly and shot Detective Buckner, but not before the detective was able to get his weapon out of the holster and get a shot off. The detective's shot hit the other man in the left arm. It wasn't bad, but enough to cause serious bleeding. The man fell back, but was able to get up quickly and stand over Detective Buckner who was shot in the chest. The detective was hurt bad and wasn't able to get up off the ground. He couldn't breathe and was bleeding out. The bullet didn't hit the Detective's lungs, but there was a burning sensation as if all of his organs were on fire. He was in such pain that he could barely speak, but as he saw the man who shot him standing over him he was able to get a few words out.

"I know you…why me."

"I didn't choose…they did."

Detective Buckner was confused. "Who are they?"

"You know the answer to the that…the men you've been getting money from at the harbor"

Fear came over the Detective as he realized who the man was talking about. He was able to gasp one more thing before his heart gave out. "McClain, they will kill you too."

Bobby McClain paused for a moment, shocked by the statement and he had to wonder if it was true, but then again, he knew for sure that his employers would kill him if he didn't fulfill his contract. He took a deep breath and shot the Detective Buckner one more time.

∞∞∞∞∞∞∞∞∞∞∞∞

Gavin, Rachel, and Alex were driving back from the Prison and talking about the information they had just gotten from Robert Grimes. All of them agreed that Robert was more of a pawn whose strings being pulled than a mastermind behind these cop killings. They all agreed that the lawyer was more capable of pulling those strings, but finding out the truth would prove impossible since they were both protected by attorney client privilege. Gavin looked at his cousin. "Okay, I fulfilled my end of the bargain, time to call your guy in internal affairs and set up a meeting."

Alex nodded yes, even though he didn't really want to. He was burning all of his favors with IAD and hadn't seen any results…just more mysteries that couldn't be solved. "I know, I call him now. When do you want to meet him?"

"Tonight, if possible."

Alex made the call, but while he was doing that, Rachel was curious about his conversation with Jimmy McManus. She had to ask. "What did Jimmy have to tell you?"

"Nothing important."

'Gavin, don't bullshit me, we should be past that by now."

He laughed. "He says he has information on our missing congressman."

"Is it real?'

"I don't know."

"But you think it is, don't you?" He didn't answer. "Come on, Gavin, I saw the look on your face when you came back to the car. It's that look when your instinct tells you something and you turn out to be right. You have good reason to believe him."

He smiled. "Wow, you are getting to know me. The problem is he wants of that prison for his cooperation so it could be a shakedown of some sort.'

"What did he say?"

"He said he knew what happened to the congressman and his proof is that Mr. Greer, not only represents Robert Grimes, but also does business with the Congressman and has been for the 15 years."

Rachel was a little shocked to hear that. "Seriously…that's a pretty big connection."

"Yes it is and now we have to check it out…unfortunately."

Rachel saw the look on his face. He was angry that it was something they had to check out. She knew him well enough to know that while he would follow up any lead to solve a case, he wouldn't do it, if it involved getting help from somebody like Jimmy…he was stubborn like that. She responded. "I know you don't want to do it because you don't want his help, but we can't let that go so I'll do it and keep you out of it until it's time to involve you. It helps us solve our case, then we'd be stupid not to follow up on this."

He nodded in agreement. "Thank You…it would be better if you do it."

Alex got off the phone. "He will be meeting with us at 10pm, he will text me the location an hour before. So, let's grab some food and maybe a couple of pints before we get bitch slapped by IAD."

Gavin couldn't help but laugh. There was truth in that statement.

∞∞∞∞∞∞∞∞∞∞∞∞

The air that night had a stifling feeling to it. It seemed to strangle every sense of good judgment that Gavin and Alex Donnelly might have had. There was no reason to be meeting with the IAD man, but the need for answers outweighed the need for rational thoughts in this case. Alex, Gavin, and Rachel waited below the tracks of one of Chicago's Elevated train. It was dark, and out of sight from anybody who might be curious. It was the perfect place for a meeting like this.

They waited for 10 minutes until finally a dark Ford Crown Victoria drove up. A man got out of the car and nodded at Alex as a way of saying hello. The man walked up to the three of them and Alex introduced him. "This is Detective Kevin Hanes with IAD."

He shook hands with Gavin and Rachel and then avoided the small talk. "Okay, why am I here…what's so important that you called in a favor?"

Gavin responded. "He called you because of me."

"Fuck, this is about FEDS…if that's true then you just wasted my time."

"This is about stopping a cop killer."

Detective Hanes gave him a dirty look as if he was trying to tell Gavin not to guilt him. "If I'm not mistaken, the FEDS aren't investigating that case…are you trying to get it all for yourself?"

"Not necessarily, but I have a case that might be connected and it involves Congressman McMahon's disappearance."

"What kind of connection?"

"Liam Donnelly was shot first by Bobby McClain and then two weeks later the Congressman goes missing…a former cop. My uncle once said that he never knew the Congressman, but for a brief period in in 1989, they served together at the 9th Precinct, according to his service jacket, why would my Uncle lie about that. Plus Bobby McClain has crossed paths with both them over the last 15 years."

Detective Hanes started laughing. "That's a big leap… are you trying to play six degrees of separation and get this case so you can get revenge on the man who shot your uncle."

[497]

"I don't care about revenge…I just want answers…no matter how small the connection is."

"So let me get this straight because your uncle lied to you and because a cop killer has a small connection to the both of them, you think these cases might be connected and want to secretly look at the IAD's files on all of them… why not get a subpoena to look at our files if there really is a connection there…make it a legitimate request and you won't have to do it in secret. "

"Because the files you would give me are digital and blacked out…I want the real ones…the hard files…the ones that aren't blacked out."

Detective Hanes gave Gavin a dirty look. "Now how would you know that?"

Gavin shook his head. "Doesn't matter how I know and let's face it the Chicago PD's servers are not that secure!"

"You hacked us?"

"I didn't, but I know what's in those files and I know that you wouldn't destroy them and I don't think you really want me to get a subpoena for those files and air out the dirty laundry of the Chicago PD."

Alex got angry when he heard that. "Hey Gavin that's not what this is about, I'm not signing off on that… if that's your intention then I won't let you."

Detective Hanes replied. "Agent Donnelly, listen to your cousin. Don't be stupid."

Gavin looked at the both of them. "Easy boys…that's not what I want…nobody here wants that, just like nobody wants Bobby McClain to get away with murder and the men who took the Congressman to get away with it either. So why don't we help each other."

Detective Hanes replied. "Only if you stop your threats and play nice. You mentioned the 9th precinct…we have a lot of stuff on them, but nothing to bring them down. There's stuff in there about the congressman. If his kidnapping has anything to do with him being a police officer, I would bet my paycheck, it has something to do with his time there."

Gavin was curious. "What do you have on the 9th?"

"Nothing concrete, it's all speculation and there's nothing we can prove, but we keep trying. And we do have stuff on your Uncle."

Both Gavin and Alex were surprised, but intrigued. Gavin was the one who asked. "What do you have on him?"

Detective Hanes smiled. "Don't worry Agent Donnelly, he's clean, but if you look him up in those files, you will probably be surprised by a few things."

"Does that mean you're going to help us?"

"I don't like this one bit...not sure, I even trust you, but there's nothing worse than a cop killer who hasn't been brought to justice. I don't know if this connection of yours really holds up, but if you can find something that will help bring him and the congressman down then yes, I'll help you."

"I'm not trying to bring the congressman down, Detective Hanes."

"But I am and maybe you can help me. I don't want to see him kidnapped...I want to bring him to justice...real justice."

Gavin didn't know what to say to that, but it didn't matter, the detective started to explain how to sneak into the place that the Chicago PD simply called, The Basement. It wasn't an elaborate plan, but it did require a great deal of deception and a little bit of luck. Detective Hanes gave them a list of times and then left. It was a list of shift changes for guards.

Alex asked. "When do you want to go?"

Gavin smiled. "Tonight...I don't want to waste time and we can make the next shift change."

"But how are going to do it?"

Gavin thought for a moment and then the answer came to him. "How about a pizza delivery when the shift changes! That should give me a minute or two to get past the camera in the tunnel below the street."

Rachel gave him a curious look. "What do mean by the tunnel under the street?"

Gavin laughed. "The basement is an old speakeasy and there's a tunnel below the street connecting it to the basement of the building across the street. It was used to deliver alcohol in secret during prohibition. Chances are that tunnel still works and they have a camera on it."

"You're joking about the tunnel under the street."

Gavin smiled. "Afraid not, welcome to Chicago!"

Rachel was surprised to hear that and all she could do was shake her head at the notion of an underground tunnel. After all, it was the kind of stuff you would read in a mystery novel. As they all started to leave, she stopped Gavin and said.

"Look, I know that I can't talk you out of this, part of me is curious to see what is in those files too, but is it worth ruining the memory of your Uncle."

Gavin stared at her for a moment. "You think my love for him will change because of what might find out about him?"

"I think you are in an emotional place and if you find something bad, then it will cloud your judgment. No matter what you find, you need to hear his side of it."

Gavin tried to smile. "It's always emotional when someone lies to you and I know there's probably something bad in those files, but it doesn't mean I'll stop loving him. You don't stop loving family just because they let you down or your perception of them changes."

He didn't say anything else…there wasn't anything else to say. He turned around walked back to the car. She knew he was right and the only thing left at this point was planing their espionage game.

∞∞∞∞∞∞∞∞∞∞∞∞

The basement was the lower part of a cop bar. The bar had, had many names since prohibition, but one thing remained the same, it had always been a cop bar and the basement was a simple speakeasy in the 1920's where cops could still do what came natural and look the other way. Sometimes the club upstairs was really busy with off duty cops, but tonight was kind of dead so when two strangers walked into the club they were easily noticed. They said hi to the bartender and then walked down stairs to enter The Basement. There was a Chicago police officer guarding the entrance. He didn't recognize the two men and asked for their ID's. Both men flashed badges and ID badges from the internal affairs department. The police officer looked at the names on the badges and then turned to the first man and said.

"Detective Byers…I've never heard of you."

"Just transferred in from New York…you can call and check on me if you want, but we are in a hurry."

"No, I don't need to do that, I can swipe your ID badge to find out about you."

The second man looked nervous. It was his first time in the field. Byers smiled at him as the officer was checking the badge to try and reassure him. Finally the officer was done. "

"Okay, Detective Byers, you check out and now I know your face. Welcome to The Basement. I'm assuming you know the rules…nothing can be taken out or emergency protocols will be taken. "

Byers smiled. "I do officer. We're only going to be here for a few minutes."

Both men went inside with hundreds of filing cabinets. They quickly found the one they were looking for and opened it up. It took a little time to gather the files they were looking for. Byers put them in

[500]

the briefcase he brought with him to the surprise of the man who was with him. He asked. "I thought we weren't supposed to take anything from here."

Byers smiled at him. "We're not, but we're going to anyway."

The second man was still confused "Won't that bring this place down?"

"Maybe, but that's not our concern."

"Then why are you leaving the one file about the congressman behind…I thought this was about destroying evidence?"

Byers chuckled. "It is, but we are leaving one thing behind…just a little bit of miss direction for a friend."

The second man shook his head with disbelief. Byers commented. "Relax Smith, you don't get to know every detail yet, or even get to know my reasons why. But put your mind at ease, there's nothing left about our involvement here in Chicago."

The second man for the first time all night smiled. He had been confused, left in the dark, and was pissed that all he could do was follow orders. But there was satisfaction in completing his first mission in the field. He commented. "You ever wonder what happens when we erase history."

Byers chuckled again. "We erase our moral compass and let the villain have free reign… after all, you can't control the world with a moral compass." Both men walked out of The Basement and disappeared into the night.

11

Alex and Gavin Donnelly stared at the steel door in the basement of the abandoned building. It was an entrance to as a tunnel that led underneath the street to the building directly across from the building they were standing in. Alex looked at his watch and replied.

"It's time, you have five minutes, did you take care of the cameras?" Gavin replied.

"I called a friend at the bureau, he and his so called girlfriend took care of that.

Gavin opened the door and shined his flashlight into the tunnel. He could tell that no one had been inside of it for a long time. Alex said one last thing before Gavin left. "It's funny to think that our bootlegger grandfather probably used this tunnel."

Gavin smiled and then got serious. "Yes, it is, but nostalgia will have to wait… we can share a pint together after this is done and talk about it. " Gavin hurriedly walked down the tunnel. He couldn't hide the fact that he was nervous. Even with the flashlight the darkness tried to swallow him as he briskly walked the 60 yards to get to the other side. But what really made him afraid was all the cobwebs that seemed to reach out to grab him and pull him into a deep demented abyss for which there was no escape. He stopped a couple of times and took a few deep breaths. He was not claustrophobic, but the tunnel was scary or perhaps it was just the situation. As soon as he got to the other side and reached the other steel door he received a text message from his partner. She was the pizza delivery girl and although the cameras would hide his existence, the steel door would make a lot of noise she was there to distract from the sounds. Also, just to have a Plan B, Gavin had W-40 and he sprayed the hinges to help mask the sounds that came from opening a steel door.

Rachel kept the police office busy who was guarding The Basement with a dispute over who ordered a pizza. She was good and kept the conversation going for a few minutes. The police officer didn't hear anything. Gavin checked his watch, he had ninety seconds left. Here counted about 50 different filing cabinets in the room and from what he could see it, it was a well-organized system. He immediately found the congressman's files should be, but didn't find anything…there was not one file in the cabinet. His first thought was that they were somewhere else and then it dawned on him…the files were taken…evidence was being destroyed. He decided to look for his uncle's files. He found one file and it was a thin file, but it was marked "9th Precinct Tour." He didn't have time to look through, but he grabbed it and ran through the steel door. He gently pushed it shut, hoping that no one would hear the sound. He didn't wait around to find out. A few minutes later he emerged from the tunnel where Alex was waiting. He asked. "Did you get the files?"

Gavin shook his head. "Only one file… there was nothing on the congressman."

"What file did you get?"

"One on your father…about his tour with the 9th precinct."

Alex was surprised and curious at the same time. "Well, what's in it?"

Gavin tightly held on to the file. "Not here, let's get my partner and then we'll see what dirt they have on him. Alex didn't want to wait, but even he knew that the basement of an old speakeasy was a bit ominous to be looking at secret files from IAD so they left disappeared without anybody knowing they had been there.

The three of them went to Morelli's Diner. Alex and Gavin wanted to look at the file together and Gavin wanted to include his partner so at least one person could be objective. He was smart enough to know that he and Alex probably would not be. They opened the file and one thing immediately jumped out at them, Detective Donnelly and Detective McMahon were partners for about four months at the 9th precinct. It was surprising, but not as surprising as to why the partnership was ended. Liam Donnelly was reprimanded for beating somebody they had arrested nearly to death according to a report. His record had been exemplary up to that point. No charges were filed against him, but he was immediately transferred to another precinct after that, which was strange. Alex commented on that and asked the question. "I don't understand, if this report is true, then he should have been brought up on charges and sent to prison."

Gavin responded. "Probably because the report is a lie…everything about this is a lie, why wouldn't this report be too. But what we really need to know is why he lied about being partners with McMahon. "

Alex replied. "Something bad must have happened for this report to be bullshit and for him to want to lie about being partners with him…when did the incident happen?"

Gavin looked at the report. "It happened in June of 1989."

A thought popped into Alex's head…he remembered a detail from of Bobby McClain's murders. "1989…a witness to the Charles Finch murder said that he overheard McClain say 'this is for 1989,' that can't be a coincidence."

"No, there's no such thing as coincidence in our cases so what are the connections between these victims, the year 1989 and the 9th precinct."

Alex smiled at the break they just figured out. "My dad and the congressman worked together in 1989, how much do you want to bet Finch worked there too?" Alex could login to the Chicago PD servers from his smart phone and he did, searching for Charles Finch's service jacket. Sure enough, he found what he was looking for; Charles Finch did a tour at the 9th precinct back then. He was a patrolman and would occasionally drive some of the senior detectives around according to reports in his file.

The three of them were not that shocked at the revelation, they were investigators who knew all too well that there was always a connection between a murderer and the victims, you had just had to find no matter how deep you had to travel down the rabbit hole. They all finished their coffee and left the diner. Rachel was curious to what Gavin's next move would be. He told her that they were still a lot of unanswered questions regarding his uncle, but he was the only one that could answer those questions. It was still a waiting game with Liam Donnelly…until he woke up the questions would have to remain unanswered.

∞∞∞∞∞∞∞∞∞∞∞∞

The men took their seats around the table and the large doors creaked as they were slowly shut. There was a lot to discuss and the situation was delicate, so everybody was at the meeting. The old man opened the meeting by saying. "The timetable has been moved up by two days. As you all know by now, the exodus project will be ceasing operations in Chicago, we had a specific date for the last shipment, but we will be moving that up by two days now."

One of the men sitting around the table asked. "Do we need to be concerned by the sudden change in the end date?"

The Old Man Smiled. "No, Mr. Roberts, this is to ensure everything goes according to plan and that by the time the FBI or Chicago PD start to figure out what's really going on, our business will be concluded there."

The rest of the men around the table nodded in agreement. The old man now turned everybody's attention to another item on their agenda. "We have a kill order in regards to this FBI agent who's investigating Congressman McMahon's disappearance. "

One of the men sitting at the table spoke up. "There's been attempts on the agent's life before and it hasn't worked."

The old man looked at him. "This is not a kill order for him, but somebody close to him. Killing him is too easy. He needs to understand that it is in his best interest not to pursue his current investigation. Are there any objections?" There were none, not even by Stephen.

The men in the room continued to discuss the current agenda. It was not meant to be a long meeting for they all had a lot to do in order to complete their plans. Time was very critical for them.

∞∞∞∞∞∞∞∞∞∞

Gavin had not slept much the night before and why Maggie tried to comfort him, it didn't help. He just couldn't shake the questions he had about his Uncle and Congressmen McMahon. He got to work early and found Rachel in their office laying out all the case files they had on the Congressman, Bobby McClain, and his victims. She laid everything out and put the important stuff on the investigation boards for the presentation they were going to have to make. He handed her a cup of coffee as they stared at the boards and discussed the connections. After a few minutes the conversation turned more heartfelt. She asked her partner. "Are you going to be alright with us talking about your Uncle as if he was a dirty cop?"

"We're not here to prove that he wasn't dirty, this is about finding the truth about why he lied and why he was targeted. I want the truth."

"Are you going to be able to live with it, if it's not what you want?"

He laughed. "One way or another I will have to."

But then Rachel gave her partner a stern look. "But, I also want to make sure that you're focused on this case and not family history."

"You keep asking me that, why."

[505]

She smiled. "To keep you focused on this case so that you can see things objectively…I'm your partner, that's what I'm supposed."

"And I didn't think you cared." She smiled at him as she finished her cup of coffee.

Two hours later AD Foster came to their office to get an update on their current case. He looked at their boards when he walked in to find information about the latest shooting victims of Bobby McClain lined up in a row next to a picture of the Congressman. He was shocked and then the feeling turned to anger. He responded in kind to his agents. "What is this, I told you that you don't get the work the cop killer case…you have your assignment and I don't see anything about the congressman except a picture."

Gavin replied. "We have this information on the board because we found a connection between the congressman's disappearance, Bobby McClain, and his victims."

AD Foster looked at Rachel. "Is that true?"

She confirmed it. "Yes, sir, it is… it may not be a big connection, but we do have one and perhaps a reason why these men are being targeted."

AD Foster wasn't entirely convinced, but he let the agents make their case. Gavin poured himself another cup of coffee and then poured one for the Assistant Director, telling him that this could take a while. Gavin started to explain what they had found.

"First, we don't know whether Bobby McClain had anything to do with the congressman, he probably didn't because it's not the same MO, but the congressman has one thing in common with McClain's five victims…they all did a tour at the 9th precinct, the one along the harbor, somewhere there together, some weren't."

AD Foster replied. "That doesn't mean anything…the congressman was a former cop, it's not unusual for these men to be stationed at the same precinct, were any of them partners?"

"No, except for my uncle…apparently he and McMahon rode together for months until my Uncle was transferred."

"How did you find that out? It's not in his service jacket."

Gavin smiled. "I figured you would check it and follow up on whether we were actually investigating the congressman's disappearance."

"I'm your boss, it's my job. So how did you come by this information?"

Gavin sighed. He didn't want to say anything, but the truth would eventually come out anyway…it was hard to keep secrets in the Chicago FBI office. He smiled at his boss and replied. "We manage to get a copy of IAD's files on the congressman and my uncle…the hard copy that's not blacked out."

"The hard copies…the ones rumored to be locked away in some secret location called the basement."

"Yes Sir"

AD Foster gave him an angry look. "You stole them, didn't you…you know the justice department won't be able use that as evidence if we can bring anybody to trial."

"I wasn't worried about finding evidence for a trial…I was looking for clues to how this was all connected."

AD Foster paused for a moment. "You will probably have to answer for that, but in the meantime…what did you find?"

Gavin was as serious as he could be in order to convey his point. "My uncle was McMahon's partner for three months until he was mysteriously transferred…there's no paperwork on why. That's the first connection to a shooting victim. Charles Finch was a beat cop at the 9th in 1989...he was known to have driven the congressman around back then. Dick Burns was the Lieutenant at the precinct that McMahon replaced 5 years before and they rode together during the transition period."

AD Foster replied. "Okay, that's 3 victims, what about the other ones."

"Harry Stanton was Dick Burns best friend, they came through the academy together, and Stanton did work at the 9th Precinct before Burns…that's the only connection. And for Tom Buckner, he went to work at the 9th after the congressman became an alderman. He was there at the same time as Charles Finch."

AD Foster stared at the board for a few moments. "Okay, Agent Donnelly, I will grant you that there is a connection, but it's not big enough to take over the Bobby McClain investigation from Chicago PD. What about leads on who might have kidnapped the congressman."

Gavin was not happy to hear that from the boss, the way he saw it, the connections were enough for the FBI to take over, but he didn't argue. Rachel told the AD Foster what they had found at Hill and Myer Research Labs and the shooting at the warehouse. He asked if there was a connection with the men at the warehouse to the congressman and the only answer Gavin and Rachel could come with was there wasn't enough information yet. AD Foster looked at the crime board and then at Gavin and Rachel. He had to ask.

"Are you sure there's no connection with the men at the warehouse and the research center. The men at the warehouse could have been hired to kidnap the congressman. Hill and Meyer has a serious motive to take the congressman."

Gavin replied. "There's no evidence of that and the only connection is they knew the congressman."

"That's enough to investigate. Follow up on this lead and stay out of the investigation into the cop killings unless you get more evidence...evidence that can be used in a court of law. You have more with the warehouse shooting and Hill and Meyer Research labs...you don't have enough with the Chicago Cops. Get back to me in a couple of days on this. "

Gavin wanted to say something, but Rachel stopped him. It's not the right time to debate the issue. Gavin slammed a file folder on his desk out of anger. Rachel chuckled and then replied. "Are you done with your tantrum?"

Gavin slowly let out a smile. "Yes, I'm done."

"I know you don't like this, but Foster is not wrong...there is a strong motive with the research labs and the connection between the labs and then the men at the warehouse is a lot stronger than you give it credit."

"Maybe, but I think Foster doesn't want to look at the real evidence with the cop killings. He's not seeing what I see."

"Because he doesn't a personal connection to it...we're FBI agents...we can't take the crimes we investigate personally."

Gavin paused for a moment. He tried to smile, but couldn't. "I've always hated when people tell us not take things personally. How can we not when it affects the people we care about or goes against that which we hate the most? Of course we are going to take it personally."

She shook her in disagreement. "You're looking at this the wrong way. We investigate all leads, all connections... that's how we do our job right."

Gavin nodded in agreement. "I won't disagree with that. You follow up on the research labs and the warehouse. I am going to follow up on my own lead...I am going to find out why these cops are being killed and what it had to do with the congressman."

Before she could say anything he walked out of their office and didn't look back. Like a dog on the scent, he was determined and couldn't let go. Time would tell if that would be a good thing.

∞∞∞∞∞∞∞∞∞∞∞∞∞

Gavin arrived at Grant Park in the middle of the day. There were always a lot of people in the park no matter what time of the day it was. Most of the people in the park who had jobs were there eating lunch. Gavin always wished he didn't stay so busy so he could enjoy lunch in the park, but in his line of work he was usually meeting

[508]

people there in order to get vital information to whatever case he working on. He walked up to the park bench and found an old man reading the paper and listening to the radio at the same time. He had bodyguards standing off to the side, watching everything all around him. They saw Gavin and slowly reached inside their coats for their weapons just in case he was a threat, but he showed his badge to them and they backed off.

The old man looked up at Gavin and smiled. "Agent Gavin Donnelly…it's been a long time…I take it this isn't a social call?"

Gavin chuckled. "Governor McGinley."

"You don't have to call me that anymore, I haven't been the governor for a long time. You can call me Ted."

"I know, but I do it out of respect and yes, this is not a social call. "

The governor put down his paper and turned off the radio. "What can I do for you?"

"You once told me that if I needed information on the Chicago PD or Politicians you would tell me the truth and now I need your help."

"And what makes you think that I can help you with your investigation."

"Because you are like the J. Edgar Hoover of Chicago…you know everything about everyone and just because you're out of office doesn't mean you've lost anything. Admit it, you still play the game when you're not betting on horses."

The governor laughed. "Guilty Agent Donnelly. Now what can I tell you…if it's about Congressman McMahon, not even I can tell you all his dirty secrets."

"I don't care about his entire past, I want to know about his dealings with the 9th precinct. In fact, I want to know why cops from the 9th are being killed. What's really going on there?"

"I don't think you really want to know all the secrets in this universe…knowing those kinds of secrets can ruin your health."

"So the killings are because of what's gone one at the 9th."

The governor laughed. "You're not that dumb for an FBI agent…you already know the answer. "

Gavin stared at the governor for a moment. It was true, he knew the answer deep down, but it was the details that he needed to satisfy his curiosity. "Tell me what goes on there?"

"Why do you think the 9th Precinct is allowed to exist despite all the budget fights where other precincts get closed…it's not even the oldest precinct that always short on resources. In fact, one might say that it has more resources than they need."

Gavin thought about it for a moment. "It's because of their location… because they cover all the harbors…so this is about smuggling."

The governor smiled. "That's only a part of it and you haven't even the right question."

"What are they are smuggling?"

"Correct Agent Donnelly and to take it a step further, what is so bad about the smuggling that they would have to publicly murder cops even retired cops."

Gavin looked at him. "Something worse that smuggling guns, drugs, or prostitutes…what can be worse?"

"Even I can't tell you the deepest secrets of the harbor when it comes to what goes in and out."

"Why not."

"Because I know enough not to know everything…like you said, I'm still in the game and knowing everything can get you killed."

Gavin sat back on the park bench trying to understand what he really meant in his cryptic messages. "But you know enough to at least lead me in the right direction."

The governor smiled and patted Gavin on the back. "I could do that, a warning is better for you…don't open up this Pandora's box…for you it will lead you to a place that you can't come back from. But if you truly want to know then there is somebody that would be willing to tell you everything you want to know…he doesn't have anything to lose now."

As the governor got up from the park bench Gavin asked him for a name. The governor simply replied. "Your old friend Jimmy…if he's still alive.

12

Gavin was walking back to his car when he felt a headache coming on. Suddenly he didn't see the street anymore. *He saw the inside of a building with guards standing around and a long corridor that led into what looked like a communal shower. He instantly recognized it as a prison, but didn't know where it was. A group of men with towels around their waist walked down the corridor and looked at the guard. The guarded nodded to them and then motioned with his eyes that there was somebody in the shower. The men walked in and took off their towels getting ready to take their shower. They started four other showers and got the water hot to where it created a lot of steam. The other man in the shower ignored them and continued to clean himself. Suddenly one of the four men lunged for the other man…he anticipated it and moved out of the way. Gavin caught a glimpse of the tattoo on his arm as he moved out of the way, but he never saw his face.*

Gavin was startled when some stranger touched him on his back to see if he was okay. He didn't see the rest of the flash and got angry at the stranger. He yelled. "What the fuck are you doing?"

"Nothing man…you looked like you were having a seizure or something, are you okay."

"Yeah I'm fine…this happens to me every once in while…its normal, but thank you.

The stranger left and Gavin was left with a fragment of his memory from the flash, not enough to give him any major clues. But then he realized something, it was the first time he had admitted out loud that his condition was normal. Suddenly he remembered the Tattoo…he had seen it before…he knew who it was in the shower.

ﾟﾟﾟﾟﾟﾟﾟﾟﾟﾟﾟﾟﾟﾟ

Jimmy stood underneath the shower, breathing slowly and trying not to be nervous. The guards were well paid to let him take a shower by himself and to avoid the usual gang rape in the shower that occurred with other inmates. It was a buyer's market in prison and those who paid the guards the most stayed safe, but even Jimmy knew that his days were running out and the money wouldn't be enough to keep him protected. As much as he tried, he still had knots in his stomach…he was still nervous and then it happened. It was the moment he had been dreading,

Four men walked into the shower and turned on more showers to make the room steamy. Jimmy continued to face forward and then let the water pour down upon the head. It didn't take long for the men to attach. One of them went for Jimmy, but he was waiting for him. He moved out of the way and grabbed the small shank hidden beneath the bar of soap he had. As the first man went for him, Jimmy moved and stabbed him in the kidney making the man fall instantly to the ground. Jimmy was able to fend off the other guys, using his shank. He took a few licks and was bleeding a little bit, but he did more damage to them before the guards finally had to come in and stop the fight. Jimmy was handcuffed and taken back to his cell. He was still wet and they didn't even bother to try and stop the bleeding. One of the guards who took him back to his cell was being paid off by Jimmy. As the guard was closing the cell door, Jimmy looked at him and said…I need a cell phone quick and I will pay double. The guard nodded in agreement and handed a cell phone to him.

∞∞∞∞∞∞∞∞∞∞∞∞

Gavin was walking back into the office when he got the phone call from Jimmy. He wasn't on the phone for very long, but Rachel could tell that he was agitated. He got off the phone and looked at his partner. "You're never going to believe who just called me and said he was ready to talk…my old friend Jimmy."

She looked surprised. "I guess he wants out of prison…what's he offering?"

"He said he could help find the congressman and help catch Bobby McClain."

"Wow…that's a tall order, you think it's Bullshit."

"Normally I would say yes, but Jimmy was in all sorts of things on the side…he knows a lot more than some two-bit Irish

[512]

thug...he could very well have something that helps is with both cases."

Rachel didn't respond to that. In the meantime, it wasn't important. She walked over to Gavin like she was going to console him. Instead, she had some important news for him. "Your aunt called... said she couldn't get you on your cell phone. Your Uncle Liam woke up."

Gavin dropped everything and drove to the hospital. Talking to his uncle was more important than anything else. It was personal. He arrived at the hospital about 30 minutes later. His family was there all packed in the hospital room not wanting to leave Liam's bedside in fear that he would slip back into a coma for good. Gavin walked into the room fearing that it would be awkward, but it wasn't. Liam smiled at him and even jokingly said to him that it was about time he showed up. Gavin was going to ask for a private moment with his uncle, but it was Liam that spoke up first and asked if he could speak to Gavin alone. Everybody cleared the room and left the two men alone. Alex was hesitant to leave, but his father told him that it would be okay.

The two men didn't speak for a moment. They were waiting for the other to say something first. Gavin finally spoke first and asked. "So how do you feel?"

Liam laughed. "Still have a headache, but the drugs they give you are great."

That was all the small talk, they could muster. Liam stared at Gavin for a moment, giving a stern a look that he had not seen since he was a rebellious teenager. Finally, he said. "Ask me what you want to ask me...you've got something on your mind."

"Do you know who shot you?"

"Alex has filled me in on Bobby McClain and the shootings."

"Do you remember what happened before you were shot...what McClain said before he shot you?"

"How do you know anything was said?"

"The FBI can pull frequencies from sound waves and form audio from a crime scene...I know it sounds like Science Fiction, but the NSA does it all the time. We got audio of your shooting."

Liam looked surprised. "So you know what Bobby McClain said?"

"Yes, but I want to know if you remember."

Liam paused for a moment. "Yes I do...he shot me because of you. Do you know why?"

Gavin sighed. "Unfortunately no, but I'm formulating s theory. You are connected to the other McClain shootings, but I'm wondering if your shooting is someone sending me a message or has anything to do with my last case. Still too many unanswered questions about that case. "

Liam chuckled. "You never quite answer all the questions in a case even when you solve it. "

"I agree, but one of those of unanswered questions for me is something I found out after the fact…a bit of a family connection. The Callon Raiders, was my father one of them?"

"What does that have to do with your last case?"

"Maybe nothing, but I still want to know more about my father and what he did in Ireland and why he had to change his name."

Liam was annoyed by the questioning, but he knew he couldn't avoid it. Gavin would eventually find out the truth. "What do you know about the Callon Raiders."

"Just stories…a group of IRA men who raided and pillaged English supply houses in North Ireland. "

Liam laughed. "Then you don't really know anything…they were an IRA unit and your father was one of them. Their job was to take out English Strongholds and cause havoc all long the country side. They got the name Callon Raiders because they liberated a prison camp along the Callon River. The English had over 100 prisoners in that camp…men, women, and children. Up until that time, we didn't know that the English had prison camps in the country where they just rounded up anybody that they saw as a threat… we had heard things like that, but it had been a myth. Your father and his unit showed us real evidence of the English's atrocities back then."

Gavin was stunned, but then the investigator in him started asking the right questions. "Why were they keeping prisoners in a camp? What were they doing with them?"

"Nobody knows for sure…none of them talked about what went on in there."

"I heard that my father was celebrated as a hero for what he did over there and also became a wanted man…is that why he changed his name?"

"He changed his name before he went over to Ireland…we both did…it was your grandfather's idea so that nothing we did over there would come back to us here. If we were going to be wanted men then they were having a hard time finding us since there was no record of the names we used…all the Brits would have, was a fake name."

Gavin smiled. "That was smart. You came back after a couple of months over there, why?"

"Your Aunt Mary… I was madly in love with her. As patriotic as we both felt, my love for her was more important so I came back and married her."

"Are you trying to tell me that he stayed for some patriotic duty?"

Liam sighed. "Yes and no…we both felt we should help the Irish cause, we had family over there that needed our help, the case was only part of it, your father also stayed because he didn't want to end up here in Chicago as a cop and felt that going to Ireland was his only way out. He was young and wanted to get out and see the world…this was his chance in a way."

"What did he do with IRA?"

"I can't answer the question because I don't know and some things are best left as secrets. I can tell you that he did some important work for the IRA. Things that made him a wanted man and the Callon River incident was one those things that made him wanted by the British government."

"Did that have anything to do with him and my mother's murder?"

"I don't know for sure, but there's no evidence that the Brits had anything to do with it."

Gavin paused for a moment and then in an angry tone asked. "Why didn't you ever tell me any of this before?

"To protect you."

"Protect me from what…the truth…don't you think I have a right to know about my father."

"You do have a right, but would the FBI ever take a man whose father was labeled a terrorist by the British Government. You had plausible deniability if it ever came up and if they never put the connection together, then it would make life easier for you."

Gavin sighed. "You could have stilled told me the truth after I had been with the Bureau for a while."

"Maybe, but they still do background checks, including lie detector tests on you and they could still find out the truth…I didn't want your career ruined."

Gavin looked at him with disdain. "Okay, you had your reasons, but now I have to wonder, what else you haven't told me and why you've lied to us about certain things."

"What did I lie about?"

"The congressman and riding with him for more than 3 months when you were at the 9th precinct."

Liam didn't say anything for a moment. "How did you find out?"

"It doesn't matter, why did you lie to Alex and me?

"You have to understand that's it's important for some things to remain a secret especially to the FBI. Some things you don't really know."

"That sounds like the excuse of a guilty man. "

Liam was angry now just like Gavin was. Gavin wanted the truth and his uncle was willing to give it to him…there was nothing to be, but angry. Liam replied. "Be careful where you go with that."

"I'm trying to figure out why you were really targeted. The only connection we have among the victims is that they all worked at the 9th and are connected to the congressman somehow and I have you lying about the time the you rode with him at the 9th. Were you into something back then that you weren't supposed to be?"

"Whether I was or wasn't, I'm not going to tell you. There are some secrets that remain with the Chicago PD. "

Gavin shook his head in disbelief. "Something's never change, I guess. But don't think that if this all goes to trial, I won't have them subpoenaed and you'll have to tell the truth in court."

Liam laughed. "Good luck with, but you won't be that lucky, this thing will never go to trial and you'll never get Bobby McClain alive. Cop killers don't come out alive in this town, but I hope you find what you're looking for. "

Gavin didn't say anything else. He knew he wouldn't get anything else out of his uncle. It always seemed that Chicago Police officers survived on their secrets. The only thing he knew for sure at this point was that he and his partner still weren't any closer to finding the truth, but it was out there somewhere. As he was walking out of the hospital his head starting to hurt, he was about to have a flash so he closed his eyes to see what was about to unfold. *It was Bobby McClain, clear as day, he could see him standing on a corner with his head down, a hoodie pulled over his head, and smoking a cigarette. He looked cool and confident, patiently waiting for his prey. An old man walked by him without noticing the man in the hoodie. Gavin tried to recognize the old man walking by and even though he knew a lot cops, active and retired, he didn't know the old man. He was assuming that the old man was a cop since McClain started walking behind him. Gavin was starting to get used to the flashes so he tried to recognize the surroundings such as signs or buildings. He still couldn't see anything, but he could see the people in the flash plain as day and then it was gone.*

Gavin was mad, he nothing to go on except that Bobby McClain was about to kill someone in 30 minutes, but he didn't know how to find him. All of a sudden, he saw a TV and it was the midday news hour on WGN, one of the newscasters said that there was going to be a news conference with Alderman Gary Rich whose section of Chicago included the 9th Precinct. He got an idea, something that might help flush Bobby McClain and his victim out into the open.

∞∞∞∞∞∞∞∞∞∞

[516]

TV and Newspaper reporters were gathered around city hall waiting for the press conference. Alderman Gary Rich chose city hall to talk to reporters so he could he could be in a place of power. It signified that he was the man in charge and important enough to be at city hall. Haley O'Brien thought to herself while standing there waiting for the press conference, this must be the Alderman's unofficial announcement that he was running for Mayor in the next election if he had to talk to the press from city hall. He was going to use the Bobby McClain Murders as a political motive so that he could show that city of Chicago that he was tough on crime and willing to do anything to catch a killer. As she was waiting, she received a text message from Agent Donnelly. She stared at the text for a moment, surprised that he was giving her questions to ask. She had never known the FBI to volunteer information, but she knew there had to be a good reason why he would text here.

The Alderman came out of city hall with one of the police commissioners. He began reading a statement, a simple statement that was supposed to make the alderman and the Chicago PD sound like they knew what they were doing despite the fact they hadn't caught the cop killer. But sounding like they knew what they were doing was just as important too. After the statement was read the Alderman took questions from the press. Finally, Haley got to ask a question and she asked was Gavin had texted to her. "Alderman, Haley O'Brien, Chicago Tribune…FBI sources have found a link between the victims and the disappearance of Congressman McMahon…they all worked at the 9th precinct at one time or another…sometimes at the same time. Do you think these shootings have anything to do with the congressman's disappearance and do you think these crimes have anything to do with what they did at the 9th precinct?

She could tell that the Alderman was pissed at the question. "Miss O'Brien we don't go by the fantasies of the FBI, its unattributed information and just because these cops might have all worked at the same precinct at one time doesn't mean, that's the reason they've been targeted by some vindictive ex-cop."

The alderman was about to take another question when Haley asked another question. "But Alderman, you have to admit that it's a big connection and more than a coincidence that the victims all worked at the 9th…wouldn't that suggest that Bobby McClain is targeting cops who worked there…is the Chicago PD investigating this?"

The Alderman gave Haley a dirty look, he was going to say something to her, but the Police Commissioner stopped him and told the group of reporters that the press conference was over. Haley had obviously gotten under their skin , but now every reporter would be writing about the connection with victims and the 9th precinct.

∞∞∞∞∞∞∞∞∞∞∞∞

Bobby McClain was hurt bad as his right hand was soaked with blood. He was trying to put pressure on his wound and stop the bleeding, but he was having a hard time. He saw the blood dripping on the concrete knew that he had to get off the street because he was leaving a trail. He flagged down a cab and handed the driver a hundred dollar bill to drive fast and keep quiet as well as the mess he was leaving in the back of the cab. He gave the driver an address and told him to get there fast. McClain was caught off guard…his victim shouldn't have known that he was coming, much less right behind him. Nobody had put the connection together or so he thought.

There had been shots fired in the area and police responded pretty quick to the scene. The body they found was already dead and since eyewitnesses said they saw a man fitting McClain's description, the lead detectives on the case were called immediately. Alex Donnelly got there late and found his partner, Detective Reilly already with the crime scene investigators. He asked the obvious. "Another murder by Bobby McClain?"

"Yes," she hesitantly answered.

"Who is the Victim?"

"Roger Stewart…retired from the job two years ago and there's something else?"

"What?"

"We have two types of blood…one of them is Bobby McClain…looks like he's injured."

Alex was stunned at the news, but also excited…it was a break in the case. The shooter was injured and couldn't go many places to get patched without getting caught. The search for Bobby McClain was being narrowed down now.

13

Agent Donnelly was barely awake, he was on his second cup of coffee and still tired as he and Agent Main drove to the Thompson Federal Correctional Facility. Agent Main commented. "Did you get much sleep last night?"

Gavin laughed. "Not much, but then again, I haven't gotten much sleep since my Uncle got shot."

"Are you sure that doesn't have to do with your affair with Maggie?"

She made the moment awkward, but Gavin got past it and laughed. "I wish that were the case…would certainly be less stressful. "

"Well, at least you still have your sense of humor. But in the meantime, I have some information for you… the details about last night's shooting. She explained everything to Gavin. He was excited to hear about the break in the case…about Bobby McClain being injured. But Gavin only had one question about the shooting.

"This Roger Stewart, did he do a tour at the 9th precinct?"

"Yes."

"That confirms the connection, he is targeting former cops from the 9th. " He smiled a little bit…not because they confirmed a connection between with the murders, but because he was finally able to use his gift to his advantage. His plan to flush a victim out and give him a subtle warning seemed to work. Perhaps he was finally gaining control of this gift. Agent Main noticed the smile. She asked.

"What are you so happy about?"

"Oh, nothing… just happy that we have a connection."

She didn't really believe the answer, but she didn't press the issue either. She got more file folders out of her briefcase and then spoke up.

"So I dug deeper into Hill and Meyers Research Labs…took a page from your book…followed the money."

Gavin laughed. "And what did you find down the rabbit hole."

"This company is incredible, especially since it's not publicly traded. The first company to synthesize AZT for the AIDS epidemic. They were the first to market a widely used Flue Shot and my favorite, invented a erectile dysfunction drug that lead to the creation of Viagra. They have profited big from some of the most widely used drugs out there. And they seem to be at the forefront of cancer research. But the strange part is while there is a usually a board of 8 to 10 people with a medical facility and they have that, they also have 39 silent partners…who has that many silent partners?

Gavin couldn't help but be a little shocked, but then again, he wasn't that surprised either. There was something strange about Hill and Meyers, nothing about them had felt right after the agent's first meeting there. It was like the underlining Scum around the edges of the toilet bowl, after a while you can ignore it, but you always know it's there. He replied.

"A company trying to hide something and people who can't afford to get caught in whatever dirt this company is sitting in. There must be a lot of important and influential people that have a stake in Hill and Meyers."

Rachel nodded in agreement. "Then let's subpoena the business records and find out who these men are."

Gavin liked the ideas, but knew that it probably wouldn't work. He replied to his partner. "We could try, but if these silent partners have any influence, then we wouldn't get anything. "

"Still worth a try!"

"Maybe, but I have another idea on how we can get that information. A Tax audit…we would be able to find out all the partners who are filing a tax return based on income from Hill and Meyers."

"What if none of these people even file a tax return from their profits with the company."

Gavin smiled. "That's a possibility, but there is still a tax record of who these people are. We just need to initiate a tax audit."

"And how do we do that?"

Gavin laughed. "For me, it's one call."

"Let me guess, you drink with an IRS agent."

"No…I just know one who owes me a favor. But let's see what can dig up."

The Agents finally arrived at the prison. They were waved in immediately because the warden wanted his say in what was about to happen even though there was nothing he could do about it. Before they could meet with the prisoner the agents had to deal with the warren and instead of arguing with him Gavin just showed him transfer documents from the Justice Department. The warden was even more angry, but he complied with the transfer. After about 10 minutes, Jimmy McManus was brought to the room to where they all were. Jimmy was surprised to see his old friend…he was betting that he wouldn't help him and still be the straight-laced FBI agent that he hated. But Gavin continued to prove him wrong and this time it was going to save his life.

There was no small talk between these old friends. Jimmy immediately asked. "What's this about, you hear to question me."

"Not exactly, you're being transferred to our custody for your corporation in our investigation."

Jimmy looked the warden, looking for some kind of confirmation, he had been in prison too long because it was the first thing instinct told him to do. He asked the warden if this was true and all he could do is tell Jimmy is ask the FBI agents.

Gavin replied. "This is not a joke; you're leaving with us today…if you can help us find Congressman McMahon then you will get transferred to another prison when our investigation is done and have a chance to reduce your sentence."

Jimmy didn't ask for too many details, he just needed to get out of jail. He dressed quickly and with a little spring in his step left with them knowing that he was alive for at least a little while longer.

As soon as they were outside the prison walls Gavin pulled a flask from the glove compartment and handed it to Jimmy who was sitting on the back seat. He smiled at the gesture, but Rachel gave her partner a strange look. Gavin responded to her. "What?"

"Whiskey, he's not on vacation."

"He may be a criminal, but he deserves some decent whiskey."

Jimmy couldn't help but laugh. "Agent Main, don't be too angry…he's not that big of a prick…at least not anymore." He took another sip from the flask. Rachel just shook her head at what must have been some kind of Irish Custom. After a few minutes Gavin looked at his friend through the rearview mirror. "Okay, now that you've had your drink, let's start talking. "

Jimmy laughed. "Are you trying to get me all liquored up and spill my secrets like a woman."

"I don't have to get you liquored up for that…I just have to put you back in Prison and see if you last the night. I was just being your friend with the whiskey."

"What do you want to know?"

"Congressman McMahon, you said you had information on his disappearance, who took him. "

Jimmy paused for a moment. "I don't know exactly took him."

Gavin was pissed. "Are you playing me just to get out of prison…if this is some kind of con then we're turning around. "

"I don't know the name of every lowlife who would kidnap him, but he has a long list of enemies that would do it. "

"Why kidnap him?"

"Because he still runs everything."

"You mean operations at the docks?"

"Yes"

"And he's still running everything through the 9th precinct…he is connected to the cops being killed from the 9th precinct?"

"Yes…his title may have changed, but he's still the man in charge."

"Is this about something in particular getting smuggled?"

Jimmy was getting agitated. "I can't tell you everything and you know that."

"I'm not asking you to betray your mob brothers, I just want a motive."

"That's for you to figure out. You're the FBI agent."

Rachel interrupted Gavin before he could reply. "Before we take you back to prison for screwing around with us, it should be noted that you still haven't given us any names yet."

"What's with the threats?"

Rachel looked him. "I don't make threats…in this job I don't have to. Now give us a name and quit wasting our time."

Jimmy shook his head "Look, I don't know who exactly took him…there's too many possible names."

Gavin was pissed at this point. He shouted. "Fuck it…we're going back" Then he pulled the car off to the side of the road so he could make a U-turn.

Jimmy got mad, but finally relented. "Okay…all I can I tell is if you want to find the congressman then you find Simon O'Connor…he's the one that connects the congressman to all these cop murders."

Gavin was a little confused. "I've heard that name before, but he's not somebody from Chicago."

"No, he's IRA…connected and is from Belfast, but he travels most of the time."

"Jimmy this doesn't do me any good… I just can't walk in Northern Ireland and find him."

Jimmy smiled. "Trust me, if these cops are being killed, then he's here in Chicago."

"Are you saying he's the man behind these murders?"

"I don't know, but if the congressman is missing and cops from the 9th are being killed, then he's here cleaning up… that's all I can tell you…the rest you will have to find out for yourself…find him and you may get the truth."

That was all the questions for now. Rachel got on the phone calling the office and asking for the files on Simon O'Conner…everything the FBI had on him. They had a new name, a new player in this sad sordid game. Gavin didn't know what to make of this new information, but his instincts about this whole case were proving right. But it also made him afraid that he and his partner were already too late…the men behind this were too many steps ahead. It was probably safer to give up, but find the truth was too important so they kept investigating.

∞∞∞∞∞∞∞∞∞∞∞

Liam Donnelly wasn't supposed to be working from the hospital, but that's what the doctors told him. He was a stubborn Irishman and thought he knew better, and telling him to sit still and heal was like telling the fog to stay out of Chicago. Officers from his precinct would periodically stop by his room and brief him. Alex came by every day to brief him the Bobby McClain situation. There was a lot at stake for Liam, a lot of deep secrets that he wanted to stay hidden. Police officers in Chicago rise and fall with their secrets. And there was nothing that made that more true for Liam Donnelly when Tommy McManus paid him a visit at the hospital. And it wasn't a social call or he would have brought flowers.

Tommy walked into the room and there were two police officers giving Liam a report. When he saw Tommy, he immediately knew that it was about business so he motioned for the officers to leave the room. Tommy told his driver and bodyguard to do the same and then he responded to his friend sitting up in the hospital bed. Three gun shots and you still lived…only your stubborn Irish Will would keep you alive."

[523]

Liam smiled. "I suppose God didn't want to have a drink with me yet, if he did then I would be dead…don't know if I should feel insulted or be glad."

"It's good to see you up and around, especially with everything that's happening, tensions are running high in this city, but at least you made it."

"We both know this not a social call Tommy, what can I do for you?"

Tommy pulled out a flask and poured some whisky into a plastic cup for the both of them. Liam didn't object, it was the kind of medicine, he wouldn't get from the hospital. Tommy replied. "This Bobby McClain Business and Congressman McMahon missing is troublesome…you probably don't realize the problems this is causing."

"I have gotten reports about an increase in violence around the docks…seems that some small gangs have started to take run at them."

Tommy shot Liam an angry look. "And some of those cops at the 9th are taking money from the people. "

Liam laughed, "What makes you think that I control that…I have nothing to do with who's on the take and who's not…my role is to turn a blind eye for the greater good."

"I know that, but that's a small problem compared to the investigation into the congressman's disappearance. I hear that your nephew is doing it and at the same time investigating these cop murders even when the FBI is not officially assigned to those cases…that can't happen."

"You're afraid that he will find out to much history….what makes you think he doesn't already know more than he should and doesn't care

"I can't take that risk and neither can you…we all have too many secrets that he doesn't need to know. We all have a history that needs to be kept hidden from the FBI. "

"And you want me to do what exactly?"

Tommy paused and took a sip of whiskey. "He needs to be reminded of what we did for him and told to step away. My People can find the congressman."

Liam chuckled. "You think Gavin needs to be reminded of that night…he will always carry it with him because he never wanted any favors from us. And my power in this town does not extend to the FBI

"But you do have influence with Gavin and we have both been in agreement that as long he works the FBI there are things he doesn't need to know even if he's an Irishmen living in our community and despite who his father was. "

"I think you overestimate how much influence I really have on him…he has always been his own man. "

Tommy Chuckled. "Then I guess he really is a Donnelly, But unfortunately, things are getting too hot around here and there's too many secrets that can spill out. You, me…. Mickey, we've held this truce together for 25 years…Kept Chicago from erupting into an all-out gang war. I won't let it end with this horseshit."

Liam tried to smile. "What are you really afraid of…the FBI knowing all your secrets or that your time as king may finally be over."

All things eventually come to end…we're old men now…maybe we shouldn't hold onto the past, but look to the future."

"I won't have our community torn apart because of some cop killer…I won't have all that we've built be torn apart because of this no matter what our alliances are. "

"Telling him to quit this case won't have the reaction you expect. You will just add more fuel to the fire. You want this fixed then find the congressman first, don't let the FBI find out any of your secrets."

"Probably both, but I'm not ready to hand over the reins yet. And just in case you think I'm being paranoid, did you know that Gavin got Jimmy out of prison today.

Liam had a look of shock. "Okay, I didn't see that coming…what do you think that's about."

"It can only be one thing…he's spilling his guts to the FBI. There's been a few attempts on his life… maybe he thinks this is the only way out now."

"Why are you questioning his loyalty…you never have before?"

"I never had too, but after his son died, he changed and not in a good way. He started making deals on the side. I wish that I could say that I trust him, but that's not the case anymore.

Liam looked at Tommy like he just figured out the piece of the puzzle and then he replied. "You put a hit on Jimmy, didn't you? Couldn't take the chance that he would talk. Your own blood!"

Tommy tried to smile. "Yes, I did, one of them at least."

"What do you mean?"

"Somebody else is trying to kill him. The man I hired was killed by his cellmate. But it proves that he's a bigger threat than I thought and needs to be put down. It's the best thing for him. And the best thing for Gavin is to look away."

Liam paused for a moment. He understood why Tommy felt that way and wasn't sure if he agreed or not. He finally spoke. "I don't like interfering with Gavin and cannot promise anything, but we'll talk to him. However, anything that has to do with putting Jimmy down… I won't be a part of."

"But you won't interfere will you"

"No…it's your business.

The two men finished the whiskey that Tommy snuck in and talked about less important things. It was small talk just to pass the time and remind them that on some level they were friends.

∞∞∞∞∞∞∞∞∞∞

Simon O'Conner was finishing his third glass whiskey and looking over reports when his bodyguard came walking into the office. Simone was already in a foul mood when he was given the bad news. The bodyguard said. "It's been confirmed. Jimmy McManus was taken out of prison by the FBI. They got him out early this morning."

Simon threw his glass of whisky across the room. "This complicates things. We have to do both shipments at once and we have 72 hours to get it done." His bodyguard was surprised and started to shake his head.

"Simon, that's not enough time. It's going to take us at least a week to just to put a double shipment together. "

"We don't have that much time. If the FBI got him out, then you know he'll talk. We got three days at the most before the docks are crawling with FEDS. "

The Bodyguard paused for a moment. "If we only have three days, then we shouldn't do a double shipment… get as much as we can."

Simon smiled. "No, they paid for two shipments and that's what we are going to give them. "

"It's too risky."

"Unless we can get to Jimmy in FBI custody, then we have to speed this up."

"What about the rest of the targets?

"Even if McClane doesn't get all of them, we'll be long gone."

His bodyguard still didn't agree, but he knew there was no use arguing with Simon when he made up his mind. He could be reckless, but it made him successful and the one man everybody knew could get things done no matter how dangerous the job could be. Even a job like this.

14

The man finished his sandwich as he sat in his car waiting for the right moment. He checked his smart phone again to confirm the information. It was his first job, he wanted everything to be perfect. He kept going over everything in his head…every detail just to be extra prepared. He didn't know how long he would have to wait, be he was prepared to be there for days if necessary.

Meanwhile Gavin and Maggi were up in his apartment about to sit down for dinner. It was the first time in a while that they actually cooked a full meal instead of getting takeout. It felt nice. As Maggie was finishing up the pasta sauce she looked at Gavin and asked. "So I heard you got Jimmy out of prison…is he moving somewhere else?"

Gavin hadn't had a chance to tell her yet. "Wow, news gets around fast in this neighborhood. It just happened today."

"Why did you get him out?"

"He's actually helping us find the congressman and in exchange for his help, his case will be reviewed."

Maggie was surprised to hear that. "You mean he could get out and come home."

"Possibly, but that's up to the justice department. She gave him a dirty look and he couldn't ignore. He had to ask a question that he always hated asking a woman. "Are you mad about this?"

Her gaze lingered to the point of making him uncomfortable. Finally, she answered. "Yes, I'm mad… I figured he still be in prison while you and I run away together so to speak. I didn't plan on running into him anytime soon. Figured I had some time before I had to talk to him. "

"I'm not trying to make this any more awkward than it already is, but I still have a job to do and if Jimmy can help us then I am going to use that even if he gets out of prison early. It's not like we weren't going to have to deal with him eventually. "

She laughed. "Yeah, and I figured it would be 10 years down the road when we've settled into our lives together. If he gets out by helping you then I need to talk to him about this and soon."

Gavin smiled. "You're right, but we should do it together…after this case is done. We both owe him the truth, I won't disrespect him like that."

Maggie smiled at him. Above all, his faults, he was still a good man and it just made her love him more. Her anger quickly went away. She walked over to where he was and kissed him long and slow, and filled with passion. They continued to kiss and he started to unbutton her blouse. She laughed a bit for she knew that it wouldn't be long before they ended up in the bedroom. She stopped and said. "While I love where this is going, let's not waste our dinner. There will be plenty of time to take advantage of me."

"Promise?"

She kept smiling. "I think you already know the answer to that, but you have to go get some more wine…we're out and you know after a bottle of wine what I am willing to do."

Gavin gave her a mischievous smile and simply said, "Hmmm!" He stole another kiss and told her that her that he would be back in five minutes. There was a corner store next to his apartment that had been there for 40 years. He had known the owners for most of his life and he was always greeted with a smile and some kind of satirical remark about life. The store felt just as much like home as his apartment.

When the man who had been sitting in his car finishing a sandwich saw Gavin go into the corner store, he got out and entered the apartment building. It didn't take him long to reach the one he was looking for. He sprayed a little WD40 on the doorknob and in cracks to stop the mechanism from squeaking and alerting his target of his presence.

Maggie was finishing up the pasta and turned the burner down on the oven off to stop the boiling water. She didn't hear the door open or even notice that a strange man walking towards her in the kitchen. It was strange luck that she knocked a spoon on the floor, bent down to pick it up, and saw the man pull a gun. But it was a stubborn instinct that made her not panic. His hand was not very steady so when he fired, the first shot missed. Maggie immediately reacted by grabbing the pot of hot water and pasta and throwing it on him, distracting him just enough to try and get away.

With his eyes shut, he fired in every direction that he heard sounds. He finally hit her. She made it to the bedroom and locked the door, then she fell to the floor in a pool of blood that dripped from her shoulder like a geyser. The man finally composed himself and made his way to the bedroom door. He shot the lock and doorknob off to get inside, as soon he opened the door and saw Maggie bleeding in her right left shoulder above her heart.   He pointed his gun at her again, but was met with a surprise. She had found Gavin's service weapon and like a seasoned pro fired it at his chest. They ended up firing at the same. She put three bullets in center mass just like she was taught, killing him instantly. He put another bullet in her, it didn't kill her, however, it was a gut shot and started to bleed profusely. She just leaned up against the side of the bed and slowly bled out, putting her hands on the two new wounds and trying to keep pressure.

Gavin was still inside the corner store chatting with the owner when he stopped in mid-sentence and said "Did you hear that...sounded like gunfire." That's when he panicked and instinct took over. He put his stuff down on the counter and ran out of the store and as fast he could make his way back to his apartment. He had his small service weapon still in the ankle holster and had it out when he entered his apartment. His heart was pounding fast to go along with the fear that took hold of him when he couldn't find Maggie. He finally saw the dead man with a gun on the ground next to him and that's when he looked to see Maggie breathing heavy and spitting up blood. She was about to pass out when Gavin rushed to her side and tried to keep her awake. She couldn't really speak from the blood she was spitting up, she kept choking on it as she too tried to say something. Gavin called 911 and gave them his badge number so they could rush an ambulance to his place, but one had already been called by the neighbors. Some of them were in the hallway taken over by their morbid curiosity. As they waited for the medics he was applying pressure to her wounds, but she was bleeding out too fast.

She kept drifting in and out of consciousness. Her body was turning cold. She kept trying to say something and Gavin kept telling her to save her energy, but she finally found the strength to get a single word out..."why." Gavin didn't know how to answer that...he knew that this had to do with him. He was gripped with guilt and could barely move. Finally, two medics and a couple of police officers arrived. The officers helped Gavin get out of the way so the medics could work on her, but the look in their eyes said it all...Gavin knew they were already thinking she was too far gone.

They worked on her a few minutes before she finally passed out. Her pulse was gone and they had to use the paddles to try and zap her heart back. They tried five times, each time at a higher voltage, but

they couldn't get her back. Finally, one of the medics was going to call
the time of death. Gavin in a fit of rage didn't want to believe it and
rushed back over, performing CPR on her. Tears were streaming down
his face. At first the medics let him work on her, knowing that it was
part of the grieving process, but after a few minutes they and the police
officers had to make him stop. Gavin couldn't let her go…he couldn't
let go of her body. He couldn't let them take her away…in those
moments, she was still his and she wasn't dead. Gavin wouldn't accept
it…after all, he didn't see it happen beforehand. It just couldn't be true.
Even one who can see the future can still have denial.

∞∞∞∞∞∞∞∞∞∞

The Old Man was sitting at his desk sipping his bourbon
quietly. The reports he was reading were not very interesting, but
necessary to his overall plans. He would have to move again, It seemed
that he was always on the move, but in his line of work, you couldn't
stay in one place for very long. He had been in Chicago longer than
most places, but in a few days he would be gone for good.
There was a knock at the door, it was his assistant. He brought
a note into the room and handed it to the Old Man. He wasn't pleased
by what he read, but as he took out a lighter to burn the note so there
was not any evidence, he commented out loud, "well, at least he killed
the girl." He looked at his assistant and said. I need a cleaner…please
make the arrangements. Our Man needs to be gone. After his assistant
left the room and called the 1st person in his contacts on his cell phone.
After one ring the person on the other end answered and the Old Man
said. "It was a success more or a less, but he's also dead, so there may
be a problem with the units. We'll have to test them and find out for
sure." The man on the other end of the simply asked. " What about the
other one…any problems?"

∞∞∞∞∞∞∞∞∞∞

Agent Main arrived to find the scene at Agent Donnelly's
apartment crowded. There were a lot police cars along with an
ambulance. She didn't know the full details yet, just that there had
been bee a shooting. And because it involved an FBI agent, a few other
agents were there as well waiting to get a statement for the office of
professional review. She finally made her way to his apartment and
found Gavin's cousin, Alex standing outside the door. He was the
supervising officer since it was a homicide. When she saw him she

[530]

knew someone was dead. There was a small part of her that feared the worst when it came to her partner.

"What happened," she asked Alex.

"Somebody broke in and shot Maggie…she held on long enough to put three bullets in the shooter, using his service weapon."

Agent Main tried to keep her composure, but sympathy washed her face. "What about Gavin?

"He's fine physically, wasn't even here when it happened?

"What do you mean he's fine physically?"

"He's still sitting in his bedroom and won't let anybody take her body. He's just been holding on to her as if she's not really dead. The paramedics tried to take the body and he pointed a gun at them. "

"Is that why I'm here?"

"Among other reasons…maybe you can talk him down. You're his partner, after all."

Rachel could feel all the eyes in the room staring at her as if she had the answer to what to do next. Nobody knew what to do with Gavin especially with a gun nearby. While everybody was waiting for her to do something about her partner, the FBI agents there were already bagging up evidence. Rachel noticed that they had her purse in an evidence bag and she asked to see it. Alex gave her a strange look and she responded. "You can tell a lot from what's inside a woman's purse… there might be a clue to the motive. ." As she rummaged through the purse, she found the sonogram with today's date on it. The professional demeanor disappeared from her and Alex and was replaced with sadness over two lives being lost that night. Rachel wondered if Gavin even new…probably not since the picture was still in her purse and not on his refrigerator or desk, and she also knew this was not the time to tell him.

She walked past everybody and entered the bedroom. Gavin didn't even look up, the shock still clung to him the decaying air in the room. She saw the gun and was smart enough to not try and take it away. She said. "Gavin, I'm sorry for what happened…is there anything I can get you?" He looked up but didn't answer.

"Gavin, this is a crime scene now. let the CSI team do their job."

He gave her a dirty look and replied. "They can wait."

"Gavin, how long do they have to wait…they can't wait all night. I know this is hard, but we're still professionals and this is a crime scene…let me help you. Tears streamed down his face. He was helpless, trying to find the answer to why this happened. But all he felt was anger…he was angry because he didn't see this happening. However, he knew deep inside what the right thing to do was …he handed the gun to his partner so she could give it to the CSI team.

[531]

Rachel helped her partner off the bed and walked him out of the room past the cold lingering eyes of Chicago cops and FBI Agents, all of whom wanted to put the blame for Maggie's Death on Gavin. She was going to take him to her place to get cleaned up and hopefully some sleep. She told the Agent in Charge that Gavin's statement could wait when the OPR meeting was scheduled. There wasn't any argument with that. As they walked past Detective Alex Donnelly, Rachel looked at him directly in the eyes as serious anybody could be and replied.

"I don't want any *jurisdicti*onal crap over this, I want both bodies sent to Dr. Kendrick at the FBI Medical Examiners."

Alex shook his head. "This is still a murder of a Chicago Resident in our neighborhood."

"Yes it is and involving an FBI agent. I can go over your head if you want to do this pissing contest, but you're not going to win."

"Maybe not, but we have to take care of our own when it comes to victims in our neighborhood…you don't understand the problems it will cause if the FBI takes over."

She paused, not wanting to relent on the matter, but she changed her tone. "I will keep you in the loop and you can tell people that you're working with the FBI."

"I guess that's good enough."

She smiled. "It's gonna have to be."

Rachel walked Gavin out the apartment building past snooping neighborhoods and members of the press that had gotten the call to cover the shooting. As Rachel was helping Gavin into the car she did notice that Haley O'Brien from the Tribune. Haley was shocked to see Gavin with blood stains all over his white button down shirt. She hadn't gotten all the details of what happened, but after seeing Gavin walk out the building she feared the worst. She tried to ask Rachel what happened, but the only answer she got was "Not now." Rachel drove off with her partner in the car. She sped through the streets of Chicago trying to avoid the storm that was coming.

Gavin still hadn't been to her new apartment and she hadn't had it for very long. She had not really settled in yet, there were still plenty of unpacked boxes in the living room. Gavin was still walking in a daze. When they walked into the apartment the first thing he noticed was the whiskey bottles on the bar area connected to the kitchen. He immediately walked over and grabbed a bottle and then started looking through the cabinets to find a glass. All he could find was a coffee mug.

He poured himself a drink and downed it quickly. Then he poured another and did the same thing trying to dull the pain that wrapped him like a cold blanket. He didn't want to feel anything.

Rachel wasn't bothered by this, even though it was rude to just start going through people's things, she understood. As Gavin was about to take another drink, she spoke up. "I understand it's easier to forget the pain with that bottle and you can do that if you want…I'm not going to stop you, but you need sleep too. " He stared at her, trying to decide if she was right or wrong about, but he didn't argue. He took one more drink and then put the bottle down and replied. "You may be right, I'll take the couch. "

She smiled. "That's nice of you, but this is my place…I get to decide where you sleep…You need a bed tonight…I don't mind taking the couch." After she said that, she led him to the bedroom and sat him down on the bed. Gavin was a little nervous. Normally in these kinds of situation he would already be kissing and undressing her. Rachel even wondered if he would try just to feel something other than pain. A part of her, deep down wanted him to and a part of him wanted it as well, but he knew that he would be crossing a line and betraying her memory. She just helped him take his shoes off and he just stared at her. That was fine with her as well. Eventually he closed his eyes and fell asleep, too tired to even take off his shirt covered in blood.

∞∞∞∞∞∞∞∞∞∞

Byers was sitting on a park bench drinking coffee. He was waiting on a phone call while looking around to see if anybody as watching him. He thought to himself… you could never be too careful these days, even though most people this time of night could care less about a man sitting alone on a park bench. Finally the phone rang. Byers answered and said. "Sir, sorry for the unscheduled call, but I think you should know. Maggie, Agent's Donnelly's girlfriend…the one still married to Jimmy McManus is dead."

The voice on the other end asked. "How?"

"Apparently an assassin was sent there to kill him, at least that's what we think, He wasn't there and the gunman killed her.

"How does this affect our plans with him?"

"Not to be cold, but this is a good thing…this is the kind of the thing that will push him closer to the edge…closer to being able to read… ready to see."

"You may be right, but let him come to you…don't rush it with Agent Donnelly. All of this is too important; he has to be ready when he finally wants to be."

Byers nodded in agreement. "I understand."

[533]

15

     Gavin finally woke up. Even being groggy and not fully awake, he could tell it was dark outside. It felt like he didn't get much sleep, but how wrong he was. He had slept 24 hours and after checking to see what time it was, he thought it must have been a mistake. When he emerged from the bedroom, he found his partner in her living room with case files and crimes photos all over the place. She had moved their office into her apartment. Gavin still felt like he was walking around in a dream. Rachel looked up from the photos she was looking at and simply said. "I put coffee on, you should make yourself a cup…you look like hell."

     He tried to smile. "What time is it?"

     "It's about 7:30."

     "I guess I got more than just a few hours of sleep. I usually wake up at 6:00am like clockwork."

     "Gavin, it's 7:30 at night"

     "You let me sleep throughout the day, why"

     She got up to pour herself and Gavin a cup of coffee. "I let you sleep because you needed it… because it might be the first good night sleep you've had in months."

     "But I need to get back to work and find out why she was killed and hopefully solve this whole fucking case."

     And you need to do that with fresh eyes…another reason I let you sleep. So if you want to get to work, then get a cup of coffee, take a shower, and we'll get to it. "

He wanted to argue with her and stay mad because she let him sleep, but the drive to find his answers made him keep quiet. He just smiled at her and took the cup of coffee she offered. He also looked at the bloody shirt that he never bothered changing from the night before and commented. "I'm pretty sure, I ruined your sheets."

She laughed. "I can always buy more…. the sheet isn't important"

Gavin did take a shower, in fact, he took a long one. The long streams of hot water felt good as if they were washing away his sins. His bloody shirt was put in the trash and he found a pair of blue jeans and a Chicago Cubs T-shirt. He felt like a new man, even if he didn't shave or really comb his hair properly. As he begins to drink a fresh cup of coffee, he looked around the room and saw the images of the victims, but there was only one question on his mind.

"Where are Maggie's and the shooter's bodies…Chicago PD didn't get them, did they?"

Rachel took a sip of her coffee. "No, I didn't have any problem with the jurisdiction, the bodies are in our crime labs. Dr. Kenrick is doing the autopsies."

"Has anybody Identified him yet?"

"No….we can't find anything

He chuckled. "Doesn't matter anyway…he's probably a ghost! Do you have anything new about the congressman and these murders?"

Rachel got out of her chair and walked towards her make shift crime board that had the photos hanging up. "There's no new information, but there is something that bothers me about these shootings and it's been bothering me for a while."

"Okay, sounds like you have a theory."

She smiled ."I do… if your aim is to execute people with a gun why tip the bullets with some kind of poison…the bullets are going to kill your victim… unless… you definitely need to make sure they die."

"Isn't the poison about torturing the victim?"

Rachel smiled. "That's what I originally thought too. But torture is about making somewhere suffer and suffer over a long period of time so that you can inflict as much pain as possible. Most serial killers get off on it. But the substance that we found acts fast…if this was supposed to be torture then it's a terrible way to do it…I don't think this is torture at all"

"Then what is it?"

"The poison is to ensure that they die if the bullet doesn't kill them."

Gavin had a surprised look, not fully understanding what she was trying to tell him. Rachel continued to tell her partner her theory.

"I looked at McClain's shooting record…he was one of the best shots on the police force." She showed Gavin pictures of shooting targets. "Look at the grouping…he's good enough to be secret service…you agree?"

He smiled as he looked at the target. "You're right… he's a marksman."

"Then why use poison if your shots are good enough to kill someone? Does he strike you as someone that couldn't kill with a single shot?.

"What are you really trying to say…spit it out.

"Either it's not really Bobby McClain or something happened to him affecting his reflexes and if the second option is true, then maybe it's something he's still being treated for."

Gavin chuckled. "And if he is being treated, then maybe we can find him if we find out where he's receiving treatment. So we start looking for medical records."

Rachel smiled. "Exactly! Because he's the one thing that connects everything…from the victims to our missing congressman and he will probably be the only one who can tell us why this is happening. It appears that we have to catch Bobby McClain to solve our own case,"

"But that also means we have to find him first because if Chicago PD does, they will kill him on sight. "

Rachel laughed. "I think you were right all along…the FBI has to take over the Bobby McClain case in order to solve it correctly and solve our case at the same time."

"However, there's something else that doesn't make sense. Jimmy mentioned Simon O'Connor as the key to finding the congressman… if that's true, then how does Bobby McClain connect to him.

"We are talking about mob connections…your friend Jimmy was connected to both of them"

Gavin paused for a moment. "It's what he was doing with them that concerns me! I don't think it was the usual business that he was in. It would have to be something really bad if Jimmy feared for his life so much that he called me to get him out of prison.

Rachel had a curious look. "What's worse than the usual smuggling and racketeering and the turf wars that go with it?"

There was a little fear in Gavin's tone. "I don't' know if I want to know the answer, but then again. I need to know the answer. "

Rachel went to the kitchen cabinet and got a travel coffee mug. "Then let's go find out. It's time your friend Jimmy earned his Keep!"

Gavin knew it was a good idea, but he was reluctant to go. He didn't want to have to tell him about Maggie yet, but like his uncle

Liam always said…the best way to get over fear was to do it quickly before you really had a chance to think about it. Other people just called it the Band Aid method.

∞∞∞∞∞∞∞∞∞∞

The Agents drove up the safe house that had Jimmy stashed in. Gavin paused for a moment, trying to delay the moment as long as he could, but eventually he knocked in the door when his partner gave him a look of urgency. Jimmy was watching the White Sox game with the marshals… the Sox were losing as usual, so he wasn't happy and didn't acknowledge Gavin when he walked through the door. Finally, Gavin said something.

"Jimmy, I need to talk to you…something bad happened."

He didn't say anything for a moment, but finally replied to Gavin. "Well…what is it."

"I hate that I am telling you this, but Maggie was killed last night."

Shock washed over Jimmy's face. "What do you mean she was killed…how?'

"She was shot…at my place."

The shock turned to rage. Jimmy could hardly get the words out…at your place…what the fuck was she doing at your place?"

"That doesn't matter…what matters is how she was killed."

"Fuck You…it does matter?"

"Somebody sent a guy to kill me and I wasn't there…she was and the guy killed her instead, but not before she put three bullets in him."\

Jimmy tried to control his rage, but couldn't and lunged laying a good right hook on Gavin and knocking him down. Rachel and the Marshals grabbed Jimmy and stopped him from doing anything. Jimmy just screamed. "This is your fault…you got her killed.

"Why did I get her killed?"

"Because of what you're investigating…that's why! I didn't think they would kill her or try a second time after I went away, but you brought her back into this when you started sleeping with her."

Gavin didn't say anything for a moment. He was surprised to hear him say that. "You knew?"

"Of course I did… I could tell the last time she visited…I guess she forgot to tell me that it was truly over."

Gavin didn't have a response to that. The shock still draped over his face. Rachel finally said something. "Jimmy…you said they…who is they?"

[537]

Jimmy didn't want to answer the question. He had been playing a good game of stalling them, but time was running out so he answered the question. "The people I used to work for."

"You mean the guy you told us about…Simon O'Connor?"

"Yes, and the people that he works for."

Finally, Gavin spoke up. "Who does he work for?"

"I don't know their names…they don't have names, that's what makes them powerful people."

"If you don't know their names then how do you know he works for these so called mythical people."

Jimmy got angry. "Because everybody works for somebody…we all have a boss…someone who pulls our strings."

Gavin paused again. "Then it's time to really start helping me. This is all about smuggling so tell me what's being smuggled?

" I can't tell you that."

"Then we're done and you're going back in."

Jimmy got angry. "Fuck you. I gave you the only name you need to know…you find him and you find your answers…believe me that's all you need."

"That's not good enough anymore."

Jimmy didn't say anything…he just stared at his friend with disdain. Rachel was going to ask a question when her phone started ringing. It was AD Foster. When she answered there was no small talk. All he told her was to come by the office that evening and to get there as quick as she could with her partner. She told Gavin that it was time to go. As they were walking out Gavin looked at Jimmy and said. "You get a reprieve, but the next time I ask what you were smuggling, you better have an answer or you're going back in." Jimmy just gave his old friend a dirty look knowing that he couldn't put him off forever. It was only a matter of time that he would have to tell Gavin his dreadful secret and even his world would be destroyed.

∞∞∞∞∞∞∞∞∞∞

It took about thirty minutes to get to downtown and arrive at the FBI building. The office was still busy even though it was at night, but like all law enforcement in Chicago at the time, they too, were on alert with a copy killer on the loose and a missing congressman, and now one of their own had murder in his own home. All hands were on deck Agent Donnelly and Agent Main walked into AD Foster's office and found that the three of them were not alone. He didn't look FBI…that was Agent Main's first impression. AD Foster spoke

[538]

"Agent Donnelly, good to see you up and around, but because of the circumstances, I have to give you limited duty until you see OPR. You can work, but you have to do from the office."

Agent Donnelly wasn't too surprised by a little annoyed. "We're still investigating the Congressman's abduction, correct?"

"Yes"

"Then how I am supposed to do my job from the office. "

AD Foster looked at both of the agents. "You two will have to figure that out."

Finally, Agent Main spoke. "We will figure out how to do our jobs, but right now I'm curious who's joining us?"

The mysterious man gave her a stern look. AD Foster answered. "This is Agent Steven Cranston…He's a customs agent…he's here to talk to you two."

Agent Cranston finally spoke up. "Agent Donnelly, Agent Main you were flagged when you tried to access the file of one Simon O'Connor. What is your interest in him?"

The agents were a bit surprised to say the least. Agent Main was suspicious, so she answered the question with a question. "Why do you want to know…he's not involved in an interagency investigation is he?"

"Agent Main, his file is very sensitive and you don't have enough clearance to see his file so answer my question…what is your interest in him?"

"How about you answer my question first?"

AD Foster was about to tell her to stop dodging the question, but Agent Cranston interrupted him. "Fine, he's a government asset, so naturally we're curious when someone is looking into him."

The agents were even more surprised to hear that about Simon O'Connor and even though they were still suspicious, they decided to cooperate. Agent Donnelly replied. "The name was given to us as part of your investigation."

"And what are you investigating?"

AD Foster explained to Agent Cranston what their assignment was. Now he was a bit surprised and so he had to ask the agents. "Why would his name come up in a missing person's case…who gave you the name. "They didn't want to answer the question, but after some prodding by AD Foster, they finally relented. Agent Donnelly responded. "An informant for us by the name of Jimmy McManus."

Agent Cranston started laughing. "Of course he would give you that name. He would sell out his own mother if it got him out of prison, but it doesn't make him very credible."

"So you say…as soon as we tried to get his file you show up…that tells he must be important."

Agent Cranston smiled. "He is important to us, but not you."

"I disagree…we need to talk to him in connection to a missing congressman."

"Well, that's not going to happen…not with our say so. Whatever reason you want to talk to him, I guarantee you that it's not important for us to let you talk to him."

Agent Main replied before partner could. "Are you trying to tell us that a missing congressman is not enough of a priority for us to get to talk to your guy."

"No…congressman come and go…that's why we have elections. And Simon O' Conner is way too important to our operations. The Intel that he provides is a matter of National Security… more important than your missing congressman."

Agent Donnelly started shaking his head. "So let me get this straight., he gives you intel and he still gets to be a criminal doing anything he wants to do! Sounds like a lot horseshit to me."

"You don't have to like it Agent Donnelly, you just have to accept it. I'm here to tell you that you are not to have any contact with him."

"And what if I just tell you to go fuck yourself…we're going to talk to whoever we have to solve our case."

Agent Cranston. "I'm sure the Irish in you will cause you to say that at first, but here's something that will change your mind." He handed each agent a copy of a court order from the Justice Department forbidding you from picking him up or talking with him. Each agent looked at the documents and pretty much had the same reaction…anger and disappointment. There wasn't anything left to say, the court order said it all. Agent Donnelly did let slip one "Go Fuck Yourself!" Agent Cranston laughed with a sense of victory and then excused himself, leaving the agent with copies of the court order and to ponder what their next move would be.

After he left, Agent Donnelly spoke up first. "What the fuck was that?

AD Foster replied. "That's a very clear message to stay away."

"Well obvious we can't"

"You have to. If you violate this court order, then not only do you get suspended, you go to jail."

Rachel finally spoke. "You guys don't find it strange that he immediately showed up with a court order telling us that we can't talk to him…He's not from customs."

Agent Donnelly replied. "What do you mean?"

"If he's an informant for another agency then he would have been flagged in the system and we would have just gotten a phone call or email asking us what this was about. The agent running him wouldn't have shown up late at night in person and with a court order saying we couldn't talk to him. I've had to question other agency's informants before and this has never happened. Simon O' Connor is protected by a more powerful agency than customs or even us."

AD Foster replied. "She's right and there's only one agency that has that kind of power…the CIA

Agent Donnelly was surprised to say the least. He had never dealt with this before. In many ways he was still inexperienced when it came to dealing with the truly horrific criminals. He only had one question. "Now what?"

AD Foster replied. "You will have to get another lead because the only way you can get a chance to talk with this guy if you arrest him and talk to him before his lawyer or the CIA shows up."

"So I guess looking at his file is definitely out of the question."

"Through normal channels, yes, but I'm sure your hacker friend can help you get around that." Both agents gave AD Foster a surprised look." Agent Donnelly replied. "How do you know about her?"

"This is Chicago Agent Donnelly…the walls are thin and filled with whispers. There's not much I don't know."

He reminded Agent Donnelly about his meeting with OPR in the morning and then dismissed. As they were walking out Agent Donnelly looked at his partner. "You think we should leave it alone?"

Her face was stone cold serious. "Absolutely not…if he's that protected by another agency then I want to talk to him and they certainly don't get to come into my house to tell me that we can't talk to him. Besides, if he's connected to the Congressman in any way, then we have to talk to him."

He smiled. "Good, I was hoping you would say that!"

"I don't always follow the rules Gavin…I just don't ignore them as much as you."

16

Jimmy was lying on the Bed watching the White Sox Game. He was entranced doing his best to ignore the clicking sounds from the Marshall's pen. It was beyond annoying. It was infuriating, but he was in no position to demand him to stop. There was a knock at the door. It was unusual to get a knock this late at night unless it was the agents and they would have gotten a text message to let them know they were coming. The other Marshall grabbed his gun and asked who knocked. A voice answered. "I'm with hotel maintenance…need to check the plumbing…we've had complaints about some of the rooms."

The Marshal replied. "We're good. You can move on."

"Sir, I need to check it now…if there's a problem and we don't fix it then we won't be able to get to it later and you're really going to be screwed."

The Marshall didn't like the answer, but he opened the door anyway. Jimmy immediately recognized the face and he tried to hide it, but the Marshal who had been clicking his pen read his poker face. Before he could do anything the maintenance guy hit the Marshal who opened the door with a Plumbers wrench knocking him out. The other Marshal tried to raise his gun and shoot, but Jimmy tried to tackle him. He wasn't very successful as the Marshal hit him with the butt of his gun and knocked him down. As he was about to raise his gun again to shoot a second man quickly entered the room and pointed his gun at the Marshall.

In a determined tone, he said. "Try it and I will blow your fucking head off." The looked down at the Jimmy. "Are you okay?"

Jimmy laughed. "Yeah I'm fine…he hits like a woman."

The Marshall responded to all three of them. "You're not going to get away with this."

"We already have, fuckwad."

The Marshall looked at Jimmy. "You run, they will gun you down."

"Let them try." He grabbed the gun from the Marshall's hand and smacked him until he fell unconscious. Then the three men gathered the Marshall's and tied them up. Jimmy looked at the two men. "Jack, Colin…thanks for coming to get me. So my plan worked"

Colin replied. "Perfects… we were able to get a tracker on Agent Main's car during the other night during all the chaos in Gavin's apartment. It was easy.

Jack spoke up. "We're sorry about Maggie. It's a terrible thing, but me and the boys put together a plan. Gavin will be dead soon and the body will disappear."

Jimmy smiled. "Thank you lads…much appreciated. But no one touches him. If anybody is going to put a bullet in his head, it should be me. Besides, he's still useful to me." The two men nodded in agreement and then they left escaping like a shadow in the night.

∞∞∞∞∞∞∞∞∞∞∞∞

The water was restless outside the porthole of the cabin Simon O'Connor was staying in. He was fond of staring out of the window. The water calmed him. It had done that ever since his childhood growing up in a fishing village off the coast of Ireland. They were behind schedule and every moment counted with the move him and crew were trying to make. It was the biggest gamble he had ever made among his criminal activities.

One of his men knocked on his cabin door. He had a message for the boss. Simone let him in and hastily took the message. Anger washed over his face. His man asked what happed. Simon replied. "Jimmy McManus escaped custody. He's on the loose."

The man responded. "What can he really do. The Marshall's and FBI will be after him. The manhunt will just be as big as that cop killers"

"Maybe, but he's more dangerous than we give him credit for. Having him loose and still alive is a problem I could do without.

∞∞∞∞∞∞∞∞∞∞∞∞

The hotel room was crawling with local Chicago PD and the US Marshal service when Agent Donnelly and Agent Main arrived on the scene. As an active crime scene they were trying to get fingerprints to see who would have helped Jimmy escape. There were no prints. One of the Marshals commented that he was surprised, he didn't

[543]

expect them to be smarter than the low-life hoods ran with. Agent Donnelly asked who was in charge. A Marshal by the name of Simpson said he was and before Agent Donnelly could ask for a status report the Marshal starting berating him.

"So you're the FBI agent who 'fubared' this situation."

∞∞∞∞∞∞∞∞∞∞

Agent Donnelly was about to say something wen his partner chimed in. "Hey, you want to blame someone, how about the two incompetent assholes you had guarding him…never let someone in unless you know them….it doesn't take a genius to figure that out."

The Marshal replied. "Well, we wouldn't have picked a place that they could easily find."

Agent Donnelly sarcastically laughed. "Now that have shown who has the biggest dick around here or is it show everybody who is the biggest dick, sorry, I get that part confused…why don't you give us a status report so we can help find the prisoner."

The Marshal flipped him off before he replied. "The status is your man's gone and we don't have any prints…good luck figuring out who did this and where they might be going."

Agent Donnelly continued to be sarcastic. "OK Mr. Helpful, then we'll actually be detectives and get answers since that concept escapes you." The agents walked over to the to where the two injured Marshals were getting patched up my paramedics. They didn't have time for small talk. They didn't have time to ask if they were alright. They simply asked. "Did you see their faces?"

One of the Marshal's replied. "I saw one of them before he knocked me out. He was about six feet tall. Had a scar on his forehead. Had a muddled Irish accent."

Agent Donnelly asked. "Did you see his tattoos?"

"Oh yeah…he had a Celtic Cross on his left arm and what looked like a fight Irishman logo on his right hand."

Agent Donnelly smiled. "Colin McKelly….bookie, drug dealer, smuggler…one of Jimmy's men."

Agent Main responded. "You know him."

"Yep…he's from the neighborhood. He's been running with Jimmy since he was fifteen. He's been seen around the Pub sometimes. Probably hit on you."

She smiled. "If he did, I don't remember."

"Oh, you would remember… his line to women is 'don't look so down, you just need to feel the luck of the Irish…I can help.'"

"What dumb broad would fall for that?

[544]

"You'd be surprised how that line actually works."

"Well, do you know where to find them?"

"I know a few places, but I guarantee they won't be there.....Jimmy's in the wind now and he's got too many people that can hide him that will definitely not talk to us."

Marshal Simpson walked over and asked if they got anything that could help them find the escaped prisoner. Agent Donnelly shook his head no. "You won't find him…I hate to say it, but he's gone for good. "

"That's bullshit… I don't accept that."

"You better learn to live with disappointment then." The Marshal didn't respond to the comment, he just told the agent that a note was left for him."

Agent Donnelly unfolded the paper and held the note out so he and partner could both read it…

"Gavin, sorry it had to be this way. Hope I didn't cause too much trouble for you. If I ever see you again, the whiskey is definitely on me. Also, meant what I said. If you find Simon O'Connor, you'll find your answers.

All of sudden a blinding light washed over Gavin and his head started to hurt, but he started to flash, something he hadn't done in a while. *He could see a desk in a small office and what appeared to be a porthole window right above. On the desk was spreadsheets with numbers, but they didn't make sense. All he saw was HMMU next to numbers, it was gibberish and just when he was about to start memorizing numbers, he felt his partner shaking him and asking if he was alright.*

Agent Main was propping her partner up as he was shaking his head. "What happened…did you have another one of those headaches again?"

"Yes…not too bad this time." He looked around and found a pen and quickly scribbled the words and the numbers he did see. "

Agent Main asked. "What is that?"

"Probably nothing."

She had a disconcerting look on her face "I was going to say…you need to see a doctor."

"I have been, but I can't tell if he's helping or not?

As they started to walk out of the crime scene, one of the Marshal's yelled and said that they can't take the note. Agent Donnelly sarcastically replied. "Request it from my office…we'll fax it back to you."

As they were getting the car Agent Main asked. "Now what?"

"Now…we find out who this Simon O'Connor really is!" He pulled out his cell phone and found a number in his contacts. The name listed was a strange one, almost like a code. He called and when the other side answered. "Hi…this is Gavin…I need to order a Pizza…Chicago Deep Dish…the works."

∞∞∞∞∞∞∞∞∞∞∞∞

Gavin's apartment was still a crime scene so he stayed at his partner's place while everything was being sorted out. He slept on the couch this time, but he didn't really get any sleep. When Rachel walked out of the bedroom to make coffee she found Gavin sitting on the couch looking through their files. The coffee was already made. She asked. "Did you get any sleep?"

He gave her a sarcastic laugh. "Not much… I got most of my sleep yesterday, so I'm good. "

She poured herself a cup of coffee. "What are you working on?"

"I'm trying to figure out how Bobby McClain is picking his victims…I can't find a pattern except that they all worked at the ninth precinct, but that's the problem…there's been thousands of cops that have worked there over the last fifty years."

"What about the cops associated with Congressman McMahon when he was a cop."

Gavin smiled. "That Narrows it down, but we still have two problems. First that's 118 cops. Second, two of the victims didn't work with him"

"So no discernable pattern"

"No and to make things worse, there's nothing remarkable about the victims or anything that stands out. They were typical Chicago cops…clean records, a few accommodations and they did a tour at the ninth."

Rachel thought for a moment. "Maybe it's not about trying to figure out how he's picking his victims. Maybe it's trying to figure out where he's going to be next."

"If I could figure out the pattern, then maybe we have a shot at that."

She laughed. "Yes…I know…but I have a better idea. Remember the substance on found on the bullet casings."

"Yeah"

"Who would make something like that…who would he go to for that."

[546]

"There's probably only a handful of people that make something like that."

"Exactly. Find that person... stake him out, then maybe we have a shot of catching McClain when picks up more bullets."

Gavin paused. "If he goes back."

"I'm not saying it's not a long shot, but I bet he has to get resupplied one or two more times before he's done. Does it feel like he's close to being done?"

"No...feels like this is just the beginning."

"Yes it does and like you said, there's a lot of cops that worked at the ninth and worked with Fitzgerald."

Suddenly there was a knock at the door. It was still pretty early so the agents were surprised to have somebody at the door. Gavin's first instinct was to grab his other service revolver. With all that he had been through the past couple of days no one could be surprised by his actions. Rachel went to the bedroom and got hers as well. Gavin, with his gun pointed at the door, asked who it was. The voice, which was female, replied. "It's the pizza lady."

Gavin and Rachel both looked surprised. After all, who would be delivering pizza this early in the morning. Finally, Gavin remembered the phone call he made last night. He opened the door and it was Janie Myers, the hacker. She actually had a Gino's Pizza box and one of their hats to look the part. She looked at the two agents.

"Sorry to interrupt your morning. Looks like you two are having fun."

Rachel gave her a dirty look. She knew how it looked... she was wearing workout shorts and an NYU T-shirt. Gavin had the same thing on except he was wearing his Cubs T-shirt. They both looked like they had gotten out of bed together. Gavin replied to here. It's a little early to be delivering this. Pizza joints aren't open yet...not even in Chicago."

Janie gave him a dirty look." I usually work at night and sleep during the day during normal hours. I'm delivering this before I go to bed,"

Gavin asked. "What do I owe you?"

"It's already been taken care of. You should put most of your money in savings and not all it in your checking account. "

"You hacked me?"

"Of course, but since you're a government employee and don't have much money, I did this cheap. Only ten grand."

He was shocked." 10 Grand, I can't afford that."

"I know. That's why I hacked the company that owns your building and paid your rent for a year. It will show that you paid a year in advance and signed another year lease."

Gavin was even more shocked. "As a government employee that kind of thing makes me look like I'm up to something illegal."

Janie laughed. "Not the way I did it. You will be fine."

Rachel started shaking her head. "I never had to do this kind of stuff until I moved to Chicago."

Janie laughed. "It's been my experience, there's no difference between criminals and law enforcement in this town…especially FEDS."

Gavin chucked. A lot of times that could be true. He replied. "Thank You for dropping this off. Want a cup of coffee?"

Janie gave him a weird look. "No, I don't want to be around FEDS any more than I have to. Besides…I don't want to be the third wheel in whatever this is."

Rachel wanted to respond to her comment about FEDS especially with her having some kind of strange relationship with an FBI Agent. Before she could say anything, Janie was already out the door. Like most hackers, she didn't socialize much and she would leave as quickly as she arrived.

17

It was early…too early for most people to be at work, but AD Foster always arrived before anybody else. He was the boss, the first to arrive and the last to leave. That was his philosophy. However, on this morning, he was greeted by two of his agents waiting in his office. It caught him by surprise. As he walked in and put his briefcase down he responded.

"Agent Main…Agent Donnelly, I hope you have something good. You should if you're here this early."

Agent Donnelly chuckled. "Yes, sir, we have a lead."

"But you still haven't found the Congressman…wait…no…you haven't or I would have heard about it on CNN this morning. Are you any closer to finding him?"

Agent Main replied. "We think so, sir, but you probably won't like the connection we've made."

AD Foster sighed. "This has something to do with Bobby McClain…doesn't it?"

Agent Donnelly gave him a sarcastic smile; it was his way of telling him yes. AD Foster replied. "Well Shit…something told me that we couldn't keep that out of our office. What do you got?"

Agent Main started to explain everything. She took the lead on this because she figured it would sound better from her.

After a few minutes AD Foster responded. "Okay, let me get his straight…the connection with the congressman, Bobby McClain, and the victims is that they all worked at the 9th precinct, but Bobby McClain wasn't there when McMahon was there. "

Agent Donnelly replied. "No Sir, but McClain moonlighted on his security team when he was an Alderman in that District…so they knew each other in that way."

"Okay, but McClain's Victims…did any of them work with the congressman at the 9th?"

"Only two Sir."

"So the rest of the victims are connected to McMahon except they worked at the 9th…that's thin. How do you connect them?"

Agent Main responded. "We still don't know how McClain is picking his victims, but know it has something to do with the 9th"

AD Foster paused for a moment. "It's still not enough to take over the McClain investigation."

Agent Donnelly replied. "I disagree and I think McClain knows where the congressman is dead or alive and I think catching him is the only way we are going to find the congressman."

"Of course you do…but I do question your objectivity in this matter…I warned you not to make it personal." AD Foster looked at Agent Main. "What do you think?"

"I agree with my partner…Congressman McMahon went missing around the same time McClain started killing cops. He was reported missing right after my partner's uncle was shot. This is not a coincidence."

"What makes you think that?"

"I don't believe in coincidences."

AD Foster smiled. "That's not good enough."

Agent Donnelly responded. "Look, we all know that cops in the 9th have protected illegal smuggling operations…what if all of this has something to do with this…what if there is some huge cargo being smuggled through Chicago and these cops all had something to do with it. What if the congressman was a part of it when he was there and help keep cops protected when he was an Alderman?"

"Okay…let's say that's true…what is the motive…to kill those who know about it…leave no witnesses!"

"Exactly!"

"The 9th has been investigated multiple times over the years and nothing has ever been found."

"Just because the FEDS never found anything doesn't make it not true."

AD Foster Smiled. Agent Main pulled out the tablet from her bag and responded. "We also have something else. The name Jimmy McManus gave that we weren't supposed to investigate. "

AD Foster replied. "Before he escaped, thank god, but I can't tell you the shit storm that caused. "

"Well, sir… it's a name that connects everybody." She opened the tablet and handed it to the Assistant Director." He started looking through the files." He was shocked and responded. "Holy Shit…I can see why the agency didn't want you to see his files."

And there it was, plain as day. Simon O'Conner's first contact in Chicago was then Detective McMahon. And then even more shocking, Bobby McClain was a bagman between the congressman and

O'Conner. AD Foster responded. "Okay, that's more than a coincidence, but his untouchable… I mean, you heard the agency man the other night. Even if you can find him, he does business all over the world, how do you know he will be back in Chicago any time soon for you to question him."

Agent Donnelly smiled. "Jimmy said he was already back in Chicago and he never lied to us…just escaped. "

AD Foster chuckled. "Okay…now you've convinced me. And as luck would have it, the US Attorney and the Justice Department have been looking for another reason to investigate the 9th again so you have that going for you, but one thing I might add…for this to work, Bobby McClain has to be taken alive…you have to question him."

Agent Main replied. "I think that goes without saying." She looked her partner. "Is that going to be a problem with Chicago PD?"

He Chuckled. "It won't be easy, but we have to be put in charge and pick the right cops for this task force…ones we can somewhat control and will take orders."

AD Foster responded. "And you know who to assign to this task force."

"I do, sir."

"Okay…then we will get all the paperwork in order today so you can start tonight."

As the Agents were leaving the office, the Assistant Director stopped them and gave them more instructions. "You will have to do a Press Conference…sooner the better, but Agent Main is the lead Agent until OPR clears you Agent Donnelly."

Gavin wasn't happy with that, but understood the protocol. At least he wasn't being assigned a desk. After they walked out of the office, Rachel stopped her partner. "You know, since we have to give a press conference, I have an idea on how we can use them to help out with the problem when it comes to figuring out who McClain is targeting. We let the press know he's targeting cops from the 9th that are connected to him and the congressman…."

The light came on, he understood where she was going with this and finished her statement. "We have a tip line and get who he's targeting to call us. Get the press to help us."

She smiled. "You're finally reading my mind. Yeah, we may get some bogus tips, but we may get at least one of targets."

"But how do we catch him."

'Still working on that. "

∞∞∞∞∞∞∞∞∞∞∞∞

[551]

Liam Donnelly was finally home. After much complaining the hospital finally let him go home, mainly to get him out their hair. He was a terrible patient and that was putting it nicely. He couldn't handle sitting around in bed too long, so the best place for him was at home. And his wife Mary was the best at dealing with how stubborn he could be. Liam hadn't been home very long when he got a phone call. The word finally came down. The FEDS had officially taken over the Bobby McClain case.

Alex had the day off and was there helping his father. Liam gave him a disgusted look still not wanting to believe what had just happened. He said to his son. "You're not going to fucking believe this. "

By the look on his father's face, he already knew the answer. "The FEDS are taking over."

"Yep! And I bet your cousin has something to do with it."

"Maybe not…we don't know for sure."

"You really believe that?"

"I want to but this would be just like him. He has a habit of thinking that his badge gives him the right to intervene in local affairs. "

Liam laughed. "That's an understatement. If he did have something to do with this then trouble is coming his way and I can't stop it this time."

"You mean cops from the neighborhood."

"No, something bigger and more dangerous. No one survives from waking a sleeping dragon, especially in this town."

Alex was taken back a little bit with his father's comment. "What do you know that I don't"

Liam smiled "A lot and that's what has helped keep both of you safe. That's all I can tell you and don't ask any questions." Alex didn't. He knew that tone from his father. He knew well enough to leave things be, no matter how much he didn't like it.

∞∞∞∞∞∞∞∞∞∞∞∞

She couldn't understand why her husband was in such a hurry. He was frantically packing and he wasn't telling her what was going on. She didn't know what to do. He kept urging her to pack the essentials, but she wouldn't do anything until he told her what was going on. He wouldn't, he just kept packing. Finally, she screamed at

[552]

the top of her lungs. It was loud enough for the neighbors to hear in the apartment building and more importantly to get his attention.

He stopped. "Honey, we don't have time for this. I need you to pack some things so we can leave in ten minutes. "

"Why…I won't do anything until you tell me why."

He paused for a moment. Knowing he was wasting time, he relented and told her. "There's a man coming to kill me. I can't tell you everything, but it has something to do from when I was a cop."

His wife was scared now. "What did you do?"

"I'll tell you everything, but I'll do it on the way." He didn't give her time to answer before he reached back in their bedroom closet and found the hidden safe. He opened it and pulled out about twenty thousand in cash and two passports. It was for him and his wife, but under false names. He handed her, the one under her fake name. She was extremely surprised. He could see it in her eye and said. "I will explain everything later, but now we have to run."

She had a ton of questions, but the only one she could get out was…"Where are we going?"

"The Cayman's… I have a couple million dollars there and we'll be safe." She was still too shocked to say anything else so she started packing. Fear gripped her in such a way that she didn't want to question anything else her survival instincts told her deep down to just start packing go with her husband.

As she was packing he went down to their car in the back parking lot of the building." He put his bags in the trunk and then went to the front seat to get the car warmed up. As soon as he put the key in the ignition and turned the car over, it exploded. His wife nearly came out of her head when heard the explosion. Then she looked up and saw the cloud of smoke out their apartment window. She knew what happened and started to cry.

Bobby McClain saw the explosion from across the street. He walked across and entered the building without noticing him as people were coming to see what happened. The pandemonium allowed him to sneak up the stairs to the man and wife's apartment building, When she opened to door to walk out, Bobby was standing there and shot her three times. She fell dead before she really knew what had happened to her.

∞∞∞∞∞∞∞∞∞∞∞∞∞∞

The Knights of Columbus Hall was packed for Maggie's wake. She was well loved and never has a true enemy. So it was not a

[553]

surprise to see so many people there for her. Gavin walked into the hall immediately felt hundreds of disapproving eyes fall upon him. He wasn't as welcomed as he should have been. There were many in the room that saw him as a traitor for sleeping with what they deemed a prisoner's wife. It was a grave offense in the Irish community. Even though she had left Jimmy McManus years ago, they were still not divorced and to serious Catholics, that was still a sin.

Gavin said hi to people, but he got the cold shoulder from most of them. Father Joseph didn't ignore him. He walked over and said. "I'm glad you could come."

Gavin smiled. "You may be the only one in this room."

"Don't worry about everybody else. You're doing what's right…you're paying your respects to the dead."

Alex came over. "Gavin, I didn't think you would actually come. Not exactly friendly territory."

Gavin tried to smile. "I know…I won't stay long and make everybody else uncomfortable."

"You're okay with me…I always have your back."

Gavin patted him on the shoulder as a way of saying Thank You. Then he walked over to the table where Maggie's parents were sitting. Silence fell over everybody. Nobody could believe the gall on Gavin. Maggie's parents stared at him for a moment, but did at least say. "Thank You for coming…it was the least you could do."

Gavin knew it was an insult more than just being polite and perhaps it was deserved. He tried to say something to Maggie's mother, but she wasn't going to be polite. She stood up from her chair and slapped Gavin. It was loud so everybody in the room turned to see what had happened. Shock took over the room, especially Gavin. He didn't know what to do. Her mother angrily said. "You killed her. Don't mistake this as some kind of tragedy, it happened because of you living in sin with her. Maybe God will forgive, but I won't." She pounded on his chest and yelled. "Goddamn you for getting her killed." She kept at it until her husband and son restrained her."

Gavin looked around the room as every eye was fixed on him He was so mortified that he briskly walked out of the hall. He knew he didn't need to be there. Alex followed after him and as they go outside yelled to his cousin. "Hey…you don't have to go. She was wrong to do that."

"No, she wasn't, Alex. She was right. I got her killed. I always thought Jimmy would get her killed, but the joke's on me…I did it. If I was God, I wouldn't forgive me. I don't deserve it.

"That's not true."

"Yeah, it is… it's the truest thing here tonight." Gavin turned around and walked back to his truck and didn't look back. The truck was parked around the corner, hidden from anybody walking into the building which explained why nobody saw the stranger sitting in Gavin's truck. When he opened the door, he jumped a little bit after seeing Byers sitting in the front seat. He said. "Besides being a man in the shadows, I guess unlocking digital car locks is part of the tools of the trade."

Byers laughed. "Yes, we took a whole course on it."

"What the fuck are you doing here?"

"Get inside, we need to talk."

Gavin looked around to see if anybody was watching and climbed into his truck. Byers continued to talk. "You've shouldn't have gotten Jimmy McManus out of prison."

"Oh, now you tell me… maybe you could have stopped him from escaping."

"Him escaping wasn't the biggest problem. Him being alive is the main problem."

"What do you mean?"

"There are a lot of people that needed him dead…not just in my organization."

"Why…what did he know?"

"More than he should have. No offense, he was a low life hustler and peddler…a small time criminal, but you already know that. About nine years ago, he got involved in some operations that were a lot bigger than he was used to…made him a lot of money, but a lot more dangerous and of course found out more than he should have about operations that have been going on for years…the kind that are too big to fail now if you get my meaning!"

Gavin gave him a dirty look. "Quit with the ominous tone and just tell it to me straight…what operations?"

Byers laughed. "You now my deal…I won't tell you all the details…you have to figure things out yourself."

"Bullshit…I don't think you now all the details and you're using me to help you find out."

"You can think that if you want, but I don't have to help you either. Now, what did Jimmy tell you?"

Gavin paused. He just stared at Byers trying to decide if he wanted to continue the conversation. Finally, Byers opened the door. "Okay, have it your way." Gavin relented.

"Simon O'Connor…that was the name he gave me."

Byers smiled. "Of course he did. Well, he didn't lie to you… he gave you a kingpin. The question is why he wouldn't give you a false name just to get out and plan his escape."

"We have his file…I know his history…he's untouchable, which means whatever his dealings are in Chicago are what you call 'too big, too fail' right?"

"Yes."

"What else can you tell me?"

"I'm sure you already know that if you want answers to the big picture, you have to catch Simon O'Connor and question him…you can't let him die."

"So he is the big enchilada so to speak?"

Byers smiled. "More than you know, but catching him comes with a price as you well know."

Gavin quickly got angry. "Fuck You…is that why she was killed?"

"I'm sorry for your loss, but I also warned you…they won't try and kill you anymore…they will kill everything you love. And you have to start asking yourself…will finding the truth be worth it? Maybe, I am partly to blame because when you started asking questions about people like the Congressman, your uncle, the 9th Precinct…she was targeted, but there are some truths that are greater than one person and worth the sacrifice."

"Like what."

Byers smiled again. "Like how you are connected to all of this more than you realize and some of the secrets you carry born into this web of lies."

Gavin was a little shocked. Did Byers know his secret? What is that obvious? "What are you talking about?"

"I won't be able to help you for a while, but keep digging Agent Donnelly…the truth will set you free."

Byers got out of the truck and walked around the corner. He pulled out his cell phone and made a call. An older voice answered. "Yeah, it's Byers sir…Jimmy McManus actually gave them O'Connor's name."

The voice replied. "Really! I wonder why?"

"I don't know, sir… it seems strange, but the Agents apparently have O'Connor's files so they're on the right path. I didn't have to lead them there."

"I guess that's something. Maybe Jimmy McManus can be an asset after all…we need to find him and see if he wants our help. In the meantime, have our friend at the FBI call me…I want a report on what they are doing to catch O'Connor. "

Byers was a little surprised…his FBI contact had never had direct contact with his boss before, but then he thought to himself, maybe he was more of an ally than he thought. Maybe he was more than an asset…maybe he would join the organization.

18

Agent Main looked at her watch again. He was late as usual. For an arms dealer, he never kept good time. Finally, his Lincoln Town Car Pulled Up to the top floor of the hotel parking garage. As the older man got out of the car, he smiled at Agent Main. His infatuation with her had never stopped from the first day they met. It was the main reason he didn't have a problem giving her information.

He walked up, shook her hand while using both of his hands just to make it more intimate. "Agent Main, it's been far too long…you never call anymore. "

"Well, I called now Pierre."

"And it was perfect timing too. I don't have a date to the Opera tonight. "

Agent Main laughed. "I'm flattered, but I'm sure there's a high priced, beautiful escort that would be glad to go with you. And she will actually sleep."

"Oh… why do you hurt me so. One of these days, you will say yes. "

She laughed. "Maybe, but until then you still get to flirt with me."

"Still a victory for me. Now what can I do for you on this fine day?"

"I'm looking for someone who makes a special kind of bullet and it's something you would probably know."

"Nice of you to think of me. What's special about the bullet?"

"This guy dips the tips in some kind of poison…acts fast and kills the victims within minutes. The substance shuts down the major organs."

"What's the substance called"

"Agent Main gave him a sarcastic look. "It's a long uninteresting name that's hard to pronounce and confuses an audience. The name doesn't matter. It's a poison."

Pierre thought about it for a moment. "There's four guys that I know of who would do something like that. One of them I know is dead. There was another one from Russia who's in prison. "

"Out of the other two, any from this area?"

"Pierre laughed. I don't have an exact address for the them. But if you are looking for one that resides close to here, then I believe he is from Kansas City."

"That's close enough…have a name?"

"I don't have a last name, but he goes by Nathan, However it's an alias, his real name is Eugene."

"I can see why he uses Nathan."

"Eugene is not a very exciting name, but even worse, everybody calls him, *The Hermit*"

"I'm assuming it's befitting his lifestyle."

"In his line of work, you don't socialize and stay in business."

Agent Main laughed at the notion. "So how do I find him?"

"If you live in Chicago there's a thrift store that you can go to and make an order. If I remember correctly, you go in and ask for a record of Herman's Hermits and they give you a number to call on their pay phone."

"Does he come to Chicago?"

Pierre Smiled. "For the right price, he will. May I ask, what he has done to deserve a visit from you?"

"He may be our only link to a serial killer. I don't care about the bullet man, but the man he's giving bullets too is a bad guy and we need him to find a missing Congressman."

Pierre looked surprised. "If this is about Congressman McMahon then it's also about Bobby McClain…the cop killer"

"How do you know about that?"

"I'm a criminal…we know other criminals and it's a well-known fact that McClain worked for McMahon. Surprised you didn't know that?'

Agent Main gave him a dirty look. "We do now. Please don't tell anybody that we talked and know the connection."

Pierre Smiled. "Never Memoiselle."

Agent Main kissed him on the cheek to make her *Thank You* a little more special. Pierre was a big flirt. He was French after all, but he was extremely helpful. And it also made him trustworthy.

∞∞∞∞∞∞∞∞∞∞∞

The conference room was so full that there weren't enough seats for everyone. It was the largest task ever assembled between the FBI and Chicago PD specially to hunt down just one man. Agent Main was put in charge since Agent Donnelly was still on restricted duty. She has also been through this before and had more experience with this kind of manhunt despite her lack of familiarity with Chicago and working with their police department. Most of the cops didn't want to be there. There were mostly heads of departments and precincts in the room, which made them less cooperative. Pretty much all of them had the attitude that they didn't need the FBI and could catch Bobby McClain themselves.

Before Agent Main got started she leaned over and asked her partner. "What happened at OPR?

He replied, "It got cancelled, which means I am still on restrictive duty."

"Cancelled…why…OPR doesn't usually cancel anything."

He shook his head. "I don't know…one of them had some kind of emergency."

"You're still allowed to be here, correct."

"Regardless of what happens, I'm not going anywhere. This is our case and with you in charge, I'm still going to be right by your side."

"She smiled. "No…I don't think anybody could pry you away from this…you'd still find a way to bother me."

Agent Donnelly laughed at the comment as his partner walked to the podium at the front of the room. She got everybody's attention and started to explain everything in detail. Right off the bat some of the cops were questioning her. She held her ground and didn't let them interrupt. Agent Main laid out the evidence they had so far from the connection of Bobby McClain to the missing Congressman and the connection with them and the victims to the 9th Precinct. Some of the Cops scoffed at the notion. Even when obvious evidence was put in from of them, they would still deny it to protect other cops. When she was done, she opened the floor to questions.

A Police Captain raised his hand to ask the first question. "Agent Main, you still haven't said what you think McClain's motive is…all you have is some connection to the 9th precinct…do you have a motive?"

She answered. "We think he was killing cops that help cover up a smuggling operation within the 9th…we don't know what it is, but he's getting rid of any link to him and this operation.

Another officer asked, "But he didn't work with some of the victims and some of them didn't work with each other…how can you be sure."

"All we know is they worked at the 9th and whatever the operation is must have been going on for decades."

"Is that how you are connecting the Congressman McMahon with this because it seems like you are reaching and just looking for an excuse to take over our own investigation."

"We all know that we look at the connections between victims and suspects and ask why to figure out the motive…we were investigating the congressman's disappearance and it happened around the same time Bobby McClain started killing cops so while you accuse the FBI of reaching…there is a connection with all of them and that's what we are looking into. We're hoping that by catching Bobby McClain, he will help us answer those questions."

Another cop asked. "Do you think McClain killed the congressman?"

"We don't know for sure, but it' possible. She didn't answer any more questions. She simply said. "The most important thing is finding Bobby McClain…alive…I can't stress that one enough. He must be taken alive. He is the one guy that connects everybody,"

An officer in the back responded. "He's a cop killer…nothing more and like a rabid animal, put them down and don't ask questions. There were plenty of cops in the room that agreed with his statement and mumbled things like," yeah" and "that's right." Agent Main replied. "Let me make this very clear, any cop that kills him will be charged with obstruction of justice and prosecuted to the full extent of federal law. That means, you will go to jail and lose your pension. He has to be taken alive, no matter what. "

Another officer was about to say something and Agent Main cut him off. "He has to be taken alive, no matter what and that's all I am going to say on the matter. 'The officer didn't say anything after that.

After that there were no more questions. The agents handed out a 3 Page document of their plan to everybody in the room for dropping a net on the city and finally catching Bobby McClain. All the precincts had clear instructions on what to do. There would be FBI agents in every precinct to aid them. It detailed what would become the largest manhunt in Chicago. Part of that plan would be having cops and agents sit on every cop that worked at the 9th with Bobby McClain and the Congressman McMahon that was still in Chicago. Between the both of them, there were sixty-six police offers, another reason they needed a lot of people in the task force.

The final thing Agent Main told everybody was that when Bobby McClain was finally cornered, her and Agent Donnelly were the first phone call anybody made so they could arrest him and finally question him. Most of the cops in the room didn't like that idea; they just wanted to find a way to gun him down, but Agent Main wasn't having any of it if she could help it.

When everybody left the room and she and her partner finally had a moment she handed him folder and said. "I have a name on who might have designed the bullets for McClain. He's called The Hermit."

Agent Donnelly laughed as he read through the file on the guy. "Catchy name…you have a way to catch the guy. "

"I do. There's a thrift shop where we can ask for his services using a code phrase and supposedly he will come to us… a one-time meeting and after that he leaves the orders in secluded places."

"So the only way we are going to meet him is pretending to make an order. It's been my experience that guys like require some kind of deposit in good faith."

Agent Main laughed. "Well, let's hope that it's not too much and we can get it okayed by the Bureau."

"Also, this should just be you and me and maybe someone else that doesn't look like law enforcement. I'm sure this guy can pick out a tail and see a sting operation a mile away if he's been doing this for a while."

"Good idea. You know who would be good for this"
"Who?"

"Any Mob guy from your neighborhood. I bet there's someone that owes you a favor."

"You know, not everybody from my neighborhood is a bad guy."

Agent Main gave him a dirty look. "But there's a lot of bad guys in your neighborhood."

He gave her a sarcastic smile. "That's just FBI profiling… you should be ashamed." He walked, leaving her with a stunned look on her face. She replied. "You're an FBI agent too you moron…that's what we are supposed to do." He was joking with her and took a little pleasure in annoying her as partners often did. Sometimes she was so straight -laced as an FBI agent that she didn't know how to take a joke.

An hour later they had a press conference outside the Justice Building in Chicago Agent Main took the lead and explained the

details of the new task force between the FBI and Chicago PD. There
were a lot of questions from the press. Too many for her to answer.
She was never good at dealing with the press anyway, so the most
common answer she had was
"No comment." But as uncomfortable as she was during the press
conference, it was not a complete disaster, they did get the tip line out
to the public and maybe, if they were lucky, they could get a potential
victim to call in and maybe help catch Bobby McClain.

∞∞∞∞∞∞∞∞∞∞

    Dr. Kenrick had been working so many hours that it felt like
she never left the FBI labs. They were behind on Autopsy's. She finally
got around to the assassin who had been in Agent Donnelly's
Apartment. There was nothing out of the ordinary in autopsy until she
started looking at some of the blood under the microscope. After all,
she was thorough. It didn't happen immediately, but at a second
glance she noticed something strange…the blood cells didn't look
right. She couldn't figure it out at first, but she had seen it before.
Finally, she remembered. It was from a blood sample of Bobby
McClain that had been sent to the FBI after Chicago PD had found
traces of his blood at a crime scene. She remembered making a note of
the sample that something was odd about it and that it might be
contaminated.
    She looked at it again under a microscope…it was the same
pattern of blood cells as the assassin's. Shock draped over her face. It
was just strange to see. In all of her years, she had never seen
something like this and then she thought to herself…could it be true.
She looked at both samples again to make sure. Dr. Kenrick paused for
a moment and then she called Agent Donnelly. He answered after a
few rings. She responded. "Gavin…I need you to come to the Lab…I
have something to show you…please come alone."
    He thought her request was strange, but he didn't argue. He
trusted her and if there was something he needed to keep from his
partner, then it must be for good reason. He told Agent Main that he
needed to check up on something and left her to go by and make the
ammo request from the Hermit. She got annoyed because he would be
expecting a man and if there were cameras at the shop he would know
something was up when he saw a woman. Agent Donnelly didn't
argue…he just told her to wear a disguise if she was that worried and
then he left. It pissed her off to say the least.

Agent Donnelly arrived at the Lab about 15 minutes later. As he walked into the lab, Dr. Kenrick motioned for him to come into the office. He sarcastically replied as he walked in. "Do you want me to draw the shades, make it more private?"

She gave him a dirty look. "Not this time…this is a serious. "

"That's disappointing. What's up?" There was a microscope in her office and he had him look through the lenses. "This is what regular blood cells look like." Then she put the assassin's blood sample under the microscope and Agent Donnelly look. "Do you see any differences?"

He looked for a moment. "I don't see any differences. "

She replied. "Look closely at the edges of the cells."

He looked again more closely. "Okay…it looks a little different, but not that much."

"That's the point…it only looks slightly different. But it's different."

"I don't get it…what am I really looking at?"

She chuckled. "Okay…blood cells can come in different sizes, right, but the edges are always the same…it's what we call their markings. Follow?

"So far."

"The edges on the second sample make the cells look like they have been copied or manufactured somehow…they don't look like natural blood cells."

"What do you mean copied or manufactured…you mean artificial cells…something made in a lab."

"Yeah…maybe."

Agent Donnelly shook his head. "Well, I've heard of smart blood…some kind of enhanced blood cells that can be tracked through vitals on a computer."

"This is not that…those have a unique look and they don't look like real blood cells so we know how to identify them… this is something else. Think of a CD that has been digitally written on then erased and then written on again, if you look closely at the bottom you will see grove, but recopy it, then you will see the grooves that don't form a unique pattern like the first time they have been copied. For blood cells that's what the second sample look like. "

Agent Donnelly gave her a strange look. "So you these blood samples have been copied?"

"Yes, that's what it looks like and somehow manufactured or enhanced."

"You mean cloned?"

"Yes…if you want to call it that."

"Is that even possible?"

"No… none that can be sustained in a human being… that's why this is strange."

"Where did you get this from."

"It's from the shooter who tried to kill you."

His gaze turned to shock. She could see the same look she had earlier on his face. "Gavin…that's not even the strangest part…I found the same thing from a sample of Bobby McClain's blood that was taken from one of his victim's crime scenes."

Agent Donnelly shook his head in disbelief. "Bullshit."

"That's what I thought too…I checked three times and it's the same pattern in the cells."

"So they've had some kind of work done to them."

Dr. Kenrick gave him a strange look. "Or they're not the same people."

"No offense…what you're saying is insane…can't be true."

"That's why I need another sample of McClain's blood to be sure. But I can't deny the facts."

Agent Donnelly paused for a moment to really take everything in. "We're talking about cloning on some level…something that's never been done with human beings…if this is true then you can't say anything."

"Are you kidding me…if I did, I would be laughed out of the building. I'm telling you because if you catch Bobby McClain then I need more samples. If he ends up dead, then the body has to come here… nobody can see this. We can't take the risk of somebody covering up the facts until we know more about how this was."

"I agree, but I'm more interested in the why. Whoever did this, whatever their purpose is, I don't think it's in the name of science.

∞∞∞∞∞∞∞∞∞∞∞

While Gavin was at the Lab, Rachel went to the thrift shop and left a message for The Hermit. As luck would have it, he was in Chicago and could meet later that afternoon. Within an hour of leaving a message, she got a message on her burner cell phone with a place to meet. It was a taqueria on the South Side without side seating and very public. It was also in a neighborhood where nobody would ask questions. They didn't have time to put much of a sting operation together. Everything happened quickly, but Gavin was able to find his friend from his neighborhood who could help.

The sting operation was small. Just three agents and Gavin's friend. His name was Roger Doyle and he was always a bit jittery, but he had the look of a lowlife and that's why they needed him. Rachel

[564]

sat with him at the table in a makeshift disguise. She was wearing a lot of bling and showed off a lot of cleavage, trying her best to look like somebody from the hood or into the gang life.

Roger couldn't stay still and started talking. "This isn't going to work… you look like a cop trying to be a gangster."

Rachel grabbed his arm. "Stop moving around so much…you let me do the talking and this will work. We just need him to sit down for a minute."

"That's not going to work…he's going to expect a man to do the talking…not the girlfriend."

"Don't worry about me… I have been trained to play the part."

He looked at her funny. "Not in Chicago honey. You're from New York, right?"

"Yes, I am."

"Well You look like it…if this guy can tell then this guy can probably tell."

She gave him another dirty look. "Just keep your mouth shut and let me do this… you're only here for the scenery.

Finally, the guy came from around a corner and walked past the other people sitting at tables. He saw where to go based on a copy of the Bible sitting on the table. That was his signal. When he met with people he asked that they be sitting with a King James Bible. He sat down and didn't say anything. He didn't do much talking way. In fact, he handed a notecard with a question…"What do you need and how much?"

Rachel asked. "What's this… you don't talk?'

The Hermit shook his head no."

She replied to the question. "We need armor piercing bullets…cop killers. Fifty boxes of nine millimeter should do it."

He nodded in agreement and then wrote down on another notecard, the price handed it to them. At the bottom of the card it said. "Half Now, Half on Delivery"

Rachel said. "We can do that." She slowly reached into her bag and rummaged around. She talked a long time and it caused suspicion. The Hermit started looking around to see if anybody was watching. Finally, he figured something was up and started to get up and leave. Rachel tried to stop, but he didn't pause. As he turned around, he was met by a bum holding a bottle in a paper bag and a gun. It was Gavin in a disguise. The Hermit tried to run, but was immediately grabbed by the 3rd agent who was Hispanic and dressed as a cook. Gavin responded. "You're not going anywhere…end of the line pal."

Roger looked at Rachel and said. "See, I told you this wasn't going to work…he would see right through it. "

She replied. "Shut up…we got the guy didn't we!"

Roger looked at Gavin. "Okay, so we're good."

Gavin smiled. "Yeah, Roger… you did good. You get a 'Get Out of Jail Free' card from me." Don't use it too quickly."

Roger laughed. "You know me, I will probably have to use it this weekend."

Gavin looked back at The Hermit and said. "Well, Eugene…we need your help catching Bobby McClain and despite what you may be thinking, you don't have a choice."

The Hermit finally spoke. He was mad enough to break the silence and it didn't matter who was listening at this point, CIA, NSA, or Homeland Security. He was caught by the FEDS. The only thing he said. "Fuck You!"

Gavin smiled. "Two Words, wow…I thought you would only have one word for me…lawyer, which you can have after we've talked."

"You can't do that…you have to give me a lawyer if I request one."

Rachel responded. "Technically you're right, but when you've been supplying ammunition to terrorists, then it's a little bit different… we can hold you as long as we want until you cooperate, welcome to Post 9/11 America." The Hermit didn't say anything after that. He knew she was right.

An hour later they had him back at FBI headquarters in an interrogation room. Normally they would have let the suspect sit there for hours without anything to drink or any bathroom breaks, a chance to let the suspect sweat a little until they were ready to talk, but they didn't have that kind of time. Gavin and Rachel both came into to the room. They brought The Hermit a cup of coffee and water." He didn't try to play any mind games he immediately took the water. He had never been caught before, so it was his first time in an interrogation room. He was nervous and the agents could easily tell.

Gavin spoke first. "We know this is your first time in this situation and normally we would let you sit until you were ready to talk, but we are in a hurry so our subtle tactics will be done away with. Here's what you're facing. Right now we can charge you with intent to distribute illegal weapons to a federal agent…that's minimum ten years. Once we search your place and find all of your 'toys' then we will have you on possession and that's another ten years, but if we hand you over to homeland security, they'll charge you with supplying terrorists and that will get you life in prison without the possibility of parole. 20 to life Eugene, that's what you're facing, but…"

He replied. "If I help then that goes away."

"Very good…first time talking with the FEDS and you get how this works."

"I think it's time for my lawyer now."

"That's the wrong answer and you were doing well so far. If that's what you really want then we have no choice to put you in federal lockup…general population and you don't strike me as someone that can handle prison well."

"You're bluffing."

Rachel replied. "We never bluff because we don't have to." She opened the door and asked for a couple of agents to escort him to nearest federal prison. When the other agents walked in that's when The Hermit got scared. It didn't take him long to take back what he said and start cooperating. He responded. "Alright…what do I have to do?"

Rachel laughed. "Simple…make contact with Bobby McClain and tell him things are getting too hot and you have to get out of Chicago and that you're leaving him the rest of his ammunition before you leave town. Confirm that he's making the pickup and you're done."

"What happens to me next?"

Gavin replied. "You become an informant for the FBI and you can go back to your life. Just give us tips on who's buying from you…you can keep the money they give you. We won't bust everybody so you can get repeat business and it won't look suspicious, but you help us bait the really big fish and you get protection from the FBI."

Again, it didn't take him long to agree. He didn't have the toughness to stand up to the FBI, plus he was smart enough to know he only had one move to make in his chess match with the FEDS.

∞∞∞∞∞∞∞∞∞∞∞∞

Stanley Dobson was watching the noon hour news and saw the report on the FBI tip line. He looked at his wife as she was on the computer emailing friends and family. He never talked much about the job with her. She was always fine with that. Her only request in forty years of marriage was that he left the work at the precinct and that the man she married and fell in love with always came home for dinner. The day before he had packed two suitcases and arranged for his monthly pension to be deposited into an offshore account.

He never wanted to leave Chicago. It was home. All of their friends and family were here, but he knew that one day he might have to. When he saw the tip line, he started to rethink his plan. He got up from his recliner and went to the phone. He called the tip line. An FBI

[567]

agent answered and he replied. "Tell whoever is in charge of this investigation that if they really want to know what's been happening at the 9th then they need to come and pick me up ASAP. I'll tell them everything."

His wife overheard the conversation and gave him a strange look. "Stanley, who did you call?"

"He smiled. "Honey, I have to tell you something…it's about the job."

"We agreed, you never had to talk about it."

"This time, I need to say what I used to do. Our lives are about to become very different and we're too old to go on the run."

A fearful look washed over her face. "What did you do?"

He tried to smile. "It's going to be okay…I promise…you believe me."

She didn't know what to say. She wanted to believe him, but instinct told her that she couldn't this time.

∞∞∞∞∞∞∞∞∞∞

While Agent Main was preparing the sting operation that would hopefully catch Bobby McClain Gavin was in their office looking through McClain's medical file. After his meeting with Dr. Kenrick he was curious. Was there any evidence of work being done on McClain! If what she was suggesting was true, then there had to be some kind of evidence. How would somebody get samples of his blood or DNA the blueprints of his genetic makeup and everything you would need to clone a person.

The file made for some interesting reading. Bobby McClain had been a part of a drug study at Hill and Meyers Research Labs. There were also notes some kind of unspecified surgeries, but that's all it said. As he was flipping through the pages, he found a small piece of paper stapled to a Hill and Myers form. It had some unusual numbers on it and he recognized them. He couldn't place it at first, but remembered his last vision. They were the same kind of numbers he saw on that list sitting on the desk in the vision. He tore the piece of paper out so he could find out what kind of numbers they were.

As soon as he tore the paper out of the folder, his partner walked in. She said. "Okay, I have a few things for you. First, The Hermit did his job. He gave a drop off location for Bobby McCain, starting in two hours and got a confirmation from McClain so we are setting up the sting operation now."

Gavin looked surprised. "Wow, that was fast."

"Yeah, we lucked out. Also, a report came in about another dead Chicago cop who once worked at the 9th. It was late coming in because he wasn't shot…car had a bomb on it. And his wife was killed too. The detectives who investigated the death wasn't sure if it was McClain or not."

"Now why would Bobby McClain change his MO."

"Maybe he's out of those special bullets, which would explain why he responded to the pickup so fast."

"Do serial killers often change their MO?"

Rachel smiled. "Not usually, unless they're trying to break the pattern and make it hard to catch them. But most serial killers have a specific reason for the MO…it's something more psychological. I think for McClain it was more out of necessity."

Gavin pondered the notion for a moment. He didn't necessarily disagree, but there was something else. Perhaps another possibility, but he just couldn't put his finger on it. His partner spoke up. "Hey, did I lose you…don't space out on me."

"Sorry…what was the other thing/"

"The tip line worked. A former police officer who worked at the 9th called in and wanted to speak to us."

"Really!"

"Yeah, AD Foster sent a couple of agents to go pick him and his wife up."

Gavin smiled. "Well more good news."

An hour and a half later as Gavin and Rachel were about to leave for the stakeout that would hopefully catch Bobby McClain, the agents who picked up Stanley Dobson and his wife finally arrived with the couple. Gavin and Rachel were already late so there wasn't any time to really question Stanley, but Gavin wanted to at least have a word with him. He told his partner that he would meet her down in the garage. Then walked over to where Stanley was sitting as the other agents were about to take down his information and said.

"Mr. Dobson, I understand you're ready to talk with me…what don't we know about the 9th. "

Stanley replied. "A lot Agent Donnelly…you think all of this is just about smuggling… it goes way beyond that."

"Like what, for instance."

"I'll elaborate more when there's an immunity deal in place."

Gavin smiled. "Didn't really come here to play ball did you?"

"Depends on the deal I get."

"And you realize if we send you home, then it's only a matter of time before Bobby McClain gets you if we don't catch him first…are you willing to take that risk."

Stanley smiled. "I was prepared to run yesterday… still can if I don't get a deal. Can you risk not knowing what I know, especially if it can help you catch Bobby McClain and the people responsible for kidnapping Congressman McMahon?"

"Alright Mr. Dobson…we will work on an immunity deal, but you can be here for a while…I have to get to a sting operation. When I get back, we'll see how much help you can be."

19

    The Hermit's drop off location was a recycling bin in the back alleyway of a strip joint on the south side of Chicago. It was a place where decent people didn't go. More importantly, it was a place cops didn't want to look. It was perfect for Chicago's most notorious cop killer to pick up ammunition. There were agents inside the club posing as customers to see if Bobby McClain would come in. Some of the Chicago PD on the task force posed as street bums at one of the alleyways and on the other there was a plumbers van. That's where Agent Main was. They had the Alleyway blocked.

    After waiting for an hour and half, one of the agents inside the club spotted McClain. He grabbed a beer and stuck a twenty dollar bill in the G-String of one of the strippers. He didn't want to look suspicious, so he looked like a typical customer. One of the agents whispered into his hidden Mic if they were going to grab Bobby McClain inside the club. Agent Donnelly replied. "No, we wait for him to go out in the alleyway and grab him there. We don't want a ruckus in here, especially if he has a gun. We don't want anybody to get hurt." The agents just watched him for about 10 minutes. McClain finally made his way to the back as if he was going to the bathroom. Gavin whispered into his Mic. "Rachel, he's coming your way."

    Bobby McClain walked out of a backdoor that lead to the alleyway. He looked around to see if there was anybody there. He did notice the bums drinking and paused for a moment. After about a minute he decided that they were harmless and then went to the recycling bin and found his package sitting behind it. As he was bent down, Agent Main gave the order. "Alright Now, close in" The two cops dressed as bums were the first to shout "Freeze, Chicago PD." They startled Bobby McClain and he immediately opened fire on them. One of the cops was hit, but he wasn't hurt. His Kevlar stopped the bullet. The other raised his gun for a kill shot, but Agent Main and two other agents were almost to where Bobby McClain and she yelled hold your fire to the cop. Bobby tried to go back inside and was immediately met by the agents who were inside of the door. He had nowhere to go, but he tried to shoot his way through the door entrance anyway.

The other cop took it upon himself to try and kill Bobby McClain during the commotion. Agent Main rushed him and punched him the face before he could shoot. "I told you, we take him alive. " The cop yelled back. "Fuck you, Bitch." She didn't say anything else to him, but said one of the agents to take his gun and badge. While that was going on, Gavin and the other agents tackled McClain before he could get another shot off. They finally had him in custody and he was alive.

Bobby McClain was put into the back of FBI Chevy Tahoe while things were cleaned up. Gavin asked his partner if he could have a moment with Bobby McClain, alone, before he was taken to a holding facility. She was the one in charge and normally she would get to talk to the perp first, but she agreed.

McClain hadn't said a word since they put the cuffs on him. Gavin got in the Tahoe and sat next to him. Before you get hauled off and questioned until you can't keep your eyes open anymore, I wanted to talk to you."

Bobby stared at him. "I'm not telling why I did this."

Gavin laughed. "We already figured out the why, but I want to know is did you kidnap Congressman McMahon?

"No"

"Do you know who did and if he's still alive."

"I don't know if he is or not at this point."

"But the same men who hired you are the ones who took him, correct?"

Bobby McClain gave him a dirty look. "What do you think?"

"I think all of this is cleanup and the same men who hired you and who are pulling the strings are getting rid of any witnesses to whatever smuggling operation you were a part of."

"Then you don't need my help…you've got it all figured out."

"Why did you really shoot Liam Donnelly…he never worked with you or was a part of anything."

"He was a name on a list and I was told to kill him…I don't ask questions, I just take orders.

Agent Donnelly thought it was a strange answer. "What do mean, if you were a part McMahons dealings, being one of his right hand men then you should know why Liam Donnelly was targeted.

Bobby McClain didn't seem to understand and for Agent Donnelly it started to make sense…maybe he wasn't really Bobby McClain, just some kind of manufactured version of him."

Agent Donnelly asked a simple question. "What is your earliest memory, Bobby? Like, do you remember anything from your childhood or when you were at the police academy?"

"No…not really…not since my surgery two years ago."

"What was the surgery for?"

"The doctor's said I had a brain injury and I had to be fixed. "

"What doctors?"

"The one at the hospital by the lake."

"You mean Hill and Meyer labs…does that sound familiar?"

"Yeah, that's the place."

Agent Donnelly paused for a moment and then thought of something else to ask. "Who taught you how to shoot a gun?"

"One of the male nurses at the hospital when I was doing my rehab."

"So you only learned how to shoot in the last couple of years and you don't remember going to the police academy?"

Bobby McClain looked dumbfounded by the question. "I don't think, I ever went to the police academy?"

Agent Donnelly had a look of a surprise, but somehow he wasn't really surprised by any of this. It was weird. He replied. "I guess you wouldn't remember, if it didn't happen for you. Where is the list of who you were supposed to kill."

"On the flash drive hooked to my keychain."

"Do you know who Simon O'Connor is?"

"No…am I supposed to?"

Agent Donnelly smiled. He got more answers than he bargained for. The pieces of the puzzle were starting to come together. He pulled something out of his coat pocket…it was a pack of gum and it only had one piece left. He looked at Bobby. "I found this, but my instinct tells me this is not really gum…this was your way out if you got caught because you can't be taken alive."

Bobby looked away and didn't say anything for a moment. Finally, he replied. "Yes."

One more question. "When you were done, where were you going to go?" If this really wasn't Bobby McClain then maybe the answer to his question could give him a clue to where to start looking next. If their smuggling operation was ending in Chicago then maybe it was being moved and he and his partner still didn't have the bigger picture. That's what Gavin was really after at this point. Finding the congressman was secondary. Bobby answered his question. "I was supposed to catch a boat to Ireland."

"Ireland…what's in Ireland?"

"Not sure…some kind of testing, I think."

"Do you know where in Ireland?"

"Someplace in the country…that's all I know."

Agent Donnelly unwrapped the last stick of gum and put it in Bobby's Mouth. "Thank You for the information. You're a cop killer and between FBI agents and Chicago's finest, I'll doubt you would make it to morning. Somebody will put you down. You answered my questions so I am going to give you your way out." He was breaking at least a dozen protocols, but he was also buying time. If Bobby McClain died at the scene of his capture then maybe his handlers wouldn't suspect him of talking to the FEDS and it would give him and his partner more to find the other so-called bad guys."

He got out of the car and Agent Main immediately asked. "Did he give you anything?

"Yes…but I will tell you in private. We shouldn't talk here." Agent Donnelly was always suspicious of who might be listening. He never used to be this paranoid until he started working in the violent crimes division and this was still Chicago…everybody was listening.

∞∞∞∞∞∞∞∞∞∞

Gavin and Rachel were driving back to the office while McClain was being taken to a federal prison. She asked him. "Now that we're alone, what did Bobby McClain tell you?"

Gavin knew he couldn't tell her everything, at least not yet so he kept it short and hoped she wouldn't see through him. "He wasn't that helpful. He said he didn't remember anything before his surgery two years ago and he couldn't remember what it was for. "

"That's all he said, you were in the car for a long time."

"No, it wasn't the only thing he said. He told me that he was given a list of cops to kill and it's on the flash drive hooked to his keychain. There should be a laptop in the back, let's bring the flash drive in and see this list."

Rachel found the computer in the back seat and inserted the drive. There wasn't much on it, but she found the word document named "Grocery List." Instinct told her that it was his code word for the list and she was right. There were lots of names on the list and a lot of names that were crossed out. After looking it over more than once, she said. "There's a lot of names on here that I don't recognize…a lot more than the victims we know about."

"How many?"

[574]

"From what I can tell, there are twelve names on here not accounted for. We've been thinking that he started with your uncle, but there are twelve names crossed out before him and it looks like he's been killing cops in the order on the list."

"How many did he have left?"

She looked at the list again. "I count eight."

"Is a Stanley Dobson on the list?"

"Yes, two down from the last one he killed. The first thing I want to ask him when he get back is how many of these cops he knew. Maybe he can shed some light on what they were covering up."

Gavin paused and thought for a moment and then finally responded. "I have a theory on what they are smuggling?"

"Oh…not guns or drugs…the two most popular things to be smuggled into Chicago."

"Guns, not, but drugs…not the kind that we are thinking of. All of this is medical related. What if the products being smuggled are some kind of drugs that are not FDA approved, but are stilling being used by Hill and Myer…there's not government oversight and they can charge whatever they want including using the drugs in drug protocols without the oversight."

Rachel thought about it for a moment. "I have to admit…it fits. The amount of money that can be made from a smuggling operation like this is astronomical. But take it a step further…black market organs. Hill and Myer is a pretty expensive place. The prices they can charge for organs would make it an extremely profitable venture, especially if you're paying off the right people to help you get it in the city."

Gavin chuckled. "And what better way to do that…get cops from a local precinct to help you including a former cop turned congressman."

"It's a good motive, but we still have to prove it."

"And I think that's where Simon O'Connor comes in." He reached inside FBI jacket pocket and pulled out a piece of paper. It was a small paper from Bobby McClain's file attached to a Hill and Myer form. "I got this from McClain's medical file. The initials HMS in the corner must stand for Hill and Myer, but I can't figure out what the numbers are, but I've seen them before and I figure this is something important."

Rachel looked at the paper and smiled. "You're wrong about the initials…HMS stands for Her Majesty's Ship. It refers to a ship from Great Britain. The numbers are container numbers. I think this refers to a ship with a container that's holding smuggled products."

"Oh…that makes sense."

"For being from Chicago, you really don't know anything about the navy and one of the largest naval bases is right here. "

"Ha Ha…I don't do boats…I like staying on land and since I don't work for customs, didn't really think I had to learn naval terms."

"You know, it is useful to know these things living in a city next to large bodies of water."

Gavin gave her a dirty look in response to her comments, but didn't respond to the comments. He simply asked. "So what does all this mean?"

"It means we have to go back to Hill and Myer and tried to find the ship that this pertains to. There has to be some kind of record of containers with the products that are supposed to go to the lab…maybe we can find the ship number too. Let's go check it out now!"

Gavin didn't argue. She was right…why wait. They security guards should be able to let them in. They broke off from the rest of the FBI cars and headed into the darkness racing through stop lights to get there as quickly as possible.

They arrived at Hill and Myer research labs about twenty minutes later. The night shift had just begun so the third shift security guards were just getting settled in. The agents walked up the front desk and immediately showed their badges. Gavin tried to play it cool and say they were there to pick up something left for them, but the head security guard didn't buy. He did what he was trained to do…he asked to see a warrant. Hilly and Myer were very serious about their privacy considering the kind of work they did. Gavin responded. "The warrant we had before is still good and a copy of it should still be in the system."

The guard looked puzzled. "I don't know what system you are referring to."

"I'm sure like most company's you have a file on your server where you keep requests from law enforcement."

Still, the guard looked confused. "We would have copies of that kind of stuff here at the desk and I don't have anything for the FBI. I think you are mistaken and I can't let you in."

Gavin gave him a stern look. "No, sir, you are… call your IT department… they can help you find it, but in the meantime, we are going to do what we came here to do."

"You will still have to wait."

"I know you have a job to do, but my partner and I don't have time to wait while you show your incompetence…if you don't let us through then you can be charged with obstruction of justice and impeding a federal investigation. Now we'll go do what we came to do, while you call IT to help you find the warrant in your system."

The guard started to get nervous. He still wanted to tell them no, but was worried that the obstruction of justice part could be true. He finally told the agents to go on through while he tried to verify the warrant, they supposedly had on their server.

As the agents turned the corner on the long hallway that faced the front entrance, Rachel said. "You know we can't really charge him with obstruction of justice."

Gavin smiled. "I know that, but he doesn't…I thought it was a pretty good bluff."

"Maybe! How long do you think we have?"

"At most twenty minutes, but we should be out of here in fifteen just to be on the safe side."

Hill and Meyer Research did have a server so that meant any computer in the building should be able to access it. The agents were looking for an unlocked office where nobody would find them. The guards would eventually figure out they were lying and come looking for them. As they were walking down the hallway they passed a room with another two men in them. Gavin motioned for his partner to stay out of sight. He noticed something strange. The men were shredding documents. Lots of documents! He looked at Rachel. "Looks they are tying up more loose ends…getting rid of evidence."

She nodded in agreement. "They know we are going to eventually raid this place, but we can't do anything about this now. Let's just get to a computer and find what ship and its containers have products for this place. Without that, it will be a needle in a haystack trying to find what's being smuggled."

They eventually found the director's office and figured it was good as any. The computer was password protected. Rachel cursed under her breath. Gavin actually had a solution. He pulled out a flash drive and said. "Put this in and run the program that pops up. It will unlock the computer." Rachel gave him a strange look. "Let me guess…she gave it to you."

Gavin smiled. "Janie doesn't hate all of us FBI…it was a gift."

The program worked. They got inside the computer. Gavin asked. "What exactly are we looking for?"

"Any list of shipping container numbers like the ones on this paper, and numbers close to these. Then we see if any of the containers on that list are on a British Cargo ship parked in the harbor." While she was searching through the server, she told her partner to look through the filing cabinet and see if he could find anything that might help their investigation. He started searching. After a few minutes she finally found shipping manifests pertaining to order for the research labs and was able to able to make a search with just part of the numbers and see if any other numbers close to them popped up. Sure enough, she found twenty containers. And even better, the name of the ship they were on was listed next to the numbers on the list. She responded. "Found it!"

Gavin replied. "Let's see if we can print it out." They got lucky again…there was a laser printer in his office. As the sheets were printing out, Gavin heard footsteps. He cracked the door a little bit and took a peak. It was security and they were checking offices. Time was up… they had to get out of there fast. The Director had a small patio outside of his office that overlooked the lake area on the property and it was low enough off the ground that the agents could climb down. That's how Gavin and Rachel made their escape. They were already on the ground below the patio when security checked the Director's office. Gavin could see the flashlight beams bouncing off the walls. Rachel thought to herself, did she turn off the computer so that security wouldn't know for sure they had been there. It didn't matter at this point. Once out of the building, security couldn't do anything. They made their way back to their car and drive away into the night.

∞∞∞∞∞∞∞∞∞∞∞∞

The Judges Chamber's was packed more than usual. Normally, only a few people would make their case for a search warrant, but this situation was less than ordinary. Agent Donnelly and Agent Main were accompanied by their supervisor AD Foster, the US Attorney and his deputy, and a US Coast Guard Captain and his Executive Office who were in charge of Patrolling the Harbors in Chicago. And just to make sure everybody was represented, two Customs Agents who were assigned to the interagency Taskforce the day before. It was a full house when the US Federal Judge Raymond Carson walked in with his assistant. He looked around the Chambers and said. "I hope everybody is comfortable…I don't think we can get more people in here and maintain some level of comfort." There were a few snickers from some of the people in the room.

The judge sat down at his desk and said. "So I understand this meeting is about obtaining a search warrant not only for the Chicago PD's 9th Precinct, but searching a British Cargo Ship in the harbor while also blocking the harbor with the US Coast Guard."

US Attorney Eric McBride spoke first. "Yes, your honor…if you take a look at the brief on your desk."

The judge cut him off. "I've already read it…it seems a little rushed, but I get the gist of the facts that you're presenting, but the main question that's doesn't seem to be answered is what's being smuggled…you don't have an answer for that!"

[578]

"Yes, your honor, but you can clearly see the connection the FBI has made with the missing congressman, Bobby McClain, and the cops he murdered, plus the list found on him."

The judge stared at him for a moment. "Yes, I see that, it's sounds like a conspiracy, but what are they conspiring to do…that's the real question." He looked at Gavin. "Agent Donnelly…what exactly do you assume is being smuggled that warrants what you're asking me to sign off on?"

"The truth is we don't know for sure, but it has to be something big in order to go to all of this trouble to hide what they're doing and you speak of a conspiracy as if it's something to be laughed at, but that's exactly what we have and if we are going to find the truth then we have to search those ships and raid the precinct to find out what they may know."

"I don't like conspiracies Agent Donnelly, but I do take them seriously, especially when evidence has been presented, but it seems like all of this hinges on talking to this Simon O'Connor who you say is linked to everybody. I'm sorry, but that's not good enough and I'm inclined to deny the search warrants because you were told by Customs that you couldn't talk to him because of his informant status and my court won't be used to grind an ax with another agency."

Gavin chuckled. "I understand your honor…but with all due respect, he's not an informant with Custom's…he's protected by the CIA."

"You have proof of this."

Agent Main pulled the tablet out of her bag and turned it on then handed it to the judge with O'Connor's File opened on the screen. The judge spent a couple of minutes scrolling through the documents on the tablet. His confident look turned to that of surprise. He replied. "Holy Shit…I'm assuming this wasn't obtained legally with an interagency request?"

Agent Donnelly replied. "No your honor, but we couldn't get it any other way. We know it's inadmissible and we know that we couldn't prosecute even if we wanted to…we just want to show you how he's really connected to everybody. And, the only thing we want to do is question him."

"Yeah, from what it sounds like, even if he's arrested, he will be let go quickly, but given enough time, you could possibly question him and get something on the record. I buy that plan. Now, what ships are you wanting to search?"

Agent Main responded. "We narrowed it down to two ships. "One is coming into port late tonight and one has been here for almost a week. We want to search both, but we think the HMS Barton is the ship we're looking for."

The Judge sat back in his chair for a moment pondering what his answer would be. He finally responded. "Okay…before I sign off on this, I want to make this very clear. First, you will notify the British Ambassador that two of their ships will be searched and why. Just because they're allies doesn't mean we don't give them that courtesy. Second, you better find evidence…this is the last time I sign off on a search warrant to raid the 9th precinct. They have been investigated time and time again and nobody has come up with anything they can be prosecuted for. They may be corrupt, but enough is enough." He looked at the US Attorney. "You get one last shot at this…make it count. " Then he looked at everybody else. "Third, you are to take people into custody, this is not an excuse to have a gun fight. And fourth: If you find Simon O'Conner…you get something on the record that can be used and can't be redacted by the CIA. Whatever you find, make sure it stops for good and that we have enough evidence to prosecute the guilty parties."

The judge pulled out the other request and then looked at Gavin. "Agent Donnelly, you have a request here to search all of Bobby McClain's possessions, including a full extensive autopsy conducted by the FBI. Why do you need me to sign off on this after the man was captured and is now dead…isn't that part of the case closed?"

"Not exactly, sir… I feel there is a lot more we need to know about him and his true role in this so-called conspiracy and if we let Chicago PD do anything about it…well, to put it simply, evidence will go missing including the body to cover up their own indiscretions. Plus an extensive autopsy will help us to understand what really happened to him at Hill and Meyer Research Labs and if they were doing more stuff than they claim."

The Judge smiled. "That's a bit of a leap, but why not, today seems to be all about hunches and theories. But the same rules apply…you better get evidence or I won't be signing off anything again.

Agent Donnelly nodded in agreement. They had their warrants. The FBI raid was a go!

ထထထထထထထထထ

As Gavin and Rachel were walking back to their car, Gavin got a call from his uncle. The conversation was short. All he said to Gavin was that it was extremely important and that he needed to meet him at the Pub. Gavin knew what it meant. It was some kind of backroom meeting. The kind of meeting that had to be done in secret because if people found out, some people would get killed. Those kinds of meetings were not uncommon in his neighborhood. He looked at Rachel and told her that he would be later and he would be back in time. She was caught by surprise, but didn't get a chance to say anything before he walked off and called a cab.

Gavin arrived at the Pub thirty minutes later. When he walked in, the only person in the room was the bartender and he motioned for Gavin to go to the back where the others were waiting for him. He entered the back room and found his Uncle, Mickey Sorano, Tommy McManus and their Lieutenants. It looked as if they were trying to scare him the same way they would with one of their competitors, but Gavin was easily rattled…he was from here and knew their methods. Tommy spoke up first. "Gavin…thank you for coming. We called you because we hoped that we could reason with you a little bit."

Gavin gave him a strange look. "Reason with me about what…I don't know what you think this is…is this about Maggie."

"No, it isn't, although, you pissed a lot of people off, but that will blow over. This is about your investigation and the raid you and the FBI are about to do."

Gavin paused for a moment. "How do you know what we're about to do."

Mickey Sorano replied. "This is Chicago, nothing stays silent for very long…we know that you came from the Justice building in Chicago where you met with the US Attorney and judge…you were getting a warrant to raid the 9th precinct."

Gavin chuckled. "Well, it didn't take your spies very long to report back."

Tommy replied. "We knew last night when the US Attorney started to put everything together for the judge."

"Okay, fine, you know; what of it."

"We're hoping you will call it off."

"And why would I do that…we're not after whatever your organizations are into. This has nothing to do with your interests."

"Oh, but it does, Gavin… more than you know."

Gavin gave Tommy a dirty look. There was only one question on his mind. "Are you working with Simon O'Connor because that's who we are after!"

The name surprised all the men in the room. Nobody expected Gavin to know it, but they shouldn't have been surprised. It was only a matter of time before the FBI found out about him and his dealings with everybody. Tommy replied. "We don't work with him. He has his own operations, but from time to time we have to get stuff from him. He's a necessary evil because he's the man that can get anything and he's allowed to operate without restriction by the council and pretty much any government in the world."

"Does your business have anything to do with him and Bobby McClain and killing cops because you know what happens next if you do?"

Mickey replied. "Absolutely not…are you kidding…the day we sign up for killing cops is the day we start a war and lose any protection we might have. We're not that stupid and you don't get to remain in power as long as have been if you're stupid. But we're also smart enough to look the other way if this involves him."

Tommy responded before Gavin could say anything. "There's a bit of a perfect balance that we have in Chicago with the 9th and Simon O'Connor…if one domino is tipped then it all goes to hell. We can't have that. If you raid the precinct and start arresting cops that are friendly to our interests, then you tip the domino."

Gavin gave him a stern look. "I understand what you're saying, but I have a missing congressman and cops being killed and it's all connect to O'Connor because of some operation that he's involved in…something big enough to kill all the witnesses. Something bigger than whatever drugs or guns or black market shit you guys smuggle into Chicago so you can make money. This is bigger than you and I want to know what's worth dozens of murders." He looked at his uncle and said. "And I would expect you to agree with me, especially since they tried to kill you."

Liam replied. "I don't necessarily disagree, as someone who has worked hard to maintain the mob peace agreement, I understand where they're coming from. You got Bobby McClain and we're all thankful for that, but isn't there a way to get what you need from Simon O'Connor to conclude your investigation and not affect Tommy and Mickey's business interests."

"You want your cake and to eat it too?"

"Yes, I do."

"And you always told me and Alex that it doesn't work that way when you wear a badge especially if it's a badge of honor."

Liam smiled. "That's true, but when you get to my age, you should be able to get both and for me, it's helping to maintain peace between mob organizations so that we don't have a street war on my watch."

Tommy replied. "And that's what's going to happen if our organizations can't deliver. Every young punk who thinks they can do better will rise up and try to take us down. Then we'll have to fight. It will be all out war because we won't go down without a fight. Is that what you want?"

Gavin paused for a moment carefully thinking about his answer. It wasn't a simple yes and no question…it never was with these guys. "Of course I don't want to see that kind of war in Chicago, but some things are bigger…the truth about what O'Connor is really doing is bigger than you so we all got to do what we have to do…don't we."

Tommy finally got mad. "You owe us…remember…you won't have a career if it weren't for us."

Gavin stared him down for a moment so he would get the seriousness of his tone. "Of course I remember…never had to be reminded, but I have paid you back time and time again. We are long past being even."

"Getting rid of a body so that you don't get prosecuted for murder is a tall order and takes a while to pay back. I'm asking you not do this with the 9th. The FBI will kill off the pipeline. Service weapons can always be found with evidence of a bad shooting."

Gavin chuckled. "And evidence of racketeering that was thought to be lost can suddenly resurface so be careful of the threats you make. I'm still an FBI agent and we will bring trouble to your door a hundred times worse that what you think you can do to me." Tommy didn't say anything. He hoped that his glare was sharp enough to make Gavin rethink his position. Gavin responded. "In all fairness, I will do the best I can to make sure your interests aren't affected too much. We're only after Simon O'Connor and anything involving his operations with the 9th precinct, especially if it involved Congress McMahon. I hope you can understand that even if you disagree with it."

The rest of the men didn't say anything. There was nothing to be said. They couldn't rely on favors this time from one of their own in the neighborhood. Gavin had to be the "by the book" FBI agent. It was the only role he could play if he had any hope in solving this case.

∞∞∞∞∞∞∞∞∞∞∞∞

Gavin made it back to the office just in time to go over everybody's role in the raid. This was the last time everybody would have the chance to go over the game plan. The raid was had to be precise, which meant that the element of surprise had to be successful for it to work. That was the hardest part in Chicago. One of the FBI task forces would lead the raid on the 9th precinct while Gavin and Rachel would lead the raid at the Harbor with the Coast Guard assisting. It would happen all at the same time, so nobody would have

[583]

time to warn anybody else. At the 9th all files and hard drives on computers would be confiscated. And two cops who were on Bobby McClain's list that still worked, there would be taken into custody for questioning. They only had one goal at the harbor, to find Simon O' Connor and search the shipping containers connected to Hill and Meyer research labs. They needed to find what was being smuggled and hopefully shut down the operations.

It was a good plan and everybody knew their part. Both Gavin and Rachel felt they would get the resolve they were looking for with this plan. After the meeting concluded Rachel pulled her partner aside and gave him a note. She said. "That former cop who came here to turn himself in before we caught Bobby McClain left after he heard the news. He left a note for us, but I don't understand it…do you."

Gavin looked at it...

"As soon as you think you know the answer, that's when you realize you know nothing. The rabbit hole goes on and on until you don't know it's there anymore!"

He replied. "Besides the Alice and Wonderland reference, I don't know what to make of it."

"It feels like a warning to me."

"Maybe! Does anybody know what happened to Mr. Dobson."

"I checked, apparently he and his wife left the country. I wonder if wherever they are going will be far enough to hide."

∞∞∞∞∞∞∞∞∞∞

Simon O'Connor was in his Cabin when one of his guys knocked on the door. He was let in and said. "The Cargo is safely in its containers. We have all of it."

"Excellent. We made it and on time. Tell the Captain to get underway."

The other guy was about to walk out when he and Simon both heard the sirens. Simon looked out his cabin window and they saw dozens of FBI cars racing along the docks. Another one of his men came running into the cabin and told him that the Coast Guard were coming up fast along the starboard side and creating a blockade. It looked as if they were about to be boarded.

Simon told his man to tell the captain to run the blockade. That was an order! The man shook his head "no" and said that it was too late. Simon picked up his gun off the desk and shot him dead and then

[584]

ordered the other man to relay the message to the Captain. Then Simon
simply disappeared into the rest of the ship.

20

6:00 PM CST.

Everybody in the car was silent. Their focus was the same to complete the job at hand. There was nothing to really say as the agents drove to Chicago's North Shore Harbor to search the HMS Barton. Agent Main had handed out the latest photos of Simon O'Connor that the FBI had so all the agents and the Coast Guard news who take into custody. Gavin spent the car ride just staring at his copy of the photo as it was going to give him some clue he didn't already have. But while he was deep in thought about the job they had to do, he decided to try a breathing exercise that he had been working on.

He held the photo in his hand and started slowing breathing in a continuous rhythm. His breathing felt more like a metronome that somebody would have during a piano lesson. He focused his thoughts on one thing…Simon O'Connor. Finally it happened, he flashed. *He could clearly see Simon O' Connor moving throughout the ship. He kept climbing down stairs until he was at the back of the ship facing a small window that was just a few feet from the water. The word "rear" was painted on the wall. Simon pulled out some kind of device from the first aid station hooked on the wall. Then he found a wetsuit that had been stashed away. That was all he saw before his partner nudged him back to reality and asked if he was okay.* Agent Donnelly nodded "yes." For the first time he was able to control his gift and will himself to see something from the future. He knew where Simon O'Connor would be in thirty minutes.

For the most part the FBI caught everybody on the ship by surprise. As the agents and the FBI tactical team boarded the ship nobody resisted. The teams swept fast throughout the ship gathering everybody on board to put in one place, The Bridge was taken first and the Captain did not resist or give any orders to do the same. Despite what O'Connor may have wanted, everybody knew that it was useless to put up a fight. One of the O'Connor's men did fire a few shots, but he was quickly shot and killed. The crew was rounded up and put on the main deck, but they still couldn't find Simon O'Connor. Nobody on deck matched the photos they had. Gavin, knowing where he was going to be, broke away from his partner and the rest of the teams to go try and find him. A few agents went with him, but he ditched them. This was something he had to do alone in order to keep his secret.

6:30 PM CST.

It took a little while, but Gavin found his way a few decks below where O'Connor should be. The map he found on the ship was more than helpful. As he looked around O'Connor turned the corner and almost caught Gavin totally by surprise, but he heard the footsteps just in time and drew his service weapon on him. O'Connor was more surprised to have an FBI agent waiting for him. He responded. "What the fuck…how did you find this place? Nobody knows about this."

Gavin smiled. "Maybe you're not as good as you think are at keeping secrets."

"Bullshit…there's no way you could have found me like this."

"No, you're just not that lucky, now put your hands behind your head. I'm taking you into custody."

Simon paused for a moment, but finally did what he was told. "You, know you won't be able to hold me. As you probably know by now, I'm protected and my handlers will have me out before you can put me in a cell."

"Who says you're going to jail…we both know that will never happen, but I am going to question you, and you're going to tell me the truth."

O'Connor laughed. " I think you Yanks call that, Wishful thinking! Never going to happen!"

"Well, that's where you're wrong. We have some Cartel Bosses that will be anxious to see you. You know the ones you stole Heroin and twenty million dollars from. I read your file and there's a contract out on you. You can stay silent all you want, but your next stop will be at one of their fronts masquerading as a bar. We'll just drop you off to them and see if you can make it through the night. I'm betting not and it won't be a quick death…slow and painful until they cut off your head."

Simon O'Connor wasn't smiling anymore. He knew Gavin wasn't bluffing and not even the CIA could rescue him from the Cartel if he was handed over. "What do you want to know?"

Gavin laughed. "I figured you'd see things my way. " Gavin got out his handcuffs and as he was about to put them on O'Connor, he had to put his gun away so he could use both hands. O'Connor took a chance. He shoved Gavin out of the way and then found a fire extinguisher to hit Gavin with. It's didn't knock Gavin completely out, but made him woozy and it was hard to get up. O'Connor pulled out his cell phone and found the correct APP. He then found his scuba gear.

Gavin finally got up and drew his service weapon again. He said. "O'Connor, freeze…you're not going anywhere.

"No…there's no way you're taking me in."

"You got nowhere to go Simon…you either come with me or take a bullet to the head.

O'Connor smiled. "That's where you're wrong FBI man…in my line of work, you always have an escape plan." He backed away from the wall and pressed the APP button on smart phone. Gavin didn't exactly know what the function of the APP was, but he rushed for Simon O'Connor, knowing that it had to be dangerous. There was a round life buoy hanging on the back of the ship near the small window located where the two men were. It started to shake after O'Connor clicked the APP on his phone. The APP started a series of small explosions that blew a hole in the ship's back wall from the outside. The lifebuoy was essentially a bomb.

The explosion created an escape hatch. When Gavin reached O'Connor, his timing was so perfect that he grabbed O'Connor and pushed him towards the big hole in the side of the ship. O'Connor wrestled with him to try and get free, but it didn't work. The momentum of the two men caused them to go forward, out the hole just as the explosion finished creating the hole. They fell out the back of the ship into the water below with parts of the back wall falling onto of them into the water. Something hit Gavin as he reached the water stunning him and knocking him out for a moment. The water brought him back to a conscious state pretty quick and then his instinct kicked in, causing him to swim up and above the waterline. When he got above the water, Simon O'Connor was nowhere to be found. He dived under the water a few times and looked for him, but didn't find anything. Simon O'Connor was gone.

6:00 PM CST.

It was shift change at the 9th Precinct. Cops were coming in the building as other cops were leaving. It was a normal day and nobody thought anything different until dozens of FBI cars rolled up to the front of the building. Most of the cops just stood there and let it happen. They weren't about to interfere with the FBI. A couple of detectives who were just leaving quickly made for their cars and tried to drive off through the back entrance of the parking lot. They didn't

make it and were met by a few more FBI cars. Nobody was getting out
that day. The Team leader got out of his car and told the officers to go
back inside. They had warrants and would be talking to everybody.
The captain came out of the building cursing. He told the FBI SAC
(Special Agent in Charge) that he couldn't do this and they had no
jurisdiction here. The SAC handed him a warrant and replied. "You
wrong Captain. Here's your warrant…we have every right to be here
and we will be taking all of your files and your hard drives." The
Captain couldn't really argue after that. Most of the cops were stunned
at what happened. The FBI SAC texted Agent Main. Arrived and
started our search. Congrats, we timed it perfectly!"

6:37 PM CST

    Agent Main was helping gather the ship's crew up on deck
when the explosion happened. It caught everybody by surprise.
Nobody really knew if it was an explosion or not. She motioned to one
of the tactical teams to go check it out. About the only they knew is the
direction it came from. The team ran to the back of the ship. While
they were doing that, Agent Main got the captain and took him with
some other agents to find the cargo containers that she and her partner
had found on the list they got from Hill and Meyer. The Captain
wasn't really cooperative, but after he was reminded that he could be
imprisoned for a long time for his obstruction of Justice, he relented
and helped her and the other agents. They weren't really after him
anyway.
    It took a few minutes, but they found the containers. All of
them were on deck level so they didn't have to climb anywhere.
Moment of Truth! Agent Main along with the Captain opened the first
container. It was dark, so they had to use flashlights. There were no
boxes. It wasn't packed tight like most containers. Finally, she saw was
in there. Aligned along the walls were Medical Chambers. It looked as
if it was some kind of Advance medical device, nothing that would be
considered dangerous or illegal. She and the other agents walked
down the container and looked at the chambers. They were pretty big
and bolted to the walls of the containers. She counted a total of 12
Chambers. Agent Main started shaking her head and responded out
loud. "I don't get it, there's nothing bad here… nothing worth killing
for unless these things, cost of millions of dollars!"
    She shined her flashlight on top of one of the chambers. There
was a window just a little bit bigger than an adult human head. And
that's when she saw it more closely. There was a person in the

chamber. Somebody unconscious and sleeping peacefully. Agent
Main caught by surprise, jumped back a little bit and shouted. "Holy
Shit!" She checked again just to confirm what she saw. Then she and
the other agents checked every one of the chambers more closely.
There were people in each medical chamber. Even the captain was
surprised. He apparently didn't know what was in the containers.

Somebody started talking through her radio. It was the team
leader of the tactical team that went to check on the explosion. He
radioed back. "We found Agent Donnelly. There was an explosion at
the back of the ship leaving a big hole. Agent Donnelly ended up in
the water."

Agent Main who got concerned, Replied. "Is he alright?"

"For the most part, but he is bleeding."

"Well, get him out the water and get him looked at. I need him
up here to see what we found. He's not going to believe it."

"A Coast Guard ship is swinging by to pick him up as we
speak."

7:30 pm CST.

Agent Donnelly walked up and down the Cargo Container
astonished at what he was seeing. Maybe it was some kind of nervous
habit, but he kept checking the bandage on his forehead that
paramedics had put there to cover up the cut he sustained when he fell
out of the ship. He just kept pacing in between the medical chambers.
He would often stop and carefully inspect a different one each time as
to reaffirm that this was real. It was hard to believe. They didn't
expect something like this and yet still a long ways away from getting
answers.

Finally, Agent Donnelly spoke. "I can't believe any of this. I
mean, sex trafficking, I get, but this a whole new level of sinister."

Agent Main nodded in agreement. "There's 112 people total,
each with their own chamber. Men, Women, and Children from we
can tell, all different ages and different races."

"So the million dollar question…what are they being used for?

"Maybe it's a secret drug trial that you can't reported!"

"But what kind of drug would require this elaborate of a
scheme. The cost to do all of this is millions of dollars and that's not
counting the risk someone would have to take to gather this many
people and put them in this state."

Agent Main paused for a moment and looked around. "I think the only thing we can say for certain is these people were going to be experimented on…that's the only logical explanation."

"And there are being taken somewhere in Great Britain, so it begs the question who could easily transport this many for some secret experiment out of the United States into the United Kingdom…I guess that's where Simon O'Connor comes in."

"But more importantly, who is he really working for? What kind organization would do something like this and how protected are they by not only our government, but other governments too. It has to be something so big with enough power that would make them untouchable in the world."

Agent Main pointed to the Small Skull Symbol next to the barcode. "Did you notice the symbol next to the barcode, we've seen it before."

"But this can't be the United Front…they're basically an anarchist group. They would rather see these people free than used for some kind of experiment."

"Are they? Maybe it's misdirection so that we don't discover their true purpose. But we do know that this symbol is a warning…a warning to stay away from whatever secret organization is behind this…whatever they call themselves.

Agent Donnelly started shaking his head. "I fucking hate secret organizations…makes me feel like I'm in an X-Files Episode. We need to have these people examined and woken up to see if they know anything."

"I already made a call. We are coordinating with the CDC and these people will be moved to one their facilities here in Chicago so they can be examined and quarantined. One of the paramedics already said that it could be dangerous to wake them up and there's a good chance they wouldn't remember anything at all depending on the drugs they were being given in order remain in this state.

"We have to at least try."

"I agree, but there's one thing bugging me. With all these cops being killed, some have been retired for over twenty years and haven't been at the 9th in thirty years including your uncle. If they are all a part of this smuggling operation…

Agent Main Finished her sentence. "Then it's been going on for decades. How can anybody keep this kind of thing quiet in Chicago?"

"Yeah! I also think your friend Jimmy knew more than he let on and I know he's your friend and all, but he's a part of this. He took part in the trafficking of human beings. This isn't running guns or drugs."

Agent Donnelly sighed for a moment. "If you're looking for me to defend him...I can't...you're absolutely right...this is bad!"

"I am only saying this because the next time you see him, you may have to put him down."

"I know and you don't have to ask if I will be able to do it. This is unforgivable...you don't get a pass for this something like this."

"I just wanted you to say it out loud."

Agent Donnelly laughed. "Here's something I want to say out loud just to do it at least once. I have a theory. This ship is meant to go to somewhere in Great Britain, what about Ireland."

"What do you mean?"

"Our last case...the supposed peace agreement that never happened...what if that was the plan all along. What if somebody engineered the tensions that are happening now between Ireland and England especially in Northern Ireland? It's no secret that England has always wanted to keep marching south and just take over all of Ireland. What if the broken peace agreement was the catalyst to start a war and England takes over. There's a lot of places in Ireland that can hide a facility where people are being experimented on or a place that an English Government can make official and nobody would ask questions about."

Agent Main gave him a disapproving look. "I know as an Irishman, England is your archnemesis, but what if somebody connected with the Irish government is engineering this. Somebody that wants to see North Ireland remain with England so they can hide a facility out of the way of prying eyes within an Irish government or an English Government that will most likely still have interests in North Ireland. And if this organization was ever caught, it would be easy to blame English interference and Irishmen in both countries would certainly believe it. And doesn't Simon O'Conner have ties to the IRA making it easy for him to move in and out of the Ireland and Northern Ireland.

"You're right about O'Connor. He's a made guy, basically untouchable."

"There you have it...just offering a different theory, but I don't disagree that this may be connected. I don't think it's a coincidence that all of this started happening in Chicago right after the broken peace accord, especially with a ship filled with people in medical chambers heading for somewhere in Great Britain or Ireland. And if this job teaches us anything, there are no coincidences just patterns we haven't figured out yet!"

Agent Donnelly laughed. "So you believe this is a part of something bigger and connected to our previous investigation."

"Without a doubt and the most important question is *Why*! Why go to all this trouble and what is these people's real purpose? I think we've only hit the surface in this investigation and we have to keep digging."

Agent Donnelly smiled. "I agree and when we get done with our final reports and my OPR meeting, there's something I need to show you that might help."

"Okay"

Jokingly he replied. "But, I disagree with your theory with the Irish government…it's always the English who are to blame."

She smiled and shook her head in disbelief. She knew he was being sarcastic even if he believed the notion at least a little bit. Agent Main responded. "We have the last two cops in custody from Bobby McClain's list, we start questioning them about what they knew and then of course the rest of the crew. We see who's a part of this whole thing and if they know where to find the Congressman.

"And if he is still alive."

"I think at this point, those chances are slim to none."

Agent Donnelly nodded in agreement. "I guess Simone O'Connor was the only person who could tell us the truth."

Agent Main Replied. "Coast Guard still hasn't found a body so until we find one he is still just a missing person, but one of the guys did say that there was scuba equipment on board so there's a chance he could have gotten away."

"Why doesn't that surprise me.

∞∞∞∞∞∞∞∞∞∞

Stephen had been patiently waiting for a few minutes to see the old man. It had been a busy few weeks and his time was valuable. Finally, Stephen was let in to see him and the old man motioned for him take a seat. He also poured himself and Stephen a drink, the kind of drink to help soften the bad news. Stephen spoke first. "Sir, we had complications with the last shipment going out of Chicago."

"I already heard."

"This is a big problem…the two agents know more about the project…they've seen too much."

The old man took a drink of his whiskey and then replied. "What do they really? They have seen small parts of a puzzle…not enough to really know anything."

Stephen gave a disapproving look. "Sir, with all due respect, I think it's time to end their partnership. We've clearly underestimated them. "

"I don't disagree with that. This Agent Donnelly has proven to be more than lucky…he's a little too good at his job. He was supposed to be a distraction to Agent Main and keep her from digging deeper, but even we can make mistakes."

"Like trying to kill him, which we have failed."

The old man gave him a stern look. "No, let's be clear…you have failed."

"Okay, but now I suggest that we separate them and transfer one of them. "

The old man paused for a moment to think about the suggestion. He responded. "As the FBI director, you can do that and it may come to that, but I have a better idea without turning their curiosity into a crusade. We are going to give you the perfect justification to end their partnership, but if they happen to get killed in action along the way then all the better. "

"And I take it that I am not involved in this."

"No…we are going to use someone they least expect."

Curiosity fell upon Stephen's face. "Is it Patient Three or Four?"

"No, clearly we still have some kinks to work out, but Patient One and Two were good test subjects in the field. You needn't worry about who we are getting for this. But there is a job for you."

"I'm Happy to Help…what can I do."

"Make sure any OPR hearings regarding Agent Main and Agent Donnelly go our way. We didn't put you as the FBI Director for no reason, but get approval before anything official is done with them."

Stephen didn't say anything for a moment. He understood the old man's tone and that this was one area, he didn't have free reign to do his job as director. It was too late for that. He did ask. "What about the FBI's role in all of this?"

The old man took another sip of his whiskey. "You won't have to worry about that. With all operations moving overseas now, it will be out of their jurisdiction. The only thing I need you to do at this point is to monitor all active investigations and make sure no one is looking into anything connected to our organization. Our projects will go on despite this mishap in Chicago. "

"And what about the bodies recovered."

"It will be handled. Eventually there will no proof of anything. Just rumors! And we have plenty of ways to distract law enforcement. Idealistic political causes are always good for that."

The old man handed Stephen an envelope. "Here are orders for you to sign and this mess will be transferred from the FBI." Stephen wasn't pleased with that answer, but he was not in a position to argue. He would sign the order and make everything official from the director's office. He would do what he was told. It was the price he had to pay to remain in power.

∞∞∞∞∞∞∞∞∞∞∞∞

Three days had gone by since the raid at the harbor and the 9th Precinct. The dust has begun to settle. As Agent Donnelly and Agent Main sat in AD Foster's office about to give their final report, Gavin couldn't help but think that somehow it was incomplete. Maybe it was. There was a lot still unresolved. The agents had been waiting about five minutes when AD Foster walked in. He didn't have time for small talk. He looked at Agent Donnelly and said.

"As your supervisor, I have been notified of the results from your OPR meeting. "You're assigned to a desk for three months…no field duty."

Agent Donnelly angrily replied. "What the hell, how am I supposed to do my job and work with my partner…they might as well as suspend me."

AD Foster gave him a stern look. "They could have relieved you of duty…be glad you still have a job. And there's plenty of work that can be done from the office. But if you don't like it, then you can always resign."

Agent Donnelly didn't say anything. His boss was right, even if he didn't want to admit it. AD Foster finally sat behind his desk and started reading their report in full. He had only skimmed it up to this point. He finally responded. "So let's start with the bodies you found. Any idea, what they are being used for?"

Agent Main replied. "We figured they are being used for some kind of experiment, maybe even an illegal drug trial…it's the only logical explanation we could come up with. And according to the CDC, they have been given plenty of nutrients to remain healthy. Also, they seem to believe the chambers were built to protect from environmental factors that could harm the exact status they're in."

"So all of this was about smuggling bodies…this is what Simon O'Connor was doing with the help of Chicago Police from the 9th precinct?"

Agent Donnelly responded to the question. "Unfortunately, it's unclear how much they really knew. According to the two detectives we picked up at the 9th and were last on Bobby McClain's list, they didn't know what the cargo was and never asked. They were being paid to help facilitate everything so O'Connor wouldn't get caught. They also implied that Congressman McMahon knew what the cargo was, but there's no proof of that."

[595]

AD Foster asked. "Do they know what happened to the congressman?"

"All they could confirm is that he was taken by O'Connor's men, but they don't know where or if he is still alive."

"I see…so they tell us what we want to know without really telling us anything and avoid prosecution by getting into the witness protection program…that seems typical of the Justice Department. But I'm curious, how long has the congressman been involved."

"They said, since the beginning…over thirty years."

"About the time Hill and Meyer Research labs opened up in Chicago…I bet that's not coincidence."

"Yes, sir, probably not."

"And how does the warehouse shooting figure into all of this.

"That is actually a coincidence. Turns out, their plan was to kidnap the congressman and use him to make some kind of gun deal. McMahon was already gone and happened upon the connection."

AD Foster chuckled as he replied. "No shit…I guess coincidences do happen every once in a while in this job. Overall, this report is good, but I have some concerns. The skull symbol…you've seen this before, but what makes you think that your last two cases are connected to this one. I understand this symbol keeps popping up, but you're insinuating there's a conspiracy by some secret organization that you don't even name."

Agent Donnelly paused for a moment to carefully think about his answer. "I don't think we have to insinuate anything…there's evidence."

"This symbol is used by the United Front and there's some evidence that Bobby McClain was part of that group as well, which may or may not be bullshit, but the fact is the only evidence we have is that the United Front uses this symbol to scare people. Did you find any evidence that they were behind the smuggling and Simon O'Connor was a part of the group?"

"No Sir.

"There you go. The skull and crossbones are known as a pirate symbol, but that doesn't mean that every pirate crew worked together and even privateers used the symbol to scare off people."

"What's your point, sir?"

"It's just a symbol that can be borrowed and used for different reasons. Maybe different criminals are using it for different reasons, but they're not connected."

"That is one possibility, but maybe the United Front uses the symbols to distract us from what's really going…that symbol is a warning, but is can also be used for misdirection."

AD Foster started shaking his head. "And you have no direct evidence of that. Your theories don't belong in this report, only provable facts!

"Then we keep investigating."

"I'm afraid not…you have solved this case about as much as you can solve it. It's been handed over to Homeland Security."

Both Agents were shocked. Agent Donnelly replied. "What…why?"

"Because this can be seen as terrorism and they asked for it. Plus, they are better equipped to investigate the real purpose behind the bodies you found."

"Pardon me, but that's bullshit."

"The director signed off on it last night. It's done and no longer your concern."

Agent Donnelly was furious over the answer he had just been given. "I would like to file an appeal…this is horseshit…I want this case back."

AD Foster stared at him for a moment. "You don't get it do you…nobody wants you to have this…the FBI doesn't want this anymore…we got our victory. You helped catch a Cop Killer, shut down a major smuggling operation with a Chicago Police precinct that the US Attorney's office has been trying to do for years, and you helped bring down an anarchist group that may have had some involvement in all of this even if you don't personally believe it. This is a victory. And no one is even concerned if you actually find the congressman…he was corrupt and in three months his seat can be filled…if anybody really cared about him, then a whole task force would have been assigned to find him, not two FBI agents. If you had found him, great, and if you didn't, you weren't going to lose your job over it. It would have been just another unsolved case. This is all about politics, whether you want to admit it or not. That's why the Director signed off of this."

"I don't care…we'll file an appeal!"

Agent Main responded. "Gavin…I agree with AD Foster…we got a win here. Let's leave it at that."

Agent Donnelly didn't know what to say. But he did respond. "There's still answers that need to be found."

AD Foster. "Sometimes you're not meant to know everything and if you can get bad guys off the streets then that should be good enough. There's no place for conspiracy theories in the FBI and that's why the final part of the report will be amended."

Agent Donnelly was going to say something. He was not protesting, but his partner stopped him and said. "Gavin…let's go, it's not worth it." She looked at AD Foster. "Is there anything else?"

"No...you two are dismissed. I'll assign something to you in a day or two that can be done in the office while Agent Donnelly's serves out his suspension from the field." That was it. They walked out of this office. Agent Donnelly was madder than hell, but even he knew his protest and appeal was a losing battle. As they were walking down the hallway from AD Foster's office, Gavin asked. "Why are you accepting this, we can appeal."

Rachel replied. "To be honest, it's not worth it and it's a fight we're not going to win anyway. We did our job, we caught most of the bad guys...that's good enough for me."

"Don't you want answers."

"Not at the cost of my career and that's what it could be for both of us if we fight this. Let homeland have this one."

"Really, would you normally let another agency take over your case?"

"No, but I am trying to keep my record here clean. I would eventually get back to Washington.'

Gavin started shaking his head. "You want to break up the band, uh. Is this because I didn't kiss you back."

She gave him a dirty look. "No, this isn't personal. I was lonely and you are a halfway decent looking guy...at the time it seemed like that's what I needed, but I was wrong." Gavin replied sarcastically. "Why thank you...glad you noticed."

She laughed. "You should already know; this isn't permanent for either of us...it's only temporary. Besides, I don't see you accepting a transfer to DC from the city you love so much."

"Probably not!"

"We enjoy it for as long as it last, but if you want to fight this battle over a case then you're on your own."

Gavin sighed. "I get it, but there is something I need to talk to you about...something that might change your mind."

"I'm willing to listen as long as it doesn't get me in trouble. "

He laughed. "Later then... I have a meeting in thirty minutes." She was a bit curious, but didn't pry. Rachel was actually looking forward to kind of a light day. She just said to him. "Tell me tonight if you're still crashing at my place. After I take a long hot bath and a glass of whiskey or two." Gavin smiled and agreed, but also told her that it would have to be after he had dinner with his family.

As she started to walk off, she remembered something and turned around. "Gavin, I forgot to give you something. We found it at your apartment the night Maggie died. It was taken with evidence, but we don't need it anymore. You should have it. "She handed him an envelope. He opened it and found a sonogram. He was surprised and then a few tears fell down his

Rachel asked. "Did you know?"

"No, she hadn't told me yet."

Rachel gave her partner the most sincere look she ever had since knowing him. "I'm sorry...truly I am. I personally believe there is a special place in hell for a person that kills someone that's pregnant."

Gavin didn't say anything. He tried to smile, but his grief was too strong. He couldn't hold back the tears and walked off to recollect his composure.

∞∞∞∞∞∞∞∞∞∞

Gavin had received a cryptic message from Dr. Kenrick early that morning. She didn't say much except that it was urgent and that she had more information about Bobby McClain. He suggested they meet in a parking garage away from prying eyes. Since there was a connection to the previous cases, he figured it would also have something to do with the Judge Files so he invited Haley O'Brian to come with. She had to find out eventually. Gavin picked Haley up at the paper and they drove to the garage. They found Dr. Kenrick in a shaded corner of the garage away from other cars. It was very private. Dr. Kenrick was already nervous and got more nervous when she saw Haley. She immediately asked.

"Who is this...I thought you were going to alone."

Gavin replied. "She's with me...you can trust her. She's a part of my private investigation and I have already told her what you told me." The doctor looked at Haley to confirm it. "Haley responded. "It's true...this has nothing to do with the paper...everything is off the record."

Dr.Kenrick was satisfied for the most part and she didn't object. She said. "I was able to conduct an autopsy on Bobby McClain's body and found something...more than I thought I would."

"Gavin replied. "What...the blood patterns were the same?"

"Yes and that's just the start.   I told you earlier that it looked like he was manufactured based on the blood, but I'm not so sure anymore."

"Why not?"

"Because his DNA genetic code has been altered...it's like someone went in and manipulated it just enough for him to look the same but be different if that makes sense."

Both Haley and Gavin looked confused. The doctor responded to their confused looks. "Okay, think of it this way... an HTML

[599]

website… you have a basic template with HTML code that looks one way…if you change just a few lines of code, it makes the site just a little bit different, but looks and feels the same. Same concept with genetic code."

Gavin asked, "Okay, before you were suggesting he had been cloned."

She laughed. "I didn't exactly say that. But if you want to use that term, sure…what I am saying now something like that with a few tweaks…something that is like the original, but has the ability to replicate and develop on its one including new memories and experiences. Let me put it this way. If cloned this person with what they did to the Genetic Clone, it would not be the exact same, but a copy that develops into its own unique identity. That's the best way I can explain it."

Haley asked. "So that means the copy would look a little different, even develop different behaviors. Like the original template would be aggressive, but the copy could be more passive, right?"

"Dr. Kenrick replied. "I suppose so."

Gavin thought of something. "Wait a minute…we got a report of Bobby McClain of changing his MO when he killed somebody. Instead of shooting them, he rigged a car bomb. He set a trap for them and killed them with an explosion instead of a bullet. That's a change in behavior. That Bobby McClain could be the replicated version of the one you autopsied, right."

Dr. Kenrick replied. "I hate to say it, but yes. I mean a little too much Science Fiction, but same principle. "

"Doc, we've already gone way past reason here…might as well explore the ridiculous."

Haley responded. "Wait…you know what means…if you're right then there's another Bobby McClain out there or somebody just like him."

Gavin asked, "Doc, is there any way to tell if the body you examined is the original or a copy?"

"She replied. "I would have to look at an original DNA Genetic code and compare, but where would you get that if we are meant to believe this is Bobby McClain. But then again the original genetic code would show signs of being altered so it would be hard to tell. You'd have to get a DNA sample from before he had surgeries…a sample from like when he was a kid."

Haley responded "How hard would it be to get that?"

Gavin replied. "It's very unlikely, according to his file, both of his parents are gone and he was an only child…finding something from over twenty years ago with his DNA on it, well, impossible comes to mind."

Dr. Kenrick pulled a flash drive out of her purse and gave it to Gavin. "All my notes and reports are on here. Homeland Security came and confiscated everything early this morning, including the body of your assassin. And they didn't even give a reason why."

"I was told this morning that this part of our investigation was given to them, signed off by the Director of the FBI because of Politics."

"What does that mean?"

"Doc, it's agency code for cover up… we don't want you to find the truth."

Dr. Kenrick gave him a half-hearted smile. "Take that information and keep digging. Officially, I can't do anything, but I refuse to completely destroy evidence of this magnitude."

She kissed Gavin on the cheek, got in her car and drove off. There was nothing more to say; nothing more she should say without getting into serious trouble. Haley was shocked by everything. She never expected in a million years to hear this kind of information. She responded with her disbelief.

"I can't believe any of this…looking into corporate corruption is one thing, but this is stuff from a science fiction novel."

Gavin laughed. "Yeah, it sounds that way, but what if it's all true…what if that which we believe is impossible, isn't? What should we do?"

"Me, personally, I'm not here to debate some philosophical question. I'm for the truth and I think people have a right to know the truth."

Gavin smiled. "Well then, let's find it. We start by looking into Hill and Myer Research Labs…all the way since they first set up shop in Chicago. We look into everything they've done, things that succeeded and especially things that failed. And more importantly, we follow the money that's been put into the research center including any parent company that they may be part of it. "

"I thought they were nonprofit?"

"Let's find out who their biggest contributor is then and start looking into why they helped fund the center"

"You think the research lab is some kind of front for something else?"

Gavin chuckled. "At this point, it's beginning to be the most logical explanation."

∞∞∞∞∞∞∞∞∞∞∞

Rachel actually arrived home at 6:00pm. It was early for her.
For the first time in a long time she was able to get home at a normal
hour. Her small apartment was still a mess with case files. She had
every intention of cleaning the place up, but she was too tired to think
about it now. The first thing she did was pour herself a glass of
whiskey, what was a left in the bottle anyway. Her and Gavin pretty
much went through the good bottle of scotch she had been saving for
something she couldn't remember.

The next thing wanted in order to relax was a hot bath. She
walked into her bedroom to undress and didn't even see it coming. All
of sudden, everything went black. She was hit over the head by a man
standing behind the door. She was trained to check behind doors
while holding her gun, but it never occurred to her she needed to do it
in her own home. She was wrong. The man wearing black pants and a
black hoodie checked her pulse to make sure he didn't kill her and then
moved her from the ground to her undone bed. He made a call with
his cell phone and only said three words to the other man on the other
end of the phone. "I've got her."

∞∞∞∞∞∞∞∞∞∞∞

It had been a while since Gavin had dinner with his family.
He'd been a little busy the past few months, needless to say. It was nice
to catch up, but it wasn't completely a social call. He and his Uncle
Liam needed to have a serious talk. It was the kind of bad news that a
good home cooked meal could make bearable. At least that's what
Liam Donnelly thought when he invited his nephew. After dinner the
two men retired to his study for a glass of twenty five year McCallum.
Gavin knew the routine and at this point he just wanted to avoid the
small talk so he asked.

"While, I appreciate the good whiskey, I know you need to tell
me something serious, so you might as well get on with it."

"You never did like small talk."

"No…wastes too much time."

"Well, you're not exactly the most popular person in the
neighborhood these days."

"What, for doing my job?"

"Yeah, the mob will hate you for that, but that will blow over.
It's mostly about Maggie."

Gavin sighed. "Is it mostly because we were back together or
that she's dead."

"Both."

"That will blow over."

"Eventually, but you know this neighborhood, people have long memories and she wasn't divorced yet. Her getting killed just made it worse."

"I see, what about you, how did you feel about it?"

Liam took another sip of whiskey. "Look, I get it. You two had been in love with each other since you were kids. I always thought you would eventually end up together anyway, but you went off to school and started a career and she married Jimmy. You both made choice and you should live with them. Sneaking around like you did wasn't right and she should have been divorced. I don't care if Jimmy was in prison…it's not an excuse…there's a right way to do things."

Gavin nodded. "I don't disagree that we handled it badly. And for what it was worth, we did plan on telling Jimmy in person before we moved further, just never got around to it with the cases I was working. I'm not making excuses, just saying that we had the best intentions."

"Good intentions only get you so far and it doesn't really make up for bad actions."

"Maybe not, but it should."

Liam smiled. "We don't live in that in that kind of World…that world is where the Chicago Cubs actually win the World Series."

Gavin laughed at the last part of the comment. "So what should I do?"

"It's been suggested that you should find a new place to live…out of the neighborhood."

"Really…I grew up here."

"I know, but maybe it's time for a change."

"What's next, I'm not allowed at the Pub anymore."

Liam gave him a dirty look. "You know better than that. It's always been neutral territory. But having to live in the area is just a reminder of what happened."

Gavin pulled out the sonogram that his partner gave him. "You may be right, but you should also know that she was pregnant and we had already planned on being married."

Liam put his hand on Gavin's shoulder. "I'm sorry… no man should have to lose a child, especially an unborn one."

"Thank You and I understand why people are mad… it shouldn't have happened, especially with me, but I think people should know the full extent of this tragedy. I lost more than everybody else and I shouldn't have to be punished for it."

"No, you shouldn't, but you know that life isn't fair."

They both didn't say anything for a while. They just pour another drink. Gavin finally asked. "With the 9th being shut down by the FEDS, how bad do you think it's going to be?"

"Bad, there's already been some mob related homicides the past few days, territory disputes. But we will get through this…we always do."

Gavin took a sip of whiskey. "I need to apologize…didn't mean to insult your honor as a police officer the other day."

"No need to apologize…you weren't wrong. I heard about what you found, the bodies that Simon O'Connor was transporting." Gavin wasn't surprised. You can't keep a secret in Chicago." Liam continued. "Here's something to keep in mind. Nobody condones what O'Connor was doing and as bad as Mickey Sorrano or Tommy McManus might be, that's a line they wouldn't cross."

"How do you do it…how do you justify your so called alliance."

Liam smiled. "Because, I don't see things in black and white. And I live with a truth that most cops don't when it comes to so called criminals. We live in their world…not the other way around. And sometimes we have to play by their rules if we are to co-exist. We'll never be able to completely stop them so the solution is to exist in their world with the fewest number of casualties. It's the main reason I support the peace agreement between the mob groups and help keep it intact. But I also don't take money and I don't break the law in doing my job. It may get bent a little, but necessary to maintain the status quo. I accept that criminals exist and if they deal in a few harmless vices like gambling, pot, and hookers, they don't cross a line in my book. To me, that's a badge of honor in the real world."

Gavin laughed. "You know most cops will not see it that way."

"And most of them don't live here, which means they can't fully understand what we deal with. The same rules apply to the FBI…remember that unless you are trying to be the director and can play politics with the truth. The police commissioner in Chicago does all the time."

Gavin couldn't help by laugh. He may not always agree with his Uncle, but he never doubted how smart he was. Gavin finished his whiskey, shook Liam's hand and told him that he would be looking for a new place this coming weekend…outside of the neighborhood he grew up in.

∞∞∞∞∞∞∞∞∞∞∞∞

On the way back to his partner's apartment, Gavin had the urge to stop by Maggie's grave. Her body had finally been released by the FBI and her family was finally able to bury her. It was his chance to visit her grave and say goodbye without making the rest of her family uncomfortable. He knew they would never forgive him, especially her mother. When he got there and walked to the grave, he found another late night visitor. It was Jimmy McManus and somehow he wasn't surprised to see him. Jimmy wasn't surprised to see Gavin either.

As Gavin walked up, Jimmy responded. "Isn't it sad that the two men she loved the most couldn't visit her grave with everybody else…she deserves better…maybe we do too."

"Then maybe she shouldn't have known us at all."

Jimmy looked at his best friend. "I don't believe that at all. I would like to think we each gave her something good…we both loved her more than anything."

"But I guess it wasn't good enough…you're tormented her and I got her killed."

"Something I could have easily done."

"Maybe, but I will agree with you that she deserved better than us…she always did."

"Yeah, she did! So are you here to take me in."

Gavin looked at him for a moment and almost reached or his cuffs, but simply replied. "No…I should take you in, but even you have a right to say goodbye."

Jimmy smiled. "I'm sorry for escaping, but it was my only shot to get out and get my life back. Sorry I used you,"

Gavin nodded. "I should be pissed, but the truth is I knew the risk. Somehow I always knew you would do something like this and I could have stopped it if I wanted to. And yes, that's how I justify it so don't try and argue."

"There'd be no point anyway. How much trouble did you get into?"

Gavin laughed. "Three month's sitting at a desk or the Bureau's version of probation. But I do have to ask you something and you owe me an honest answer!"

Jimmy laughed. "It's the least I can do."

"Did you know what Simon O'Connor was doing…what he was smuggling?"

"Yes…I helped him get people.

Gavin was stunned. "Fucking Christ, Jimmy! Why?"

"The money was too good and I was looking for a way out for my family, when my son was born, I knew I had to get out of the life and Simon offered me a job with lots of money. The money was too damn good and It's hard to turn down a job that pays that well"

"Do you know what they were being used for?

"No and never asked. I was given a list of what to look for and a date of when they had to be delivered." Jimmy paused for a moment and regret could be found in his voice. "To be honest, I didn't want to know."

"So if this was all about money, how much did you get?"

"Twenty Grand a person."

"Holy Shit…how much money did you make?"

"In Five years, I made Five Million dollars…that's enough for a new life and my way out. You can understand that, right."

Gavin gave him a disapproving look. "No, because at the end of the day you were kidnapping and smuggling people…there's no excuse for it because it's a line you just don't cross. I never cared about what racket you were in, but this is unforgivable."

"Spare me your righteous indignation; I already know I'm going to hell. I made peace with that a long time ago. For me, it was about my family and until you have a wife and a child, you won't understand. "

"That's where you're wrong." Gavin showed him the sonogram. "Maggie was pregnant when she was murdered."

Jimmy was filled with rage. While Jealousy would be a normal reaction considering Gavin has been sleeping with the woman who was still his wife, he felt sad for his best friend because he had been there before. "I'm sorry Gavin…looks like we've both lost a child with the same woman, but if it's any consolation, she always loved you more. No matter what I did or how nice I was to her, she always "

"Nice of you to say, but it doesn't take away the pain."

"And there's nothing that can…that's the harsh truth. All you do is learn to live with it each day."

Jimmy pulled a piece of paper out of his pocket. "Look, I can't give you answers on what the people are being used for. But if you really want to know, I can point you in the right direction, maybe this can help, hopefully, it will lead in you in the right direction."

The piece of paper only had numbers…

N-53-59-45.1   W-6 37 17.5

12-14-16

"What does this mean?"

"I don't know, but I bet you can figure it out "

Gavin nodded in agreement. "Thank You, I'll look at it more closely another day since I'll have more time on my hands." He laughed to himself and then he changed the subject.

"Well ,at least we can say goodbye to Maggie."

"And remember her for who she was…for how beautiful she was." Jimmy took a flask out of his jacket pocket and took a sip. He handed it to Gavin, who took a sip as well. In their own small way, it was a toast to the woman they both loved…the woman they would mourn for the rest of their lives. Gavin was about to say something when his phone started ringing. The Caller ID said it was his partner. He Answered.

"Rachel, what's up!"

A thick Irish Accent answered back. "I'm not your partner, but she is here with me. Do you know who this is?"

Shock hit him like a two-by-four. There was fear in voice as he replied. "Simon O'Connor…you're not dead."

"You're not that lucky boyo"

"Where's my partner?"

Simon started laughing. "You took something of mine, so I took something of yours."

"You know, if you kill her there will be no place to hide…I will find you and all the protection won't keep you safe from me. "

"Agent Donnelly, I'm not going to kill her… I am going to do something far worse."

"What do you want?"

Simon started laughing. "Nothing you have or can give me. There's no point in negotiating. I just wanted you to know who has her and why."

"Fuck You. Know this, you son of a bitch, I will hunt you down to the ends of earth to get her back."

Simon started laughing again. "I thought you'd respond like that…so boyo, let the game begin."

To Be Continued in Book 5.…